Linguist, polit... ...an, BBC
Television Prod... ...s Boyd's
life took man... ...author.
His fascination with the fine art world began while working on
a BBC series about Sotheby's of London, for which he visited
many private collections and discovered the lengths certain collectors are prepared to go to own works of art they covet. *The
Fiddler and the Ferret* is his fifth novel.

Also by Douglas Boyd:

THE EAGLE AND THE SNAKE
THE HONOUR AND THE GLORY
THE TRUTH AND THE LIES
THE VIRGIN AND THE FOOL

THE

FIDDLER

AND THE

FERRET

Douglas Boyd

WARNER BOOKS

A *Warner* Book

First published in Great Britain in 1997
by Little, Brown and Company
This edition published by Warner Books in 1998

A CIP catalogue record for this book
is available from the British Library.

ISBN 0 7515 2186 8

Typeset in Sabon MT by M Rules
Printed and bound in Great Britain by
Clays Ltd, St Ives plc

Warner Books
A Division of
Little, Brown and Company (UK)
Brettenham House
Lancaster Place
London WC2E 7EN

To Sue, with love

Acknowledgements

One of the pleasures of fiction writing is finding how many friends, acquaintances and total strangers are prepared to make available their specialist knowledge to an author. Among those who have thus helped with research for this book, I should like to thank Atarah Ben-Tovim (music), Caroline Currie (fine art sale rooms), Wilfred Franc de Ferrières and Jean-François Jannoueix (wine), Florence Palmer (a thousand small points), Peter Ritchie (surfing), Jennifer Weller (art), Harold Yauner (medicine).

At a time when all is a-changing in the world of publishing, I'm lucky to have had Hilary Hale as editor of my last three books. And where would I be without Mandy Little, my agent and trusty jungle guide, with whom it all began?

Un grand merci à tous!

PART I:
Melles-sur-Mer,
South-west France – April 1945

With each snip of the scissors Céline felt a severed lock of hair fall onto her bare shoulders and slide off. She wanted to pull her blouse together and protect her bare breasts from the leers of the crowd, but her arms were pinioned behind her. A boy, who could not have been more than fourteen, grabbed a handful of the dark curls from the sandy ground and thrust them into her mouth. He threw back his head and laughed, mouth wide open so that she smelled the garlic on his breath. She spat out the hair and wondered how long the torment could go on.

A mirror flashed the sun in her eyes, blinding her – but only after she had seen the roughly hacked tufts of hair remaining and the patches of scalp between. The local barber was enjoying his moment of fame. People laughed and jeered at his victim as he slapped a brush loaded with shaving foam over her head and face, deliberately getting some of the soap in Céline's eyes. Conscious that he was the centre of attention, he drew his cut-throat razor from the front to the back of her scalp again and again, wiping it with a flourish each time on the towel that was draped over his left arm, until finally her head was as bare of hair as a billiard ball. A cloud now covered the sun. The breeze blowing off the sea was cold on the exposed skin of her scalp.

A woman with a pot of some dark paint-like substance in her hand pushed through the crush. One of the two uniformed gendarmes who were holding Céline in the barber's chair forced her head down until her chin was on her naked chest. She felt the paintbrush cold and wet on the shaven skin as the sign of the swastika was roughly daubed on her scalp. The mirror was thrust in front of her face again and a hand beneath her chin jerked her head roughly upwards so that she could not avoid seeing her reflection.

The barber was yelling at her to open her eyes. She remembered his voice from her childhood. So many times she had accompanied her father to the little salon behind the church for his daily shave when the family was in Melles-sur-Mer for the summer holidays. The same man who had given her sweets from a glass jar, which stood on a shelf among the massage oils and perfumes, was now presiding over her humiliation, shouting, '*Regarde-toi, putain!*' Look at yourself, you whore . . .

Opening her eyes, she saw a hairless stranger down whose forehead and cheeks trickles of some dark viscous liquid were running. A familiar smell teased her nostrils. Tar? Yes, it was tar.

She watched almost with indifference as the woman with the paintbrush dipped it into the pot again and drew another swastika across Céline's breasts, neatly ending two of the arms of the ancient device with a small circle around each of her victim's nipples. A harsh chorus of laughter rang out. The older gendarme said to the women, '*Alors, ça suffit, n'est-ce pas?*'

Perhaps they will let me go now, Céline thought dully. What else could they do? As long as her lover was safe, nothing else mattered.

They had lain in bed late that morning, lulled by the rumble of the waves on the rocks below the villa and luxuriating in the miracle of being able to throw open a window and let sunshine into the bedroom after so many months of hiding in the perpetual gloom of a cave and coming out only after nightfall.

Caresses had turned to love-making, so that when the noise of the sea had been drowned by the roar of an angry crowd, they had not at first heard. It was the rattle of stones on the wooden shutters which finally roused the lovers.

With no time to get dressed properly, Céline had just pulled on a blouse and skirt, then gone out onto the balcony. In the mass of upturned faces below, all disfigured by hate, the barber's was not the only one she had known since she was a child. Even when the first stone caught her on the elbow, numbing her arm, she had still not been afraid.

Dietrich had pulled her forcibly back into the bedroom and closed the shutters. He wanted to go downstairs and confront the mob, arguing that he had done nothing wrong, but if they caught him obviously hiding, it would be only human nature to treat him like a criminal. Overruling him, Céline led the way up onto the roof of the villa, where she showed him how to squeeze between two tall brick chimney stacks. She and her sister had hidden there once as children, and caused a panic when the servants could not find them at dinner time.

'Whatever happens,' she said, 'don't come out until I tell you it's safe.'

Face white with anxiety for her, Dietrich argued, 'You're not well. I can't leave you alone to face these people.'

They heard the splintering of wood downstairs, where the ground-floor shutters were being crowbarred from their hinges. Next came the smashing of glass and the pounding of feet as the mob poured into the old wooden house, smashing and looting their way from room to room.

'I'll be all right,' Céline insisted. 'I'm French. They have nothing against me.'

She shut the trapdoor that led to the roof and hurried downstairs to meet the ringleaders on the floor below.

'Where is he?' they shouted. 'Where's the dirty *schleu*? Where's your German lover-boy?'

'He's gone,' she cried, desperate that they should believe her. 'I'm alone.'

Angry at finding only one victim where there should have been two, they grabbed her, wrenching her arms behind her back. Fists punched her. Hate-filled faces loomed towards hers, spitting. Hands pulled her this way and that, plucking at her clothes, tearing at her blouse until the buttons popped and it was pulled down over her shoulders and roughly knotted there to pinion her arms behind her. Fists struck her in the face, on her arms, on her breasts, on her back. She tried to bend double, to protect the child in her womb. A blow more vicious than the others connected behind her left ear and nearly knocked her unconscious. She fell and, as she was roughly pulled to her feet, someone shouted out that she was wearing no knickers.

But for the hands grasping her arms so painfully tightly, she would have fallen again and been trampled underfoot. As she was pulled outside the house, Céline lowered her head, to avoid seeing the lust in the faces of the men leering at her from all directions. Even worse was the vicious glee of the women witnessing her degradation.

A few of the men wore FFI armbands and items of uniform, but most of the mob were civilians who had spent the past four or five years peacefully employed by the Organisation Todt as paid labourers, working alongside the German soldiers on the construction of the blockhouses and other fortifications of the Atlantic wall that guarded Hitler's Fortress Europe.

Two uniformed gendarmes pushed through the throng. Céline thought they had come to rescue her. Only when they grasped her arms and forced her onwards did she realise that they were part of the crowd. Its noise was like the sound of an ocean of hatred in turmoil, tearing at the minuscule island of humanity which was herself.

No, Céline corrected herself. Nature was never so cruel. The clamour of the mob was an infernal chorus, conducted by the devil himself. As the orchestral conductor hears every instrument among the hundred or so in front of him, so her musician's ear insisted on distinguishing individual voices in this hymn of hate. On her right there was a man with a voice as low as a tuba. He was roaring, 'Fuck the whore! Let me get my hand up her skirt and I'll show her how a loyal Frenchman cures a Boche-lover like her!' A woman close to him cackled with laughter, as though it was all just a dirty joke. On Céline's left, the barber was yelling repeatedly in his tenor voice of trombone register, 'String her up! String her up! Rape's too good for her sort of trash.'

Close behind Céline the contralto voice of a middle-aged woman was calling for a branding iron. No viola in hell had ever sung this song. 'Not paint,' she was screaming. 'The whore will just wash it off. Heat some metal and brand her for life! Brand her on the mug and brand her on the tits.'

Further away was a soprano cadenza of hatred coming from the lips of a teenage girl crying, 'Strip her naked! Let's all see what she's got that was so special. Let's see the lollipop her German lover-boy was licking all these last five years!'

Unwilling to open her eyes and see the hatred that surrounded her, Céline stumbled onwards, wondering where they were taking her – and why. The important thing, she kept telling herself, was that they were heading away from the house, away from the hiding place where her lover was safe. But why was this happening to her? Neither she nor Dietrich had done anyone any harm. Who could have betrayed them? For what motive?

And then she saw the even bigger crowd ahead, baiting a pathetic line of women who had already been humiliated before her. Heads shaven, breasts exposed, they were tied one to each lamppost along the street. A few were proudly defiant, some had their heads bowed in shame, some were weeping, but most were gazing blankly in shock. At the end of the line stood a priest in his black cassock, biretta on his head, laughing at some joke being told by a group of men which included the mayor, resplendent in his tricolour sash of office.

When it was Céline's turn, the gendarmes forced her down into the single bentwood chair, behind which the barber stood waiting. Nothing matters, she told herself, so long as Dietrich is safe.

The crowd was growing restive. There were rules even for this sort of barbarity. In the presence of the gendarmes, the priest and the mayor, the humiliation of the victims who had already been dealt with could go no further.

Then heads began to turn at the sound of another mob approaching. When the wall of bodies divided in front of her, Céline wanted not to look at the beaten, bloodied man they were holding upright, two paces away from her. Dietrich was naked to the waist. His chest was covered in bruises and cuts, over which someone had painted a crude approximation of the SS runes. One of his eyes had been torn out and hung like a bloody jellyfish on his cheek. The other stared unseeingly straight ahead.

Céline tried to wrench herself free from the hands that held her, wanting to throw her arms around him, cradle his beaten head to her breasts and protect him. With an animal howl of anguish, she screamed, 'Let him go! Let him go! He is innocent! Let him go!'

The few nearby who heard, laughed. Dietrich's single eye focussed briefly on the shaven, painted victim in front of him. Could he recognise her? Céline wondered. A woman pushed her way between them and viciously brought her knee up into the groin of the new victim, whose mouth opened in a scream of pain, to show split lips and bleeding gums where teeth had been knocked out.

Like a flock of birds wheeling together on some hidden signal, the crowd pivoted en masse to get a better view of the next act in the drama. Above the mob, Céline saw a man on top of a ladder, dressed in blue work overalls and with a black beret on his head. There was a half-smoked cigarette dangling from his lips as he calmly knotted one end of a rope around the top bracket of a lamppost.

On the fringe of the mob, a man in uniform was fighting his way through the throng. He wore the insignia of a sergeant in the British Intelligence Corps, and was shouting in poor French that the victims should be handed over to the proper authorities for justice. Since the surrender the previous day of the stay-behind German troops in the Royan pocket, armed French soldiers had repeatedly rescued surrendering Wehrmacht soldiers from mobs who were beating them up. Here, there was little that one foreigner armed with a service revolver could do against a crowd, many of whom had automatic weapons in their hands.

Below the man on the ladder, people made way for a *gazogène* – a wood-burning flatbed farm truck which was being reversed up to the lamppost. Eager hands lifted the German onto the bed of the truck. Because his arms were tied behind his back, he fell awkwardly and had to be pulled to his feet by the two self-appointed hangmen, before being turned through 360 degrees so that everyone could see what boots and stones and spades could do to a human face. Like a conjuror holding up the rabbit to show that there was no deceit, one of the men on the truck held up the noose for the crowd's roar of approval before slipping it over his victim's head. The knot was pulled tight. As a final touch of viciousness, in order to prolong his death struggle, the rope binding his arms was cut and his left arm was raised on high to show to the crowd the scar beneath his left armpit.

'That's where his SS blood group was tattooed,' someone said.

'No, no!' Céline screamed. 'He got that scar years ago. He was never in the SS, believe me!'

She wanted to close her eyes, but kept them open in case her lover's single functioning eye should see her face. At least, she prayed, let him know that there is one person in all this senseless cruelty who cares . . .

She struggled to break away from the two gendarmes, and go to him. Unable to free her arms, she hacked with her heels at the shins of the men holding her. When that did not work, she managed to bite one of her captors, drawing blood from his hand and earning herself a hail of oaths and a brutal cuffing. The two volunteer hangmen jumped down to the ground. One of them slapped his hand against the side of the *gazogène* as a signal to the driver.

'No!' Céline screamed. 'Oh God, no!'

But God was not listening, and His priest had his back to her, watching as fascinatedly as the others. In a cloud of choking blue exhaust fumes, the truck jerked forward. The lone man standing on it – high above the crowd, so infinitely alone – made a small jump as it pulled away, whether to delay for a millisecond the inevitable moment of his death or to try and bring it closer, no one would ever know. Then the truck was gone and the mob, suddenly quiet, closed together after its passage, all faces gazing up at the dying man, who dangled like a broken puppet on the rope that twisted and jerked as his legs scissored and scrabbled, seeking any support for the weight of the body that was choking him slowly to death.

His arms flailed the air above his head. First one and then the other found the rope and clung uselessly to it. The steel-tipped heels of his shoes played an uneven drum roll against the metal lamppost. There was distant shouting from people on the fringes of the crowd complaining that they could not see well enough. Among them the foreigner's voice was still raised in argument.

'Hang me! Hang me too!' Céline screamed. At that moment she wanted more than anything else for them to bring back the truck, produce another noose and hang her beside Dietrich. With complete indifference she let herself be dragged to the lamppost beneath his still twitching body and tied there with another piece of the same rope they had used to hang him.

Her legs had no strength in them. She slumped down, letting the bonds take the weight of her body. The gendarme she had bitten twisted her right ear between his thumb and forefinger to pull her head back against the sun-warmed metal of the lamppost, forcing her to look up. Her field of vision was filled by the silhouette against the cloudless sky of the man slowly dying above her. She saw that both of Dietrich's shoes had fallen off in his death throes. He was wearing a pair of socks she had darned several times during the months of hiding. There was a hole in one through which the big toe poked. As the sphincter relaxed, the contents of his bladder trickled down his legs. Drops of urine formed on the big toe, and dripped from there onto her shaven head.

PART II:
Guéthary, Basque Coast –
November 1996

.1.

The beach of Guéthary, a small surfer's paradise on the Basque coast which played host to the 1996 World Longboard Championships, lies just to the north of the Spanish border, where a deep submarine canyon channels the full force of Atlantic storms onto the glorious few miles of the Basque coast.

In summer, whenever the conditions are right, the sea is dotted with surfers. On a cold and grey November afternoon, Ken Scott was the only person out on the water. Hands and feet numb from the cold despite the protection of a 6 m.m. neoprene and titanium wet suit with hood, gloves and boots, he rode what he reckoned would be the last worthwhile wave of the day. It left him a hundred metres from shore, fighting his way through the vicious rip current that seemed intent on dragging him onto the rocks. Seaward, the surf was dying as the offshore wind dropped with the dusk. Heavy black clouds closed like curtains across the Bay of Biscay, shutting off the last light of the day.

Ken beached in water up to his knees, wondering how many all-year surfers had died because their brains were literally numb with cold. The water temperature was just above eight degrees centigrade. Eastwards, the sky was already dark above the mass of the land. To the south and west twinkled lights that were in Spain. To the north-east, the light on the Virgin's Rock at Biarritz flashed its warning seaward, where a few side-trawlers bobbed their way homeward to the fishing port called Hendaye by the French and Hondarribia in Basque.

Ken hefted the board under one arm and walked up the deserted beach. The Goofy Food café, where he had been hoping to buy a hot drink, was closed. There were several vehicles parked on the gravel track that led up to the main road. Through the open windows came the smells of cooking and sounds of radio voices in a dozen different languages. Some of the cars and vans were new arrivals, but others had been parked there for a week or longer, inhabited by surf addicts from all over the world who were hoping to catch a ride on the Big One – a freak wave that was rumoured to arise like the Kraken from the bowels of the Atlantic during the first real winter storm each year and outclass anything seen on the North Shore of Hawaii.

Ken's lovingly polished Harley-Davidson FXRT was chained to the rear of a large Mercedes camping van with Dutch number-plates, guarded by two Alsatians who wagged their tails at his approach. Above the dogs hung a Honda Goldwing that belonged to their owner, suspended from electric davits. Ken leaned the board against a fence, took off the neoprene gloves and opened one of the rear panniers of his bike to find a couple of dog biscuits for the canine Mafia. As they crunched them happily, wagging their tails, the door of the van was thrown open and the Flying Dutchman stuck out his green Mohawk haircut and said something. He was a huge man with a beer-belly, clad in jeans and a singlet, whose arms were tattooed from wrist to shoulder with an encyclopaedic collection of motorcycling insignia.

Ken eased the drawstring of his wet suit hood and slipped it back so he could hear. 'I'm bribing your dogs,' he said, 'with a view to future favours.'

'You are one crazy old man,' said the girl standing in the doorway behind the Flying Dutchman. Her blonde hair was dyed in orange, gold and brown streaks to match the paintwork on the Goldwing.

'I think too,' the Flying Dutchman said. 'One day you are staying out so long the cold gets you – and we get to keep the Harley for ever, Ken.' He laughed and closed the door.

Ken peeled off the sticky wet suit and rolled it down his body and legs. Immediately the wind cut through his moist skin, chilling him to the bone. Naked, he moved into the lee of the camper, rubbing himself down vigorously with a rough towel, to get the circulation going again. Some faces stared at him from the windows of a three-car local train on the line above. His naked body belied his age; it had the spare toughness of the all-year surfer; only in the lines on his face was his age written accurately. With skin still numb, he dressed in sweater, jeans and trainers, then went for a half-mile warm-up run past the launching ramp where the fishing boats were laid up.

'Wanna cuppa tea, Pom?' a voice asked from one of the other vans on his return.

Endless Winter was the name painted on the sides of the vehicle in joking reference to a famous surfing film. The atmosphere in the ancient British-registered Bedford camper could have been bottled and used as evidence. Ken climbed inside and chatted while the kettle was boiling, about waves and boards and wax and the advantages of five fins over three. They were the only topics of conversation he had in common with the two golden youths from Queensland. Their real names were Dave and Chaz, but they were known on the surfing grapevine as the Wizards from Oz on account of their daring and skill when riding the waves.

'You're welcome to a toke of the herb superb,' offered Dave, who was making the tea.

'You know I don't smoke.' Ken felt the generation gap open wide beneath him. He sat near the small catalytic gas radiator and took the mug of scalding fluid gratefully, sipping it to put life back into his body.

'You're a living legend, you know,' remarked Chaz. He was lying on one of the bunks, eyes concealed behind dark glasses, determined to get the last hit from his roach. 'We heard about you first on the North Shore of Hawaii. An old bloke, but game as Ned Kelly, they said.'

'Even so,' said Dave, 'staying out for five hours on this coast in November is asking for trouble at your age, man. What are you trying to prove?'

Ken took the good-natured ribbing as the price of a hot drink and stayed to play a few hands of *belote* – a French card game which the two Queenslanders had picked up locally. They told him that a storm was forecast far out in the Atlantic that night. Having travelled all the way from California to Europe in the hope of riding the Big One, they intended giving up next day if it did not arrive – and heading somewhere warmer.

Ken's board was too long to take with him on the Harley. He left it with a friendly local shopkeeper, bought some food for an evening meal and headed home through the monotonously flat pine forests of Les Landes. The road was one he could have driven blindfolded. The bike cruised effortlessly at speeds way above the legal limit, its 1340cc engine throbbing away comfortingly. Although criticised by some hard-line Harley-Davidson fans for looking too Japanese, with its triangulated frame design around the battery box, the FXRT was a dream for which Ken had gone overboard the first time he rode it, trading in his 883cc Harley Sportster on the spot.

In the high beam from the Harley's single headlamp, the road stretched straight ahead for miles without a bend, the trees rushed by, the white lines flashed past and the world was somewhere else. The Harley came equipped with a superb stereo which was feeding Ella Fitzgerald's version of *Summertime* into the headphones of his helmet. Life was not the way he had planned it, but Kenneth Wilson Scott was not complaining. While he could not echo her sentiment that the living was easy, his fiftieth year was turning out to be more fun than he would ever have dreamed, during all the time he worked in MI5. Whenever he felt bitter at the way the Security Service had treated him, he rode the Harley to the beach and forgot everything except the waves and staying alive.

Le Farou, the half-derelict complex of buildings in which he lived, was a fourteenth-century fortified manor house which he had bought three years before with the copper handshake of redundancy and the intention of converting the extensive outbuildings into lettable holiday apartments, to compensate for the heavily discounted pension he received from Her Majesty's Government.

The buildings stood on a low rise in the valley of the

Dordogne, not far from the town of Bergerac. They were in the form of an easily defended hollow square, with the living quarters facing the only entrance, which was a large archway, high enough for men on horseback or loaded waggons to pass comfortably through. Beneath the newly rebuilt roof of the three wings that had accommodated the stables, the dairy and the hay barn, there was enough space for a dozen or more family-sized self-catering apartments. On the plans, which Ken had drawn up himself, the courtyard area was dominated by a large swimming pool with terrace and a poolside bar. The artist's impression pinned to the wall of Ken's kitchen showed bikini-clad waitresses serving drinks to happy holidaymakers at tables beneath Campari sun-umbrellas.

With less than six months to go before the hoped-for arrival of the first paying guests, the reality was a sea of mud, broken by a few islands of building materials protected by plastic sheeting flapping in the wind. Building costs in France had escalated and the pound sterling was worth less, not more, than when Ken had started the project. Only grim determination made progress possible. To cut costs, Ken worked as labourer to the building tradesmen on the site, digging ditches for drains himself, carrying tiles up ladders to the roof in order to avoid hiring machinery, mixing cement for the masons, laying concrete floors, fetching and carrying, and doing most of the plumbing and re-wiring on his own.

There was no money for the pool, but much of the structural work was finished and the first two apartments would at least be habitable the following summer. Gambling that he could make enough money from letting them to part-finish two more for the year after – in a self-financing programme that should see the whole project through to completion in ten years' time – Ken had thrown all his remaining capital into the first pair, with the exception of a small advertising budget which he had put on one side. The hard work enabled him to forget, most of the time, the ignominy of being made redundant from a job at which he was better than most – and for a reason which still made him angry.

He parked the Harley in what had been the hay barn, beside

his Toyota Land Cruiser. His own living quarters had few mod cons apart from some new plumbing and a few UK-type electrical sockets that he had installed. The kitchen fire, banked up in the morning before he left for the coast, had gone out. The house was cold, damp and unwelcoming. Ken arranged some vine twig kindling in the hearth with progressively thicker logs on top, and threw in a match after spreading his wet suit inside-out to dry over a couple of chairs.

Retrieving a bag of shopping that he had left in a pannier on the Harley, he was halfway back across the yard when he saw, through the archway, a light in one of the row of small cottages where the farm workers of Le Farou had lived before mechanisation drove them all off the land.

There was an unspoken pact between Ken and the tenant of the cottage that neither would ever assume they were automatically welcome in the other's home, so he knocked on the cottage door and waited. In the darkness a pair of baleful yellow eyes watched him from a distance: Satan the all-black cat did not like men – perhaps because of the local vet, who had done him permanent damage. Inside the cottage, the facile patter of a DJ on *France Inter* was turned down and a rich Irish contralto voice called, 'You can come in. It's not locked.'

Satan slipped inside and took up a defensive position on the bed before Ken was properly into the single multi-purpose room. He had knocked out the dividing wall which had originally separated the kitchen and bedroom, in order to make a combined studio and living room/bedroom for his tenant. Boldly coloured abstract landscapes done in oils on canvas covered most of the available wall space. The cheap wooden furniture was painted in the same bright primary colours, but the brightest thing in the room was the slim, auburn-headed woman with green eyes who was seated at an easel.

Catriona O'Riordan rested her palette and brushes on her knee and looked pleased to see Ken. 'You're home early. What happened? Did the sea dry up?'

The painting in front of her was a head-and-shoulders portrait of Ken. It showed a man just on the right side of fifty, whose quizzical smile was at odds with his flinty grey eyes and grizzled hair cut very short and close to the head.

'Haven't you finished my picture yet?' he asked.

'What do you expect? Since you keep disappearing as soon as there's a wave big enough to drown a mouse, I have to work from memory most of the time, don't I?'

Ken pulled Catriona to her feet, to feel her warm body against him. Even in a pair of old jeans and her paint-stained cotton smock, she was a stunningly beautiful woman. Standing five-foot-ten, her face was nearly level with his. He kissed her on the lips and buried his face in her red hair, sighing, 'I must be crazy to spend the whole day on a fibreglass surfboard in cold salt water when I could have been lying in a warm bed with a hot-blooded woman like you.'

'Who gave you the option, I'd like to know?' she challenged him, her hands still occupied with brushes and palette.

'I love your perfume, Mrs O'Riordan.'

'I'm not wearing any, Mr Scott.'

'Turps,' he said. 'In twenty years' time, the smell of turps will still remind me of you.'

'When I'm long gone out of your life? Is that what you meant?' She elbowed him roughly down onto a chair. 'Now just stay still, damn you, while I work on your eyes. I can't get them right.'

'They look fine to me,' Ken protested.

'Oh, it's the way you look,' she agreed. 'But it's not the way I see you. Those are two very different things.'

He poured himself a drink from the bottle of Jameson's on the table and toasted her. 'Just as well you were born Irish. Only a Celtic brain could handle thoughts like that.'

She worked with intense concentration, gripping between her teeth the brushes she was not using. Ken let the warmth from the stove seep into him. He had long ago stopped using the word *home*, but he felt good around Catriona. Sometimes they went for three or four days without more than waving to each other across the field, yet when she was not there Le Farou seemed to him a very lonely place. Despite Satan's habit of making the point from time to time that he was an intruder by jumping onto his knee and deliberately digging his claws in, Ken felt more peaceful in the cottage of this unpredictable Irish redhead than he had with any of his three wives or the women he had known in between.

Half an hour later, Catriona sat back looking satisfied.

'What have you done?' Ken asked.

Cleaning oil paint from her hands with a turps-soaked rag, Catriona looked from model to picture and back again. 'What I'd painted from memory were maybe a copper's eyes, looking at the world and seeing sin and secrets everywhere. Now, with those last few deft touches of my brush, so to speak, I've managed to turn them into your eyes, looking at me.'

'It's good,' he decided. 'People pay fortunes for good portraits. Why don't you stick to doing them?'

'They pay money for portraits that flatter them,' she corrected him.

'Isn't that the same thing?'

'It is not, Mr Scott. Lacking the technique to tell lies on canvas, I paint my sitters as I see them, warts and all.'

'And those?' He pointed at the wall, covered in the big pictures she called abstract landscapes. 'If that's what you see when you look out of the window, you must need glasses.'

'People buy them,' she said.

The smell of turpentine filled the room as she stood up, stuffed the cleaning rag into a plastic bag and grabbed Ken's glass, to swallow the inch of whiskey remaining. He came to stand behind her and put his hands around her slim waist. 'Have you got any food in the house, Cat?'

'Food?' She tore her eyes from the portrait.

'Enough to fill the belly of a hungry man?'

'I'm nobody's wife, Mr Scott. If you're hungry, look in the cupboard to see what the mice have left, while I get cleaned up.'

The shower cubicle was at the end of an obstacle course: the last paintings for Catriona's show which opened in London in a few days' time were stacked against the wall, drying. She picked her way around them with a towel and some clean clothes over her arm. About to pull the curtain of the shower cubicle, she saw Ken watching her and thought about the message she could read in his eyes, then shook her head with a smile.

'After a day spent slaving over a hot easel, I need to shake the kinks out of my spine with a good shower first. So you'll have to wait, Mr Scott.'

She swirled the curtain closed behind her. Ken threw a couple of logs into the stove and opened the draught; after spending half a windy November day in water with a temperature of around eight degrees, he needed to feel heat on his skin and food in his belly.

The wind was making the shutters bang. Leaning out of the window to close them, he realised that the fire he had lit in his own house would soon burn out. He thought briefly of running across the field to build it up for the night, but he could hear Catriona singing an Irish folk song under the shower. While he did not understand the language, he did recognise the symptom: it was unlikely he would be going back to his own house that night, so what did it matter if the fire went out?

'An omelette?' Catriona sat down at the wooden table which Ken had scrubbed clean of paint. It was cramped between the easel and the stove but in the light of the two candles he had lit and the glow coming from the open hearth, it looked warm and welcoming. 'Can't you cook anything else, Mr Scott?'

'All you had in the pantry was a bit of cheese and some stale bread. Luckily I did some shopping at Guéthary before setting out on the way home.'

'So what have you put in this?'

'*Cèpes*,' he said. 'I fried them in butter with parsley and garlic first.'

'*Cordon bleu*,' she announced after the first mouthful. She closed her eyes and inhaled the bouquet of the wine he had brought with him. 'And where's this nectar from, I'd like to know? St Emilion or the Médoc?'

Ken laughed. 'It's from South Australia, Cat. I won it at Guéthary in a game of cards with two surf bums from Oz.'

'The French had better watch out.' Catriona swallowed, put

down her glass and opened her eyes. She put out her hands to Ken and intertwined her fingers with his. 'Sometimes I think I almost know what being loved is.'

'What's it like?' Across the table from him, Catriona's auburn hair glowed in the candlelight, her green eyes sparkled, and the freckles on her cheeks stood out. Her only make-up was a dash of orange lipstick. The ankle-length plain brown woollen dress, belted at the waist and gathered at the wrists, was absorbing the candlelight, concentrating Ken's eyes on her softly lit face and her hands. The long fingers which were interlocked with his ended in wide, spatulate nails with traces of paint still lodged beneath them.

'It's maybe having a man arrive with a heavenly bottle of wine at the end of a long day's painting,' she smiled. 'And him cooking a great omelette and looking at me across the table like he hadn't had a woman in years.'

She leaned forward, studying Ken's eyes. 'You know something, dammit? Your portrait will never be finished, because your face changes so much. I'd sell my soul if I could put on canvas the way you're looking at me right now, Ken.'

The phone rang. It was an extension of the line from the farmhouse, which Ken had rigged up to save Catriona having to pay for a line of her own.

'Leave it,' he said.

'It might be important. I have to confess, I left the damned thing unplugged all day while I was painting.' She listened for a moment and then held out the receiver. 'It's for you. Someone called Ivor Morgan.'

'Never heard of him. Tell him I'm not in.'

She listened, then covered the mouthpiece with her hand. 'Someone's died. A Mrs Prescot, who used to teach your son the violin. Mr Morgan's her solicitor. I think you'd better talk to him.'

'You're not asleep, Ken?'

'I'm thinking.'

'About that poor old lady being knocked down?'

'Not so much about her. More about Irving.'

'Have you really never met your own son face to face?'

'Oh, I've been to hear him play many times. Even with cloth ears, I remember being stunned the first time – although Mrs Prescot had told me how good he was. He played the Elgar Violin Concerto with the Merseyside Youth Orchestra in the Liverpool Philharmonic Hall. He must have been fourteen at the time, and the newspapers were talking of another Menuhin.'

'And yet you never made contact?'

'I thought about it,' Ken sighed. 'But, knowing Marlene – his mother – I could imagine the stories she must have fed to the kid.'

'Like what, for example?'

'That I deserted her when she was pregnant and never gave her any money. That sort of thing.'

'And would they have been true, these stories?' Catriona wondered.

'I was nineteen when we got married, Cat. Marlene was only eighteen. I didn't even know she was pregnant until after the boy was born. And when I did find out, there was no particular reason to suspect that Irving was my child. That's why we broke up. That and the drink. Marlene grew up in a pub run by her father in Wallasey. She drank like a fish before I even knew her. I suppose that's what happened to the money I used to send her for the boy.'

'And will you go back to England for the funeral?'

'Apparently Mrs Prescot particularly requested it in her Will. It seems mean not to go, after all she did for Irving.'

'Well, perhaps the funeral will give you the chance to get to know your famous son at last.'

'I don't even know what kind of man he is.'

.2.

Eyes closed, the swimmer back-stroked his way up the open-air pool on the roof of the Intercontinental Hotel in Abu Dhabi, replaying in his head the last few bars of the Brahms Violin Concerto. At 1.30 a.m. local time, he was the only person in the water.

The performance that evening had been given by an under-rehearsed Japanese orchestra conducted by a Frenchman with an English soloist, playing German music for an audience from every corner of the world. And yet the audience had applauded wildly and brought Irving back for two encores. Probably only the musicians in the orchestra had appreciated that the entire concerto had been a battle of wills between him and the con-ductor, with Irving pushing the tempo to what he knew was right, while the man with the stick tried to drag the orchestra back to his leaden tempo at every opportunity.

Swimming after a performance usually relaxed Irving's brain and muscles, but tonight the inner tension would not subside. It was a compound of overtiredness and anger with himself for not having played better, despite all the problems. He had caught the plane from Singapore to Abu Dhabi twenty hours ago, to arrive at the magnificent new concert hall and find the orchestra sitting on the platform, patiently waiting for their parts and instruments which had gone astray somewhere between Tokyo and the Gulf.

At the end of a three-week global tour, spending more time in aircraft seats than hotel beds, Irving could have done without that kind of problem. The concert had been saved, literally at the last moment, by the promoter sending his private 747 to Karachi where the music had been offloaded by mistake. As usual, the public had never even known of the drama backstage.

Making a mental note to call his agent in the morning and refuse to work ever again with the French conductor, Irving heaved himself out of the pool. The Lebanese pool attendant handed him a hot towel. Irving glanced at the woman reclining on the poolside lounger, sipping a glass of iced Pepsi. In her early forties, with a full figure, dark good looks and hungry eyes, she had been in the front row at the concert, dressed in ball gown, necklace and tiara. Beside her had been sitting a little man, the lapels of whose evening coat were covered with medals. At the diplomatic reception afterwards, she had cornered Irving and revealed that she was the wife of a Latin American consul. It had not surprised him when she turned up at the hotel shortly after he got back there, this time in a red satin cocktail dress, with an evening shawl draped over her shoulders, in deference to Arab sensibilities.

Rich and bored women of her sort often pursued famous musicians – not that Irving was complaining. Each one he bedded was a mile-post, recording how far he had travelled up the social ladder from the backstreets of Liverpool where he had grown up.

The consul's wife, who had not said a word since arriving at the poolside, let her gaze slide down Irving's well-muscled arms and chest to the bulge of his crotch, revealed by the clinging wet bathing shorts. The haughty look in his dark brown eyes she recognised as the arrogance of a man used to getting his own way most of the time. When she crossed her legs, the rasp of her stockings rubbing against each other carried clearly across the still water of the pool. Any minute now, Irving thought, she's going to start purring.

'Mr Bradley, sir.' The attendant spoke with the lack of urgency of those used to serving mega-buck clients, for whom there was never any reason to hurry. 'The switchboard is holding a call for you. Will you take it here or shall I tell them to keep it on hold until you get back to your room?'

'I'll take it here.'

The attendant padded away and returned with a cordless phone. The Scouse accent at the other end had to have originated in the area of Liverpool where Irving had grown up. To outsiders, all Merseyside accents sound the same; to a native, each is specific to a particular part of town. Trying to put a name to the voice, Irving faced away from the woman across the pool, whose hungry stare was beginning to turn him on.

'Who's calling?' he asked.

'Ivor Morgan's the name. You probably don't recall me, but we used to go to school together.'

'I remember. What are you doing in Abu Dhabi, boyo?'

There was an echo and delay on the line. 'I should be so lucky, Irv. I'm calling from darkest Merseyside.'

'What can I do for you?'

'I'm Mrs P's solicitor. I've been trying to reach you for hours. I got the number of the hotel from your agent in London. There's some bad news for you: the old lady was knocked down by a car, late last night.'

'Is she badly hurt?'

'I'm afraid she was killed outright.' After thirty seconds of silence, Ivor Morgan asked, 'Are you still there?'

'Yes.' Irving was stunned. His brain kept repeating the message: Mrs P is dead. Mrs P is dead.

'I know how important she was to you, and I'm truly sorry to have to give you this news.' Morgan cleared his throat. 'I've fixed the funeral for the day after tomorrow, to give you time to get here. Is that all right?'

Irving glanced at his wristwatch. The only person in the entire world for whom he truly cared, was dead. It seemed a mammoth problem to work out how long it would take to get from Abu Dhabi to Liverpool. *Mrs P is dead.*

'I'm due in London tomorrow evening,' he said at last. 'That's the first plane, so I can't get there any earlier. I'll call you for the details of the funeral as soon as I touch down at Heathrow.'

In the respectable Merseyside suburb of Crosby, Morgan put down the phone.

'How did he take the news?' his wife asked from the other side of the bed.

'Badly, I'd say. The old lady was like father and mother to Irv. Until she started teaching him the fiddle, he was just another street kid, forever in and out of trouble with the police.'

'Well, you can relax now. Come to sleep.'

Morgan yawned. 'I didn't bother to tell Irv that the old lady's home had been broken into as well.'

'Had they taken much?'

'As far as I could see, nothing. The only things of value she had were her instruments, and they hadn't been touched.'

'If it was kids, they'd have just taken her cash.'

Morgan laughed. 'She didn't have much.'

'What about all those famous pupils of hers? Didn't they pay for her lessons?'

'Some did. Mostly she taught – as we used to say – for love.'

On the bedside cabinet, that day's edition of the *Liverpool Daily Post* was folded open to show the obituary notice:

Mrs Madeleine Prescot, well known as the violin teacher who produced more than twenty professional players during a teaching career that spanned fifty years in Liverpool, was knocked down and killed in Sefton Park last night by a vehicle which did not stop. The accident occurred near the junction of Lark Lane and Croxteth Road at 10.12 p.m. The police are appealing for witnesses, or anyone who may have information about a dark car with one shattered headlight, which could have been in the area at the time. Mrs P, as she was universally and fondly known to generations of pupils and their parents, was born in France. But little is known of her early life before she arrived in Liverpool as a war bride. Her husband, Geoff Prescot, a professional photographer, set up his studio in Lark Lane after being demobbed from the Intelligence Corps in 1946.

Mrs Prescot left no known relatives. Her most famous ex-pupil, Irving Bradley, was not available for comment, as he is currently on tour in the Gulf States.

Morgan switched out the bedside light. 'Irving's going to be mad as hell at me when he sees Ken Scott at the funeral.'

'So why did you invite Scott?'

'It was written into the Will. Mrs P wanted them both to be there.'

'Why?'

'Don't ask me to read my clients' minds. My job is to carry out their instructions. But actually, she said when I was drawing up the Will that Scott paid for Irving's lessons and was, I quote, a good man, unquote. I had the idea that she thought the quiet moment at the graveside might be a good time and place to reconcile them.'

'Perhaps it will,' his wife yawned. 'At Irving's age, it's a bit stupid still to hate your father because of a divorce that happened before you were even born.'

'Irv's not the sort to forget a grudge. At school he had a temper that made him a killer. And I doubt if all the pressures of a soloist's life have made him any more easy-going.'

Four time zones to the east, Irving Bradley finished drying himself. The night air was mild. He slipped into the bath robe which the attendant was holding out.

Mrs P is dead. Mrs P is dead.

As he walked past the table where the consul's wife was sitting he held his key so that she could see the room number on the tag. He did not want her for sex, but he needed to talk to someone like a stranger on a train or in a plane: she would do. When she pushed the door open a couple of minutes later, he was sitting on the bed, his head in both hands.

'The phone call?' she said. 'You had some bad news?'

As the sky lightened with the dawn and the heat and humidity built up outside the air-conditioned hotel, Irving was still telling her about growing up in a damp, rented house with broken windows, where the electricity was cut off for half the winter because his mother had spent the money for the bill on bottles of cheap wine from the corner off-licence.

The word was not in the vocabulary of a diplomat's wife.

'*¿Qué quiere decir* off-licence?'

'A take-out liquor store,' Irving explained.

'And was your father a drunkard as well?'

'He left before I was born.'

'So you were brought up by another man?'

'Men. My mother went through quite a few.'

Irving's childhood had been good preparation for the concert platform, with its daily cut and thrust during rehearsals, which the audience never saw, and the clashes of naked will-power between conductor and soloist in the green room. As he talked, the woman beside him tried to reconcile conflicting images of this strange man with whom she was spending the night. They ranged from the street kid, growing up in grim poverty, to the jet-set soloist in white tie and tails, applauded by the glitterati on every continent.

'In the programme notes last night,' she said, 'I am learning that you studied at the Juilliard School in New York. So what is this story of a little music teacher in Liverpool?'

'Mrs P was my first teacher. Before going to New York, I spent six years at the Mozart School for prodigies in Birmingham. But without Mrs P, I'd never have got to the Mozart. Come to that, I'd never have touched a bow, or tucked a fiddle under my chin either.'

He was remembering the years at the Mozart School when he had gone back to Liverpool each weekend and walked ten miles from Lime Street station and back, just so he could spend a couple of hours with her, going through everything he had learned that week. Even at the Juilliard, whenever he had flown back to England, he would head north to play all the new pieces in his repertoire for her opinion.

'She's the keeper of my musical conscience,' he said. 'And now she's dead.'

The ambassador's wife was kneeling in front of him on the floor, her fingers undoing the belt of the bathrobe. Why not? Irving thought. Sex was as good a way to forget as any other.

Afterwards, he lay thinking of the day when, aged thirteen, he had been caught by the police, organising a gang of boys to steal from local shops. At the juvenile court hearing, it had been Mrs P as character witness who kept him out of Borstal.

The probation officer had been a tired and disillusioned man of the old school who did not believe in being messed about by young hoodlums. He had been quite explicit: 'Miss one appointment with me or one lesson with Mrs Prescot and I'll wash my hands of you, Bradley. Then you'll be in deep shit. Is that understood?'

What had scared Irving most was not the probation officer's threats, nor the judge's warning. It was Mrs P saying quietly in her French accent, 'If you do anything like that again, I shall not give you another lesson, ever.'

By then it had been unthinkable to stop learning from her. But how had Mrs P guessed in the first place that a young neighbourhood scruff, whose only previous ambition had been to become a latter-day Merseyside Al Capone, wanted to learn the fiddle? More importantly, how had she known he had the necessary talent?

It was just after his ninth birthday that he had been looking into Geoff Prescot's photographic shop in Lark Lane, trying to work out how to steal a camera from the window display. An upstairs window was open and through it he heard the sound of the violin for the first time in his life. The piece Mrs Prescot was playing was one that Irving was to perform many times – the Bruch Concerto in G Minor – but that morning the music had had no name for him, just a strange, almost sexual compulsion.

Geoff Prescot had come out of the shop, intrigued by the expression on the face of the pale-faced boy in dirty, ill-fitting second-hand clothes who was listening so intently to the music.

'D'you like the sound, lad?' he had asked.

Irving had glared at him, uncertain how to handle normal civility. 'It's a'right,' he admitted gruffly.

'You'd best come in.' Geoff Prescot held the shop door open. 'You'll hear a lot better than from out 'ere in't street. But I'll not ask you again. Make your mind up.'

Seeing it as an opportunity to make a reconnaissance of the shop and its contents, Irving squared his shoulders, and said, 'All right then, mister. I'll come in.'

The maisonette above the shop seemed like luxury to him

and the strange couple living there – the big man with the gentle Lancashire voice and his diminutive wife with her foreign accent – were like aliens from another planet. When Irving walked out two hours later, he was carrying his first violin in a case under his arm.

'Worravyer got there?' a gang of older boys had shouted threateningly as he was crossing some wasteland on the way home.

'Keep yer 'ands off,' he had yelled back at them. 'It's a fiddle and it's mine. Touch it and I'll smash yer faces in.'

. 3 .

In the strong westerly wind that was driving the drizzle horizontally, slowly soaking the clothes of the few mourners, one of the undertaker's men was having difficulty holding an umbrella over the priest's head. At the thanksgiving service in the local church, several hundred people had been present, but only a handful had followed the hearse to the cemetery, where Ken stood beside Ivor Morgan, sharing his umbrella.

Irving was a little way off, in the lee of a Victorian Gothic tomb whose angels had been decapitated by local vandals. He was taking shelter not for himself but for the violin. In the church he had played 'Air on the G String' and the Meditation from *Thaïs*, which had moved many in the congregation to tears. But this was a private farewell. At the end of the unaccompanied Bach partita, he lowered the violin and placed it in its secure flight case, then turned back to the scene at the grave, where the priest was walking away, with Ivor Morgan and the other mourners following. Only Ken still remained, bareheaded beside the mountain of red and white carnations which was Irving's offering, watching the grave-diggers remove the green plastic imitation grass mats and expose the wet mud, preparatory to filling in the hole.

When they had been introduced by Morgan in the vestry at the church, Irving had refused point-blank to let Ken stay for the service until reminded by the solicitor that it was Mrs Prescot's expressed wish that they should both be present at her funeral.

Well, since you're here, Mr Scott, he thought, you might as well make yourself useful.

He picked up the violin case and walked between the graves, right hand outstretched in apology. 'I went over the top when we met. I wasn't expecting to see you here.'

'Forget it,' Ken replied. 'That yell had been waiting a long time to be let out.'

They stood face to face in the drizzle, two hard men, neither of whom was used to backing down. The resemblance ended there. Ken's face was tanned by wind and weather, while Irving had the soft complexion of a musician who spends long hours indoors throughout the year, performing and practising. In contrast with his shock of long black hair, the pale skin of his face seemed nearly white.

The clothes echoed his natural colouring: a white Hugo Boss trench coat over a black polo-neck sweater from Pierre Cardin and black Armani trousers. Extremely clothes-conscious, he was distinctly unimpressed by the way Ken was dressed. Having thrown away most of his suits, shirts and ties on beginning his new life in France, Ken was wearing the only garments he had left which were suitable for a funeral: a nondescript dark grey overcoat and a well-worn grey suit which was a relic from his time as a wage-slave with MI5.

'I didn't even know you knew Mrs P,' Irving said.

'I kept in touch with her over the years.'

'Morgan told me on the way here that you paid her for all the lessons I had.' Irving glanced down at the coffin, now half-covered with shovelfuls of yellow mud. 'Mrs P used to say that I had a mysterious benefactor. I suppose she got that idea from *Great Expectations*.'

'She got it from me,' Ken said. 'I thought that if you knew who was paying you might have gone right off music. And I didn't want that to happen.'

'You were right,' Irving admitted. 'When Marlene wanted to bad-mouth someone, she did a thorough job. I suppose I was still looking for the horns and tail when I sounded off at you in the vestry.'

He handed a £20 note to each of the grave-diggers and led the way in silence towards the exit from the cemetery. Ken was wishing that he knew enough about straight music to make some intelligent remark about what Irving had just played. Would that have bridged the gap between him and this son he had never known?

The rest of the cortège had already departed. They got into the single black Rolls which was still waiting. To break the silence, Ken said, 'I suppose you'll be heading back to London after Morgan's read the Will tomorrow morning?'

Irving nodded. 'I've got a full concert schedule for the next week and then a big recording session for my new label spread over the following ten days. Frankly the reading of the Will is a nuisance. I could do with getting back to the Smoke today. There's nothing to hang around for, is there? But Morgan was adamant. We both have to wait here until tomorrow morning. It was Mrs P's wish, so I'll go along with it, out of respect for her. But frankly, I can't see what she had in mind.'

For several minutes as the Rolls glided smoothly back towards the city centre, neither man spoke. The driver was taking the least congested route into town, through Sefton Park. Near where the accident had occurred, they drove past a police notice board appealing for witnesses to come forward.

'I want that bastard caught, you know,' Irving said.

'The driver who knocked her down?'

'Yes.'

'At ten p.m., he was probably slewed and shit-scared when he realised what he had done.' Ken looked at the tense, pale face beside him. 'Frankly, it's pure chance whether they catch a hit-and-run driver when there's not even a number plate to go on.'

'Fuck the police,' said Irving. He studied Ken out of the corner of his eye. 'If I want something done, I pay for it myself. Supposing I write a cheque here and now for whatever your weekly fee is, will you do it?'

'I'm not a private investigator.'

'Marlene told me when I was a kid that you worked for MI5. If you were any good at all at catching spies, I should think finding a hit-and-run driver would be a push-over.'

'It's not the same job. The local CID . . .'

'How much?' Irving asked. Influenced by Ken's cheap clothes and unassuming manners, he halved the sum he had been going to offer: 'Is a thousand a week okay?'

The Rolls crawled up the ramp of the Adelphi Hotel, where a liveried doorman opened the door for Irving to alight. Taking his time, he used a gold Parker pen to write a cheque for £4,000, which he handed to Ken. 'Four week's work. If you need more for expenses, just let me know. I'll see you at Morgan's office in the morning.'

Ken was by no means certain that he would have any better luck than the police in tracing a hit-and-run driver. He was about to hand back the cheque when he changed his mind. From what he had seen of Irving Bradley so far, he had all the arrogance of an international tennis-player or Olympic athlete. There were probably few ways through the defences of such a person, but the affection he obviously felt for his old teacher might be one.

'It's a deal,' Ken said. 'But I don't want your money.'

'Don't mess about.' Irving grabbed his hand and shook it with a surprisingly hard grip. 'Frankly you look as though you could do with the cash. And you'll be doing me a big favour, taking this job on. Find the bastard who killed Mrs P and I'll consider the cash well spent.'

Ken stood on the rain-lashed Pier Head, from which a handful of the once numerous ferries still plied their way across the ebbing Mersey. On the Wirral side of the estuary where he had grown up, nothing seemed to have changed in the grey murk. On the Liverpool side of the water the Albert Dock had been converted into a tourist complex, with a restaurant overlooking the quayside. Only the huge ugly bulk of the Liver Building seemed untouched by the hand of progress.

Inside the new Merseyside Police Headquarters, a harassed traffic superintendent wanted to get rid of his visitor as swiftly as possible. He hardly looked at Ken's out-of-date ID card.

'We've got the car,' he said. 'A black Ford Granada. That was the easy bit. It was stolen in Southport three hours before the old lady was run down – and abandoned right afterwards. Joy riders, probably – kids who'd had a few drinks. The damage corresponds and the blood groups match those of the victim and her dog.'

There were, he said, no fingerprints. Whoever had driven the Granada had been wearing gloves, and left nothing inside the vehicle. But there were a couple of other leads: two black youths who had been running in the park had arrived on the scene within seconds, as the driver was reversing back towards the body, and . . .

'There's an old codger who lives a few doors away from the victim. He memorised the number of a blue Rover he saw leaving the scene of the accident at speed. Trouble is, it was the wrong car. The driver was a printer's rep from Wallasey by name of Dewhurst.'

'Why didn't he stop?'

The superintendent chuckled. 'His passenger was his boss's wife, who was supposed to be somewhere else at the time. Dewhurst didn't want to risk her husband getting to hear what he had been up to.'

Ken drove his Land Cruiser through the tunnel under the Mersey to Wallasey. At the printing works, the receptionist had the same name on her desk as the proprietor, so Ken guessed that she had been the passenger on the fatal night. Dewhurst, she told him, was out making calls and not expected back for an hour or so. Since she already looked sick with worry and her husband was prowling suspiciously in the background, Ken left her alone and killed the time by driving into Birkenhead. He walked along the streets near the Cammel Laird shipyard where he had been apprenticed on leaving school at sixteen. Apart from the accent in the voices, there was nothing to remind him of his childhood. The house in which he had grown up had been demolished.

After three years as an apprentice in the yard where his father and grandfather had spent all their working lives, Ken had been eager to get away from the grime and the poverty. Finding his wife in bed with his best friend had been simply the last straw which drove him to enlist. Now, even the recruiting office where he had signed on for five years in the Army – and unwittingly taken his first step towards a career in MI5 – was closed and boarded up.

Dewhurst proved to be a prematurely bald, chain-smoking man of thirty-five who confirmed his statement to the police that he had been driving in the opposite direction to the car which hit the old lady, and was approximately a hundred metres away at the time of impact. He was plainly terrified of losing his job if called to give evidence at the inquest, and added little to what he had already told the Merseyside police.

'I can't afford to be called as a witness,' he pleaded with Ken. 'I've got a wife and kids. I need my job.'

'Then help me, and I'll disappear like a bad dream in the morning.'

He and the woman had had a few drinks, Dewhurst admitted. That was another reason he had not stopped. His reactions slowed by alcohol, he had not realised what he was seeing until he had already driven past the body lying in the road. The car that hit the old lady was a new black Granada Ghia, with one white male passenger; the driver was also a white male. No attempt had been made to avoid the little old lady and her dog.

Back on the Liverpool side of the Mersey, Ken headed for the address of the two youths who had been running in the park. In the area of town that he remembered as Granby Street, the old slums had been knocked down and the residents re-housed, more or less in the same spot, in some urban planner's idea of better housing. Neither runner was at home. He tracked them down in an echoing Victorian cotton warehouse at the bottom of Parliament Hill, where they were working out in a gym with not a single white face in sight.

'We already made a statement,' they told him sullenly.

'This is different. I'm not a copper.' Ken led them over to a bar selling soft drinks in one corner and took two £20 notes from his wallet, laying them on the counter. 'I'd like to know what you didn't tell the boys in blue.'

'What makes you think there is anything else?'

Ken turned up his Merseyside accent. 'Since when did you guys ever talk to a white copper, then? Or a black one for that matter? If you want my money, tell me what you actually saw – and don't piss me about.'

The taller of the two said, 'It wasn't much.'

From the interaction between them, Ken thought he was the dominant one, so he ignored the other. 'The car was a blue Rover, right?' he prompted.

'Nah, it was a black Granada Ghia.'

'Did you see the number?'

'Couldn't. The number plates was covered with mud.'

'Did you get a look at the driver?'

'Nope.'

'That's all?'

'Yeah.'

Ken could smell collusion, stronger than the pungent odour of sweat and liniment in the air. He grabbed back the two bank notes.

'Hey, come on!' the taller one protested. 'You said . . .'

'I said not to piss me around.' Ken put away the two twenties and pulled out two £50 notes instead. 'Does this make a difference?'

A look passed between the two, then the taller one said, 'We go out for a run in the park most nights. We'd see that old lady always taking her pooch for a crap at the same time – ten o'clock, give or take a few minutes. And, like, we reckoned the two blokes in the Granada had been waiting for her to cross the road.'

'What makes you say that?'

'They was parked in the lay-by a couple of hundred metres away. And when the driver accelerated from a standing start, he sort of skidded in the wet leaves, like. We was wearing our Walkmans. It was the revving of the engine that made us look that way in time to see him run her down. Otherwise we wouldn't have seen nothing.'

'Why didn't you mention any of this to the police?'

'If you was us, would you get involved?'

Ken handed over the two banknotes. 'Thanks, lads.'

'You'll keep that to yourself then, boss?'

Ken nodded.

In the early dusk, the street lighting was just coming on as he pulled up where Mrs Prescot had died. With a photocopy of the police plan in his hand, it was easy to visualise the scene as it had been. There was only one street lamp in working order in two hundred metres. If the Granada had been parked in the lay-by, as the black runners had said, it would have been practically invisible to passing cars. The lay-by itself was actually a turn-off for a road across the park that had never been made. Judging by the number of used condoms among the piled-up wet leaves, it was used mostly as a lover's lane.

From the tool kit of the Land Cruiser, Ken took a torch and used it to search among the piled-up dead leaves and refuse. It was hard to be certain, but one set of tyre tracks, which were deeper than the others in the damp leaf mould, belonged to a heavy car with new tyres, and could have been made by the Granada. There was a small pile of soggy cigarette stubs near where the passenger door would have been, when it was parked. They were all Marlboro Lights.

Ken backed the Land Cruiser into the lay-by and parked level with the stubs. Accelerating from a standing start, he found that even the all-terrain Desert Dueller tyres on the Land Cruiser skidded at first in the damp leaf mould, before getting a grip on the cobbles beneath – which bore out the runners' story.

The moist tobacco smell of the stubs in his palm made Ken yearn for a cigarette for the first time in months. If the accident that had cost Mrs Prescot's life had not been an accident, perhaps the burglary of her maisonette was not what it seemed, either . . .

The words GEOFF PRESCOT, *Industrial and Portrait Photography* were still visible in faded black sign-writing on the shopfront above the poorly lettered silk-screened poster stuck across the boarded-up window that read *Ace Rentals – Latest Adult Videos. Rent One, Get One Free!*

The door leading up to the maisonette where Mrs Prescot had lived and taught for fifty years had a new pane of glass with fresh putty showing round the edge. Ken had hardly parked his car outside when the neighbour who had reported the break-in was giving him a complete account.

'I 'eard 'em breaking in,' he was saying. 'It must have been about half an hour after the accident.'

'Why didn't you call the police then?'

'I thought it were some kids smashing a street light, you know what I mean? It was only when I was going out to get me ciggies next morning, that I noticed the glass in Mrs P's front door was broken, like.'

'Any idea who did it?'

'Aye. It was them kids that hang out in the park at night, sniffing glue, smoking pot and shooting up in the empty house at the end of the road.'

'D'you know what they took?'

'They'd be after her cash – to buy drugs, like.'

Ken drove back to Merseyside Police Headquarters, down by the old docks. At the end of her long working day, the female detective who had been called to the break-in still had the shrewdness to try and get a closer look at his ID. He put on a superior-officer brusqueness and slipped the card back into his wallet. She had worded her report to suggest that the incident was a routine breaking and entering by local kids.

'Don't shit me,' Ken said. 'I spoke to the neighbour who reported the break-in. He says he heard broken glass about thirty minutes after the accident. If it was kids taking advantage of the old lady's death, they were damned fast off the mark, weren't they?'

'Give me a break, Mr Scott.' The DC lifted a pile of incident report forms several inches thick from her desk. 'That's just this week.'

'Off the record,' said Ken.

'You're right,' she shrugged. 'If it had been local kids, they'd have nicked the telly and the hi-fi – and probably crapped on the old lady's bed or in her underwear drawer. Whoever did this job was a pro. In and out in five minutes or less.'

In a quiet pub at the south end of the Dock Road, Ken bought a pint of bitter and a packet of Silk Cut cigarettes. For the first time since he had been fired by MI5, he realised that he was hooked again – both on smoking and on the peculiar satisfaction of ferreting out the hidden details of people's lives. If the high from cigarettes came with the first one of the day, the kick in his work was harder to achieve and even harder to define.

But it was a drug, and he did not want to become dependent again. He tried to tell himself that the two black youths had warped imaginations and must have made up the story in order to get money out of him.

But that left the timing of the break-in unexplained. If Mrs Prescot's death had been an accident, it was a hundred to one that the hit-and-run driver would have left the area immediately, and not hung around to burgle her maisonette while the police were still drawing up their plan of the skid marks on the road only three hundred metres away.

.4.

Ivor Morgan practised law with three partners in a converted supermarket, due for demolition in the near future. Like most of the buildings still standing in the area, it had windows covered by vandal-proof small-mesh grilles and heavy padlocks on the solid plywood door.

The building smelled of dry rot. On the other side of the thin plasterboard partition wall, a woman was complaining in a Caribbean accent to one of the other solicitors about police victimisation of her twenty-year-old son: 'He wouldn't even know where to buy crack, never mind sell it. He's a good boy, but they keep picking on him.'

Morgan seemed not to hear her voice, or the sound of a man with a hacking cough who was whining about unpaid Social Security payments in the office on his other side. He took the Will from the fireproof wall-safe and spread it on his desk.

'This won't take long.' He sounded apologetic. 'I'm afraid Mrs P's estate boils down to the lease on the maisonette, which has only fifteen years to run, some money in a building society – and not much else.'

'Then why am I here?' Ken asked.

'Because you are both named as beneficiaries.'

The news made no sense to Ken, who had not seen Mrs Prescot for years.

Morgan spread his hands. 'Elderly clients have funny ideas sometimes. They get confused and think their few precious possessions are valuable – or else die intestate and leave a million.'

He read the simple one-page document: the entirety of Mrs

Prescot's estate was bequeathed to various musical charities, with the exception of 'my favourite picture', which was left jointly to Ken and Irving, on condition that it be sold and the profits divided between them.

'What is this picture?' Ken was registering the fact that the Will had been made only three weeks before Mrs Prescot's death.

'It's a piece of chocolate box art that hangs over the mantelpiece in her living room,' Irving explained.

'Was Mrs P confused in her last months?' Ken asked.

'Absolutely not.' In a white cashmere polo-neck sweater and black wool trousers with black, handmade suede shoes, Irving looked severely out of place in the shabby office. 'I called her from Seoul, a week ago, after I'd performed the Elgar Violin Concerto. I won't bore you with the details – because they wouldn't mean anything to a non-musician – but I'd always played the opening in a certain way. That night, for some reason I did it differently. After the concert, I played it over the phone to Mrs P. She stopped me after two bars and said never to let her hear me play such arty-farty rubbish again.'

He stood up and looked out of the dirty, mesh-protected window, so that neither of the other men could see his face.

When Ken asked, 'Did you often call her from the other side of the world for advice like that?' Irving nodded without turning round.

'And would you say she was as lucid as ever, when you spoke to her from Seoul?'

Another nod.

'Mr Morgan . . .' Ken turned to the solicitor. 'Was this Will substantially different from the previous one?'

'Previously, there was no mention of the picture, and the musical charities were to receive everything.'

'There's no mention of relatives in either case?'

'So far as we know, Mrs P had none since her husband died five years ago.'

'In-laws?'

'None still alive, to my knowledge.'

*

Ken pulled up behind Irving's car – a showroom-condition black Lexus GS 300 saloon. Following him up the stairs to what had been Mrs Prescot's home for fifty years, he could feel Irving's anger at the sight of the slashed upholstery and the mess everywhere.

The contents of every drawer and cupboard had been emptied onto the floor. Padded armchairs had been slashed, the foam stuffing pulled out and thrown aside. Dark patches showed on the wallpaper where a few pictures had been hung. A broken china ornament crackled under Ken's foot. Irving picked up some of the photographs, many with smashed glass, lying on the floor. Most of them were of former pupils in evening dress on concert platforms, or shaking hands with the great and good. The handwritten dedications were all on the same lines: *To Mrs P, without whom* . . . His face was a mask of stone.

'Which is the picture we're supposed to sell?' Ken asked.

Irving jabbed a finger angrily at a dark patch above the mantelpiece in the living room. 'It's not here. That's where it used to hang.'

'Can you describe it to me?'

'Does it matter?'

'Try.'

'It was a picture of two women in Victorian dresses, picking flowers in a garden. I told you, it looked as if it had been copied from a chocolate box.'

'Do you suppose whoever broke in here could have taken it?'

'How the hell do I know?' The anger and grief in Irving welled over. 'You're supposed to be the one who answers questions.'

'You're right,' Ken agreed calmly. 'Do you want to know what I've found out so far?'

Irving nodded. He sat on the arm of a slashed armchair and listened without comment to the concise résumé of what Ken had learned, before saying, 'Are you trying to make me believe that there was some plot to murder Mrs P and steal that bloody awful painting?'

'I'm not trying to make you believe anything. You asked me what I'd found out. I told you.'

Irving was finding it hard to breathe. His life had taken a new direction in this room to which he had returned so many times over the years, to visit his old teacher. He would have liked to get his hands on the man or men who had killed her – and thrash whoever had broken into her home and made it look like a junk shop. But murder? There was no way he could buy a theory like that.

He stood up, deciding that it had been a mistake to get involved with Ken. 'I think you're paranoid. You've spent too long making midnight rendezvous with shabby little agents on bomb-sites on the wrong side of the Wall in divided Berlin. All those floodlights and barbed wire have affected your judgement.'

'That wasn't my job at all.'

'You know perfectly well what I mean. People don't go around murdering little old ladies who teach the fiddle, just to steal their favourite picture.'

'Then where is it?'

'There's probably some perfectly rational explanation.'

'Such as?'

Irving shook his head. 'I have a concert tomorrow, and haven't practised for two days. It's time I was heading back to the Smoke.'

Ken took the cheque out of his wallet and tore it up. 'I thought you really cared.'

'Oh, I care all right.' Irving's voice was harsh. 'But you didn't know Mrs P very well. All she ever thought about was the fiddle and her pupils.'

He pointed to three overturned drawers from a filing cabinet, from which spilled bundles of letters held together with elastic bands. 'She might have had no relatives, but she wrote every day to two, three, four of her old pupils. She remembered their birthdays, the names of their kids, and the details of their jobs. They were her family. Like me, when they had a problem – I mean a musical one – they wrote or called her for advice. She never made any enemies, so there's no reason anyone would have wanted to kill her. So forget the conspiracy theory. Lee Harvey Oswald had nothing to do with this.'

*

Catriona was sitting up in bed, propped up on a pile of gaudy cushions, writing a letter to her grown-up daughter, when Ken knocked on the door. She closed the writing pad and opened a bottle of Bushmills Whiskey – the last of a dozen with which she had been paid for a painting by a summer visitor – to keep him company, glass for glass, while he talked and she listened.

'What did Irving mean,' she asked at last, 'when he talked about you standing on bomb-sites, meeting agents in Berlin?'

'It was sarcasm. He knew perfectly well I worked for the Security Service, not SIS.'

'You told me you had been a claims adjuster for an insurance company.'

'Editing the truth gets to be a habit in my job, Cat,' Ken apologised with a half-smile. 'Especially when talking to people with accents like yours.'

Catriona nodded at his portrait which was hanging on the back wall, between two of the abstract landscapes. 'You didn't fool me. Look at those eyes. I knew all along you were a copper of some kind.'

'Do I talk in my sleep?'

'You don't need to. I'd have been a good portraitist if I stuck at it. Everything's written in the face – not when you're twenty years old, perhaps. But by your age, your whole life is there. And – I'll tell you something – I'm surprised you gave up.'

'Gave up? Irving asked me to make some enquiries, and then changed his mind.'

'But didn't you want to find out what really happened for your own satisfaction?'

Ken did not reply. The answer to Catriona's question was yes, but with the qualification that he wanted never again to be hooked on the peculiar pleasure of prying into other people's lives.

At Guéthary next morning, the sea was what would have been described in California as 'corduroy to the horizon'. The heavy swell and the strong off-shore wind were creating regular sets of waves with the wind blowing back a curtain of spray as each one broke: perfect surfing conditions beneath a leaden sky. Ken felt like a medieval knight beholding the Holy Grail on some lone vigil. The Wizards from Oz had moved on. The Flying Dutchman, with his colour-coded girlfriend and bike, and the assortment of Day-Glo boards on the roof of his van, was gone too. The café was closed, with the windows protected by pad-locked sheets of marine plywood against storm damage. Car park and beach alike were deserted.

Ken collected from the friendly shopkeeper the larger of the two boards he kept at Guéthary, a nine-foot-plus nose-rider, built on the other side of the Atlantic for championship surfing. Lying on it, he paddled seaward, thinking about nothing except the waves he could see waiting for him. They were far bigger than he had thought when standing on terra firma. As his board rose on the crests and slid down into the troughs he saw no other surfers. The only sign of life, human or otherwise, was a small side-trawler rolling crazily as it hastened homeward to the port of Hendaye. Even the gulls, it seemed, were staying indoors that day.

The voice of reason inside Ken's head whispered that there was still time to head back to shore. Ignoring it, he paddled on through waves bigger than he had ever been in before. Some were over five metres high and the big ones farther out looked to be twice that size. There was fear in the pit of his stomach long before he reached them, but stronger than the fear was the anticipation of the thrill that lay ahead. By the time he reached the break point, he was sliding up waves as high as the ridges of two-storey buildings and hurtling down them to paddle desperately out of the trough before the tons of water spilling down from the next house-high crest could thrust him down to a watery grave.

Half a kilometre from shore, there was nothing to break the mid-Atlantic fury of the sea. The puny weight of man and board was flung around like a fly in the slipstream of a Jumbo jet. The wind was playing strange tricks with the spume from the crests, slashing whip-like strands of stinging salt-water spray across his face, blinding him when he snatched a look behind to see nothing in any direction but waves and spray.

And then he saw the Big One. It was no legend, but real life, although probably closer to death. The whole set of waves bearing down on Ken was huge, but the second wave in the set was a freak. He negotiated the front-runner to find himself looking up nine or ten metres at the heaving grey mass of water which loomed above him. There was time for one thought only: I must be crazy. After that, there was no choice but to ride the monster or die lying down.

Even the board seemed alive and frightened, bucking beneath his booted feet. He scrambled upright, manoeuvring his body weight to gain speed and trying to stay ahead of the tons of grey water that wanted to smash him, crush him beneath their weight, drown him and spew him out, a bruised and useless mess of flesh held together by the neoprene wet suit. He felt, rather than heard, the crest starting to curl and come at him with the speed of an express train from the right, going far faster than he could travel. He angled left and down the wave, crouching to gain speed. A glance over his shoulder showed the tube of water, which looked as solid and lethal as steel, gaining on him inexorably.

Had this been a normal wave, there would have been a choice of staying in the tube or twisting left and going over the top to safety. In a sea like this, such a manoeuvre would end with him flying through the air ten metres above the following trough and almost certainly losing his board – which would mean death. Without its flotation, he would never make it back to shore.

Ken willed himself faster and faster down the sheer slope. The sky vanished as the tunnel of water overtook him. Inside the sealed and insulated helmet, the roar of the curling water, now surrounding him on all sides except right ahead, was terrifyingly loud in Ken's ears. Tantalisingly, the tube seemed to be slowing down as his brain, spurred on by desperation, worked faster than ever before, trying to find a way out where there was none. Finally the light went, apart from dead ahead, where the hole at the end of the lethal moving tunnel taunted him with its inaccessibility, receding faster than he could travel towards it.

Usually a surfer, once tubed in a breaking wave, would trail his inside hand against the wall of water to slow himself down and stay in the tube for as long as possible. But this was different: for the first time in his life, Ken crouched low and kept his arms close to his body like a skier trying to reduce the wind resistance of his body to the minimum. But will-power and skill meant nothing against the sheer brute energy of the wave. He grabbed a last lungful of life as the small hole of grey light at the end of the tube vanished to a point and then was gone.

The world turned upside down and inside out, pummelling the air from Ken's body. Somewhere in the whirling vortex that was several million tons of water in motion, the tip of the board connected with the back of his head, nearly stunning him despite the titanium and neoprene helmet that broke the force of the blow. Whirled and spun in several directions, he was no longer sure which way was up but fought towards a faint glimmer of lesser grey. His brain screamed for oxygen. He felt the leash of the board cut against his gloved right palm as the wave tried to yank it away, and instinctively closed his fingers around the thin cable, grabbing it tight just before the heavy-duty Velcro collar around his ankle gave way.

Breaking surface with bursting lungs, he saw the following wave towering above his head and gulped a few mouthfuls of air before it submerged him. The good news as the water closed over his head was to see that the Big One had brought him nearly all the way back to the beach, which was only a hundred metres away. The bad news was that he was in the rip current, fighting his way through water churning in every direction that was carrying him sideways onto the jagged rocks. Without the board he would have drowned. Even lying on it, paddling like mad, the odds were still on the sea winning. Overworked muscles in his chest and shoulders were screaming for oxygen. Don't cramp, he prayed. Don't cramp on me now.

And then he had a different, but still potentially lethal fight on his hands. On shore, the waves were still three and four metres high. With the undertow dragging him back each time a wave knocked him down in the wind-whipped white foam, he clawed his way inch by inch up the beach until at last he reached the high-water mark, where he crouched on all fours with lungs heaving and every muscle in his body refusing to do another iota of work until it had some oxygen. Like a balloon deflating,

Ken crumpled onto the sand and lay prone, unable to move and with only one thought in his head. *I did it!*

Getting dressed on the gravel track beside the Harley after a swig of brandy had brought some warmth back into his numbed limbs, Ken did a brief victory dance, naked in the cold wind, challenging it to freeze him to death. The Wizards from Oz, the Mohawk from Holland and all the others had left just a few days too soon. He, Kenneth William Scott, crazy old man of the sea, had been the only surfer to ride the Big One that year and probably for many years to come. And he was alive to tell the tale, just. But he would not tell it, because no one would ever believe the sheer size and monstrous force of the wave – and certainly no one still alive would be able to share that do-it-or-die blend of terror and exhilaration that he had known in the tunnel of grey water.

The storm chased him all the way home, winds gusting up to a hundred kilometres an hour and more, with torrential rain that made Ken wish the Harley had a windscreen less decorative and more functional.

He parked the bike in what had been the dairy, and set about getting the house warm and cooking a meal for himself. He was still eating when Catriona came across the field to tell him that Ivor Morgan had called with the news that there had been another break-in at Mrs Prescot's home.

This time, it could have been some local kids taking advantage of the maisonette being unoccupied, except for one detail: the proprietor of the video shop downstairs had been knocked unconscious by the intruders and tied up. To Ken, that smelled like the same team who had broken in on the night Mrs Prescot died. And if they had come back, that meant they had not found what they were looking for the first time.

. 5 .

At dusk the following day Ken collected a key to the maisonette from Ivor Morgan and let himself into Mrs Prescot's maisonette. He could see at a glance why whoever had done the job had knocked unconscious the man in the shop downstairs. This time, the waist-high panelling had been ripped off the walls, fitted carpets pulled up and floorboards removed. Even the loft space was a mess of piled-up fibreglass insulation.

Ken talked to the man who had been attacked. He had heard a noise at the rear of the premises, gone outside to have a look, and recovered consciousness two hours later. The regulars and bar staff in the local pubs were not much more helpful. Nobody, it seemed, knew much about Mrs Prescot, except that she was 'the fiddle teacher with all them prodigies-like on the telly'.

Despite the mess, the maisonette was warm from the central heating. For food and drink, there were several restaurants nearby, and both Indian and Chinese take-outs within walking distance. Rather than checking into a hotel, it made more sense to Ken to stay where he was and work on through the night.

The job of building accurate psychological profiles of people – by analysing their choice of books, diet, clothes, personal habits and hygiene, telephone bills and the rubbish in their garbage bins – was one Ken had done many times before. Often he had been working in haste during an illicit break-in, where he had to take care not to disturb anything and keep one ear on the telephone for the two rings that meant the target was returning home unexpectedly. This time, there was no hurry. He took his time, clearing up the mess on the floor, re-hanging photographs where they matched the dark patches on the wallpaper so far as possible. The patch above the fireplace mocked him silently.

The houses on either side were unoccupied. The absence of neighbours made the maisonette very quiet, except for the occasional noise from the video shop downstairs, such as a car driving up or a door slamming. Ken could understand why Mrs Prescot had kept a dog for company. He collected up the hundreds of records, cassettes and CDs strewn on the floor and stacked them on a shelf, putting on the hi-fi a CD of Irving playing Prokofiev with Previn and the LSO. As the music began, he carried on cleaning up, trying to get the feel of the woman who had chosen to make this place her home.

Pinned to a door of a wall cupboard, the lists of examination results showed that all Mrs P's pupils achieved distinctions. In addition to the piano, there were several violins and a viola in cases. A cello stood in one corner. None of the instruments had been taken.

On the bedroom floor in a shattered frame lay a photograph of Mrs Prescot's late husband. Ken remembered him as being an unremarkable grey-faced man, stooped and aged by bad health, who had borne little resemblance to this broad-chested, smiling soldier in battledress with the Intelligence Corps flash on the shoulder and a face that showed a tough resourcefulness and quiet strength of character. Face-down on the dressing table was a photograph of the same big, gentle-looking man posing awkwardly in a smart suit outside a Register Office with his bride. She was a petite brunette with delicate features and intensely intelligent eyes, dressed in the hour-glass fashion of Dior's New Look, with a hat that could have been borrowed from a Chinese coolie.

Ken removed the picture from the frame and found written on the back, as he had hoped, a date and a place: *Liverpool Register Office, 2nd April 1947.*

A portion of chop suey and spare ribs and a couple of beers later, he finished leafing through Mrs Prescot's personal papers, having learned that she had £57,512.75 on deposit in a building society cheque account, from which she made monthly withdrawals of differing amounts, always slightly less than the accrued interest. Crawling around the small bedroom which had served as her office on hands and knees, he rescued medical forms, insurance policies, the accounts and tax returns for the photography business in which she had been a partner – putting in date order all the minutiae of life that were stepping stones to the past.

Two-thirds of the way across the river of time, they stopped. The first one that was missing was her marriage certificate. Every piece of paper prior to 1947 related to her husband. His army paybook, call-up and demobilisation papers were there. So were his school reports and school leaving certificate, even his birth certificate. His life on paper was complete, yet it was as though his wife had been a woman with no past on the day she married him.

Ken felt an old and familiar frisson. Madeleine Prescot's documented past was like that of a spy whose legend began with the marriage. Was it remotely possible that she had been infiltrated into post-war Britain as an illegal or a sleeper? The idea seemed at first as laughable to him as the suspicion that she had been murdered had appeared to Irving. Yet, as Ken knew better than most people, among the hundreds of thousands of refugees and DPs – displaced persons from all over Europe – who had been let into Britain to fill the labour shortfall after the Second World War were a surprisingly high number who came as spies and betrayed the country that had welcomed them, working for Moscow throughout the Cold War either voluntarily or under pressure. If Mrs Prescot had been one of them, had the Intelligence Corps sergeant she married known about it, or had he been an unwitting dupe?

Fighting his way through the surf on the beach at Guéthary, Ken had promised himself never to touch another cigarette. Hurrying to the nearest off-licence before it shut for the night, he compromised: just one packet . . .

On the way back through the park, he saw the police notice boards appealing for witnesses. Where *had* Mrs Prescot come from? Speaking with a French accent was no proof of anything, for accents could be learned. Even if she had been born in France, it was quite possible that she had been one of the hard core of French Communists who spent the war years in Moscow. When she came to Britain she had not been old or fragile, but a forceful, resourceful young woman. Who knew what lay behind that enigmatic smile outside the Register Office?

Locking the door for the night, Ken noticed a security bolt as well as the Yale lock and a sliding chain. They were normal precautions for a woman living on her own, but the chain and bolt looked new – the metal shiny and unscratched. He used a kitchen knife to remove a couple of screws and found that the wood in the holes was fresh, which confirmed that the bolt and chain had been fixed recently.

In the bedroom he studied the wedding picture. Character, intelligence . . . By the look of her, Geoff Prescot's bride had had those qualities in plenty. She was, if not stunningly beautiful, a poised and attractive young woman who wore her fashionable wedding-day costume with a confidence that betokened a middle-class upbringing or better. So what was she doing in those class-conscious years, marrying a working-class man who had spent five years in uniform and risen no higher than sergeant? Of course, if she had been a spy in the era of microdots, before satellites and burst transmitters, the choice of a professional photographer as husband/partner in espionage made sense. Geoff Prescot would have had the equipment, the chemicals and the expertise to reduce a whole page to the size of a full stop and to enlarge the replies for her to read.

For the second time, Ken disciplined himself to put on the brakes. Why, he wondered, would the Comintern have installed an agent in Liverpool in 1947? Although the labour force in the huge and thriving docks had constituted a ripe target for Communist agitation at a time when many thought that Merseyside would be the cradle of the British Revolution, that would not have called for an illegal on the spot. However, dotted all over the north-west of England were strategic targets of interest to Moscow at the start of the Cold War. There were the dock installations themselves and the Cammel Laird shipyard across the Mersey. The big Royal Ordnance factory at

Leyland was only a few miles away, as were the Ferranti works at Moston where the guidance systems for the ultra-secret Bloodhound guided missiles were designed. At Wharton airfield, English Electric had done much of the development work on the Lightning bomber and the TSR2.

The longer Ken thought about it, the more dots appeared on his mental map of the north-west – each one representing another high-priority Cold War target. He put down the photograph, accusing himself of professional paranoia.

Yet there was certainly something very odd about Madeleine Prescot's past, or lack of it. And why had she chosen – fifty years after coming to Britain – to appoint Ken Scott, of all people, a beneficiary under her Will? Had she perhaps known that Irving Bradley's father worked for MI5 and *wanted* him to investigate her past after her death? If so, she would have left a clue of some kind for him to find.

Ken left a message on Irving's answering machine. It was well after midnight when the call was returned and Irving yawned, 'What are you doing in Merseyside? I thought you'd gone back to France.'

'Just clearing up a few loose ends.' Ken made it sound casual. 'I was just wondering whether you have any idea why Mrs Prescot wrote me into her will?'

'None.'

'Did you ever mention to her the line of work I was in?'

Irving laughed, 'Mrs P and I talk – that is, we used to talk – about technique and repertoire, not much else. A non-musician would probably think we were talking gibberish.'

'That's more or less what I thought. It was only a long shot. Sorry I bothered you. Good night.'

.6.

With a pot of strong black coffee at his elbow, Ken tackled the bundles of correspondence which had been pulled out of the drawers in the filing cabinet. In each bundle, the letters were in date order interspersed with handwritten copies of her replies.

As Irving had said, his old teacher seemed to have known everything about her ex-pupils' health, relationships and jobs. She had remembered their anniversaries and the birthdays of their children. It was indeed a family correspondence; the woman who had no child of her own was spiritual matriarch to a musical tribe that was spread across the globe. The ex-pupils lived in Japan and India, Iceland and Brazil. They were everywhere musicians could earn a living by playing or teaching the violin. Any one of them, Ken reflected, could have been a postman, forwarding correspondence to Prague or east Berlin. Any one of the thousands of yellowing letters that spanned the years of the Cold War could have been in code, or have had microdots stuck over full stops.

Her own letters said little about herself beyond, 'Geoff and I are both in good health, thank you.' Even during the weeks when her husband was in hospital dying, instead of talking about herself, Mrs Prescot had painted well-constructed, vivid pen-pictures of life in Lark Lane, from which her neighbours emerged as large as life and twice as interesting. She was a born writer of short stories, Ken concluded. Her side of the correspondence was a joy to read – and made him appreciate to what extent the art of letter-writing had suffered from the invention of the telephone.

Were these the letters of a spy? There was no telling. Gordon Lonsdale aka Konon Molody had been a highly successful businessman with a large circle of friends who thought they knew him well. The Krogers had been widely respected antiquarian book dealers. The best spies worked harder at their cover identities than most people did at real life.

Ken opened a window. The night air was colder than the coffee in the pot but he needed another cigarette, and smoked it feeling apprehensive about what he might discover in the bundles he had deliberately left until last. They were labelled and numbered in Mrs Prescot's neat old-fashioned hand: *Scruff No 1, Scruff No 2* and so on, Scruff being the nickname by which she had called Irving.

It was easier to start by reading the latest letters and postcards than to go to the beginning of the correspondence which had lasted through the best part of two decades. Ken was nervous of the boy, not the man. Most of the current correspondence was professional chit-chat. Irving would send a cassette of his playing from Rio or Sydney or Hong Kong with a brief note asking for Mrs Prescot's advice on the interpretation of a passage. Without understanding the technical points involved in her succinct replies, Ken could appreciate how much Mrs Prescot's opinion had been valued by her star pupil. He wondered whether many top-flight soloists kept up such a relationship with their old teachers.

At last, uneasy about what they might reveal of the child he had never known, he turned to the earliest bundle. The letters began when Irving first went as a boarder to a specialist music school in Birmingham. Another boy might have poured out to his mother the anguish of a lonely and insecure pre-adolescent from an underprivileged home trying to adjust to the hothouse atmosphere of a school where most of the other pupils came from middle-class families. To each of Irving's cries for help, the childless teacher had known the right reply: sympathetic but firm, and always encouraging by holding out the prospect of success that lay ahead.

*

Of course you're lonely, Scruff. The others sense that you have something extra. One day they'll all be proud to say that they were at school with you, and probably tell people they were your best friends, whereas your best friend will always be your violin . . .

In the second year, Irving seemed to have settled in. His letters became, for the most part, requests for musical advice. When he disagreed with one of the teachers at the school on a point of technique or interpretation, he had the sense to keep his mouth shut, voicing doubts only in the privacy of his correspondence with Mrs Prescot. Contemporary newspaper cuttings in the file about 'the new Menuhin' showed photographs of a pale, rather haunted face beneath the shock of jet-black hair that was already Irving's trademark.

Later came letters about friendships and girls that hinted at loneliness unassuaged by the reputation he had already earned by the time of his sixteenth birthday.

Both Fred and I are competing for the leader's desk in the first quartet, Mrs P. This is his last year at the school so, if he won, I'd still have two more chances but this is his only one. I wanted him to win the audition because he needs this on his CV. But when the chips were down, I played to beat him hollow. I could see his face in the audience: he felt I was betraying him. He was the only real friend I'd made since coming to the school. Now he doesn't talk to me any more . . .

Later:

I knew Tracey would go with Darren if I didn't take her to the disco last Saturday, but I was working on the Beethoven quartets and honestly had no idea of how time was passing. It was past midnight when I remembered that I was supposed to be going out. Now she says that I can't care about her and it isn't true. Why can't she understand?

*

And later still, when Irving was at the Juilliard School in New York, he had written:

About the tape I sent you of the Bartók quartets, you're right as always: I was fighting the second violin. Her name is Lucy Poon. She is Chinese – from Shanghai and very beautiful. She's also my only serious rival here. The other strings students are top class but they couldn't catch Lucy or me if you gave them a ten-mile start. At Tanglewood, after staying up all one night working on the Bartók, we slept together – just the once. I like her but she's a competitor, so I undermine her confidence whenever I can. I hate myself for it, but what can I do?

It was dawn before Ken closed the file and sat back. He stubbed out the last cigarette from the pack, feeling for the first time that he knew his son as a person, not just a public figure. The human image was not very likeable, but was Irving to blame that he had turned out such a ruthless, ambitious, driven man? If one had prodigious talent, what choice was there but to push for the top and trample over competitors by any means possible?

Perhaps, Ken accused himself, I should have taken the boy away from Marlene when I saw the lush she was turning into. It was only the fear that she would carry out her threats to commit suicide which deterred me. But that was no excuse, because I knew her to be incapable of bringing up even a kitten properly. My duty lay with the kid once I had decided he was mine. Yet, what sort of home life could I have offered the boy, even when I came out of the Army? Neither of my other wives wanted children of their own, let alone to bring up another woman's son. Given the circumstances, could I have done more than send Marlene money for Irving's upbringing, and pay for his music lessons? Who knows? And anyway, I'm not here to find Irving. He's done all right for himself. It's Mrs Prescot I have to concentrate on . . .

He shut the window and dozed off watching the sky lighten above the trees in Sefton Park. When he awoke, cold and cramped in the chair, he tried to recapture the elusive thought that had roused him. This time, the phone was picked up on first ring.

'Irving?'

'Jesus Christ! What do you want now?'

'Did I wake you?'

'Just remember that musicians go to bed late and get up late. I've got a long day ahead of me.'

'I'll bear that in mind,' Ken promised. 'Answer me one question. Think back a few years. When you were a kid, did you discuss me with Mrs Prescot – you know, my job and . . .'

'You already asked me this.' Irving let the irritation show. He was tempted to hang up.

'It's not the same question,' Ken persisted. 'I'm talking now about when you first came here for lessons – or when you went away to school and used to unburden yourself to the old lady at weekends.'

'You've been poking through her correspondence.'

'Did you?'

There was a long pause before Irving said, 'There wasn't much point talking to Marlene even when she was sober, was there? There wasn't anyone else I could talk to.'

'Thanks,' said Ken. 'Sorry I woke you up.'

He went into the bedroom, where the eviscerated mattress lay useless on the floor. Placing several layers of blankets over the springs of the brass Victorian double bedstead, he lay down and gazed at the papered-over cracks in the plaster ceiling which Mrs P had seen on going to bed and when waking up, every night and morning for so many years. He had to admit to himself that he was no closer to knowing who she was or where she came from than when he had started. But there did seem a fair probability that she had made him a beneficiary of the Will in the full knowledge that he worked for MI5. That would have been a strange thing for a spy to do – unless, of course, she had wanted to be investigated posthumously for some reason.

The clerk in the Register Officer was a bright Pakistani girl with a Merseyside accent, wearing western clothes, but with a headscarf completely enveloping her hair. She was impressed by Ken's MI5 identity card, over the expiry date of which he was careful to keep his thumb. The card was three years out of date, but that did not worry him too much because he had always found that people tended to concentrate on comparing the photograph with his face and never read the details.

After he had explained what he wanted, the girl left him alone in the basement with a thick ledger in which were recorded marriages solemnised during the first six months of 1947. There were twenty-four entries for 2 April 1947, none of them bearing the name Prescot. Ken searched forward to the end of the month and backwards to the beginning of March with similar lack of success.

Had the Register Office photograph been stooged by Geoff Prescot? If so, why? How many wives kept a fake wedding photograph by their bed for nearly fifty years? Each question spawned another, until he worked out what was the one obvious thing he had not checked.

Ivor Morgan was in court, so Ken had to wait until the lunch recess to drive him to police headquarters and claim the handbag that Mrs Prescot had had with her at the time of her death. Back at the maisonette, he emptied the bag and ran his fingers round the satin lining. On the writing desk in front of him was a Post Office Savings Bank passbook, a pension book, a block of rosin and some coiled violin strings, a spare pair of spectacles, an ancient kidney donor card, a purse containing coins and some small-denomination notes, and a couple of stamped letters which Mrs Prescot had been going to post, when knocked down.

He opened the letters and read them through, but there was no clue there. Some small change jingled in the purse. He opened it and tipped the coins out. Tucked into the back pocket of the purse was something that no provident, self-respecting old lady like Mrs Prescot would be expected to have: a Day-Glo orange pawn ticket date-stamped on the day of the accident.

.7.

The pawn shop was a short bus ride away from Mrs Prescot's maisonette, in the area of Liverpool known as Dingle. Like Morgan's offices, it was waiting to be demolished.

When Ken walked in, a middle-aged man in a grey overall was standing behind the counter, heavily protected with anti-bandit screens, watching the racing news on television. He took the orange ticket without a word and shambled along the shelves, keeping one eye on the screen, until he came to a brown paper parcel which he unwrapped on the counter to reveal a small, rather dirty oil painting of a flower-filled garden in which two women wearing crinolines and holding Japanese parasols were walking towards a white wooden latticework belvedere. Ken repaid the loan of £5 plus the minimum of one week's interest and walked out of the shop with the parcel under his arm.

'The old lady ill, is she?' the man asked.

'That's right,' Ken confirmed. 'You remember her?'

'Could hardly fail to. She came in each week, didn't she?'

'To pawn something?' That didn't sound to Ken like the woman he thought he knew from all the correspondence.

'To pawn the picture,' the man said. 'She paid the interest and re-hocked it each time.'

'Why would she do a thing like that?'

'You tell me, boss. Behind this counter, you see everything sooner or later.'

Ken nudged a fiver across the counter. 'When did she first bring the picture in?'

'Three weeks ago.'

The framed painting fitted exactly the unfaded patch on the wallpaper above the mantelpiece in Mrs Prescot's living room. There was nothing tucked in the back of the frame and nothing written on the wrapping paper. As to the picture itself . . .

'I suppose the frame might be worth a bob or two,' said Ivor Morgan when Ken placed it on his desk later that afternoon. 'Are you sure you want me to lock it up?'

Ken nodded. 'On second thoughts, don't put it in your safe. Put it in a bank vault.'

'It seems a bit excessive.'

'Just do it.' It was easier for Ken to bark an order than to explain to the solicitor why he thought it was worth putting in a very safe place the picture which Mrs Prescot had first pawned on the day she changed her Will.

Harry Tilson could not have been more different from Ken in temperament or looks. Buying him a drink among the coppers and crooks at the Prince of Wales pub in Lant Street, south of the river, Ken wondered whether he would have eventually turned into a replica of the other man, if by the grace of God he had not been sacked from MI5 prematurely. Like Tilson, he had drunk and smoked far too much for years, living on sandwiches, hastily snatched hamburgers, and ersatz coffee in plastic cups.

It seemed another lifetime.

A layer of dandruff peppered the collar of Tilson's jacket. His shirt was grubby around the neck and cuffs. The old soak looked more disreputable than ever – if that were possible. His cheap off-the-peg suit had needed a trip to the dry cleaners when Ken had last met him two years previously; now it needed incinerating.

'Long time, no see.' Tilson sounded pleased to see an old chum. 'Best thing that ever happened to you was getting the push, Scottie. You look ten years younger.'

'And you look a hundred and ten, Harry.'

For years, Tilson had exploited the greatest organisational flaw in MI5: the fact that the Service was split up, with staff in nine different buildings – B and K directorates, responsible for

personnel and secretariat, in Curzon Street while G Branch was in Gower Street, and so on. Whenever he was found to be missing from one set of offices, Tilson always had an alibi for being in another. That should have all changed at the end of 1994 when the Security Service was at last united in the ugly grey stone bulk of its new headquarters in Thames House, within walking distance of its political masters in Whitehall. Yet Tilson had apparently survived the move.

'How come they haven't sacked you yet, Harry?' Ken asked.

Tilson stuck out a well-furred tongue. 'See that brown stain? Whenever a new arse appears above me, I lick it.'

They chatted about old acquaintances, Ken buying two drinks for his guest to each one for himself, although Tilson had obviously got in a few before he arrived. It had always been a mystery to Ken how such a confirmed alcoholic managed to find his way back to work after lunch, never mind juggle all his alibis for being in the wrong place.

After two hours' hard drinking, they parted. In the Underground, Ken unfolded Tilson's *Daily Telegraph* which he had picked up off the bar. The crossword had been completed in an uncharacteristically neat hand. Apparently Tilson timed himself. In the margin was written: *4 min, 37 sec.* Between the middle pages lay a facsimile copy of Geoffrey Prescot's marriage licence. It seemed fair exchange for the £50-note Ken had tucked into Tilson's breast pocket as a thank-you.

Had Mrs P's husband served in any other unit of the British Army, his Second World War personal records would have been pulped long ago. Luckily, as Ken had remembered from his own service in it, the Intelligence Corps had its own way of doing things. According to the licence, Sergeant Prescot had married his French bride nearly two years before the date on the faked wedding photograph – in the early summer of 1945. The wedding had been solemnised not at Liverpool Register Office but in the chapel of the British Embassy in Paris. The witnesses were a captain and a second lieutenant, both in the Intelligence Corps. The bride's name was given as Madeleine Lasalle, with an address at Royan, a French seaside resort north of Bordeaux.

On 20 May 1945, the war in Europe had just ended. Millions of refugees and displaced persons were on the move all over the Continent. Eisenhower's allied armies confronted Soviet forces all along the cease-fire lines. The world stood poised on the brink of a fresh confrontation. Yet three British soldiers were taking time out in the British Embassy chapel in Paris to celebrate and witness a wedding.

As Tilson had commented, 'Either Sergeant Prescot was on exceptionally good terms with his CO, Scottie – or else he was very persistent. It wasn't easy for a bloke in uniform to get permission to marry a French girl in 1945.'

Ken knew that the Army had usually done everything in its power to obstruct the course of true love, suspecting that any local woman who wanted to marry a soldier was on the game. The usual device had been to post the man home or to another theatre of operations. As Alice might have said, the quest for Mrs Prescot's past was growing curiouser and curiouser.

Eight hundred miles south of Liverpool, the November weather was pretty much the same in Royan. Rain swept in from the Bay of Biscay. The address which Geoffrey Prescot's bride had given to the British Embassy chaplain had ceased to exist on 5 January 1945, thanks to Arthur Travers Harris and his men of RAF Bomber Command.

Fortified by the Wehrmacht as a pocket of resistance for the purpose of interdicting Allied use of the Gironde estuary and the port of Bordeaux after the Normandy landings in June 1944, Royan had literally been levelled to the ground by a series of RAF and American bombing raids in the first quarter of 1945. By the end, of two thousand three hundred civilians in the town, more than five hundred lay dead in the ruins, with several hundred others shocked and injured. German casualties totalled forty-seven, for the loss of six aircraft on the last mission alone. With the war in its last stages, the raids had been strategically pointless. The German army had already long since withdrawn from the region, and the troops in the pocket were resigned to the prospect of surrender within a few weeks. The total destruction of the town in the final American raids served only as a rehearsal for the Dresden raid the following month, in which Harris also played a key part.

Among the other losses were all the records of the *état civil* – the register of births, marriages and deaths. British and American bombs had made Royan a good place in which to base a legend, for anyone could reasonably claim to have been born there prior to the town's destruction in 1945. Was that coincidence or corroboration, Ken wondered? Time would tell.

A helpful woman in the Syndicat d'Initiative directed him to a private museum outside the town that was dedicated to telling the story of the Battle of the Pocket. There Ken wandered among tanks and armoured vehicles from both sides, uniforms and weapons – all displayed in lifelike settings. It was an impressive collection, lovingly assembled by a couple of enthusiasts. There were radios and guns that had been air-dropped by the RAF to the local *résistants*, together with the parachutes and containers that had been used. Among the vehicles on display were two ancestors of Ken's FXRT. The first was a Harley Davidson UA, with a two-cylinder, four-stroke 1200cc engine and the other was the similar WLA. In each case, the letter A stood for Army. Some 88,000 of these bikes had been produced during the Second World War for communications, scouting and military police duties. Painted GI olive drab, de-tuned and given eighteen-inch wheels plus extended cooling fins on the cylinders and heads, one third of this number had been supplied to Stalin and used by the Red Army as a veritable cavalry on two wheels in the final push to Berlin. The ones on display in the museum, with their worn leather pannier bags and dented skid-trays, the leather holsters for a Thompson sub-machine-gun on the front forks and front and rear blackout lamps, had obviously seen heavy service during the fighting in France.

Ken moved on to the collection of false papers and maps used by the local *maquisards*, and the photographs they had taken clandestinely of themselves. If men had done most of the actual fighting, women had played their no less dangerous parts as couriers and radio operators. Among the many photographs was one of a group of young people in civilian clothes with FFI armbands, showing that they belonged to the Forces Françaises de l'Intérieur. Few of them were older than twenty. All were brandishing firearms and trying to look fierce, like a boatload of unblooded young Vikings psyching themselves up for their first raid. In their centre, a tall blonde girl seemed more interested in smiling at the boy beside her than in killing Germans. She was wearing sandals and white ankle socks, and had an FFI armband sewn incongruously on the right sleeve of her flowery summer frock. In her left hand, held proudly above her head, she held an air-dropped British Sten gun. In faded ink on the bottom margin of the picture, she was identified as Madeleine Lasalle. Her face bore not the slightest resemblance to Geoff Prescot's petite brunette bride.

Flashing a visiting card which he had printed for himself, using a machine on board the cross-Channel car ferry, Ken introduced himself to the custodian of the museum with the story that he was a freelance reporter, working on a feature about women in the Resistance for a British woman's weekly. The custodian was a bearded middle-aged man, whose own personal souvenir of the war was a heavy limp, collected as a child during one of the Allied raids on the town. He used a thick walking-stick to lead his out-of-season visitor to a carefully hand-lettered roll of honour. Halfway down the line of freshly re-gilded letters, Mademoiselle Lasalle M. was recorded as having given her life for France on 11 April 1945 – one week before the Germans in the pocket capitulated.

'Can you tell me anything about her?' Ken asked.

'It was a bad business. From the date on which she died, I can tell you that she was one of those killed in the only massacre that took place around here. The local *maquis* were asked by radio from London to sabotage the installations of the Atlantic Wall. They were made over-confident by a widely believed rumour that thirty thousand American paratroopers were to be dropped that day in the south-west.'

'But the paras didn't arrive?'

'There never were any airborne troops to spare for this part of France. Every available man and piece of *matériel* was already committed to the drive into Germany at that time. The rumour was just disinformation, designed to confuse *les Boches* when it came to their ears. However, thinking that the war was as good as over, this particular *maquis* group set out to blow up a radar station on the coast with more than usual carelessness. Over half of them were killed in the first minutes of the attack. A dozen or so survivors surrendered under a white flag. Despite the fact that they were wearing FFI armbands and various items of uniform, they were shot out of hand by the Indian troops guarding the radar station.'

'Indian troops?' Ken thought he had misheard.

'There were a lot of Hindu soldiers among the Wehrmacht units along the Atlantic Wall. Some joined up after being taken prisoner in Allied uniform; others found their own way to Europe because they wanted to fight the British. These were Sikhs.' The custodian pointed to a photograph of a bearded and turbaned figure behind a .50 machine-gun in a one-man Tobruk strong-point. 'Marooned so far from home, I suppose they were feeling desperate as the end of the war drew near.'

'How can you be sure that anyone was killed at a particular time?' Ken asked. 'The keeping of records must have had a low priority in all the confusion of the Liberation.'

'In this case, it's easy,' was the answer. 'After the massacre, the bodies were recovered from the sea and buried by local people who knew all the victims personally. They wouldn't have got a name wrong. There's a memorial to the victims at the place where they were killed.'

Ken had seen the little wayside shrines all over France with names engraved on them under the catch-all title *Morts pour la France*. Usually the date below the names was in the summer of 1944, when Liberation hysteria prompted otherwise perfectly sane men and women armed with hunting rifles, Stens and a few hand grenades to tackle battle-scarred veterans of the Wehrmacht and Waffen SS who had heavy machine-guns, tanks, flame-throwers, field guns and aircraft on their side.

The custodian produced a large-scale IGN map of the area. On it he circled a spot on the coast about fifteen kilometres to the north of Royan. 'It's easy to find,' he said. 'You leave your car on the main road and follow the footpath. It's called the *chemin des douaniers* and was originally for customs officers keeping a watch on the shipping in the estuary. If you get lost, use the local name for the *lieu-dit* where the memorial is sited. It's called the Villa Céleste, after a house that used to stand there.'

There was nothing very heavenly about the salt-lashed promontory with a gale-force, on-shore wind scouring the sand off the beach and whipping the stunted bushes and salt-resistant evergreen oaks that crouched low with their backs to the sea. The memorial was a simple marble column, broken off two metres above the base to symbolise youth cut down in its prime.

Ken recalled the custodian saying something about the average age of *résistants* killed during the Occupation being only twenty-two. According to the inscription on the plinth below the column, most of those who had been mown down at this spot on 11 April 1945 had been even younger. Madeleine Lasalle and her brother Yves – was he the boy at whom she was smiling in the photograph? – had been twenty-one and nineteen respectively.

On the tip of the headland, still defying the elements, stood the three concrete blockhouses. The metre-thick reinforced concrete of the largest one was still blackened by fire in places where the weather had not scrubbed it clean. The thick metal door on the landward side hung crookedly on one hinge, bent by the heat of an explosion. The aerial array on the roof of the largest blockhouse was gone, reduced to some short stumps of rusty metal and a few corroded cables which projected from the concrete. Inside the blockhouse, whose horizontal slits gave a view of the beaches on both sides of the headland, some German tourist had written on the wall in thick felt pen: *Auch wir erinnern uns an Euch!* We too remember you. Outside, on the seaward side of the blockhouse, a French admirer of the Wehrmacht had aerosol-painted the legend: *Honneur au soldat allemand!*

Ken climbed onto the concrete roof, undamaged by time and the elements, and stood there with the wind wrapping his overcoat tightly around his legs and salt spray pickling his face. Below him, on the sheltered side of the rocky spit against which the waves were breaking, were the remains of what had been a stone jetty.

He turned his back to the wind, trying to picture the scene on that spring morning in 1945 when the band of young *maquisards* had crept through the bushes to surprise the German sentries. Some of the raiders would have been cool and calm; some would have been almost paralysed with fear. None of them would have guessed that before midday they would all be dead.

Among the stunted bushes and trees inland, Ken saw the outlines of brick and concrete foundations, and wandered over to investigate them. The quality of workmanship was not up to the standards of the Organisation Todt. This had been a pre-war holiday home like the ones he could see, half-hidden in the pines that grew down to the beach on either side of the headland. For the most part they were large Edwardian villas, built for the families of prosperous middle-class families from Paris and Bordeaux in the early years of the century. Perhaps this one had been levelled to clear a field of fire, although there was no reason that he could see why anyone should have done that, because all the firing slits of the bunkers faced seaward and the remains of the villa were on the landward side.

Ignoring the chill wind, Ken tried to picture the Villa Céleste as it had been before the memorial was erected and before the blockhouse was built. He imagined a spacious family villa, surrounded by well-laid-out gardens – and perhaps a boat moored by the little jetty. On a summer's day, it must have been an idyllic setting for the prewar holidays of some rich French family.

PART III:
At the Villa Céleste –
September 1939

.1.

Yvonne Picard shut her copy of *Marie-Claire*, the most popular new women's magazine of 1939. Married to a rich husband, with all the money she wanted to spend on clothes, make-up, jewellery and travel, she epitomised the smart, rich *modern* women who peopled the pages of the magazine.

They had no vote – indeed, Article 213 of the *Code Civil* still denied married Frenchwomen any legal status in their own right – but continued to influence the course of their country's politics in ways that had not changed since medieval times. In Paris at the salon of Madame de Crussol, mistress of Edouard Daladier, France's dour premier, and at that of Madame de Portes, who was mistress of his dapper and far more entertaining rival, Paul Reynaud, the privileged could hear the latest political gossip and scandal *before* it was known in the Chambre des Députés.

In that ostrich summer season, French society seemed determined to outshine itself with bigger, more extravagant parties and balls that required entire hotels to be refurbished in colours that would harmonise with the dress which the hostess wanted to wear and *concours d'élégance* where the silk-stockinged legs of the lady drivers counted for as much in the eyes of the judges as their enormously over-powered, custom-built motor cars. Daisy Fellowes and Elsa Maxwell threw parties that cost more than hospitals. Another American, Lady Mendl gave a ball with music by not one, but three orchestras: a black American band playing *le jazz hot*, another from Cuba which specialised in the newfangled tango and a Hungarian all-woman orchestra that played only waltzes.

Some people had problems: it took Lady Deterding's ultra-chic clique three weeks of deliberation before they could agree to meet for cocktails each afternoon at the bar of the Crillon, rather than the Ritz. And why? As Paris correspondent Janet Flanner explained to her avid readers in *The New Yorker*, Emile the barman at the Crillon just knew how to mix the most divine Martinis, Sidecars, Manhattans, White Ladies and Bronxes.

When England's newly installed King George VI and his wife paid a state visit, the not untypical menu of one banquet began with caviare, followed by melon with sherry to drink; trout in a crayfish sauce with 1926 Montrachet; lamb mignonettes with 1915 Hospices de Beaune; stuffed quails with 1919 Corton-Grancy; duck with cherries and 1918 Mouton-Rothschild; salad; a sorbet made with 1921 Lanson champagne; supreme of chicken with 1904 Latour; baked truffles; iced mousse with 1921 Château Yquem Sauternes . . . and lastly a peach dessert with 1911 Pol Roger champagne for those who were still feeling peckish.

It was all – for the lucky few – a way of forgetting the cold, wet weather that had lasted through most of the summer and the uncomfortable fact that next-door neighbour Herr Hitler had reoccupied the Rhineland and the Sudetenland, declaring all Germanic peoples to be *ein Volk, ein Reich*, which needed of course *einen Führer*.

Drowsy with all the sunlight and heat she had absorbed, Yvonne dropped her copy of *Marie-Claire* onto the warm sand, and rolled over to lie face-down on the large beach towel which was spread in the lee of the private jetty. She opened her legs wide to let the sun stroke the insides of her thighs and between her buttocks, like the hand of a phantom lover. From head to foot, her skin was tanned in the new outdoor-girl look only recently made fashionable by socialite Coco Chanel – before whom brown skin on a European body signified the degradation of manual labour or the shame of a recent illness for which the treatment had included a period of convalescence in the mountains or by the sea.

The silence on the beach was broken only by the lapping of the wavelets in the rock pools and the occasional cry of a gull wheeling on a thermal above the naked woman lying on her beach towel. Only inches from Yvonne's face a school of tiny silver fish swam into a seaweed-edged pool which made a natural aquarium for them. The crystal-clear water looked so cool and inviting that she reached out lazily with one hand and dipped her fingers in. As the shadow of her arm hit the surface of the pool, the fish turned as one and disappeared like an optical illusion.

Yvonne dozed. Each time she opened her eyes, she was tempted to get up and go for a swim to cool herself down, but a profound ennui kept her lying on the beach towel, moving only to rearrange herself on the towel from time to time, and thus ensure the evenness of her tan. Her husband had gone on a business trip to the United States on the glamorous new *SS France*, leaving her behind in charge of his property, which included ten hectares of the most valuable vineyards in the world. With the *vendanges* only a few weeks away, she should have been at his chateau in St Emilion, making sure that the preparations were going ahead in his absence. But her father had spoiled the moment of long-awaited responsibility by asking her to spend a few days at the Villa Céleste, the family's seaside summer home where her sister Céline was awaiting the most important phone call of her life.

The wind changed direction and was blowing from the house to the beach, carrying with it the sound of a violin: Céline was practising. Yvonne sat up, the drowsiness gone, and shook back from her face the long blonde hair she had inherited from her Alsatian mother, holding it back by slipping her sunglasses upwards onto the top of her head. Then she closed her eyes against the sun and began rubbing coconut-scented oil into the skin of her breasts and shoulders, which had started to burn.

The gurgling of the water flushing through the rock pools with each incoming wave was a sound that always made her feel sexy. Or was it the sun? Or simply being naked in the open air – something impossible at home in St Emilion, where all the time she was watched by her servants and the *domestiques* who worked in the vines?

Yvonne was tempted to go back to the cool privacy of her bedroom, but that would mean asking Céline once again, with pretended sympathy, 'Any news yet?' Lying down again, she shut her eyes against the brazen disc glowing through the shimmering heat haze. A storm was forecast, she remembered hearing on the radio at breakfast time. A good storm would be a relief from the heavy, cloying humidity . . .

'Well, what have we here? A mermaid?'

The red light burning its way through Yvonne's closed eyelids turned dark. She opened her eyes to see the black, haloed silhouette of a man standing between her and the sun. He was clad in a pair of wet bathing trunks from which water dripped down his legs. She grabbed a corner of the towel and pulled it awkwardly in front of her to hide her nakedness.

'Can't you read?' she gasped. 'This is private property.'

Pulling the towel around her with one hand, she stood up. It was impossible to see the intruder's face clearly against the glare bouncing off the waves behind him. Her sunglasses slipped down and got in the way, so she took them off and used her free hand to shade her eyes. The first thing she noticed was his mocking facial expression. He was tall, well-muscled and of about the same age as herself: twenty-four or twenty-five. She was aware of his eyes dwelling on the swell of her breasts, forced upwards by the towel, and that her chest was heaving from the effort of getting suddenly to her feet after lying flat in the sun for so long.

He spoke a perfect French, with just a hint of an east-of-the-Rhine accent that went with his short blond hair and blue eyes. 'A naked native girl,' he mused, 'lying on the beach? For a moment I thought you were something much more exotic – a stranded mermaid, at least.'

'I suggest,' Yvonne said coldly, 'that you leave before I call someone to have you thrown out.' The threat was pure bluff; the cook and the maids had already left the Villa Céleste at the end of August. Only the gardener was local and, at this hour of the afternoon, would be sleeping off his lunch in some shady corner.

'You're trespassing on a private beach,' she repeated. 'Can't you read French? There's a notice on the path warning people to keep out.'

Her voice was that of someone used to giving commands to servants. Waiters, mechanics, shop assistants – all hurried obediently to serve her. Why didn't this irritating foreigner know how to behave? Why didn't he just apologise and go?

'I didn't come along the cliff path,' he said casually. 'I swam here. None of the fish I met warned me to keep away.'

'Well, now you know.'

'D'you own all this?' he asked, lifting both arms to encompass the beach, the sea and the sky.

'A lot of it.'

'And is that your house?' He pointed at the villa.

From where they stood, neither he nor Yvonne could see the ground floor, which was hidden by the low cliff. In the open bow window of the first-floor salon, her father's glittering brass telescope pointed seawards. The louvred shutters on the second-floor windows were closed, allowing the breeze to penetrate into the bedrooms while keeping out the sun's heat. Under the projecting wooden gable on the floor above, the windows of the servants' rooms were less than half-size, as though to ration the view for their menial eyes.

'It's one of my family's homes,' Yvonne said.

He whistled. 'I could live in a place like this, you know. It is so clean. Just the wind and the sea and me . . .'

'If you owned the place,' she agreed. 'But you don't, so I think you should leave.'

'Sepp!'

The shout startled half a dozen gulls scavenging at the water's edge. They lifted off, screaming, and skimmed away seaward just above the waves. Yvonne turned and saw, on the top of the cliff beside the notice board, the figures of two young men in *lederhosen* and white singlets, holding bicycles.

'Sepp! We've been looking all over for you,' one of them called in German.

'At least your companions are literate and know how to behave,' she said in the same language. 'Is that your name, Sepp?'

'Sepp Müller.'

Before she could stop him, he took hold of her shoulders, turned her to face him and raised her right hand to his lips. As the towel started to fall open, Yvonne had to drop the sunglasses and hold it closed with her other hand. Seeing the wedding ring on her finger, he murmured, '*Kuss die Hand, gnädige Fräu.*'

He laughed at her confusion, took one step backwards and sprinted across the narrow strip of sand, to launch himself in a shallow dive into the narrow channel which led to the open sea.

'There are rocks!' she called. 'Be careful . . .'

The warning was too late. He surfaced with blood staining his right arm, but seemed unbothered. Now that he was in the water, Yvonne could see that his tan was even deeper than hers. She watched him swim, using a powerful overarm crawl, in a wide semicircle that ended on the rocky beach below the two other young men with bicycles standing by the notice which read, *Propriété Privée – Passage Interdit.*

For a moment as he scrambled up the cliff to rejoin his companions, she thought of inviting them all to use her private beach. It would make a nice change from being stuck here with only Céline to talk to, for she would only talk about the violin and the job for which she had just auditioned. The three Germans would almost certainly jump at the chance, because the private beach was the only swimming place on that stretch of the coast. Elsewhere, notices warned of sharp rocks and dangerous currents. But the sun had slowed Yvonne's brain. Before she could make up her mind, the three young men had mounted their bicycles and ridden away laughing together, without a backward glance. A gust of wind blew her magazine into the water. Yvonne walked carefully across the rocks, slippery with seaweed, to recover it. She stood, swathed in the towel, watching the water gurgling its way from one pool to the next.

'Sepp,' she said several times with only the gulls to hear. The name had a hard, brutal sound. It could not have been more different from her husband's, Antoine Saint-Xavier de Saint Brieuc. The men's names were as different as their bodies, she thought: the one so pale and soft that it was like a girl's, the other hard, tanned and uncompromisingly male.

A sailboat was running before the fitful wind offshore, parallel to but well clear of the rocks. Carried on the shifting breeze, Yvonne heard the skipper's shout of warning to the two girls who were crewing for him, just before it gybed. Then the boom swung across with a vicious slap of the sail and the boat picked up speed on the other reach, foam creaming beneath its bow. The heat haze was building up and up. From the house came the sound of the violin.

.2.

The patrons streaming out of the little cinema in the family seaside resort of Melles-sur-Mer that evening were animatedly discussing the film they had just seen. The cinema, as Lenin had said, was the most important of the arts in those years before television, and Jean Renoir's *La Grande Illusion* was one of the most important European films of 1938. Its story of the French prisoners-of-war in Germany during the First World War and their relationships both with each other and with their captors was still gripping cinema-goers' imaginations in the first week of September 1939. Whatever optimistic pronouncements Daladier in Paris and Chamberlain in London might make publicly about their dealings with the Reichskanzler, a more accurate gauge of the political temperature had been the issuance of sandbags to Parisian householders and the appearance on notice boards outside every *Mairie* and *Hotel de Ville* in France of posters recalling reservists to their regiments.

Yvonne and Céline walked out of the cinema, dressed in similar short-sleeved cotton frocks with calf-length skirts, and identical sandals on their feet. Physically, they could not have looked more different: one tall, languid and blonde, the other a petite, intense brunette.

'You didn't pay any attention to the film, did you?' Yvonne asked, not expecting any reply. 'I could see you staring at the screen and not taking anything in.'

'I'm sorry,' Céline apologised. 'Was it that obvious?'

'I'm going home to St Emilion tomorrow.' Yvonne had made her decision in the cinema. 'Whatever Papa thinks, you might just as well be alone here – so what's the point in me staying on, to be ignored by you? You've hardly said a word to me since I arrived.'

Céline caught her arm. 'I am grateful to you, Yvonne. I really am. But how can I concentrate on a film or a conversation when I'm waiting for a telephone call that may change my whole life?'

'*Bonsoir, mesdames.*'

Yvonne did not recognise the man who had spoken from the shadows. He was clad in white tennis shirt and white slacks. Behind him stood two other young men, similarly dressed. Before she could walk on, the one who had spoken stepped forward and gave a slight bow. 'Sepp Müller, *à votre service.*'

The contrast between his insolence of that afternoon and the smoothness of this greeting put Yvonne off her guard.

'Herr Müller,' she explained to her sister, 'invaded our private beach this afternoon.'

Müller smiled at Céline. 'I'd dived into the sea to cool down and surfaced in a mermaid's grotto, unaware that there was private property in King Neptune's realm.'

'You didn't excuse yourself this afternoon,' Yvonne pointed out. 'I might have reacted differently if you had.'

'Might you?' Müller's smile indicated that he did not care either way. He waved an arm with the same grand gesture he had used on the beach. 'Allow me to present my better-mannered companions, the brothers Dietrich and Helmut Bohlen.'

The other two men bowed slightly in the same formal manner. The elder, Yvonne saw, was tall and dark-haired, with a narrow, sensitive face, while the younger brother was slim and fair, with rather long hair. All three men were very good-looking.

Fancying a little flirtation before returning to the stifling correctness of her life as Madame de St Brieuc in St Emilion, Yvonne ignored Céline's unspoken disapproval, and shook hands with the men, introducing both herself and her sister, and proposed that they all go for a drink.

There was no problem finding a table on the terrace of the little bar overlooking the beach of Melles-sur-Mer in the first week of September. Apart from a few foreigners and the residents, the resort was nearly empty. Traditionally, the French middle classes locked up their holiday homes at the end of August and left the best weather of the summer for the seagulls and any foreign tourists who were less ritualistic about their holidays.

Yvonne had expected her sister to make an excuse and return to the villa. She was amused to see Céline laughing at some remark of Dietrich Bohlen's. Within minutes, conversation had divided the group in two: Céline talking with the brothers about films like Renoir's *La Règle du Jeu*, which had been banned for its portrayal of the corrupt upper classes of French society, Yves Mirande's *Derrière la Façade* and Marcel Carné's *Quai des Brumes* and *Le Jour se Lève*, while Yvonne argued with Müller about the film they had just seen. Against her opinion – which she had borrowed straight from the pages of *Marie-Claire* – that the film had an important message of international understanding, he argued that it was a bourgeois irrelevancy, made for the box office. The two principal characters, he said dismissively, were aristocrats whose behaviour to each other was dictated by traditions of class that happened to override their patriotic differences.

His masculine pomposity grated with Yvonne. 'Are you a Communist, Herr Müller?' she asked. 'You certainly talk like one.'

He leaned forward and parted his hair, inviting her to examine a scar as long as a finger that bisected his scalp. 'You see that? I got it fighting the Communists in Berlin. I am a National Socialist. I can assure you it's a very different thing.'

'Then you're a supporter of Herr Hitler?'

'Of course. All right-thinking Germans are.'

'And do you march about,' she teased him, 'in one of those ridiculous brown Boy Scout shirts festooned with badges, waving your arm in the air and shouting *Heil!* whenever he tells you?'

'I do all sorts of things, when I want to.'

Müller stood up, the same insolent smile on his face that had intrigued her that afternoon. 'Right now, I'm on holiday. And when I am on holiday, I don't do what anyone tells me.'

He walked out of the café without excusing himself. Beneath one of the streetlamps on the promenade between the terrace and the beach, he stopped and lit a cigarette. Across the table from Yvonne, the conversation between Céline and the two brothers had moved on to Darius Milhaud's *Scaramouche*, a piano duet recently premiered in Paris, and Salvador Dali's sur-realist exhibition at the Galerie des Beaux Arts. They were not Yvonne's sort of topics. She stood up and followed Müller out-side.

'Supposing I were to order you to join my sister and me for supper on the beach?' she asked. 'Would you refuse because you are on holiday?'

'Of course.' He blew a smoke ring at the moon.

'In that case, I shan't bother to invite you.'

'In that case, I accept.'

Yvonne laughed. 'Are there many men like you in Germany, Herr Müller?'

'Millions,' he said calmly. 'We are the strongest, most vital nation in Europe.'

It was not the evening air that made Yvonne shiver and hug her bare arms around her, but the way this stranger had of looking at her, ignoring her or talking to her when it suited him and generally taking her for granted in a way no man of her own age ever had done before. Plainly he knew how to behave, but chose not to. She could not recall who had written about Lord Byron that he was 'mad, bad and dangerous to know', but sensed that the description might just as reasonably be applied to Sepp Müller. She knew that she ought to back out of the con-versation before it went any further, because there were people in the café who knew her family. It was not done for a married woman of her class to pick up total strangers like this. Supposing news of her behaviour should get back to St Emilion?

At the table on the glassed-in terrace, Céline was still talking with the two brothers. That, Yvonne decided, was her alibi. If anyone asked, she would say that she had invited the Germans to join them as a way of cheering up Céline and taking her mind off that damned phone call which never came. Müller had walked on ahead, forcing her to half-run after him. He ignored the sound of her heels on the paving flags of the promenade, continuing at his own pace.

'We have a couple of crayfish in the pantry,' Yvonne said when she had caught him up. 'And some fresh prawns my sister bought at the fish market in Royan this morning. I suppose a *Wandervogel* like you would know how to cook them over a bonfire on the beach, Herr Müller?'

'Can't you cook?'

'Of course not,' she laughed. 'I have servants for that sort of thing.'

'So let them do the cooking.'

'They went back to the property at St Emilion at the end of last month. I only returned for a few days to keep my sister company.'

'Then I shall have to give you two Frenchwomen a lesson in *l'art de la cuisine*.'

They had walked beyond the pool of light from the last streetlamp. Müller stopped and turned to Yvonne. He was standing far too close for politeness. She felt his physical nearness pressing against her body. For a second she thought he was going to kiss her. She would slap his face, of course . . . not too hard, and only the first time he tried. Then he flicked the stub of his cigarette away onto the wet sand, making an arc of sparks through the darkness, and started walking back in the direction of the café, leaving her feeling curiously numb.

'It's a pity about the others,' he said.

.3.

At dusk the sea had turned into a flat calm. With not a breath of wind, the air was hot and clammy. In their summer dresses, Céline and Yvonne were as near to being cool as the fashions of the day permitted them. Once on the beach, the men took off their shirts and everyone went barefoot. There was no need to light the hurricane lantern which they had brought from the villa – the full moon was huge in a cloudless sky. Diffused through the haze, it silvered the sand, turned the rocks and trees into black shapes and made the flat surface of the sea look like a slowly rippling sheet of steel.

Dietrich, the older of the two Bohlen brothers, opened the first of the bottles of cooled white wine from the icebox in the villa. He chinked glasses and chatted with Céline and her sister against a background of light music. As her contribution to the ambience, Yvonne had brought along her portable wind-up gramophone and a dozen 78 rpm records by Tino Rossi, Charles Trenet, Edith Piaf and Yves Montand. As one record ended, she put on the next, ignoring the protests from Céline, on whose musician's ear the distorted sound of the gramophone grated painfully.

At the fold-up table that Helmut had set up on the sand, Müller made a great ritual of his preparations, chopping up the herbs and preparing a sauce for the prawns. He made occasional jokes in Plattdeutsch, which neither Yvonne nor Céline could follow, although they both spoke fluent German. Helmut always laughed at the jokes, but Dietrich looked uncomfortable.

The relationship between the three men intrigued Yvonne. From Dietrich she had found out that, at the end of the holiday, he was to start work as an assistant curator at the Gemäldegalerie in Berlin-Dahlem. His younger brother Helmut was only seventeen and still at high school. Dietrich had met Müller while he was studying art history at Leipzig University and Müller had been majoring in French and Russian. Müller's job was something political, about which the others did not talk.

The Germans made an odd threesome, Yvonne decided. She had never known a boy like Helmut before. Slim and fair-skinned, forever brushing his long fair hair back from his face, he watched Müller's every move and spent most of the meal hovering on the edge of the firelight, only too pleased to jump up and run errands back to the house, to fetch more driftwood or to strike a match for his idol's cigarettes.

After the fish had been consumed, Müller sent him on a two-mile run along the beach to where the Germans had set up their tents, to fetch some cheeses and fresh bread which they had been going to eat for their evening meal. Whilst the boy was gone, Céline took Dietrich back to the villa to select two bottles of her father's 1935 vintage red wine from the cellar. Several times whilst they were alone on the beach, Müller's eyes met Yvonne's but he said nothing to her, despite attempts on her part to make a normal conversation. Instead of angering her, his smouldering silence intrigued her.

When the others returned, it was, on the surface, a relaxed and casual meal: five young people eating *al fresco* on a beach, listening to the popular music of the day, enjoying good cheese and a marvellous red wine from St Emilion. Yet on shore as at sea, there were that night undercurrents which were quite at variance with what was happening on the surface.

Normally Céline did not touch wine. That night she had a glass of white and two of red. Yvonne was surprised to see her dancing a foxtrot with Dietrich and laughing with him at the difficulty of moving gracefully in bare feet on soft sand. A blur of white trousers further along the beach showed where Helmut was paddling in the shallows to keep cool. But where had Müller gone? Yvonne looked round and could not see him.

There was a brief glow against the dark blur of the pine trees that grew down almost to the high-water line and then another arc of sparks through the darkness. Yvonne got to her feet and felt the grains of sand between her toes as she strolled up the beach towards the glowing cigarette end. She kicked sand over it and walked on. Among the trees, it was dark, the moon's light blocked by the interlacing branches.

The music and laughter from the bonfire sounded very distant. Across the sand carpeted with pine needles Yvonne moved like a sleepwalker, feeling her way forward in the gloom. Müller was waiting in a small clearing, seated on a fallen tree trunk that was resting across another. He did not say a word as she stepped into the moonlight, but motioned her to come nearer, the same sardonic smile playing on his face as when he had intruded on her that afternoon. Yvonne stopped two paces away.

'Closer,' he said, refusing to get up or reach for her.

She took one pace, then another, and watched his hands reach up to undo the bodice of her dress. He lifted her breasts out of her bra and weighed them like ripe fruit. Then one strong arm was around her waist, pulling her closer still so that she had to lift up the full skirt of her dress and spread her legs, straddling his. Eyes closed, she felt his lips on her breasts. His teeth bit on her nipples until she was uncertain whether it was pleasure or pain. His hands slid higher up her legs until they were kneading and pulling the skin of her buttocks through the thin silk that covered them.

Yvonne arched herself towards him, seeking the hardness of his breastbone and ribs against her belly. Her small moans of pleasure turned to a gasp as his fingers gripped her labia and tugged in the same rhythm as a farmer milking a cow. She felt her strength draining out of her with each tug. And then he was gone, leaving her gasping and holding the tree for support. She felt his strong hands grasp her waist and push her face-down across the trunk. With one hand he held her there while unbuckling his heavy leather belt. He bundled her skirt out of the way and grabbed the wasitband of her panties, pulling them down to her knees. And all the while a part of her mind was wondering, What am I doing here with this animal?

She knew it would hurt when she felt the size of him, thumping against her labia until he could hear her moistness and decided she was ready. He entered her and pulled her head back at the same moment, arching her spine and twisting her head so that he could kiss her lips and stop the cries she could not restrain. Yvonne wanted to cry out in pain but her mouth was too busy devouring his. She wanted to tear his hands away from her breasts because they were hurting her too, but her arms had no strength. She wanted to stand on her own feet but they would not reach the ground. But when Müller thrust her roughly down across the tree trunk in the moonlight, and used her like a female beast in the forest, it was impossible to think any more.

The weather was changing rapidly as the storm massed black clouds in the darkness of the western sky and the wind gathered strength, preparing to assault the slumbering land. Lightning danced on the sea and the thunder was getting much louder. On the beach, the music ground to a halt as the gramophone spring finally unwound. Helmut stood in the shallows, staring at the tree-line, certain that he had heard someone cry out above the swishing of the wind in the branches. By the fire, fanned into new life by the sudden gusts of wind, Dietrich and Céline were laughing together so loudly that they did not hear the cry when it was repeated.

Helmut ran up the beach, his feet slipping in the dry sand. He stopped in the gloom beneath the trees, feeling the pine needles beneath his bare feet, hearing only the beating of his heart in his ears as he groped his way from trunk to trunk. Hearing another cry, quite near, he groped his way forward in the gloom until he reached the edge of the clearing. The first clouds were already obscuring the moon. In the half-light he saw Müller's naked form bent over and thrusting. Beneath him was a blur of white dress across the dark trunk of the tree. As Müller climaxed and withdrew shuddering, Helmut saw Yvonne's buttocks and the backs of her legs, with her panties still around her knees. The rest of her body was hidden from him by the tree trunk, across which she lay, moaning rhythmically.

Helmut closed his eyes and stumbled back through the pine trees, twice tripping over protruding roots and crashing to the ground. 'Sepp,' he sobbed. 'How could you?'

Then he was on the beach of silvered sand beneath the hazy moon, running and running until he could dive into the clean, clean sea.

'What did he say?' Céline asked as he ran past.

Dietrich shook his head. 'I couldn't hear. Where are the others?'

The beach was deserted, apart from themselves. As the first storm cloud blacked out the moon, Céline lit the hurricane lantern with difficulty; gusts of wind kept blowing out the matches. They stood looking at each other for a moment, listening. The wind blew a shower of sparks from the cooking fire across the beach and bent the tops of the trees. Shutters banged in the villa.

'I must go and close the windows,' Céline said, closing the lid of the gramophone and starting to tidy up. 'These sudden autumn storms can cause damage.'

She was halfway to the steps that led up to the villa when Dietrich shouted. He was down by the water, staring seaward to where a shaft of moonlight, shining through a gap in the clouds, illuminated Helmut, several hundred metres out and still swimming away from the shore.

Again Dietrich called out, 'Helmut, *komm züruck! Ein Sturm kommt!* Helmut!' He pulled off his shirt and started undoing his belt.

Céline cried out a warning, 'Be careful. There are currents and rocks offshore.'

As the squall hit, the waves were growing higher by the minute. Dietrich waded into the water in his white cotton undershorts. There was no sight of Helmut but, from Céline's vantage point higher up the beach, a line of breakers showed where the rocks were, just beyond where they had last seen him.

'What's going on?'

Céline turned when she heard Müller's voice behind her. 'Helmut came rushing down the beach a few minutes ago and ran into the water. He didn't come out, so Dietrich has gone in after him.'

'The fool,' said Müller. 'The crazy young fool.'

He cupped his hands and shouted both their names, but his voice was lost in the noises of the squall: salt spray and cutting sand stung their faces, the wind tore at the tops of the trees. All the towels had blown away and the table fell with a crash of breaking glass and china, then went bowling along the beach faster than a man could run. Müller pulled off his trousers and ran naked into the water just as the storm hit.

Stunned by the speed at which everything had happened, Céline ran after the windblown debris, collecting things up and carrying them into the shelter of the steps that led up to the villa. It seemed like half an hour but was only ten minutes later when Müller reappeared, staggering through the breakers with one arm supporting a retching Dietrich. Both men were naked. Céline ran into the water to help them onto dry land, was knocked off her feet by the undertow and found herself pulled roughly upright by Müller and dragged out of the waves.

'Has Helmut shown up?' he shouted, as the three of them collapsed on the dry sand above the waterline.

'I haven't seen him,' Céline gasped, coughing up salt water.

Dietrich broke free from Sepp and tried to go back into the water. Müller wrestled him to the ground just above the water line. With foam washing around them both, he shouted in the other man's ear. 'He's playing games, that crazy little brother of yours. You know he is. He must have doubled back to the beach while we were looking for him out there. In fact, he's probably watching us right now and laughing his stupid head off.'

'Has your brother done this sort of thing before?' Céline asked.

Dietrich looked at Müller. 'Yes,' he admitted. 'He has.'

As he got to his feet, a shaft of lightning struck the sea so close that the flash and the crash of thunder were simultaneous, imprinting on Céline's retina the red stain on her dress and the wound under Dietrich's left arm where a wave had hurled him onto the jagged rocks. And then they were staggering with the lantern towards the steps up to the villa through wind and rain that hit them with the force of a fire hose.

.4.

At 2 a.m. the doctor left after dressing Dietrich's wound. The storm was at its height. Salt spray and hailstones were drumming on the closed shutters; the wooden frame of the house vibrated with each shock of the waves on the solid rock in which its foundations were anchored.

Yvonne had ignored the drama downstairs and gone straight to bed. After changing into a warm woollen dress Céline went to knock on her door, and opened it when she received no reply.

'You can't be asleep,' she said, standing in the doorway of the darkened room.

'I'm thinking.'

'Dietrich had to have several stitches. He'll have a scar.'

'They all have scars,' Yvonne murmured from the bed. 'Remember those German clients of father's with their duelling scars? Müller has one on his scalp. And now Dietrich has one under his arm.'

'Are you all right?'

'Why do you ask?'

'You sound strange. There's still no sign of Helmut. I'll put the light on.'

'No! Leave it.'

'I can't send the Germans back to their tent. It's probably blown away by now. Even if it's still there, they'd get soaked to the bone, walking that far in this weather. So I thought I'd put them in one of the servants' rooms, if you agree.'

'Do what you like,' Yvonne said. 'Just close the door and leave me alone.'

In the salon, after Müller had gone upstairs for the night, Dietrich stood playing with the brass telescope. His left arm was in a sling and the clothes he was wearing had been borrowed from those which Céline's father kept at the villa for winter sailing: thick brown cord trousers and a white polo-neck sweater, with the sleeve slit all the way up, to make it easier to put on without tearing the stitches under his arm.

'Please go to bed,' he said. 'Only one of us need stay up, so let it be me.'

Céline knew that she would not sleep a wink that night, and offered to keep him company despite his protestations that it was unnecessary.

'Is it true that Helmut could play a trick on us all like this?' she wondered. 'I mean, it's one thing to swim out to sea and double back to land in normal weather, but surely he'll realise how worried you are, on a night like this?'

Dietrich pushed his dark hair back and stretched. 'You shouldn't blame my brother too much. It's Müller's fault. He's always had this effect on Helmut – right from the beginning.'

Sensing that Dietrich wanted to talk, Céline stayed silent. The information came in half-sentences, disjointedly. During their first vacation from Leipzig University, Sepp had come to the Bohlen home to borrow a book. The house, in a suburb of Berlin called Gatow, was a small and unpretentious wooden villa on the banks of the Havel lake, with no telephone. Dietrich and his mother – a widow from the First World War – had been out at the time. When they returned that evening, there was a note from Helmut, saying that he had gone for a beer with Müller at one of the lakeside beer gardens. The boy had only been fifteen at the time. He reappeared after midnight, drunk. Both his mother and Dietrich had tried to stop him seeing Müller again.

'. . . but every now and again, they seek each other out and there's always trouble of some sort.'

'So why did you invite Müller to come on holiday with you?' Céline asked.

'I didn't.' Dietrich sat down on the *canapé* beside her, wincing at the pain. 'Sepp had some plan to take that foolish brother of mine climbing in the Schwabian Alps, but Helmut has never done that sort of thing before and Mother was terrified he'd have an accident, because he has no sense of danger. So I planned our bicycling tour as a way of getting him away from Müller.'

'And?'

Dietrich kept to himself his suspicions that Müller was on some kind of intelligence-gathering mission, for which he had insisted on changing the originally planned itinerary to include the ports of Brest and La Rochelle as well as the estuary of the Gironde. 'For some reason, Sepp decided to come with us.'

'You could have told him he wasn't welcome, if you felt that strongly about his influence over your brother.'

'I did,' Dietrich said wretchedly. 'Müller just laughed that he didn't care either way. It was Helmut who insisted that Sepp should come with us.'

'It'll be all right,' Céline said, to comfort him. 'In the morning, when the storm has blown itself out, you'll see. Nobody would have swum out to sea in this kind of weather. When the sun's up, we'll find Helmut sitting in your tent and laughing at the worry he has caused us all.'

The four figures on the beach were well spread out. Céline and Yvonne were wearing shorts and pullovers, for the temperature had dropped fifteen degrees overnight. Checking out the larger tidal pools, they had espadrilles on their feet, to walk more easily over the sharp and slippery rocks. Half a kilometre to the north, Müller trotted along in the shallows, diverting every so often to examine piles of seaweed and pieces of flotsam from the storm. To the south, Dietrich was walking along the sand at the water's edge, poking at each pile of debris washed up by the storm that was large enough to conceal a body.

'Helmut!' Céline cried for the hundredth time since dawn. And again, 'Helmut!'

It was the sound of the gulls that drew her attention to the cleft above which they were circling. She shaded her eyes against the glare from the sun, which was barely above the horizon and tried at first to persuade herself that the object half in and half out of the water was a rock. But rocks do not float. Nor was this a mass of seaweed.

The body floated in the shallows face down, seemingly undamaged, until a wave larger than the others lifted it over the threshold of the rapidly emptying cleft between the rocks. As the water receded, leaving it momentarily high and dry, the corpse rolled over onto its back, displaying deep gashes in the torso and legs caused by repeated dashing against the needle-sharp rocks. Apart from a few shreds of skin, the penis and testicles were missing, either amputated by the rocks or eaten by fish or gulls. By a freak chance, the pale, ivory-coloured face was untouched, its expression almost mischievous, as though Helmut was smiling to himself at the bother he had caused.

Céline scrambled over the rocks and waded into the cleft until she was standing in knee-deep water, staring at the naked body that was lifted up towards her on each wave. Beneath it, a bed of red sea anemones waved their tendrils in the water around his head. How beautiful they looked in their element, and how ugly when the water receded and left them like glistening lumps of excrement smeared on the rock. So it was with Dietrich, who had been so beautiful in life, and was now just a lump of clay . . .

She was aware that she ought to call the others, but did not wish to turn their nebulous fears into the awful knowledge of Helmut's death. Better, she thought, to leave them in ignorance for a few more seconds. She concentrated on the sounds in her ears. Close to, there was a scuttling of crabs and the lapping of water. Further away was the sound of the disturbed gulls screaming above the wave noises. And from far out on the flat waters of the estuary came the contrapuntal *putt-putt-putt* of a diesel engine in a fishing boat chugging seaward with the tide.

A scream made Céline look up. Yvonne was standing on a high rock, with one hand across her mouth. Above the hand, her eyes were wide in horror, staring at the mutilated body in the water. In the distance, alerted by her scream, the small figures of the two men were standing still on the empty beach. For a moment, none of the living stirred. Only the corpse lifted and rolled back, a little less with each wave as the tide receded.

*

The *pompiers* had removed the body on a stretcher, the gendarmes had left after laboriously typing out their *procès-verbaux*, the statements from the four people who had last seen Helmut Bohlen alive. Yvonne departed in her slinky red Peugeot 402B tourer and Sepp mounted his drop-handlebar bike to ride slowly away in the direction of the main road. Dietrich was required to be available until after the inquest; Céline had told him that he could stay in the villa for the two or three days until his passport was returned.

The house was quiet. When the phone rang, Céline picked it up, expecting to hear the doctor or someone from the gendarmerie or the *caserne des pompiers*. Her father's voice sounded foreign: everyone outside the small group who had shared in Helmut's death was a stranger.

'Is something the matter?' he asked. 'Céline, are you there?'

'Yes, Papa.' Feeling remote, as though it had all happened to someone else, she told him about the drowning.

He listened for a couple of minutes before interrupting: 'A tourist, you say?'

'Just below the villa.'

'But a German tourist is nothing to do with us, *ma chère fille*. You must forget all that and concentrate. I just had a call from the Opera. They wouldn't tell me the result of the audition, but I don't think they would be making a long-distance telephone call just to say that you had failed to get the job. So I've given them the number of the Villa Céleste. They should be calling any minute now. Phone me back immediately you have spoken to them.'

After he hung up, Céline sat by the telephone, looking at Dietrich's back. With his good hand, he was turning the adjustment wheels on the telescope, winding the tube purposelessly in and out – and staring at the sea which had taken his brother's life.

The phone rang and another remote voice, calling from Paris, told Céline that she had been given the job.

'I'm delighted,' she said mechanically. 'When can I start?'

She listened to her father laughing with pure delight when she called back to give him the news. 'I'm so proud of you,' he kept saying. 'Number Five is a marvellous position – on the outside of the third desk. You'll be seen by the conductor and the audience. They must have been very impressed with your audition. Now all those years of work will bear fruit. At last I can say that my daughter is truly a musician.'

'*Oui, Papa*,' she said.

They stood side by side on the platform at Royan station, watching the undertaker's men load the coffin into the luggage van beside the two bicycles. Dietrich was insisting that he would repay the money Céline had advanced for the expenses.

'It doesn't matter,' she repeated. 'I feel we were all to blame for what happened. I only hope it will be some consolation to your mother that Helmut can be buried in the local cemetery.'

Doors were slamming. The guard put the whistle in his mouth. Dietrich climbed aboard and put his head out of the window.

'All innocence is dead,' he said.

Céline wanted to ask him what he meant, but the train was already moving. She stood on the platform until it was out of sight. When she walked out of the station the newsstand was displaying that day's continental edition of the *Daily Mail*. There was a picture of Prime Minister Neville Chamberlain beneath the headline BRITAIN PRESENTS ULTIMATUM. Thirty-six hours later, Europe was at war.

PART IV:
Dordogne, France –
November 1996

. 1 .

Old spooks never die, they only go to live in France.

Ken had learned the truth of the adage one morning at Bergerac market while he was getting to know the area and looking for a suitable property he could afford to buy. After wandering around the picturesque old quarter of the town in the heat of midsummer, he paused to take in the busy market scene over a cup of black coffee at a pavement café. The street was nearly blocked by stalls. Traffic threaded its way with difficulty through the throng of hustling market traders, local people doing their shopping and camera-laden tourists.

An elderly man in a denim shirt with rolled up sleeves was buying cheese from a rosy-cheeked countrywoman at her stall in front of the café, carefully tasting a sliver of each before deciding to buy. Although his face was shadowed by the wide brim of a *chapeau de paille*, the traditional summer headgear of the region when working in the fields, he was no local peasant: his height alone distinguished him from the other shoppers. Standing over six foot, despite a slight stoop, he towered over the locals of both sexes.

Intrigued by a memory that refused to be identified, Ken dropped a ten-franc coin on the table and followed his quarry as he moved from stall to stall. By habit, he started checking off what he did know. Age: anywhere from sixty-five upwards. Two: the man was probably a widower or bachelor, because he knew too much about different cuts of meat, and which seafood was good that week, for someone who was just running errands for his wife. Three: he was no stranger to Bergerac market, for the traders greeted him as a regular customer, while he called several of them by name. Four: although dressed in an old denim work shirt and vivid blue cotton trousers of the type worn by workmen all over France, with espadrilles on his feet like many of the locals, he was not French. He spoke the language fluently, but with a light transatlantic twang.

After a complete circuit of the market, the man in the straw hat sat down with his back to Ken at a table on the terrace of the café where it had begun. He ordered a pastis and, without turning his head, asked in English with a New England accent, 'Do we know each other, son?'

Ken still did not have any idea whom he had been following. Then the straw hat came off, revealing a leonine head of thick, swept-back silver hair. A large red polka-dotted handkerchief was used to mop the perspiring forehead, and an image surfaced which had been stored in Ken's memory bank on a visit to Langley, Virginia, years before.

'Now there you have one of the founding fathers,' his conducting officer had announced, pointing out the tall man getting into a black chauffeur-driven limousine in the CIA staff car park. 'Erich Hallstatt, in person.'

The name was a legend among Ken's older colleagues on both sides of the Atlantic. When he expressed surprise at seeing a ghost, his CIA guide had explained why this ghost was still intermittently in harness. Alan Dulles and Wild Bill Donovan had not believed in putting too many things down on paper for the politicians on Capitol Hill to use against them. In those days there were no computer data bases and no Freedom of Information Act. But Hallstatt, who had been at the sharp end in Europe during the Second World War and the early Cold War years before rising high in the intelligence hierarchy, had a photographic memory and instant recall. Whenever the CIA wanted to find a useful precedent that could not be contradicted by the man in the White House, Hallstatt was called back from retirement.

Across the car park, the distinguished, grey-haired man with the Harry Truman bow tie and the matching red polka-dot handkerchief spilling out of the breast pocket of his Brooks

Brothers suit was shaking hands with a posse of senior executives and getting into the limousine.

'He'll never be signed off,' the conducting officer had told Ken. 'E.H. knows too much, ever to be let go.'

Yet there the living legend was, sitting two tables away in Bergerac market with his straw hat on the table and an old raffia shopping bag on the cobbles beside him.

Ken apologised, 'Excuse me. I didn't mean to embarrass you, sir.'

'You followed me from the cheese stall, young man.' Hallstatt did not look round.

'I knew I'd seen you somewhere before. It just clicked where. Again, my apologies.'

'Join me.' Hallstatt turned with a grin and pulled a chair forward. He raised a scrawny, liver-spotted hand and snapped his fingers so loud that a passing waiter nearly dropped his tray. '*Garçon*,' Hallstatt boomed at him, '*un autre pastis pour mon ami.*'

He raised his glass to Ken. 'I guess we were in the same line of business. So who are you snooping on at the market, apart from me? I thought the French were your allies.'

It still hurt to say it: 'My contract was terminated. I was put out to grass a little prematurely.'

'What did you do? Steal the Crown Jewels? Anyway, you can relax. I know how it feels.'

Ken shook his head. 'Oh come on, sir. I don't think . . .'

'And don't call me "sir".' Hallstatt glared from beneath bushy brows. 'Makes me feel like a centenarian. Right?'

Ken lifted his glass. 'All the same, the idea of you being pensioned off . . .'

'Langley is run by accountants now,' growled Hallstatt in his deep voice. 'Some kid with a degree from Harvard Business School hit on the bright idea of saving a few grand by getting me and a few other old relics off the payroll at last.'

'And you settled here?'

'My wife was French. I promised her we'd come back here to live when I retired. Each summer we visited our farm just north of here for a month or so – not that I was ever left in peace that long, but she'd stay on with the kids after I'd been called back to Langley. And when they'd grown up and had families of their own, she'd usually bring over one of the grandchildren to keep her company. Each fall, when she returned to the States, she'd ask when I was going to make the break – and I'd stall her by saying we couldn't leave the country permanently, in case the Director needed me in a hurry. A coupla years back, she died of brain cancer. Three months later, they finally put me out to grass. So who's the fool?'

Underestimating how lonely he had been, during the years since he had settled in France, Hallstatt blamed Ken for making him talk too much. 'Does everyone open up to you like this on first meeting?' he growled.

'A lot of people do.'

'And your people let you go?' Hallstatt shook his head. 'Pray to God the other side is just as stupid. What's your name, son?'

'Ken Scott. People call me Scottie.'

'Sounds like a fricking dog,' Hallstatt guffawed. 'You call me Erich and I'll call you Ken.' The town-hall clock was striking noon. 'D'you eat *boudin*, Ken?'

'I don't know what it is.'

'Blood sausage. Full of fat, cholesterol and everything else the doctors tell you not to eat.'

'Sounds good to me.'

'And *andouillette*?'

'Fill me in, Erich.'

'Guts sausage. Made from all the bits they probably throw away in England.'

'I'll give it a try.'

Hallstatt stood up. His joints seemed to be giving him pain and his back was not as straight as it had been when Ken had last seen him. 'Join me for lunch,' he ordered. 'On market days I eat at that little café across the square. It's where all the stall-holders take lunch after they've packed up. Those guys always know the best places to eat.'

When Ken offered to carry the loaded shopping bag, Hallstatt snatched it away from him, 'I warned you. Stop treating me like an old man.'

'So long as you stop calling me *son*.'

'It's a deal, Ken.'

They consumed two *boudins* each and a large *andouillette*, with mashed potatoes and apple sauce, washed down with endless glasses of *vin de pays* for which there was no charge – and the conversation flowed as easily and naturally as if they had been friends for years. Most of the market traders had eaten and hit the road long before they staggered out of the café after a leisurely cheese course and several brandies with their coffee.

Before parting, Hallstatt scribbled directions to his home on the back of the till slip and said, 'Come and see me if you want any advice on buying a house. Meantime I'll put out a few feelers for you – now that I know the kind of property you're looking for. I may have a hell of a Yankee accent when I talk French, but I know my way around this goddam country. Should do, I've been coming here since Thirty-nine.'

Old spooks get lonely, even the ones who never danced on tables all night in their youth. Unlike other senior citizens, they can never relax over a drink and bore their new friends and golf partners with tales of their professional lives. After listening to other people's anecdotes, they are unable to contribute in kind. Some fall back on a repertoire of jokes as their share of the conversation, but Hallstatt was not one of them. Being a spook had been his whole life and there was nothing else that interested him very much.

After Ken moved into Le Farou – a property he found with Hallstatt's help – they got into the habit of spending an evening together once a month. Cagily at first, and then with greater freedom when he found that Ken's mouth stayed shut except when they were together, Hallstatt opened up about his past. Without ever betraying current secrets, he and Ken traded stories – not so much of their triumphs as the laughable failures. And because their sessions went on late into the night, with a prodigious consumption of alcohol, they got into the habit of staying over – and were never in a hurry to say goodbye the next morning. It was the sort of friendship that only happens once or twice in a lifetime, with neither man aware of the thirty-year age-gap that separated them.

With wry humour, Hallstatt explained one night that he had been brought into OSS not because anyone thought he had a talent for killing Germans, nor because he had worked in Paris right up to the commencement of hostilities and spoke fluent French. 'The initials of Wild Bill Donovan's organisation were often taken to mean Oh-So-Social. I just happened to have the right background because my mother's side of the family were in banking in a big way, back home in Boston. That's why Donovan wanted me.'

'What exactly were you doing here before the war, Erich?'

'I was eighteen in 1939 and expecting to go to Harvard in the fall, majoring in French. But my father saw the way the wind was blowing in Europe and sent me to work for one of his correspondent banks over here instead. By VE Day there was no way the young warrior king I had become at the age of twenty-four was going to settle back to his studies, so I never got to Harvard. Maybe that's why I still have a chip on my shoulder about younger guys with more education than I got.'

Hallstatt had been in Paris right through the phoney war and stayed on until four days after Pearl Harbour, leaving only on 11 December 1941 when Washington declared war on the Berlin-Rome-Tokyo axis.

'To prolong my stay,' he had explained to Ken, 'my old man had gotten me accredited to the Embassy, where I worked in the Consular section, fixing Uncle Sam seals to deed boxes and bundles of bonds in French bank vaults attesting that they belonged to neutral US citizens. In theory, that should have guaranteed their inviolability. Of course, it didn't – but that's another story. All in all, it was an interesting job for a young fellow of nineteen.'

The most fascinating anecdotes as far as Ken was concerned came when Hallstatt reminisced about his times with OSS in France during the war. After being parachuted into the south of France, he had conducted clandestine strategic sabotage operations before the Normandy landings, then emerged after D-Day as chieftain of a ragtag army of three thousand young men who tore around the Rhône valley in requisitioned civilian vehicles with FFI painted on the side. Their job had been to harass the German troops of General Wiese's retreating

Nineteenth Army after Operation Anvil – the joint American-French landings on the Côte d'Azur between Cannes and Toulon. It was quite a war for a young man who had still not seen his twenty-fifth birthday when it ended on 8 May 1945.

'Trouble is, Ken, that I couldn't settle to anything else afterwards. When they wrapped up OSS after VE Day, I was on the street. I tried banking for a while because my mother wanted me to, but I'd had more experience by then in robbing banks than working in them. To give him his due, my grandfather made me the family trouble-shooter, which could have been a challenge for somebody else, but it sure as hell wasn't my bag. I must have been a bit scary to have around. Today, I guess they'd say I was suffering from post-traumatic stress, and give me counselling and a pension.

'Let's say I just didn't fit into normal society. So when the National Security Act of September 1947 set up the peacetime CIA, I was one of the first to knock on Admiral Hillenkoetter's door for a job, the day after he was named boss of the new outfit. I guess my family breathed a sigh of relief to see me go back where I belonged.'

. . . all of which was why Ken decided to drive past Le Farou after leaving the Villa Céleste, and head up-river to talk to Hallstatt, a man who knew from personal experience what life in Occupied France had really been like.

The converted farmhouse where he lived was built of honey-coloured stone in the Perigord style, with a steeply pitched roof. It stood on a grassy knoll with a fine view of a crook in the Dordogne, edged by limestone cliffs. Hallstatt came to the door, his face flushed from cooking. A man of huge, if passing, enthusiasms, he had recently discovered the delights of making food, as well as eating it. He was wearing a blue and white checked barbecue apron on which some grandchild on the other side of the Atlantic had cross-stitched with more enthusiasm than accuracy the legend *Hail to the Chef!*

A gusty westerly wind was threatening to shut the door in Ken's face. He shrugged off his anorak and accepted a glass of *marc*, which he and Hallstatt had distilled together in an illicit still they had made for fun.

'What can I do for you?' Hallstatt asked. 'You look like a man with something on his mind.'

He listened without comment to the story of Mrs Prescot's death, the burglaries and the painting.

'I need to have some idea of what things were like in France during the Occupation and the Liberation,' Ken said. 'I've read as many books about the period as most people, but I can't buy the simplified picture they present of heroic British agents, garlic-chewing *résistants*, brutal Germans and sadistic *miliciens* . . . What was it really like, Erich?'

'First thing,' said Hallstatt, sipping his own glass of *marc* appreciatively, 'is that you've got to forget all that crap about the Resistance being set up by either the Reds or De Gaulle. It was Pétain who created the *maquis* by instituting Le Service de Travail Obligatoire, a system of conscription under which men of military age were conscripted to work in the Reich – to replace the German men who were all away in the army. To escape that, tens of thousands of young men went underground, hiding out in forests and remote areas all over France.

'And you can forget all that Chairman Mao shit about the guerrillas being the fish who swim in the sea of the population. These guys hadn't read the little red book. Most *maquisards* were young thugs on the run who lived by knocking on people's doors at night and threatening them with loaded guns. "Give us food and clothes," they said, "and we'll give you a receipt which will be redeemed by De Gaulle after the Liberation." Of course everybody knew that the IOUs were worthless, but what would you do, threatened by armed men in the middle of the night?'

'Hand over what they wanted.'

'Right. Which did not exactly make the Resistance the flavour of the month, as far as most people were concerned. Of course, no one warned me about all this. I had to find out the hard way when I was parachuted into the Alpes Maritimes in the spring of 1943 and discovered that my first job was to get the leaders of the different gangs of young hooligans to talk to each other, never mind agree to accept my authority in something like a disciplined clandestine army.'

.2.

'*Qu'est-ce que vous faîtes là?*' Catriona peered suspiciously at the man bent over Ken's Harley Davidson, his face invisible in the gloom of the old dairy.

'A friend. Don't shoot.' Irving straightened up. The silhouetted figure standing in the doorway with hands on hips could have been that of a tall boy, apart from the contralto voice. He put up his hands in mock surrender and walked into the light spilling through the half-open wicket door.

It was typical of his impulsive nature that, after the first few moments of incredulity listening to Ken's voice from a phone box at the Villa Céleste, he had decided to cancel a publicity photo-call and caught the first Bordeaux flight from Gatwick Airport. As Catriona backed away from the doorway to let him out, he saw her face clearly for the first time, and was struck by its Celtic beauty.

'Oh, it's you.' As he emerged into the daylight, she recognised him from record and CD covers. To her artist's eye, Irving's looks were even more stunning in the flesh than through a camera lens. The pale skin, the almost jet-black hair, and the intensity of his dark brown eyes . . .

Remembering Ken as he had been in Liverpool, Irving had been expecting his father's companion to be an equally nondescript grey fiftyish wife, not this radiantly smiling woman who looked hardly older than himself.

'Who are you?' he said.

Catriona turned away to point across the meadow. 'I'm the tenant of the little cottage over there.'

'I was looking for the door key when I saw the Harley. Is it Ken's?'

She nodded.

That bike? That woman? Irving was trying to fit them in with the image of the man in a grey suit and collar and tie standing at Mrs Prescot's graveside.

'What you're looking for is just inside the barn door,' said Catriona. 'Reach out with your right hand and you'll feel it.'

He weighed the heavy old iron key in his hand. 'You still haven't introduced yourself.'

'The name's Catriona.'

Seeing the surfboards stacked against the side wall of the dairy, Irving asked, 'Are those Ken's too?'

She nodded.

The woman, the bike, the surfboards? Irving shook his head. Ken Scott was *not* the man he had thought him to be.

'If it's dangerous, Ken does it,' Catriona smiled. 'Now, I've always wondered whether these things are genetic, Mr Bradley. You, now . . . What do you do for kicks?'

'Me, now?' He mocked her accent. 'I play the fiddle, sure I do.'

'That's not exactly a blood sport, is it?'

Irving grinned. 'That just shows how little you know about the life of a solo musician. Think of me as a musical high-wire artiste. Some fans want to see me reach the other side; others come to see me fall and die. There's no safety net in my business: I'm only ever as good as my last performance. I don't need dangerous hobbies because my professional life is one long adrenaline trip. Can you tell me when Ken'll be home?'

'No idea. I'm not his keeper.'

Irving was irritated at the thought of being kept waiting, albeit unintentionally. It was usually he who wasted other people's time.

He was dressed from head to foot in black: black polo-neck sweater, black jeans and black suede shoes that were already spattered with mud from the yard. Against the dark background of the doorway, his pale musician's face floated in nothingness. I have to paint this man, Catriona thought. It was a long time since she had felt such a strong compulsion to capture a face on canvas.

'While you're waiting for Ken to turn up, come over to my cottage,' she offered. 'You'll be a whole lot warmer than in his house, that's for sure. And . . . I'd like to paint your portrait, if that's all right by you.'

'Just like that? I'm leaving tomorrow morning, you know.'

'Ken has plenty of photographs of you I can use for reference – record sleeves, that sort of thing. I can probably manage with just one sitting, if I work fast. And don't worry . . .' She took both his hands briefly in hers and let them go. 'Painting's my job. I won't let you down.'

'D'you offer to paint the portrait of everyone you meet?'

'No.' She studied him from several angles.

'Then why?'

'I could say it's because you have good bone structure, Mr Bradley. You've a fine mouth and eyes that are hard to look away from. Or I could say it's because you have the face of a great artist. And all that would be true.'

'But actually?'

She could not say, *Because I have to.* So . . . 'I'll be honest, Mr Bradley. You're famous. Now, I have a show coming up in London in less than a week's time. The more red dots I get on my pictures at the private view, the more money I make. It's a penny to a *punt* that some snob will buy the portrait of a celebrity like you.'

'Your honesty is disarming.' Perhaps the afternoon waiting for Ken would not be so boring after all, Irving thought. This strange artist with looks that many women would have traded for a fortune, one way or another, was beginning to intrigue him.

'I'll get my fiddle from the car, and come over,' he said.

'I was going to ask you if you'd mind holding it as though you were playing.'

'I shall be playing. I can sit there practising while you paint me. That way, the afternoon's not wasted.'

'Can you bear to go on for as long as a couple of hours?'

Irving laughed. 'I practise between two and ten hours out of every twenty-four, depending on what else I'm doing that day.'

After Catriona had gone, he took his time looking around Ken's living quarters. There was not a trace of comfort, nor a single feminine touch anywhere. The paintwork was worn and the wallpaper faded, yet everything was arranged with almost military tidiness. There were no dirty dishes in the sink. In the bedrooms, the beds were made with clean sheets and the clothes either folded in drawers or hung in the wardrobes. An orderly man, Irving thought.

Back in the kitchen, he noticed two clipboards by the telephone: one was for writing down messages, the other for shopping lists. An entire wall of the kitchen was taken up with temporary shelving made from planks laid over breeze blocks. The books on them were all in alphabetical order. Judging by the neatly arranged collection of 78s, LPs, cassettes and CDs, Ken's taste in recorded music – apart from a comprehensive sub-collection of Irving's own recordings from the first to the most recent – was mainly jazz-orientated.

Spread out on the kitchen table, made from a plywood-faced door laid across a pair of trestles, were a series of blueprint drawings, on which work completed was marked in green ink. On the wall above the table hung a watercolour sketch of the farm that Catriona had done. The pencilled title read *Le Farou – After*. The view through the window was so different that Irving felt a twinge of sympathy for the man who was trying to make a vision come true in stone and mortar.

By contrast with Ken's quarters, Catriona's cottage was a warm, comfortable confusion of colour and noise. The radio was on so loud that she had to shout for Irving to hear her invitation to enter. He examined the picture of Ken, which was still on the easel.

'It's very good.' He turned off the radio, which was hurting his ears. 'Is this for the show, too?'

Catriona was hunting through the pictures stacked against the rear wall for an unused primed canvas. 'No, that's a present, in lieu of rent. You know what artists are like . . . paying their trivial debts with pictures that are worth a fortune after they're dead.'

Satan was sitting on the bed. Irving tickled him between the ears, to be rewarded with bared teeth. Hastily he retracted his hand and sat down with the violin tucked under his chin. Catriona was squeezing oils onto her palette. The smell of turps and the sight of the pure unmixed colours always gave her a sensuous thrill.

'Play us a tune if you like,' she said. 'But don't talk.'

Irving shut his eyes to concentrate and began playing through one of the Ysaÿe unaccompanied sonatas.

'Oh, great,' Catriona said. 'I'll call this picture *The Blind Fiddler of Le Farou*. Would you mind keeping your eyes open, sir? Shutting them changes the whole of your face.'

'I always practise like that,' he objected. 'That is, if I'm not reading the music.'

'Just for me,' she pleaded. 'The eyes are the focal point in the landscape of a face. Without them, it's a wasteland.'

The music meant nothing to her but the paint flowed mystically from tube to palette to canvas, so fast that she prayed he would not speak and break the spell. *If only I can capture, not just the male-model good looks, but also the arrogance of the man . . . and the contrast between the gentleness of the music he plays and the violence I can sense lurking behind those brown eyes of his . . .*

An hour later, the daylight was nearly gone and Catriona sat back, exhausted. No one else could have seen it yet, but she knew already what the finished picture would look like. The intensity of emotion swirling inside her was as strong as if she had been touching her sitter's face all the time she had been scanning it with her eyes – as though she had stroked every square millimetre of his skin with finger tips, explored it with lips and tongue. Embarrassed by painting women, she was always turned on by the intimacy of getting a man's face onto canvas. But this was something more . . .

Aware that Irving had spoken, she looked up.

'Is there any food in this house? I'm feeling peckish, having skipped British Airways' lunch on the plane.'

'I don't make a practice of feeding strange men,' she said. 'Nor stray cats, for the same reason. But there's probably some biscuits somewhere. And there's a packet of arabica on the shelf above the sink. I don't know about you, but I could do with a shot of caffeine.'

She blocked in the dark background while Irving boiled a kettle and made coffee for them both in silence. Now that she was not looking at him, the inner turmoil subsided gradually to a tolerable level. The face on the canvas, she told herself, was just that – a face, no more. Their relationship was simply that of painter and sitter; the illusion of intimacy would fade. And when she put down her brushes and knew it was finished, the umbilical cord or whatever it was would be severed and this man's face that was obsessing her would be that of a stranger once again.

Irving had munched several biscuits before he realised that the crumbled edges were where mice had been nibbling them. Catriona ignored the complaint, sitting back with a sigh of relief as he handed her the mug of coffee.

The portrait was going to be good, she decided. The essentials were all there; the rest of the work she could do at a pinch from memory and photographs. Because the stove often burned out when she was painting, she had filled it with logs before starting. It was hot in the cottage, with the door and window closed. She put down brushes and palette and pulled her smock off over her head, dropping it onto the floor behind her as Irving began playing the sixth and last sonata.

'You could light me a cigarette,' she said. 'There's a pack on the table behind you.'

'I don't smoke.'

'If you'll set fire to it and stick it in my mouth, I'll do the inhaling myself. That way, you'll save me from daubing paint on everything I touch.'

Irving leaned forward to put the lit cigarette between her lips. As she moved to take it, the low-necked singlet hung loosely in front of her, so that he found himself looking down the inside at her small, firm breasts – with the musky odour of her warm body floating up to his nostrils.

The Harley, the surfing, and this beautiful and presumably available woman . . . Ken Scott must be at least two people,

Irving decided: the grey man and the guy who had everything going for him in secret at this out-of-the-way French farmhouse.

Hallstatt was carving slices off one of the home-made sausages he was smoking in the chimney above the open fire. 'Taste that,' he ordered Ken. 'No sodium glutamate, no saltpetre, not an E in sight!'

Ken agreed that it was the best garlic sausage he had ever eaten. 'So ninety-nine per cent of the French population came to some accommodation with the Germans during the Occupation?' he said.

'D'you blame them? They reckoned it was the politicians who had got them into the mess, and that their personal duty was to family and self. A few hundred misguided idealists got involved helping downed Allied fliers and escaping prisoners. A lot of them paid with their lives – and not just their own. Whole families were shipped off to the camps on the principle of *Sippenhaft*. D'you know how many of those fliers ever flew in combat again? I think it was nineteen. So all that suffering didn't shorten the war by a second.'

'You said there were several different Resistances, in addition to the one De Gaulle's people ran from London.'

'Oh sure. A lot of the time they were fighting each other. But that's another story. Perhaps the best way to explain what the war did to perfectly ordinary French people is to take someone you know, like the mayor of St Martin and his three brothers.'

Hallstatt placed on the kitchen table a plate of sliced sausage and fresh bread. 'Those four men spanned the gamut of wartime French politics. Gaston, who's run on the Gaullist ticket for mayor ever since the war, simply ran away to join the *maquis* in order to avoid being sent to Germany under the STO. And Louis, the second son, just chose Vichy to spite Gaston – so neither was exactly a political choice.'

'So Louis was a traitor?'

'Wrong,' Hallstatt corrected. 'At the time – and even *after* the Allies landed in Normandy in June of Forty-four the lawful government of France was in Vichy. Marshal Pétain was the constitutional President of the country and De Gaulle was a renegade officer with a price on his head and no political following. So legally Gaston was the traitor, not Louis. Makes you think, doesn't it?'

As they ate their way through the sausage, washed down with draughts of *marc*, Hallstatt's account continued: 'Louis took a job in what they called the army of the Armistice, patrolling the demarcation line between the occupied zone and the so-called *zone libre*. The line was effectively an international border, with French soldiers on one side and the Wehrmacht on the other. One night Louis was asked to look the other way when Gaston's group were bringing some refugees across the border.'

'And he didn't?' Ken guessed.

'There was an ambush, people died and young Gaston nearly lost an arm. Louis had an alibi, confirmed by his mother: he was in bed at home that night, sick. But nobody believed the ambush was not his fault, so after the Liberation he was given two years in jail. His wife and her sister started the café in the square while he was still doing time.'

'What about the other brothers? You said there were four of them.'

'Number three is Armand. He's a recluse who lives in the old water mill outside the village where he runs a timber business when he's sober. He comes into St Martin once or twice a month to buy supplies. You've probably seen him around. An alkie with a gaunt, haunted face, and three fingers missing from his right hand? Like everyone else, you probably assumed he fell against a saw blade when drunk.'

'But he didn't?'

'Frostbite. Armand Gallot spent the war fighting in the LVF – the French volunteer battalions that saw combat in German uniform on the Russian front. I guess he joined up to spite law-abiding Louis and Gaston who was in the *maquis*. Whatever the reason, after basic training in France, the poor sonofabitch found himself wearing Wehrmacht uniform and swearing an oath of loyalty to Adolf Hitler – probably at the huge Wehrmacht base in Kruszyna in Poland, where they went to learn the tricks of anti-partisan warfare.

'However good the training was, it can't have matched up to the reality of fighting in temperatures of minus fifty degrees centigrade, with motor transport immobilised all winter. The uniforms of the LVF were completely unsuited to those temperatures. Food supplies were often non-existent for days on end and many men lost their lives simply because they ran out of ammunition. When a position was overrun, it was the rule to shoot any non-walking wounded rather than let them fall into partisan hands. Armand Gallot ended the war fighting in the Charlemagne Division, which suffered eighty per cent casualties in the final hopeless defence of Berlin. The survivors were marched to Siberia – and I mean marched there, all the way on foot – in whatever they happened to be wearing when captured. That's how Armand lost three fingers and most of his toes. He didn't get back to France until 1958 – and he was one of the few to return at all.'

Hallstatt left the table to take a phone call from one of his daughters in America. Not listening to the family chat, Ken wandered around the house, digesting the information he was being given. The walls of the old farmhouse were lined with bookshelves, crammed with books and magazines. Hallstatt had collected most things ever published about the secret world. Nearly every page was annotated in an illegible scrawl with his own personal comments. But the sort of conversation they were having was worth a million printed pages to Ken.

'The fourth brother,' he prompted when the phone call was finished. Time was going on and he wanted to be back at Le Farou in time to light some fires and make the place comfortable for Irving's arrival.

'His name was Victor,' Hallstatt said.

'And where is he now?'

'In the churchyard. He was hauled out of the Dordogne, just below the bridge. His mother died of the shock.'

'What were his politics, this brother who died?'

'He was a Doriotist.' Seeing the blank look on Ken's face, Hallstatt added, 'Doriot was a French politician whose followers marched around in brown shirts with swastika banners, generally embarrassing all but the nuttiest Nazis. Victor turned up here just after the invasion of Normandy with a truckload of his kind, to massacre the Jews in St Martin.'

'I'm surprised there were any.'

'The south-west was full of refugees from all over France. Victor and his boys murdered a handful of old men, women and kids – and departed singing marching songs like *En Passant Par La Lorraine* and *Auprès De Ma Blonde*, as though they had carried out some valiant action against an armed enemy.'

'So how did he come to drown?'

'I didn't say he did.' Hallstatt finished the last slice of sausage. 'He'd been strangled before he was thrown into the river.'

'How do you know all this?'

'My wife was a Gallot, a cousin of the brothers. Gaston and I keep in touch. That's how I knew Le Farou was for sale.'

Like a gun dog scenting game, Ken froze. Instinct told him that Hallstatt had not recounted the whole story.

'Who killed Victor Gallot?' he asked softly.

Hallstatt looked down at his large hands on the table. With his fingers interlocked and the thumbs pressing inward, they were still strong enough to throttle a man. 'After the Liberation,' he said, 'like a lot of other guys who'd backed the wrong side during the war, Victor enlisted in the Foreign Legion under an assumed name. He got himself taken prisoner at Dien Bien Phu and turned up at St Martin again after being repatriated in the autumn of Fifty-four.'

'And who killed him?'

'I was here on leave. Gaston reckoned Victor's return was going to cause problems for the family. He gave me the job of luring his brother down to the river, thinking that he was less likely to suspect a foreigner. I pitched Victor some story about wanting him to show me how to catch lampreys. When Gaston showed up, Victor knew what was coming, and went down on his knees, pleading. But we did the job all the same.'

Ken stood up and put an arm around his friend's bony shoulders. 'Thanks for telling me all this, Erich. I appreciate it.'

Driving back down-river to St Martin, he was glad he had confided in Hallstatt. He was used to working as part of a team; having just one other person to whom he could talk made all the difference. And one thing was certain: if the story of the mayor and his brothers was anything to go by, the conventional media depiction of life in France during and after the Occupation was a gross simplification of the truth.

.3.

Two neon restaurant signs competed with each other in the single street of St Martin. Irving, who had insisted on driving into the village in his rental car, stopped at the first one by the bridge over the Dordogne, outside which were parked several expensive cars, until told by Ken to drive on until they came to the local café in the tiny village square.

They walked through the smoke-filled bar and sat down in a shabby little room at the back, which was badly in need of a coat of paint. The only other customers were a group of men in jeans and work shirts who were staying the night in the cheap rooms above the bar. Brought to such a grungy establishment, Irving wrote Ken off as a tightwad, until the food changed his opinion. There was no choice of menu; they were offered the same fare that local tradesmen and truck drivers passing through had eaten at midday, cooked by two fat ladies forever laughing in the kitchen. The plates were not so much placed on the paper table cloth as dumped in front of each diner by Louis Gallot, the man who had betrayed his own brother during the war. He was a lecherous little man with grizzled hair who badly needed a shave and could not keep his eyes off Catriona's low neckline.

The meal began with a *potage* that any farmer's wife in the region might have made for her menfolk a hundred or two hundred years ago. This was followed by a *salade landaise*, with slices of smoked *gésier* and *magret* of duck lying on a bed of fresh lettuce, decorated with pine nuts and dressed with nut oil.

It was, as Catriona remarked, 'Almost too pretty to eat.'

The main course was the most succulent *confit de poule* that Irving had ever tasted, with sauté potatoes cooked with garlic, parsley and mushrooms, and *haricots blancs* cooked in goose fat. The wine, a 1992 from the local *cave cooperative*, went equally well with the cheese course – the board invisible beneath half a dozen varieties of France's second most famous product, not one of which Irving had ever tasted before. The dessert, carried in by one of the fat ladies from the kitchen, was three king-size *crèmes brûlées*, which could have been made in heaven.

Ken was mellow: sharing a good meal was not a bad way of getting to know someone. Irving's eyes flicked from his face to Catriona's. It was hard to put aside thirty years of prejudice in one evening, but he wanted to make a gesture of reconciliation, and insisted on paying for the meal.

Back at Le Farou Catriona refused to join the men for a nightcap, on the excuse that there were things she wanted to do in the cottage. So Ken and Irving seated themselves in a pair of old but comfortable armchairs in front of the open fire in the kitchen with cups of strong black coffee and glasses of the *eau de vie de marc* that he had made with Hallstatt.

Irving coughed on the first mouthful, which felt like liquid fire in his chest. He took another, more cautious sip.

'Now tell me why you didn't want to talk in front of Catriona.'

'Habit.' Ken did not elaborate; it was hard enough for him to share with Irving what he had found out so far. It helped that the son had something of his father's ability to listen without interrupting. He sat completely still, with the exception of his dark eyes which wandered idly around the room.

'It sounds unlikely,' Ken summed up. 'But there it is. Your Mrs Prescot – this little old lady who was a much-respected fiddle teacher – had been living a lie for the past fifty years. Whoever she really was, she was *not* Madeleine Prescot, *née* Lasalle. Whether her husband knew that when he brought her back to Britain as his bride, is another matter altogether.'

'And you think this is relevant?'

Ken shrugged. At this stage everything was relevant. Unfortunately, like most amateurs, Irving was in a hurry to get results.

'It's only fair to warn you that I've dug up a Pandora's Box,' he said. 'We might open it to find that Mrs Prescot was a Comintern spy. Or she could have been a collaborator during the war, who took the name of that poor girl gunned down at the Villa Céleste, to escape the summary justice of the Resistance in the period known as *l'épuration* or "the cleansing" after the war. And those are just two possibilities she could have been running away from.'

'We might equally well find that she was a Resistance heroine,' Irving argued.

Ken disagreed: 'Changing your identity involves a lot of work for someone without a support infrastructure. I can tell you from experience that individuals only go through with it if they have some very compelling reason to do so – like running away from a crime or a marriage.'

'The truth can't hurt Mrs P, where she is now,' Irving decided. 'If you're right and the way to trace whoever killed her is by unearthing her past, let's do it. This time, don't tear up the cheque. Just looking around this place, it's obvious you haven't much cash to spare.'

He wrote a cheque for £5000 and stuck it on the mantelshelf over the open fire. 'I'd like to be more involved, but I'm pretty tied up for the foreseeable future. So you put in the time, and I'll provide the finance. Is that a deal?'

'It's a deal.'

There was a long silence in the old kitchen, broken only by the crackling of the logs in the hearth and the scratching of a small field rodent behind the wall panelling.

Ken got up from his chair. 'Time for bed. I've heated up the spare room.'

Irving stood up and stretched. 'I'm not staying the night. I said I'd drive Catriona back to London with some of the paintings for her show. Since I have a rehearsal early tomorrow afternoon, that means leaving now in case the Chunnel's not working and we have to take a ferry from Calais.'

Ken had completely forgotten that he had promised to drive Catriona back to London the following day, with the last few paintings for her exhibition. At first he resented the fact that Irving was doing the chore for him, then he felt relieved that it left him free to pursue his trail. Irving's money would make things easier, but even without it, he could not have stopped now. Without putting the thought into words, he was aware of having felt more *alive* the last few days than he had since losing his job.

When Irving had said, 'Am I allowed to know why you were sacked from MI5?' Ken had answered quietly that things had changed after the end of the Cold War, and his face did not fit in the re-styled Security Service.

He could have explained without infringing the Official Secrets Act that when the Berlin Wall came down in 1989, a lot of smart-ass politicians had asked what Britain needed SIS and MI6 for. With the old enemy prostrate at our feet, they asked, from whom are we protecting ourselves? The mandarins at the top of the intelligence and security services had had to think up a new rationale to justify their salaries and keep intact their intricately contrived power structures. 'The KGB may have temporarily stopped trying to steal our military secrets,' they told their masters in Downing Street. 'Now they're after our commercial secrets: chemical formulae, research reports, export contacts, boardroom negotiations. They have a lot of catching up to do and will stoop to any tricks. Only we know how to outwit them.'

Since it was becoming increasingly obvious that Yeltsin had ordered the KGB, reborn as the SVR, to give commercial espionage the highest priority, they were listened to – and Ken was told by his colleagues that he was lucky still to have a job.

'But I came into this racket to protect my country,' he argued when MI5's internal *perestroika* started, 'not to act as watchdog for the fat cats. I don't approve of spending the taxpayers' money defending the secrets of Ford and General Motors and ICI and the other big names on the Stock Exchange. Companies like that have enough money to look after themselves.'

Each time he found another appalling example of sloppy

security and loose mouths – whether in the boardroom or on the factory floor – he insisted on putting everything in his report and refused to change a word. Nor would he feed into the shredder, as ordered, the result of six months' work proving that the chairman of one of Britain's most prestigious conglomerates was regularly showing classified information to his girlfriend – a whore who lived in Shepherd's Market – and frequently left papers in her apartment overnight, where she photocopied them on a machine paid for by one of his companies, which he had given her as a present. Since some of the papers were Government property, Kenneth Wilson Scott recommended a prosecution under the Official Secrets Act. Stubbornly, he refused to change a sentence in the report, nor alter the recommendation even when ordered to do so.

It was a stalemate: although he had written off his own chances of further promotion, Ken would have continued to be employed by MI5 if he had not subsequently taken matters into his own hands, and leaked to a journalist whom he trusted the gist of his report. From there it was picked up and used by several national newspapers until Ken had the satisfaction of seeing charges brought . . . three days before he was sacked, ostensibly as just one more victim of the ongoing rationalisation programme inside the security service.

At first he had been angry, but not worried. With his knowledge, contacts and experience, he had thought it would be only a matter of time before he found a job in the private sector. He never found out whether he had been blacklisted by MI5, or whether there had been no need for them to play tricks, for the message from one personnel selection company after another was, 'If you're over forty-five, forget all about finding a new job, invest your severance pay sensibly and move somewhere cheap to live.'

Ken poured himself another glass of *eau de vie* and toasted the portrait. He took Irving's cheque from the mantelshelf, in case it fell into the fire. It seemed ironic that his first paying employer since MI5 had kicked him out was the son who had never spoken to him until less than a week before.

.4.

'If it's some kind of contest, you should tell me the rules,' Catriona said.

Irving was concentrating on the motorway ahead, where a Spanish truck was jack-knifed across the carriageway, surrounded by flashing blue lights. As they drove slowly past in the line of single-file traffic, they could see an elderly Peugeot station wagon being cut away from the tractor of the artic by firemen with oxy-acetylene equipment. Several suitcases from the overloaded roof rack were strewn across the roadway, their contents getting soaked by the drizzle, while a group of North African men were arguing with the police. An ambulance was just departing.

'What was that?' Irving asked.

'It's over an hour since we left Le Farou and you haven't said a word to me – just grunted a couple of times.'

'I usually travel long distances alone.'

'Is that a hint I should shut up?'

'I was thinking. Tell me about Ken. I find it hard to talk to the guy – and you must know him as well as most people.'

'Let me ask you a question first. What do you make of him?'

'It was a bit like meeting the devil,' Irving confessed. 'My mother bad-mouthed him so much when I was a kid that it's hard to see the man as a human being.'

'Did she hate him that much?'

'Marlene was half-gypsy, always having vendettas with people. According to her, Ken was Attila the Hun reincarnate.'

'Real gypsy?'

He nodded. 'My Romany grandmother came to stay once and told me she had never slept more than one night in the same place. As a kid of eight, I was so impressed that I ran away from home for the first time, the week after her visit.'

'So you did it more than once?'

He ignored the question. 'She was an old witch who told fortunes. She clutched my hand and gazed into my eyes – it was very creepy. Then she said that one day I would be very rich and famous because of music, so maybe she was psychic. At the time, I'd rather have had a present.'

Catriona saw in her mind's eye the portrait she had been working on. Despite the pallor of Irving's complexion, gypsy blood explained the black hair, the dark brown eyes. 'What did she look like, your mother?'

'There was a picture of her and Ken, taken at New Brighton funfair soon after they got married. I can see why he fell for her, although they must have been as compatible as oil and water. She had that overblown Mediterranean beauty that fades early. Big earrings, flashy clothes, a lot of make-up. The kids in the street used to call her Bradley's tart, until I got big enough to stop them.'

'Bradley was your step-father?'

'He was the local bookmaker.'

'He didn't beat you up, or anything? You know, the ugly step-father . . .'

Irving moved in his seat to get more comfortable. 'They split up when I was six. After that there were a succession of men I was supposed to call Uncle.'

'Did they treat you all right?'

'If anything, it was me that was the pain in the arse. I was into all sorts of trouble before I got involved with the fiddle. It sounds dramatic, but you could say that Mrs P and the violin saved me from a life of crime.'

Catriona lit a cigarette. 'The way I heard it, Ken did his best for you, given the circumstances. Did you look at my portrait of him?'

'Of course.'

'No, I meant *look* at it, Irving.'

'Probably not in your terms. I'm not very visual.'

'Well, the next time you go to Le Farou, try really looking at a painting for the first time in your life.'

'And what will I see?'

'Oh, I'm not God. I can't peer deep into anyone's soul. But I'll say this: it's an accurate picture of the man I know.'

'If it's not a rude question, Catriona . . .'

She laughed. 'They always are when they begin like that. So let me guess. You were about to ask what on earth a beautiful woman of thirty-something is doing with a man nearly old enough to be her father? Of course, if Ken was rich and getting richer with every turn of the wheel, you wouldn't think of asking me a question like that. Rich old men are allowed younger lovers.'

'Precisely,' said Irving drily. 'Ken doesn't exactly buy you a good time, so far as I can see.'

They slowed down and stopped at the *péage* outside Tours – a third of the way to the Channel coast.

'Ken and I have two things in common,' Catriona said as Irving accelerated away from the toll booth. 'We're both Celts and we both decided for different reasons a few years ago to do what the hell we want and let everybody else go fuck themselves.'

'Which means?'

'In Ken's case, it meant thumbing his nose at wage-slavery, respectability and a mortgage. It meant deciding to get fit after years of too much booze, too many cigarettes and too little sleep – by buying a derelict farm in France and converting it into lettable holiday apartments, doing a lot of the work himself. It meant trading in his boring saloon car for the Harley and the Land Cruiser. It meant doing things he'd never had time for – like surfing, at which he's pretty good, so they tell me.'

'And fooling around with crazy Irish painters?'

Catriona did not reply. What did she feel about Ken? Because he never manoeuvred her into expressing her feelings, she did not really know.

'In his case,' said Irving, 'I can see he left Britain to escape the stigma of being fired by MI5. What are you running away from, a marriage?'

'Someone else's marriage, maybe.'

'That sounds Irish.'

Catriona pushed in the cigar lighter and watched the glowing tip until it was black and she had to push it in again.

'I was acting the part of someone else,' she said. 'My husband is an ophthalmological surgeon with rooms in Fitzwilliam Square, Dublin. We had a five-bedroom stockbroker Tudor mansion at Foxridge with three cars in the garage – his latest-model BMW, my Volvo estate car and a Land Rover to pull my daughter's horse box to gymkhanas at the weekends. I used to paint pretty watercolours which were sold at charity auctions, and sit on the board of an orphanage, and act as hostess for my husband's dinner parties. You don't know what Dublin's social round is like: more stiflingly English than anything in London. The only Irish accent I ever heard was my own and that was dwindling year by year as my soul shrivelled inside me.'

'All the same, it must have taken a lot of guts to leave.'

'I thought to myself, my daughter's a woman now. A year older than her, I was pregnant. As Ken might say, it was time to climb aboard the next wave or stay out there for ever.'

'Do you still keep in touch with them?'

'If I send my husband a postcard, he replies with a lawyer's letter. He'll never forgive me for turning into a person. Being Catholic, the poor fellow can't get married again until I die. And he'd never run the risk of scandal, so I've complicated his life considerably.'

Irving chuckled. 'No hostess for all those smart dinner parties . . . It must have taken guts to leave, all the same.'

'One day I realised that I was out of my depth and drowning in respectability. So I threw myself a lifebelt.'

He laughed at the image that conjured up. 'Tell me about your daughter. How old is she?'

'Twenty-one.'

Irving shot Catriona a sideways look. 'You don't look old enough.'

'Thank you for the compliment, sir,' she murmured. 'Pray disregard my blushes. Remember that Ireland's a Catholic country. At least, it was when I was twenty years old and in love.

Or maybe I was just burning to discover sex. Probably the latter, after all those years at the convent boarding school, wondering about the strange animals called boys who roamed wild on the other side of the boundary wall . . .'

'Hold on,' Irving interrupted. 'Twenty plus one plus twenty-one, does not add up to thirty-something.'

'A gentleman would not have noticed the discrepancy.'

'What's your daughter's name?'

'Siobhan.'

'D'you keep in touch?'

'We ring each other a couple of times a week. When I left her father, she wrote me a letter, saying how much she admired me for it. That took a load off my mind, I can tell you. She's a wonderful person, who is all the things I wish I'd been at her age. She's a fiddler of sorts, too.'

'Professional?' Irving was curious.

'Indeed.'

'Maybe I've met her. I've played with all the orchestras in Britain, so we've probably crossed tracks somewhere.'

'Oh, you were her idol for years. But you wouldn't have met Siobhan in the flesh. She plays what she calls Celtic Revival music in a folk-rock group out of Belfast, with one of those little microphones glued inside her instrument, to amplify it.'

'A pick-up, you mean.'

'She sings like an angel too – and sometimes like a she-devil from hell. Mind, you probably wouldn't rate her kind of music at all.'

Irving was pulling into a service station. 'D'you want a coffee before driving?'

At the all-night counter, Catriona sipped hot coffee from a plastic cup. 'You surprise me,' she said. 'I had you marked as one of those men who never let a woman get behind the wheel of a car because it threatens their masculinity.'

He flexed his fingers. 'After driving for twelve hours solid with my hands locked on the wheel, I wouldn't be able to play for days. How did you and Ken meet?'

'You really want to know?'

'I wouldn't ask otherwise.'

'Well . . . After my narrow escape from death by drowning in Dublin, I hit the hippy trail, back-packing round Greece and Turkey before I realised that the other guys had all gone home. But I had fun doing some of the things that more courageous women do before they get married and have kids. Then, one day I was painting down by the river in Bergerac. Not one of the big landscapes I do now, but a watercolour sketch to sell for food money. And I heard this man's voice behind me say, "How much d'you want for it?" I asked him how he knew I was English, without hearing me speak. "You're from Dublin," Ken said. "And you're on the run."'

'How did he know?'

'That's Ken for you.' Catriona shrugged. 'I named a low price because I could see he wasn't loaded, but he insisted on paying me double, because he could tell I was hard up. We had a drink or two. When I woke up next morning, he said I could live in his cottage rent-free if I wanted to. Two years later, I'm still there.'

She had thought that Irving would stay awake, criticising her driving with his eyes, if not his mouth. Yet, five minutes down the road, after complaining that her canvases stopped his seat back from going all the way down, he was asleep. In the spill of light as they went under a bridge, she stole a look at his face, comparing it with Ken's, whose tanned skin was a network of fine stress lines, while Irving's nearly white complexion had all the smooth perfection of youth, apart from a few crinkles around the eyes. Ken's greying hair was kept short; Irving's dark mop was so long that he had continually to brush it back from his brow with a slender hand whose fingers were long and tapering – so different from his father's powerful, square hands with fingers cracked by physical labour and too much time spent in salt water. Even their voices were different: Ken's – except when he was making love, or wanted to – was hard and clipped, with few traces of his Merseyside upbringing, while Irving's Liverpool accent was far more pronounced.

There was a blare of air horns and a flashing of headlights.

Christ, I'm in the wrong lane!

Adrenaline pumping, Catriona veered sharply to the right as a black Mercedes saloon with German plates passed her, doing two hundred kilometres an hour. Concentrate on the road, girl! she told herself.

Irving had not woken. The white lines flashed past in the headlights. What am I doing here? Catriona wondered. Why invent this urgent need to take some canvases back to London two days early? And why had Irving fallen in with it and agreed to drive her back, instead of just taking the morning flight as he had planned? She had a sneaking suspicion that he had just wanted to get her alone, so that he could learn about his father.

. 5 .

Ken awoke to find himself slumped in one of the fireside chairs. Daylight was pouring through the kitchen windows; he had forgotten to close the shutters. The bottle of *marc* on the table was empty and there was a roaring in his ears which took him a moment to recognise as the noise of a powerful diesel engine. In the yard outside, a ready-mix concrete truck waited to disgorge six cubic metres of molten hard work. He had ordered it the previous week and – like the promise to Catriona – forgotten all about it.

He pulled on his work clothes and grabbed a quick coffee. Fighting the concrete level on a bed of steel reinforcement mesh and tamping it down with a long plank was a painful but effective cure for a hangover. Despite the icy wind blowing in through the high doorway of the old dairy, he was drenched in perspiration long before the job was finished. At midday he put down his tools and stood looking at a perfect four-car garage floor.

He showered, changed and ate a snack lunch before going back to pull a sheet of building plastic across the concrete, so that it would cure properly and not dry out too quickly. The pristine surface was not as he had left it. Satan had walked across it from corner to corner and again from end to end. Catriona's cat sat in the middle of its handiwork, staring up at a bird sitting on one of the beams. Ken swore, but it was too late to do anything about it.

The telephone was ringing. He sprinted to the kitchen and heard the voice of the notary in Royan whom he had asked to investigate the ownership of the ruins of the house known as the Villa Céleste.

It had burned down, he learned, on 18 April 1945. No one knew how it had caught fire, but it had not been the result of military action, because all the German troops in the pocket had surrendered the day before. The notary had no other information – except the name and address of the owner, who had chosen not to rebuild her seaside home after the fire.

'I've never seen musicians at work before,' Catriona said. 'I wouldn't have missed this for the world.'

She had spent half the rehearsal sitting silent in the third row of the darkened auditorium of the main concert hall in the massive Barbican Centre, sketching details of the scene on the platform: a hand and a part of an instrument, the play of light and shadow, a glance from one musician to a neighbour, the conductor wiping the perspiration from his bald head with a small towel which he wore around his neck, like a scarf.

Irving was dressed in a black tee-shirt and black jeans. He put down his violin and bow on an empty seat nearby and plucked the sketch pad from her hands. 'May I have a look?'

'Help yourself.'

The house lights came up and cleaners began hoovering between the seats. The platform was emptying rapidly as the musicians disappeared to other commitments, with the exception of one group where the leader of the double basses was in a huddle with the rest of his section, discussing bowing marks. Stage hands were resetting the rostra for another orchestra which was giving a different concert in the hall that evening. In the middle of the hubbub a rather portly middle-aged French horn player was still sitting on his rostrum, blowing muted notes and looking worried.

'You're all so matter-of-fact,' Catriona said. 'Like a load of civil servants who've been at a meeting and have to catch the six-thirty from Waterloo. I'd thought to see temperament and passion, hair torn out and souls revealed, hysteria and tears. Instead, the only excitement was the shop steward's fight with the conductor about when to have the tea-break. And you don't even play the music right through – just a few bars here and a few bars there.'

'It's a job. You have to remember that we don't write the music. Mozart did the hard part.' Irving was flicking over the pages of the sketch pad. 'Are these for sale?'

Catriona gave a wistful smile. 'If I thought anybody would give money for them, they would be. I'm not Picasso.'

'I'd like to have one.'

'Choose whichever you like.'

One simple line drawing of himself, with the leader of the orchestra and the conductor in the background, had caught a moment of concentration that had lasted no longer than a blink – and yet it captured the essence of the *ménage à trois* between soloist, conductor and orchestra. Irving tore it out carefully and asked her to sign it.

A man in chauffeur's livery was hovering nearby, making discreet hurry-up signs.

'I'll have to say goodbye.' Irving put the violin away in its case. 'The Beeb have sent a car. I'm due to record *Desert Island Discs* in half an hour. The Gramophone Library – as they insist on calling it – had a bit of a job finding a recording by your daughter's group.'

'Meaning?'

'I've included one of Slieve Gullion's tracks in my selection for the programme, to give her a plug.'

'You did that?' Catriona ran the length of the row, threw her arms around Irving's neck and kissed him on the lips. 'I'm amazed you had time to think about Siobhan.'

'I think about lots of things at rehearsal,' Irving smiled. 'During a concert, it's different. Then I wouldn't notice if the Bomb dropped.'

'You're taking a risk on my recommendation. Maybe she's a rotten player and you'll hate the music.'

'I'll take the chance.' Irving tucked the violin case under his arm and turned to head backstage for the artists' exit, the chauffeur hurrying ahead to open doors for him.

Catriona was halfway up the gangway to the public exit when she heard him call her name. He was walking back towards her. Behind him, in the spill of light from the platform, the BBC driver was looking unhappy.

'I want an invitation,' Irving said, 'to your private view.'

She found a card in her shoulder bag and scribbled his name on it. 'I should warn you. Despite the posh address and name, the Szabo Gallery, just off Bond Street, is not known for generosity. Ziggy – he's the crook who owns it – decides how many bottles of booze, and what kind, by calculating the probable profit of the show. Since I'm the sort of also-ran they slip in between more important exhibitions, all they serve at my *vernissages* is red and white plonk.'

'I can't wait.' Irving placed his hands lightly around her waist and kissed Catriona on both cheeks. She hoped he was going to suggest a meeting after he had recorded the radio programme. Then he was walking away from her, towards the driver holding his violin case by the door.

'Have fun on the island,' she managed to call after him.

Irving waved a hand without turning round. 'I always have fun.'

Feeling weak at the knees, Catriona sank into a seat on the pretext of collecting together all her sketches. On each sheet of paper, Irving's sardonic smile mocked her.

'Grow up!' she told herself. 'You're behaving like a teenager. You're the wrong side of forty. There are some things you just can't have any more.'

The sign at the roadside read *Vente à la propriété. Dégustation gratuite.*

Ken drove slowly up the drive that led to Chateau Magnus, one of the *premier grand crus* of St Emilion. The home of the woman who owned the ruins of the Villa Céleste was an elegant Second-Empire *gentilhommière*, built in the local honey-coloured limestone. It stood on the escarpment to the east of St Emilion, overlooking the Dordogne valley. The gardens were immaculate in the French style: weedless gravel paths, low, precisely trimmed hedges, well-mulched rose beds. A sign in three languages directed visitors to the *chais* behind the house where a pretty local girl in her early twenties was obviously bored at the lack of business on a grey November afternoon, and quite happy to chat to a man who liked listening.

At a shopping centre in Libourne, the nearest big town, Ken had computer-printed some cards for himself, with the description *Purchasing Director* above the name of a fictitious chain of British wine shops. Hinting at a big order to come, he took his time sampling several vintages, finding out from the girl about her employer. Madame Yvonne Picard, he learned, was an old lady with a bad heart, who was currently undergoing treatment at a thermal spa in the Haute Savoie. Even when at the chateau, she never saw visitors and rarely left the house, except to keep an eye on the fermenting wine at the time of the *vendanges*.

Ken gathered that she was a tyrant who ran the property with a rod of iron. He left a visiting card and expressed an intention of returning the following day, then sauntered around the yard, talking with some of the work-force, who were getting ready to go home after a day's pruning in the vines. Madame Picard, they told him, had inherited Chateau Magnus from her father. Nobody had heard of the Villa Céleste, but one of the labourers remembered that there had been two sisters: Madame Yvonne and a girl whose name escaped him. He thought she had died during the Second World War.

Back at the sales counter, Ken looked through the album of publicity photographs featuring celebrities who had honoured Chateau Magnus by drinking its wine. He recognised two past French presidents and several other faces – familiar from films and magazines – shaking hands with the tall, rather angular woman who owned the chateau.

In the album devoted to the history of the property were drawings of the house and gardens as they had been when first built. There was a geological description of the *terroir*, which consisted of eleven hectares of Günz era gravel, all that remained of a hill of quartz-bearing clay, eroded and covered during the Mindel glaciation by a layer of fine sand and a few pebbles. The resultant low-fertility soil would have suited few crops, other than the mixture of Merlot and Cabernet Franc vines, many of which were approaching the end of their useful life.

The section covering the Picard family, who had owned the property since founding Chateau Magnus in 1831, began with an engraving of the founder. Then came a stiffly posed daguerreotype of his successor, followed by photographs of the subsequent owners down to the present day. The two last in line were Monsieur Adrien Picard – who had died in 1942 – and Madame Yvonne Picard, the present owner. Included in the family pictures were wives, children, favourite dogs, horses and expensive cars. The Picards were plainly a family that had lived well off the few acres of poor soil that suited grapes and little else. But neither in the photographs, nor in the family tree that followed the Picard line through six generations, was there any mention of the owner's sister.

Next morning, using the freelance reporter identity that had been so successful at the museum in Royan, Ken visited the offices of the regional daily paper in Bordeaux. *Le Sud Ouest* had microfilmed its more recent back issues, but the archives for 1939–45 were still copies of the original daily editions, with slip pages for the various districts, kept in a dusty warehouse at the rear of the printing works on an industrial estate outside town.

There, Ken ploughed through the cardboard boxes of old newsprint. He had no clear idea of what he was looking for, but it seemed as good a way as any of pursuing the hunch he could not have put into words. He worked backwards from April 1945 – when the real Madeleine Lasalle had died in the attack on the radar station – scanning the paragraphs of local news, and trying not to be distracted by the fascinating insights into life in the south-west of France during the German occupation and the Liberation which were hidden between the lines of the main news items. At midday, he had still not got anywhere.

At 2 p.m. when the archives re-opened after lunch, he restarted his quest at the month of December 1940. His patience was rewarded less than an hour later. In the issue dated 14 June 1940 was a display announcement of a marriage. Less than a month had elapsed since the Wehrmacht had put an end to the phoney war by walking, cycling and driving round the western end of the Maginot Line. It was less than a fortnight since the evacuation at Dunkirk had ended. The German army was in Paris, a quarter of France's population were homeless refugees and at St Emilion Monsieur Adrien Picard was proud to announce the marriage of his daughter Céline to Monsieur Feliks Kandinsky.

On 23 June, in the same edition which gave full details of the Franco-German armistice signed at Compiègne the previous day, there was a photograph of the happy couple. Even with the poor definition of half-tone printing, the details of the bride's features and the way she held herself made it almost certain that the new Madame Feliks Kandinsky, wife of the resident conductor of the Paris Opera, was the same woman who had stood outside Liverpool Register Office seven years later to stooge the fake wedding picture which had stood on Mrs Prescot's bedside cabinet for half a century.

With the elation of a hunter getting his first clear sight of the quarry, Ken paid for photocopies of the marriage announcement and the wedding photograph, then drove fast to St Emilion – heading not to Chateau Magnus, but the Hotel de Ville, where his journalist's credentials gained him access to the records of the *état civil*. Consulting the register of marriages for 22 June 1940, he found the signatures of Céline Marie Picard and Feliks Kandinsky.

The bride's handwriting was identical to the scrawled *Madeleine Lasalle* on Mrs Prescot's marriage licence. The clincher was a peculiar flourish – a kind of double curl – at the start of the capital M in *Marie* and *Madeleine*.

Another photocopy went into the thickening file in Ken's briefcase.

The evening was fine and warm for the time of year. A brilliant sunset flooded the sky with red and yellow light. Behind the high clouds blowing in from the Atlantic the sun was just balancing on the horizon. Ken walked from the Hotel de Ville to the terrace by the church at the top of the town, where he stood looking down at the patterns of the tiled roofs, and the few out-of-season tourists taking their aperitifs at tables in the cobbled square below.

Had Mrs Prescot, before she became Madeleine Lasalle –

and was still Madame Céline Marie Kandinsky, *née* Picard –
stood on the same spot and looked at the same view? Maybe
she had sat at one of those tables in the square, sharing a drink
with her fiancé on a fine summer day in June 1940? The demarcation line which gave the Wehrmacht jurisdiction of the
Atlantic coast all the way to the Spanish border had run a few
miles to the east of the town, so any tourists in the square that
day would have been German.

Whose side had Céline Picard been on? Ken wondered.
Kandinsky could have been a Frenchman, but the spelling of his
first name suggested that he had been a naturalised Pole or
Russian. In those days, so soon after the Spanish Civil War
when the Comintern was taking advantage of the leftist sym-
pathies of artists and intellectuals throughout the world, it was
quite possible that he had been either a fellow-traveller or sus-
ceptible to pressure because of relatives living in the Soviet
Union. After all, Kim Philby's clandestine career had started
with his marriage to a Viennese Jewess who had become a
fanatical Communist after seeing the massacres that ended the
abortive Austrian worker's rising of February 1934.

And why was there absolutely no trace of Céline Kandinsky,
née Picard in the copious records of her family at Chateau
Magnus?

PART V:
Paris – September 1939

. 1 .

An opera house is a fantasy world at the best of times; in Autumn of 1939 when Céline moved to Paris to take up her new job in the orchestra pit of the Paris Opera, the Palais Garnier – its home – was doubly so. As the whole world hung poised on the brink of war, only faint echoes of the international tension penetrated to where Céline sat playing her violin, half-hidden beneath the stage.

In the first few weeks of her career as a professional musician, she had more immediate worries on her mind. Jules Prévert, the man with whom she shared the third desk of the First Violins, had recently been moved down from the second desk, and blamed the arrival of women in the orchestra for his demotion. On her very first day in the Palais Garnier, he took pleasure in telling Céline with a knowing leer that she had been 'given the job because Kandinsky wants to get his greedy prick up your tight little arse'.

No one had ever spoken to her like that before. Not knowing how to react, she blushed but said nothing – and tried not to let her feelings show when he played every dirty trick in the orchestral musician's book to put her off her stride: from altering bowing marks to turning the music they shared at the wrong moment in the hope that she would lose her place. From remarks passed in the women's cloakroom, which had been made by knocking together two disused broom cupboards and was devoid of toilet or washbasin, Céline gathered that she was not alone in suffering this sort of harassment.

Yet Prévert's unpleasantness could not spoil for her the magic of making music in one of the most magnificent opera houses in the entire world. Although only one of seventy or more musicians in the orchestra pit, she felt, while playing the music of Mozart and Massenet, Beethoven and Bizet as though subsumed into their genius, so that she became a figment of their creative will. Nothing else, she told herself, was important.

At that time, the women were not the only ones to suffer harassment. The Palais Garnier contained in miniature all the tensions of the Third Republic: the communists hated the fascists, the fascists hated the Jews, the xenophobes hated the many foreign players. The orchestra included refugees from all over Europe, who fought among themselves: Russian against Balt, Hungarian against Pole. Locked together for eight or ten hours a day in intimate musical communion, they had little time to form relationships outside the incestuous community of their work. As a result, love and hatred flared up all too easily.

As the phoney war dragged on through the winter of 1939, the gossip in the women's dressing-room was about one of the back-desk violas. Anna Cluny was the raven-haired Italian wife of Albert Cluny, the communist shop steward of the orchestra. Her husband was a bitter, frustrated little man who had been Principal Trumpet until losing his embouchure and being demoted to Second and recently Third. On her first day in the Palais Garnier, Anna's submissive beauty and generous figure had caught the roving eye of Feliks Kandinsky, whose hawkish face, piercing blue eyes and mane of prematurely grey hair sweeping back from his high forehead dominated the orchestra for every hour of the working day. The son of a taxi driver who had been a White Russian landowner before the Revolution, Kandinsky had fought his way from poverty and obscurity to become one of France's best-known conductors by his thirtieth birthday.

To conduct for the opera requires an ability to dominate the orchestra and yet remain an accompanist to the singers who are the real stars. Kandinsky had that rare gift. Yet when the orchestra played concerts outside its operatic engagements, he showed a different side of his complex personality: demanding, flattering, bullying and praising by turns to get his own way – and dazzling the audience with his performance 'from the back' as musicians say. The critics prophesied that he would have a great future. Like the majority of the other players, Céline admired him unreservedly for his total dedication. If the conductor she idolised had feet of clay where women were concerned, she consoled herself with the thought that even Popes had been proven fallible in that regard.

She had been at the Opera for six months when her idol spoke to her off-stage for the first time. Kandinsky had noticed in rehearsal that she was playing with a heavier bow than usual, which tended to skate off the strings when playing staccato. By then, she so worshipped him that it was like being addressed by God. She blushed and stammered that her best bow was being re-haired and that she would have it back in time for that evening's performance. He congratulated her on her playing, said that it had improved greatly since she had joined the orchestra – and told her that the leader was considering moving her up to the second desk.

The brief exchange lasted a minute at most. But nothing passed unnoticed in a hotbed of gossip like the Palais Garnier. Downstairs in the dressing-room that evening before the concert, one of the other women said to Céline, 'He'll be buying you presents soon.'

And Anna Cluny remarked bitterly, 'At first flowers, then perfume and underwear. Lastly, jewellery. It's always the same pattern with *nostro maestro*.'

Céline had never been kissed by a man before Feliks Kandinsky took her in his arms one night after a performance. How she came to be alone in his dressing-room with him, she could not afterwards remember. He fixed his piercing eyes on her, and said, 'Come to me, Céline. Don't be afraid.'

She took the four steps that separated them in a blissful haze of unquestioning adoration – like a nun in the act of marrying Christ. Whatever he had asked of her at the moment, she would have done willingly.

Kandinsky regarded all the female players in the orchestra as his sexual property. If he tried to be discreet with the married ones, the unmarried women were used and discarded as publicly as garments with which he had become bored. Céline would soon have gone the way of all the others, except for the chance of her affair with him coinciding with the end of the so-called *drôle de guerre* in the summer of 1940.

Three million men had been mobilised by France's generals, to make what they told the nation was a fighting force without equal in the world. There were plans to conscript three million more. With the German army marking time on the far side of the allegedly impregnable steel-and-concrete Maginot Line, and 'the mightiest army in Europe' standing guard between the capital and the enemy, no one in Paris took the war seriously. Even calling it *une drôle de guerre* made the whole business seem a joke. People planned their summer holidays as usual, the cafés and theatres were full, white ties were worn at the Opera and British officers on leave from the static front walked the streets in uniform.

The war stopped being a joke when Hitler changed the rules in May of 1940. After crossing the Meuse, the Germans cut to pieces the waiting French armies in just three days of Blitzkrieg. In Paris, three million civilians took to the road, mostly heading – like the government, which outran them all – to the south and west, away from the advancing Germans. On the way, the columns of refugees swelled as a large part of the population of every town through which they passed joined in the mad rush towards Bordeaux. Some rumours said that President Lebrun and Prime Minister Reynaud intended to make a last-ditch stand there. Others had it that destroyers were waiting in the port to evacuate them to safety in Britain or America, leaving their nation to its fate.

The journey was a nightmare, even for the privileged rich like Kandinsky who were travelling in the luxury of their own vehicles. Broken-down cars, trucks and even farm carts were stranded along the way, blocking traffic. Many of them had bullet-holes in the bodywork from strafing attacks further north. So many children, separated from their families, stood bewildered and weeping at the roadside that for months afterwards newspapers ran advertisements from devastated parents, asking for news of children and even babies last seen at Orleans,

Blois or Poitiers on a date in June 1940. Corpses of old people and children lay where they had died at the roadside, the faces sometimes covered to keep off the flies, and sometimes not. Occasionally, army officers tried to restore some kind of order to enable a convoy to head north, but most army vehicles were also fleeing away from the front, and added to the confusion.

Kandinsky's custom-built Delage tourer had only two seats, because the dicky was completely full of his baggage. He had arrived without notice at the house on the Left Bank where Céline rented an attic room. Given only two minutes to get ready, she had brought nothing except her two violins and a small toilet bag.

The journey to Bordeaux took four days. Each night they slept in the car because no hotel rooms were available. For four hours in Poitiers, Kandinsky visited all the garages for miles around, bullying, cajoling and bribing the owners in order to get enough petrol to reach Angoulême, the next major town.

In Bordeaux, the chaos was total. Not only was every hotel room taken, but government ministers and ambassadors were openly fighting for bedrooms in private houses. They held court in doorways and on staircases. Even Marshal Pétain, whose hour this was, had to sleep between sheets taken from the trousseau of the concierge of the house where he was staying. It did not suit Kandinsky's ego to compete for living space in that bedlam. The main reason why he had brought Céline with him was the proximity of her family home in St Emilion – to which he now invited himself. The last drops of petrol in the tank of the Delage were sucked into its greedy carburettor five kilometres short of Chateau Magnus, leaving them to finish the journey on foot.

Céline's father would have been a professional musician, except for the hazards of the First World War, in which a splinter of German shrapnel on the Somme in November 1916 had severed the tendons of his left hand. All his frustrated ambitions had been put into his younger daughter's musical education.

Within minutes of his arrival, Kandinsky, still dust-covered, hungry, thirsty and footsore from the unaccustomed exercise of walking along country roads for an hour in his polished two-tone shoes, was being toasted by his host with a glass of chilled Moët et Chandon champagne in the elegant Second-Empire salon where Napoleon III had taken refreshments on one of his many trips to Biarritz. Céline's father took his guest on a tour of the house, to show off the time and money he had spent in furnishing and decorating the whole house in the style of that period. The effect was lost on Kandinsky, who cared only about music and himself.

After dinner, at which each dish was accompanied by a great vintage wine from the family's private cellar, Adrien Picard adjourned to the music room with his guest, suggesting that Céline pay a visit to her sister Yvonne and her husband at their home on the neighbouring property of Chateau La Treille. Returning just before midnight, Céline lay in bed, listening to her lover playing the Bechstein grand in the salon.

Before the week was out Kandinsky, bored with country life, was spending hours each day on the telephone to Paris. The Germans, he was assured by all, were model conquerors, polite and courteous, eager to pay for whatever they wanted. His exaggerated fears were due to having been born while his mother was taking a cure at Karlsbad in the area Hitler had renamed the Protectorate of Bohemia and Moravia. Understanding the problem, friends suggested that it would be prudent for him to return to the capital protected by marriage to a French citizen.

The available French citizen was Céline. In between two phone calls, her idol communicated to her the startling news that he had decided to marry her and that her father had given his consent. Céline felt as overwhelmed and honoured by this annunciation as the Virgin Mary must have felt by hers. Kandinsky was, if not the Almighty, at least a god in her pantheon of music. It seemed the proper way for a god to behave.

.2.

Paris was strangely quiet, abandoned by most of its inhabitants and taken over by tens of thousands of impeccably behaved tourists in uniform. Already road signs in Gothic lettering were fixed to lampposts. There were so many on the Place de l'Opera where the Kommandantur von Gross-Paris was situated that the Palais Garnier was almost hidden from view by them. At major intersections helmeted German military policemen were on traffic duty, their polished breastplates glittering in the sun. On the kerbside, uncertain how to behave, the familiar figures of Paris policemen stood to attention and saluted the passing military convoys.

And everywhere there were posters depicting a German infantryman gazing tenderly at a child in his arms. The slogan beneath read: *abandoned people, put your trust in the German soldier*. The shopkeepers were already putting their trust in his money, convertible at an inflated rate, fixed in Berlin. Officers and men – together with the female auxiliaries known as *Blitzmädchen* – filled the shops, buying everything in sight. Their leaders had chosen guns over butter years before, and they simply could not believe the wealth of luxuries that Parisians took for granted after nine months of war.

One by one, the members of the orchestra returned from their various bolt-holes and the events of the outside world became once again merely the backdrop against which was played the real life inside the Palais Garnier. There, the hero of the hour was not Marshal Pétain or the new Prime Minister, Laval, but Glouglou the concierge, who had been the only member of staff on duty early in the morning of 23 June – the day after the signing of the Armistice at Compiègne – when Adolf Hitler compensated himself for the political inadvisability of a grand victory parade down the Champs Elysées by making a lightning tour of the architectural wonders of the French capital.

After conducting his VIP visitors around the recently refurbished interior of the Palais Garnier, and switching on the stage lighting for them, Glouglou became the first Frenchman – and probably the last – to decline a tip from a German to whom he had rendered service. Impressed by his visit, the Führer departed to visit Napoleon's tomb at Les Invalides, muttering that he had decided, after all, not to destroy Paris because he wished it to stand as an example of what had been considered the most beautiful city in Europe before the building of his intended federal European capital at Linz, which would outshine it by far.

In the orchestra pit, the drama of the Battle of Britain during the summer of 1940 passed largely unnoticed, so busy were the musicians with the rehearsals for *The Damnation of Faust*, which was due to open on 24 August. The ballet company under its brilliant new director Serge Lifar was in the final stages of a new production of Délibes' *Coppelia*, of which the first performance was scheduled to take place four days later. The orchestra burst into spontaneous applause when it was informed at rehearsal one morning that advance ticket sales for both the opera and the ballet were five times better than expected, thanks to the presence of so many culture-loving Germans in the capital.

Kandinsky's brief depression after his flight from Paris turned to a sustained elation when he discovered that the Germans had ordered life in the capital to return to normal as soon as possible, placing particular emphasis on the continuity of cultural events. Among the many high-ranking officers he cultivated was an opera-loving general who invited him and his new bride to the races at Longchamps with Serge Lifar.

Although a few Jewish faces were missing, *le tout Paris* was there, elbow to elbow with Germans of all ranks. Invited with her husband and Lifar into the box of the President of the Republic, Céline found herself being toasted in champagne by the first Kommandant von Gross-Paris, General von Vollard-Bockelburg.

For a few weeks, bathing in Kandinsky's charm, she felt the most adored woman in the whole of Paris. Presents of silk stockings, expensive lingerie and model clothes were lavished on her. Walking along the Rue de Rivoli or the Champs Elysées on her husband's arm during the first days of her marriage, Céline caught the envious glances or rich and beautiful women aimed in her direction. At rehearsals and in the dressing-room, it was a different story: she got the message from the other women in the orchestra that she had broken some ancient rule which prohibited concubines from becoming wives.

Kandinsky had no time to listen to her problems, even had she dared to bother him with such trivia. When not on the podium, he hustled from office to office, making contacts with the many German cultural organisations that sprang up in occupied Paris like the mushrooms for which the city was famous, competing for events which could be sent on tour to the great cities of eastern Europe in order to demonstrate to the subject nations that the Thousand Year Reich already stretched from the Black Sea to the Atlantic Ocean. One dressing-room rumour had it that the entire company and orchestra were to be booked for a tour of occupied eastern Europe promoted by the Ahnenerbe – the cultural department of the SS. Reassured by the new career opportunities which he sensed opening up ahead of himself in a Europe united under Berlin, Kandinsky began within weeks to regret the apparently unnecessary insurance of his marriage.

The first rule of his relationship with Céline remained unchanged by wedlock: what he did and where he went were his business alone, whether he came home in the small hours or stayed out all night. A hyperactive who slept only three or four hours a night, Kandinsky might come in at two o'clock in the morning and hustle her out of bed because he was wide awake and wanted to play a duet. Or she might hear him return after midnight and find herself dragged out of bed long before dawn for a one-to-one master class. It was a bizarre apprenticeship, but as the months drew on, the combination of long practice and Kandinsky's forceful teaching methods lifted Céline's playing up to new levels. She told herself that the privilege of being his sole pupil made up for everything else that was lacking in her marriage. After three months of living with him, she realised that she had never once called her husband by his first name, even in bed. She accepted this as the way things should be, for to a god all things are permitted.

Often she rehearsed in the orchestra all day without sharing a word in private with Kandinsky, and returned in the evening alone to the imposing but frigid apartment on the Rue Mozart in the ultra-chic sixteenth arrondissement, where the large salon was lit by gilt wall sconces and dominated by a mint-condition Pleyel concert grand piano. There she immersed herself in that unending therapy of unhappy musicians: practice, practice, and more practice. Her reward came when the male players who had been conscripted began returning after the Armistice. One by one, the less able female players were paid off until the women's numbers had dwindled from eighteen to five. The men still missing were either dead or prisoners in Germany, so there was little risk of Céline losing her job. Yet still she drove herself in the grinding, fun-less routine which the French call *Métro-bobo-dodo*, meaning train-work-sleep.

Her home life presented few distractions. The resident cook and maid were a pair of elderly unmarried sisters who had grown up on the Kandinsky family estate in Russia. They slept in a windowless cupboard off the kitchen, hardly long enough or wide enough for them both to lie down – which was not unusual for servants in those days. Neither of them spoke enough French to hold a conversation with Céline. Dressed in mourning black, with black headscarves, they flitted around the apartment cleaning and polishing, twittering quietly in their mother tongue, putting Céline in mind of two caged black crows. In their master's presence they were usually silent, scurrying serf-like to do his bidding whenever he snapped his fingers or shouted a command.

Sometimes Kandinsky's arrogance had startling results. One

chilly morning in November 1940, shortly after the government in Vichy had promulgated racial laws more draconian than Hitler's own, the musicians were wearing overcoats to rehearse in the unheated Palais Garnier, when two Gestapo men in leather coats came to arrest a Hungarian cellist, whose papers were not in order. He was one of several victims of Cluny's Communist clique in the orchestra who, at that time, were pro-German, and had allied themselves on several previous occasions with the pro-Vichy faction in denouncing to the Gestapo non-French players who were living in Paris on false papers.

'Get out!' Kandinsky raged at the interlopers. 'You have no business being here. Get out, you scum!'

To everyone's surprise the Gestapo thugs turned tail and ran, with him in pursuit, hurling abuse from the pavement as they drove away in a black Citroen. A few days later, the Magyar failed to arrive at rehearsal and was never seen again.

On a later occasion the pro-Vichy members of the orchestra denounced a Polish Jew who was the deputy leader of the violas, married to a Frenchwoman. When two blue-caped Paris policemen came for him in the middle of rehearsal, he stood up in his moth-eaten old fur-collared coat and, with great dignity, thanked the orchestra for the privilege of making music with them. Then he handed his instrument and bow to the leader and said, 'I shall not need these again.' This time, Kandinsky stared silently at the score on his music stand as the man was led away.

After Germany declared war on Russia, many Reds were in their turn arrested and shot in Paris, or sent to concentration camps. Somehow Cluny survived. There was a rumour in the orchestra that he owed his immunity to his wife's new liaison with an officer of the Gestapo, based in the Rue des Saussaies. For a while André Malromé, the leader of the orchestra, insisted on bicycling to work from his apartment on the Left Bank with two fishing rods (*deux gaules* in French) tied to his cross bar. In the orchestra, opinions were divided as to whether he was indeed an undercover Gaullist or simply a show-off, far too vain to run any real risks.

In January 1941, Céline was promoted to the second desk of the first violins on merit, and not through Kandinsky's influence. For her, that was the major event of the year. She was aware that old people and children were dying from hunger and cold in the poorer quarters of the city that winter, but the Kandinsky household had all the food it needed, purchased on the black market. The only problem that worried Céline was the shortage of horse hair for restringing her bow, because all the horses in France had been requisitioned by the Wehrmacht.

At first accepting of the way Kandinsky treated her – which was only a little more demanding than the way her father had behaved – she slowly began to rebel. Since the one way to make her husband respect her was through music, she formed a clandestine string quartet with a couple in the orchestra who were of about her own age – a second violinist and his wife, who was a viola-player – and an equally young cellist. They practised secretly in each other's homes on free mornings or evenings. Only when her husband was out of town did Céline dare invite her three friends back to the apartment on the Rue Mozart.

One day Kandinsky returned unexpectedly and found them rehearsing in his salon. The cellist was convinced that the two old crones in the kitchen had betrayed them, but Céline thought it more likely that someone in the orchestra had given them away. Seeing the quartet as a conspiracy against himself, Kandinsky flew into one of his rages and fired all three of Céline's companions on the spot. After they had gone, she stood up to him for the first time, telling him that while she did not care how he punished her, he must reinstate her three friends, or risk Cluny calling the orchestra out on strike. Kandinsky was so stunned that he agreed.

The electricity had just failed, due to an air raid in progress somewhere in the suburbs. He threw open the floor-to-ceiling windows to let in the moonlight and sat down at the grand piano. Céline recognised the beginning of the Kreutzer sonata and realised that he was offering an apology in musical form. Against the background of distant explosions, they played the entire sonata from memory in the half-light without a single false note or second of phrasing that could have been bettered.

At the end, Kandinsky stood up, pulled Céline to her feet and embraced her.

'That was sublime,' he said, stroking her hair and kissing her face. 'You must never leave me. Never.'

The highlights of their relationship were the occasional blissful evenings spent playing chamber music together. Only another musician could possibly understand that this seemed to Céline infinitely more precious than the normal joys of matrimony would have been. In recognition of the radical improvement in her playing, the attitude towards her in the orchestra was changing. Players came up and congratulated her after a particularly good performance. Even Prévert raised her hand to his lips one night at the end of Strauss' *Heldenleben* and murmured, '*Mes hommages*, Madame Kandinsky.'

Just occasionally the outside world intruded, as when Céline received a letter from her sister, Yvonne, whose husband, taken prisoner in June 1940, had died of wounds in a German military hospital. Under French law his property – Chateau La Treille, where Yvonne was living – was automatically inherited by his brother, whose home in Alsace had been destroyed during the German advance. Since no special provision had been made for Yvonne, she received not a penny from the estate.

When the new owner brought his family to live at Chateau La Treille, he gave his widowed sister-in-law just two hours in which to pack her clothes and leave the house. Yvonne returned to live with her father at Chateau Magnus. A month later he was arrested because someone had informed the Gestapo in Bordeaux that there was a clandestine radio transmitter in the attic. Locked up in the Fort du Hâ prison in the centre of Bordeaux, he ceased to exist under the *Nacht und Nebel* decree. The elegant house at Chateau Magnus was confiscated by the Germans and converted into a convalescent home for wounded soldiers. For the second time in a few months Yvonne was homeless, and had to move into one of the labourers' cottages among the vines on the estate of Chateau Magnus.

.3.

Yvonne was at first numb with shock. The comfortless little hovel with its flaking lime-washed walls and terracotta tiles laid directly on the earth, was cramped, dark, cold and damp. There were no luxuries like electricity or running water. Every drop for washing or drinking had to be hauled up a well and carried fifty metres to the house in pails suspended from a yoke over her shoulders. She had never appreciated before how heavily two full buckets of water could weigh at the end of a day's hard physical work. From bathing twice daily, she was reduced to washing herself piecemeal, using a kettleful of water heated on the smoky wood-burning stove.

Up at the chateau, as the Germans settled in, the elegant Napoleon III furniture was looted or smashed up in horseplay or for firewood. The wardrobe of expensive and fashionable clothes which Yvonne had been obliged to leave behind on evacuating her home at thirty minutes' notice, was sent back item by item to Germany, to grace the wives of the convalescent men, while their rightful owner wore shapeless dresses and old coats borrowed from her own tenants. From the cottage windows, Yvonne could see the chateau dominating the escarpment which overlooked the Dordogne valley. Around it, the wired-off gardens were patrolled by armed guards with dogs day and night.

After a few weeks Yvonne realised that she had spent the whole of her life being told what to do by a man. Deprived of father, husband and most of her possessions – she felt strangely elated by the realisation that she was free to take charge of her destiny for the first time in her life. She told herself that the war would go on for ever, and that it was time to prepare for the future, not bemoan the past. What, after all, did a house matter? It could be refurnished, or even completely rebuilt if necessary. The most important thing about Chateau Magnus was the land, which was still hers.

Perversely, the vine thrives in poor soil. There is a saying: the harder you make it work, the better it repays you. Forced to search deep below the impoverished topsoil for nutrients, the vines of Chateau Magnus produced the powerful sap that makes the best claret. Benjamin Franklin, on his tour of Gironde in 1787, had noted in his journal that the three principal desiderata for producing fine wine were 'old vines, poor soil and little manuring'. The soil chemistry of Chateau Magnus fulfilled these conditions perfectly. As to the vines themselves, her father had been talking for years of pulling them up and replanting, but had never got round to it.

The vineyards were overgrown with weeds, the vines unpruned. There were no male labourers for hire, nor had Yvonne much money to pay for labour, so she recruited girls who had just left school and mothers who needed cash to feed their children – paying them on the black. To keep them working meant becoming a slave driver and labouring alongside them, for as soon as she was absent, the pace of work slackened. If the labour was hard for her employees, it was doubly so for *la patronne*, who had never known what it was to handle a hoe or a pair of secateurs for longer than a few minutes.

With France running on Berlin time – two hours ahead of the sun – Yvonne rose before dawn and laboured in the vines until dusk. Most of the farm machines had been requisitioned for scrap, to be melted down for the German war effort. To pull the single plough and harrow which remained, there were only two slow, stupid oxen which had to be fed in their stalls at four o'clock each morning, so that they would be ready for work four hours later. Knee-deep in mud, Yvonne drove the oxen with shouts and a whip, heaving the plough round at the end of each furrow with sore and cracked hands and aching muscles. She fell into bed each night so tired that even the outbursts of rowdyism in the chateau could not wake her.

On 22 June 1941, Hitler launched Operation Barbarossa, a sneak Blitzkrieg attack on his ally, the Soviet Union. Mobilising the French Communist Party to switch sides overnight, Moscow ordered it to start a terror campaign, which was bound to provoke the Wehrmacht into savage reprisals against the population – which in turn would force Berlin to keep in the West troops that might otherwise be committed to the Russian front. Thus ended the honeymoon period between the mass of the French nation and its German occupiers. In Bordeaux, Châteaubriant and Nantes the first ninety-eight hostages were executed in retaliation for the unprovoked killing of a German naval sublieutenant in the Paris Metro. In Vichy the ageing marshal who was France's President signed his long-trumpeted Charter of Labour, which was to be the first step since the Revolution towards a classless society, with a guaranteed minimum wage for everyone. In St Emilion, Yvonne was summoning her courage to tackle the hardest job of all, for – with very few exceptions – the art of *vinification* was a jealously guarded masculine mystique.

It was widely believed in the Dordogne that a menstruating woman just walking into a *chai* could turn all the wine stored there to vinegar. No one could think of a precedent for a woman making a wine that was worthy of a St Emilion Grand Cru like Chateau Magnus, but Yvonne put her trust in another piece of folk wisdom. Good wine years were supposedly always divisible by three, which boded well for 1941 . . .

The result of all her hard work was not a *premier vin* nor even a *second vin* that was worthy of the chateau's name. In order to get money to pay her small work force, Yvonne was forced to sell the two indifferent *cuvées* she had been able to produce as common or garden *vin ordinaire*.

The following summer brought eight weeks of drought. Leaving half the property to go wild, Yvonne concentrated all her efforts on the two best fields, watching the vines for traces of disease known as *coulure* and for the onset of mildew, like a mother watches over a sick child. Getting in that year's grape harvest was achieved with a labour force of half a dozen women, some schoolchildren and a couple of wounded ex-prisoners, just returned from camps in Germany. By work-ing day and night – with only the help of a retired *maître des chais* who had worked for her grandfather before retiring years before, bent and crippled with arthritis – Yvonne man-aged to press enough grapes to fill two of the huge concrete vats in which the first fermentation was done. It was a pitiful harvest, compared with before the war.

Gaston Lagrange, the old man, was blind in one eye and had a cataract growing across the other too, but his palate was sound. His verdict after tasting the contents of the larger one seemed to bear out the superstition about women and wine. He spat the mouthful out on the earthen floor, and exclaimed, '*Merde! C'est du vinaigre!*'

Yvonne took a mouthful and closed her eyes to concentrate on the taste. Something had failed in the delicate biochemistry of fermentation, with the result that the wine was no better than it had been the previous year. She spat it out on the floor and ordered Lagrange to sample the other *cuvée*. Shoulders slumped with disappointment, she was standing in the great arched door-way of the *chai*, looking despondently at the pile of must left over from the pressings, and still tasting the bitter flavour of defeat in her mouth, when she heard him shout, '*Venez vite, madame!*'

Thinking that he had fallen from the rickety ladder she had placed against the side of the vat for him to climb up, she ran inside to find the old man standing in a pool of light made by a single shaft of sunlight from the bull's eye window, high up in the end wall. He was swilling the sample from the second *cuvée* around his glass and holding it up to see the colour, muttering about '*une belle robe pourpre*' and something about 'fourteen degrees, if I know anything about wine'.

She took the glass from him and tasted, inhaling at the same time in order to spread the perfume of the wine.

'It's not bad,' she said uncertainly.

When he told her that the wine promised to be as good as the famous vintage of 1929, which her father had always said would never be improved on, Yvonne sat down on an old cask and let the tears of relief flow. One vat of good quality wine was a mil-lion times better than none at all . . .

'Not here,' the old man shouted. 'For God's sake, don't cry. A woman crying can ruin everything!'

Tears turning to laughter, she let him half-pull her out of the *chai*. Together they sat on the ground in the thin November sunshine, drinking the still effervescent *bourru* until they were both too drunk to stand up.

'If only we had oak barrels for it,' speculated the old man, 'I think this wine could be even better than the vintage of 1929.'

Not wanting it to be looted one dark night by black marketeers from Bordeaux or confiscated under the law that enabled the occupying power to requisition any agricultural produce for the Reich, Yvonne swore Lagrange to silence about their triumph, and made a point of selling off unbottled to a wine merchant in Libourne all the wine of indifferent quality, in order to allay her neighbours' suspicions.

New barrels were unobtainable. Learning that the cooks in the SS canteen were chopping up for firewood a stock of unused ones which her father had purchased in 1939, Yvonne arranged to swap what remained of the barrels for a waggonload of oak logs and a live pig, bought on the black market from a neighbour. The next problem was where to hide the wine while it was maturing in the oak casks. Lagrange remembered a man-made cave beneath the chateau, from which the stones of the house had been quarried two centuries before. He had played in it as a boy, until it had been walled up after another child had been injured when part of the roof caved in after heavy rainfall. With his help, Yvonne broke through the wall. Behind it, there was enough space to mature ten vintages – dry, well ventilated and with a temperature that remained constant, summer and winter.

Now came the labour of filling the barrels and moving them there by horse and cart under the noses of the sentries. After the vintage was safely stored behind the wall, the bricking up had also to be done by night, with Lagrange painfully wielding the trowel in his gnarled hands and Yvonne mixing the mortar herself.

A small crawl-hole was left for the necessary periodic inspections, concealed behind piled-up faggots of vine prunings, which were stored in the entrance to the cave for use as kindling. At the end of the herculean labour, Yvonne felt exhausted but triumphant. None of her neighbours had had more than seven or eight degrees of alcohol that year, but she had fourteen. Their wine would not keep and would have to be sold for current consumption; hers would last until peacetime, when the lack of accumulated stocks would send postwar prices soaring sky-high – or so she hoped.

The problem of procuring bottles – again, there were no new ones available – was solved by bribing the cooks in the chateau with half a black-market pig to let her cull some of the thousands of empties from the vast pile behind the house. To avoid awkward questions, Yvonne cleaned each one herself with bottle brushes and cold water from the well, working late at night after the *domestiques* had all gone to bed.

Getting hold of corks proved more difficult. New ones were simply unobtainable and used ones had to be scrupulously cleaned, to avoid contaminating the wine. She presented the cooks with another illicit half pig carcase, and spent night after night inside the guarded perimeter, picking over the kitchen garbage heap by hand. Mouldy corks had to be thrown away; the others she boiled to sterilise and swell them up for re-use. On some nights, after counting the few she had saved and the thousands still needed, the only thing to do was to go to bed and weep.

Long before 1941's wine had been laid down in the cave beneath Chateau Magnus, the back-breaking, muscle-murdering, tendon-teasing job of pruning the thousands of vines by hand for the next year had been finished – with a work-force even further reduced by the exigencies of the Service de Travail Obligatoire which caused most young men to join the *maquis*, rather than be shipped off to work in the factories of the Reich.

Yvonne's hands were by now as calloused as those of the women who worked in the vines beside her. Her muscles were as tough as a man's and her brain was as sharp as those of the wine merchants who arrived from Bordeaux and Libourne to take advantage of the wine-growers' bad luck. On winter days, when the cold and the wet chilled her to the bone and her back ached with more pain than she had ever known, she would straighten up for a moment and take strength from the view of the chateau through the driving rain, promising herself that one day she would live there again and be rich, dependent on no man ever again.

.4.

Because music is so assessable an art form, it was obvious to everyone in the orchestra that Céline was ready to move on to a new career in chamber music. Even without using her husband's name and relying on her own talent, she could not have failed to succeed. As Céline Kandinsky, she would have gone even farther, so she chose what seemed a propitious moment to tell Kandinsky her plans and hopes, asking for his help with introductions.

They were sitting in Goering's personal armour-plated Mercedes, being driven home with a motorcycle escort after giving a private recital of a Beethoven sonata for the Reichsmarschal himself on one of his many visits to the city. Refusing to listen to what his wife was saying, Kandinsky's mellow mood changed to the anger that could hold a whole orchestra in thrall.

'I made you what you are,' he thundered. 'Help you? You must be mad, even to think of it. If you leave my orchestra, you betray me. In return, I should see to it that you never played again professionally, anywhere in the world!'

The tirade went on and on as they were driven through the darkened streets. For days afterwards, Céline's hands shook too much to hold the violin and bow. Pleading illness for the first time in her life, she stayed in bed, numb with the realisation that, as far as Kandinsky was concerned, she was an acolyte, dedicated for life to the service of the god who had made her what she was.

Such was her life when Dietrich Bohlen came back into it, one evening in the summer of 1942.

The opera which had just been performed was Mozart's *Entführung aus dem Serail*, one of the many German works in the repertoire during the Occupation. After the final curtain, Kandinsky had muttered something about a dinner engagement with Serge Lifar. It was rare for him to make an excuse. In the cramped ladies' dressing-room, as she got changed into her street clothes, Céline could not help seeing the expensive new lilac-coloured satin and lace underwear his current girlfriend was wearing. It was not so much that Kandinsky was generous to his mistresses, but rather that he wanted to dominate the way their bodies looked and felt and smelled, even when he was not with them.

There was a distant air raid in progress. During the performance the *crump!* of bombs far off and the harsh coughing of the anti-aircraft batteries had intruded on the music. In the last interval, someone had said that the RAF was bombing the Renault factory at Boulogne-Billancourt, where the production lines were turning out military vehicles for the Wehrmacht. To Céline, the people dying on the ground and in the air just a few kilometres away were less real than Mozart's characters on the stage with their preposterous adventures and improbable loves in the seraglio. However, as the last chords died away even a musician with her head in the clouds had to pay attention to the real world, for missing the last Metro home meant being trapped by the curfew at midnight. Unlike Kandinsky who had a pass issued by the Kommandantur von Gross-Paris, she had to hurry.

She used the pass door to go into the front-of-house, looking for anyone who might be able to give her a lift home. A concierge in the cloakroom was asking patrons with a single train to catch, to stand aside and let those who had to change trains en route collect their coats first. There was a party of German officers in uniform standing at the crowded first-floor bar. One of them, who had had too much to drink, pursued her through the crush, trying to catch her sleeve. Flustered, she bumped into another officer, knocking his arm with her violin case. At first she did not recognise the man wiping the spilled champagne from his uniform jacket, taking him for one of Kandinsky's many German contacts when he spoke her name.

Leutnant Dietrich Bohlen was a most unlikely soldier. Although his hair was cropped short and his face leaner than it had been when they last met, he wore his uniform with an air of apology quite inappropriate to an officer of the army which was master of all Europe.

He gave a small bow and repeated his name.

'You must forget all that,' Céline's father had said.

With her musician's ear, it was the voice she remembered first, and only then the face.

Dietrich told her that he had arrived in Paris that afternoon and come straight to the Opera deliberately to meet her at the stage door after the performance. Only at the last moment he had wondered whether she might be embarrassed to be seen with a German officer in uniform. Since his civilian clothes were still in transit, he had come upstairs to the bar instead, intending to return another night. She reassured him that Parisians were no longer being worried about having German friends in or out of uniform, and accepted his offer of a lift home.

Her usual routine after a performance was to eat a light snack, left ready for her by the two crones, follow this with two or three hours' practice, and then fall into bed, tired out. That night, she seemed to have two left hands, and put away the violin after only a few minutes. There was no heating and the water was turned off as a result of the air raid. Unable to sleep, she lay half-awake, wondering where Kandinsky had taken his girlfriend. To a hotel or some love nest? Was the girl still wearing her new satin and lace underwear? That he liked making love to a woman wearing the clothes he had bought her, Céline knew from experience. Was Kandinsky already growing tired of his new conquest? There were at least six other women in the orchestra with whom he had had affairs. Did he say to them all at the end, 'You must never leave me, or I shall see to it that you never make love again . . .'?

*

Dietrich had arranged to meet Céline the following week when Kandinsky was due to conduct in Lyon. They met by the lake in the Bois de Boulogne, she dressed in the clothes she had been wearing at rehearsal, and he in casual civilian clothes. Strolling along in the thin winter sunshine, Dietrich did most of the talking, unburdening himself about the night his brother had committed suicide: he had never dared to tell his widowed mother about Helmut's homosexuality. She felt strangely at peace with him, and wondered whether this was how women felt who had brothers or male cousins to whom they were close. When it was time for her to hurry back to the Palais Garnier and get changed for the performance, Dietrich scribbled a telephone number in her diary, saying that it was a direct line, on which she could call him at any time.

Since her availability was dictated by the orchestra's rehearsal schedule, Céline chose for their increasingly frequent meetings places where none of her colleagues would have any reason to be: by Bizet's tomb in Père Lachaise cemetery, or in the Montparnasse graveyard where Saint-Saëns was buried. When the weather was bad, they met in darkened cinemas, and sometimes under bridges down by the Seine. Dietrich was almost always able to fit in with whatever time and place she proposed. Although they had to meet in secret like lovers, apart from kissing her hand when he arrived and when they parted, he never made any overtures – even when he began to understand how unhappy she was.

One day he asked her out of the blue, 'Do you love your husband?'

Céline replied that she respected Kandinsky and shared a great deal with him through music. 'He has helped me more than I can explain. In return, I would do anything for him. Isn't that love?'

'What you describe is slavery.'

'Perhaps what people call love,' she replied defensively, 'is really nothing more than voluntary emotional slavery.'

'If you are right,' he argued, 'it should be mutual. Would your husband do *anything* for you?'

Céline smiled at the very idea of Kandinsky caring about or

for another human being. Music, she told Dietrich loftily, was his one true spouse, to whom he was never unfaithful.

Then she burst out laughing at the pomposity of what she had said. The innocent rendezvous, at which she laughed so much, became more and more important in her life – until, if a week went by when it was not possible for them to meet, she felt a sense of loss like a Catholic who has missed Confession. When Dietrich was out of town, she slept badly, wondering where he was and what he was doing, for he could never telephone her long-distance because the lines were monitored by the Gestapo. Without being aware of it, Céline was falling in love for the first time in her life.

After one trip to Berlin, she asked what he had done there, and whether he had had time to look up old friends. Although he did not go into details, she could sense what life in the German capital was like. He told her that the Party fat cats, nicknamed *die goldene Fasanen* – or golden pheasants on account of their splendid light-brown uniforms – strutted about looking important, and that there were still plenty of businessmen driving about in big cars. But, except for the cripples and the dead, all the men of his own age were in uniform somewhere else. The only friend he had met was Sepp Müller, convalescing after losing a hand in the battle of Kursk where thousands of German tanks had been destroyed in three days by the Red Army, now on the offensive.

Sepp had accompanied him to lay a wreath on Helmut's grave. Dietrich said how magnificent he had looked in his black SS tanker's battledress, covered in decorations for valour. He passed on Sepp's typically cynical remark that even a dozen Iron Crosses First Class, like the one he wore at his neck, wouldn't compensate for the loss of a finger, never mind a whole hand.

'And yet,' Céline questioned, 'he had volunteered to cut short his convalescent leave and return early to his unit. Why?'

'He told me that he had never felt so alive in his life, as when under fire.'

'No woman will ever understand the paradox of men wanting to live and yet going eagerly off to war.'

'Some men,' Dietrich corrected her. 'Believe me, I am not one of them. I would never dare to admit this to anyone else, but I think I should kill myself rather than accept a posting to the Ostfront. Life there is hell.'

Neither he nor Céline had any inkling how the chance encounter with Sepp Müller was to change both their lives.

.5.

'*Wach auf, Hauptsturmführer.* On your feet! We've got to get you out of here.'

Someone was slapping his face hard – knocking hell out of him. Sepp's eyes were stinging. When he tried to open them, he could see nothing except a red mist. He closed them again and was aware remotely and academically that he had not breathed for some time. The knowledge seemed about as relevant as Pythagoras' theorem until the reptilian cortex took over and he heard a deep, rasping inhalation as his bruised rib-cage was forced to expand. A lungful of the acrid smoke that curled around him left him choking and gagging on the all-too-familiar smell of burning rubber, hot motor oil and roasting human flesh.

Sepp wished that whoever was hitting him would go away and let him sleep. It was months since he had slept for a whole night. Didn't the bastard know?

'*Du Arschloch,*' he mumbled. '*Hau Dich ab.*' Fuck off, you arsehole.

The day had begun badly, with the driver's periscope of the brand-new Tiger tank – properly called the PzKpfw Tiger AusfE – being shot away soon after the attack went in. Why they were attacking in this Godforsaken place had been a mystery to him and his men from the start. It was something to do with not letting the Ivans cut the railway line which led to the bridge over the River Bug at a town with yet another unpronounceable Slavonic name. But the Tigers each weighed in at over forty-two tons, and would be too heavy for the bridge, already weakened by shelling – even with their super-wide tracks spreading the load. Whoever else walked or rolled across the Bug dry-shod, the men who had paid the price in spilt blood, torn flesh and shattered bone would have to use the amphibious capability of their tanks to swim across under fire.

It was three months since *der Giftzwerg* – the poison-dwarf Josef Goebbels – had admitted on Berlin Radio that the main line of defence on the eastern front had been shattered by Stalin, so this counter-attack, like all the others which cost hundreds of thousands of men, was simply to buy time. And the time was paid for largely by the men of the Waffen-SS, like the Division Das Reich to which Sepp Müller belonged, body and soul. And why? Because the Führer had so little faith in the mere humans of the Wehrmacht that he tended more and more to hand impossible jobs to the supermen who wore on their collars and lapels the double-S device, for designing which a graphic designer had been paid exactly two and a half Reichsmarks in lieu of copyright. When the twentieth century lay dying in the mud of ages there would be no more widely recognised symbol of terror in the whole world than the sacred SS runes, but few of the men who had worn them would be there to know.

Sepp's ribs felt as though half the Moscow State Circus had been using them as a trampoline. His belt buckle was digging into his diaphragm. With his good hand, he tried to undo it, fingering the engraved motto: *Meine Ehre heisst Treue*. Despite everything, loyalty was his honour. It was simply the German way of saying, as Englishmen had in the previous war, 'My King, sir. My country, right or wrong.' No more, no less.

Führer, command and we will obey . . . The creed of total, unquestioning loyalty still held good, although in this year of war 1944 the average age of an Untersturmführer in a Waffen-SS formation was twenty and his life expectation on the eastern front only two months at most – and despite the fact that less than fifty per cent of Waffen-SS men were German. Casualties had been replaced by Balts and Slavs, men from the Balkans and the frozen north. In Sepp's tank – which was the most 'Germanic' of the whole squadron – he had a Romanian gunner, a Volksdeutscher loader from the Sudetenland and a Ukrainian driver.

To celebrate *Sylvesterabend* and welcome the New Year three days earlier they had drunk looted Polish vodka and captured Georgian champagne, but ended sober after hearing the news that the Red Army had retaken Kazatin, south-west of Kiev in the Ukraine, pushing back Army Group South under von Manstein to the Ukraine's pre-1939 border with Poland. Hundreds of thousands of Axis troops had been abandoned to their fate on the Crimean peninsula in another mini-Stalingrad at Kamenets Podolsky, where SS Division Das Reich was nearly wiped out to the last man. The survivors owed their lives to the naked bravery of their comrades in SS Hohenstaufen and Frundsberg who fought and died to hold open the closing Soviet pincers long enough for them to escape the trap. Yet when they tried in turn to do the same for the remnants of SS Viking Division, entrapped in the Korsun-Charkassy pocket, the vastly superior numbers confronting them forced them to abandon the encircled men to their fate. Those taken prisoner were shot on the spot because the Russians made no distinction between 'grey' and 'black' SS formations – the grey being elite combat troops and the black being the Einsatzgruppen and Police Divisions which operated concentration camps and specialised in the massacre of Jews, partisans, and political commissars.

The second piece of bad luck for Sepp that day was a momentary humanitarian reflex on the part of the driver of his tank, who should have known better. Seeing a movement and part of a human body half-hidden by the front left shoulder of the hull as he negotiated the tank between vast heaps of rubble, he had swung the light powered steering – the Tiger was too heavy for the traditional clutch and brake-steering of previous, lighter tanks – towards a man foolhardy enough to get so close, only to swing away again when he saw that he was bearing down on an apparently unarmed Russian female medical auxiliary, whose face was transfixed with fear at the monster bearing down on her.

A chance shot through the driving slit had removed the

bridge of the driver's nose and both eyes. Seeing stars as his head slammed against the bulkhead of the wildly slewing tank, the radio operator/gunner sitting in the right front seat had managed to defy the centrifugal force sufficiently to hurl himself sideways in an attempt to heave the screaming Ukrainian out of his seat. His own face was only centimetres from the open driving slit when the Russian *partisanka* recovered her nerve and tossed the Molotov cocktail she had been holding behind her back in an awkward underhand throw. The brief fireball wrapped itself around the front drive-wheels of the Tiger's left track and her body. Flames whipped in through the driving slit, lasting only a few seconds but intense enough to roast into crackling the skin of the radio operator's face and leave him also blind.

There was nothing the three men in the turret could do except brace themselves as the Tiger drove straight into a brick wall ten metres high which collapsed, partly burying the hull under tons of masonry and steel girders. Had the driver still been at the controls, the 694-horsepower Maybach engine could still have pulled them free, but with both the wounded men thrashing convulsively in the confines of the two front seats, no one else could get near the controls. The engine stalled. Their ears ringing, the three men in the turret heard above the screams of their comrades the hoarse cheer of triumph which went up from the platoon of Red Army infantrymen crouching in the ruins of the factory on the other side of the collapsed wall.

The loader opened the turret hatch and stuck his head out, only to fall back inside, his face reduced to a lump of shredded meat by fragments of a Russian hand grenade. Despite his inert body partly shielding them, fragments of a second grenade tore into the gunner's arm and Sepp's scalp and leg, the blast stunning them both. The gunner recovered consciousness first. He heaved the body out of the way, but it was impossible to re-close the hatch because the hinges were jammed. To stay in the tank was certain death. Once outside, there was at least one chance in a thousand of staying alive, so he hauled and shoved his still unconscious commander up through the hatch during a lull in the firing and rolled with him off the hull and into a depression in the rubble.

'Wake up, Hauptsturmführer. On your feet. We've got to get you out of here.'

The first lucid thought in Sepp's mind was that most of the enemy fire which was pinning them down was coming from two Russian Tommy-gunners, firing alternately. Given the short range of the weapon, it was time to go. But what was he doing outside his tank? What fool had opened the hatch when Red infantry was so near?

With a tremendous effort of will he forced himself to sit up and remember where, when, why. Kneeling beside him, the gunner was trying to tie a tourniquet on his own arm to staunch the flow of blood which jetted from a torn artery, using a length of uniform webbing held taut between his other hand and his teeth.

'Let's go,' he gasped. 'You'll have to walk. I can't carry you. I'm bleeding like a pig.'

Sepp wiped away the blood running down his face from a scalp wound, which was making it hard to see. His right leg looked as much a mess as the gunner's arm: the pea-pattern camouflage overtrousers, made from captured Russian ground-sheet material, were a dark red from thigh to ankle, through which crimson flesh and white bone showed in places.

He locked his left arm around the gunner's neck and heaved himself into a low crouch. It was almost funny to note that his artificial hand was reduced to a stump of shining metal and charred leather; at least that could not hurt, unlike his bastard leg, the excruciating pain of which was threatening to put him out again.

Before they could move, a huge shape loomed closer through the smoke and dust, accompanied by the most welcome sound in the world. With a crunching of rubble and grinding of tracks and steel drive-wheels, another Tiger from Sepp's squadron manoeuvred itself to the top of the mound of masonry, under which his own tank was trapped. To keep the Tommy-gunners' heads down, its twin MG34s were spreading a fan of 7.92 mm. death above the two wounded men in black SS tankers' jackets who were lying in the rubble.

Inside the second Tiger, a voice Sepp recognised was shouting, 'Move your arses!' The driver did not want to stay for a second longer than necessary in such a vulnerable position, with the tank's less thickly armoured underbelly exposed to any captured Pak anti-tank gun the Russian infantrymen might be aiming at him. Incoming rounds pinged off both Tigers, whining away to bury themselves in the shattered remains of the factory, now reduced to a series of gaunt chimneys and roofless walls reaching for a grey, smoke-laden sky.

And all the while the 88 mm. gun in the Tiger's turret was traversing and firing HE shells into the factory at point-blank range, rocking the entire tank back on its suspension and making the air even more unbreathable with brick dust so thick that visibility was reduced to a few metres. Even with minimum elevation, the shells were passing high over the heads of the Russians crouching in the rubble. Give them a few more seconds, Sepp thought, and the bastards would realise that the danger from the big gun was more psychological than real.

Somehow the injured gunner heaved and pushed his commander onto the rear of their rescuer's hull, where they lay in the narrow space between the huge cylindrical Feifel air filters and the cup-shaped grenade throwers. Russian bullets ricocheted off the single piece of bent 80 mm. steel which made up the sides and rear of the turret. With a shout of *'Um Gottes Willen, festhalten!'* from inside, the Tiger lumbered off, reversing away from the factory.

For God's sake, hold on . . . Sepp's good hand was locked around the flange of one of the air filters, his other arm wedging his body between the filter and the turret in an attempt to reduce the movement of his injured leg.

They were twenty-five metres away – and already out of sight in the choking smoke- and dust-laden air – when a second Molotov cocktail curved through the air and landed inside the still open hatch of the abandoned Tiger, barbecuing the three crewmen still inside. Ammunition started cooking off. Unable to see what was going on, but recognising the noises, Sepp wondered whether his men had known anything about it.

He remembered the driver screaming in his pidgin German, *'Hilfe! Hilfe! Kann ni' sehen!'*

A moan of agony escaped Sepp as the turret swung slowly round, squeezing his injured leg against an air filter. The gunner was aiming at a window in a shell-shattered apartment block from which he had seen a sniper firing. He fired a sighting burst with the MG34 in the mantle, which was operated by the pedal under his right foot, leaving his hands free for elevating and traversing the cannon. A body flopped forward over the window-sill and tumbled to the ground. But the gunner had not been born yesterday. Knowing that some Red snipers kept a dead comrade beside them to use as a decoy, and wanting to make sure he had got the right man, he loosed off a single round of HE from the 88 mm. cannon and blew away the entire corner of the building for good measure.

His good hand now clenched around the radio aerial, Sepp clung to the lurching Tiger, hoping that the gunner would remember the two men clinging to the hull, and not try to rotate the turret any further – which could well brush them right off. He took consolation in the knowledge that the turret traverse on a Tiger was extremely low-geared. The design defect that would give the more lightly armoured Shermans in Normandy a chance to get in quick side and rear shots, was for the moment working in his favour.

Sepp turned his head to the Romanian who had saved his life. The man's face was white, his eyes upturned. Through the open mouth, a last trickle of blood was oozing onto the vibrating metal on which they lay. Even a dead comrade could save one's life. Sepp pulled the Romanian's body closer, hauling it across him to act as a flesh and blood sandbag, and then passed out.

. 6 .

'You're going to lose the leg, Hauptsturmführer.' The Army surgeon in the bloodstained white coat did not bother to wrap up the bad news for the man on the stretcher, who had survived two hours of being bumped over rubble on tanks and half-tracks, been manhandled at the casualty clearing station, crossed the Bug on a lurching Schwimmwagen which was loaded to the gunwales with other wounded men, and had then been driven another hour in the back of a three-ton truck to reach the forward field hospital.

'Am I fuck!' Sepp replied. The injection they had given him at the dressing station had worn off long ago. He was cold from all the blood he had lost, but the wounds in his leg were tongues of fire that licked up his spinal cord and into his brain. He lifted his head to see the leg, from which the field dressing had been removed, and fell back exhausted.

'Listen,' he croaked at the man leaning over him. 'You're scared of me getting gangrene, right?'

'I don't think I can save the limb anyway.' The surgeon was impatient. *Triage* was a word that had originated in battlefield hospitals, where the injured had to be divided into three groups: those who must be operated on immediately, those who could wait for attention, and those who had not a chance and were left on one side to die.

Sepp was in the first category but, even so, the time the surgeon could give him was limited – and it did not include minutes spent arguing with a patient who should be unconscious. Yet there was something about the hard-eyed Hauptsturmführer that demanded a reply.

'My professional opinion is that you have already lost too much tissue,' he said. 'It's a miracle the arteries weren't severed. If I ablate the damaged muscle, there'll be nothing but bone left. And the grenade fragments in your tibia and fibia, not to mention the smashed kneecap, make it unlikely you'll ever walk again. So why take the chance of dying from gangrene?'

Sepp pulled the 9 mm. Luger automatic from his holster. The Feldgendarmen at the hospital had tried twice to take it from him, but he had kept it for this moment. He was so weak that it was necessary to brace the weapon on the stump of his left wrist – at some point the damaged artificial hand had been removed – in order to align the sights midway between the surgeon's eyes.

'Because it's my fucking leg, doctor,' he snarled feebly. 'That's why. If I haven't bled to death in all this time, my professional opinion is that I can keep my leg. So I'm ordering you to clean it up but not cut it off. If you won't agree, I'll shoot you dead.'

The clouds of morphine thinned and the nurse's face came into focus, blurred and became sharp again. He wondered whether she was an angel, but was dimly aware that no Waffen-SS man ever went to heaven.

There was only one question: 'My leg, nurse?'

Sepp's mumble was unintelligible, but all the men on this ward asked the same thing, so she knew what he meant. She scrubbed his arm with alcohol and raised the syringe, voiding the air for his injection.

'They didn't cut it off. You still have two legs,' were the last words he heard before the morphine flooded his brain.

In the dream, he was running on two strong, whole legs.

I am running. Running along a Black Sea beach, splashing in the shallows with a blonde-haired, golden-skinned Ukrainian girl, whose name I have forgotten – if I ever knew it. She was laughing as she tried to escape, and still laughing as I pulled her down onto the sand . . .

I am running. Running on the beach at Hendaye, at the end

of the long, hot drive through France in the summer of 1940.
The SS Verfügungsdivision, as we were called then, had been
refused tanks by the Oberkommandantur der Wehrmacht,
which wanted to keep all available armour for regular army
units. So I had commandeered a captured Polish armoured car,
equipped it with two stolen MG34s, and we did the trip in
that – all the way from our jumping-off point on the Dutch
border, through Belgium and France to the Spanish border,
where the guards in their tricorn hats cried 'Arriba Alemania!'
when they saw us arrive.

And we shouted back, 'Arriba España!'

God, but it was bliss to stretch our legs after the long,
cramped drive in the heat. Maybe Poles have shorter legs than
ours . . . The few civilians on the beach kept their distance. A
squad of half-starved French conscripts marched up, saluted
and asked where they could surrender their weapons. I told
them to chuck the hardware into the sea.

Then I let my men strip off and wash their stinking clothes in
the salt water, spreading them out to dry on the sand. Without
even posting sentries, we spent the rest of the day running races
and playing football on the beach, dipping into the sea from
time to time to keep cool. At dusk, we used some of our hastily-
printed invasion francs to buy wine and bread, charcuterie and
cheese. Lying around on the beach afterwards, waiting for the
war to catch up with us, I ended up wrestling naked with Hansi,
which led to other pleasures . . .

I am running. Now, where in hell is this white desert? I
remember. We were almost within sight of Moscow – just before
the start of the big retreat in Autumn 1941. The name of the
division had been changed to SS Deutschland, but that was too
much like the Army's Grossdeutschland Division, so it was
altered to SS Reich – and finally to SS Das Reich, the name that
will go down in history. Our numbers were only five per cent of
the manpower the Wehrmacht could boast, but we had twenty-
five per cent of all the Panzer divisions, and were quite simply
the best elite soldiers in the world. And then, overnight, the
temperature dropped forty degrees Celsius, freezing the oil in
every vehicle that had not been left switched on all night long.

But why was I running? Ah, yes.

Our flak had winged a Yak-1 fighter, which crashed only a few hundred metres away from the laager. The pilot parachuted down and landed nearby, but tried to run away instead of surrendering. Like a pack of hounds, my boys gave chase and brought the pilot to the ground, wanting vengeance for their comrades who had just been cooked alive by a hail of 82 mm. rockets fired from the Yak.

The smoking tank that smelled of roast pork was still billowing black smoke, so I wasn't surprised when the lads started knocking the Ivan about. The surprise came when the pilot pulled open his flying jacket and flaunted a pair of tits, the like of which we had not seen for months. None of us could understand the words she was spitting out, but her meaning was plain. Defiantly, she pulled off her helmet and revealed long chestnut hair and a face like Marlene Dietrich.

The guys who had been hitting her forced her to her knees in the snow. She was half-naked by now. Hansi put his Luger to her head and got out his tool. He fired one shot within an inch of her head, to show that he was not joking, so she closed her eyes and let him go ahead. Just as he was coming, the bitch twisted her head sideways and bit off one of his testicles before he could press the trigger. Then she dived between the legs of the men watching and took off like a sprinter, heading for the plane wreck.

The guys were falling about, laughing their heads off, but I guessed she had some kind of weapon in the cockpit . . . and that's why I was running.

The others joined in the chase – except for Hansi One-Ball staring in shock at his own testicle, lying in a patch of red snow. I caught the pilot, kicking and scratching like a wildcat, tussling with her in the snow, and pulling off the rest of her clothes. Then I let her go in a game of cat and mouse. Each time it took four men to hold her down while another fucked her, making sure not to get his flesh within range of her teeth. The game ended with Hansi stuffing into her mouth what she had bitten off, and pulling the trigger to blow her head away before the medics carried him off.

'Oh God, my leg!' Sepp groaned.

A male orderly was replacing the stinking ersatz rubber bag, full of urine from the catheter tube, with an empty one. Each day the morphine dose had been reduced because supplies were running out and had to be reserved for the most urgent cases. Now it had reached the point where it had almost no effect on the pain, making it impossible to sleep at night.

'What about it?' the orderly asked. He had not slept for three nights; only vodka kept him going.

'Show me,' Sepp ordered.

Wearily the orderly pulled the sheet back. Beneath the bent metal cage, Sepp saw two legs, one pathetically thin and covered with red- and yellow-stained paper bandages and the other of normal thickness, clad in a white woollen sock that reached from toe to crotch. The wonderful thing was that each leg ended with a foot.

'I'm going to run again. One day, I'll run again.'

Despite the pain, Sepp started laughing and continued until tears were streaming down his face.

.7.

So many German generals found an excuse to visit the flesh-pots of Paris that a Wehrmacht joke had them all travelling by the JEIP tourist agency – the letters being an acronym for *Jeder Einmal In Paris*, meaning: Everyone Gets To Paris Once. Conductors seemed to have the same idea. For Wagner's birth-day in May 1941 von Karajan conducted *Tristan und Isolde* at the Palais Garnier. Kempff, Jochum, and Engelberg jumped on the same bandwagon. Only Furtwängler had the courage to refuse to come to France until he was invited to conduct for his talent and not just because of the Wehrmacht's presence. For this, he earned the gratitude and respect of an entire generation of French musicians.

Just after Easter 1943, Kandinsky was invited for the first time to conduct the Vienna Philharmonic and Dietrich sug-gested that Céline take advantage of her husband's absence to steal away for the weekend with him. Sensing that it marked a watershed in their relationship, she put off making the confir-matory phone call to him until the rehearsal break at Friday lunch-time. Some urgent problem at work had come up, Dietrich said. He might be late. If so, she was to wait for him on the embankment of the Seine, near the Louvre museum.

The afternoon rehearsal dragged by. Luckily it was music Céline had played many times – *Ein Heldenleben* by Strauss. At the end of rehearsal, she hurried home to leave her violin and collect an overnight bag. Leaving her instrument behind was something she had never done before: since she was five years old it had gone everywhere with her, so that each day she could do her quota of practice. Resenting this tyranny, she wanted to be free to explore her developing relationship with Dietrich without wasting a single minute on music.

She arrived early at the rendezvous on the embankment of the Seine, and sat on one of the stone benches, listening to the lapping of the water on the stones of the quay. Excited at the thought of the coming weekend, she forgot to keep moving, which was a precaution that had become second nature for everyone in occupied Paris.

A black Citroen swept down the cobbled ramp from the upper level. Thinking it was Dietrich, Céline stood up. Two Germans in leather coats got out and demanded her papers. Whilst one was checking them, the other lifted her suitcase onto the bench. He ferreted through her clothing and toilet articles, held up some of her underwear and accused her of trying to sell it on the black market.

Before she could even protest, Céline was shoved into the rear seat of the car, with her right wrist handcuffed to the chrome grab-rail on the back of the front passenger seat. There she sat in a panic as her case was thrown onto the seat beside her. Then – like a miracle – a second black *traction-avant* drove down the ramp. Dietrich parked deliberately across the front of the first car, ignoring the shouts of the man at the wheel.

He was wearing a linen sports jacket, tweed cap and tweed golfing trousers. When he showed his identity papers, the attitude of the Gestapo men changed immediately to one of respect. A small crowd had gathered on the upper level, peering over the stone balustrade at the drama below. As the handcuffs were unlocked and Céline was allowed to get out of the car, she thought for a moment that she recognised among the people peering down at her one of Cluny's clique.

Dietrich took Céline in his arms and kissed her on the lips for the first time. When he released her, she looked back up at the balustrade and saw no familiar face there. Hoping she had been wrong, she said nothing about it.

'You should have kept moving.' Dietrich tried to make light of her experience as they drove away. 'Apparently someone reported you for loitering suspiciously.' He had a friend in the

Abwehr, based in Grenoble, who had told him that over fifteen million anonymous letters had been received by German security organisations since the Armistice – all of them written by neighbours, friends and relatives of the people being denounced.

As he accelerated across the almost deserted Place de la Concorde with its sandbagged monuments, Céline was trying to work out whether the tightness in her chest was fear of the two Gestapo thugs who had been going to arrest her or the turmoil stirred up by the feeling of Dietrich's lips against hers.

It was a beautiful evening, with the leaves still on the trees in every shade from red to yellow to green and black. They drove out of Paris and up-river along the Seine through the multi-hued countryside. Dietrich had booked two single rooms for the weekend at the Auberge du Soleil, a small but exclusive country inn, which had been a riverside haunt of the Impressionists after the extension of the railways towards the end of the nineteenth century made day trips possible from Paris that, previously, would have been out of the question by horse-drawn transport. For years he had wanted to see it with the right companion.

At the hotel, there was a sprinkling of well-fed and very prosperous-looking French businessmen who were entertaining German civilians with whom they were concluding deals. Most of the other guests were German officers living it up with their tarty French girlfriends. At dinner, two tables were occupied by elderly middle-class couples who had been coming to the hotel for years. They called the staff by their first names and totally ignored the intruders, French or German.

All the food in the restaurant came from the black market. The only pretence of legality in the whole weekend was when the head waiter politely asked for everyone's bread coupons at dinner on Friday night. While most of the population of Paris was living on a diet of turnips, they dined off *foie gras* with a sweet white wine from Monbazillac, followed by oysters with an Alsatian Gewürtztraminer and then venison for the main course with a bottle of Pomerol. With the *omelette surprise*, they drank a 1928 Sauternes, and rose from the table with that glow of well-being which true haute cuisine produces in those lucky enough to afford it.

And still Céline did not understand her own emotions enough to put a name to them. In the dream world of music where she lived, everything was dominated by the sombre shadow of Kandinsky. It never entered her mind that the delicious whirl of lightness and freedom which Dietrich aroused in her was what was called being in love.

After the meal, they danced to a small band with a singer in the hotel's ballroom, made by covering an outdoor terrace with a tarpaulin because of the blackout. The musicians were local semi-pros and not very good. They played hits of the day like Tino Rossi's *Roses of Picardy* and Charles Trenet's *Menilmontant*. The repertoire was exactly the sort of music Céline normally detested, but that evening it fitted her mood exactly. After dancing for two hours, she wandered away hand in hand with Dietrich along the moonlit tow path on the banks of the Seine.

There, they discovered an overgrown and very dilapidated wooden belvedere, right by the water, which Dietrich recognised as the one depicted in a painting by Mary Cassatt, about which he had been arguing with one of Goering's minions only that afternoon.

There was a mist rising off the river, which made the trees, the houses and the masts of the boats seem to float on nothingness. The moonlit scene was so beautiful that Céline did not want to go indoors, despite the chill in the air. Cocooned in a couple of blankets from the bedroom, they spent the night in the belvedere talking, and went to their separate rooms just before dawn.

The following day passed in a blur of confidences and silences. After dinner – at which Céline ate very little – the same orchestra was playing. This time, they did not dance, but sat and talked in the belvedere for an hour or so, holding hands. Céline could feel how much Dietrich desired her. She was puzzled that he did not take the initiative, and disappointed when he retired to his room after one chaste kiss by her bedroom door. The music and laughter from downstairs had stopped long before she heard the knock on her door.

By dawn, she had discovered physical passion. With Kandinsky, she had done whatever he wanted because he wanted it. Yet when Dietrich touched her at last, all her senses went out of control. Her whole body sought to devour him in every possible way. At first taken aback by her sexual voracity, he became swept up in the same tempest that left them, shortly before dawn, stranded in a tangle of bedding and whispered tenderness, from which there was no going back.

Looking at him across the breakfast table, Céline wanted never to let Dietrich out of her sight again. And yet, perversely, when he tried to talk her into staying at the Auberge du Soleil for one more night, she refused. She was terrified not so much that Kandinsky might return early to Paris and discover her absence as of the way in which desire for Dietrich had changed her into another person altogether. If she spent a second night in his arms, or so she reasoned, it would be impossible ever to share her husband's bed again.

As they drove away after lunch on the Sunday, Dietrich promised that, after the war was over, he would take her back to the Auberge du Soleil for a honeymoon. Céline spent the journey in a daze of happiness, not even noticing which towns they passed through until they arrived in the suburbs of Paris. Then the enormity of what had happened dawned upon her.

As lovers do, she convinced herself that Kandinsky was unlikely to ask what she had been doing that weekend. She totally overlooked the fact that there were people in the incestuous world of the orchestra who kept a closer eye on her comings and goings than did her husband.

.8.

The gymnasium was part of what had been an expensive private school in the Black Forest, requisitioned as a rehabilitation centre for severely wounded SS men. Sepp had used up all his energy arguing with the panel of SS doctors, who were already moving on to assess the next invalid. Other men with missing eyes, hands, toes had been passed fit for combat, but Sepp Müller had been rejected as useless. He had shown the doctors what he could do, and they were not impressed: 'You have to face it, Hauptsturmführer. You'll never walk again without crutches. Oh, if you keep at it and have the determination, you may manage with a single stick eventually. Think yourself lucky that your good hand's on the right side. Next man!'

Sepp let go of the parallel bars and clenched his fist in anger. He *knew* he could command a squadron of tanks better than most men in Europe. He *knew* that the Americans and the British would soon launch their long-threatened invasion and that Germany would need every last soldier to drive them back into the sea within hours, or at most, days, if she were not to lose the war. SS Das Reich had been withdrawn from the eastern front shortly after the battle in which he was wounded and sent to south-west France to re-equip and prepare for the anticipated landings, while SS Viking and Totenkopf had been left to face the Red Army outside Warsaw. In the Balkans, SS Prinz Eugen was now the backbone that stiffened the German retreat, supported by some second-grade, locally-recruited Moslem *Handschar* formations who devoted most of their energy to wiping out partisan groups that belonged to neighbouring races with whom they had been practising ethnic war for centuries, trading rape for rape, murder for murder, atrocity for atrocity, massacre for massacre.

Sepp had talked to other tankers in various hospitals who had fought with Rommel against the Americans and the British Eighth Army in North Africa. They told him of the over-whelming quantity of armour Montgomery had been able to range against them. Each Allied Sherman destroyed had been replaced by five new ones the next day, or so they swore.

'Damn it, the Fatherland needs every man like me on whom it can get its enfeebled hands. I'm not a cripple,' he shouted at the doctors. 'Look! I'm not holding onto anything. Put me inside a Tiger and it won't matter how many legs or hands I've got!'

Sepp fixed his eyes on the clock high up on the gymnasium wall and forced what remained of his leg muscles back to work. A white-coated orderly held out his crutches, which he knocked aside. They fell to the parquet floor with a clatter. He put his weight on the stick-leg that would never bend again and moved the other foot forward cautiously, transferring his weight slowly onto it. Then he pulled the stick-leg forward, centimetre by centimetre until he was clear of the bars. He had moved twenty centimetres in all.

Sweat ran down his scalp and the veins in his temple stood out. 'Look at me,' he shouted. 'I can walk, you bastards! I can walk!'

In the Wehrmacht by this stage of the war, few men argued when told they were no longer fit for combat duty. SS doctors, however, were accustomed to the fanaticism of indoctrinated men like Sepp Müller. Unimpressed by his display, they did not even bother to turn round. Only one of the panel even turned his head when they heard Sepp fall to the floor and lie there sob-bing over and over again, 'I can walk, I tell you. I can walk.'

He was still on the floor after they had gone, staring at the hated crutches, which lay just out of reach. 'Fuck 'em all,' he said at last. 'I gave the bastards everything during four years of hell on tracks. From now on, Sepp Müller will look after him-self and no one else.'

*

Using a pair of Zeiss binoculars borrowed from another officer, Sepp had spent days watching the distant figure, adrift in a sea of green foliage. If he had delayed so long in making the approach, it was because it had taken two weeks of the good food and unlimited wine at Chateau Magnus to give him the energy to walk as far as the boundary fence. And then he had had to bide his time until a day when Yvonne came into the adjacent field to remove the *pampres* – the useless growth that sapped energy from the grapes, if not removed.

She nodded good-day to him without speaking and turned her back to start the next two.

'You don't recognise me?' Sepp asked.

She straightened up, with a hand in the small of her back, pressing against the pain in her spine that came from bending over all day long. It was not at all unusual for convalescent Germans to come to the wire and try to chat her up. Despite the lack of expensive clothes, make-up and perfume, she had now a vitality and facial beauty which came from physical exercise and fresh air and more than made up for the missing artifices of femininity.

'Oh, but I do,' she said, cold and unsmiling. 'You're the man who's been watching me through binoculars this past week.'

Sepp glanced back at the glassed-in conservatory where the confined-to-bed cases lay, among whom he refused to number himself. 'You must have good eyes.'

'The sun glints on the lenses.'

'I should be ashamed,' he grinned. 'After four years of war, I ought to have known that.'

'You'll have to excuse me.' She went back to her work, tugging the *pampres* off the vines and tossing them to the ground.

'That's not very hospitable.'

'There's a lot to do.'

'And you're fed up with being bothered by German soldiers with nothing better to do than chat up a pretty Frenchwoman?'

Yvonne straightened up again and looked him in the face. 'You're living in my house, monsieur. There's nothing I can do about that, but I don't have to talk to you as well.'

She walked away, angry at herself for showing emotion, and damning this persistent man with the artificial hand and the limp. Why wouldn't he leave her alone?

'I'm not just another *Boche*,' Sepp called after her. 'I'm the stud who gave you the best fuck of your life!'

She felt her cheeks redden with anger. If there was one thing she did not have to put up with, it was insults. The one-eyed aristocrat who was commandant of the convalescent home was very strict about what he called *le comportement correct de mes officiers*.

'I'm going to report you,' she said, keeping her back to Sepp. 'At least have the decency to leave me alone now.'

'That's the one thing I couldn't do,' he called. 'I've come a long way in more than one sense to see you again, Yvonne.'

She turned as he removed the black tanker's forage cap with its metal death's-head beneath the German eagle and swastika. The well-tailored all-black tanker's uniform with silver piping made him look like all the other men in the chateau. The double-breasted jacket fastened with concealed buttons and worn with the black leather belt outside, the Das Reich sleeve flash, the Iron Cross on its ribbon at his throat, the silver tank battle badge . . .

She knew the voice now, but the face that went with it was of a man twenty years too old, until Sepp smiled. She walked back to the fence, seeing clearly the artificial hand in its leather glove and the stiff leg so thin that the wind was whipping the cloth of his trousers around it, like a stick in a paper bag. My God, she thought, what's happened to you?

They looked at each other for a long moment without speech. Then she grasped the wire between the barbs with both hands and asked, 'How did you get here?'

Sepp replaced the cap, to hide the scar on his scalp where the hair would not grow. Yvonne was slimmer than when they had last met, and kept her hair cut short for practicality. She was wearing no make-up. Instead of a blouse, she had on a man's shirt. The wind was blowing her thin cotton skirt back between her legs, so that it resembled a pair of baggy Caucasian trousers. She could have been a boy, Sepp thought.

'I ran into Bohlen once,' he said, 'when I was on leave in Berlin.'

'Bohlen?' She had forgotten the name.

'The brother of the kid who drowned. Dietrich has some cushy posting to Paris, where he met your sister. He told me that your house was being used as an SS convalescent home and, since my division had been posted to the south-west of France, I managed to wangle my way here.'

Sepp's leg was giving him hell. The walk from the house to the fence was the longest he had managed since the ride on the tank protected by the dead gunner's body, but he could handle the pain for a while longer without giving in. Instinct told him that everything was going to work out; it was important that Yvonne should not see him as a cripple. A wounded soldier was one thing, a cripple something else.

'Why?' she asked.

'Why did I travel three thousand kilometres to be here?'

She nodded.

'Because I gave a large part of my body and probably all of my soul in the service of *Führer und Vaterland*. What's left is for me and the rest of the world can rot, for all I care. After what I've been through, I'm going to make a point of having every single damned thing I want, for the rest of my life. I lay on one hospital bed after another, from the River Bug to Warsaw to Berlin and then the Schwarzwald – and all the time I thought, if I get out of this God-awful mess alive, what's the one thing I want above everything else?'

'And what was it?' Yvonne asked.

He felt almost sorry for her. What did one more lie matter? 'You,' he said.

PART VI:
Paris – November 1996

. 1 .

Eighteen hours after finding Céline Picard's marriage certificate in the Hôtel de Ville of St Emilion, Ken was parking his Land Cruiser at a motel on the outskirts of Paris, chosen because it was near to a Metro line. After the recent bomb outrages, there was a heavy army, CRS and police presence both on the trains and in the stations. By the time he got out at the Place de l'Opera, Ken's briefcase had been checked three times by uniformed men with Alsatian sniffer dogs.

He used his journalist's visiting card again to gain admittance to the reference library of the Palais Garnier. In the reverential hush of the large, airy, modernised room at the rear of the building, musicians and musicologists were pursuing their various lines of research. Claiming to be working on a newspaper feature about French cultural life during the Second World War, Ken asked to see programmes for the 1940–41 season. From them, he learned that the resident conductor for the season had indeed been Feliks Kandinsky. Among the players in the first violin section of the orchestra was listed Céline M. Picard. The conductor's wife had obviously kept her maiden name for professional purposes.

The librarian was a quietly spoken, rather dreamy man in his mid-forties. Kandinsky, he informed Ken, was still alive. He no longer conducted, but had become France's most influential music critic. A recluse, known as *l'hermite de la Rue Mozart*, he emerged from his apartment only to attend a performance and then scurried back to write his pieces. Occasionally he came into the library of the Opera to use the archives or consult a score that was not easily obtainable elsewhere. But he never gave interviews to the Press.

As for the first violinist, Céline Picard . . . The librarian consulted a computer terminal, which showed only two entries against her name. 'She joined the orchestra in September 1939 and left in June of 1944. There are no other details.'

Of the other women whose names were on the back of the programme, four were still alive. Against the promise that his paper would happily pay them for an interview, he elicited their current addresses from the librarian. At the first two, he drew blanks: a former second violinist and a cellist both recalled Céline Picard, but could add nothing useful to what Ken already knew. Number three on Ken's list did, however, succeed in identifying Geoffrey Prescot's bride as the woman she had known as Céline Picard.

The last port of call that afternoon was a cramped third-floor walk-up apartment in the Marais district. Ken jabbed the bell-push beside the small brass plate which announced that Madame Amandine Lafont, former sub-principal viola of the orchestra of the Opera de Paris, gave private lessons on the violin. The elderly lady who came to the door was visibly overcome when he came straight out with, 'I wonder if you can help me. I'm making enquiries about a musician called Céline Picard.'

She ushered Ken inside her apartment, which reminded him of Mrs Prescot's home. Here too, the walls were covered with photographs of pupils, young and old. The furniture was comfortable, but not new, and the room smelled similar: potpourri of rose petals and rosin predominating.

Without giving Madame Lafont time to compose herself, he switched on the mini-recorder he had bought as a prop for his reporter persona. The old lady was clearly flustered. She and Céline had joined the orchestra on the same day in September 1939. All the women got to know each other quite well because they were forced to band together against the hostility of the male players . . .

'At first we thought that as soon as the Armistice was signed, we would be out of a job. But some of the men who were prisoners did not come back from Germany until the end of the war, so a few of us were kept on until after the Liberation.'

'Including Céline?'

'She had a privileged position, being Kandinsky's wife. Also, she was a wonderful musician. It's possible that the orchestra would have kept her on, even after the war – if things had turned out differently.'

'Did she make many other friends in the orchestra?'

'Céline was very withdrawn when she first came to Paris. People used to say that she was stuck-up – especially after she became Madame Kandinsky. The truth is that she was actually a very shy person. She'd had a sheltered childhood, with few friends of her own age – which is not uncommon for a musician. I only really got to know her myself when she invited me to play in her quartet . . . Are you a musician, Monsieur Scott?'

'I'm afraid not. Just a humble journalist.'

'Then perhaps I should explain that playing chamber music together imposes a kind of intimacy on musicians. I came to know Céline better in a few months of rehearsing in her group than in a lifetime of playing in the orchestra with her.'

'And did she confide in you?'

'I think I was the only person to whom she ever talked.'

'She had a sister in St Emilion.'

'Oh, they didn't get on at all.'

Frustratingly for Ken, the doorbell rang to announce a pupil who was arriving for a lesson. He left after Madame Lafont had agreed he might return the following morning, when she would be freer to talk. In the Metro, heading back to his motel, he went through the contents of his briefcase. The latest addition to the growing file on Céline Kandinsky/Picard were a studio portrait of four musicians, which he had promised to return to Madame Lafont after having it copied. In the slightly faded photograph, Céline's quartet looked very young and earnest, sitting with their instruments at rest.

The other picture Ken had borrowed was a street photographer's snap in which a fair-haired, pipe-smoking man in his mid-twenties was walking along a Paris street, with a pretty girl on each arm. He was wearing plus-fours and an open-necked, short-sleeved shirt. The girls were dressed in light summer blouses and skirts, with the piled-up hairdos fashionable in the Forties. A distant swastika banner on a public building in the background dated the picture sometime during the Occupation. The youthful Amandine Lafont was smiling at the camera, but Céline Picard was looking radiantly into the eyes of the man, with whom she was obviously in love. The quality of the photograph was a great deal better than the halftone reproduction of her wedding picture in *Le Sud Ouest*. It made clear beyond any doubt that Céline Picard and the young Madeleine Prescot were one and the same person.

'Is this Kandinsky?' Ken had asked, pointing at the man in plus-fours.

Madame Lafont had laughed. 'No, that is Céline's lover, Dietrich Bohlen.'

'A German civilian?'

'Dietrich was an officer. But he was an art historian, and not really a soldier at all. My father was wounded in the First World War and brought me up on horror stories of what the Boche had done in northern France and Flanders. Getting to know Dietrich was for me quite an eye-opener.'

'Did you often go around as a threesome?'

Eyeing the photograph in Ken's hand, Madame Lafont had shaken her head. 'Céline and Dietrich had to meet in secret, which was difficult because orchestral musicians worked very long hours in those days and Dietrich's duties often took him away from Paris for weeks at a time. So when they could be together, they wanted to be alone. I used to lend them my apartment sometimes.'

'This apartment?' Ken had queried.

'It was my parents' before becoming mine,' Madame Lafont had explained. 'I never married, so I never moved out. Yes, this is where they used to meet.'

I'm getting closer, Ken thought.

Hallstatt stepped off the first TGV of the day, which had brought him to Paris. At a coffee bar in the Montparnasse mainline station, he was impressed by the file Ken had already built up. 'I don't see why you need to bring out of retirement an old war-horse like me. You seem to be doing pretty well on your own, *fiston*.'

'I wasn't even born when all this drama was going on, Erich. I want you to use your background knowledge to chat up this old lady who knew Céline Picard, and explore all the angles. There's a lot more to this story than I thought. For example, why is there no trace of Céline Picard at Chateau Magnus, where she grew up? Somebody's hiding something down there, that's for sure.'

'And you think it's all connected with the murder of this old lady in Liverpool?'

'It could be important. It could be a waste of time. But since I want to catch an afternoon flight to London in order to be at Cat's private view tonight, I'm hoping we can wrap up this end of things by lunch-time.'

Madame Lafont was no longer the flustered old lady of the previous evening. Nor was she alone. Backed up by the concierge of the building – a formidable black-clad Portuguese woman in her fifties with suspicious eyes – she made it clear what was on her mind. The newspapers were full of stories about men gaining admittance to old people's flats and mugging them, so she wanted to see some identification . . .

Hallstatt roared with laughter. 'Do I look like a teenage *voyou*?' he grinned. 'Or a con-man trying to cheat you out of your savings?'

'*Non, Monsieur. Vous n'en avez pas l'air. Je m'excuse.*'

When the concierge had gone, Madame Lafont accused Ken of taking her unawares the previous day. 'I've wondered so often what happened to Céline, that when you knocked on my door out of the blue, I was unable to think clearly, and did not even ask how you had come across her name.'

'More than her name,' said Ken. 'I knew her personally. She was alive and well in England until last week.'

'That's impossible,' Madame Lafont interrupted. 'There is no question that, if Céline had been still alive after the war, she would have contacted me somehow. We were as close as sisters, Monsieur – except that perhaps that's not the right expression in this case, because Céline did not get on at all with her own sister.'

'Take a look at this.' Ken held out Mrs Prescot's wedding picture, keeping his thumb over the groom's face. 'Is this your friend Céline?'

Madame Lafont tried to take the photograph from him. The style of Dior's New Look told her that it had been taken after the war.

Ken removed his hand. 'The man standing beside Céline is her English husband. His name was Geoffrey Prescot. For fifty years, Céline Picard lived in Liverpool as his wife, claiming that her maiden name was Madeleine Lasalle. Why do you think she might have done that?'

'I haven't the slightest idea.' Madame Lafont blinked as one picture succeeded another in front of her eyes and Mrs Prescot aged ten years at a time.

Receiving a nudge in the ribs from Hallstatt, Ken let him take over. He had never seen his old friend put on the charm before. Quite the lady-killer, he thought, as Madame Lafont's faded rose-petal cheeks flushed with the recollections of her youth triggered by Hallstatt's apparently guileless chatter about life in Paris at the beginning of the Occupation. She perched on the edge of the piano stool, eagerly interrupting his recollections with memories of her own – from which a picture gradually emerged of Céline Picard as her closest female friend had known her. Like a photographic print in a developing tray, it was at first fuzzy, then sharpened and became full of detail. Himself no slouch at confessing people, Ken sat back and admired Hallstatt's technique.

Céline Picard, he learned, had been one of the unsung heroines of the Resistance.

'Are you sure?' Hallstatt questioned. 'A lot of people *said* they were in the Resistance. Perhaps she was just boasting?'

'Not Céline.' Madame Lafont had no doubts. 'She wasn't a person to boast about anything. I only learned afterwards that, for eighteen months before the Allied invasion in June 1944, she had been travelling regularly between Paris and Lyons, which was the capital of the Resistance, carrying messages hidden in her violin case.'

'And after the invasion?' Hallstatt queried.

'I said goodbye to her on the morning of 10 June, four days after the landings. As far as I know, from that moment Céline vanished off the face of the earth.'

'For which underground organisation was she working?' Ken asked.

'For the Communists.'

'You're sure of that?'

'Quite sure.'

The pieces were falling into place, Ken thought. One: Céline Picard/Kandinsky works for the Communists during the war. Two: after the invasion, job done, she vanishes. Three: in 1946 she re-surfaces as Madeleine Prescot *née* Lasalle, the wife of a British ex-serviceman, in the city which many had thought would give birth to the British Revolution.

It was a classic KGB agent history. As in life, so in death. Had Irving's old teacher perhaps been killed because she knew too much about some ex-KGB operation in the United Kingdom that was now being run by the SVR? Stranger things had happened.

.2.

Like religious and political converts, late-starter cooks tend to bore their friends with the intricacies of their new enthusiasm. Over lunch in a little *restaurant de quartier* near Madame Lafont's apartment, Hallstatt – who had never even boiled an egg while his wife was alive – insisted on giving Ken a full rundown of how to prepare the dish they were eating.

'*Lamproie à la bordelaise* is a work of art,' he boomed. 'You have to bleed the beast for fifteen minutes via an incision made ten centimetres from the tail. The blood is put on one side. Next, you gut it and thrust it whole into a cauldron of boiling water. That's to make it easier to pull off the inedible skin. Chopped into three-centimetre slices, the flesh is then lightly fried to seal in the flavour, while you bring a litre of wine to the boil in a second pan. In a third pan, chopped white of leeks – but not the green – are fried until golden. The leeks and the lamprey are then placed in the cooking dish and covered with the boiling wine. Of course, it must be good wine, because the next thing is to flambé the whole thing. Only then do you start cooking – which takes two hours on a low burner. You remember I said we had to keep the blood?'

'I remember, Erich.' By now, Ken was losing interest in eating what was on his plate.

'You add some wine to it and a few chopped shallots, then pour it into the dish, to thicken the liquor. Ten minutes later, you have a meal fit for a king.'

Ken pushed his plate away, and watched Hallstatt finish both portions. He had chosen a table that was awkwardly jammed between a corner and the door into the kitchen because there they were isolated from the other diners by the comings and goings of the waiters.

He pressed the Play button on the mini-recorder, and listened to Madame Lafont's voice: 'I don't think even Céline knew exactly what Dietrich was doing in Paris, but once when she could not meet him and asked me to pass him a message, I was put through to some switchboard at the Louvre museum, and a woman's voice said, "*Kunstschutz. Wer spricht?*" Is that any help?'

'What was the Kunstschutz, Erich?' Ken asked.

'An anomaly.' Hallstatt finished soaking up the gravy with a piece of bread. 'In the First World War, when the Western Allies were putting it about that Kaiser Bill's troops spent their whole time raping Belgian nuns and shooting innocent English nurses, the Wehrmacht actually had an impeccable record of protecting works of art. That probably surprises people who've read stories about the Nazi loot in World War Two, but it's due to an extraordinary little outfit called the Kunstschutz, or art-protection. It was staffed by civilians mainly and was independent of local commanders, so could report straight to the Oberkommandantur der Wehrmacht.

'In World War Two, the system did not work because the Kunstschutz's work was hampered from the start of hostilities by the Third Reich's parallel command structures: the army took its orders from the OKW; the Waffen-SS reported directly to Himmler; the Luftwaffe was Goering's private army and the Kriegsmarine talked to Hitler himself. If Dietrich Bohlen did work for the Kunstschutz, he must have had a pretty frustrating war, watching the SS divisions loot their way across eastern Europe while Himmler's Ahnenerbe organisation carried off anything of so-called cultural value and Goering's men looted everything their boss might take a fancy to.

'Worst of all was the Einsatzung Reichsleiter Rosenberg, whose teams began in France by looting works of art and ended by expropriating soap dishes, pots and pans and used underwear from all over the country, packing them into cardboard boxes – which were sent as starter kits for families bombed out of their homes in Germany's major cities.'

Hallstatt's crude research was leavened by anecdotes about characters like Rosenberg, the Party ideologue who sought to prove that not only the great German cathedrals but also Greek architecture and the Italian Renaissance were likewise achievements of the Aryan Nordic race. His mammoth book *The Myth of the Twentieth Century*, was called by Hitler 'the worst book I have never been able to read'.

'The ERR,' Hallstatt explained, 'was a vast bureaucracy employing thousands of people, created in a typical Third Reich manoeuvre expressly to circumnavigate the Kunstschutz, whose boss was Count Franz Wolff-Metternich – a descendant of the statesman who played such an important part in restructuring Europe after Napoleon. The count was a civilian – an art historian who had more balls than some generals I've met. His first official act in Paris was to place an embargo on any work of art leaving France. By sheer nerve, he actually made it work for a while.'

'But you never met this Leutnant Bohlen?'

A shake of the leonine head. 'I guess I left Paris before he hit town. But I met Goering many times. At the height of the Battle of Britain during the summer of 1940, when he should have had better things to do, Fat Hermann frequently took time off from the Adlertag forward headquarters near the Channel coast for art-buying trips in Paris, usually with a German dealer by the name of Bornheim in tow as his adviser and bagman. They were popular as hell with French art dealers, on account of paying top prices in untraceable and therefore untaxable cash. It was estimated that they spent over fifty million dollars in today's terms. Taking into account that it was the buyers' market of the century, with everything practically being given away at knock-down prices, fifty million bucks must have bought a heck of a lot of art to grace the walls of Carinhall.'

'You're very clued-up about all this.'

'I was dashing young Erich Hallstatt, the gentleman spy, remember? Every week I sent a report through the diplomatic bag to my father, updating him on important Third Reich figures who showed up in Paris.'

'What was Goering like?'

'He was several different people – and I'm not talking about his weight. Our paths crossed again in 1946, when I came to have quite a lot of respect for the guy. But to the young wise-guy I was in 1940, Fat Hermann was frankly a comic figure of avarice. In November of that year, when the Battle of Britain was finally lost, he ordered a private view of works from collections which had been earmarked for confiscation by the ERR. The Louvre itself was so crammed with looted works of art by then that the far smaller Jeu de Paume museum had to be used for his private exhibition.'

Hallstatt drew a vivid word-picture for Ken of the scene at the Jeu de Paume on 3 November 1940, where officers from all the several services involved, aware how much the Reichsmarschal loved pomp and ceremony, donned their best ceremonial uniforms and found themselves seriously over-dressed when Hitler's deputy appeared in civilian clothes. Perhaps, Hallstatt mused, he was hoping that his lack of uniform would incline people to forget that he, as head of the Luftwaffe, was responsible more than any other single person for losing control of Germany's one real chance of a quick victory – when his much-vaunted ME 109 had been matched against the Spitfire over the fields of Kent that summer, and found wanting.

In a soft hat and enormous ankle-length overcoat, Goering looked like a mobile tent rolling across the priceless carpets and between the potted palms, admiring the assembled works of art. So excited was he by the experience that he stopped for neither lunch nor dinner. Two days later, he was still there, having selected from the wealth of choice available, twenty-seven major works for himself. They came principally from the home of Edouard de Rothschild, and included Rembrandt's *Boy with a Red Beret* and Van Dyck's *Portrait of a Lady*. Having had his knuckles rapped over a similar incident in Austria, the Reichsmarschal refrained from purloining the famous Rothschild Vermeer known as *The Astronomer*, which he allocated instead to the Führer's collection, destined to embellish the Führer's home town of Linz when it became capital of a unified Europe at the end of the war.

To get around the Kunstschutz transport embargo, Goering moved the loot in his own train – bizarrely named *Amerika* – which was operated by the Luftwaffe transport command. An expert at confusing issues, he also legitimised in advance his seventeen future art raids on the French capital, in which he personally acquired some six hundred works, by issuing a decree that all works of art in conquered France should be divided into five categories.

First came the Führer's choice. Next were 'objects which will serve to complete the Reichsmarschal's collections at Carinhall'. Third were items selected by the ERR to corroborate Rosenberg's bizarre cultural theories. The fourth group was to be despatched by the ERR to German museums. Anything left was to be sold and the profits donated to French war orphans – who never actually received a penny. In a piece of neat Third Reich footwork, Goering had the astuteness to claim that he would personally obtain Hitler's approval of the arrangements immediately after returning to Berlin, which meant that his decree had the effect of law from the moment that it was set down on paper.

To these categories, the ERR added one of its own: 'degenerate, Jewish or modern' art, which was to be destroyed. Paintings by Klee, Miró and Dali, among others, were slashed and burned. Paradoxically, many of these 'degenerate' artists, including Braque and Picasso, continued working unmolested in their Paris studios throughout the Occupation.

In all, the ERR despatched 4,174 crates of art treasures eastwards to the Reich between April 1941 and July 1944, filling 138 sealed railway waggons which could certainly have been better used by the army for much-needed military supplies. All this was in addition to the road and rail convoys of trucks transporting Goering's loot, as well as the personal trophies of the tens of thousands of individual officers and men who 'liberated' works of art on their own initiative – as their Allied counterparts were to do later on.

'The organs of Vichy France were powerless to do anything on an official level,' Hallstatt concluded. 'So the only organisation actively trying to combat the art drain was ironically the

Wehrmacht's own Kunstschutz. Those guys worked their butts off trying to keep track of the road and rail shipments even after they arrived in Germany and were moved from museum to flak tower to remote castles and even remoter salt mines, in the endeavour to keep them out of the way of the Allied bombing campaign. It was due to their efforts that so much of the loot was traced and recovered after the war.'

'. . . which explains why a junior officer of the Kunstschutz like Leutnant Dietrich Bohlen had such freedom of movement,' Ken guessed.

A nod. 'Metternich's officers had to use both caution and guile, in order not to run foul of Himmler, Rosenberg, Goering and Hitler himself – to whom they were not exactly the flavour of the month. I was even told – but I never had proof of this – that they sometimes used false identities, impersonating SS officers and members of the Gestapo in order to gain access to prohibited areas where looted art treasures had been taken, and check exactly what was there.'

'You're a mine of information, Erich,' Ken said in genuine gratitude. 'I can see why the DCI used to take you with him to those monthly briefings in the Oval Office at the White House.'

'I was rarely asked to speak. Mostly I just went along for the ride and sat outside in the corridor, waiting to be called. But I got a kick out of being there, all the same.'

'I bet.'

'Now, I wouldn't give a shit.' Hallstatt squared his shoulders to face the afternoon. 'You know, Ken, every year on my birthday I get a visit from two guys in grey suits working out of the Embassy in Paris. They bring me a dozen bottles of Jack Daniel's as a present from the current DCI. Very politely, one of them manages to bring into the conversation a warning not to divulge to anyone the knowledge I accumulated in Uncle Sam's service. His buddy usually spends some time poking through my bookshelves, to make sure there's no restricted material there. As if I'd be so stupid . . .'

'And how do you react?'

'I accept the whiskey and tell them to go fuck themselves.'

Ken checked his wristwatch. 'It's time I started heading for the airport, if I'm not to miss the opening of Catriona's show in London.'

'Have fun,' said Hallstatt. 'You can leave Madame Lafont to me. And give that beautiful Irish girlfriend of yours my love, when you get to London.'

.3.

Hallstatt watched Ken's taxi drive away. Despite the cold wind, he was sweating. For fifty years he had avoided being alone in Paris with time on his hands. There were two hours to kill before Madame Lafont was free to continue her conversation: she had apologised that it was not possible to cancel all the lessons arranged for that day.

Hallstatt had choices. He had seen the tourist sights too many times to do them again, but there were museums, art galleries, exhibitions. Cinemas were open for matinée perform-ances, but not for him. The cinema he had to visit was in his head, and it was playing a scratched and gritty old print of a black-and-white film he had watched too many times. He found himself heading, as he had known he would, for the Gare du Nord, remembering step by step how it had felt on the day he was arrested there, less than a week after he had parachuted in to join up with the *maquis* in the Rhône valley.

'I was a cocky young know-it-all,' he muttered under his breath. 'I deserved everything that happened to me. With an accent like mine, I shouldn't even have been in Paris, where any one of a thousand old acquaintances might have recognised me.'

The instant he had opened his mouth that day, they had known what he was – probably even who he was. So he had got the full treatment: the drownings, the hanging upside down on a rod, the electric shocks in the places that hurt most. The moment of truth came when he found himself locked up alone in a cell, with the promise of worse to come. Up to that second, he had been bluffing all his life and getting away with it because he had the self-confidence that came from being the only son of rich and respected parents. Alone, in the pain and dirt and darkness, what he had thought was his personality blew away like cobwebs in a gale, leaving not very much behind.

At the time and afterwards he had rationalised that a live coward was more use to the Allied war effort than a dead hero. Years later, he had found in a poem by A.E. Houseman the couplet, *Life, to be sure, is no great thing to lose/But young men think it is and we were young.*

The inescapable truth was that he had cracked – and people had died as a result. Rescued at gunpoint two days later while in transit from Paris to Marseille, where the local Gestapo wanted him to identify some prisoners they were holding, Hallstatt had been fêted as a hero by the jubilant *maquisards* who had carried out the rescue. After he had resumed his role as the young hero from across the sea, no one had ever pointed the finger of suspicion at him.

He had tried to atone for what he had done by taking insane risks that he would never have asked of anyone else. But, like the Ancient Mariner, he found himself condemned to watch others dying while he went on unscathed and became eventually the living legend his men called *Erich pare-balles*, or bullet-proof Hallstatt.

Ken supposed his old pal would have done the same: it was hard to ignore the teaching that things should be kept in watertight compartments so far as possible.

He had reached Irving on his mobile phone in between rehearsal and concert the previous evening, after deciding to appeal to his vanity: 'I have a problem, with which I think you can help. Mrs P's marriage to Geoff was bigamous.'

'You're kidding!'

'She was married under the name of Céline Picard in the summer of 1940 – to a French conductor by the name of Feliks Kandinsky.'

'Are you having me on?'

'I'm giving it to you straight, Irving. I need to talk to Kandinsky. The problem is that he doesn't return my calls. But if a famous musician like you were to ring him up . . . Can you spare the time to pop over to Paris tomorrow?'

When his taxi drew up at the corner of the rue Mozart where Ken was waiting, Irving stepped out. Dressed entirely in white – white windcheater, white chinos and white trainers, he looked like a male model on the way to a photo assignment. Over a coffee in a side-street bar, he filled Ken in about the man they were going to see: 'Kandinsky was never in the Karajan class. But he was good. I've heard some of his recordings.'

'What did you tell him when you spoke yesterday?'

'I used the line you gave me, said I was in Paris doing some research for my autobiography, and had been surprised to learn in the library of the Opera that my old fiddle teacher had once been married to him.'

'What was his reaction?'

'At first he argued that Mrs P – he called her Céline – had died during the war, and said I must be mistaken. So I laid on the flattery pretty thick. It always works with conductors. People think a soloist is vain, but I can tell you the man with the stick has an ego twice as big as any of us. When I told him that I wanted to pay an adequate tribute to him in my book as the teacher of my teacher, it worked like a charm.'

The man who opened the door of the apartment in the rue Mozart was stooped and bird-faced. The doyen of French music critics was a hypochondriac, terrified of draughts. Kandinsky closed the door behind his visitors, then bolted it and hurried ahead of them into the salon: a gnomish figure in green tracksuit trousers and felt slippers, wearing a green velvet smoking jacket, with a long red scarf wound round his neck. Unusually for someone who had lived so long in France, he did not offer to shake hands with either of his visitors.

Age had faded the eyes which had held the orchestra of the Opera de Paris in thrall sixty years before. They were now a baby-blue colour, peering shrewdly at Ken and Irving over the top of half-moon spectacles. What had been a shock of prematurely grey hair was now reduced to a few wisps around a bald pate, but there was still an angry energy in Kandinsky's gestures and movements.

Inside the salon, Irving obeyed the instruction to close the door behind him, and put his violin case down on the only chair that was not covered in paperwork.

Kandinsky's accent was a cocktail of many ingredients. A serial killer of grammar, he confused *tu* and *vous* continually, switching from English to French and back again, interspersing both with phrases from Russian and German. The only tense with which he seemed comfortable in any language was the present: 'Of course I am remembering you, Monsieur Bradley. You are playing the César Franck sonata in A Major in Studio 106 at the Maison de la Radio.'

'And you wrote a very kind piece, *maestro*, about my performance in *Le Figaro* next morning,' said Irving.

'I don't write kind reviews,' Kandinsky snapped. 'If you play good, I say so. If you play bad, I write that too. *Qu'est-ce que je peux faire pour vous?*'

Irving spoke fast. 'Since Céline Picard was the most important influence in my early development, I need to know something of her background, *maestro*. She was always very vague about her life in France, before coming to Britain, so I wondered if you could fill me in.'

'I advise you to leave the business of writing books to *alte Männer* like me, Mr Bradley. At your age, a player of your talent does better to concentrate on playing and nothing else.'

Ken was checking out the room. It felt like a museum. If Mrs P had walked into it, the only visible change that would have met her eyes was the double-glazing that dulled the noise of the traffic in the rue Mozart and the bookshelves that now covered the walls. The permanent lack of ventilation and the hundreds of old books and music scores on the shelves and piled up on the furniture and the floor gave the room a library-like mustiness. On the Boulle-work writing desk by one of the windows was an old-fashioned upright typewriter in which was an unfinished crit of a recital at the Salle Pleyel the previous evening.

Kandinsky seated himself at the piano. 'After hearing you play last year, I was purchasing of your recordings several, Monsieur Bradley. Your style, phrasing, interpretation were intriguing. All were immediately familiar to me. It was like hearing an echo of Céline herself.'

'Yet you didn't think of coming up to talk to me at the time, or of contacting me afterwards?'

'Monsieur Bradley – ' Kandinsky was cracking the joints of his fingers, willing arthritis away – 'if you are seeing in the street this afternoon a girl whose face remind you of your grandmother as a young woman, are you chasing after her and calling out that old lady's name? So far as I can know, Céline is dead twenty years before you are born.'

'I only knew your wife as a middle-aged woman, *maestro*. What was she like when she was young . . . when you married her?'

Kandinsky seemed not to understand the question, so Irving put it another way: 'What kind of person was she?'

'I've no idea.' The question was irritating the old man; he had never been interested in Céline as a person. For him she had always been first and foremost a musician.

As though doodling at the keyboard, Kandinsky fingered the chord of B Minor, followed by a B natural and a D. Irving recognised the pattern as the opening of the Franck sonata. By the violin's entrance in bar five, he had his instrument tucked under his chin and came in on the beat, tuning his instrument later during the piano's solo passages.

The first movement of the sonata was a mutual exploration via a series of challenges; Kandinsky had the printed music in front of him, but Irving refused to look, wanting to play from memory. His eyes were closed, his brow furrowed in concentration.

The second movement, marked *allegro*, was a naked contest between the two players, with Kandinsky testing Irving's ability to follow him dynamically and rhythmically. For a man in his eighties, his fingers were amazingly nimble on the keys.

By the time of the recitative in the third movement, the duet was an equal match, the music moving fluidly from piano to violin and back, the two instruments blending as one. And the last movement – the *allegretto poco mosso* – was as free and relaxed as the chit-chat of a couple of friends who had known each other for years, strolling side by side in the park on a sunny day.

As the music ended, Kandinsky's eyes were moist. Was that, Ken wondered, just the natural rheuminess of an old man's eyes?

Irving was no Hallstatt. Control of the conversation was mainly with Kandinsky. Ken sat on the sidelines, unable to find a chance to intervene until Kandinsky finished a tirade against Charles de Gaulle – who, he said, had ruined his career by banning him from playing or performing in public because he had been working for the Communist Resistance right through the Occupation.

'We understand that Céline was also involved in this underground work,' Ken said.

Kandinsky snorted. 'Céline was what you call double agent. Really she works for the Germans all the time. One day they arrest her in Lyon. The next day she is free.'

'And how did she explain that?'

'I don't know.'

'Why would she work for the Germans?'

'Women! You can never trust them. They meet a man and *paf!* they betray their husband and desert their children . . .'

'She was having an affair with her German handler, then? Is that what you are saying?'

'Of course.'

Ken exchanged a glance with Irving. Could Dietrich Bohlen's job with the Kunstschutz have been merely a cover for an officer in the Abwehr or the Gestapo? In Paris at that time, anything was possible. 'How did you learn that she had been freed?' he asked. 'Did Céline return to Paris?'

'She could not. The Communists would have executed her.'

'That's what I thought. So how did you find out that she had been released?'

'Cluny told me. The Reds knew everything. Two days after Céline is arrested, they let her go free. She disappears with her German handler. So soon after the Normandy landings, everything was in chaos, you can imagine. They just disappeared. Later, I hear a rumour that man has stolen much valuable paintings, so I am thinking maybe they escape to South America. That is where all the rich ones were supposed to be, after the war, *nyet*? Then, as years go by, I am knowing she is dead.'

'How?' asked Ken.

'You are not musician. But I . . .' Kandinsky laid a hand on his heart. 'I know that life without music is not possible for someone with Céline's gifts. She plays like you have to breathe. It is her life. And if she plays, then sometime I am coming across the sound that only she could make – on a record or in a radio programme.'

'Tell us about the last time you saw her,' Ken prompted.

Eyes closed, Kandinsky was remembering the day after - and the bowel-emptying fear that she would incriminate him, which had caused him to leave the rostrum half a dozen times during the rehearsals for *Die Meistersinger*. Returning from a trip to the lavatory in his dressing-room, he had just regained his position on the podium when a screaming figure in German uniform was attacking him, in front of the orchestra.

'A real Nazi,' he said in answer to one of Ken's questions. 'He knows who I am, of course. He asks me, "*Wo ist Céline?*" He says to answer his question, so nothing will happen me. I tell him she was arrested in Lyon the previous day.'

'This German officer . . .' Ken flicked through the photographs in his briefcase and pulled out the three-shot of Dietrich Bohlen and the girls. Keeping his hand over their faces, he asked, 'Could this have been the man who came to the Palais Garnier that day?'

'How can I say? It's a long time ago.'

'Yet you remember the music you were rehearsing that day, Monsieur Kandinsky!'

'Music I never forget. People . . .' The old man made a gesture implying that they did not count. 'Now you must go, both of you. I have work. *Mnoga rabota, mnoga.*'

'He's lying,' said Irving, when he and Ken were outside again, on the rain-slicked pavement.

'About what?'

'About Mrs P being a double agent. She was too up-front for

that. You wouldn't understand this, but one musician can't lie to another. Oh, maybe with words one can, but not when we're playing.'

'Then how do you account for Mrs P living a lie all the years you knew her in Liverpool?'

'Whatever you think, she never lied to me. I'm a hundred per cent sure of that. And don't look so sceptical. Playing with an orchestra, I know who's having an affair with whom, who hates whom, who's in love with someone else who doesn't love them - it's all in the sound, in the way we play together, or don't. But only another musician can hear it.'

'What about Kandinsky? You just played with him. Was he lying to us?'

'I don't know.' Irving shrugged. 'I only played one sonata with Kandinsky, whereas I played duets with Mrs P over twenty years.'

'You never had any inkling that there was anything unusual about her?'

'Are you kidding? I realised long before I made it to the Juilliard that she must have been an amazing performer, when young. She had all the technique and musicianship for a solo career, but an accident had damaged two fingers on her left hand unfortunately – after which she could only teach.'

'And did Mrs P ever talk about it?'

'The accident? No. I asked her a couple of times, but I suppose she didn't want to remember.'

'It's time we were getting out to the airport,' Ken said, 'if we're not to be late at Cat's private view.'

'You look unwell,' said Madame Lafont.

'Something I ate at lunch.' In her bathroom, Hallstatt had caught sight of his haggard face. *Get off your butt, Erich! Stop feeling sorry for yourself. There's a job to do and Ken's relying on you to do it.*

He switched on the mini-recorder, which Ken had left with him.

'Céline gave me this letter,' Madame Lafont was saying. 'She told me to hand it to Dietrich when he returned to Paris. I asked her why . . .' There was the sound of the doorbell on the tape.

'Let's take it from there,' Hallstatt said, pressing the Record button. 'You asked her why she couldn't give it to Dietrich herself, presumably.'

'Yes. I could see she was terribly upset about something, but I thought it was the Leader's threat to throw her out of the orchestra because her playing had declined catastrophically. I tried to help but all she would say was that she had a problem she could not discuss. It was stopping her eating, she couldn't sleep . . . Well, I was ill myself that day – after four years of poor food, people were ill all the time – so I hurried home with some medicine I had been able to buy on the black market, and went to bed early, selfishly thinking no more about it.

'The next day was a day off. When Céline did not arrive at rehearsal the following morning, I still did not guess what had happened. Not even when Kandinsky came in. He looked terrible, as though he had a fever. Worse than that, he looked hunted. And he kept staring at me, as though I knew something. The rehearsal was a farce. Several times Malromé, the Leader, had to stand up and correct Kandinsky's mistakes – something which had never happened before.

'In the break, I had a sudden premonition that something terrible had happened to Céline. I went into a toilet, to open the letter she had written for Dietrich – and could not believe what I was reading. I thought I had shared all Céline's secrets, because I was the only person she had ever told about Dietrich. I had to re-read the letter several times before I understood that she had been leading a double life for the past eighteen months, acting as a courier for Cluny's network. It didn't seem possible that the woman I knew would get involved in something as dangerous as that - until I realised how she had been tricked into it.

'I walked out of the rehearsal without giving any excuse. That may not sound much, Monsieur Hallstatt, but it was an unthinkable thing to do. From a public telephone in a bar, I called Dietrich's office. He said he was busy, and would meet me that afternoon, but I managed to convey to him that Céline was in great danger. Fifteen minutes later, he arrived in uniform.

Inside the building, I showed him the letter and he went pale with anger. Until then I had only ever seen him as a very gentle person. He became a different man, shaking me by the shoulders and shouting accusations that I had hidden the truth from him. He was so violent that I was afraid. But somehow I managed to make him believe that Céline had told me nothing.

'He strode along the corridors of the Palais Garnier like a whirlwind, hauled Kandinsky off the podium in mid-bar and grabbed Cluny by the neck, marching them at gunpoint backstage and into the conductor's dressing-room. The orchestra sat there, too stunned to do anything. I stayed on guard outside the door of the dressing-room, which was sound-proofed so that the noise of the piano would not reach the stage when Kandinsky was taking a singer through an aria in private. Yet, through the door, I could hear what sounded like blows, and Dietrich was screaming at the two men to tell him exactly what had happened.

'When he came out, Cluny had blood on his face and was moaning. Kandinsky was sprawled on the floor. I thought he had had a heart attack. Dietrich had tears in his eyes and was shaking all over, from fear or anger, I couldn't tell. I asked him what he was going to do.

'"I can't abandon her," he said. "I must go to Lyon and see what can be arranged."

'I never saw either Céline or Dietrich again, Monsieur Hallstatt. A week later, I had my own problems. Just after the Allied invasion of Normandy, I was informed by the management that my services were no longer required in the orchestra. Luckily I had a few pupils and I could let the large bedroom, to make a few *sous* – enough to get by.'

'I know how it was,' Hallstatt said. 'Did you make any enquiries about Céline, after the Liberation, when it was safe to do so?'

'I didn't wait until then. A few days after that awful morning, I called Dietrich's office at the Jeu de Paume. When a man's voice asked me to identify myself I put down the phone, and walked home past the museum, loitering as long as I thought safe. There was no sign of Dietrich, but several obvious Gestapo types were hanging around, so I did not stay long. I thought of going to Lyon, to try and pick up Céline's trail. But whom could I trust? How could I know who was a *résistant* and who an informer? I would have been sticking my head into a noose.'

'But you knew Céline had been working for Cluny. Didn't you ask him what had happened?'

'Cluny was arrested two hours after Dietrich left the building. Two carloads of Gestapo arrived and hustled him away. He was deported and never returned. You'll find his name on the plaque in the Palais Garnier commemorating members of the Opera who died in the war. It's out of alphabetical order, because at first the Gaullists would not allow the Communists who had died to be included in the roll of honour.'

So the girl had talked, Hallstatt thought. Of course, everyone talked in the end – some sooner than others, that was all. He felt a great kinship with Céline Marie Picard, the woman he would never meet. It was as close as if they had shared neighbouring cells at the same address in hell.

'And Kandinsky?' he asked. 'Why was he not arrested that day?'

'The men who came for Cluny were looking for him too, but by then he had gone. He went into hiding immediately after Dietrich left the Palais Garnier. No one saw Kandinsky again until several weeks after Paris was liberated. He walked into the Palais Garnier one morning and asked for his job back, telling some story about having been working underground for the Resistance. But the Gaullists were in power by then. They gave most men who had worked for the Communists the choice of being thrown in prison or of being conscripted into the army instead. Kandinsky was relatively lucky, just to be banned from conducting. Businessmen, singers . . . even writers were put up against a wall and shot in those days.'

PART VII:
Paris – June 1944

.1.

Signal, the pro-Vichy picture magazine, had a lead story about the mass funeral service for the victims of British bombing raids on Paris. It had been attended by Marshal Pétain in person, and enthusiastic crowds of supporters had brought his motorcade to a halt, with thousands cheering his speech on the balcony of the Hôtel de Ville. The invasion of Normandy that had begun four days previously was relegated to a few paragraphs on an inner page, which implied that German forces were in the last stages of mopping up the Allied bridgehead.

Céline sat throughout the whole three-hour journey from Paris to Lyon staring at the same page of the magazine, without reading a single word. From her seat in the second-class compartment, she could see Kandinsky standing in the crowded corridor. His face was white, his tie crooked, he had cut himself while shaving and there was cold sweat on his brow, which he kept mopping with a white linen handkerchief. She wondered why he was so nervous this time.

The train lurched and swayed its way through a marshalling yard that had been bombed by the RAF the previous night. There were twisted rails and damaged rolling stock everywhere. Parties of Russian prisoners who were relaying the tracks stood aside as the train passed. Strutting like Charlie Chaplin in *The Great Dictator*, one of them mimed a warning of German soldiers on the platform ahead. Several packages of black-market food were tossed out of the train windows by nervous travellers. Despite shouted threats and the loaded rifles of the skinny teenage boys in Wehrmacht uniform who were guarding them, a group of prisoners more desperate than the others darted forward to catch the parcels. Looking down, Céline saw missing teeth and staring eyes in faces like skulls with thin layers of skin stretched over them.

The train clanked and clattered into the platform at Lyons-Perrache station, where she saw armed German soldiers lining the platform. The fear clutching at her stomach made her wonder whether she would be able to walk as far as the end of the platform without soiling herself. Kandinsky had vanished, pushing his way along the crowded corridor to put as much space as possible between them. She got out of the train, trying to concentrate on a Bartók study, but the notes kept repeating themselves in her memory, like a gramophone record that was stuck in the groove.

Slowly the queue inched its way towards the ticket barrier where papers were being checked by two men in black leather coats. Behind them a dozen armed Feldgendarmen stood watching. There were four people ahead of her in the queue, then two, then one. She stepped forward and presented a set of false papers which she had not used before. One of the Gestapo men turned to the soldiers behind and barked, '*Sie ist es*,' as though they had been expecting her.

A tidal wave of fear welled up inside Céline. Her legs felt weak. The cramps in her stomach made it seem impossible to walk any further. As they marched her across the concourse, some travellers averted their eyes, while others stared in fascination.

She was pushed through the baggage entrance of the station hotel, through which porters had wheeled travellers' luggage in happier times. Numbly, she watched a deskbound SS man sign for her. The Feldgendarmen disappeared and she was given a new escort of two SS men in uniform, both armed with machine-pistols. One in front and one behind, they marched her through the lobby with its inlaid marble floors, gilded mirrors and exquisite panelling. The Hotel Terminus had merited four stars in the *Guide Michelin* before the war.

Céline asked to be allowed to go to the lavatory, both because she badly needed to and in the hope that she could somehow flush away the papers hidden in the rosin pocket of her violin case. The escort paid no attention to her request. At another checkpoint, she heard them say that Hauptsturmführer Barbie was expecting her, but the name meant nothing to her. She was marched into a third-floor office which had been the hotel's presidential suite, where she was made to stand facing a desk behind which was seated a man with his back to her, speaking quietly in German on the telephone. It had always been her best foreign language, and she often conversed with Dietrich in it, but fear had frozen every cell in her brain, so that she understood not a single word.

Barbie was wearing an immaculate black uniform, of which the cap sat on the desk, with its shining death's-head insignia. The woman standing at the window, checking her make-up in the mirror of a powder compact, was an obvious professional from her fashionable piled-up hairdo to her high-heeled wooden-soled platform shoes. She gave the prisoner one bored glance, then snapped her compact closed, put a German cigarette into a long tortoiseshell holder, and lit it. The office was silent except for Barbie's voice. He had still not turned round. The only movement was that of the cigarette smoke wreathing its way out of the large sash window, which was slightly open at the top.

At last, Barbie put down the phone and spun round in his chair. Without bothering to look up, he riffled through the contents of Céline's handbag, spilling them onto the desk, then with a lazy gesture indicated that she should place the violin case also on the desk. He opened it, lifted out the violin and pinged the strings, commenting that she must be a professional musician to have such a good instrument. Céline was trying to remember the details of her fictitious identity. Was she supposed to be a musician on her false papers? If not, how could she account for the instrument?

He laid the violin down and reached towards the rosin compartment, where the papers were, took them out and asked her – still in the same mild voice – where she had got them.

By now, her heart was beating like a kettle-drum; it seemed that all the people in the room must hear it. She blurted out something about a stranger pushing them into her hands as the train drew into the station. 'Seeing the soldiers outside, I panicked and hid them in the only place I could think of.'

The smile playing on his face could have meant anything. Against the light from the window, Céline could not tell whether Barbie's pale eyes were grey or blue. Like all musicians, she had an acute sense of time and was normally able to measure fractions of seconds in her head. Now, time was a blur, jerking forward one heartbeat at a time.

The whore sat on Barbie's knee, fondling him. It was a technique he used to disconcert and worry his victims, especially the female ones. He slid one hand up the whore's skirt and kissed her on the lips. Without raising his voice, he told Céline, 'You have ten seconds in which to decide whether you are going to identify for me the person who gave you these papers or not.'

Céline watched him undo the woman's blouse while she lit two cigarettes and put one in his mouth. Time became elastic, measured now by the length of the ash on his cigarette. He stubbed it out half-smoked and pressed a bell-push on the desk. Céline heard two more people come into the room behind her, but did not dare look round. A woman's heels clattered on the parquet floor and a uniformed Blitzmädchen placed a correspondence blotter in front of Barbie, who pushed the whore away and initialled several signals.

Without looking up, he said, 'Strip!'

'In front of all these people?' Céline stammered.

'You heard.'

She took her time, hoping that he was bluffing. Finally she stood naked, trying to conceal herself with her hands and feeling the flush of embarrassment and terror spreading from her cheeks, down her neck and across her chest. Two of the men behind her were sniggering. A second woman, in civilian clothes, entered the office and searched her clothes, item by item, before thrusting them into a cotton laundry bag and taking them away.

When this was finished, Barbie said quietly, 'You will remain here until I return.'

He snapped his fingers for the whore to follow, and left the room through a second door. Without daring to turn her head, Céline heard the other men troop out of the office, leaving her alone, with the roll of papers on the desk mutely taunting her. The station clock struck one o'clock, then two, then half-past. From the other side of the door through which Barbie had gone, she could hear the sounds of love-making: Barbie's murmurs and the whore's pretended ecstasy.

The sun poured in through the barred window and burned the skin on the front of Céline's body. The air got hotter and hotter, making her more and more thirsty. Frightened she was going to faint, she sat down on a chair, only to have the main door thrown open within seconds and hear the sentry bark, *'Steh auf! Debout, debout!'*

The clock had just struck three-thirty when Barbie walked back into the office, minus his uniform jacket and doing up his fly buttons. He tossed the papers into a drawer and asked Céline again where she had got them.

Her throat was so parched, that she could hardly speak. 'A man thrust them . . .'

All her attention focussed on Barbie, she was unaware that the guard had come back into the room. The blow from the metal butt of his Schmeisser machine-pistol knocked her clean across the room, to land sprawling on the floor below the window, looking at the blood dripping onto the polished parquet from a gash above her left ear.

'Aufstehen!' he shouted. *'Debout, debout!'*

His steel-tipped boot connected just under her left arm with an explosion of pain that made her fear he had ruptured her heart. It did not seem to be working properly, because she could not breathe or see clearly. Slipping in the puddle of urine she had made on the floor, Céline struggled to her feet but it was hard to stay upright without holding onto something.

Barbie finished the cigarette he was smoking and crushed it carefully in the ashtray. The bully had turned back into the schoolteacher giving advice to a backward pupil. 'It really makes no difference,' he said mildly. 'In the end, you will tell me everything.'

Abruptly, he left the room. Another half-hour passed until a guard appeared with a dress of coarse grey fabric on which were several dried bloodstains. It smelled of vomit but Céline put it on, grateful not to be naked at last. For a moment she forgot to be afraid, and followed the guard, with another armed man behind her, along corridors and down stairs to the basement. To cling to some kind of sanity, she counted the footsteps and each stair – as though keeping a tally of bars' rest in the orchestra in order to make her next musical entrance correctly.

In the basement, one of the SS men threw open a cell door and kicked her in the small of the back, so that she landed sprawling on all fours on the stone-flagged floor. The door thudded shut and bolts slid into their sockets. When Céline picked herself up, an eye was watching through the Judas-hole. Behind a wire grille above the door was a dim bulb, hardly brighter than a child's night-light. There was an open latrine pail in one corner and two narrow concrete benches, hardly wide enough for an adult to lie on.

On one, a blanket-covered form was curled up, twitching and whimpering. Warily, Céline approached and saw a woman in a dress identical to the one she was wearing. Her face was covered in dried blood, her hair matted with vomit. One eye was puffed up so much that she could only see out of the other. She could have been any age.

By the latrine pail was a chipped enamel mug of water with a dirty plate, on which were two crusts of brown bread. Céline thought of dipping the corner of her dress in the water and washing the woman's face, but felt ashamed that she could not bring herself to do it.

The woman tried to sit up, using the heels of her hands and flinching as they touched the concrete of the bench. The ultimate horror for Céline was to see that all her fingernails had been torn out, leaving each finger a swollen, bloody stump. She forgot the thirst, the hunger, the gash in her scalp and the pain from her fractured ribs. Worse than all these was the realisation that if they did to her what they had done to this moaning, broken creature, she would never be able to play the violin again.

.2.

As the leaden hours passed, Céline went over and over in her mind how she had come to be in the cell.

She rarely listened to the radio news bulletins and never read newspapers, and so had made no connection with what was going on in the rest of the world when Kandinsky asked her to carry the first message to Lyon. He was expecting no argument, and said, 'I'm too obvious, too well known there. They watch me the whole time, so you will have to do this.'

He had been working on a score, seated at his inlaid Boulle-work writing desk, which was a wedding present from her father. From the secret drawer, intended for lovers' letters, he took an identity card in the name of Monique Duval which had Céline's photograph pasted on it, together with a handful of documents and letters addressed to the same fictitious person.

She knew then that it had never entered his head that she might refuse. He explained that Cluny's people had a lot of experience in false papers, and that she had nothing to fear, so long as she learned by heart her new date of birth and a few family details – in case she was questioned.

When she asked what he was doing, working with the Communists who had killed his grandparents and turned his parents into penniless exiles, Kandinsky said he was still a Russian in his soul. White? Red? What did the colour matter? Millions of his people were dying in the fight against Germany . . .

She could not believe that someone so egocentric was prepared to act the hero. Then it dawned on her that her husband was expecting her to take all the risks. He would travel on the same train, but first class. If she was caught, there would be nothing to connect Monsieur Feliks Kandinsky with Mademoiselle Monique Duval.

'How can you ask me to do such a thing?' she said. 'I'm no heroine – just a selfish musician who wants nothing but to play her violin. I can't do this. Not even for you.' She threw the false papers on the floor and locked herself in the bedroom.

After the rehearsal at the Palais Garnier that morning, Cluny pulled her into the stage doorkeeper's cubby-hole and hissed, 'Kandinsky tells me you are making problems.'

He took from his pocket a handful of photographs which he had been keeping for that moment, and Céline realised that the whole idea of using her as a courier had been his from the start. The first picture showed Dietrich kissing her on the lips, that day on the Seine embankment when she had so nearly been arrested. Céline recalled the glimpse of a familiar face, looking down from the balustrade. There were other pictures that had been taken of her meeting him in cemeteries, outside cinemas, and going into the doorway of Amandine Lafont's apartment building. There was even a shot of the two of them walking hand in hand along the river bank by the Auberge du Soleil.

She felt soiled and exposed, wondering numbly whether someone from Cluny's network had followed her to every clandestine rendezvous. In all the secret moments of happiness when she had thought herself alone with Dietrich, had there been an enemy nearby, spying on their every act?

'If you don't do this for us,' Cluny threatened. 'I shall give the whole file to Kandinsky. You can guess what his reaction will be.'

During the concert, Céline 'came in' wrong and played wrong notes. There was no one with whom she could talk about her dilemma. It would have been unfair to involve Amandine and even if Dietrich had been in Paris, how could she have talked to a German officer about this problem? Sitting on the train to Lyon next day, with a tightly rolled bundle of papers nestling in the tiny compartment in her violin case where she normally kept a block of rosin and some spare strings, she thought how ironic it was to be conspiring with Cluny against Kandinsky, and sharing with her husband a secret that she must never tell to her lover.

At Lyons-Perrache station, she joined the queue of travellers going through the identity check at the end of the platform and tried to keep calm by playing through in her head one of the Isaÿe studies. By concentrating totally on the music, it was just possible to keep fear at bay. She left the small package behind the cistern in the toilet of a café near the station, as instructed, and caught the next train back to Paris, immensely relieved that her ordeal was over.

It was only beginning . . .

On his return to Paris the following day, Kandinsky embraced Céline for the first time in months.

'You were wonderful.' He held her tightly. 'I watched you walk through the barrier when the train arrived at the station. The way you did it was perfect.'

She tried to avoid his embrace, because his touch made her flinch. She prayed for the telephone to ring, or one of the crones to knock on the bedroom door, or a visitor to arrive, but nothing happened to stop him unbuttoning her blouse, and fondling her through the silk of her slip.

It was months since Kandinsky had touched her. She wanted to scream, 'Leave me alone. I love another man!' But how could she tell him the truth?

As her skirt slid down her legs to the floor, she saw their images in one of the wall-mirrors. His hand fascinated her as it undid her stocking suspenders and touched the skin of her thigh. She was thinking, This is rape, and I am doing nothing to stop him. All she could do was close her eyes and hope it would soon be over. She tried her father's formula that had worked in so many different situations: *You must forget all this.*

But this time it had no effect because Dietrich's gentle loving had taught her body to feel. So she tried imagining that the man lying on her, kissing her lips, caressing her body and thrusting his flesh into her, was the one she loved – only to find herself betrayed by her new appetites. Afterwards she felt sick when Kandinsky murmured triumphantly, 'I always knew that one day I should make you climax.'

He had brought back a present from Lyon – some underwear and perfume – which he insisted she put on, to go to dinner at the Lido on the Champs Elysées, surrounded by high-ranking German officers who had come there for the floor show. Looking at *les poules de luxe* at the other tables, Céline told herself that she was as much a whore as they were.

On the next courier trip – which took place two months later – Céline spent the whole journey planning how to tell Kandinsky that he did not have to reward her.

'Just leave me alone,' she was going to say. 'I'm doing this because I owe you so much, not because I love you.' But the words were never said, so she had to suffer the presents and the love-making again.

Worse than his advances were her own responses. And worst of all was the fear of being caught, which grew bigger on each trip, growing inside her like a giant foetus-worm gnawing away at her intestines. As the tide of war turned inexorably against the Germans with the defeats on the eastern front, in the Middle East and in North Africa during 1943, the Resistance sabotage grew more widespread, with the result that security checks on the French railways became more frequent and more strict.

On the four trips which Céline made to Lyon during that year, she saw dozens of men, women and children hauled off the train by police, *miliciens* or plain-clothes Gestapo men, or stopped at the barrier for no obvious reason. Some of their offences were trivial – papers out of date, a packet of black-market butter found in a suitcase – but the terror in their eyes finally brought home to her the reality that Cluny's little packages could land her in a concentration camp, or worse.

When she and Dietrich managed to get away for a night together at Christmas 1943, the strain was telling on Céline physically: she had lost a lot of weight and had no appetite. Yet to all his questions, she replied that everything was all right. How could she involve him in this nightmare?

She watched his face as he slept, and traced the lines of his brow, his nose and his lips with her fingertips, thinking how beautiful he was. While she was near him, there was no other reality.

Despite her protestations, he must have guessed something of what was afoot, because he reversed the car after kissing her goodbye at a suburban Metro station on the way back into Paris, and said, 'If anything ever happens to you, you must call on me for help, come what may.'

By the first week in June 1944, Céline's playing had suffered to the point that André Malromé, the Leader, yelled at her in front of the whole orchestra during rehearsal, 'You're letting down the standards of the orchestra. I don't care if you're married to Jesus Christ, I won't have it! One more poor performance and you're out!'

In the break, Céline went to Cluny and pleaded with him to explain to Malromé why her playing had declined. Cluny ranted on about the intention of the well-armed Communist underground organisations to take control of Paris, the moment the Germans withdrew, carrying out a coup d'état in the power vacuum before the Allied armies arrived. Then, he promised, Malromé would be hanged from a lamppost, together with all the other Gaullist traitors who wanted to hand the French people over to the Anglo-American capitalists.

Distraught, Céline burst into Kandinsky's dressing-room where he was discussing the score with a German tenor. After Kandinsky had hustled the man out of the room, she screamed at him, 'Look at me! Twice during performances this week, I've lost my nerve completely and had to stop playing altogether. Can't you see that I cannot go on like this any longer?'

Yet the following morning – it was a free day for the orchestra – she found herself once again on the hated train to Lyon, with a bundle of messages hidden in her violin case, staring at a copy of *Signal* for three hours without seeing a single word on the page in front of her.

PART VIII:
London – November 1996

.1.

A fat little man in a burgundy velvet smoking-jacket with a navy-blue cummerbund was leading Catriona across the gallery to meet a new client. Wearing a black silk shirt, tucked into black velvet pants, with black patent-leather boots, she looked very sexy, Ken thought – although she had hardly glanced at him since he arrived.

Zygmunt Szabo was glowing with self-importance as he whispered in Catriona's ear, 'I've sold the portrait to Mr Bradley.'

Arm around her waist, he introduced her to the new client and chatted for a few minutes before greeting a Swiss collector who had bought several of Catriona's abstract landscapes over the years. There was a ritual to be observed, she knew. Before deciding to buy, this client always liked to give her a lecture on Expressionism and she had to agree with his analysis as he told her in detail what her paintings meant. As he gestured at the canvases, the back of his hand kept brushing against her breasts. That too was a part of the ritual.

'You fool,' she said to Irving later when the crowd had dwindled to a few of her friends and some drinking cronies of Szabo. 'You could have bought the portrait from me for half the price after the exhibition. Ziggy takes at least a hundred and fifty per cent mark-up on everything that's sold here – even more when I'm not around.'

'I guessed that,' he said. 'But *a* it looks good for you with a red sticker on it and *b* I didn't want to chance someone else buying it.'

Catriona planted a kiss on his cheek. 'Why don't I have more clients like you?'

'I've had several portraits done,' he said. 'But none of the others is a tenth as good as . . .'

She followed his eye-line to the door, where a late arrival was signing the visitor's book, at the insistence of Ziggy's exotic Brazilian wife, who was all make-up, dangling earrings and bangles. The latecomer was a tall, slim redhead in a silver jumpsuit and matching high-heeled boots. When she waved hello at Catriona, Irving said, 'Now that has to be Siobhan, your popstar daughter.'

Catriona sensed the instant electricity that flickered between them as she made the introductions. When they wandered away to the far end of the gallery, talking together, she said a few goodbyes and came to stand beside Ken at the bar. He was looking smarter than she had ever seen him before, in a new denim suit bought in honour of the occasion.

'Thank you for being here,' she murmured.

Ken blinked. It was a remark she might have addressed to a stranger. 'Are you satisfied with the sales?'

She ignored the question. 'Seeing my daughter with Irving makes me feel old.'

'Are you going to introduce me to her?'

'Siobhan's not interested in anyone except Irving. He was her idol for years, before she got involved in the stuff she plays now.'

Ken gripped Catriona's chin firmly, turned her face to him and accused her of being jealous of her own daughter.

'Maybe I am.' Her eyes challenged him. 'Is that a crime?'

Spending Irving's money by staying in a smart and comfortable London hotel made a pleasant change for Ken from curling up in a sleeping bag in the Land Cruiser, parked on a roadside verge. It brought home to him the extent to which he had been living on a shoestring since being sacked from MI5.

He took the second double gin and tonic from the bar up to his room and relaxed in a hot bath. Eleven of Catriona's fifty-odd canvases had had red stickers on them before the end of the evening. Flushed with the success of the private view, she had gone off in a taxi with her Swiss client – who was taking her out to dinner – without even saying goodbye to Ken.

In the course of the evening he had seen her touched by several men in ways that indicated familiarity, if not actual intimacy. Ziggy, the gallery owner, had a habit of holding the hands of women to whom he was talking and gazing passionately into their eyes, presumably as some kind of sales technique if one could judge by his wife's total lack of reaction. With Catriona he went further: planting a lingering kiss on her lips when they had met and said goodbye, frequently putting an arm around her waist and idly sliding one podgy, well-manicured hand down her flanks while they stood side by side talking to clients.

Ken reminded the man in the bathroom mirror that Catriona was not his property. Who she was with and what she was doing, were none of his business, unless she chose to make them so. As with all advice, it was easier to expound wisdom than act on it. He lay on the bed and zapped the local TV channels, then sampled CNN, a German and a French channel before dipping into a Spanish-language quiz show in which all the expensively dressed contestants kept repeating each other's words and screaming hysterically.

According to Directory Enquiries, there were six numbers for subscribers identified as O'Riordan, S. He dialled them in turn on the off-chance that Catriona was spending the night at her daughter's apartment. At the last one he heard an Irish accent on the line, but was disappointed to realise that he was listening to Siobhan's answering machine: 'I can't come to the phone at the moment, but if you'd like to leave a message . . .'

In the dream, Catriona was confused with Céline Picard. She was living in Paris during the war and having an affair with Dietrich, who was Swiss and very rich. Ken wanted to warn her of the dangers she was running, but the telephone was ringing and he had to answer it . . .

He grabbed it off the wall-hook, dropped it and scrabbled on the floor for it. In the half-light coming through the drawn curtains, the bedside alarm clock showed 0615.

Irving's voice was tense and angry: 'I just got in and found my place ransacked.'

Ken was as alert as if twenty years had dropped away: the early morning call, the ice-cool brain examining an unexpected development, using instinct and experience in equal measure to work out where exactly it fitted among the multiplicity of possibilities.

'Anything taken?' he asked, guessing what the answer would be.

'That's the odd thing. My fiddles are still in their cases. They're the most valuable things I own.' Irving's voice was agitated. 'I'm only here to shave and change my clothes before catching the shuttle to Edinburgh for a BBC lunch-time concert. Can you get over here and handle this? I'll leave a key in an envelope for you at the porter's desk.'

'Was there a night porter on duty?'

'He says he didn't see anything, or hear the alarm going off.'

'Give me your address,' said Ken. 'I'll get over there straight away.'

Irving's prestige apartment was in one of the Barbican towers, with an impressive view across the roofs to the dome of St Paul's cathedral. Every item of upholstered furniture had been slashed, the fitted carpets had all been lifted and hundreds of books and records and CDs pulled off shelves and thrown to the floor. There were seven violins on the grand piano. Not one had been touched, indicating that the intruders had known the size of what they were looking for. The trademark on the job, Ken thought, was that of the same firm who had been through Mrs Prescot's maisonette in Liverpool.

There was no obvious damage to the entrance door but it would not close properly, so he phoned for a locksmith, and then occupied himself until the man arrived by tidying up as best he could, replacing the more obvious items on their shelves and in cupboards and wardrobes.

He took advantage of the opportunity to give the apartment a good once-over. Everything about it was expensive, from the mint-condition Scandinavian furniture to the kitchen equipment and the state-of-the-art Bang and Olufsen hi-fi with speakers in every room, including the lavatory. The celebrity photographs on the wall of the entrance hall all featured Irving – shaking hands with the Queen, standing with the Prime Minister and the Minister for the Arts, playing with Menuhin, discussing a score with Previn . . . All the famous faces were there. It was an impressive display for a boy from the Dingle to have assembled entirely by his own merits.

The bedroom held a large double bed, slashed to pieces. There were no women's clothes in the heap that had been torn out of the wardrobe and thrown on the bedroom floor – from which Ken deduced that Irving did not have a live-in girlfriend. A photo album lying in one pile of his belongings was filled by a collection of pictures in each of which he had his arm around a different beautiful girl. If the data-back dates were anything to go by, none of them had lasted more than a few weeks.

Hanging up in the king-size fitted wardrobe the clothes which had been strewn all over the floor, Ken noted all the fashionable labels: Hugo Boss trenchcoats, Armani jeans, Versace blazers, Christian Dior shirts. The stage clothes were hand-tailored, all either black or white, but Irving's other clothing was also mono-chrome. It seemed that he wore no colours ever. Even his underwear and the towels in the bathroom were all black and white.

The spare bedroom had been sound-proofed and equipped as a miniature recording studio. The damage was worst here, because the acoustic panelling had been ripped off the walls and heaped up in the middle of the floor, although the equipment itself did not appear to have been touched.

Imagining the apartment as it must have been before the break-in, Ken thought that it fitted Irving like a glove. It was the home of a man dedicated to three things in life at the expense of all else: the violin, style and success.

After a multi-point locking system had been fitted on the door of the apartment and a couple of extra gadgets added to the alarm system, Ken put the new keys in his pocket and walked the three miles back to his hotel. Handing over the elec-tronic room card, the receptionist gave him a strange look, which made sense when Ken walked into his bedroom and found a house detective and the duty manager standing in the second shambles of slashed foam mattress and lifted carpet which he had seen that morning.

.2.

The gallery was empty, apart from a rather debby girl with long blonde hair at the desk, who was holding a telephone conversation with her boyfriend about which house party to go to that weekend. Recognising Ken, she waved him past the walls lined with Catriona's paintings. Behind a partition was a metal spiral staircase leading down to the cramped basement office belonging to Zygmunt Szabo. There, among the stored canvases, wrapping materials and reference books, Catriona was seated at a desk covered with art books. Mrs Prescot's painting was on an easel under a powerful fluorescent light. She looked up at the sound of Ken's feet on the stairs and gave him a tight-lipped nod.

'How are you getting on?' He had more or less abandoned the idea that the picture was important, but since it was something that had to be checked out, he had arranged for it to be brought to London by a special Securicor delivery while he was in Paris with Hallstatt and Irving.

'By the condition of the paint,' Catriona said, 'it's got to be about a hundred years old. That's the first thing. Then there's the subject: two ladies strolling in a flower garden. Then there's the style – which is obviously Impressionist, with hints of Degas. Of course, it's not signed, which is unusual.'

'Meaning that you think you know what it is?'

'I did a project at art school on the female Impressionists.'

'And?' Ken lifted the painting off the easel.

'Ziggy agrees with me. He was salivating with excitement, until I got rid of him this morning.'

'Over this?'

'Over that. What you and Irving thought was a kid's copy of a chocolate-box lid, happens to be a genuine Mary Cassatt. At least, Ziggy and I are pretty certain it is.'

It still looked like a chocolate box to Ken but, guided by her tone of voice, he set the picture down with a little more respect. 'I never heard of Mary Cassatt.'

'She was the daughter of a banker from Pittsburgh, Pennsylvania. When she arrived in Paris around 1870, she made friends with several of the Impressionists, largely because she could introduce them to rich American collectors who were friends of her family. Male painters at that time did not take the women like Berthe Morisot and Cassatt seriously because they tended to paint only other women and children in domestic or informal situations – like what you're looking at right now.'

'What I called chocolate-box art . . .'

'Degas, on the other hand, thought Cassatt could really paint. It was he who invited her to exhibit at the salon of, I think, 1879. There was a very strong rumour at the time that she and that grumpy old misogynist were having a wild affair, but nothing was ever known for certain. Am I boring you?'

Ken shook his head. 'What's it worth?'

'In Ziggy's words, Cassatt's pictures are very collectable.'

'What would that mean moneywise, Cat?'

'We're not talking Renoir, but put it this way . . . Last night was the most successful private view I've ever had, but I'd need to carry on painting for about three thousand years to gross what one picture by Mary Cassatt is worth now. Ziggy made a few phone calls. The consensus was that it wouldn't be too ambitious to ask around £250,000.'

Ken whistled. 'For that!'

'For that.'

'Thanks, Cat.'

'Oh, it's all part of the service.'

Ken pulled her to her feet and kissed her on the lips, but Catriona did not respond. 'Did you know,' she said, 'that this is the first time you've looked at me since all this business with Irving's teacher began?'

It was an echo of the complaint made by each of Ken's wives at some time or another: 'All you ever think of is that damned job of yours, Ken!'

'I'm sorry,' he said. 'I've had a lot on my mind.'

She pulled away from his embrace. 'D'you want to know the rest of it? I mean, I might as well be useful.'

'There's more?'

She pulled a thick and glossy art book across the cluttered desk. It was a comprehensive survey of Mary Cassatt's known work, with each painting named and dated, and attributed to this or that private or public collection.

Ken sat down and leafed through the book until he came to a full page reproduction in black and white of Mrs Prescot's painting. Catriona had highlighted the text in Day-Glo orange:

At the Auberge du Soleil. 60 cm × 53 cm. Probably executed in the summer of 1877 when the artist spent several weeks in the company of Degas, staying at this country hotel, just outside Paris, where both artists painted many local scenes. Property of Baron Etienne de Selincourt. Disappeared from his Paris home during World War II. Present whereabouts unknown.

'You've been amazing, Cat,' Ken said.

She stood up and saluted. 'Glad to have been of service. I don't suppose you're going to tell me where you've been or what you've been doing. So I'll be off.'

'Where are you going?'

'My business. I've been used and ignored by one man. That's enough for my lifetime.'

Ken had not taken in what she said. He was re-reading the paragraph. For *disappeared*, read *looted* . . . Catriona's information changed everything, because no Comintern agent would have brought an identifiable stolen or looted painting to Britain with her. So, forget that line of enquiry and concentrate on Kandinsky's hint that Céline and her German lover had made off with some valuable paintings. Perhaps the motive for the murder was simple greed? No, nothing about this business was simple. Why had Mrs Prescot changed her Will three weeks before her death and specifically left to him and Irving – with the provision that it had to be sold – a picture which had been hanging on her wall like a cheap reproduction certainly for twenty years and probably for fifty? Was the legacy a message from beyond the grave? Had she known, or at least feared, that she was in mortal danger? In which case why had she left no more explicit clues?

The bell on the gallery door dinged twice and the door slammed shut. Ken raced up the iron spiral staircase to the ground floor, in time to see Catriona on the pavement outside, lifting a large suitcase into a taxi.

He caught up with her as the taxi started to move and yanked the door open. 'What are you doing?'

'Going. Don't let me disturb you.'

'I'm sorry. I was thinking . . .'

'Then you won't be lonely, will you? Oh, if you're worried about re-letting the cottage, I'll be back in a few weeks to clean my stuff out.'

The narrow street was blocked. Several motorists behind the taxi were hooting.

'When you've quite finished,' said the driver.

Ken stood back and watched the taxi disappear. Perhaps, in view of what he had just learned, it was better for Catriona to remove herself from the line of fire . . .

Ken remembered Harry Tilson's lecture on the induction course. It had been years ago, before Tilson was a complete lush – and before almost everything could be accessed on a computer screen, without moving from one's desk.

'What are the two most important assets we have in this work?' he had asked the trainees.

The answer was, feet.

Ken hoofed it around the corner into Bond Street, where he bought a Polaroid camera. With several pictures of the painting in his pocket, he went to Sotheby's and Christie's and from there did the rounds of the lesser-known fine art salerooms, asking the same questions in each place: 'We're trying to trace this painting. Can you help?'

Towards the end of the afternoon, he entered an imposing doorway in Bond Street. Hill and Clark were a new auctioneers. 'New and pushy,' one of their competitors had labelled them.

Ken followed a long corridor that led through to the other side of the block, where the real premises were. The door and corridor were simply a way of getting a Bond Street address. In the main auction room a sale of carpets was in progress. To rest his feet, Ken sat down and watched the action for a few minutes – taking in the unemotional voice of the auctioneer, the way his sharp eyes picked up the little nods and signs that were bids, the ripple of interest when a price went higher than expected – before concluding that the more worn a carpet was, the higher the price it would fetch.

The woman who came to the paintings counter at the rear of the building was wearing a rather severe but expensive black woollen business suit, relieved by a colourful silk scarf knotted around her neck. She had the classic haircut, cool gaze and sort of voice to acquire which parents send their daughters to an English boarding school. Introducing herself as Sarah Field-Cavendish, Director of Nineteenth-Century Paintings, she let her frigid manner convey the suspicion that a man walking in off the street, dressed in an off-the-peg suit like Ken's did not have the sort of money to be a worthwhile client.

After a hurried glance at his ID card, she ushered him into the seclusion of a private viewing room where the presence of a policeman would not embarrass clients, and returned a few moments later with a brown manila docket in her hand. It bore the date of the day before Mrs Prescot had first pawned the painting.

'A little old lady brought the picture in,' Ms Field-Cavendish remembered. 'She'd seen a programme about the female Impressionists on television. We always get a flood of hopefuls after that sort of thing, and usually have to disappoint them. But I was pretty certain that her picture was a genuine Mary Cassatt – not just because of the style but for other reasons too. So I told her that it would probably fetch above £200,000, if she wanted to sell.'

'And what was her reaction?'

'She seemed altogether a little confused, even before I mentioned the money. In fact, I realised that she thought she was in Sotheby's.' Ms Field-Cavendish gave a sly look, quite at odds with her quasi-aristocratic manner. 'Our doorway's often mistaken for theirs.'

'May I?' Ken took the docket. On it were Mrs Prescot's name and address, and a description of the painting and its condition.

'I left the room for a minute,' said Ms Field-Cavendish, 'to find a colleague who could give me a second opinion on the painting. When I came back, Mrs Prescot had gone.'

Ken handed back the docket. 'How many people would have seen this?'

'Normally, only me and my assistants. But in this case, I had an odd feeling. So I did some research. When I found that it was listed in the Art and Antiques Loss Register . . .'

'What's that?'

'You're obviously not from the Art and Antiques Squad at Scotland Yard?'

'Different outfit altogether,' Ken smiled self-deprecatingly. 'You're dealing with a total ignoramus, I'm afraid.'

'It's an international record of all major works of art stolen, missing or looted in war. When I found the Cassatt listed, I circulated a routine in-house memo – in case it turned up again.'

'But you didn't think of telling the police?'

Ms Field-Cavendish was gathering up her papers.

'You've been very helpful.' Ken rose to go. 'Any idea who might have read your in-house memo?'

'All the directors, the security people . . . anyone, really.'

'Quite a few people, then?'

'Quite a few,' she agreed.

Eleven hours after his early morning phone call to Ken, Irving paid off the taxi that had brought him all the way from Gatwick Airport to the Barbican. He had not slept the previous night, and started walking on auto-pilot across the complex in the direction of his apartment block. At the entrance, he stopped and retraced his steps to where Ken was waiting in a nearby pub with the new set of keys.

'Cat's not just a pretty face,' was Irving's comment, when he learned about Catriona's contribution to the day's progress.

Ken grunted. 'It puts a different complexion on things, that the picture's worth so much money. And I think Mrs P intended us to find out.'

Irving's mobile phone beeped. 'Oh no,' he said, after listening for a moment. 'Does it have to be now, Max? I've had a long day. Can't this wait until the morning?'

.3.

Max Grayson's outer office was empty, his secretaries gone for the day. In the vast oak-panelled sanctum overlooking Baker Street, the doyen of London's straight music agents and impresarios was seated behind a massive desk with a cluster of telephones at one end.

Grayson was a cherubic little man, whose baby face concealed a brain like a cash register. Without ending either conversation, he put down the two phones on which he was talking and rose with a smile of welcome when Irving came into the room. 'How was Edinburgh?'

'Fine.'

'And Mendelssohn?'

'He was well when I left him.'

Grayson mentioned the other works in the programme and enquired after the conductor, the BBC Radio producer and the leader of the orchestra all by name, to show how much he was involved in the life of this client who might one day be hailed as the world's premier violinist. Sitting down in one of the large comfortable armchairs in the conversation end of the office, Irving accepted a glass of Perrier and watched the agent mix himself a large gin and tonic.

Grayson took a sip of his drink and toyed with a string of amber worry-beads. 'I had a call from Sir Terence Savage. He wants to meet you.'

'I've met him,' Irving replied. 'Slimy type, always hovering around the royals at charity galas.'

'Don't underestimate slime. Terry's a personal friend of

half the Royal Family. He's on the board of Covent Garden and the BBC Music Panel, and involved in several of the major festivals.'

'So?'

'He has an instrument he thinks you might be interested in.'

'What kind of instrument?'

'A Strad.'

'A good one?'

'That's for you to say.'

'I haven't that kind of money, Max.'

'Apparently, there may be a way round the problem. Have a chat with Terry.'

'I'll give him a ring sometime.'

'He'd like to see you this evening.'

'Max, I've had a long day.' With another busy day ahead of him – planning the repertoire for a new album with the record producer – Irving had been intending to go straight home from the airport and sleep for twelve hours solid.

Grayson looked out of the window at the evening traffic build-up that was blocking Baker Street. 'He sent a car for you. It's the black Rolls parked on the double yellow lines down there. If you're in any doubt that you're getting into the right Rolls, the number plate is TS1.'

Above the statue of Pallas Athene, the reproduction of the Parthenon frieze spread from side to side of the building. Ever since the Athenaeum was founded in 1824 by Boswell's editor, John Wilson Crocker, it had prided itself on being, 'an association of individuals known for their scientific and literary attainments, artists of eminence in any class of the fine arts and noblemen and gentlemen distinguished as liberal patrons of science, literature or the arts.'

Famous men who had worked in the Athenaeum's library included Macaulay, Matthew Arnold and Trollope. It was an imposing high-ceilinged room into which a couple of modern town houses could easily have fitted. The walls were lined three storeys high with fine leather-bound volumes. A brass-railed staircase led to walkways on two upper levels, avoiding the necessity for anything so plebeian as a step-ladder to reach the higher shelves.

The friend of half the Royal Family was alone. He stood in one corner, leafing through a copy of *The Field* on a polished mahogany lectern. A well-preserved fifty-year-old, standing just over six feet tall, he was – from the well-cut curling grey hair through the dark-blue pinstripe suit and regimental tie to his hand-made black leather shoes – the epitome of establishment man.

'My dear Bradley,' he murmured in a hushed voice. 'I'm so glad you could come.'

Irving felt naked without his violin case, which he had carried into the club under one arm – against the advice of the liveried driver of the Rolls – only to find himself relieved of it by a club servant in tail coat and black tie who had assured him soberly, 'Your box will be quite safe with me, sir.'

He shook the peer's clammy hand; it was like holding a piece of cod that happened to smell of aftershave.

'Drink?'

'No, thank you. Max Grayson said you have a Strad. I might as well tell you that I haven't the money to buy a good one, and the other kind I don't need.'

'Then why are you here?'

'Because I'm always curious about instruments.'

'Precisely.' Sir Terence moved away from the lectern, allowing Irving to see for the first time an open violin case lying on the low bookcase behind it.

Irving moved forward and lifted the instrument from its bed of green velvet, tapped it with a knuckle, then flicked a nail across the strings. It was untuned and, judging by the sound, had not been played for a long time. Intrigued, he held it close to one of the shaded reading lamps and peered closer.

The proportions were exquisite, the balance perfect. By squinting through the *ff* holes he could read the maker's signature on the label pasted inside. It was quite clear, if a little faded by time: *Ant°. Stradivari*. Of itself, that meant nothing: many stringed instruments have fake labels pasted inside them.

Sir Terence interrupted the examination by clapping his

hands once. The same club servant who had taken Irving's instrument appeared in the doorway with it in his hand. Like a priest performing the liturgy, he placed it carefully on one of the reading tables and walked out, closing the double doors behind him.

Irving took the bow from his own case, tensed it and nestled the other violin between chin and collar-bone. He took his time tuning the Strad, getting to know it, and then played the first bars of the slow movement of the Mendelssohn violin concerto which he had performed for the BBC in Edinburgh just a few hours before. Despite the deadening acoustic effect of all the book-lined walls and the high ceiling and carpeted floor, the instrument he was holding sang with the voice of an angel. The sound made the hair stand up on Irving's scalp and down his spine. Eyes closed, he felt his entire body vibrating as if to a lover's caress.

It took a conscious effort at the end of the movement to lift the bow from the strings and end the sheer bliss of such a perfect sound.

To a violinist, every great instrument has its own personality. Irving was as intrigued by the one he was holding as he would have been by a brilliant and beautiful woman he had just met for the first time. It was not just any Strad. The surviving instruments from the workshop of the greatest luthier of all time varied tremendously in quality. If the best were aristocrats among instruments, this one was a queen. He held it under one reading light after another, and caught a movement in the corner of his eye. Sir Terence was getting restive.

'Well, Bradley? I imagine you have a rough idea how much a violin is worth. And you're wondering how to get your hands on that kind of money. Am I right?'

Irving nodded.

Sir Terence sniffed and pulled a monogrammed white linen handkerchief from one sleeve, making a pantomime of blowing his nose on it before returning it to his cuff. 'It's possible that you can become the owner of this instrument without any money passing. I'm told there's a painting in your possession that was stolen some years ago.'

'Go on.'

'I'll put my cards on the table, Bradley. The picture in question is by a minor Impressionist. Prices are not so high as they were a few years ago, but I brought along a catalogue from the last sale at Christie's when a painting by this artist came up for sale, so you can see what sort of money it would fetch at auction.'

Beside the copy of *The Field*, was a sale catalogue with prices marked in the margin. According to them, two Cassatts had been sold, making £195,000 and £214,000 respectively.

'The Strad is worth a great deal more than that,' continued Sir Terence. 'But the owner would like his picture back without any publicity, so you're in a seller's market.'

Irving was convinced that the Strad was worth several times the value of the painting, but that was not his problem . . . By saying yes to Sir Terence's offer, he could become the owner of one of the greatest violins ever made. He replaced the Strad in its green velvet bed, and asked, 'With all due respect, Sir Terence, how do I know this instrument's kosher? Supposing it were to turn up on a police list, or something embarrassing like that?'

'You have my word.' The implication was that no member of a London club which every bishop and archbishop of the Church of England had the right to join without the potentially embarrassing ritual of election would ever break his word as an English gentleman.

'And how,' Irving continued, 'do you suggest that I account publicly for getting my hands on an instrument worth – as you say – a great deal more than a minor Impressionist painting?'

'You'd want to play it – and not simply keep it as an investment?'

'Of course.'

Sir Terence closed the sale catalogue. '"Loaned by a benefactor who wishes to remain anonymous." That's what one usually says in these circumstances.'

It was all too good to be true. Irving knew that, if he were to make a sane and rational decision, he should not even look again at the Strad, the echo of whose siren song was provoking an irresistible desire to possess it. Like Ulysses' sailors, he ought to stop up his ears, avert his eyes and hurry from this place of temptation, telling Sir Terence that he needed time to think. But it was impossible to be sane and rational, confronted with such a choice.

He watched his hand reach out to caress the violin and lift it. Totally absorbed in what he was hearing and feeling, he bowed single notes and chords, testing the instrument for weakness anywhere in its register. There was none: the purity of sound held good throughout. He played scales from the top note to the bottom and then some brief extracts from the more difficult solo passages. For ten minutes that seemed like seconds he was alone in eternity with the sublimity of the purest sound he had ever made. His skill and talent allied with the potential of the instrument he was holding would, he knew, make music as good as that of Haifetz, Menuhin in his prime, Perlman . . . Instead of being one of the twelve best violinists in the world, Irving Bradley would be *the best*.

He lowered the Strad slowly, reluctant to break the spell of its sound. 'It's a deal,' he said. 'The only complication is that I don't have the painting actually in my possession.'

'My driver will take you wherever you wish,' Sir Terence offered. 'You can give the picture to him. He's totally reliable. The chap's been with me for years.'

Another sniff was followed by the same elaborate play with the handkerchief. 'Well, Bradley?'

Irving replaced the Strad in its case and ran his fingertips lightly across its glowing surface. Who cared whether the secret of the Stradivarius sound was in the composition of the varnish, the perfect proportions of the instrument, the seasoning of the wood, or the selection of the trees to be used while they were still growing in the forest? What was the point of trying to analyse perfection? By comparison, he thought, Dr Faustus had got a very poor price for his soul.

Ken looked around the lobby of the hotel he had moved into after the burglary. It was over-priced and nasty, near to Euston station. Most of the clients were Africans, who looked dazed, as though having problems reconciling this expensive squalor with the tourist images of London bobbies and Big Ben.

Obsessed with the thought of getting his hands on the Strad, Irving had hardly listened to his argument. 'Savage's driver is waiting outside in the Rolls right now, with the Strad,' he said. 'All I have to do is hand over the picture to him and the most wonderful instrument in the world is mine.'

'You can't be serious.'

'And you don't understand the deal I'm being offered. For me, having such an instrument will be like being granted the gift of walking on water for the rest of my life. You can't expect me to throw away a chance like this.'

'Listen to me! Apart from confirming for us exactly what the painting is, Savage told you a pack of lies. He's not acting for the legal owner. All Baron de Selincourt would have to do, is go to the police, and they'd seize the picture for him. I don't know who's behind Savage, but it's not the rightful owner.'

'Ken, be reasonable. Sir Terence is an important figure in the arts world, for Chrissake, not some cheap hoodlum from a late-night movie who'd send a couple of heavies up to Liverpool to kill an old lady, just so he can get his hands on a painting.'

'Did he say how he knew we'd got it?'

'Probably somebody called him from one of the auctioneers you went to.'

Ken placed a restraining hand on Irving's arm. 'I admit I can't yet prove that Mrs P's accident was attempted murder. I can't prove that the same men turned over your apartment this morning. And I do understand you wanting this Stradivarius so badly. But haven't you wondered for just a moment why Sir Terence and whoever is behind him are prepared to pay so far over the odds for the painting? If I know one thing about the rich and famous, it's that they never pay a penny more than they have to for anything. So why the generosity?'

Irving shook himself free. 'They probably don't know what the Strad's worth. Only a musician could really tell how good it is. A bargain like this only comes once in a thousand lifetimes. I'd be a fool to pass it up.'

'. . . unless by doing the deal you'd actually be giving these people something much more valuable than the painting itself.'

'Like what?' Irving asked sarcastically.

'I don't yet know. But I have a feeling that you and I have been treated with kid gloves so far because the people behind Sir Terence don't know where the picture is. Once you hand it over . . .'

'You're seeing tigers behind every bush.'

'In my professional life,' said Ken drily, 'I have observed that many people who scoff at paranoia end up as tiger's breakfasts.'

Irving stood up. His patience was exhausted. 'Legally,' he said, 'the painting is half yours and half mine. I'll meet you at Szabo's gallery tomorrow morning when it opens and give you a certified cheque for your half. What I do with it then, is my business. Right?'

Watching him walk out of the lobby, Ken was thinking how much easier life had been in the days when he had the power to threaten people with the Official Secrets Act. Legally, Irving was quite right: if he wanted to buy Ken out, the picture was his, to do with as he liked.

For a woman close to fifty who had had a very long working day, Liz Blantyre looked good. Thrice weekly work-outs with a personal trainer contributed a lot to the youthful way she moved; her thirty-something figure was due to a ruthless diet, and Nature had been kind in giving her facial skin that did not wrinkle. All in all, Ken thought as they embraced, his second wife had worn extremely well.

She held him at arm's length and studied his face. 'You've changed.' Her low and husky voice, like its owner, was never quite sure on which side of the Atlantic it belonged. After growing up in Vermont State, overlooking Lake Champlain, and majoring in journalism at UCLA, she had spent most of her working life based in Britain.

Ken kissed her on both cheeks, recognising her perfume. Dune, it was always Dune. 'It's the erosion of the years,' he murmured.

Liz's home – a large apartment in a modern block overlooking Hampstead Heath – was warm and comfortable, well furnished and decorated with souvenirs of her globe-trotting brand of journalism: carved African masks, Australian aboriginal and Inuit art . . .

She had a lithe grace as she walked ahead of Ken down the hallway. From her dark hair and facial tan – she claimed to be one-eighth Huron – to the tips of her varnished toe-nails she was the same mixture of femininity and toughness that had always turned him on. The way she walked managed to endow the cream-coloured satin housecoat over matching silk pyjamas with a sense of style.

'Drink?'

'Thanks.' Ken took his eyes off her nipples, twin peaks pushing through the cloud base of the thin layers of material.

'Whisky, neat?'

He nodded. 'You look like a million dollars.' He wished he had come up with a more original greeting, but meeting Liz always had that effect on him.

She handed him the glass and moved away, kicking off her shoes and curling her legs beneath her on the red Thai silk settee in a gesture Ken remembered.

'And you,' she said, sizing him up, 'look almost human. What's made the difference? Is it the current woman in your life? Are you married at the moment? I forget.'

'Not married.'

'But living with someone?'

'More or less.'

'What's her name?'

'Catriona.'

'Cat-ri-ona? Is that how you say it? Are you in love with her?'

Ken looked away. 'Cat and I have a relationship in which I don't have to ask myself that kind of question.'

'And doesn't Cat-ri-ona ever ask?'

'No, she doesn't.'

'She must be a very extraordinary woman,' Liz purred.

'She is.'

This was not the conversation Ken wanted. But he needed Liz's media experience. Her access to people at the top of newspapers and television organisations made her one of the few people in London who could possibly outflank Sir Terence Savage.

So calm down, Ken told himself. 'How is . . . I've forgotten his name?'

'It's over. Has been for months. So tell me to what I owe this pleasure. And make it snappy. You're lucky I hadn't switched the phone off for the night. I leave for Brussels early tomorrow morning.' Liz put her hands together, as though praying. It was another gesture Ken remembered. I am listening to you, it said.

He was uncertain that he had done the right thing in coming. 'I need your undivided attention for half an hour. Is that possible?'

'Absolutely. Shoot.'

'Do you still have a valid NUJ card?'

'It's no longer necessary. The union packed up years ago. My last two year's subscriptions went into some guy's private account. That's how bad it was.'

'But you do still work in Fleet Street?'

'I don't believe this,' Liz laughed. 'You're not going to try and sell me another exclusive story, Ken – what they used to call a scoop?'

'Actually, I am.'

'Boy, you've got a nerve!' she exploded. The how-nice-to-see-you-after-all-this-time mask slipped and revealed an angry woman. 'Your last exclusive favour cost me a job and cost my employer a million bucks in an out-of-court settlement of the libel suit. Or have you forgotten?'

'It didn't have to end that way,' Ken protested. 'Your paper's lawyers chickened out – or were bought by the other side. If they'd stood firm, we'd have won the case.'

'We?' she snapped. 'The story was over my by-line, Ken. I lost *my* job. You'd already lost yours.'

'Was it MI5 who brought the pressure to bear on your editor?'

'If I knew, I wouldn't fuel the fires of your paranoia.'

'Well, as it turned out, I didn't do you any harm.' Ken waved a hand at the decor. 'Three years later, you're obviously not counting the pennies.'

'The next time I want to relocate professionally, I'll do it in my own time and my own way.' Liz checked her wristwatch.

'This is just like old times. You've been in this room exactly five minutes – and already I feel like screaming at you. If I remember right, the first fight of our brief marriage happened on the way from the Register Office to the reception.'

Ken held up his hands in surrender. 'Give me a break and let me start at the beginning. You remember that my son Irving learned the violin from an old lady in Liverpool?'

'Vaguely.' Liz was swallowing her anger. Why did Ken always do this to her? 'I heard him play at the Festival Hall last month. He was shatteringly good.'

'Since when are you a music critic?'

'Get on with it, Ken.'

Thirty minutes later, Liz stood up and faced away from him, looking out onto the darkness of the heath. You bastard, she thought. You still know how to press my buttons.

'I don't think you know what you're getting into,' she said. 'D'you remember the Quedlinburg Gospels?'

'The name rings a bell.'

'When they recently resurfaced in Texas, fifty years after being privately liberated by an American officer in Germany, estimates of their value varied between $30 million and $200 million. Whatever, they were known to have been stolen at the end of the war, but when they were actually left with Christie's in New York for three months – for purposes of authentication and sale – it appears that no one thought of telling the police. And Sotheby's in London also knew they were being offered for sale, but nobody there blew the whistle, either.'

'So?'

'These guys invented networking long before there was a word for it, Ken. If he went through *Who's Who*, it would be quicker for Terry Savage to tick the people with whom he's not on first-name terms, than the other way round. My advice to you is: disengage now. Take your cash, let Irving hand over the picture, then go back to your farm in France and forget about the whole thing.'

'So you won't help?'

'Ken,' she said quietly. 'Didn't you learn anything from that last shit-storm you stirred up? The Holy Grail isn't really there;

it's just a laser-effect in the sky, dreamed up to sell a new rock group or brand of detergent. You're sitting in the Siege Perilous polishing your plastic Excalibur replica, while Sir Gawain and the Black Knight are speculating in derivatives. Without hard proof, their expensive lawyers will enrich themselves considerably while demonstrating that your story is just another fantasy from the paranoid imagination of Kenneth Wilson Scott.'

'That's more or less what Irving said.'

'Well, bully for Irving. The editor of any respectable rag would agree with him. Now, if you'll excuse me, I need to sleep.'

At the door, Liz held both Ken's hands in hers, moving in close, body to body, before planting a kiss on his lips.

'Take care,' she said huskily. 'You're my favourite ex-husband . . . and black doesn't suit me.'

.4.

'Strictly speaking,' Ivor Morgan had said on the phone, 'I ought to have that bloody awful painting valued for tax purposes, but having seen it, I can't imagine it's worth much, and the rest of the estate is way below the Inheritance Tax threshold. If Irving wants to buy you out, so he can keep the picture for some sentimental reason, there's no objection from me.'

Ken had thought of telling Morgan the true value of the Mary Cassatt painting and having it impounded by some official body – presumably the Inland Revenue for the time being, until the original owner proved his title. But where would that get Kenneth Wilson Scott? On Irving's blacklist for life, that was certain. And he had still not come up with the slightest shred of what a lawyer would call proof that Irving's old teacher had been murdered. Suspicion alone was insufficient reason to hang on to the painting and prevent Irving acquiring the instrument which, he was convinced, would enable him to become the greatest violinist of all time. And anyway, Ken told himself, giving up the picture did not necessarily mean giving up the trail too.

For the second time in twenty-four hours, he stood on the pavement outside the Szabo Gallery and watched a taxi turn the corner into Bond Street and disappear. In his pocket was a certified cheque drawn on Irving's bank for £125,000. The money would come in more than useful for doing up the holiday apartments at Le Farou.

The driver of the black Rolls with the tinted windows had

compared the painting carefully with a photograph he had brought with him, before handing over the Strad to Irving. About to drive off, he wound down the window and called to Ken, 'If I can give you a lift, sir? It'd be no trouble.'

Ken shook his head. 'No, thanks. I'll walk.'

In the taxi crawling through the mid-morning traffic along Pall Mall, Irving opened the violin case on his knee and caressed the Strad. By daylight, it was even more lustrously alluring, and seemed to glow with the promise of a secret power which was his to master. That it was the bargain of his life, he had no doubt. A painting, however valuable, could only be hung on a wall for some rich and lonely collector to gloat over. What he had got in return for it was a musical miracle.

To find out how much of a miracle, he paid off the cab near Leicester Square. Walking through the square itself, he stopped on the edge of a crowd of tourists listening to four music students who were playing a Mozart quartet in the open air. The second violin and the cello were good. The viola player had an appropriately agonised face and made a nice sound, but the girl playing first was not up to it.

'Sell your fiddle,' would have been the best advice Irving could give her. Instead, feeling magnanimous, he walked up to the open instrument case into which people were tossing coins, and threw in a £20 note.

'Did you see who that was?' the viola player whispered to the others as he turned away.

In the middle of Chinatown, Irving walked into a red-painted doorway between two Cantonese restaurants, from which smells of cooking were already coming. Going up the grimy, uncarpeted stairs two at a time, he had to make way for several tough-looking Chinese men coming out of one of the several rooms in the building from which came the clicking of mah jong tiles, night and day. On the third floor was one of the strangest shops in London. It had no shop front, nor even a sign outside, and relied entirely on word-of-mouth publicity.

With a tape measure round his neck, Emmanuel Rabinovitz would have landed a walk-on part from any casting director looking for the typical East-End Jewish tailor. He had begun life in the city of Lodz and, after sixty years in Britain, his speech still had the sing-song lilt of Yiddish and was larded with my-life-already clichés. He lived in a respectable semi-detached house in Golders Green, had never pronounced the letter *r* in his life, nor gone bareheaded. He never locked up his shop, believing that his Chinese landlords provided better security than the best alarm system money could buy – this despite the fact that, each night, he left tens of thousands of pounds' worth of stringed instruments in all stages of repair, lying on his work-bench, hanging on the walls or simply sitting in their cases on the cluttered floor, waiting for his expert attention.

Rabinovitz was, in Irving's opinion, not just the best repairer of fiddles in the world, but also far more knowledgeable about stringed instruments than most of the musicians who played them. In waistcoat and shirt-sleeves, with a yarmulke on his head and green baize armlets protecting his cuffs, he was hunched over his bench, working on a violin which he had invisibly repaired by grafting a patch of wood of the same age, taken from a write-off. He put down the instrument and the knife with which he had been matching the detail of the original pur-fling – the delicate detail round the edge – and removed the watchmaker's spectacles.

'Irving,' he said. 'What a pleasure.'

The respect was mutual: Irving was one of the rare musi-cians to whom the old man was polite. Most of the others he regarded as clumsy buffoons whose main activity in life was sitting on, standing on, dropping and generally abusing their delicate instruments - and then expecting him to work miracles so that they could be restored to playable condition against the clock.

Irving opened the violin case. 'Manny, I want you to look at a fiddle for me.'

'That's the story of my life, Irv. No one ever comes in here and says, "Manny, I want you to look at this beautiful girl I've brought along." It's always . . . What have you got there, my boy?'

He took the Strad in his hands. The clicking of the mah jong tiles next door was the loudest sound in the room. Unlike

Irving, Rabinovitz did not want to hear the instrument; to him, everything was in the wood. He turned it over, sighted along the grain, felt the varnish, weighed the instrument in his hands. 'Where did you get this beautiful thing?' he asked.

'None of your business, Manny. Is it kosher?'

'Are you buying or selling?'

'It's mine, and I'm certainly not selling.'

'How can you do this to me, Irv?'

'What do you mean?'

'You walk into my shop with the most perfect instrument I have ever seen in my life. And you're not going to sell it to me – not that I could afford it, even if my wife sold all her jewellery and the car. And it doesn't need mending, so you've come to gloat.'

'Manny, I may be a *goy* but I'm not *meshugganeh*. Stop the refugee-from-the-ghetto act and tell me exactly what I've got here. I'm right in thinking that the label's genuine, aren't I?'

Rabinovitz grunted scorn at the question. 'More to the point is, when was it made? It's not an early Strad, made when the master was still influenced by Amati, under whom he served his apprenticeship. Look at the varnish, Irv.'

The colour told him a lot. The greatest of all Cremonese luthiers had used an oil varnish over a spirit varnish. Ever seeking new heights of perfection, Antonio Stradivari changed the formula in 1684, producing a darker hue, with rich amber and red overtones. From the quality of the detail in the cutting of the *ff* holes, the carving of the scrolls and the exquisite precision of the purfling, Rabinovitz was sure that this instrument must have been made long after 1684.

'And it's not a long Strad,' he mused. 'That's what we call the slightly longer instruments, which Stradivari made when he first shrugged off the yoke of Amati. So, it was made after 1690, when he reverted to a slightly shorter length.'

Rabinovitz had handled two of the best-known violins from the most famous of Cremona's workshops. They were the 'Pucelle' and the 'Viotti', both made in 1709. This one had been made after them, he felt sure, yet it was not a late instrument.

'You see,' he explained, examining it in close-up through the watchmaker's spectacles, 'after 1730 the shaky hand of an old man was apparent in the smaller details. But there's no shakiness here. Everything's clean-cut, decisive. Beautiful. Beautiful. Beautiful.'

'So what are we left with?'

'I'd say this fiddle was made some time between 1710 and 1720 – at the peak of Antonio Stradivari's powers. How did you get your hands on it, Irv?'

'Never mind that. I want to know where it came from, Manny. Do you recognise it? Is it one of the known ones?'

Rabinovitz shook his head. 'I've seen them all. This one's been hidden away in someone's collection for years, maybe a century or more.'

'Isn't that unusual?'

'Unusual? The word has no meaning when you talk of such an instrument. Unique, maybe. The 'Messie' Strad spent fifty years in Count Cozio de Salabue's collection unplayed, and was then hidden for thirty years in an isolated farm in Italy. Who knows, my boy, perhaps this instrument has a similar history?'

'You can do better than that, Manny.'

'I need time. Leave it with me,' Rabinovitz pleaded.

'I can't. But I need to know what it's worth.'

'Whatever the seller wants to ask.'

'Sure, but give me a figure, however rough.'

'The price of a Strad varies widely, depending on the year in which it was made and other factors . . . I was in Sotheby's in June of last year, Irv. You remember when Tom Jenkins' Strad – which was made in 1667 – was knocked down for £340,000?' Rabinovitz was finding it hard to talk. The excitement was such that his body kept forgetting to breathe; it was like a steel band tightening around his chest. 'And four months later, the Dickinson-Stuart Strad fetched only £200,000.' He peered at Irving over the tops of the heavy spectacles. 'Yet when Erica Morini's was stolen in New York, the insurance company paid out over $3 million.'

'I'm not talking about them, Manny. I want a value for this one.'

'More.'

'More than $3 million?'

'Double that, and add the number you first thought of.' Rabinovitz held the violin across both hands and offered it back to Irving with all the tenderness of a mother holding out her new-born child. He replaced the watchmaker's glasses with a pair of thick-lensed spectacles and shuffled to the book shelves that lined one wall of his shop, where he started leafing through volumes full of detailed drawings of violins, violas, cellos and basses, while Irving played some Paganini variations quietly by the window.

'I've got it,' Rabinovitz said, ten minutes later.

He put down the book and took the Strad from Irving, nodding to himself as one minuscule detail after another confirmed his judgement. His normally pale face was flushed and he was too short of breath to speak, so Irving had to be patient while he washed down a couple of pills with a glass of water and sat down on the only chair in the shop.

'I could be wrong,' he said at last.

'You could be right. Just tell me what you think, Manny.'

'I think you have the San Domenico Strad, my boy.'

'Never heard of it.'

'That's because it was never sold. It was named after the church in Cremona where Stradivari was buried in 1737. According to his third son by his second marriage, Giuseppe, who became a priest, the instrument was made in 1720 as a twin to the Piatti violin . . .'

'I've heard the Piatti. I was even allowed to play it for a few minutes. This one's better.'

'Many people think the Piatti was Stradivari's greatest achievement, but it seems that he thought otherwise, Irv – because, according to his son, he refused ever to sell the twin and presented it to the church of San Domenico in Cremona shortly before his death, in return for masses to be said and sung in perpetuity for his soul. There's been no trace of that instrument since the destruction of the church in 1869.'

'Where are you going?'

'Home.'

'At this time of the morning, Manny? Are you ill?'

Six thousand years of yearning were in Rabinovitz's eyes as he tore them away from the instrument in Irving's hands.

'To you,' he said, 'that fiddle you're holding is just a tool to make music and earn money. To me, seeing it today was like looking into the face of God.'

He waved his hands in a gesture encompassing all the other instruments in the shop. 'I feel like smashing the whole lot up for firewood, Irv. If I stay here, I might just do that, so I'm going home.'

After putting the old man into a taxi and paying his fare all the way to Golders Green, to stop Rabinovitz getting out at the first Underground station in order to save money, Irving hailed another cab for himself. The three-mile journey back to the Barbican seemed to take hours, so strong was the anticipation of putting his bow to the strings again and hearing the exquisite sound that no other luthier had ever quite achieved – not the Guarneri family, not even Amati who had taught both them and Stradivari.

Like an adolescent bursting to tell someone about a new girl-friend, Irving was aching to tell someone about the Strad, but in whom could he confide? Only another violinist would understand what the Strad meant to him. Only another violinist would even have the vocabulary to share in the joy of this wonderful instrument . . .

There was a face that seemed to be staring at him from every poster hoarding the taxi passed. Siobhan's group was doing a gig in north London. She would understand about the Strad. He had been wondering how to find an excuse to contact her again, so perhaps he could kill two birds with one stone?

At 2 p.m. he arrived at the venue where Slieve Gullion were due to perform that night: a converted railway maintenance shed in North London with a couple of reconditioned steam engines at the sides of the platform and all the glitzy ambience of a motorway service station at three o'clock in the morning. It was the height of the get-in. On the stage, the band was doing a sound check, with riggers tapping microphones and snaking cables across the floor. The auditorium was occupied territory, where humpers in Hell's Angels' leather gear sat on flight cases, swigging beer from cans and smoking own-rolled cigarettes. Overhead, a team of four athletic girls in black leotards swung like monkeys from the scaffolding lighting rig, calling each other by names like Fred and Jack.

To Irving's unpractised eye, it seemed impossible that a public event could materialise out of such chaos within a few hours. The shouts, the crashing of heavy equipment and a persistent howl-round on one of the massive banks of speakers hurt his ears. In the centre of the platform, apparently legless on a cloud of carbon dioxide smoke, about the quality of which two technicians were arguing over the PA, stood Siobhan. With no make-up, dressed in an old sweater and jeans, she was unmistakably the pivot around which everything else revolved.

In her hand was a radio microphone, which was giving problems, and over which she was threatening to emasculate some invisible sound technician, her voice alternately booming and fading on the speakers. When the microphone was replaced, she turned her attention to the musicians. Irving heard her insisting on her way of singing a song, holding out against the rest of the band until she won.

A tough lady, he thought. She's obviously used to getting her own way. Do I know what I'm doing, chasing after her like this? Since spending the whole night talking with Siobhan, he had not been able to stop thinking of her for long.

The house lights dimmed and sequencers washed red, green, yellow and blue over the fantasy land on-stage. Irving walked down to the front row of seating and called Siobhan's name. When she took no notice, he realised that the powerful fold-back speakers aimed at her must stop most of the audience reaction ever reaching the platform, and that the twin follow-spots which locked onto her every movement blinded her when she looked outward from the stage.

Two hours later, the roadies and humpers were gone, the auditorium was empty and the musicians were still arguing on-stage.

'My God, I could do with a drink,' Siobhan said.

Irving thrust into the spotlit circle of light where she stood a chilled can of Coke that he had just bought from a dispenser at the back of the hall. 'Will this do?' he called.

Assuming that the arm and hand with the Coke belonged to one of the roadies, she reached for it with a curt word of thanks, but he held on tight.

She shaded her eyes to see him better. 'What are you doing here?'

Irving scrambled up onto the stage, aware that it was hard for Siobhan to fit him inside a horizon that excluded everything irrelevant to the rehearsal and the gig that night. He made a joke of introducing himself: 'Irving Bradley. We met a couple of nights ago.'

She swallowed the cold Coke and took a deep breath. 'But what are you doing here?'

It was not the moment to tell her about the Strad. He held both arms out wide. 'I wanted to see how you work. All this is very different from my scene.'

'I suppose.'

The musicians had stopped arguing and were staring in their direction. Irving felt stupid and exposed. 'I have a free evening,' he explained. 'I thought I'd come along to the show, if that's all right with you.'

'It's a public event,' she said.

'I'll buy a ticket.'

'No need.' Siobhan turned away and clapped her hands to get the musicians' attention. Over her shoulder she added, 'Ask backstage for a Welsh girl called Sian. She'll give you a house seat. Tell her I said so.'

Irving walked off the platform, wishing he had not come. The girl called Sian pulled a wad of tickets from the hip pocket of her jeans. 'You want two, three?'

'One's fine. Thanks.' He took the ticket, having already decided that he had made a mistake and would not be coming back that evening.

.5.

In his room at the motel just off the boulevard périphérique, Ken listened to Madame Lafont's voice on the mini-recorder, which Hallstatt had left for him in a sealed envelope at the reception desk. The tape ended with an apology: 'Sorry to crap out, old buddy, but I have *la grippe*. So I'm heading home by train. So long!'

Ken was about to press the Stop button, when he caught Hallstatt's afterthought, which echoed a doubt in his own mind: 'It's worth bearing in mind that this boyfriend of Céline's could have been working for the Abwehr, or even at a pinch for the Gestapo. Had you thought about that? It would explain why, according to Madame Lafont, Céline could usually reach him on a private line that didn't go through any military switchboard, why he was able to slip away from his duties at short notice to be with Céline, why he had a private car, why he was nearly always in civilian clothes. And so on. Supposing she was working for him and had penetrated the Communist network as a double agent? Think about it. Good hunting!'

Southbound traffic on the A10 motorway out of Paris was dense. It was the evening rush hour and Ken used the Land Cruiser's air horn, lights and bull-bumper to tailgate other drivers and bully his way through the jams in an uncharacteristic display of aggressive driving. Past Orléans, the traffic thinned and he played the tape through again several times. Hallstatt had done a good job.

Doing a hundred and fifty kilometres an hour, he wound down the driver's window and let the wind lash his face. There was time to wonder where Catriona had gone. She had already walked out on him a couple of times before, but this was different. He had picked up the odd vibes between her and Irving, but Irving had the hots for her daughter, so what did that mean? And was she serious that he should have paid more attention to her, with all this on his mind? Why did he never learn? Like a bloodhound with its nose to the scent, he had hardly even looked up when she threw at him that line about being used and ignored by one man already. Only now was it sinking in that he was going to miss her a lot, when this business was over.

Bloodhound? Ken remembered his third wife once calling him an unlovable ferret. 'I could take you ignoring me all week, while you poke and pry into other people's lives,' she had said. 'I could be a dutiful wife and housekeeper – and probably even convince myself I still loved you – if I at least existed for you between six o'clock on Friday evening and seven o'clock on Monday morning.'

Siobhan's concert began while Irving was sitting in the staff canteen on the top floor of Broadcasting House in Portland Place, chatting with a pony-tailed BBC television producer wearing an open-necked shirt and old jeans, whose hair was a different colour each time they met. He was having problems getting the channel controller's approval of the budget for a documentary film he wanted to shoot of Irving's upcoming Latin American tour. There were twelve months to go, but already he wanted to talk of Irving playing on an Amazon steamer, in an Indian village, among rubber tappers on a plantation . . .

Toying with a plateful of stewed rabbit in mustard sauce, Irving found himself looking at his watch every few minutes. Despite the astutely timed massaging of his ego, the conversation was boring him. Like a lover in unsought company, he wanted to be alone with the Strad, which sat in its case on the chair beside his.

After the meal, he accompanied the producer across the road to the Langham Hilton, where they had a couple of drinks. At 9.30 p.m., after being introduced to several senior BBC executives, Irving was fed up with being shown off as a trophy and walked out, intending to drive straight home. Instead, he found himself at the wheel of the black Lexus, heading north through Regent's Park towards the venue where Siobhan was playing.

The violin was in its case belted into the passenger seat. Irving could feel its presence reaching out to him. If Rabinovitz was right – and Irving knew intuitively that he was – then whoever owned the Strad could name his own price for it. Five million sterling would not have been too much. So Ken had a point: it seemed worryingly implausible that Sir Terence's principal would have given away the most valuable musical instrument in the world in return for a painting worth only a fraction as much.

There was a security cordon at the artists' entrance of Siobhan's venue but one of the bouncers who also worked at the Albert Hall, was a fan of Irving's and waved him through backstage. The interval was nearly over. In the main dressing-room a clutch of photographers and reporters from the pop music magazines were clustered, wielding flash-synchronised cameras and waving mini-recorders at her.

For the second time that day Irving decided that he was in the wrong place. He pushed his way out into the corridor, where one of the two Irish fiddlers in the band stopped him to ask for an autograph. Sian, the Welsh stage manager who had given him the complimentary ticket, appeared, wearing radio headphones and shouting at the Press hounds to leave because the second half of the programme was already late in starting. As they trooped out, Irving was pushed along with them. Already in the corridor, he felt Siobhan's heavily made-up eyes fasten on him, and turned to face her.

'I thought you'd changed your mind and decided to give the show a miss. What did you think of my playing so far?'

'Great,' he said. 'You were fantastic.'

She caught his hand with slender but strong fingers. 'You weren't even in the house. I looked at the row of seats that Sian was giving away. You weren't there.'

He could hardly breathe, this close to her. The cloying smell of perspiration – hers mixed with that of a thousand other performers who had touched the ground here briefly, reduced momentarily to the status of mere mortals in this motley dressing-room – was in his nostrils. In her heavy stage make-up, wearing a glittering caftan-top over glitter-pants and high-heeled boots that looked as though they were made of red steel, Siobhan was a witch, holding his gaze and stopping his mouth. All he could think of was licking the beads of salt sweat from her neck, stripping her clothes off and plunging himself into her warm flesh, to stay there for a very long time.

The stage manager was back, shoving Irving roughly out of the way. 'Now, Siobhan!' she shouted. 'Not in ten effing minutes. The rest of the band is on!'

Pulling Irving with her, Siobhan ran along the black-painted corridor towards the wall of sound from the stage: the intro to her first number. Grabbing her fiddle from the stage manager, she shouted at him, 'You stand right there till I come off-stage, y'hear?'

Hidden from the audience by the black drapes, Irving stood in the darkness at the edge of the stage, pulsating with wild Celtic rock – a fusion of plaintive runic melodies with fast, driving rhythms. The musical boss of the group, he thought, was a good musician. If the core of the band was sometimes the rhythm section of electric guitar, bass and drumkit, most of the time the Celtic instruments – bodhrans of different sizes, fiddles, penny whistles and above all the Uilleann pipes, which sounded so different from Scottish bagpipes – gave the group an unmistakable style of its own which said, We're Irish and to hell with you.

Siobhan sang in the third number, putting down her fiddle to detach the vocal mike from its stand and coming to sing on the corner of the stage, just two paces away from where Irving was standing. He recognised the lyrics about which she had been arguing during the rehearsal and wondered how he had not guessed earlier in the show that she was the musical brain of the group. So she was young . . . But hadn't he at her age tussled with and dominated conductors and orchestras? As one pro to another, he gave a double thumbs-up of congratulation, which she acknowledged with an ironic half-bow.

She was singing at him, ignoring her twelve hundred fans out in the hall. He could not understand the words, because they were in Gaelic but her eyes seemed to be flashing the message: 'I know you want me, but you can't have me.'

She came off-stage forty minutes later, looking as though she had just been under a shower. Grabbing a can of Diet Pepsi from the stage manager she gasped at Irving, 'What did you think?'

'You were fantastic.' It seemed to his own ears a feeble tribute, after what he had been listening to.

Siobhan dropped the can on the floor and reached for him. Thinking that it was for a spontaneous embrace in the mood of the moment, he allowed her to pull him towards her, only realising that he had been tricked when she led him on-stage. In the darkened auditorium, the audience was whistling and slow-clapping, hungry for more. Accustomed to seeing the audience in a well-lit concert hall, Irving felt momentary stage fright in the unfamiliar environment. Siobhan took her violin and bow from one of the fiddlers in the band who had been looking after it for her since she ran off the platform.

'Play a duet with me,' she said, half a little girl pleading, half a woman in command.

'I can't.'

'Haven't you got a fiddle in that case under your arm, Mr Bradley?'

'Yes, but I don't know your material,' he shouted at her.

The mascaraed eyes were mocking him again. 'We'll make it up as we go. Just a jig.'

'That's not my sort of music.'

'Any fiddler worth his salt can play a jig,' she taunted.

It was crazy to take a Strad onto that stage, but not much crazier to play it, so he put the case on a speaker, opened it and tuned hurriedly.

Just a jig, she had said. Siobhan danced away from Irving musically, waiting just long enough for him to start catching up and then hiding in a sequence of chords where he could not follow, showing herself and flitting away again.

To hell with this, he thought, catching the grins of the band out of the corner of his eye. He shouldered Siobhan away from the centre-stage mike and bettered her last phrase, stepping back to let her show him another. Each time he beat her at her own musical game, the band musicians loved it, following first him and then Siobhan as they took it in turns to push the tempo faster still. And the audience loved it too, dragging them all back on-stage to play another jig as punishment.

'I'd say that was a draw,' said one of the sweat-lathered fiddlers in the band backstage afterwards. 'Great playing, Irv. If I ever need to put in a dep, I'll give you a call.'

'That was a lousy trick,' Irving said to Siobhan, angry that she had outmanoeuvred him.

She was so hoarse that he had difficulty hearing her reply, with his ears still ringing from the noise of the PA.

'I thought it was what you came for.' She gulped Pepsi from a can, high on adrenaline and the buzz from the audience that had come to hear her and was going away still wanting more. Irving knew what it felt like. Yet, although it was absolutely the wrong time to do it, he could not stop himself from asking her to dinner.

At their first meeting Siobhan had summed him up as a man who usually got what he wanted from girls far too easily. 'I'm not free,' she said. 'Sorry.'

'Tomorrow night?'

'Not tomorrow either.'

.6.

Irving parked the Lexus in his reserved space in the warren of underground parking within the Barbican complex. About to wish the man on the security gate goodnight, he noticed that the usual attendant – a Trinidadian with a rich baritone voice who sang in the chorus at Covent Garden – was absent.

'The regular bloke's ill, guv,' said the pale-faced Cockney sitting in his place. He seemed more interested in the flickering screen of the portable television on the counter than in looking at Irving.

There were two men in suits waiting in the subterranean passageway that led to the stairway and lifts, both built like the bouncers at Siobhan's gig. They had their backs to Irving as he walked past, so that he would have thought nothing of it – so obsessed was he with the violin he was carrying – except for the wording of Ken's last warning: *Watch your back!*

He felt the hairs on the back of his neck prickle as they had not done for years. Sensing violence in the air, he turned just in time to see a third man getting out of a car parked at the end of the passage, and recognised the man who had been driving him in Sir Terence's Rolls. The strange parking attendant had come out of the kiosk, which made four of them. At the far end of the passage, the metal doors were closed, an illuminated arrow showing that the lift was thirteen floors above. Knowing that it would not arrive before the men caught up with him, Irving stabbed the call button and turned to face them.

The child is father to the man; this man was the child of the defiant street kid who had shouted, 'Touch it and I'll smash yer faces in,' the very first day he had carried a fiddle. Unlike many people, Irving was not shocked helpless at the imminent prospect of physical violence, because it had been an everyday fact of his childhood. Aggression, in his book, was best handled by retaliating immediately, upping the violence one notch at a time without getting excited about it.

As the two heavies came towards him, he stood with his back firmly against the metal lift doors and the violin case cradled in both arms. The men obviously knew who he was; this was no casual late-night mugging. From their relaxed stance, Irving judged that they were not expecting an effete musician to give any trouble. At the end of the passageway, Sir Terence's driver was waiting beside the parking attendant.

The taller of the two bouncers said quite politely, 'Just get into the car with us, please, Mr Bradley.'

For a musician, the problem with any of the conventional methods of self-defence is that he cannot afford to use his hands, even defensively. However he delivers or parries a blow with them, the damage to himself, although slight, can prevent him playing for days or even weeks. After being mugged in New York during his time at the Juilliard school, and losing a violin that represented most of his worldly wealth at the time, Irving had determined never again to fall victim to any cheap street criminal. He had set himself to learn what is perhaps the most difficult form of self-defence for someone who is not an athlete: kick-boxing. This was the first time in years he had needed that peculiar skill.

The toe of his right shoe connected with the left knee of the man who had just spoken and dropped him to the ground in agony with the patella bone shattered. Then the second bouncer got to grips, his sheer body weight crushing his victim against the lift doors with an echoing thud. A blow from the short, black rubber cosh in his assailant's left hand missed Irving's right ear by millimetres. More worried for the Strad than himself, Irving clutched it tight.

As the bouncer's arm went back to deliver a second blow, he saw his target slide down and to the right faster than should have been possible, even without the encumbrance of the violin case. At the edge of his field of vision, Irving appeared to fall and recover his balance. As his trunk went forward, his right foot came up to head-height and jabbed savagely backwards, the steel edge of his shoe heel connecting with the bouncer's third cervical vertebra, nearly severing the spinal cord, in the classic reverse roundhouse kick *gyaku-mawashi-geri*. At a karate competition he would have lost points for not gripping his opponent's right arm and pulling him into the blow, but the effect was almost the same. As his attacker crumpled unconscious to the ground beside his groaning comrade, Irving heard the lift arrive and the doors open.

'You'd do better to get into the car, Mr Bradley,' called the driver in a South African accent. His unemotional, business-like voice, at another time and place, could have been that of a bank manager or an accountant saying, 'You'd do better to hang onto your gilts for the time being.'

'Up yours, wack,' Irving shouted back.

If he had not had the Strad to look after, he would have been tempted to take on the two remaining men. As it was, discretion seemed the better part of valour. He leaped inside the lift and stabbed the button, willing the doors to close fast. There were fists beating a tattoo on the metal panels before the lift had moved more than a couple of feet, and he could hear the sound of feet on the concrete stairs that ran around the lift shaft. Four floors up, Irving hit the open-door button, leaping out as the doors closed again behind him.

Using the fire exit on that level would set off the alarm system for the whole building, but that was not his problem. Leaving the bells and the flashing lights behind him, he headed at a fast walk along the deserted concrete walkways of the Barbican towards the nearest all-night cab rank.

Irving had been waiting in the street outside Siobhan's cottage in the mews cul-de-sac just off Queensway for two hours by the time she arrived home by taxi. Startled, she jumped visibly as he walked out of the shadows of the doorway to the next house before she could shut her door.

'Are you all right, miss?' the cabbie called, reversing back along the darkened mews. He had one hand on the microphone in front of his face.

'Tell him, yes,' urged Irving.

'I'm not sure I should.' Still in her stage make-up, Siobhan did not look pleased to see him. 'You really don't give up, do you, Mr Bradley?'

'I'm in trouble.'

'That's not my fault.'

'This is not a try-on,' he pleaded. 'I badly need a bed for the night.'

'Haven't you got any friends?'

'It has to be somewhere that no one would think of looking for me.' As he said the words, Irving realised how impossibly melodramatic they sounded.

'Well, that's a line I haven't heard before.' Despite her suspicions, Siobhan smiled. 'You're a real trier, Irving. I'll give you that.'

'Can I come in?'

'Are you having problems?' the cabbie asked, with his head out of the window.

'No,' Siobhan called. 'But thanks anyway.'

The taxi drove off. She stepped aside, to let Irving through the door, and locked it after him with the warning, 'I may be Irish, but I'm not the sort on the building site who takes the wheel off his barrow, to make it lighter to carry. You've got five minutes to convince me why I should let you stay the night on my futon. And I am not, repeat not, going to sit up all night talking to you again.'

The white lines flicked by. At least, Ken thought, he could now forget about the possibility of Irving's teacher having been planted in Britain as a Soviet agent and killed by the SVR because she knew too much about some old KGB scenario which had been resuscitated. Under whichever of its many sets of initials, Moscow Centre trained its agents to be grey people. None, to Ken's knowledge had ever got involved in even petty crime, let alone been crazy enough to steal a painting worth £250,000.

Then why had Mrs Prescot changed her identity on coming to Britain? Kandinsky had hinted that more than one valuable work of art had gone astray when his wife vanished with her German lover. If Geoffrey Prescot and his new bride had brought a hoard of paintings to Britain with them, that might have been sufficient reason to change one's identity in the hope of throwing pursuers off the trail. But Mr and Mrs Geoffrey Prescot had lived very modestly above the shop in Liverpool, without the slightest indication they had had the sort of money that came from selling works of art. There was nothing to suggest that either of them had known its value before Mrs Prescot had seen the television programme about the female Impressionists.

But Leutnant Dietrich Bohlen of the Kunstschutz would have known a Mary Cassatt painting when he saw one. So had he not told his lover? And what had happened to him? Where had he and Céline been between the second week of June 1944, when he left Paris to rescue her from a Gestapo cell in Lyon, and April 1945, which was the earliest she could have assumed the identity of the girl who had died in the massacre at the Villa Céleste?

Deep in thought, Ken almost missed the turn-off for Royan. He hauled the Land Cruiser onto the exit ramp, paid the toll and parked by the *péage* booth, to grab a few hours' shut-eye in a sleeping-bag on the back seat. Shortly after dawn he was walking, bundled in thick cord trousers and an anorak, along the top of the low cliff at the Villa Céleste, on the path known as the *chemin des douaniers*. Below him, the sea was grey and three-metre waves were breaking on the jagged rocks, sending curtains of spray high over the old Atlantic Wall bunkers.

Ken ignored the weather, trying to see in his mind what the place had looked like on 18 April 1945, just before the house had burned down. On the beach, a line of metal stumps reminded him that the coast from the Rhine estuary to the Spanish border had been littered with Rommel's asparagus, the welded triangular anti-tank obstacles. Almost certainly, the beach had been mined as well, with skull-and-crossbones notices warning *Achtung! Minen*.

He turned and faced inland. At that time, the house was still intact and the bunkers empty because the Wehrmacht soldiers – Russians, Romanians, Hindus, Mongols, the sweepings of the Third Reich's military reserves – had all surrendered the previous day. The fire had not been the result of enemy action. So who had burned down the Villa Céleste, and why?

PART IX:
Paris – June 1944

. 1 .

Céline spent the night in the cell listening to the groans of the woman on the other bunk. Every time footsteps approached along the flagged corridor, she pressed herself back against the cold, damp wall, as though she could hide in the cracks like the bugs which came out to feed on her body. Because of the pain from her broken ribs, even walking across the cell to use the toilet bucket required a major decision. Men in adjacent cells moaned and screamed in their sleep, but sleep eluded her. She lay wondering whether she would end in front of a blood-spattered wall, and whether dying hurt more or less than torture.

How brave would she be?

What was it like, to be at the mercy – if that was the word – of men whose daily job was to inflict intolerable pain on other people?

She could have asked her cell-mate, but it seemed grotesque to put such questions into words.

It was almost impossible to imagine that within a few hours, she would be in the hands of the men who could do to her body what they had already done to the woman moaning on the other side of the cell. How would they start? Would they hit her, whip her, kick her? Would they shout at her or work in silence? Would she be tied up first? Would they strip her naked or let her keep at least the dignity of the soiled prison dress? Would there be at least the semblance of officialdom, with that frightening, quietly spoken Obersturmführer Barbie in charge, or would she be handed over to a pack of faceless sadists, more intent on their own pleasure than applying just enough pain to make her talk?

Breakfast was two mugs of water and a couple of crusts thrust through the food flap at the bottom of the door. So many of the other woman's teeth had been broken that she could not eat the bread. Yet she mumbled that Céline must eat and drink, to keep up her strength. The fluid was warm and brownish, with no taste at all. The crusts were almost inedible. In France at that time all bread was made from flour mixed with sawdust to make it go further; this bread seemed to be all sawdust and no flour. Each mouthful Céline managed to swallow made her thirstier.

She soaked the other crust in some water and fed pieces of the pap to her cell-mate. Then she moistened the corner of her skirt and wiped the mass of dirty bruises that covered the woman's face, wondering whether their roles would be reversed in a few hours' time. Yet there were limits to her practical sympathy: even had there been anything useful to be done for those obscenely swollen and mutilated fingers, Céline could not have brought herself to touch them.

The woman whimpered when Céline's arm brushed against her breast. 'It burns,' she mumbled.

'What does?'

'They call it the telephone. One man winds the handle, but instead of ringing, it gives you shocks and burns you here and here.' She indicated her breasts and between her legs.

Oh God, will they do that to me?

Céline stopped talking after learning that her cell-mate was only nineteen and had been in the cellars of the Hotel Terminus for two days. It was beyond belief that men could reduce a healthy young woman to a wreck like this so quickly.

There were some things it was better not to know.

The bath was of the old type, made of cast iron, with lion's feet supports. It was full of filthy water, in which large lumps of ice floated. Barbie was wearing a neat grey double-breasted civilian suit and sitting, smoking a cigarette, on the corner of a desk. He asked Céline the same questions, but seemed bored and irritable, compared to his malign playfulness the previous day. The other two men in the room were fat, like wrestlers gone to seed, and wore espadrilles on their feet which enabled them to approach her from behind soundlessly.

The first time they picked her up and ducked her head under the icy water, she felt so weightless and puny that there was no logical point in struggling. But the body is not logical. Céline's body spasmed, her arms and legs flailed – but to no avail. Lifted bodily out of the water and allowed to take a few breaths, she made the terrifying discovery that she could not inhale because of the scream that went on and on, from the pain from her broken ribs where they had bent her over the edge of the bath. Thrust back into the bath, mouth still wide open, she swallowed vast quantities of the filthy water. More questions and another drowning. Each time her head was plunged into the water she thought her whole body would explode with the pain.

When Barbie was called away to take a phone call in his office, the two men dumped their soaking, retching victim on the floor and sat on a couple of chairs in one corner, smoking cigarettes, drinking coffee and taking no notice of Céline. Their matter-of-factness seemed to imply that she had no existence except when they were at work on her. A telephone rang in the corridor. One of the fat men dragged into the middle of the room, facing the desk, a heavy chair that jingled from all the buckles on the restraining straps for the head, the legs, the torso, the arms of their victim.

He gestured to Céline to get up and sit in it. She struggled to her feet, the wet dress clinging to her body, and walked unsteadily to the chair. When he tightened the strap around her ribs, she screamed. Again she told herself that resistance led only to greater pain, but her arms and legs seemed to have a mind of their own and fought the men off until a hail of blows to her head left her sobbing impotently as the straps locked her biceps, her forearms and then her head to the oaken bulk of the chair. Her legs were forced apart and secured at the thighs and calves to the widely spread chair legs.

A thick leather gag that smelled of vomit was forced into her mouth and tied behind her neck. When the only parts of her body that she could still move were her hands, it seemed impossible these men could restrain her any further. Then each of them lifted one of her hands, flattened the fingers and forced them into metal devices screwed to the end of the chair arms, with grooves into which the thumbs and fingers fitted. The matching top half of each hand vice was swung up and over, locking into position with a split pin, to hold Céline's fingers immobile, with just the tips poking out. What brain, she wondered dimly, could invent and make such a hellish contrivance?

One of the men pulled up a stool and sat in front of her. 'Time for your manicure,' he said.

Barbie was back, bending over Céline to watch her eyes for the reaction when he said, 'I think we'll start with the left hand.'

Behind the gag, she tried to scream a protest. It might just be possible to play with an injured bowing hand, but if they damaged the fingers of her left hand, she would be unable to stop the strings: it would mean the end of her career. Unable even to move any part of her body, she could only watch helplessly as the fat man on the chair selected a scalpel from the top tray of a trolley like that of a garage mechanic, on which several rows of tools were neatly arranged.

The blade was like fire as it cut into the quick below the nail of her little finger, to give purchase for the pliers. But the pain from the pliers, once he started pulling the nail out by its roots, was unlike anything Céline had ever experienced. Frightened of drowning in her own vomit behind the gag, she felt her body make the only protest possible. Wetness flooded out of her. She could hear the drips falling onto the floor and attempted to throw herself backwards, trying to move both her own body weight and that of the chair away from the man with the pliers. The second man, who weighed more than twice what she did, was holding the back of the chair, so that it hardly moved.

Constricted by the chest strap, her broken ribs produced a

high soprano scream of agony in her brain, against which the new pain was a deep bass rumble. It seemed impossible that the swinish grunting she could hear coming through the gag was made by a human. It seemed impossible that such agony could come from so small an area of her body. It seemed impossible that the pain could continue any longer without blowing a fuse in her brain.

Head locked back against the wood of the chair, with sweat pouring down her face, Céline stared down at the bloody stump at the end of her left little finger in disbelief and horror. The fingers of her right hand were bleeding too, where the metal grips were cutting into them. Between the pain from her ribs and the gag which seemed to be filling her mouth and growing ever larger, she could not breathe. How much longer could this go on?

The man seated on the stool facing her said, 'One done. Nine to go.' He removed the bloody, torn-out nail from the pliers and laid it on her lap, then started on the next finger, cutting away the quick for the pliers to do their work. The different pains swirled in Céline's brain like the colours of petrol spilt on water, blending and merging until the agony from the second pulled nail overwhelmed all the others and dragged her down and down into blackness.

She came to, drenched with cold water from the bath, to find that the gag had been removed. The last two fingers of her left hand ended in bloody stumps, from which shafts of fire tore through her whole body. Barbie was bending over her. It was hard to hear his quiet voice, through all the roaring in her head.

'I will tell you anything you want to know,' she pleaded. 'Anything.'

'You will tell me lies.' He smiled, the gentle schoolteacher once again. 'It's always lies for forty-eight hours. Isn't that what you're told to do?'

Céline could feel the pain coming back, like a tidal wave that would wash away her ability to talk. So she had to talk fast, to make this quiet-voiced man in the grey suit understand that there was no need to hurt her any more.

'Very well,' he said. 'Tell me for whom you are working.

But remember, each lie you tell me will cost you another nail.'

The pain came in waves, flooding Céline's brain and then receding as the endorphins made room for a million other nightmares to flit through her mind. She changed her position a thousand times. Each turn gave only slight relief for a few minutes. When the guards came for her again, she could not stand up: her leg muscles refused to carry her body back for more pain.

'*Courage*,' called her cell-mate, as the two SS men hauled Céline out into the corridor.

In an office on the ground floor of the Hotel Terminus, a man was waiting. He seemed to be a prisoner, but had a first-aid box with him. Céline thought she must be hallucinating as he cleaned her face and hands with a piece of lint soaked in some disinfectant and then bandaged the two injured fingers. He left without having spoken a word, leaving her alone, nursing her left hand, until Barbie appeared and asked why she was not dressed in her own clothes.

An SS guard arrived with the laundry bag containing Céline's clothing, and led her to a toilet in the corridor, where she pulled off the stinking prison dress and cleaned herself up as best she could, with the door held open by the guard's booted foot.

'*Schnell*,' he kept saying. '*Dépêche-toi. Schnell.*'

She came out, still awkwardly doing up the buttons of her blouse; every movement of the left hand caused another jolt of agony in her brain. In the corridor window, she saw that it was dark outside. The reflection staring back at her was that of a madwoman, one side of her face dark with bruises, her hair plastered to her head. Only the clothes seemed to belong to the person she had been before walking into the Hotel Terminus so few hours before. Was she being moved to another prison or sent to a camp? Or was she to be shot already?

Barbie returned. He seemed tense, kept looking at his watch. 'Follow me,' he ordered curtly. 'And don't do anything stupid. You're being released.'

There were guards at the checkpoints, who jumped to

attention and saluted at his approach, the doors being held open for Céline to follow him through. She wondered whether this was some new game, or whether she was dreaming. Only the pain was real.

In the street outside the hotel, it was raining. Barbie pulled his peaked cap further down on his head and the collar of his ankle-length greatcoat further up, and strode ahead, with Céline half-running to keep up with him, short of breath and with the pain from her ribs stabbing into her brain at each pace.

I should run away, she thought dimly. But the uniformed, jack-booted figure seemed endowed with all the power in the world. He had said, 'Follow me,' so she had to.

Hardly aware of her surroundings, she followed him into a sordid *hotel de passe* at the back of the station. There was no one at the desk. Barbie took the stairs to the first floor and stopped outside a room, where the door was thrown open at his first knock and Céline saw Dietrich standing there in civilian clothes.

His eyes travelled past Barbie and settled on Céline's face. He winced at the sight of the bruises and her bandaged hand held in front of her. 'Are you all right?'

She nodded, too weak to speak, and let him pull her inside the room and sit her down on a chair. Her whole body was trembling in fear or relief and she could do nothing to stop it.

At the other end of the room was a large dining-table, on which stood a pair of leather suitcases. She watched the two men bend over them, and heard Barbie muttering, '*Mein Gott, das ist so schön!*'

The catches clicked on the cases and Barbie was gone with them. As the door closed behind him, Dietrich was already urging Céline to hurry.

'I don't understand,' she said. It was all too much to take in.

'You don't need to,' he whispered. From another suitcase under the bed, he took two Luftwaffe uniforms, and made her get dressed as a female communications auxiliary, while he put on that of a senior NCO.

Much later, when she was sitting beside him in the jerking, jolting Luftwaffe truck, she asked, 'How did you persuade that terrible man to let me go?'

'I bought you from him.' Fighting the wheel over the bad road surface of a minor road, Dietrich's face was bitter. 'Those people know the war is lost. They are all preparing for afterwards.'

Céline did not understand. 'You bought me? With what?'

'My honour.'

.2.

By dawn they were a hundred kilometres to the south-east of Lyon, driving along country roads that wound from village to village which had hardly changed since the nineteenth century. At the only German roadblock they had encountered, Dietrich had shown some papers and tossed out a carton of black-market cigarettes as a bribe to the men at the barrier. When one of them had asked about Céline's injured face and hand, he had said something about her being his girlfriend, who had been injured in a British bombing raid.

That day, they stopped twice to eat food which Dietrich bought from peasants at isolated farmhouses, far from the nearest telephone line. The night was spent trying to get some sleep, with the truck concealed in woods near the road. For Céline, Dietrich fashioned a rough sleeping area in the rear of the truck, between the stacked packing cases and jerricans of petrol. After four days of driving on country roads, they arrived at Chateau Magnus, to find the house empty, the wounded SS men having just been evacuated back to Germany.

It was widely expected on both sides that the Allied armies would swiftly break out of the Normandy bridgehead and sweep right through France in a matter of days, but there were still large formations of German troops moving about in the area, so Yvonne at first refused to let them stay. Because Céline was intermittently delirious from the infection in her injured hand – and also because he had already used up enough luck talking them through Feldgendarmerie roadblocks with his false papers, Dietrich insisted they were going no further. As a compromise, Yvonne insisted they live not in the chateau but in the cave beneath the house where Sepp Müller was already hiding, having gone AWOL to avoid being repatriated to Germany with the other wounded men.

A first priority was to ditch the truck; if it were found on the premises, everyone at the chateau would be arrested, or possibly shot on the spot. Before that could be done the crates had to be unpacked, each one being broken open by Dietrich and Sepp to reveal world-famous paintings which had been immobilised in the marshalling yards at Lyon by Allied strategic bombing raids while waiting for a Swiss-bound train to take them across the border to neutral Lucerne.

With the paintings safely installed in the cave before dawn, and Céline being attended to upstairs in the chateau by the Picard family doctor, Dietrich drove the truck away and ditched it in a small lake not far from the house. Exhausted, he fell asleep, to be awoken just before midday by Müller, with the news that a patrol of German military police had found the broken packing cases floating on the surface of the lake, and hauled the truck out of the water. They had surrounded Chateau Magnus and were questioning everybody on the property.

An hour later, Yvonne came down to the cave where the two men were hiding, with the good news that the Germans had left in a hurry because the Fort du Hâ in Bordeaux, where Resistance prisoners from all over the south-west were locked up, had been surrounded at dawn by local *maquis* units, demanding that the doors be thrown open and all the prisoners released.

Feverish, Céline slipped in and out of consciousness, nursed by Dietrich. During her lucid moments he promised her that the war was nearly over. Six weeks later, he was still promising the same thing when she was able to go for a first look round the chateau. The house had been stripped bare of furniture and furnishings, except for one walnut sideboard that had been built in situ in the dining-room and was too large to get out. The reception rooms were filled with tiers of wooden bunks, strewn with items of cast-off German uniform. The silk wall-hangings were torn, the elaborate plaster-work all chipped and bullet-scarred. In every room there were huge red swastika banners hanging on the walls.

As Céline slowly regained her strength, she became increasingly desperate to get out of the cave, which reminded her of the cell in the Hotel Terminus. But Yvonne refused to let Dietrich into the house, saying that the local Resistance were killing lone Germans on sight and even ambushing lightly armoured Wehrmacht columns. No longer the passive, acquiescent woman Céline remembered, she ran the chateau and its work-force with a rod of iron. Only Sepp seemed able to make her do whatever he wanted.

For a while, the local Resistance installed itself in the chateau above the heads of the three people hiding in the cave below their feet. Then a German column arrived and the *maquisards* fled. It was a time of widespread violence, when all sorts of scores were being settled. Reluctant to leave Dietrich's side for more than a few minutes at a time, Céline stayed in the cave with him. Their days were shared with Sepp, but at night – after he had sneaked out to sleep in the chateau – they were alone.

August went by, with them all living on food supplies which the Germans had left behind. But Céline's first improvement was not maintained. She could not sleep, and had no appetite. Every noise outside the cave made her jump. Dietrich did what he could to comfort her, and their love-making grew more careless – with the result that she found herself pregnant.

The lack of proper food, sunshine and medical care, had their inevitable result when she lost the child during the grape harvest in late September. Yvonne was furious, as though her sister was deliberately causing her problems at such a busy time.

Shortly after Christmas, Céline was pregnant again. And still the war dragged on. With the Allied Forces driving eastwards into the Reich, the liberation of the south-west of France was left to the various Resistance movements known as the Forces Françaises de l'Intérieur. This made Dietrich all the more determined to stay in hiding until he could hand over the paintings in his care to an appropriate Allied organisation. He looked pale and worn after all the months of living underground, but Céline looked worse.

Winter became spring. On 14 April – ten months to the day after they had arrived at Chateau Magnus, six days before Céline's twenty-eighth birthday and with the Russians already in Berlin – they heard a dull rumble in the air, coming from the north-west.

In the chateau, Yvonne was listening with Sepp to the radio in her father's study. The wet-cell battery was getting low, making reception of the medium-wave FFI station in Bordeaux capricious, but they could make out just enough of the newsreader's voice to understand that the US First Tactical Air Force was continuing in daylight the murderous night-time RAF air raids on the town of Royan. For the first time in history, napalm was being used. The fading voice from Bordeaux predicted surrender of the German forces in the pocket any day. Negotiations had already begun between plenipotentiaries of the two sides meeting under a flag of truce between the lines . . .

This was the moment for which Sepp had been waiting. He had discussed with Yvonne many times his plan to get rid of her sister and Dietrich, so that they could keep the paintings for themselves. 'Fifty million people have died in the last four years,' he said. 'Who cares about two more?'

But Yvonne had refused to be party to a double murder. Now, Sepp argued persuasively, they had a God-given chance to get rid of the two people who stood between them and a fortune, without raising a hand against either Céline or Dietrich. If previous form in the region was anything to go by, there would be reprisals when the German troops in the pocket finally surrendered. News of the massacre of *résistants* at the Villa Céleste reinforced his belief.

'All we have to do,' he concluded, 'is persuade Dietrich that Céline needs to be moved to the villa for the sake of her health and that of the child . . .'

On the 17th, the German troops in the pocket surrendered, and the south-west was completely liberated at last. There was a mood of celebration in the air. Yvonne had hoarded a few litres of petrol which, she said, would be enough to drive her

sister to the Villa Céleste, where she could get healthy again with the sea air and the sunshine. At first, Dietrich argued that it would be better to stay where they were until regular Allied military units, which had reached as far as Angoulême, took over the area. What finally convinced him to go along with Yvonne's plan was the fear that Céline's mind would not hold out for much longer in the cave. She sat there for hours on end, staring at the Mary Cassatt painting and dreaming that one day they would go back to the Auberge du Soleil together.

For Céline's sake, Dietrich agreed. Before leaving the chateau, he gave her the painting, much as a parent gives a child a favourite toy or a comfort blanket for the journey. Even if the car was searched at a roadblock, he thought it unlikely that anyone would recognise a Mary Cassatt for what it was. Everything else was left behind at Chateau Magnus, in Sepp's care for the time being.

After all the months cooped up in the cave, the journey was unreal: through lush countryside bursting with all the greens of spring. Nearing Royan, they drove past long columns of weary, disarmed German soldiers and huge piles of discarded equipment and weapons, from which local people were helping themselves.

At the FFI roadblocks Yvonne said that her two passengers were prisoners who had been released from the Fort du Hâ prison in Bordeaux when it was captured by the *maquis* – and that Dietrich was unable to talk, having lost his voice as a result of being tortured.

The Villa Céleste was like an oasis of peace. There were minefields all around, so that the beaches were dangerous; barbed wire was strung across the garden, but the house itself was undamaged and had not even been looted because it lay within the forbidden coastal zone, where civilians had been allowed only under escort during the past five years. There were Wehrmacht seals on the doors and windows, and a notice threatening with a court martial any military personnel found damaging the property.

Because of the widespread violence all around, it seemed prudent to try and keep the house looking unoccupied. Yvonne had forgotten to bring a key, so Dietrich had to shin up a drain-pipe and break in through a first-floor window, where the damage would not show.

When giving the Judas kiss as she left them, Yvonne felt Céline's burning cheek against hers and thought, My God, how thin she is. No wonder she lost the first child . . .

'You'll soon be better,' she lied. 'Just stay in the villa for a few days until de Gaulle's men take over the administration, then you can come out. Meantime, get plenty of rest and fresh air.'

In a hurry to be gone, she climbed out of a ground-floor window, leaving Dietrich to close the shutters behind her. The sunset sky was clear over the sea, although inland a huge cloud of dust and smoke from the three days and nights of bombing rose high into the cloudless sky. There was still time to change her mind.

Like a sleepwalker, she headed back through the dusk to the main road where she had parked her car because it was unsafe to bring it any nearer: white tapes strung between stakes marked only the footpath as being free of mines. She picked her way over shell-casing, cast-off items of German uniform, all the debris of an army in retreat. A small crowd of civilians were remonstrating with some French soldiers in uniform, who had arrested for their own protection a couple of miserable-looking Russian boys of eighteen in German uniform, caught hiding in a bomb-damaged bunker in the hope of making a getaway after dark.

Among the civilians, Yvonne recognised the dapper build and carefully-cultivated moustache of Delmas, the barber. He was the most vociferous of the group of men locked in argument with a uniformed tanker captain who had a Breton accent.

'Come on, captain,' Delmas was shouting. 'Hand the Russian swine over. We know what to do with turncoats.'

The French soldiers' loaded rifles were to keep the crowd back, not to stop the prisoners escaping. When the two nervous Russian boys were led away, having suffered nothing worse than a few stones thrown at them, Delmas began shouting that it was 'time we gave the Jerry-bags what's coming to them'. One or two other voices were raised in agreement, but the crowd split up when a rumour went around that a military canteen had been set up at the Mairie to provide a basic meal to the civilian population.

Yvonne knew that she ought to drive back to St Emilion and tell Sepp that she could not go through with his plan. It had not taken her long to realise that he was more interested in men's bodies than hers. Before the convalescent unit decamped, she had found him several times with soldiers in the fields and behind the wine *chais*. When she had finally accosted him about it, he had laughed in her face and told her that the real reason why he had come back to Chateau Magnus was that he had learned from Dietrich how rich the Picard family was. To a man who had grown up in a working-class slum in Berlin and had already had a bellyful of sacrifice for the Fatherland, Chateau Magnus had seemed the ideal place to sit out the rest of the war.

And yet, despite everything, Yvonne needed him. In the daytime, she was the tough, no-nonsense *patronne* of Chateau Magnus. At night, she was Sepp's slave. She cooked for him, she washed and mended his clothes, she serviced his lust in whichever way he wanted. And she was frightened of him.

Instead of heading back to her car, and facing up to his anger when she got back to St Emilion, she waited outside Delmas' salon for him to come out. After five minutes, she promised herself that if he had not come out by the time she had counted to one hundred, she would go away and brave her lover's anger.

With thirty seconds to go, the door of the salon opened and Delmas came out with a soup plate, cup and spoon in hand. She remembered him as a repulsive little man, forever brushing against her and Céline and making snide remarks when they accompanied their father for his daily shave during the holidays at Melles-sur-Mer. Standing near him made her stomach churn, but it was as easy as Sepp had said it would be. An SS man on the run, she said, was hiding with his mistress in the Villa Céleste . . .

After Yvonne had left them, Céline made supper for herself and Dietrich, using some cans of food still intact in the pantry from before the war. They had brought bread and some coffee with them and, as going-away presents, Yvonne had contributed a small piece of butter and Sepp a bottle of schnapps. There was no electricity in the house, so they went to bed early. After all the days and nights spent in the damp, stuffy cave, it was a miracle for Céline to be sleeping in a room with the window open, seeing stars in the sky and breathing fresh dry air.

Next morning they lay in bed late, lulled by the rumble of the waves on the rocks below the villa and luxuriating in the sunshine that flooded into the bedroom. They made love and dozed off again, which is why they did not hear the noise of the sea change to the roar of an angry crowd until it was too late. Céline pulled on a skirt and blouse and stepped out onto the balcony, to see what was happening. She was not afraid, for she was in her own house and the war was as good as over. So what was there to fear?

The garden – or rather, the part that was not wired-off – was a seething mass of faces staring up at her. Céline recognised people she had known since she was a child, coming here on holiday each year: the grocer, the barber, the postman. Even when the first stone was thrown and caught her on the elbow, numbing her left arm, she was not really afraid because she had no idea how far they would go.

PART X:
Royan, France –
November 1996

.1.

Ken was waiting on the doorstep of the museum when the doors opened at ten o'clock.

He explained to the custodian how hard it had been to find anything in Paris bookshops about the period known as *l'épuration* – the settling of scores in the weeks that followed the Liberation, when no less an authority than the current Minister of the Interior had estimated the number of people executed in France without trial at one hundred and fifty thousand.

The custodian was not keen to talk about it, either, but Ken got him to admit that there were some records kept under lock and key, being considered unsuitable for public display. If Monsieur would be prepared to treat what he learned as being off-the-record . . .

A school party claimed the man's attention for the next hour. After the children had left, he limped into his private office and unlocked a metal filing cabinet. One entire drawer was full of written accounts and photographs of atrocities: eyewitnesses telling of German soldiers beaten to death with spades or tied up with a lump of concrete and thrown alive into one of the many oyster-farming creeks. There were photographs to match: grisly black-and-white shots of surrendered soldiers, dead and alive, showing appalling injuries inflicted by the civilians alongside whom they had been living for five years without any trouble on either side. As the custodian remarked, the atrocities were all the more puzzling in an area where not a single French citizen had been killed by the Germans throughout the war.

Ken ploughed through the gallery of horror. In an old manila envelope marked *Melles-sur-Mer, 18 April 1945*, there was a series of professionally taken photographs which told the story of the public humiliation of the women. Céline – in the picture taken before her hair had been cut off, while she was still recognisable – was being held between two gendarmes. She looked ill, thin, worn out – and more dazed by what was happening to her than frightened. She was trying to hold her blouse together. In the next picture, with half her hair hacked off, she stared blankly ahead with her breasts uncovered.

Ken went back to the beginning of the sequence, seeing her forced to sit on a bentwood chair in the centre of a jeering, jostling mob. The barber – a little man with a Salvador Dali moustache and slicked-back black hair – was obviously enjoying every moment, as he started to hack her hair off. Then came the final flourish of the cut-throat razor and the victim being daubed with the sign of the swastika on her shaven scalp. The gendarmes were laughing, the priest was pretending not to see, and the mayor was actually pointing at the spectacle.

So far it was all predictable stuff.

Then the pictures took a turn for the worse: a man defending himself from a mob armed with sticks; the same man on the ground, hands and legs held so that he could not defend himself while two men attacked his face with spades; the man dragged upright, one eye hanging out of its socket, his mouth a bloody mess of smashed teeth and torn lips.

Ken went back to the first picture in the sequence, where the face of the victim was still recognisable as that of the smiling pipe-smoker who had walked along a Paris street on a sunny day with two pretty girls on his arm.

He followed the action, shot by shot: Céline, shaven-headed and with her blouse torn open, struggling with the gendarmes when confronted with her beaten and bloody lover; Céline, her mouth open in a desperate shout of protest, being hit by one of them; Dietrich being hauled onto a flatbed truck; the noose placed around his neck; the truck being driven away, leaving the body twisting on a rope that seemed too thin to hold a man's weight. In the last shot, Céline's head was raised to the sky beneath the suspended corpse of Leutnant Dietrich Bohlen, her mouth open as though cursing God Himself.

Ken laid the picture down and then picked it up again. He had been so focussed on the corpse and the shaven woman that he had almost missed another detail. In the bottom right corner of the frame, a man was forcing his way through the throng, back to the camera. He was bareheaded, but wearing a British army battledress blouse, on which were an Intelligence Corps' shoulder flash and a sergeant's stripes.

Remembering his role as a journalist, Ken said, 'Some of the people who participated that day must still be alive. I'd like to talk to them.'

The custodian looked uncertain.

'This man . . .' Ken tapped the picture in which the barber was finishing the job of shaving Céline's head. 'The mayor, for example?'

'He's dead.'

'The two gendarmes?'

'Both dead.'

'What about the barber?'

'Monsieur Delmas? He's still alive.'

'It looks to me like he was the ring-leader.'

'Delmas was a typical *résistant de dernière heure* – a bitter little man who jumped on the bandwagon of violence that day to work out all the grudges he held against the world in general.'

'Do you think he'd chat to me – off-the-record, of course?'

'He might. But for God's sake don't mention that I gave you his name. He's a very respected senior citizen.'

On the way to the Maison de Retraite – the old folks' home at Melles-sur-Mer – Ken braked the Land Cruiser and stared at a street corner. He was about half a kilometre from the Villa Céleste. Among the pines stood holiday homes, some prewar, some modern, and all discreetly set back from the road. Smoke rose from a few chimneys, but most were closed up for the winter, with doorways blocked by wind-drifted piles of dead leaves.

What had caught his eye was a distinctive old-fashioned cast-iron water pump on the pavement, which he recognised from the photographs. This was where Céline and the other women had been humiliated . . . and there was the lamppost on which her lover had been lynched. Ken took out of his briefcase two photographs he had filched from the museum collection. There was no doubt about it: this was the place where it had all happened.

The Maison de Retraite was noisy with the clatter of crockery and cutlery as the remains of the midday meal were being cleared away. There was a stale smell in the day room: a compound of equal parts of boredom and frustration with a few undignified additives. The residents sat in a row around the edge of the large, sunny room, watching a children's cartoon on television. Many had blankets over their shoulders or knees, although the room was warm.

'*Un visiteur cherche Monsieur Delmas*,' the voluntary helper called out. 'Does anyone know where he is?'

A few pairs of eyes left the screen. One of the women thought that Delmas was in the garden. He was having one of his better days, she said.

'Okay,' said Ken to the helper. '*Je me débrouillerai. Merci, madame.*' I can look after myself.

Outside, it was a relief to breathe clean air. In the well-planted, tidy garden a couple of elderly men were playing chess on a concrete bench in the sun. They pointed out a clean-shaven man, almost completely bald, who was sitting alone in a wheelchair at the end of the path nearest the sea, watching the gulls wheeling in to snatch in mid-air pieces of bread that he had thrown for them. Beyond him a section of the cliff had fallen in the last storm, leaving a fresh scar and a sheer drop to the rocky beach thirty or so feet below. Ken introduced himself, trying to see in this shrunken figure with one leg amputated at the knee, the dapper, moustached barber who had shaved Céline Picard's head, all that time ago.

'A journalist, you say?' Delmas' left hand was busy with a cigarette, his right one perpetually rolling small pieces of bread into pills, in a sort of nervous tic.

'. . . doing an article about the Liberation and *l'épuration*,' Ken said.

The old man's eyes narrowed. 'How much do you people pay?'

Ken took out a 500-franc note and pressed it into his hand.

'What do you want to know?' Delmas growled.

'I'd like to get across to readers who weren't even born then how decent men and women got swept up in something they maybe regretted afterwards.'

'Why?'

'After what's just happened in Yugoslavia, I think there's a lesson for us all in knowing what happens in these situations.'

Ken's point had obviously not registered, because Delmas laughed. 'I meant why d'you think they regretted what they did?'

'It was just a supposition.' Ken sat down on the nearest bench. 'You were the barber, Monsieur. I'm told you shaved the women's heads.'

Delmas chuckled. 'You ever watched an amateur trying to shave someone's head with a cut-throat razor? Those women would have been scalped if I hadn't done the job properly.'

The day of the women's humiliation had been a public event, he declared, a spot of fun for the lads. He had done nothing to be ashamed of, and did not regret a moment of it. Why, the priest had given absolution afterwards to everyone who asked for it. And even the men who had strung up the lousy *schleu* had never been charged with any offence . . .

The man in the wheelchair was enjoying his conversation. It was a long time since anyone had asked him a question more stimulating than, 'What do you want for dinner?' And plainly the memories that Ken's questions were stimulating were a source of pleasure for him, not shame or regret.

They chatted in general fashion about the peculiar situation of the Royan pocket, where no French citizen had any reason to bear the Germans a grudge. Why had the mob been so violently anti-German on 18 April 1945? Delmas retorted that the whole event had been a spontaneous gesture of anger at the massacre of the young *maquisards* who attacked the radar station – which gave Ken the opening for which he had been waiting.

'The women whose heads you shaved had not killed any *résistants*, had they? So who picked them out for the ordeal?'

'They got what was coming to them.'

'What had they done that was so evil?'

'They were little *putes* who had slept with the *schleus* in return for favours.' Delmas threw some pellets of bread to the gulls, which came screaming in to catch them in mid-air.

'But everybody here had had dealings with the Germans. Did you refuse to cut German hair? Or did you just refuse to be paid?'

'That was different. It was business.'

'So it was all right for a whore to go with German soldiers, but not for a girl who fell in love with one? As far as I can see, those were the ones you punished.'

Delmas looked at the 500-franc note in his hands, as though in two minds about handing it back. Ken hurried on: 'The girl who was with the German soldier they lynched. Do you remember her?' He passed across one of the photographs from the museum. 'I'm told her name was Céline Picard.'

'That's right.'

'You knew her personally?'

'Her people were stinking rich. They used to come here every August. They owned the big villa on the headland and behaved as though we were all peasants, to be ordered around like the servants they brought with them.'

'And can you tell me how the Villa Céleste came to be burned down?'

'The girl did it herself.'

'You mean, she went mad?'

'I suppose so.'

Ken took four more 500-franc notes out of his wallet. 'I want to know everything that happened that day.'

Half an hour later, he stood up. According to Delmas' version, Céline Picard had been liberated by a sergeant from the Allied Press base at Angoulême, about twenty minutes after watching her lover lynched. She had disappeared in the sergeant's jeep, apparently going back to the Villa Céleste with him. No one knew why. Shortly afterwards, the house was seen to be ablaze and the carbonised remains of a woman were found in the ruins.

The most chilling thing had been when Ken asked, 'How did you know Céline Picard and her lover were hiding in the villa that day?'

Delmas' reply was: 'Her sister told me.'

'Yvonne Picard told you?'

A nod. Ken listened with incredulity, but despite cross-questioning Delmas for half an hour, he could not shake the man's story.

'Do you think she had any idea what would happen the next day?'

Delmas chuckled. 'Oh yes, she knew all right. That's why she came.'

'Why would she want to do a thing like that?'

'You work it out,' said Delmas.

Ken turned away without saying goodbye. As he walked back towards the buildings, the man in the wheelchair patted the money in his pocket, stretched out his right hand, palm upwards, and gave his visitor the finger.

.2.

In June 1944 Céline and Dietrich had been in Lyon. In April 1945 they were at the Villa Céleste. Ignoring postwar road construction such as motorways and by-passes, Ken used his Michelin map book to trace the most obvious route from A to B. It almost touched St Emilion. Since they were both on the run, it seemed probable that they had spent at least some of the time hidden there.

Hallstatt knew what it had been like. Ken thought he might handle Madame Yvonne Picard better than he could himself. It was late afternoon when they rendezvoused at the end of the drive, leading up to the chateau and he asked, 'How's the flu, Erich?'

Hallstatt got out of his ancient Citroen 2CV and grunted something inaudible. Ken put the taciturnity down to the after-effects of a bug, but gradually Hallstatt's mood changed, as he turned over in his mind the thousand possibilities of Ken's update.

Seeing the photograph of Sergeant Geoffrey Prescot pushing his way through the mob, he exclaimed: 'That guy must have had balls. The mood those mobs were in, he could have gotten himself lynched alongside the Kraut.'

He took a deep breath and put aside the old ghosts. 'I got one more piece for the jigsaw right now, Ken. You wanna know why Yvonne Picard shopped her sister and the boyfriend to that little shit of a barber? I'll tell you. Under French law, on the death of their father in 1942, Chateau Magnus would automatically have passed equally to the two sisters. If Céline died without children, Yvonne would also inherit her share. People have killed their kin for a lot less than a half-share in a chateau like that one up there on the hill.'

Several vehicles – ranging from modest-but-not-new to old-and-clapped-out – were parked at the rear of the house. They belonged to the staff who could be seen working in the fields. A man on a tractor was ploughing between the rows of one vineyard. In another, several men and women were pruning the vines. In a third, a couple of women were pulling the cut branches away from the wires on which the vines were trained and throwing them into a rusty metal incinerator on wheels, from which a thin plume of blueish smoke rose straight up in the still, cold air. It was a peaceful, idyllic scene of rural prosperity which – apart from the tractor and the cars – had changed little from the way the property must have looked when Céline Picard had last been there.

Ken drove up the immaculate, weed-free gravel drive, to park in front of the house. With Hallstatt beside him, he mounted the semi-circular flight of stone steps leading to the front door. Even close-to, there were few visible changes in half a century: an electric coaching lamp on either side of the front door, the bell-box of an intruder alarm system fixed under the eaves, a cluster of television and radio aerials clamped to one chimney.

Hallstatt pressed the bell. A housekeeper appeared and asked who wanted to see her employer. Madame Picard, they learned, was not in good health and rarely saw casual visitors. If *ces messieurs* wanted to buy some wine, they should ask at the office in the yard . . . Obeying Ken's instruction, Hallstatt replied they were old friends of Madame Picard. On holiday in the area, they wanted to pay her a surprise visit.

While they were being kept waiting, Ken looked around the entrance hall and the reception rooms. Yvonne Picard had taken great pains to replace all the original furniture with similar pieces; her father would have approved. A large portrait in oils of him holding a glass of wine in his right hand was given pride of place on the chimney-breast above the open fire of oak logs. The walls were covered with rows of framed certificates and diplomas awarded to Madame Yvonne Picard of Chateau

Magnus at wine fairs all over the world. As in the Press books down at the sales office, there was no picture anywhere of her sister.

The tall, thin woman who walked in after keeping them waiting for ten minutes was leaning heavily on a walking-stick. Years of heavy toil in the vines had taken their toll on Yvonne Picard's joints, and arthritis made any exercise painful for her.

'I was told there were two old friends to see me,' she said, peering over a pair of half-moon reading glasses at Hallstatt. 'Have we met before?'

'I'm afraid not,' said Ken. 'You were away when I called last week. I wanted to ask you some questions about your sister, Céline Picard.'

'Who are you?'

'We're friends of hers.'

'You're making a mistake.' Yvonne looked at Hallstatt, standing in the background. 'Him, maybe, but you can't possibly be. You're far too young. Céline died in the war.'

'How did she die?' Hallstatt asked.

'There was a fire at the family's seaside house. Her body was found in the ruins.'

Ken shook his head. 'This is going to come as a surprise to you, Madame Picard. Your sister is alive and well.' He held up the picture of the shaven woman tied below the hanged man, indicating the figure in the bottom right of frame. 'Thanks to this man, Céline Picard wasn't lynched with her lover at Melles-sur-Mer. She was rescued by Sergeant Geoffrey Prescot, who got her to Paris, married her and took her to live in Britain as his bride.'

'This is a fantasy.' Madame Picard looked outwardly calm as she seated herself on one of the elegant Second-Empire chairs. 'It's a case of mistaken identity, surely.'

Ken exchanged a look with Hallstatt. He had expected a stronger reaction, or none at all – anything but this measured curiosity.

He pulled up another chair and put his briefcase on the polished table, taking out the photographs of Mrs Prescot that had so impressed Madame Lafont in Paris and laying them, one by one, on the polished surface. 'This is your sister on her wedding day in Liverpool. You can see the likeness? Here she is a year later . . .' He ended with a picture of Mrs Prescot that had been taken within the last six months. It showed her in the courtyard of Buckingham Palace, standing beside Irving who was holding the OBE, with which he had just been honoured by the Queen. 'And this is how she looks today.'

'Why now?' The question was almost inaudible.

'I beg your pardon?'

Yvonne Picard was running her fingertips over the photographs on the table, as though they had texture. 'Why did she send you now?' she asked wonderingly. 'After all these years?'

'She's very ill,' said Ken. His lie seemed to be working. 'She wants to sort out everything – a kind of stocktaking, you know. Particularly, she wants to know what happened to the paintings.'

Yvonne Picard's eyes flitted from his face to Hallstatt's.

'She took one with her,' Ken continued. 'It was a little picture by Mary Cassatt. The rest were left behind. And she'd like to know where they are now.'

He felt Hallstatt's hand on his shoulder. 'Go take a walk *fiston*. This is my scene.'

When he was alone with Yvonne, Hallstatt began, 'If it makes it any easier, Madame, we know all about your visit to Delmas, the barber at Melles-sur-Mer.'

There was a long pause before Yvonne said, 'I haven't been to confession since April of 1945, you know.'

Just as quietly, Hallstatt said, 'We all did terrible things in those times.'

'You?' she said sharply. 'What does an American know of *those times*?'

'Plenty,' he said. 'I was in France then. I didn't betray a sister but I caused the deaths of my comrades by my own cowardice. I guess only St Peter could weigh your sin and mine, and tell us which was worse.'

The story came out in disjointed sentences. The daylight was going, but Yvonne did not put on the lights. It was easier to talk in the confessional gloom; her father's portrait on the wall took on something of the aura of a picture of Jesus with right hand raised in blessing, and Hallstatt's quiet empathy was not unlike that of a priest who had heard everything before.

'Perhaps,' Yvonne wondered aloud, 'I had always been intending to betray Céline. I remember thinking outside the barber shop that, by keeping me waiting, God was giving me a chance to think again. But what kept running through my head was a phrase of my father's. So often in my childhood he had said, "I am disappointed in you, Yvonne." However hard I tried to please him, I could never do anything right, while Céline was a paragon of virtue.'

Hallstatt sensed that the woman sitting across the table from him in the darkened room wanted to talk about many things, given the right cue. With an angler's patience, he let her run, and then reeled her in, sentence by sentence. 'We have to know what happened to them after Dietrich was hanged and Céline disappeared in the chaos of the Liberation. I took a look around the chateau and the farm buildings this afternoon. The whole place is extremely well-appointed and obviously well-run, but there's no evidence of wealth over and above what comes from being one of the top *appellations* in St Emilion. It doesn't look to me as though you sold the paintings. What did happen to them, Madame Picard?'

'Sepp sold them.'

'And what happened to the money?'

A long-case clock was ticking by the fireplace and the logs were settling into the embers. Yvonne closed her eyes. There was something hypnotic about this quiet American, who seemed content to listen to her for ever.

Hallstatt was one of the few people in the world to understand the story she told him. She had bought some false papers on the black market in Bordeaux for her lover. There was a thriving trade at the time in new identities for former collaborators – and Sepp's French, although accented, was good enough for him to pass as an Alsatian. After the Liberation, he travelled all over the south-west of France, posing as a *mutilé de guerre* from Strasbourg. In this guise, he visited all the POW camps where men from the SS Regiment Das Reich were locked up, taking food for them, carrying messages and posting letters. Conditions in the camps were appalling and the men were dying like flies.

Another man might have thought that Yvonne was making the whole thing up, but Hallstatt was aware that four million German POWs in the French and American zones of occupation at the end of the European war – who were theoretically entitled under the Geneva Convention to the same rations as base area soldiers in the victorious Allied armies – were kept for months after surrendering in wire enclosures without shelter from the elements, deliberately starved and even denied water in certain camps.

Although sugar, meat and some fats were certainly in short supply in Europe, as far as the Western world as a whole was concerned, the war effort had increased wheat production in North America significantly – more than offsetting the acreage lost due to the ravages of war. The prisoners' rations were, however, as low as one twentieth of what was being issued to Allied soldiers – and far below even what the undernourished German civilians were subsisting on.

The situation was made legally possible by a stroke of administrative sleight of hand by the US Provost Marshal's department, in which one and a half million POWs were transferred to the status of DEF, meaning *defeated enemy forces*. By the juggling of six letters, these men no longer had any entitlement to anything, for the invented term DEF had not figured in the Geneva Convention.

The prisoners were denied tools with which to build shelters for the coming winter, or even to dig latrines. Bare hands were used to burrow into the infected earth of the cages, where a cut brought death from tetanus or septicaemia to men already weak from starvation. That winter, only the sickest were even given sheets of cardboard to cover their sleeping holes. They died of typhoid fever, pneumonia and just about every scourge that follows in the wake of severe malnutrition. The International Committee of the Red Cross was denied access to the camps. When Canadian Prime Minister Mackenzie King had the courage to protest about the barbarous treatment, pressure from both Churchill and Eisenhower forced him to desist.

General de Gaulle asked the Americans for three-quarters of a million German prisoners as reparations labour to clean up war damage in France. Six hundred and forty thousand men were handed over, enfeebled by starvation and exposure. A quarter of a million died before the year was out. Though of men in their prime years, the corpses weighed on average less than fifty kilos when committed to the earth. The lucky few survivors were used as slave labour. Working outside the camps enabled them to beg, borrow or steal food and clothing for themselves and their comrades. The majority of the German prisoners never saw the outside of the barbed wire that surrounded their camps. As marker stones in German military cemeteries all over France still testify, they continued dying throughout 1946 and 1947, even as late as 1948. And one man – Sepp Müller, the unlikely Scarlet Pimpernel – had been outside the wire, trying to do something about it . . .

'He would have done anything to help those men,' Yvonne finished. 'So when this Englishman showed up out of the blue and offered to buy the pictures at – I think it was £1000 each – Sepp agreed. He told me that the money would enable him to save many thousands of men's lives.'

'Hold on,' said Hallstatt. 'What Englishman are we talking about?'

Yvonne opened her eyes. By now the room was virtually dark. 'A major.'

'What was he doing here?'

'Looking for the pictures. He knew they were here.'

'How had he traced them to Chateau Magnus?'

'We never knew. He just arrived with two jeeploads of British military police.'

'When was this, Madame Picard?'

She had to think for a moment. 'We had just completed the *écoulage* – siphoning the wine off from all the *marc* – so it would have been just after the middle of November 1946.'

'D'you recall the major's name?'

'I remember that it sounded German. I thought at the time

how strange it was for an English officer to have a German name. But, of course, lots of French generals have had German names and vice versa.'

'Did you see him, face to face?'

'Once.'

'What kind of man was he?'

'Tall, thin-faced, arrogant and sly. I warned Sepp not to trust him. I had known Englishmen like that – clients of Papa's before the war with grand names who ordered wine and never paid for it.'

'But Sepp did trust him?'

'They were both the same kind of man, if you see what I mean. I suppose that was why.'

Hallstatt was working out why a British army major would have offered a German soldier on the run even the derisory price of £1000 per painting in 1946. Having tracked the paintings to Chateau Magnus, he could simply have sequestered them – if all had been above board. The fact that he offered money proved that the major was not acting for the legitimate authorities, nor for the legal owners of the pictures.

'And did they do the deal?' he asked.

'I don't know exactly what happened. One day I was away in Bordeaux on business. Afterwards I wondered whether Sepp had sent me on that errand deliberately, to get me out of the way. When I returned, the *domestiques* told me that the English officer had been here again – this time with a truck and some armed soldiers in British uniforms. I hurried down to where the pictures had been hidden, to find them all gone.'

'And Sepp?'

'Gone with them.'

'Did he come back?'

She shook her head. 'He left a letter for me.'

'Have you still got it?'

'It's in the drawer of the night-table by my bed.'

'I'd like to read it, if I may,' Hallstatt said gently. 'This could be rather important.'

He followed Yvonne along the red-carpeted corridors and up a flight of marble steps to her bedroom, where she opened a drawer and took out a faded First Communion prayer-book, a posy of dried-up spring flowers, some ribbons and old photographs. Beneath, there was a false bottom. In the slim cavity below lay an Iron Cross with oak-leaf clusters, a silver SS tank combat badge – and the letter.

Hallstatt unfolded the yellowed sheet of paper carefully and read it in the light of the bedside lamp.

Dearest Yvonne,

I wish things could have been different between us, but I am the way I am and there is nothing to be done about that. Perhaps it is some consolation to know that if I had been able to love a woman, or anyone exclusively, it would have been you. You have all the qualities I admire, but admiration is not love. Not even the alchemists could change one into the other.

You were right about Major Arthur Brandt. The tricky swine was supposed to bring the cash with him today. Now he says there was some delay in its transmission from London, because it's hard to move so much money in these times, with all the regulations. So I have to go with him, to collect it from a bank on the way. With four armed men to back him up, there's nothing I can do except go along with the change of plan. I have my Luger and can look after myself. My men are dying and I am the only one who can save them, so I have to grab the one chance there is of getting some money, or kiss their arses all goodbye. One thing is certain: if I survive, I'll be back here sooner or later and we can see how things work out.

Look after yourself. Sepp.

.3.

In south-west France, the vendange of 1996 had brought too much wine, of very variable quality – thanks to the rainy summer. Much of the surplus had been trucked immediately to local distilleries, there to be converted into industrial alcohol. The new modern *chais* of Chateau Magnus were lined with shiny stainless-steel fermentation and storage vats, each full to the top. The place was more like a factory than the picturesque scenes of peasants treading grapes, on which tourism thrives.

After leaving Hallstatt to confess Yvonne Picard, Ken sauntered through the buildings, greeting the workers as though he had every right to be there. In the maturing *chai*, long lines of oak barrels, their tops daubed with the colour called *lie de vin*, stood in precise rows, stretching away into the shadows. It was a sight to impress wine buffs from all over the world. But what Ken was looking for was not here. He was fairly certain that Céline and Dietrich could not have risked hiding above ground for ten whole months. In St Emilion, 'going underground' meant exactly that. The town itself and most of the outlying chateaux were built of local stone quarried from beneath the vineyards and the buildings, to leave vast caves where the constant temperature and humidity made the best storage conditions possible for wine until the advent of modern air-conditioning systems.

The daylight was already going when he found the walled-up cave beneath the chateau. The front part had become a dump for the rubbish that collects on farms – of which fertiliser sacks, obsolete machinery and old clothes and boots were the most obvious. Picking his way through the rusted metal and junk, Ken discovered a padlocked man-height metal door in the stone wall, which looked as though it had not been opened for ages. He used a rusting piece of iron from some old farm machine to prise the hasp out of the wall, and walked inside.

The air was stale but dry, and the cave was far more spacious than he had suspected: there was enough room for several families to hide there for months on end. Because the feeble light entering through the door was insufficient to do more than throw a faint glow on the cluttered floor near the entrance, he returned to the Land Cruiser to fetch a torch. Through the glass front doors of the house he could see the shadowy silhouettes of Hallstatt and Yvonne Picard in the front reception room. They looked as though they had not moved since he left them.

In the cave, the powerful beam of the torch illuminated piles of rubbish, the largest of which was a small mountain of dusty old bottles – the last remnants of Yvonne's carefully amassed stock, built up during the Occupation, and left there when new ones were available. In another corner, ancient oak barrels, some damaged and some intact, were stacked up, three and four high.

There were small niches carved into the walls at head height for candles and much larger ones lower down for sleeping in. The people who had excavated the stone and carved them must have been short; Ken tried one for size and had to bend his knees and twist his neck, in order to fit inside. The bottom ledge had a stone lip, to retain a layer of hay or straw bedding. Presumably, labourers or house staff had lived in the cave after the stone had been quarried from it.

Against the wall furthest from the entrance stood a roughly-fashioned sleeping platform, large enough for two people side by side. Another single platform stood not far away. And behind them . . .

'Bingo!' Ken shone the light on a stack of picture frames. Broken, dusty and worm-eaten, they were the sort one sees in museums: heavily carved and gilded. He shone the torch back to the two crude beds. One piece of wood on the smaller one bore stencilled markings in Gothic script. Bringing the light close, he could decipher the words *Eigentum der Luftwaffe* and *Öffnen strengstens verboten.*

Putting the torch down on the floor, Ken picked up an old barrel stave from the floor, and battered at the beds until they disintegrated in a cloud of dust and dried rat-droppings, to lie in termite-eaten fragments on the ground. Sneezing the dust from his nostrils, he turned over a sheet of plywood, and found pasted to the back the yellowed remains of a French railway consignment note dated 6 June 1944. The consignee's name was written by hand in faded ink: Hans Wendland, c/o the Lavranchy forwarding agents in Lausanne, Switzerland.

Ken switched off the torch. The darkness gave him the illusion that the weight of the rock over his head was pressing down and down. After ten months in this oppressive place, Céline must have felt relieved to be going to the villa in April 1945. And Leutnant Bohlen? What would have been on his mind, when the two of them left here? To have achieved what he had, he must have been a brave and resourceful man, aware that he might not make it safely home. Surely he would have left some kind of message or sign?

Ken played the torch slowly around the vertical walls, chiselled in the native rock. Above the bed-alcoves were small recesses at head height, in some of which old candle stubs could still be seen. But one was much higher than the others: a good four metres from the floor of the cave. Had the dwarfs who carved those short sleeping niches climbed on each other's shoulders every time they wanted to put a new candle in it?

The Disneyesque image was intriguing. But so was the niche. It was shallower than the others and smaller – also less well-carved. It could have been a sand martin's nest before the wall had been built across the cave.

The staff appeared all to have gone home. Ken scouted around the *chais* until he found a light aluminium ladder leaning against a vat. He carried it into the cave, climbed up to the mystery hole, and reached inside. The packet which his groping fingers felt was wrapped in oilskin and about the size of a man's wallet. He climbed down and carefully unwrapped the oilskin.

The first document was a German army paybook in the name of Dietrich Bohlen. The face in the ID photograph was clean-cut, almost noble, Ken thought. Bohlen did not look like a candidate for lynching.

Next came twenty or more sheets of closely-written manuscript, which began: *An alle die es angeht.* To whom it may concern . . .

In the torchlight, Ken read the sloping Gothic script slowly: '*Der untergezeichnete, BOHLEN, Dietrich, bestätigt hiermit wie folgt.* I, the undersigned Dietrich Bohlen . . . hereby certify as follows . . .

There was a complete schedule of the hundred and forty-nine paintings, with a description of each, its attribution, size, condition and legal ownership. Degas, Monet, Renoir, Toulouse-Lautrec, Cézanne . . . The list would have made a core collection for a respectable museum of Impressionist art in any capital city of the world. No. 149 was listed as: *At the Auberge du Soleil, 49 cm x 34 cm, oil on canvas, painted by the American artist Mary Cassatt circa 1879. Removed from Musée Marmotan, Paris, by ERR on (date unknown).*

In a footnote, the writer, Leutnant Dietrich Bohlen, confessed that, on 10 June 1944 in the city of Lyon, he had given ten of the listed works of art – including a Renoir, a Toulouse-Lautrec, and a Sisley – to Obersturmführer Klaus Barbie in exchange for the release of Mademoiselle Céline Picard.

The accompanying letter declared that the paintings had been stockpiled by Goering at the Jeu de Paume Museum in Paris for exchange by Swiss dealers against pictures by German, Flemish and Italian Old Masters, which were considered more desirable in the Third Reich. Shipped to Lyon when the first news of the Allied invasion came in, they had been in a Luftwaffe storage area, waiting to be loaded on a train to Lausanne, when removed by the undersigned Leutnant Bohlen, Dietrich, acting on behalf of the Kunstschutz.

The finder of the document was begged to communicate his discovery immediately to the US Monuments Commission, or any other Allied military unit. Both the list and the letter were signed *Bohlen, Dietrich, Leutnant im Dienst des Kunstschutzes* and dated 17 April 1945. The signatures had been witnessed by Céline Picard.

Ken refolded both schedule and letter, placing them and the paybook back in their original wrappings. Taking a pace backwards, he instinctively saluted the memory of the man who had thought of everything except his own safety. One hundred and forty-nine less ten, less one, made one hundred and thirty-eight of the most valuable paintings in the world – gone missing. At last Ken knew why Mrs Prescot had been murdered. The next question was: by whom?

Forty feet above his head, in Yvonne Picard's bedroom, the only sound was the rustle of paper as Hallstatt refolded the letter written by Sepp Müller. Under the pretence of replacing everything in the drawer as it had been, he slipped it into his jacket pocket.

'I never saw Sepp again, from that day to this,' said Yvonne. In the light of the bedside lamp, Hallstatt saw that her face was grey. She sat down abruptly on the edge of the bed, her clenched right fist pressing against her breast-bone.

'Are you okay?' he asked. 'Can I get you something?'

'I have some pills,' she gasped. 'The housekeeper knows where they are. And a glass of water, please.'

. 4 .

Within thirty minutes of reaching home, Hallstatt had snatched a quick meal and was hard at work. There were few libraries or archives in the world where he was as likely to find what he needed as in his own house. The first job was to track down Hans Wendland in Lausanne, to whom the paintings had been consigned. That took only minutes. A German-born lawyer who became resident in Geneva in 1941, Wendland had moved a number of consignments of what the Nazis considered 'degenerate art' into Switzerland during the war, there to be discreetly exchanged by Swiss galleries and dealers for more acceptable works by German, Flemish and Italian Old Masters. He was known to have worked closely with a Berlin art dealer named Walter Hofer who was Goering's right-hand man in the German capital.

Hallstatt took a deep breath. That tallied with Dietrich Bohlen's account.

On to the next question: who was the mysterious Major Arthur Brandt, who had removed the paintings from Chateau Magnus in November 1946, and how had he tracked them down?

Even using side roads whenever possible on the illicit journey from Lyon to St Emilion, the truck would have had to pass through some Feldgendarmerie checkpoints, where its passage would have been logged. It was entirely possible that the visit of the Luftwaffe police to Chateau Magnus, which resulted in them finding the truck in the lake, surrounded by floating broken packing cases, was not chance at all but part of a specific search operation. Immediately upon arrival they had begun interrogating everybody on the property – and only left after news arrived of the FFI attack on the jail in Bordeaux. After which, nothing had happened until some time in the middle of November 1946. Why then?

The date was nagging at Hallstatt's memory. He had spent the autumn of '46 as aide-de-camp to his old boss Wild Bill Donovan, who himself had just been appointed special assistant to Justice Robert H. Jackson, United States chief prosecutor at the Nuremberg war crimes' trials. From the day Donovan arrived in Nuremberg, there had been a sustained battle of wills between the two men. Jackson – a trained lawyer – wanted to base the prosecution case on the incontrovertible evidence of the vast mass of captured enemy documents, carefully preserved by the Nazi bureaucracy. Donovan, on the other hand, had been secretly charged by President Truman with the staging of a more vote-catching spectacle, which could be exploited by the nascent media of the day: the print and radio reporters, the newspaper photographers and newsreel cameramen. A feature of this plan was to use big close-ups of harrowing personal testimony from witnesses who had suffered from the Nazis' political, military and economic decisions, with the impassioned victims confronting the men in the dock responsible for their suffering.

Wanting to please Truman, Donovan had gone behind Jackson's back and set out to persuade the charismatic Hermann Goering to go through the motions of defending himself, instead of refusing to plead and ignoring the court, as most of the other accused had decided to do. With Hitler and Goebbels both dead in the bunker and Himmler having committed suicide after his chance capture by the British, Goering was the biggest fish still in the net. Hitler's former deputy was to be the star of the show.

Hallstatt recalled the scene in the former Reichsmarschal's cell before the trial opened, when he had accompanied Donovan to make an offer to Goering which he would not refuse. Having lost a third of his body weight and been weaned of his addiction to 150 paracodeine tablets a day, Goering's brain was working well.

'Colonel Donovan,' he smiled. 'What you are in effect asking me to do is to be your chief witness *against* Adolf Hitler. If I agree, what's in it for me?'

'A soldier's death.'

Donovan promised that, if Goering put up a good show, he was empowered by Truman personally to arrange the ex-Reichsmarschal's death by firing squad with full military honours, instead of the hangman's noose which was the fate planned for the other accused.

To Hallstatt's surprise, Hitler's extrovert deputy agreed enthusiastically, despite knowing already what the outcome of the trial was to be. So important to him was his public image that he was prepared to go through a totally pointless pantomime of defending the indefensible excesses of the Third Reich – for the benefit of a posse of cameramen and reporters – in return for being granted the privilege of dying the so-called 'soldier's death'.

Unfortunately for the ex-Reichsmarschal, by the time the trials ended in October 1946, Donovan had long since fallen out irrevocably with Jackson and departed from Nuremberg for good. Having fulfilled his side of the bargain, Goering was appalled by the realisation that the promised honourable execution was to be denied him – and that he would die by hanging, like all the others. Yet, around midnight on 11 November 1946, within two hours of the time secretly set for his execution – and of which he was not supposed to know – he cheated the noose by committing suicide with a cyanide capsule which had been smuggled into his cell by a person or persons unknown.

As Hallstatt leafed through the report of the subsequent enquiry, he thought – not for the first time – how extraordinarily slipshod, or else deliberately misleading, it was. The report concluded that a letter found in the dead man's hand, claiming that he had had the poison with him all along, proved that no one was to blame.

At the time, Hallstatt had thought that writing such a letter was a strange way for Goering to occupy his last hours, particularly since he detested Colonel Andrus, the American commandant of the prison, whom the letter appeared to exonerate from any charge of lax security. Fifty years on, Hallstatt was left wondering whether the letter had been intended to exonerate someone else who had smuggled the poison into the cell and insisted on this kind of exculpation. He made a hot drink for himself and settled down to some more serious reading, working his way through one book after another from his shelves.

Within an hour he found what he was looking for. It was a list of persons who had had access to Goering in the week before his death, which had been published as an appendix to the report of the original three-man investigating Board of Officers, appointed by General Eisenhower on the day after the suicide.

The log showed that on 10 November – just thirty hours before Goering swallowed the capsule – a British officer by the name of Major Anstruther Bennett, had had a private conversation with the former Reichsmarschal in his cell. Major Bennett's unit was shown in the record as 'attached SHAEF'.

Being attached to Supreme Headquarters, Allied Expeditionary Force, could mean anything. But was it coincidence that the rank and initials of the officer who had visited Goering were the same as those of the mysterious major who had appeared at Chateau Magnus a few days later?

Hallstatt fell asleep, the report still in his hand. He awoke with his brain sharp after two hours' sleep, to start hunting anew through his library, on the track of another mysterious British major who had appeared briefly above the intelligence horizon in the US zone of occupied Germany in the early summer of 1945. The incident had occurred at Schloss Kronberg, near Frankfurt, the seat of an aristocratic family descended from Queen Victoria, whose temporary head was Countess Margaret of Hesse. At the time, the castle was being used as an American army club.

This British major had tracked Countess Margaret down to a farm labourer's cottage where she was living near the castle, and persuaded her to write a letter to the American colonel running the club, instructing him to release to the bearer several boxes of family papers which were stored in the attic. Rightly unimpressed, the colonel refused to release, in his own words, '. . . so much as a single sheet of toilet tissue'. However, while he was telephoning for instructions, the British major and an aide made their way upstairs and illicitly removed the papers, as well as Queen Charlotte's crown, family jewellery and other items.

Safely back in Britain, the major was rewarded with his sovereign's gratitude – ostensibly for having brought back the correspondence from Queen Victoria to her eldest daughter, wife of Frederick of Prussia, and more recent letters from members of the House of Windsor, including Queen Mary, the Queen Mother, to their close German relatives. Their recovery had saved King George VI the potential embarrassment of seeing the warm and friendly letters published so soon after the war in American newspapers, which were unfettered by the British Official Secrets Act.

Or so the published wisdom went . . .

But Hallstatt knew that there had been more to it than that. The true aim of the undercover mission had been to remove from Schloss Kronberg and possible discovery by the Americans, the private diaries of Prince Philip of Hesse who had acted as intermediary between Hitler and the Duke of Windsor, the King's own brother, during the '30s – plus the secret correspondence that had passed between them. If published, these papers would have been infinitely more embarrassing for the British Royal Family, since they revealed that the former King Edward VIII and his consort, the American divorcee Wallis Simpson, had been prepared to act as puppet king and queen of the United Kingdom after a successful German invasion of the British Isles.

What Hallstatt was looking for now, was the false name used by the British major who had outwitted the American colonel at Schloss Kronberg, and stolen the papers while he was on the phone.

Shortly before dawn, he found it: Ashby Blythe.

The sound of the jackpot rang in Hallstatt's ears.

In his own career, he had many times overruled the deep-rooted tendency of people involved in clandestine operations to keep their own initials when choosing false names for an under-cover operation.

Ashby Blythe's real name was Anthony Blunt; the record was clear about that. At the time of the little errand for King George VI, Blunt had been listed as a major in MI5, but he had actually been attached to SHAEF at Fontainebleau in his capacity as expert art historian – as part of Britain's contribution to the recovery of looted art treasures after the war. Wearing another hat, he had also been a member of the Royal Household, by virtue of his recent appointment as Surveyor of the King's Pictures.

In the circumstances, it seemed more than a reasonable prob-ability that Ashby Blythe, Arthur Brandt and Anstruther Bennett were one and the same man, which meant that the major who had taken Goering's pictures from Chateau Magnus in November 1946 was none other than Anthony Blunt, traitor and Knight of the Realm who retained his post in the Royal Household for fifteen years after his confession in April 1964 to having been a Soviet spy during and after his service with MI5. At the time of Mrs Thatcher's forced revelation of his treachery to the House of Commons in November 1979, one or two cyn-ical people had wondered why the Queen had continued to protect and employ Blunt for so long after being advised of his treachery in 1964. The insider whisper was that Blunt – whose IQ was in the genius bracket – had prepared an insurance against his own downfall by not handing over all of the mater-ial removed from Prince Philip of Hesse's castle on that secret mission in 1945.

Which hat had Blunt been wearing during his two-hour long discussion with Goering? Hallstatt wondered. By that time, MI5 had no legitimate interest in the ex-Reichsmarschal, even if Blunt had used his security clearance to gain access to the death cell. His background, his official function with SHAEF at the time, as well as his post in the Royal Household, all indicated that the subject most likely to have been discussed in the death cell was the whereabouts of Goering's untraced loot.

After the accumulated treasures had been shipped elsewhere, Goering's palace at Carinhall had been dynamited by the Luftwaffe to prevent the advancing Red Army from capturing it. Most of that loot had been traced and was accounted for in Germany. But supposing – and it was a reasonable supposition – that the Luftwaffe police who had searched Chateau Magnus had reported back to their master that they had found the truck which Dietrich had hijacked? The Reichsmarschal would have had more pressing problems to deal with in June 1944, but the knowledge of the missing pictures' probable whereabouts could well have been filed away in his wily brain as a trump card to be played at the very end of the game.

Was that the knowledge which Goering had traded with Blunt in the death cell, receiving in exchange a filed-down cartridge case containing enough cyanide to kill ten men?

To get his hands on a hundred and thirty-eight of the most valuable paintings in the world, Blunt must have killed, or had killed, Sepp Müller – the only witness to what he was up to. Had the four British soldiers who had been with him also met an untimely end, or had they been unaware of what was going on? How many other people had died because of the pictures?

It was far from what a trial judge would call proof, but intelligence work required very different thinking. Off the top of his head, Hallstatt could think of a dozen covert operations that had been mounted – at a cost of many millions of dollars spent and scores of lives lost – on far less convincing evidence than what Ken and he had dug up between them.

And what had happened to the paintings since 1946? If Sir Anthony Blunt had disposed of them and they were scattered far and wide at the time of his death, there would have been no reason for Sir Terence Savage or anyone else to arrange a fake accident for Irving's teacher when she surfaced out of the blue with her Mary Cassatt . . . which made it highly probable that the collection was still more or less intact . . . which in turn explained why someone was prepared to offer Irving a violin worth £5 million in exchange for a painting worth less than a tenth as much. What would a hundred and thirty-eight Impressionist paintings be worth in the inflated market of today? A billion dollars? Hallstatt had no informed idea, but the answer was obvious: more than enough to make it worth Savage's while to rub out a little old lady whose memories could lead to the exposure of the biggest single art heist of the century.

Hallstatt sat back, yawned and stretched. Through the windows he saw the dawn tingeing the low clouds with red edges. There was a noise of cackling outside. Nature's burglar alarm – his flock of geese – were announcing the arrival of a car. Hallstatt went to the door. There was a car at the end of the track leading to his house. At that distance he could not discern the make or model, but it looked as though two men were sitting in the front seats.

. 5 .

Before leaving Le Farou to head home for the night, Hallstatt had had the natural courtesy to call Chateau Magnus and enquire how Yvonne Picard was feeling.

A male French voice had answered and said that she was not available. Who was calling? A friend who had been with her that afternoon, said Hallstatt. Another man's voice came on the line. Would Monsieur like to leave a number where he could be reached? Hallstatt rang off. During the two hours he had spent in the house, he had seen only three or four female staff and the two men on the line did not sound like doctors or nurses.

Long unused reflexes were fine-tuning his hearing as he listened for a moment and put down the phone. 'I think,' he said, 'the bad guys are catching up with us.'

After he had left, Ken made his preparations for the night. One of the reasons why the Land Cruiser had won over lighter and sportier four-wheel-drive vehicles, was that he could persuade the Harley, just, to fold itself into the rear after the extra seats had been removed. That done, he went through the store of useful oddities which – like most people in intelligence work – he had laid in over the years. From one cache he took passports in three different names and a well-oiled Browning 9 mm. service automatic with a full magazine, which he had claimed to have lost during an operation with Special Branch years before. He disliked firearms because of the way they concentrated the mind on violent solutions to a situation, but there were times when it would be stupid not to have one – and this was one of those times. From another hiding place, he took a set of spare number-plates for the Land Cruiser. It was cash that was going to be the problem; he had the feeling that it might be quite a while before he would want to use a credit card again.

While he was sorting out the items he might need and replacing the others in their various hiding places, the telephone rang once. In case it was Hallstatt, Ken picked it up and heard a man's voice apologising for a wrong number.

Outside, there was no sign of life. To anyone not professionally paranoid, the night was normal. To Ken, the silence, the leafless trees in the moonlight, the frosty clarity of the night sky were all whispered warnings.

Let the dog see the rabbit, he thought. That way, the rabbit would know which dog was on his trail. Yet prudent bunnies made sure there was more than one exit from their warrens, so he backed the Land Cruiser out of the garage and drove cross-country without lights to the deserted holiday home of some German neighbours, where he parked it in the barn and walked home, senses all alert.

Standing in the archway of Le Farou, he strained his ears and eyes one last time. There was the sound of a distant train on the single-track railway that ran along the valley on the other side of the Dordogne. Very faintly from the direction of the village, came the sound of music. It was the night of the weekly disco in the *salle des fêtes*.

After hauling the solid oak doors closed and heaving the bars into place, Ken made himself comfortable in one of the kitchen armchairs, fully dressed and with his boots on. It was a relief that Catriona was not around, but somewhere safe and sound. Not wanting to light the kitchen fire, he had brought a duvet from his bedroom and sealed himself inside this – with the Browning, fire selector on *safe*, within reach of his right hand.

During the last week he had had only two nights' reasonable rest. Within seconds of shutting his eyes, he heard himself snore, then jerked awake as the thought occurred that he had not checked his mail. Perhaps Catriona had sent a postcard with an address . . .

He groped his way across the starlit courtyard and into the pitch darkness of the stables, where one of the arrow-slits enfilading the gateway served as a ready-made letter-box. Without putting on the light, he scooped up the pile of junk mail lying on the cobbled floor below the slit and carried it back to the kitchen, where he could sort everything out behind closed shutters.

In the pile of glossy, personalised offers from hi-fi dealers, furniture stores and supermarkets, there were only three letters: a final demand from France Telecom, a credit card statement and a folded handbill with a list of places and dates, advertising *The First-Ever Continental Tour of Slieve Gullion.* Slieve Gullion? An Irish mountain gone walkabout? It took Ken a moment to work out that the name was that of Siobhan's group. Someone had written on the back of the handbill in pencil: *A job's a job for a' that.*

The message was unsigned, but Ken recognised the handwriting as Irving's. He stuffed the handbill into his hip pocket and went to sleep, the only concession to comfort being to let out his belt a few notches.

The telephone rang again at midnight and at 2 a.m. – with no one on the line either time. The next time Ken was jolted awake, his ears were filled by the roaring of the concrete lorry. It was daylight. Had he forgotten ordering more concrete? No, Jesus, this was not sunlight pouring in the windows, but the light of flames! And the noise was the roar of burning timber, punctuated by the shattering of a thousand tiles as part of the roof gave way.

He leaped out of bed, and tried to call the fire brigade. The line was dead. Browning in hand, he threw open the kitchen window. The conflagration could not have been going on for more than a few minutes. To have got such a hold already, it must have been set by professionals. While he was taking it all in, his eye was drawn to where some kind of Molotov cocktail had just landed on the cobbles inside the archway. With a dull *whoomf!* flames spewed out of it and licked hungrily at the inside of the oak doors. He could see now that the fire had several centres. Still another fire bomb was arching over the walls. Whoever was outside had an Olympic-standard throwing arm.

Ken had never liked Satan. The antipathy was mutual, but

man had conceded to feline an honourable truce on the day when Catriona's cat had appeared inside the locked courtyard, hunting the small rodents that lived in the outhouses. By keeping the doors locked and trailing Satan to an ancient pile of faggots in a cellar below the house when it was the cat's suppertime, Ken had found the hidden entrance to the tunnel which Hallstatt had told him must be somewhere. Every dwelling of that period in and around St Martin, or so he said, had an underground bolt-hole or escape route dug by the original inhabitants, as a way of escaping the murderous onslaughts of raiding parties, during the wars of religion. St Martin being a Catholic outpost in Protestant territory, even the houses in the village had interconnecting cellars which led to the crypt of the church, where everyone took refuge in times of bloodshed.

Offering up thanks to Satan, Ken took the waterproof torch from its recharging unit by the fuse-box and made his way down to the cellar. Wanting to keep the fire-setters guessing as long as possible, he spent a couple of minutes awkwardly rearranging the bundles of vine prunings behind him before kicking open the half-rotten iron-bound oak door and scrambling into the tunnel which had been chiselled through the solid limestone. Had he known what lay ahead, he would not have bothered with this finesse.

In places the roof of the tunnel was high enough for a man to stand; in others, Ken had to bend almost double. The tunnel led downwards, roughly following the contours of the land above. Approaching the lowest point, he saw water ahead. Usually the tunnel was dry, but the recent rains had been heavy. Ken took off his anorak, rolled it up with the Browning inside, then waded into cold, muddy water which rose to his knees, his waist, to his chin. By the time it was nostril-high with his head scraping the roof and the anorak already soaked, he had to face the fact that his escape route was blocked.

When excavating the rubble from the lowest point in the tunnel, he had come across a complex of subterranean rooms and roughly cleared them out. Through one ran a subterranean water course which flowed summer and winter. According to Hallstatt, whoever had constructed the warren must have kept their animals down there in times of danger, to prevent them being driven off by raiders if left above ground. The water supply and the extra storage rooms for fodder made this *souterrain* rare but by no means unique. Some boulders must have been dislodged by the unusual flow of water and blocked the narrow outlet duct of the stream, flooding the complex. How much of it was under water, was impossible to say.

Abandoning the anorak, Ken buttoned the Browning inside his shirt, gripped the torch in his mouth and dived. The beam of light lit up the walls and roof of the flooded tunnel for a few metres ahead but water was pouring into his mouth, so he turned and re-surfaced, coughing water out of his lungs and swearing at himself. The cold was already eating into his muscles. A few feet above his head, the titanium and neoprene wet suit hung uselessly on a hook in the kitchen.

The only thing to do, was hand-hold the torch – which was going to complicate swimming. Ken took several deep breaths, expelling as much carbon dioxide as possible from his lungs each time, then snatched a final not-too-deep breath and dived again. The beam of light lit up the low roof of the tunnel. With only one hand free for swimming, it was impossible to keep his head from scraping against it. Counting the seconds since his last breath, he fended himself away and swam on.

It was impossible to orientate himself. Under water, every room looked the same: a succession of chisel-marks on the walls, niches in which candles had been stood, and the occasional crudely-carved religious image.

Ken swam through one room, then a second and a third. He had never bothered to memorise the layout, but surely he had never walked through four rooms in order to pick up the tunnel on the other side? His muscles were screaming for oxygen and it was hard to think straight. There was a pulse hammering in his brain. It was tempting to execute a 180-degree panic turn, but he had nowhere near enough air left to make it back to the dry part of the tunnel, so he followed the wall on his left.

From the training he had put himself through when he took up surfing, he knew that he could swim underwater for ninety seconds maximum. But these were a long way from optimum conditions. If the choice was wrong, he would run out of air in fifteen seconds at most.

Eighty-five, eighty-six . . . On the count of ninety-five he saw the small pool of light on the stone roof ahead of him change to the reflection of the beam on the underside of an unbroken surface. His head came free and his lungs gulped air. Coughing and spluttering, he crouched beneath the low roof in ten inches of air space and peered ahead, to find that he was not in the tunnel, but in one room of the complex whose roof happened to be slightly higher than the others. He had been saved by a pocket of air, trapped there as the water level rose. There was nothing for it but to rest a few minutes, inhale as much oxygen as possible, and try again.

The longer he rested, the better for his lungs but the greater the chance of the cold bringing an attack of cramp, which would be fatal. Ken rubbed his arm muscles, unable to get any warmth into them. He tried drawing a mental map of the warren. He had swum through seven rooms, so he must have inadvertently chosen the wrong direction at the start of the complex. Since he had hugged the right-hand wall on the way in, all he had to do was keep right on the return journey and he would find the way out.

The theory sounded fine, but on this dive the water felt colder than ever, the ubiquitous chisel-marks on the walls and roof mocking him with their uselessness as points of reference. He could feel himself swimming more and more slowly as the oxygen ran out and the cold attacked his muscles more and more deeply. After eighty-one seconds underwater, the swimmer's deadliest enemy chose its moment to strike. Cramp hooked itself inside the muscles of his right thigh, locking the knee in a full bend.

Ken dropped the torch and tried with both hands to knead the spasmed muscles, which were hard as iron. An involuntary grin of pain forced his lips apart. Bubbles of air escaped through them and water started pouring in. As he rolled over, trying to fend himself away from the roof, the beam of the torch – which was falling gently to the floor – hit a crudely-carved figure of Christ on the wall, with one hand raised in blessing. It was like a miracle. Ken knew where he was. He gave up trying to swim and clawed his way along the roof, somehow hauled himself under a stone lintel and emerged in the tunnel, where he surfaced, thrashing the water in agony from the spasmed muscles but gulping air, delicious air, into his lungs.

The leg was like an alien creature, refusing to obey his brain. Even now, it tried to drag him down. He went under and seemed to fall a long time before his rump hit the floor and he could get enough leverage to propel himself to the surface a second time. In total darkness, he splashed and thrashed his way into shallower water until at last he could sit half in and half out of the water, massaging his leg until it allowed him to stand. Groping his way by touch alone, he limped onwards and emerged from the tunnel in the old cart shed behind Catriona's cottage, which she used as a junk store. Shivering in the night air, he crouched there, listening to the roar of the fire and trying to persuade his leg muscles to do their job.

In front of the cottage were parked three cars. Inside one of them, a couple of men with their backs to Ken were listening to a VHF radio tuned to the local fire service frequency. Beyond the car, Ken could see several figures – one carrying what looked like a FAMAS assault rifle – silhouetted against the flames. One of the men in the car was using a walkie-talkie radio to communicate with the men staking out the blazing farm. Bent double to avoid suddenly appearing in a car mirror, Ken sneaked closer, and heard him talking in a South African accent. A flash of light as part of the roof caved in and flames shot skywards revealed the face of Sir Terence Savage's driver.

It seemed that the whole of Le Farou was burning, with flames leaping fifty or sixty feet into the night air. Ken's entire life savings were going up in smoke: no French insurance company would pay out for a fire that had so obviously been started deliberately.

He had vowed on leaving MI5 that he would never again let his temper get the better of him. So much, he thought bitterly, for good intentions. The Browning was still safe inside his shirt. He took it out, and thought, to hell with the consequences. But halfway to the car, he stopped. It was just possible that he could kill all the armed men, if he took them by surprise one at a time, but where would that lead, except to the possibility of a long spell in prison? And, on his own, there was no chance of capturing one of them and making him talk.

The intelligent thing – however hard it was to do – was to walk away while he still could. Reluctantly, Ken moved the fire selector to *safe* and walked carefully backwards until he had the cottage between him and the men in the car. The others were no threat, he decided, because they must be night-blind from staring at the flames.

He loped unsteadily across the fields in the direction of the Germans' house, and there spent a couple of minutes changing into dry clothes. The number-plates on the Land Cruiser had belonged to a Dutch-registered beach buggy that had been totalled as a result of being driven at a hundred and fifty kilometres an hour down the largest sand-dune in Europe by a very stoned friend of the Flying Dutchman. The Harley was concealed from casual view in the rear of the Land Cruiser, beneath what looked like a load of camping gear. The driving licence and passport in Ken's pocket were in another name. With the Browning Velcroed securely behind the dashboard, he headed cross-country, following farm tracks to join the main road miles away from the village, just after two fire engines had roared past.

The contours of the dark landscape hid the buildings at Le Farou from sight. A last look back showed only the tips of the flames visible above the dark horizon, making it look like the rim of a volcano in eruption.

.6.

As Hallstatt recognised Ken's car, he called, 'Boy, have I got news for you!' He was so full of what he had learned during the night that he failed for a moment to see Ken's white and strained face.

'Now take it easy,' he cautioned, when Ken had finished telling him about the fire. 'If I've learned one thing in a long life it's to start a bad day with a full stomach. For the next thirty minutes, I'm in charge. I'm ordering you to get shaved and have a long hot shower, while I pack an overnight bag and rustle up the biggest English breakfast you've eaten in years.'

Over a gargantuan fry-up of bacon and sausage and eggs and steak, washed down with mugs of hot strong coffee, Ken digested Hallstatt's research. At last, the puzzle was complete, except for three things. One was the connection between Blunt and Sir Terence Savage. The second was why Mrs Prescot had concealed her true identity during all those years in Britain. And the third? He could not recall. His brain was in a skid.

'My guess is, she didn't know who the hell she was,' Hallstatt said. 'After a trauma like what had happened to her, it's a thousand to one that the poor woman lost her memory. Maybe that's why the Intelligence sergeant took such good care of her. There doesn't have to be anything more sinister in it than that.'

'And the body found in the ruins at the Villa Céleste?'

'Who knows? A looter, maybe. At a guess, Céline took Prescot back to the villa to collect the painting that meant so much to her for some reason. Maybe her memory didn't go until afterwards. Or maybe the picture was the only thing she did remember, without even knowing why it was important. Amnesia's a weird and unpredictable thing. I ought to know: I spent an hour during the night reading it up. We'll never know whether Céline set fire to the house, or whether it was burned down by the woman whose body was found. And it doesn't actually matter – except academically. The important thing is that we do know who set fire to your place.'

'What are you doing, Erich?'

Hallstatt was lying on the kitchen floor, reaching beneath the heavy carved oak dresser for something that was clipped to the underside.

'What does it look like?' He scrambled to his feet. 'I'm checking the action.'

'Is that a Walther?'

'Uh-huh. The TPH model – made under licence by my friends at Interarms in Alexandria, Virginia.' Hallstatt held the automatic two-handed and sighted down the barrel at a rabbit sitting on the lawn outside. 'This little toy was a present from an old hunting buddy who came to stay a while back and thought I was rather vulnerable, a guy with my background, living here all alone. It's a good choice: only six rounds in the magazine, but the short barrel – 57 mm. as against 83 mm. for the PPK model – makes it easy to carry around in your pocket. On a man of my age a shoulder holster looks ridiculous, don't you think, Ken?'

Outwardly everything appeared normal at Chateau Magnus. The only difference from the previous day was that – since it was Sunday – there were no figures working in the vines and no staff cars parked around the *chais*. Even so, Ken felt uneasily exposed as he drove the Harley slowly through the entrance gates.

Not a soul moved in the neatly-ordered rows of leafless vines that stretched away in all directions to the horizon, hidden here and there by sporadic pockets of cold, clinging ground fog. The only colour in the otherwise monochrome brown-grey landscape were the few late-blooming roses – the traditional early warning system for mildew attacks on the vines – that clung to the bushes planted at the end of each row. Catching Hallstatt's eye as he clung to the grab-handle behind the pillion seat, they brought to mind one of the simplest yet most enduring images of death and grief: *In Flanders fields the poppies grow/between the crosses, row on row.*

Up the drive with the throttle almost closed: a nearly silent approach. Ken parked the Harley in front of the large glass entrance doors. Fast in, faster out, was his plan. Leaving Hallstatt to guard the bike while he was inside, he shouldered open the unlocked front door and walked straight into the house without removing his gloves or helmet. He moved quietly but quickly up the stairs and along the red-carpeted landing to the main bedroom, counting the seconds since switching off the engine of the Harley.

Yvonne Picard was lying in bed with a transparent plastic oxygen mask over her nose and mouth. Hallstatt had been right about the heart attack. Her face looked grey and corpse-like. There was a bowl of some porridge-like substance lying untouched on the bedside table, and a carafe of water.

It was hard to walk quietly in steel-shod biker's boots on the bare polished floorboards of the bedroom. The noise of Ken's footsteps brought a man in a white nurse's overall from the en suite bathroom. From the unemotional way his eyes took in the Browning and he stopped dead in his tracks, Ken guessed he knew more about firearms than bandages and bedpans.

'One sound,' he hissed, 'and you're dead.'

The man nodded, and faced the wall to be frisked. Ken removed a chrome-plated 9 mm. Beretta from his hip pocket, and pushed him into the bathroom, closing and locking the door. Then he did the same with the door leading from the bedroom into the corridor.

After removing his helmet, he put his face close to that of the woman in the bed and spoke in French. 'Madame Picard, we need your help.'

Yvonne's eyes opened. She had spent a sleepless night in the company of ghosts: Sepp and Dietrich, her father, Delmas, as well as herself and Céline as they had been half a century before.

'I wouldn't let them move me,' she mumbled indistinctly. 'What's the point? I told the doctor I'd rather die in my own bed.'

'Céline needs your help.' Ken removed the oxygen mask, to hear her better. 'You can make amends for what happened.'

'You shouldn't be here,' she said feebly. 'Major Brandt's men have come back.'

'I know.' Ken could hear voices coming from the ground floor, where men were shouting to each other. The element of surprise was gone. He thrust the Browning inside one of the weatherproof breast pockets of his leathers and took out a photograph which Hallstatt had torn from a book. It showed Anthony Blunt in the uniform of a lieutenant in the field security police at the time of his posting to France in 1939.

'Is this the English officer who removed the pictures and took Sepp Müller away with him in November 1946?' he asked, trying not to sound impatient. 'Please look at the picture, Madame Picard.'

Yvonne opened her eyes and took the photograph from him with a hand that shook. 'My glasses,' she said. 'I can't see a thing without them.'

Ken handed her the reading glasses from her night table. There were feet pounding up the main stairs from the ground floor. It was hard to be patient, but if he flustered the sick woman, he would be throwing away the whole point of coming to Chateau Magnus. A glance through the window showed Hallstatt standing by the Harley, his hand poised over the horn button.

'Take your time,' Ken said calmly. He left Yvonne gazing at the photograph while he heaved a chest of drawers in front of the door into the corridor. The ancient trick was still one of the most effective ways of obstructing entrance to a room.

The woman in the bed took a deep breath from the oxygen mask and peered at the picture. 'I can't be sure.'

Ken pulled out a handful of other photographs of Anthony Blunt, removed from the same book. They showed Blunt at school with Louis MacNeice, Blunt with Andrew Dow, the Cambridge classics don who had been his mentor, Blunt at a gathering of the Apostles, Blunt in a Bloomsbury garden with the bearded Lytton Strachey, Blunt with a group of students at the Courtauld Institute, some time in the 1950s.

Yvonne's gaze travelled from one to another as she summoned energy to compare them. Through the half-open window, Ken heard one blast on the Harley's horn. A large black car was being manoeuvred across the entrance to the chateau's driveway, while a farm tractor had been parked in the drive that led round the side of the house, effectively blocking the two main gaps in the dense yew hedges that surrounded the garden.

He was wondering desperately how to prod Madame Yvonne Picard into action. 'Do it for Sepp,' he said, on the spur of the moment. 'You owe him that. Is this the man who killed him?'

Her eyes cleared for a moment. She stared at the photographs. 'Yes,' she nodded. 'That's Major Brandt.'

Like a lawyer visiting a client on his deathbed, Ken had the statement already written out and the ball-pen in his hand.

'Sign this,' he said tersely. 'You don't need to read it. It merely confirms that the man in the photographs is the person who removed the paintings from Chateau Magnus in November 1946.'

With agonising slowness, Yvonne's hand pushed the point of the ball-pen across the paper, making a shaky signature.

'Come on, come on,' Ken muttered to himself.

Fists were hammering on the door that led into the corridor, shoulders thudding against the panel. The wood of the jamb was already splintering at the lock. A hand came through the gap, to feel what the obstruction was. With furious anger, Ken barged his full weight against the chest, slamming the door closed. There was a satisfying crunch as bones snapped, flesh tore and blood oozed down the clean paintwork.

A scream of agony came from outside. 'Oh Jesus, my fucking hand!'

The respite would be measured in seconds. Yvonne's grip

slackened, allowing the sheet of paper to flutter to the floor. Ken stooped, grabbed it, stuffed it and the photographs into his pocket, and tugged the zip closed, aware that the piece of paper was useless, if he didn't get safely away with it.

.7.

Ken threw open the casement window, below which was a sheer drop to a rose bed twenty feet below. It was too late to go back for his helmet on the other side of the room, so he scrambled onto the sill, let himself down as far as he could by his hands and dropped the rest of the way to the ground. He heard Hallstatt start the Harley. Thorns tore his cheek but the recently dug and manured soil gave him a soft landing. The Harley was twelve paces away. He scrambled to his feet just as two dog-handlers in civilian clothes came round the side of the building.

The man standing by the black car shouted, 'Head them off.'

Sprinting across the gravel, Ken recognised the South African accent. He was in the saddle, gunning the beautiful 1340cc engine and shouting at Hallstatt to get aboard a split-second before the two dogs were unleashed.

'You go!' Hallstatt hit him on the shoulder hard. 'Don't argue! You need me to run interference.'

There was no time to talk. As Ken accelerated and shifted into second gear, the Doberman was on him. Ignoring the static target presented by Hallstatt, it turned to the man on the moving bike, fangs bared, going for Ken's face. He clouted it in the muzzle with a gauntleted fist, nearly lost balance and skidded on the loose gravel. The dog fell away, its yelping inaudible under the revving of the Harley's engine as Ken straightened up and headed for a gap in the privet hedge between the courtyard and the kitchen garden.

Hallstatt threw himself flat on the gravel, his hands empty

and in full view. The Alsatian showed more intelligence than the Doberman: instead of running after its target, it was heading diagonally to cut Ken off from the hole in the hedge. Halfway there, he saw a man in green gardener's overalls manoeuvring a large metal refuse barrow into position, to block the gap. Ken cut behind the Alsatian and changed direction again for a circuit of the courtyard, looking for another way out. Both the dog-handlers had drawn handguns. To give them something to worry about, Ken wheeled round and accelerated straight at them, making all three leap for their lives and end up flat on the ground.

'Yo, buddy!' Hallstatt yelled as he drove past.

Too busy trying to get a clear shot of Ken, the gunmen were paying no attention to the grey-haired man lying flat on the gravel. In concentrating on them, Ken let the Alsatian get too close. It feinted and lunged sideways as he roared past, tearing the right knee out of his leathers and drawing blood. Side-swiping the animal viciously with the rear wheel, Ken straightened up to see the man in green overalls in the act of taking from his barrow what looked to be a sniper rifle with telescopic sights.

He changed direction yet again, opened the throttle wide and headed straight for the middle of the privet hedge, yanking the front wheel off the ground to burst through the greenery into the kitchen garden. Swearing at the gash on his knee and a cut on his cheek where the hedge had got its revenge, Ken wrenched the handlebars round and headed across the vegetable patch, rear wheel skidding in the soft earth and splattering a shower of clods behind it that made it hard for the man with the rifle to take aim.

Then Ken was clear of the garden and into the first vineyard, roaring between the rows of vines. A glance back over his shoulder showed the man in green overalls at the far end of the row, down on one knee and taking careful aim. The vines were attached with plastic ties to heavy-gauge galvanised wire strung between firmly implanted stakes, which made an impenetrable barrier. With only a metre and a half between the rows, it was impossible to do anything except ride in a straight line and keep low by hugging the tank. Head almost level with the handlebars, Ken changed down and accelerated with the throttle wide open.

Through the Swarovski sight on his Ruger Mini 14/5R, the marksman had a close-up rear view of the man hunched over the Harley. The bike was bucking slightly on the irregular ground but holding a straight line. It was a nearly perfect target. A twist on the gnurled focusing ring and the back of Ken's head lined up as crisply as a studio portrait. If the marksman had been aiming for a killing shot, Ken would have died at that second. But the order was to stop him, alive.

There were five 7.62 × 39 Russian service rounds in the staggered box magazine of the Ruger. The whitening finger squeezed the trigger once.

Before there was time for a second shot, a slug from Hallstatt's Walther caught the kneeling man in the right shoulder, paralysing the whole arm. Ken grabbed a look over his shoulder as the marksman spun round and fell to the ground, the weapon flying from his grasp. Behind him, frozen for ever in Ken's memory was the figure of Hallstatt standing, feet braced apart and holding the Walther two-handed.

Involuntarily, Ken screamed, 'Get down!' But it was too late. Behind Hallstatt, the man with the South African accent loosed a short burst from a Scorpion machine-pistol, throwing the tall grey-haired figure bodily forward to fall like a wet red rag across the wounded marksman.

Too late, Ken remembered the cliff above the cave where the paintings had been hidden. At the end of the rows of vines, he saw space opening up ahead of the Harley's front wheel, but he was going too fast to stop or turn. He grabbed a lungful of air, stood high on the foot-rests with his knees bent, braced his body from head to toes, tightened his grip on the handlebars and closed the throttle in mid-air to avoid wheel-spin on landing. He sailed over a pile of rocks and a stack of upside-down, sharply pointed, two-metre-long stakes that bore the wires on which the vines were grown – landing neatly between the rows of vines in another vineyard below the cliff.

He owed his life to the local custom of ploughing the soil in every alternate row. If the Harley had returned to earth on moist ploughed earth, after a leap of ten metres and a drop of roughly the same distance, it would either have dug itself in or gone into an uncontrollable skid. But Ken's luck held, bringing him back to land on *terra firmissima*. The shock nearly dislocated his neck, but somehow he managed to keep both the bike and himself upright, going gently on the throttle until he was sure the Harley was mechanically none the worse for his unplanned aerobatic display.

Thanks to the legendary Willie G Davidson, the company's Head of Design, the FXR series of bikes were stronger than most which bore the famous name, their frames being cast and forged, rather than stamped and welded. Ken was thinking that he had got away scot-free when he felt a blow on the back of the head and snatched a glance behind to see another clod of clay soil spinning up from the rear wheel. The mudguard had been completely torn off and was lodged on the last of the pointed stakes. Death had been that near.

There was no going back for Hallstatt. At the end of the vineyard, on the first left turn, Ken smelled petrol, and found that impalement was not the only untimely end he had just narrowly missed. One round of 7.62 mm. ammunition had pierced the tank twice, after gouging a ten-inch slit in the leather of his trousers on the underside of his left thigh, grooving the skin and missing his vitals by centimetres only. Exploring the damage, his hand came away dripping blood. On each turn, petrol slopped over his torn flesh. He consoled himself with the thought that it was probably antiseptic. By jamming his knee against the tank, it was possible to more or less plug the entry hole, but the exit hole was out of reach at the front. It was only a question of time and turns before the Harley ran out of juice.

'Who the hell are you?' The wounded marksman had the twangy accent of Marseille. On his feet again, clutching his paralysed right arm, he delivered a vicious kick to Hallstatt's ribs.

It was very cold, lying on the gravel, but peaceful. Hallstatt could feel a trickle of blood from his mouth running down one cheek, but not much else – apart from the cold. He looked up at the angry eyes of the men bending over him, and murmured inaudibly, 'They call me *Erich pare-balles*.'

No one laughed. Hallstatt was not surprised: a joke that has been waiting fifty years to be told is liable to fall flat. The faces got further and further away and there was a great silence.

Ken avoided metalled roads, nudging the Harley along farm tracks and across vineyards while keeping one eye on the sky as he came out of each pocket of fog, in case the opposition had included a helicopter in their plans. To reduce the rate of fuel loss, he had to take the bends slowly. In the empty, frosty Sunday morning landscape, he seemed to be the only living creature – until he turned the corner of a copse and found himself fifty metres away from two men with guns. The anger on their faces gave him a bad moment, until he realised they were weekend huntsmen, furious that the noise of the Harley's exhaust had put up a magnificent stag they were stalking.

Its winter coat was as much grey as brown. For a split second the wise old brown eyes met Ken's through the undergrowth at a distance of a few paces. He thought he heard the echo of a rebel yell, 'Yo, buddy!' Then the great greying beast bounded away, leaping effortlessly over a man-high fence and clearing a four-metre wide sunken road in one soaring leap that was as clean and perfect as a poem.

After ten minutes with no sign of pursuit by the men at the chateau, Ken's bare head was frozen. It was time to risk using the roads and heading fast for where he had left the Land Cruiser at the unoccupied holiday home of some Swiss friends. There he dumped the Harley in the barn, together with his ruined leathers, and staunched the bleeding from his leg with some rapid first aid from the box he kept in one of the rear lockers of the Land Cruiser for surfing mishaps.

Beneath the passenger seat was Hallstatt's overnight bag. About to dump that too, Ken undid the zip and looked inside first. There was a large white envelope with his name on it in Hallstatt's bold handwriting. He tore it open to find a list of the books Hallstatt had used, with page numbers for reference and a sheaf of rough photocopies of the relevant passages which he had made on his fax machine during the night. A notelet pinned to the last sheet read, *Just in case, pal. Use it well.*

From the single frozen frame that kept flashing into his mind, Ken thought it unlikely that Hallstatt was still alive. But he stopped at the first public telephone box to make an anoymous phone call to the local gendarmerie, telling them that a man had been shot at Chateau Magnus. To get any more involved would mean a delay, probably of days, so he put down the phone fast.

Ignoring the pain from his leg, Ken settled himself behind the wheel of the Land Cruiser and began the long drive north in a cold controlled rage with one aim in life – to nail to the wall the man who had shot his best friend.

PART XI

.1.

At ten o'clock on a cold and wet Monday night, the Belgian city of Ghent looked like a film set after the crew and actors have gone home. There were few cars and no pedestrians in the streets. Reflections of streetlamps glittered on the water-ways between the picturesque wood and stone house-fronts which had no signs of life behind them.

According to the dried-out handbill on the dashboard of the Land Cruiser, Slieve Gullion was performing in a converted medieval canalside wool warehouse, to which Ken got direc-tions by walking into an Irish pub on the main street and calling out, 'Where's the gig, Paddy?' at the man pulling the pints of Guinness and Murphy's behind the bar.

On-stage, Irving was unrecognisable in a cheap patterned caftan, an old and worn pair of jeans and open sandals. His black hair was cropped short and dyed blond. A dark three-day stubble and a gold ring in the right ear completed the transfor-mation. Ken had seen many less effective disguises. The change from long-haired classical soloist to hard-drinking on-the-road showband musician, told him that Irving was a perfectionist not only when playing a fiddle.

He waited backstage for the concert to end. High on the per-formance, Siobhan stalked off first in her glitter-dust stage make-up, her eyes looking twice as large as nature had made them. She was breathing deeply, as if she had run a couple of miles.

Never, Irving was thinking as he waited for her to reappear, had a Strad been so hammered for a few hundred half-stoned fans to dance a jig to. He was beginning to appreciate the downside of owning the most valuable musical instrument in the world: until it had a twenty-four-hour bodyguard, he could never let it out of his sight.

In the auditorium, the audience was still clapping. Behind the black drapes, Siobhan licked dry lips and grabbed a Diet Pepsi from the stage manager, pulling the tab and upending the can to rehydrate her vocal cords. Perspiration glued the silk shirt to her moist breasts. Catching sight of Ken, she glared, 'What the fuck are you doing here?'

'They're waiting, Siobhan,' the stage manager said.

With another glare in Ken's direction, she bounded back on the stage, and launched straight into the encore: a ballsy, up-tempo romp that Cecil Sharp would never have recognised as being a version of *The Boys of Malin*. The regular musicians were aware that it was a duel to the musical death between her and Irving, which he won only because half a dozen strands parted on Siobhan's bow. As they came off-stage after the number, she grabbed another drink of Pepsi and accused Irving of pulling his punches at the beginning of the tour.

'Until tonight,' he admitted. 'But that was real, what we just did out there.' Although the repertoire of Slieve Gullion lacked intellectual weight as far as he was concerned, playing with and against Siobhan on her own ground had been exhilarating – and very erotic. She still had no idea why he had offered to deputise for the second fiddler in the band, whom she had sacked just before leaving Britain because he was using hard drugs.

The stage manager cued the house lights to go up. Irving moved in closer to Siobhan, who was standing with her back to the unplastered brick wall. There was an amplified clonk as their violins collided; the pick-up on hers was still live. Her arms locked around his neck, her battered old fiddle resting lightly against his spine. He jerked his head away as her teeth closed on the pierced lobe, which was still sore. Siobhan's legs, clad in Day-Glo-green Lurex tights, squeezed his thigh. Irving felt a tap on the shoulder.

'I'm sorry to break up the party,' he heard Ken say. 'But it's time we hit the road.'

'What took you so long to get here?' Irving asked without turning round.

'I've been busy,' said Ken.

Siobhan's eyes were half-closed, her lips parted in anticipation.

Irving released her and turned. 'You look like shit,' he said when he saw Ken, pale-faced and with eyes red-rimmed from the long drive north.

'You don't look much better,' was the retort.

The Land Cruiser was parked in the shadow of a giant TIR articulated truck with Turkish plates, waiting for the dawn ferry at the Hook of Holland. Ken changed his position on the seat, trying to get comfortable. The glands in his groin were swollen, the lymph system fighting an infection in the wound, which was growing more painful by the hour, the flesh around it being hot to touch, swollen and discoloured.

The good news, Ken thought, was that Irving no longer used expressions like 'tigers behind every bush'. He still intended to keep the Strad, come what may, but in every other respect he was a changed man, determined both to avenge Mrs Prescot's murder and punish whoever was behind what he called 'the opposition's latest move' – the cancellation of the two-week recording session for his new label, against which all his agent's remonstrations and threats of legal action had proved useless.

There was a white-hot anger in the words: 'Nobody fucks with my career like that and gets away with it, Ken. We have to screw these bastards right now.'

The big problem, as Ken pointed out, was that although he had, with Hallstatt's help, assembled a sequence of circumstantial evidence that led to Sir Anthony Blunt in the year 1946, there was still nothing to connect it with Sir Terence Savage and whoever was behind him.

Against this, Irving had riposted that what he called 'the opposition' was obviously getting very worried, to resort to overkill like the fire at Le Farou and the violence at Chateau Magnus . . . which meant that Ken must be closer to the end of the trail than he thought.

He was very cagey about what he had been doing in Britain before crossing the Channel. From hints he let drop, it sounded to Ken as though he had been raising a small private army. Irving had attended – when he was not playing truant – one of the worst comprehensive schools in Merseyside. The pupils called it the Pen, meaning Penitentiary. The girls ended up as hookers, or got pregnant before they were old enough to leave school. And the most legitimate job any of the other boys in his year had landed was running a nightclub that laundered drugs money. From time to time, as he said ambiguously to Ken, his old classmates had been as useful to him as any old-boy network from a public school.

'What are you intending to do?' Ken queried. 'Take Sir Terence's house by storm and hold him hostage?'

'Have you got a better idea?' was Irving's rejoinder. 'We can't go to the police with what we know. Savage would just take refuge behind a screen of expensive lawyers. And the guys who killed Hallstatt and Mrs P won't think twice about wiping us out when they catch up with us, so we must get them first.'

Ken blamed sheer tiredness for making him disclose the hiding place of the Browning. Irving tugged it out of the Velcro cradle beneath the dashboard and toyed with it, enjoying the feel of the weapon in his hand. It was unpretentious, work-manlike, solid, well-balanced. After he had been beaten up in New York, he had taken handgun lessons at a National Rifle Association firing range in Connecticut. And when he was a kid looking for trouble in Liverpool, he boasted to Ken, he had been able to take out a streetlamp with an air rifle at two hundred metres, first shot.

To Ken, he looked – with the gun in his hand, that haircut and those clothes – like an undercover cop in a television movie. As far as he was concerned, an amateur with a loaded firearm was a potential own goal.

'Firing at a cardboard target is one thing,' he cautioned. 'Putting a bullet into a living, breathing person is something else, Irving. Elite military units spend a lot of money and time deprogramming the Sixth Commandment in order to turn recruits into automata who'll shoot straight in a firefight and not crack up until years afterwards. Savage's men are pros. During the fraction of a second's hesitation while you're grappling with the taboo against killing, the other guy will have pressed the trigger. So forget the Browning.'

Cars were starting to drive onto the ferry. Irving slipped the automatic back into its home beneath the dashboard. 'Let's get one thing straight,' he said, turning the key. 'You may have a lifetime's experience of dirty tricks, but oddly enough I think you're probably a nice guy inside, despite what I was brought up to think about you. Conversely, I may have zero experience of shooting guns at people with intent to do them permanent harm. However, you should get it into your head right now that, notwithstanding my public image as a pampered idol of the concert platform, I'm a really nasty bastard underneath the thin veneer of civilised musician.

'I thought your hypothesis about Mrs P being murdered was way over the top, because I had no idea of the motive. Now, when I meet the guy who killed her, I'm not going to have any hesitation about blowing him away. Your job is to get me to him and make sure the circumstances are right, because I do not intend to end up in prison.'

He hauled the wheel round and jumped a queue to get on the boat more quickly. Ken gritted his teeth with pain as the Land Cruiser bumped up onto the loading ramp.

'I have to know one thing,' Irving said. 'I've been straight with you from the beginning, Ken. You might not agree with the way I think, but you know *what* I think. So tell me, what's in this for you?'

It was a good question. Until the shoot-out at Chateau Magnus, Ken would have replied, like the professional he was, 'I want to see justice done.' He had faced a man before with a loaded gun in his hand and not pulled the trigger. This time, he did not know what his decision would be when he confronted the man with the South African accent who had killed Hallstatt. But he did know from experience that only in Hollywood westerns did the good guy draw first as the sun went down. In real life the bad guys usually got their shot in first; only afterwards did the men on white horses turn up and grab the villain – or watch him get clean away for lack of evidence that would convince a jury.

As Irving parked on the ferry, there was shouting and the clanging of metal on metal as the ship's crew secured trucks and cars to the deck with tensioned chains. The weather forecast was rough. Unable to face climbing all the stairs to the passenger decks, Ken told Irving to bring him a hot drink, some aspirin tablets and something to eat in three hours' time, then wrapped himself in a couple of sleeping bags and stretched out on the floor of the car, to find that even the heat of the ship's engines, after the loading doors had been closed, could not stop him shivering.

The smell of diesel fumes filtered into the car and the crashing of heavy seas against the hull made the whole vessel reverberate. As they came out of the harbour and into the North Sea, the pitching and rolling grew rapidly worse, throwing Ken from side to side of the car. Half-asleep, he wondered whether he had fed sufficiently the curiosity of his ex-wife. A lot depended on that.

One particularly bad shock made him yell with pain from the leg wound. Drenched in sweat from head to foot, he hauled himself up onto a seat and saw to his amazement from the dashboard clock that he had slept for six hours solid, despite all the motion, the smell, the heat and the noise.

Through the driver's window, Irving was grinning at him. 'I let you sleep on,' he shouted through the glass and over the noise of the storm. 'You look a bit better for the zizz.'

The ship was still lurching heavily from side to side and shuddering from stem to stern as the bow plunged into the heavy seas. He opened the door, keeping his balance with difficulty on the wet metal deck, and shouted, 'You had me worried, sleeping through a Force-Eight gale like this one.'

Ken took the styrofoam cup of coffee and jumbo hamburger, leaving both Irving's hands free for him to scramble into the car. He felt weak, but no longer feverish: the crisis had passed. 'I had me worried too,' he said.

.2.

Embracing Liz, Ken was acutely aware that his ex-wife had put on some flesh in the right places since they had lived together. In a cotton blouse and the skirt of her dark-grey business suit, most women of her age would have looked tired at the end of a long day, but she managed to look fresh and crisp.

After a shower and shave, and with a total of ten hours' sleep on the boat and the drive from Harwich to London, he was feeling ravenous.

'I had a hell of a day,' Liz said. 'There was just time to grab a couple of ready-cooked dishes from Marks and Sparks on Oxford Street. Is that all right? You used to like duck.'

'I still do.' Ken peeled off his anorak. Liz had always hated proper room lighting. In the warm glow of the reading lamps, he saw the table set for two.

Loading the microwave cooker, she called from the kitchen, 'There's a bottle of bubbly cooling in the ice bucket. Pour one for me too.'

Ken carried her glass into the kitchen, and watched her chopping up herbs for the salad.

'Switch on the hi-fi,' she murmured. 'I put a cassette in, ready.'

The soothing voice of Frank Sinatra came out of the speakers, inviting them to fly away with him to Acapulco. The album was one which Liz had often played when they lived together, because Ol' Blue Eyes was one of the few singers to whom they could both listen without arguing.

Ken watched her reflection in the window glass as she struck a match and lit two candles on the dining-table before switching off the lamps and coming to join him, looking out at the blackness of the heath.

She took a drink from his glass; hers was still in the kitchen. 'Now tell me what's been going on, over there in la belle France.'

'The last time I talked with you, you said you weren't interested in getting involved in my story. But this afternoon, on the phone . . .'

Liz looked him in the eyes. 'I never said no, meaning no, Ken. I said no, meaning let me think about it. While you were away, I've had time to do a little digging. I've unearthed a few nuggets, which could be gold. Or they could by pyrites. So you tell me what you've dug up, and I'll see how my dirt pans out.'

'And the soft lights, sweet music and champagne?'

She kissed his ear and moved away. '. . . are just my way of relaxing after a long day's work, honey.'

'I remember your idea of relaxation after a long day's work.'

'I'm listening, Ken.'

Listening was something at which Liz was good: the résumé of how a Mary Cassatt painting worth a quarter of a million sterling had found its way from a rich man's home in occupied Paris to a humble maisonette in Liverpool, kept her silent for half an hour. The microwave had pinged unnoticed by either her or Ken.

Liz glanced down the list of works of art written in Dietrich's careful Germanic hand. 'Renoir, Toulouse-Lautrec, Sisley, Gauguin? This lot must be worth a zillion dollars. We have Dietrich Bohlen's signed trilingual statement, a French railway consignment note naming Goering's Swiss forwarding agent . . . Sepp Müller's letter to Yvonne Picard, and a piece of paper signed by her identifying Sir Anthony Blunt as the man who removed the collection of pictures from Chateau Magnus in 1946. I'm impressed with the work that you and your pal Hallstatt have put in, in such a short time, but where are the pictures now, Ken?'

'No idea.' He wondered why Liz was looking smug.

'And who was Terry Savage acting for, when he swapped the Strad for this old lady's painting?'

'You tell me.'

'Given his connections, he'd only take a risk like that for the Queen or someone very near to her.'

'D'you think she's involved?'

'On the face of it, the question is ridiculous, but why *did* HMQ keep Blunt in his Palace job for fifteen years after being informed of his confidential confession to MI5? It wasn't to help them keep in place a burned agent and use him to feed disinformation to the other side because Blunt's espionage activities are supposed to have ended in 1946, if we believe the official version. There are plenty of theories why he was protected, but none make so much sense as Hallstatt's: that Blunt was blackmailing the Royal Family with his knowledge of the Duke of Windsor's ties with Adolf and Co – and had kept back some of the documentary evidence for his own purposes.

'However, it's also possible that he set up a second line of blackmail by sharing some of Goering's loot with certain members of the House of Windsor. But . . . and it's a big but . . . if we open up that can of worms, my editor's going to get cold feet. Unlike the guy in the White House, the lady in the Palace is unimpeachable – and don't you forget it! So let's work on the second hypothesis: that Savage is acting exclusively for Terry Savage.'

Ken was staring into his drink, half-listening.

Liz leaned forward and placed a hand on his arm. 'I'm sorry about your friend Erich. Truly sorry. He sounds a great man. Are you sure he's dead?'

Ken met her eyes and looked away. 'Hallstatt took a burst in the back from a machine-pistol at short range. People don't get up and walk away from that.'

'And you blame yourself?'

'For getting him involved, yes. It was one thing to consult a pal for research, but why the hell did I let a man of his age convince me into letting him come to the chateau?'

Liz held up the sheet of paper on which was written, *Just in case, pal. Use it well*. Her voice was gentle. 'It sounds to me as though this old boy might just have chosen to go out in a burst of glory. At his age, it's possible.'

Aware that pain cannot be reasoned away, she took Ken's glass and put it down on the low table which was covered in the paper and photographs that made up his file. Sliding her hand inside his sweatshirt, she felt the tight muscles and the ribs beneath. He was a lot fitter than most of the men she knew.

'This won't work,' he said, looking at the up-tilted face and the lips so invitingly close to his.

'I think you need a bit of loving.'

'Since when were you in the business of sexual charity?'

Liz licked her fingers and ran them round Ken's lips. 'Not being able to live with you is one thing – wanting you, quite another.'

He closed his eyes to enjoy the feel of her hands on his skin; the unspoken offer was tempting. Liz and he had either been fighting or fucking most of the time they had spent together. She knew how to move against him and where to touch.

On the hi-fi, Sinatra was loving Paris in the springtime. Ken smelled Liz's hair, her make-up and a discreet touch of the perfume he remembered from his last visit. Underneath it all was the vital, earthy smell of the woman herself.

'I need you!' Her lips closed on his. She moulded herself to his body. There was a momentary resistance, then she felt his arms go around her and knew she had won. One of his hands was on her breasts, the other tracing each vertebra, moving lower and lower. Nuzzling, groping, caressing, they slid down on the settee until Liz was lying in the cushions, with Ken on top.

This was not a time for lengthy seduction, she decided. Ken needed a quick catharsis to let out the pain of grief. She parted her legs and felt his hardness against her, where it should be. His mouth was hard on hers, hurting her lips and prompting her to dig her nails into the flesh of his back, raking the ribs. She felt herself moisten and wished she had changed out of her skirt and into something looser before he arrived – but at least she was wearing stockings, not tights. One of his hands was busy with his zip. She waited with eyes closed as he shrugged out of his jeans and kicked them away. Then he had her skirt up around her hips and, without even removing the French knickers she was wearing, was inside her.

She gave a tiny moan – half surprise, half pleasure – then everything felt right. Her muscles gripped his flesh, matching his rhythm. Ken raised himself above her, his face still lined with pain, and Liz thought, Hold on, this is for him. She lay still, accepting his thrusts, then slid her hands inside the sweatshirt to find his nipples and squeeze them rhythmically between thumb and finger. It was all going to be too fast, but that did not matter. And when he came and lay sobbing on her, she caressed his shoulders, his neck, his ears – and wondered why they had spent so long apart. Despite everything, she thought, he's the only man I truly care about.

Sinatra was on the move, this time to Old New York. Liz wondered whether Ken was asleep. One arm was getting cramped; she gently flexed her fingers to restore the circulation without disturbing him. When Sinatra began extolling the pleasures of the second time around, Liz knew there would not be one. It was unlike Ken to be satisfied after a single orgasm, however climactic. One long night that lasted into the next afternoon, they had made love thirteen times. Or was it fourteen? She recalled popping a contraceptive pill from its wrapper on the bedside table after each orgasm, so that she could keep a tally – and being so shaken up next day that she was unable to drive a car, or even handle a phone call without sounding like a spaced-out zombie.

Ken was stirring. Liz disengaged herself and sat up, smoothing down her rumpled skirt and pouring them both another glass of champagne. 'We could give it another try, you know,' she murmured.

'Give what another try?' He sat up, trouserless, and took the glass from her.

'Living together,' she said. 'We're older now . . .'

'. . . but no wiser.' Ken felt that a great tension had gone out of him; his brain was his own again. 'You know how long it would last, Liz? A week, a month, and then what? The same midnight scenes endlessly replayed . . .'

'Listen!' One of her fingers closed his lips. The song just starting was her favourite: *The Lady Is A Tramp*.

The candles had nearly burned out. In the spill of amber light from the streetlamps, reflected off the low cloud-base, Liz watched Ken crawl away on all fours, looking for his clothes. His tight buttocks, pale in contrast with the rest of his tanned body, made her hunger to slip her hands between his thighs and grab the flesh that she could make so hard, but this was not the moment.

Sinatra was into *The Wee Small Hours*. 'In case you're wondering,' she said, 'I didn't plan that, Ken. It just happened.'

When he stood up with his back to her, to pull on his jeans, she saw the skin-coloured plaster on the inside of his thigh for the first time, and suggested he let her call a doctor.

'Later,' he said. 'Now tell me what you found out.'

Liz changed her tone of voice from bedroom to newsroom. 'Give me five minutes, partner,' she said briskly. 'I need to take a shower and change into some clean clothes. Meanwhile, see if the duck's still edible and open another bottle of bubbly. You'll find one in the fridge.'

She picked up her shoes and her wristwatch, which were lying on the floor beside them. In the bathroom, she left the door open a few inches – despite knowing the invitation would not be taken up. For a moment, before getting into the shower, she stood naked in front of the mirror, wishing there had been time for Ken to undress her and admire her trim figure. With no stretchmarks and no flab, she was in as good shape as when she had first met him, aged twenty-seven. Well, almost . . .

Her hands pressed hard against her flat belly, nails scarlet against the white skin and black pubic hair. Clenching her muscles to recapture the sensation of holding Ken's flesh inside her, Liz closed her eyes and stepped under the hot water to let it caress her skin the way he had not had time to do.

She wondered why she had let him go. Let him go? He had walked out. Or had she? And why did they always end up fighting? The two of them made such a damned good team. Was it her fault or his that they always fell out? Perhaps now that Ken's Irish girlfriend had walked out on him, they could make it work . . .

.3.

Liz was curled up on the red silk settee, wearing a grey jogging suit, her dark hair tied back in a pony-tail. She finished eating a leg of over-cooked duck with her hands and wiped her greasy fingers on a tissue. The second bottle of champagne was nearly empty.

'Tell me all you know about Savage,' Ken said.

'He's a complex character. Irving would not have guessed when they met – unless he recognised the tie – but the good Sir Terry began life in the Guards. He had the right background: no money to speak of, but a good family and public school. There was a well-hushed-up scandal involving a young guardsman keeping him warm in a sentry box on a cold winter night when he was the inspecting officer. Afterwards, Savage resigned his commission and decided to study art history at the Courtauld Institute, considering it a safer bet for someone of his talents and inclinations.'

'So Savage and Blunt knew each other?'

'Ultimately, intimately.'

Ken smashed his right fist into the palm of his other hand. 'And that's why you've been looking so damned smug all evening!'

Liz held out her glass for a refill. 'At Sherborne, Savage was known as the school tart. He may look a bit raddled now, but when young he apparently had the looks of a Greek god. From the day he enrolled at the Courtauld, according to my sources, Blunt was trying to get the new boy's pants down – which was unusual, because he didn't normally mix his separate lives. By day he prowled the corridors of the Institute in the guise of an ultra-establishment professor of art, and popped across to Buck House or down to Windsor to chat to the Royals about plans for exhibitions and so on. By night he brought the most astonishing collection of rough trade up to the apartment overlooking Portman Square, where he lived above the Institute, but the students knew nothing about all that.'

'With the exception of the young Terence Savage . . .'

'Wrong. Savage resisted Blunt's blandishments until 1974, which was three years after he had left the Courtauld – and the same year that Blunt confessed, and was given immunity from prosecution.'

Liz took a sip of her champagne. 'The old queen – and I am not speaking of the dear Queen Mother – was head-over-heels in love, and straining at the leash after pursuing his beloved for six years. He kicked his long-term boyfriend out of that famous flat above the Courtauld . . . and in moved our future knight: absolutely not the kind of lover for whom Blunt usually went overboard. All his other liaisons, whether one-night stands or live-ins, were working-class blokes, with whom he could feel superior – and get away with beating them up when the mood took him. They were sailors, truckers, dockers, factory hands. He picked them up while cottaging in a public toilet at Hyde Park Corner or in Russell Square, where Tom Driberg MP – remember him? – was regularly to be seen with his raincoat over his arm.

'So perhaps this was true love on Blunt's part. Whatever, I sense a more mercenary motive on the other side of the bed, because within weeks Savage had persuaded his protector to introduce him into the Royal Household. He worked in the library at Windsor Castle in an honorary, unpaid capacity for two years, charming all the Royals and worming his way into the inner circle of those who come and go freely in the royal residences. It was widely understood that Blunt was grooming his young lover to replace him on retirement. But, once bitten, twice shy: Her Maj decided not to give Blunt's job to his boyfriend.'

'Hold on,' said Ken. 'Could it be that you think you know where the pictures are?'

'I'm pretty certain I know where they *were*, at one time. But I'll come to that later.' Liz was enjoying the way she had Ken hanging on every word. 'By the way, do you know why the Queen surrounds herself with so many gays?'

'Tell me.'

'They play charades. Now and again even a cynical time-served Grub Street hack like me can be taken by surprise. I didn't believe my ears when my source at the Palace told me how, on evenings with nothing better to do, HMQ unwinds with a game or two of charades after dinner. It seems that most of her loyal but married servants go home in the evening to their wives and kids, but the gays are prepared to hang about until she's had her nosh. Then raid the dressing-up box to give their employer a good laugh. Apparently the royal giggles in the private apartments can be heard halfway down Pall Mall on some nights.'

Ken wanted to know what had been meant by that *I know where they were*, but there was no hustling Liz. She would tell him in her own good time, and not before.

'My guess is that Blunt never sold a single one of those pictures,' she continued. 'Firstly, he was far too clever to make such an elementary mistake, and secondly, he never had any interest in money, so far as I found out. Even your former colleague Arthur Martin, who interviewed him for MI5, commented how spartanly the man lived. Terry Savage, on the other hand, lives like a Renaissance prince. And nobody knows where his money comes from. The family are what used to be called fallen gentlefolk, on this side of the pond. Mama still lives in a draughty Queen Anne country house on the Fylde estuary in Lancashire. So Savage's money is not inherited wealth. I'd say – but it's pure guesswork – that he has sold a few of Goering's Impressionist paintings.'

'If we could trace one . . .'

'Not a chance. You can take it from me that none of the purchasers is going to testify against him, and the pictures will never have shown up in a sale room.'

'Unless a purchaser sold them on.'

Liz laughed. 'Guys who are in the market for a Toulouse-Lautrec or a Renoir which they can't talk about or show off to their golfing partners don't ever get down to their last million bucks. And even if one of them did have such rotten luck, there was probably a buy-back clause in the original deal.

'And one other thing you should know is that Savage has surrounded himself with more protection than the Mafia by dint of doing favours for the right people. He finds paintings and other works of art at prices nowhere near their current market value. And the whisper is that certain people – the Royals and others in positions to be useful to him one day – never get a bill for their latest acquisition.'

'Tell me about his home,' Ken said.

'His house in Brownlow Square, Belgravia – only five minutes' comfortable stroll from the Palace – is stuffed with works of art.'

'Have you been there?'

'The question's flattering,' Liz grinned. 'I don't exactly move in those circles, but I've spoken to someone who does. The building alone is worth a few million, given the land it stands on, which is large enough to fit in a classy small hotel. The garden has more unbroken Greek and Roman statuary than the British Museum, if you leave out the Elgin marbles. Inside, the house is more like a museum than a home: Chinese porcelain in the entrance hall, Old Master paintings on the stairs . . .

'But one thing's interesting. Apparently, when Sir Terry takes a small party of intimates home after the opening night of a new opera, there are always some rather well-built gents in dinner-jackets who politely but firmly discourage the guests from going upstairs.'

Liz took a leisurely sip from her glass of champagne, enjoying the long-forgotten pleasure of stringing Ken along. 'And,' she said, 'Sir Terence has at least one Swiss bank account.'

'Can you find out how much is there?'

'Not a chance. I only know about it because, after Blunt's death in 1983, Terry was apparently very cut-up.'

'Were they still living together?'

A shake of the head. 'No. By then they were sisters – pals but no longer lovers. Perhaps remorse made Savage unwary for once. Whatever, he contacted two of the dear departed's former boyfriends, and paid them a monthly allowance out of his own pocket in fulfilment apparently of some last-minute promise to Blunt. For five months, the money came direct from Switzerland. Now it comes from a London solicitor, but a hacker source of mine in Threadneedle Street says that the payments are covered by equivalent amounts in Swiss francs which arrive every quarter from Zürich.'

'Amazing,' Ken murmured appreciatively.

'You ain't heard nothing yet.' Liz put down her empty glass and stretched out a hand to turn up the dimmer on the lamp beside the settee; she wanted to see Ken's face as she played her best card. 'D'you remember the fire at Windsor castle in November 1992?'

'A wing of the castle went up in smoke, is that right?'

She tossed him a folder that was lying on the settee. Ken took out half a dozen Press cuttings. At 11.37 a.m. on Friday 20 November fire broke out in the Private Chapel of Chester Tower. Flames engulfed the State Apartments in the north-east corner of the Upper Quadrangle, destroying most of the roof and seriously weakening the structure of the Brunswick Tower and St George's Hall. Household servants, led by Prince Andrew, formed a human chain to pass valuable paintings to safety. Twelve hours later, firemen were still damping down the blaze and questions were already being asked in the Press as to who was going to find the millions of pounds necessary to repair the damage.

'The story fizzled out,' Liz said, when Ken had finished reading. 'I smelled something funny at the time because there was never any blame attributed, and usually these fires start at night, when there's nobody around to smell smoke. That's how they get a hold. But at midday? In a national monument, packed with art treasures, that is also a royal residence? With all the security staff, intruder alarms and smoke sensors there must be in a place like that, it didn't seem likely.'

Ken's pulse was racing. 'And where did that line of thought lead you?'

'To Slough fire station, where I talked with a gorgeously athletic young man who was on the first vehicle to arrive at the scene of the fire. He told me that they have a permanent contingency drill worked out for Windsor Castle. Yet on the vital day, they lost several minutes – which might have made quite a difference – because there was some kind of argument going on when they arrived between Prince Andrew and a man who, from the fireman's description, could only have been Terry Savage.'

'And this disclosure led in turn to . . . ?' Ken knew there was no point in getting tense; it was Liz's style, to make him work for each titbit.

'It led to an insurance investigator who came to interview my hunky fireman a few days after the event, and left that.' Liz pointed to a visiting card, stapled into the file cover. The name on it was Jack Belasco, with an address in Camden Town.

'You've talked to this Mr Belasco?'

'Briefly, on the phone. He hung up on me.'

'And?'

'It was just a vibe I picked up, Ken – after I mentioned Savage's name.'

'What kind of vibe?'

'Jesus! You know what I mean. A pause that's a fraction of a second too long. A change in inflexion of the voice. Belasco didn't want to talk on the phone, but it's a dollar to a dime he knows something – you can take it from me.'

'I'll call him first thing in the morning.'

'On which note, as Mr Pepys said, let us to bed. It's one-fifteen and although my editor is bullying me to get our story ready for this Sunday's edition, he also insists I still do chores like popping over to Brussels on the breakfast flight this morning, to interview some EMPs about the single currency.'

Ken stood up and stretched. 'Do you have some blankets? I'll kip down on the settee, if that's okay.'

'It seems a mite unfriendly: you out here and me in the bedroom.' Liz stood up, scanned Ken's eyes and kissed him on the lips. In the bedroom doorway, she stopped and undid the pony-tail, shaking her hair out in a gesture Ken recalled, and holding out a hand to him.

'There's no commitment,' she murmured.

.4.

The street was one of those in Camden Town which had been slum property thirty years earlier. Restored, the terraced houses were now desirable Yuppie residences – as demonstrated by the BMWs and Volvos lining the pavement. Ken parked his rental car with difficulty and limped up the six white stone steps to the glossy red front door of Belasco's house and lifted the polished brass knocker.

The blonde Polish au pair who opened the door was carrying a boy of about three with Down's syndrome on her hip. 'What do you want?'

'Is Mr Belasco in?'

'Is necessary an appointment, to see him.' Her deadpan eastern European accent matched the grey murk of London's winter.

'Tell him I'm here on police business,' Ken said.

'What is it, Marisha?'

The stocky, ruddy-complexioned man of about forty in check shirt and cavalry-twill trousers who stuck his head out of the front room had to be Belasco. His accent could not have been acquired east of Plymouth. He would have looked in place seated on a harbour wall, mending nets. Ken could almost smell salt in the air and hear the cries of gulls.

'This man want to see you,' said the girl in the same sullen voice.

'Police business?'

'That's right,' said Ken.

'Come right in. What can I do for you?'

The front room was equipped as an office, with a Packard Bell Pentium computer, a Canon laser printer, a modem and a fax machine. The walls were decorated with scale drawings of sailing ships, with meticulously carved and varnished semi-hulls to the same scale glued beneath them. Each bore the initials J.B. Mr Belasco, it seemed, was a boat-lover.

'Beautiful, aren't they?' he beamed.

Ken waved his MI5 ID card, which Belasco took before he could put it away. Checking the face, he said, 'It's out of date.'

This was not a man to bullshit. 'You're the first to notice,' Ken grinned.

'In three years?'

'I don't use it that often.'

'Scott? That your real name?'

'It is.'

The card was handed back. 'Now you've gone private?'

'Not really. Let's say I retired prematurely and involuntarily, but circumstances have kind of overtaken me.'

'Tough,' Belasco said.

'I won't waste your time.' Ken talked fast. Once Belasco had made up his mind, it would be too late to change it. 'I want to talk about the fire at Windsor Castle three years ago. You interviewed a fireman in Slough shortly after the blaze.'

'Ah,' Belasco sighed. 'You're something to do with that high-powered Press bitch who tried to bulldoze me into an indiscretion a couple of days ago.'

'The bitch was working for me – on a long lead. She told me that you didn't want to talk about Sir Terence Savage – and I think I understand why. I'd like to ask you a few questions and I give my word you won't be quoted.'

'Mr Scott, I don't want to be offensive. It's conceivable you're an honest man, whose word can be trusted, but I've nothing to say. And right now, I'm going out.' Belasco grabbed a Gannex weathercoat from a hook behind the door and picked up a well-worn briefcase.

'I need your help. I want to nail Sir Terence to the wall and you're the best lead I've got.'

'What's he supposed to have done?' Belasco asked.

'Killed two innocent people – one of them a very good friend of mine. And . . .' Ken took a gamble, based on his assessment of Belasco. '. . . sold an unspecified number of very valuable paintings that didn't belong to him.'

'You're talking about a personal friend of the Queen.'

'If you say so.'

'Do you object to a body search, Mr Scott?'

'You think I'm carrying a wire?'

'People say I'm a prudent man.'

Ken took off his anorak. Belasco put down the briefcase and coat, then ran his hands carefully over Ken's body from head to foot, missing nothing.

'You're an ex-copper,' guessed Ken.

'Her Majesty's Customs.' Belasco straightened up. 'My grandfather was a smuggler, so maybe I was redressing the balance. I did three years opening suitcases at Heathrow.'

'Usually people avoid the most obvious place.'

'You'd be amazed what I've found between men's legs in my time, Mr Scott.' Belasco was methodically feeling along the seams and in the pockets of Ken's anorak.

'If you quote a single thing,' he said, dropping the anorak on a chair, 'I'll deny it – and sue you into the bargain.'

'That's fair,' Ken agreed.

'And what makes you think I've anything to tell you about Sir Terence Savage?'

'My partner's instinct during the brief telephone conversation you had with her.'

'Give her a raise. She must be good at the job.'

'She is.'

Belasco filled two plastic cups with coffee from the filter machine on the window ledge, and handed one to Ken. 'Tell me what you know, then I'll decide.'

'I can't play it that way,' Ken said. 'I just want to talk about the fire. You started an investigation, told the fireman you'd be back to take a sworn statement, and never reappeared. Why?'

'Because I went to the castle and started asking questions. Dealing with the Royal Household is trickier than Downing

Street, but I discovered that a snap inventory had been taking place on the morning of the fire. It was something to do with some royal property that had been found to have gone astray during a bomb scare the previous month. I pricked up my ears when I heard that, because it wouldn't have been the first time that a major fire had been started as a cover-up, and then got out of hand. In my business, two and two often make four – although people spend a lot of time and energy trying to persuade me otherwise. Since Sir Terence was among the small number of people who had been in the right place at the right time to start the fire, I asked to interview him and a few others on the off-chance.'

'And did you talk to him?'

'For a few seconds. He gave me a brush-off, said he was busy and made an appointment at his house for the next day.'

'What happened then?'

'Nothing. I was retained by a company which insured part of the loss, Mr Scott. Forty-eight hours after the fire, I was pulled off the case. The chairman of the group called me at home and told me to drop the investigation.'

'Then why are you telling me all this?'

'Because I'm an awkward bastard who doesn't like being paid off not to pursue a man I know was up to something fishy.'

'I know how it feels.'

'I think you do, my dear.'

Despite the rich Cornish accent and the 'my dear', the jolly Jack Tar image was misleading, Ken realised. He wondered how many people had made the fatal mistake of writing off the man in front of him as a slow-witted provincial.

'Mr Scott, I don't go looking for trouble. But I knew after my ten-second chat with Sir Terence Savage that, whether or not he had started the fire, he was up to some mischief that day. His blink rate was way over the top, he was sweating despite the cold, damp weather and he was stammering slightly – which I gather is not usual.'

'Why d'you leave the Customs, Mr Belasco?'

'Money. I've got a wife and three kids. One of them has special needs. He costs us quite a bit, as you can imagine.'

'Well, thanks for talking to me.'

'I didn't,' said the Cornishman. 'You came to see me. I was too busy to fit you in without an appointment. You waited in the kitchen –' He checked his wristwatch – 'for precisely nine minutes. Then I told you to piss off. Marisha will bear me out, if necessary. She doesn't want to be sent back to Warsaw before she's saved enough hard currency to get married.'

'Thanks all the same.'

Ken was halfway out of the front door when Belasco pulled him back inside. 'If you get close to Sir Terence, watch out for his minder, a deceptive little thug called Kurt Servus.'

'Can you describe him?'

'A bit on the short side, careful about his appearance, dark hair – and a quiet voice with a South African accent.'

Ken's face gave away nothing of the elation he felt at having a name for the man who had shot Hallstatt.

'Why didn't you tell me about Servus earlier?' he asked.

'I didn't think you'd need to know. Now I reckon maybe you will.'

'What else can you tell me about him?'

Belasco hesitated. 'I knew him when he worked for Freight Security at Heathrow as a dog-handler, about fifteen years ago. There were whispers that he was on the take. It was a bad period for pilfering. Some stuff even went missing from the Bonded Warehouse, but that was hushed up. Shortly after the big bullion robbery, Servus resigned, one step ahead of an investigation by C1. The next I heard – via the Customs' grapevine which covers the entire globe – was that he'd gone back to South Africa and was recruiting mercenaries for some little war or other.'

'Anything else?'

'Later, he spent time in Colombia. What he did there, is anyone's guess. Our paths crossed again when I went to Sir Terence's house before I was told to drop the enquiry. Sir Terence was too busy to waste time on a minion like myself, so I found myself talking to his driver cum bodyguard. I don't think Servus recognised me, but I was – to put it mildly – surprised to learn that a man with his record was driving freely in and out of Windsor Castle, with and without Sir Terence in the back seat.'

'Thanks for the warning.'

'That's not all, Mr Scott. One of the first things I did on the day of the fire was to check the gate log at Windsor Castle. It showed that a Mr Service had driven a Ford transit van out of the main courtyard thirty minutes before the fire brigade was called. At the time, I didn't connect, because the name in the log was spelled S-E-R-V-I-C-E. Once I knew who we were talking about, the timing did seem interesting, to put it mildly.'

'Thank you, Mr Belasco. I've a feeling you've just answered a whole lot of questions that I wouldn't even have been able to ask.'

'I don't see how, my dear,' Belasco beamed. 'I kept you waiting in the kitchen for a quarter of an hour and then told you to piss off. Good luck, Mr Scott. You'll need it.'

.5.

Either I'm tired, or I'm out of practice, Ken thought. He had been unaware of any surveillance until the driver got out of the black Escort GT that was blocking the Land Cruiser in.

A man of about thirty, wearing a grey suit and sunglasses, he stood waiting on the pavement in a relaxed stance with his hands in his pockets. 'Someone would like to talk to you, Mr Scott,' he said.

Warily, Ken stooped and peered inside the Escort. Seated on the rear seat was the crumpled figure of Harry Tilson, who invited him to take the weight off his feet.

Ken got in and took the visiting card Tilson handed him. The embossed copperplate print read: *Alasdair McIntyre KBE, Holm Brae, Crieff, Stirlingshire*. On the back, in a spiky hand which he recognised, was the typically economical message: *'I'd like a word, Scottie.'*

'The McIntyre wants to see me?'

'Looks like it, Scottie.' Tilson sounded glum, but that could have been because they were driving past pubs that were already open.

Ken pocketed the card, reflecting that wild horses would not normally have been able to drag the reclusive Scot who had been his boss for fifteen years away from the Perthshire hunting tower, the grouse moors and the salmon rivers to which he had dedicated his retirement. If someone like Sir Alasdair McIntyre had been brought to London and kept on ice for this moment, Savage was even better connected than Liz had realised.

Thanks to the rain, traffic was even worse than usual in the

West End, but the driver clamped a blue flashing light to the roof, used his police siren, and pushed aggressively through gaps where even a cab driver might have hesitated. He did not look at his passengers once, but kept his eyes on the road and whistled tunelessly between his teeth.

They inched along Regent Street and round Piccadilly Circus, which was even more congested. The half-mile journey along Pall Mall to the twin gateposts labelled simply IN and OUT took five more minutes of dodging from one small gap in the gridlock to the next.

Like most London clubs which have managed to survive the decline of the gentry, the Naval and Military has had to open its doors far wider than the original members would have tolerated. At various times, it has absorbed the Ladies' Carlton, the Cowdray Club, the Junior Naval and Military, the Canning Club – most of whose members were businessmen with Argentinian connections – the Goat Club with its membership of one thousand naval officers, the Constitutional and, for a while, the Royal Aero as well. Of all these, perhaps the most exclusive was the Portland Club. Recognised as the most authoritative bridge club in the world, and generally accepted as the final arbiter in any dispute about the rules of the game, the Portland enjoys its own private card room at the In and Out.

After turning off the siren and removing the blue lamp, the driver parked on a double yellow line outside the club's side entrance in Half Moon Street. He got out and held Ken's door open. Harry Tilson was staring out of the window and did not say goodbye. Ken followed the driver inside the building, across an enclosed courtyard and along a corridor to a mahogany door on which was inscribed in gilt letters *PORTLAND ROOM – MEMBERS ONLY*.

There he knocked and listened.

'Come.'

Sir Alasdair's meanness with words was legendary. Inside the card room, the lighting was low. At the far end Ken saw a gaunt, grey-haired man with the humourless face of a Victorian highland laird. He was playing a complicated game of patience on one of the green baize tables. A decanter of whisky and a glass jug of water stood by his elbow, together with a couple of glasses.

'You've been a bad boy, Scottie,' was the terse greeting.

Sir Alasdair's voice had been likened by one lowland Scottish colleague of Ken's to that of an Edinburgh judge. 'It has all the warmth of an iceberg,' she had said. And yet the Director-General who had worked night and day so that he could disappear on the overnight train to Scotland each Friday evening and not return until Monday morning had not been unpopular with his subordinates. In his day they had been mainly male. Among them, his reputation had been: tough but fair. It had amazed everyone when a woman – Stella Rimington – was appointed to succeed him.

Ken had never before seen his old boss dressed other than in a well-pressed blue pinstripe suit. Sir Alasdair's tweed suit with leather cuffs and leather patches at the elbows said more clearly than words: I am retired and not being paid for this. I am off-duty.

He neither stood up, nor offered to shake hands. Refusing to remain standing like some ghillie being hauled over the coals, Ken sat down on the other side of the table and took the glass of single malt that was pushed across the baize towards him. He recognised the game being played as Battalion, probably the most difficult of all games of patience.

The whisky in the glass was diluted fifty-fifty with lukewarm water, and tasted like a weak infusion of peat smoke. For several minutes Ken watched the game play itself out in silence.

It was Sir Alasdair's habit always to keep his subordinates waiting until they felt so uncomfortable that they initiated the conversation. The game finished, he collected the cards, shuffled them together with gnarled and liver-spotted hands, and replaced them in a silver card case, which he returned to his pocket. Then he sat back to look at Ken as though sizing up a man he had never seen before.

'What can I do for you, sir?' Ken asked. It was easier to go along with the old man's quirk than endure another five minutes of silence.

'It's what I can do for you, lad.'

Sir Alasdair poured himself another small dose of whisky and water, which he sipped as though it were some priceless nectar. Many of the in-house jokes during his term of office had revolved around the minuscule drinks he offered his staff during the frequent evening conferences at the top of Leconfield House, which went on into the early hours without any break for refreshment.

'I've been asked back by the new boy as consultant,' he said. 'The poor wee man's sorting out the mess that woman left on his desk. One of my briefs is to look into the case of former officers who have reasonable cause to feel that they have been hard done by insofar as their pension rights are concerned.'

'Including Kenneth Wilson Scott?'

'I've been through your personnel file, Scottie. I can read between the lines. If I'd been in charge at the time, I'd have rapped your knuckles early on, when you stepped out of line. Then things would never have got to the pass they did.' There was a misogynistic implication that, with a chap at the top, the other chaps would have rallied round the chap who had stepped out of line before any harm had been done. One way or another, he seemed to be inferring, it was all that woman Rimington's fault . . .

'You're not the type to go ratting to the gutter press.' Sir Alasdair shook his head sadly. 'If I'd heard about this earlier, I'd have bent a few ears in Leconfield House, I can tell you that.'

'You were always very straight with me, sir,' said Ken slowly. 'I'd like to know what exactly prompted this meeting.'

Sir Alasdair put down his drink and stood up to warm his back in front of the open fire in the grate, hands thrust deep into jacket pockets. 'When Peter Wright wrote *Spycatcher*, the Iron Lady told me privately that she thought it a national scandal to treat loyal servants as shabbily as Wright had been treated. "Something must be done," she said, "to stop more of them cashing in by publishing their memoirs outside the jurisdiction of the English courts."'

'But nothing was done,' commented Ken. 'Counter-intelligence officers always have been under-paid and over-worked, compared with their colleagues in SIS.'

Sir Alasdair talked over him. 'What would you say to full restitution of your pension rights and an ex gratia payment of £25,000 in compensation for . . . I'll not call it wrongful dismissal, but rather, a misunderstanding that cost the Service one of its best officers?'

Ken said nothing. By MI5's parsimonious standards, it was a very generous sum.

'. . . and full pension rights,' continued Sir Alasdair, 'instead of that miserable pittance you've been receiving.'

'It's certainly worth thinking about.'

'Personally, I'd like to make the ex gratia payment higher, but that would mean going before the Select Committee. Once we get involved with MPs . . ' Sir Alasdair's gnarled hands were raised theatrically, as though to fend off the fiends of hell. 'I think it's better done this way, out of the Secret Vote.'

'On the other hand,' Ken said thoughtfully, 'compared with the sort of compensation that civil servants are awarded for wrongful dismissal these days, what you're offering is not a fortune.'

Sir Alasdair gave a thin smile. 'I had it in mind to recommend additionally that you be given some consultancy work from time to time, Scottie. The Treasury wants cut-backs, and on paper it looks clever to employ former staff by the week, or the month. In your case, such work will be paid at the going rate, on top of everything else.'

'Anything else I should know?'

A shrug of the tweed-clad shoulders. 'I'm informed that you're carrying out some private investigation, Scottie. That must stop immediately. Moonlighting is out of the question. You know the rules. And incidentally I understand that a valuable musical instrument, stolen from a friend of mine, is either in your possession or that you have knowledge of its whereabouts. That must be returned. I can't recommend the re-employment of someone against whom criminal proceedings are pending.'

Ken stood up. There was a sour taste in his mouth, which did not come from smoking too many cigarettes, or Sir Alasdair's mean measure of whisky.

'I'll let you know, sir,' he said. 'There are other people involved.'

'Don't take too long to make up your mind, Scottie.' Sir Alasdair thrust his head back. He was taller by three inches than Ken, and managed to appear to be looking down at him from an even greater height. The gaunt face was only half-lit by the low shaded lamp above the card table. 'The owner of the instrument wanted to handle this differently, Scottie. I suggest you get in touch with me after you've chatted to who-ever else is involved. Call me here before midnight. I'll be staying in the club and I'll let the porter's desk know where to reach me.'

There was the briefest moment of eye contact. 'Before mid-night,' repeated Sir Alasdair. 'Understood?'

At the door, Ken looked back and saw his old boss breaking out the cards to deal himself a fresh game of patience. In the corridor, the driver of the Escort was balancing on the balls of his feet, like an old-time copper who had been pounding the beat all day. The car was still parked outside, but Tilson had gone.

Ken ignored the single taxi that was waiting on the rank by the club and headed on foot along Piccadilly towards Green Park Underground station. Halfway down the steps, he turned and ran back up them, three at a time. According to an elec-tronic display on a shop front further along Piccadilly, the temperature was eight degrees centigrade. Through the curtain of drizzle floating across St James' Park opposite, he could see lights in the upper windows of Buckingham Palace.

But what had caught his eye was a Dillon's bookstore on the other side of the road. In a copy of Who's Who, Ken looked up Sir Alasdair McIntyre and the chairman of the insurance group who had whistled Jack Belasco to heel. They had only one thing in common: collecting paintings.

Ken had never visited Holm Brae, but former colleagues had described it to him as a bleak, comfortless pile of grey stone, cold in summer and freezing in winter. One visitor had singled out the unheated bedrooms, while another talked of Sir Alasdair's silent grey drudge of a wife and the small portions of badly-cooked food she served at table. But everyone who had been there had mentioned the impressive collection of eighteenth- and nineteenth-century portraits which hung on the bare stone walls – a collection of which Sir Alasdair was so uncharacteristically proud and about which he was so strangely reticent.

.6.

A smell of incense pervaded Siobhan's home. Like all the other bijoux residences in the mews, just off Queensway, with their freshly-painted front doors and the regulation potted bay trees flanking them like sentries, her cottage was tiny. The ground floor was completely taken up by the garage and staircase. Stacked around the walls, with only inches to spare between them and a battered Transit van, were racks of band equipment in aluminium flight cases.

In the cramped first-floor living-cum-dining-room, Irving was practising. From the violin in Siobhan's hand when she came to the door and the two music stands in the middle of the room, Ken assumed that she and Irving had been playing a duet before his arrival. It seemed a strange thing to be doing at a time like that, and made him realise that he did not understand the first thing about how Irving's mind worked.

After letting him in, Siobhan ignored him and went into the minuscule kitchen to make a phone call, closing the door behind her.

'Catriona called half an hour ago,' Irving whispered, under cover of the sound of his violin. 'I don't know what she said, but right now you're public enemy number one around here.'

There was silence for a moment from the kitchen. Then Siobhan's voice resumed talking. The words were indistinct, but the lilting Irish accent was too familiar for Ken to ignore the sound. Irving resumed bowing odd notes, constantly retuning the violin.

The living-room was decorated with Tibetan woven rugs and

instruments hanging on the walls – a family of the flat, Irish single-skinned drums known as bodhrans, three fiddles, penny whistles and a flute. A framed Japanese scroll hung over the mantelshelf and, in one corner, a small bronze Buddha on a wall bracket was watching the smoke curl upwards from a joss-stick. Patchwork cushions were strewn on the futon settee. The cluttered, comfortable, colourful confusion reminded Ken of Catriona's cottage at Le Farou. Hanging on a hook by the kitchen door was a coat of many colours, which looked like one of hers.

He summarised the events of the day for Irving, ending: 'But Belasco had it the wrong way round. My guess is that the fire was started, not to conceal something that was missing, but to cover up the removal of things that had no right to be in the castle in the first place. It's a dollar to a dime, as my Yankee ex-wife would say, that Kurt Servus and Sir Terence Savage were sweating blood as they loaded Goering's pictures into the hired van on the morning of the fire.'

'You have to admire the nerve of these guys.' Irving put down the Strad. 'If you're right, first Blunt and then Savage actually stored Goering's pictures in the bosom of the royal collections. Sheer genius!'

'There couldn't have been many safer places in the world to hide them, in Blunt's day,' Ken agreed. 'Probably even the Queen had to ask his permission before she could poke around her collections. Well, how did your day go?'

Irving pulled the tabs on a couple of cans of Grolsch, passed one to Ken, and subsided into a pile of cushions on the futon. 'I spent most of the time with an old school chum called Prince. You remember all those Liverpool nicknames? Diesel fitter? The guy who was always dropping crates of women's clothes on the dockside to burst them open and grabbing a pair of knick-ers for his wife, saying, "Dese'll fit 'er. Dese'll fit 'er."'

'Spare me the Merseyside humour, Irving. I grew up there too, you know.'

'Well, Prince got his name because he was already into the whole Rastafarian thing when we were only ten years old, set-ting fire to empty houses for kicks. He declared to the whole school in assembly one morning that he was descended from some Ethiopian king in the Bible. His family lived in a condemned house, somewhere in darkest Granby Street, but he was into smart clothes and Afro haircuts, so they called him Prince – short for Black Prince. Once I escaped from the Pen and went to the Mozart School, I didn't exactly have a lot in common with my old classmates, whose idea of a good time was to sit around smoking ganja or shooting up in squats down by the Rialto, using the money their girlfriends made on the game. But Prince had style, so we kept in touch.'

Ken was being patient. 'And just how is the Black Prince going to help us?'

'He's an expert at getting into other people's houses. The Savage residence is a fortress with ten-foot high brick walls, topped with razor wire. The alarm system is state-of-the-art and connected to a security company. Infra-red beams crisscross the garden and every exterior door and window is covered. Lucky for us, Prince likes a challenge.'

'So how do we get in?'

'We wait until Sir Terence comes home, and the alarm's switched off.'

'I said I wanted to explore the house when no one was at home.'

'Then you'll have to lump it. Prince says it's never left unattended. By doing some door-to-door canvassing, he found out from the neighbours that there are a couple of other men who live in the house with Savage. One of them answers to the description of this man Servus. The other is a young guy, who spends a couple of hours in the garden every afternoon, pumping iron, come rain or shine. An ex-naval cook, the neighbours said – except for a retired colonel who lives a few doors away. He called him "Savage's bum-boy". Oh, and there's canine security too: a couple of Alsatians roam free in the garden at night when the alarms are switched off.'

They were sitting in Liz's Saab convertible in which she had just driven back from Gatwick airport after her day in Brussels. The Black Prince had put his days of sartorial exhibitionism behind him. He had a tidy haircut and wore a smart mid-grey off-the-peg suit beneath a dark-blue overcoat, making Ken and Irving in their jeans, black trainers and dark polo-neck sweaters look cheap. Prince's haircut was neat, dreadlocks long gone. Even the too-identifiable Scouser talk had been replaced by a middle-of-the-road London accent and usage. In the Underground, Liz thought, with his laptop bag and a copy of the *Guardian* tucked beneath his arm, the polite, self-effacing young black man with polished leather shoes and black pigskin gloves, would have been taken for an ambitious and hard-working shop or office manager – not a professional criminal.

A pro, Ken thought, watching the gloved hands smooth out the ground-floor plan of Sir Terence Savage's Kensington house – which Liz's source had drawn from memory – and compare it with his draughtsman-quality plan of the exterior of the house and garden. The light of his pocket torch reflected off the paper, lighting Prince's intelligent face.

'Piece of cake,' he drawled, folding the plan up and passing it back to Liz.

'How are you going to get them inside?' she enquired.

'Crowbars and jelly, ma'am.' The white teeth flashed in the black face. 'Not scared of bangs, are you?'

'I've got used to Irving's sense of humour,' said Ken heavily. 'A double act is going to be hard to take.'

'I'm using a silenced helicopter.' Prince enjoyed his joke.

'And where are the other men?' Ken asked. 'You said they'd be here.'

'Relax.' Prince patted his knee. 'All will be revealed.'

Across the street from where they were sitting ran the side wall of Sir Terence's garden. On top of it, the razor wire gleamed in the light of the streetlamps. The metal supports were insulated, so Ken presumed that the wire carried at least a voltage sufficient to give a warning if it was cut. On the far side of the wall, the rear of the house looked dark and uninviting. Ken opened a pack of rubber gloves and passed a pair to Irving.

'How much do you get for a job like this?' Even in such bizarre circumstances, Liz was still the reporter, wanting to know all.

Prince sounded pained. 'I wouldn't take money from an old pal like Scruff.'

'You work for nothing?'

'I didn't say that.' Another grin exposed the perfect white teeth. Prince tapped the laptop on his knee. 'A black guy walking along a street at this time of night with a holdall gets stopped all the time by the boys in blue. The way I'm dressed, and with the scent of a good brandy on my breath – don't worry, I just rinse my mouth out with it – they're more likely to salute me. The trick is to learn to walk as though the bag doesn't weigh anything.'

He pointed across the road. 'In a house like that, there's bound to be a few trinkets to reward me for my trouble. Miniatures, snuff-boxes, netsuke, vinaigrettes . . . You'd be amazed how many I can scoop up in thirty seconds flat. I'll be back outside quicker than you can blink.'

A party of Arab men in their twenties, wearing white robes, were coming out of one of the other houses in the street, talking excitedly as they got into a pair of black chauffeur-driven Mercedes stretch limousines.

'Now that lot, they'll be off gambling or whoring in Mayfair,' Prince announced as the cars drove off.

When Ken asked how he could tell, he answered, 'It's the repression.'

'You mean, recession?'

Prince chuckled. 'No, the repression of the Islamic way of life. Those young blokes go crazy when they're let off the leash here in London.'

'I didn't know you were a philosopher,' Irving remarked.

'I'm a professional at me job, Scruff. Just like you are at yours. You have to know how the punters live. That way . . . Ah, here he comes – the best dockside crane jockey I ever met.'

A burly man in a navy-blue donkey jacket with *SITE MANAGER* stencilled in white on the back was walking along the pavement towards the car. As he drew level, his voice floated back to them in the quiet street with the unmistakable accent of Liverpool. 'How you doin' there, girls? Ready to go, are we?'

Leaving Liz sitting in the car to await a call on her mobile, telling her that the coast was clear, Ken hurried after the other men, wondering whether he was insane to put himself into the hands of jokers like Irving's friends.

At the end of the cul-de-sac, a wired-in observation platform overlooked a building site where two houses had been demolished to make room for a block of prestige apartments. The nails down one side of the panel of shuttering next to the platform had been removed, allowing the panel to hinge like a door. Once on the other side, the crane jockey went into a huddle with two more men waiting in the shadows, who handed dark-blue donkey jackets to the newcomers. From his laptop case, Prince took a throwaway paper boiler-suit and pulled it on to protect his clothes before taking the last donkey jacket.

Someone put a white hard hat on Ken's head and a gas mask was thrust into his hands. Looking to any sleepless local resident like a night crew working on the site, the six men picked their way in the moonlight and the spill from the streetlamps between piles of building materials to where a huge steel bucket sat in the centre of the site. From it, a cable led upwards into the darkness, to where the boom of the crane could dimly be seen, 150 feet above. There was a pile of breeze-blocks beside it, up which Irving clambered. The strapped-up tear in Ken's leg made him wince as he scrambled into the bucket. Prince and the two other men followed. In silence, they squatted low, keeping their heads below the rim.

The crane jockey was halfway up the ladder inside the tower of the site crane, moving with the agility of long practice. Once at the top, they saw him insert a key in the lock of the driver's cabin, and then vanish inside. The low-pitched whirring of the electric motor was inaudible at ground level, but they felt the bucket lurch as the cable tautened and the bucket left the ground. The boom began its swing and the trolley tracked along the rails.

Ignoring Prince's hissed instructions to keep down out of sight, Irving half-stood to peer over the rim, catching a vertiginous panorama of the cul-de-sac where Liz's car was parked and the roofs of the neighbouring houses from the spinning bucket. Two streets away he could see the roof of Ken's rental car. Then the spin stopped, the cable was paid out, and the bucket was descending apparently straight into the flagged and terraced garden of Sir Terence's house, where Renaissance fountains stood cheek-by-jowl with classical statuary between cypress trees that could have been growing in Rome.

'There's a dog in the garden – a big one, having a crap by the look of it,' he whispered to Prince.

'There should be two, Irv.'

'I can only see one.'

'Has it seen us?' Ken asked.

'Not yet.'

'Well, don't worry about the pooch,' said Prince. 'We're getting off at Edge 'ill.'

Edge Hill being the station before the mainline terminus at Lime Street, the Scouser expression meant to practise coitus interruptus. Its present relevance was made clear to Ken when the bucket stopped with the rim level with the balustrade of the balcony outside the master bedroom, only inches away from it.

Seeing the strange object descend from the sky, the dog started to bark. Prince and the other two men were over the top before the bucket had stopped moving. He tossed a canister of CS gas from his briefcase towards the dog below, which started to whine and whimper, pawing its eyes and gagging on the fumes that were spreading rapidly as a grey mist across the whole garden. With a flat strip of plastic, he opened the French windows as quickly as if they had had handles on the outside and stood for a moment, listening, before vanishing into the house, followed by the other two.

Ken helped Irving to clamber out of the bucket, then ducked his head instinctively below the rim as a shaft of light cut a swathe across the garden below. The kitchen door had opened and a voice was calling, 'What is it, Bruno? What's the matter, boy?'

Alone on the balcony, Irving watched the heavily-built man in the garden approach the dog and kneel down to see what was wrong with it. Hearing the scrape of metal on stone as the bucket brushed against the balustrade, he glanced up and saw Irving's face looking down at him.

More in surprise than anger, he shouted, 'What the fuck are you doing up there?' The next inhalation had him choking and fighting for air like the dog, as his lungs filled with gas.

Two figures wearing gas masks ran out of the kitchen, grabbed the choking man and the dog, and dragged them inside. It was as slick as a well-rehearsed military operation.

Prince reappeared on the balcony, rearranging the contents of his laptop bag. In the excitement of the moment, he reverted to pure Scouse: 'You should be a'right on the upper floors, lads. That stuff's marginally heavier than air. Just for info, there's only two blokes in the house, the owner and the guy you saw coughing his guts up down there in the garden, like. His boss should be having similar problems by now, because I chucked another canister down the main staircase at him, to stop him using the telephone. So don't go downstairs without the masks on – or you'll be sorry like, youknowworramean?'

He scrambled into the bucket, pulled off one glove and held a hand above his head, pink palm upwards as a sign to the man in the sky. With a muted whine, the bucket spun back skyward.

.7.

They found themselves in the master bedroom, dominated by a Tudor oak four-poster bed at one end, flanked by matching iron-bound chests. The vast room doubled as a gallery for a dozen or more life-size marble statues of male nudes in mostly suggestive poses, each subtly spotlit from above.

Ken drew the Browning and hurried onto the wide landing which ran round three sides of the entrance hall at first-floor level. At the bottom of the main staircase Sir Terence was lying inert by the ormolu and marble telephone table. In the open air, the riot-control gas first synthesised in 1928 by two mild-mannered research chemists named Carson and Staughton is unpleasant enough. In a confined space, it can kill the old, the young and the infirm by exhausting the muscles of the heart.

Pulling on his gas mask to follow Ken down the stairs, Irving ran down to help the choking owner of the house. Before he had reached the bottom step, the eyepieces of the gas mask had fogged up. It was like running through a Turkish bath. Irving fought down the momentary panic that he was not getting enough of the rubber-tainted air through the rasping, farting filter. The gas was starting to itch his exposed skin.

Slumped immobile on the floor, Sir Terence was not even breathing visibly. Wanting him conscious and talking, Ken tore off his mask. The rubber strap came loose from the buckle. Rather than waste time trying to fix it, he held it over Sir Terence's face with one hand while using the other to lift his head, with Irving carrying the legs. They staggered up the stairs, one step at a time, Ken with eyes closed and a pulse hammering in his head until he could stand it no longer and had to open his mouth and gulp air, no matter what the cost. As the gas hit the mucous membrane of his throat and lungs, he stumbled and almost fell, but somehow managed the three additional steps that put his head above the level of the gas layer.

The first lungfuls of uncontaminated air were like cool water in the desert.

'Jesus!' gasped Irving, dragging off his mask. 'To think the SAS do an assault course wearing those things . . .'

He made to throw his away, but Ken, still unable to speak, stopped him by a gesture. He did not know how long CS gas kept its potency, but with Prince and his crane jockey friend gone, the only way out was down the stairs and through the grey mist to the front door, where one of Prince's friends was already waiting to let Liz in, with a spare mask in his hand for her.

Ken gestured to Irving to help him carry the unconscious man into a first-floor sitting-room, where they placed him in a maroon leather wing armchair by an open fire. Irving pulled off the Guards' tie and loosened his shirt collar, while Ken checked the pulse in Sir Terence's neck and found it rapid but strong and reasonably regular. When he pulled back an eyelid, the pupil reacted to the light.

'You stay here,' he ordered Irving. Certain that both the cook and the bodyguard had been in the house when the raid commenced, he wanted to know where Servus was. On the ground floor, the only point of interest was the kitchen, where a row of black-and-white monitor screens replayed pictures from the surveillance cameras around the outside of the house. But of the bodyguard there was no sign. Ken spent the next ten minutes moving cautiously up each flight of stairs and checking out every room of the house in turn.

Sir Terence's home was the private museum of one very greedy man, each room on the first and second floors devoted to a different speciality of his eclectic collection. Only the bathrooms and toilets were devoid of decoration. In one former bedroom, empty display cabinets testified to Prince's lightning progress through the house. A handful of miniature portraits lay scattered on the silk Persian tree-of-life carpet, together with an unused gas canister, which Irving's old school pal had thrown out of his bag to make room for more valuable loot. Ken picked it up and stuffed it into a pocket. The label read *Home Office – for Police use only. Not to be used within one metre of face, or permanent eye damage may result.*

The third floor, which extended only over the front rooms of the house, appeared to be where Servus and the cook lived in two self-contained suites, equipped with ordinary modern furniture. In the first one – which had to be the cook's – the magazines and photo blow-ups pinned on the walls were all of nude body-builders in ambiguous poses, exhibiting enormous, steroid-enhanced muscles bulging beneath their well-oiled skin. In the other apartment, which was as immaculately clean and tidy as a sterile operating theatre, girlie mags ranged from *Playboy* to ultimate SM and bondage. Their main theme was the abduction of frightened underage girls, who were forcibly stripped, tied up, gagged, whipped, sodomised and confined naked in cages.

The blood, burns, weals, bruises and knife-cuts on their bodies looked real. On a shelf above the bed were some photo albums of similar material – mainly Polaroid shots in which Servus was the main participant. The cover of one had a type-written label inside, to the effect that it was made of human skin taken from a sixteen-year-old Zulu girl. Since most of the pictures in the album were of a young black girl being savaged by two large dogs, Ken thought the label probably true. He let the book drop to the floor and picked up a cigarette carton out of the waste-paper bin. Marlboro Lights . . .

There was a locked door, which Ken barged open. The box-room in which he found himself was a gun-room, which smelled of metal and oil. Weapons ranging from flick knives to a Kalashnikov assault rifle were clipped to a perforated board that covered one wall, arranged like a mechanic's tools in a garage. Around each one was drawn an outline in felt pen. There were photographs of Servus in various macho poses with each weapon. The outline of the one that was missing was labelled Scorpion – Intratec, USA. Ken removed an Israeli Uzi assault pistol from the board for Irving, and inserted a loaded 20-round magazine.

He was tempted to take a mint-condition Calico M-900 for himself. With a fifty-round magazine, it outclassed the Scorpion. But against that, he had never handled the weapon, and the good old Browning was like an extension of his own hand.

Working his way back down through the house, Ken stopped in one of the second-floor rooms. It was atypically bleak, devoid of furniture and smelled of turpentine. In the centre of the room stood a robust-looking artist's studio easel beneath a full-spectrum overhead light, like that in a dentist's surgery. On a plain wooden table beside the easel were rags, tubes of paint, jars of varnish and jugs full of brushes. There was a palette and a selection of knives for oil painting. The picture on the easel nagged at Ken's memory. It showed a crowd of young men and women in nineteenth-century costume dancing or sitting and talking in an open-air restaurant. The men had wing collars and bowlers, boaters or top hats; the women wore crinoline dresses and velvet chokers.

Ken thought he had seen a reproduction of the picture before in an art book. He glanced at the copy of Dietrich's list that he had brought with him. No 37 was itemised as: *At the Moulin de la Galette, painted 1876 by Pierre-Auguste Renoir. Oils on canvas. 131 cm x 175 cm. Removed from the Museum of Impressionism at the Louvre, Paris by Einleitung Reichsleiter Rosenberg on 15 December 1941.*

The painting on the easel could be a copy, of course. But some of the paint was cracked by age and, in the lower right corner, the dash of red suggesting the drink inside a tall glass on the green wooden table was fresh. Ken touched it. The dab of oil paint which came away on his finger made him understand one very practical reason for Sir Terence to keep the paintings in his own home, rather than a bank vault. There must be a need for constant monitoring of their condition, and restoration jobs to be done from time to time. Who better to look after all that side of things than a man who had been trained by a former Surveyor of the Queen's Pictures?

But where were the other hundred and thirty-seven paintings? Ken was backing everything on the hunch that Savage had brought Goering's paintings to his own home during that panic on the day of the fire at Windsor Castle, and that they had never been moved elsewhere because of the risk involved. If they were not there, he had failed.

His wristwatch read 0.15. Twenty minutes earlier they had been sitting in the car, waiting for the crane jockey to arrive when Prince's sharp eyes had picked out two air-conditioning units sticking through the masonry on second-floor level, one at each end of the house. 'Not the sort of thing you're normally allowed to do to a listed building,' he had commented.

The sentence echoed in Ken's mind, until he realised that the central corridor which appeared to run the length of the house, was actually shorter than the sum of the rooms which ran off it. Lit in daytime by a long skylight, it ended in two blank walls which gave off a dull thud when hit. Ken noticed a narrow crack in the wallpaper along the top, bottom and sides, suggesting that the end walls were doors of some sort. But there was no trace of a keyhole or a button-pad.

In the first-floor drawing-room, Sir Terence was moaning softly and seemed to be on the point of recovering consciousness, while Irving paced the room impatiently. Ken handed him the Uzi. 'Be careful. I put it on single shot.'

Irving took the weapon warily, and watched Ken go through everything in Sir Terence's pockets, placing each object on the oval drinks table beside the chair: a silk handkerchief from the breast pocket of the Savile Row pinstripe jacket, a gold hunter fob-watch on a chain from the waistcoat, a bunch of car and house keys from one trouser pocket, but no small change. From one inside breast pocket Ken took a wallet containing £200 in twenties, an American Express Gold Card and several other credit cards. In the other was a gold note-case with matching miniature ball-pen.

'The keys,' said Irving.

'There's no keyhole,' Ken snapped. 'I told you.'

Irving tutted infuriatingly. 'That bastard snoring over there never even gets into his Rolls unless there's a driver at the wheel. So what's he doing with a Ford bleeper on his key ring?'

Ken snatched up the keys. 'I'd tell you that you were brilliant if you didn't already know.' He raced up the stairs four at a time.

'Humiliating, isn't it?' Irving called after him.

Ken stood in the corridor, pressing the button and pointing the bleeper at one end wall, and then the other. Nothing happened. He was about to throw the keys down in frustration, when he heard the whine of heavy-duty electric motors coming up to speed. Both end walls slowly pivoted, revealing themselves to be metal multi-point locking doors thick enough for a bank vault. The mirror-image spaces behind them made a combined storage place par excellence for more than a hundred of the most valuable paintings in the world. The custom-made racking system held each one upright with enough space for air to circulate between it and the next canvas. As the doors stopped moving, the only sound was the hum of the air-conditioning units.

He walked into the nearest storage room. A hygrometer and a thermometer were fixed to the wall. It was a tight squeeze, with just space for him to move sideways between them and the paintings. Recognising Mrs Prescot's picture in one of the smaller racks above the air conditioner, he knew that he was looking at works of art that had not been seen by the public for half a century, during which time they had cost the lives of three people: Sepp Müller, Mrs Prescot and Hallstatt. The pictures in these two small rooms represented enough wealth to pay off the national debt of one or more Third World countries.

Ken spun round at the sound of feet coming up the stairs. Sir Terence lurched unsteadily into view. He was breathing with difficulty, wiping his brow with the large silk handkerchief and leaning heavily on the arm of Irving, who was holding the Uzi well away from his body and had a look of intense distaste on his face.

'You must be Scott,' Savage gasped. 'Whatever you do, don't touch anything, for God's sake.'

'Don't tell me what to do,' Ken rapped.

Sir Terence pushed past him. Ignoring both the Browning and Irving's Uzi, he began touching the frames, as if to make sure that none were missing. 'You can't take them away, Scott. You wouldn't know what to do with them. They must stay here. They absolutely must!'

'They don't belong to you.'

'They belong to humanity. I've cared for them. They're in better condition than many national treasures in the world's greatest museums. I know what I'm talking about.'

'You talk about humanity?' Irving put down the Uzi to grab Mrs Prescot's picture off the rack and thrust it into Sir Terence's face. 'What about the old lady you had killed in Liverpool, to get your hands on this? Wasn't she human?'

'And what about a man called Erich Hallstatt?' said Ken. 'He was shot by your thug Servus two days ago at St Emilion. Wasn't he human?'

Sir Terence was not listening. He was remembering a wet Friday afternoon in the winter of 1964, when Sir Anthony Blunt – still high at having won his battle with MI5 – had locked them both in a disused stock-room at Windsor Castle with half a dozen bottles of Moët et Chandon, some oysters and a quarter kilo of caviare.

'I have something to show you, Terry,' he had said archly.

They had been having problems. It was the old story of the younger man wanting more freedom and fun. Blunt, for the first time in his life unwilling to use physical violence on a recalcitrant lover, had decided instead to offer the biggest bribe the world had ever known. Without any warning, he had whipped the dust-covers off first one painting, and then another and another. By the end of the afternoon his young lover had felt dazed and raped by the experience.

'God, Anthony,' he had said, when at last he was able to talk without relapsing into helpless giggles every few words. 'You can't keep all these. Who else knows they're here?'

'Only you.' Blunt's adoring eyes had been more on his young lover than the paintings. 'And what are you suggesting, Terry? That I besmirch my reputation as one of the greatest art scholars of the twentieth century? Or should I abandon these wonderful objects on the doorstep of their legal owners, like foundlings on the hospital steps? What on earth would be the point?'

Blunt had been ecstatic, as he always was when gloating over his hoard – with the bonus that at last he could share his great secret with another very special person.

'Would you have me hand this Renoir or that Van Gogh or the Gauguin back to the Louvre, to be hung on walls for the gaping hordes to file past with their nasty little guidebooks in their hands and those irritating, twittering little headphones on, telling the fools what their ignorance prevents them seeing for themselves?'

He had put on a simpering mock-female voice that had amused the Queen at their last session of charades: 'Oh, that's the Mona Lisa, Gladys. Look at her smile. She must have been such a nice person. And isn't that Renoir pretty? And Day-gah . . . (They always say "Day-gah", have you noticed, Terry?) Isn't it clever, the way he paints the dancers' dresses?

'Terry, my dear, allowing the tourist hordes to gape at and breathe all over wondrous paintings will be seen as one of the cultural crimes of our populist era in the not-too-distant future. Unfortunately, most of us who are equipped to appreciate a great work of art haven't the money to own it. Thanks to me, you're one of the rare exceptions.'

'I'm talking to you.' Ken grabbed Sir Terence by the shoulders and shook him. 'Where's Servus?'

'I don't know.' Sir Terence looked vague. 'It's his evening off. I don't ask my staff where they go to amuse themselves.'

With a Scorpion machine-pistol? Ken let that go. 'I counted the pictures,' he said. 'There are a hundred and fifteen, including the one on the easel. That makes twenty-three missing. Where are they?'

'In good homes.' A wary look came into Sir Terence's eyes. 'You'd be very surprised, Scott, to know some of the people who owe me favours. Indeed, if I were in your shoes, I'd be a truly frightened man at this moment in time.'

Irving was prowling around, looking as though he wanted to

hit someone. 'I think we ought to shoot the bastard right now,' he said. With his bovver-boy haircut and the earring, he looked capable of killing Sir Terence with his bare hands.

'That would save the taxpayer a lot of money,' Ken agreed.

A telephone started to ring downstairs on the first floor. When it had been ringing for five minutes Sir Terence said, 'That just might be Kurt Servus. If it is, I think you should listen to what he has to say.'

. 8 .

Ken allowed Sir Terence to pick up a cordless phone on the table by the easel. Whoever was on the line, he could not cause much harm, with the muzzle of the Browning pressing into his forehead and Irving listening in on a downstairs extension.

After a moment's silence, Savage said, 'Don't hang up, Kurt. Mr Scott is right here with me. I think he ought to know the situation.'

Ken took the phone in his left hand.

'Congratulations,' Servus said. 'You move fast. But I move faster.'

'We have the paintings,' Ken said. 'We have your master. And metaphorically we have you too. When the police see your bedtime reading and the weaponry in your room, there'll be a warrant for your arrest within hours.'

'No, there won't.' The nasal South African voice sounded unworried. 'Just listen to this voice, man.'

There was a rustle at the other end of the line and Ken heard Liz say his name. More faintly, Servus' voice was urging her to tell him what was happening to her.

'This man's holding a gun against my head.'

Liz sounded calm, but Ken felt sick, knowing that she was in the hands of a man who kept photo albums bound in human skin by his bed.

'Hang in there,' he said. 'Don't panic. We'll sort this out.'

'Oh, will we?' It was Servus back on the line. There was another rustle and a clonk, as though the handset at the other end had been dropped in a struggle. Ken heard Liz scream, 'Next door.' Then there was a dull thud and Servus said faintly, as though the phone was nowhere near his mouth, 'Fuckit.'

'Hello?' Ken said. 'Talk to me.'

The line went dead.

Ken spun round and jammed the Browning into Sir Terence's throat, forcing his head back against the wall. The brief conversation had not sounded as though it came from the car where they had left Liz.

'Where's he taken her?' he shouted at Savage. 'Where's Servus taken the woman?'

'I don't know.' Sir Terence was plainly frightened by the rage in Ken's face. His eyes were trying to climb out of their sockets, magnetised by the whitening knuckle of the trigger finger only a couple of inches from his face.

'Next door!' shouted Ken. He was prepared to pistol-whip the man in front of him, to make him talk. 'What the hell does that mean, next door?'

'I . . . I . . . I . . .'

Irving was back. He grabbed Ken by the shoulders. 'Ease off. You're frightening the cowardly bastard so much, he can hardly speak.'

Ken recalled Belasco telling him about the stammer on the morning of the fire at Windsor. He let Irving back him off a couple of paces. There was a red mist in his head, he wanted to kill this man, but that would not help Liz.

In a calmer voice, he said, 'You've got five seconds to tell me where Servus is.'

Sir Terence swallowed to moisten the bruised vocal cords. 'I . . . own the neighbouring . . . property. There's a connecting door . . . in the kitchen.'

Through the window, Ken saw a grey car drive up the ramp from the basement garage and accelerate away down the street with a screech of tyres. Leaving Irving with the Uzi, he raced down the stairs to the ground floor, grabbing his gas mask as he went and collaring the man on guard in the front hall, to come with him. Together they ran into the kitchen, to find the connecting door locked shut. For the second time that night, Ken barged open a door. The other house was silent. He kicked the door to behind him and tore off his gas mask, inhaling the smell of paint and new plaster. There were trestles and dust sheets everywhere. He stepped through the doorway into a hall, which led to a dining-room in similar throes of redecoration. Further along the hallway a smashed telephone handset was swinging at the end of its cord. There was a reddish mess sprayed over the new wallpaper from floor to ceiling and a thin trail of blood leading into the front room.

Ken walked in cautiously. Liz lay crookedly on the Persian carpet, one arm bent awkwardly behind her. Her face was ashen beneath the tan. There was a neat black hole in the centre of her left ear, without even a trickle of blood coming from it. Ken turned her over, and groaned involuntarily. The right side of her skull was gone – blown completely away, leaving an empty cavity where Liz's brains had been. On entry, the single .22LR bullet from the Scorpion had set up a hydraulic shock-wave at approximately the speed of sound in water. It had lasted for no more than a millionth of a second, but in that time the compressed matter of the brain itself had literally blasted the other side of her skull to atoms before the bullet even reached it.

'Jesus,' said the man behind Ken.

Ken heard him sicking up on the floor. He laid Liz's head back on the carpet. Instinctively he straightened her limbs and closed her eyelids. Facing right, she looked so peaceful that he had a momentary delusion of her opening her eyes and saying, 'Ken . . .' Then slowly the unbalanced skull rolled over on its other side. Very gently, Ken wedged a cushion from the sofa in place, to stop it happening again.

It was a time for vengeance, not grief. He tore open the front door and ran along the road to Liz's car. It was empty, and Ken's briefcase in which she had had all the laboriously gathered evidence, was gone.

Siobhan's recurrent nightmare was the price she had had to pay for the success of her group's first album *Slieve Gullion Awakes*, from which she had made enough money to buy the mews cottage and live alone in the solitude she needed to work on her music at any hour of the day and night, as the mood took her.

In the dream, she came home alone late at night after a gig, to find an intruder hiding in her bedroom. The man, whose face was never distinct, had a gun in his hand, and made her strip naked while he watched. What he wanted was never spelled out completely because the nightmare ended in mid-step as he came towards her and reached out to place his hand on her bare skin. At that moment, she always woke up, pulse racing, sure that she had heard a noise, a creak on the stairs, a man's voice downstairs . . .

The reality was much more brutal.

She had been sitting on the bed in the spare attic bedroom, talking to Catriona who was half-asleep after deciding on the spur of the moment to catch the next flight from Florence back to London. They were discussing intuitions and how different Ken and Irving were, and yet how equally impossible. Because Ken had insisted on keeping things watertight, neither woman knew exactly where the two men had gone, nor why.

At first, Siobhan ignored the intermittent ringing of the front-door bell. Ken had told her not to answer the phone or the door. But, after a couple of minutes, not wanting the other residents in the mews to be disturbed, she kissed Catriona goodnight, closed the bedroom door, went downstairs to the ground floor and called out, 'Who is it?'

'Thank God you've come at last,' the man outside whispered through the letter-box. 'They've run into trouble. Scottie told me not to use the phone. I can't talk out here – unless you want the neighbours to hear everything.'

Siobhan slipped off the security chain, unlocked the Yale deadlatch, and was hurled back against the stairs as Servus barged his way in with surprising force for such a small man. The matt-black Scorpion machine-pistol in his hand did not look like any weapon Siobhan had ever seen, but it was so functionally ugly that she knew it was real, even though she had no idea of the appalling damage which the twenty-nine remaining .22LR bullets in the long, thin magazine could do to a human body.

Seeing her mouth opening in a panic reflex, Servus slammed the muzzle of the Scorpion hard into her solar plexus. 'One word,' he hissed, 'and I'll blow you in half, darling.'

There was a personal-attack button beside the door, connected to the burglar alarm. Siobhan could have stretched out her arm and reached it, but it might just as well have been a mile away. Servus whistled between his teeth. An Alsatian dog shouldered its way through the open doorway. He kicked the door closed and locked it with one hand, while keeping Siobhan covered with the other.

'Now walk up the stairs very slowly,' he said. 'And don't be stupid.'

She was too stunned by the speed of his attack to do anything else but obey. As her head came level with the top step, she saw the dog waiting for her.

'Just walk past it,' Servus said. 'It won't touch you until I say so.'

His eyes flicked around, taking in the decor. 'Now, take off your sweater and drop it on the floor.'

Siobhan was hoping the noise of the fracas would have reached Catriona, two floors above them. There was a second personal-attack button beside her own bed. All Catriona had to do, was creep down one flight of stairs and press it. But of course, she didn't know it was there . . .

Her mouth was too dry to speak. She licked her lips. 'I haven't got anything on underneath.'

'Good.' Servus was screwing a silencer into the muzzle of the machine-pistol. 'I'm more of a buttock and thigh man myself, but it's nice to combine work and pleasure.'

'No,' Siobhan said. 'I'm not going to.' *He won't dare to shoot me – the neighbours will hear.*

One moment, she was standing up and the next she was flat on the floor. She thought he had hit her. But it was the dog which had leapt on her, teeth grabbing her right arm and using sheer weight and momentum to bear her to the ground.

'Don't ever say no to me,' Servus warned in the same calm voice.

Siobhan sat up, rubbing her forearm. It was badly bruised by the dog's teeth, but the skin was not broken. The Alsatian was back at heel, watching her, tongue hanging out.

'Now take off the sweater,' Servus ordered. 'And not on the floor, darling. I want to see you do it. Stand up, so that I get a good view.'

Siobhan stood and pulled the sweater off over her head, holding it in front of her.

'Drop it on the floor,' he ordered. 'Now take off your jeans.'

I'm going to wake up. This isn't really happening . . .

'So you don't have any illusions about the dog . . .' Servus pulled out a pack of Marlboro Lights. He stuck one in his mouth, lit it one-handed, using a lighter from his pocket, and studied Siobhan's breasts through the smoke. '. . . I'll tell you how I trained him. None of that crap they do in Britain, with a bloke running round in an enclosure, thrusting out his padded right arm for Fido to grab. In Zaire, I used kaffirs – black girls, to you – as bait. We worked in the open, because it gave them further to run. It took a lot of practice to get everything dead right, because both the dog and me got worked up. But, by the end, I had him trained to go for the tits, the buttocks – or any other body part I tell him to.'

The hand with the cigarette fondled the Alsatian's head between the ears. 'He's never bitten a white female yet. I don't know if the body smell will make any difference. Now, get those jeans off. And do everything I tell you, fast. Next time, I'll order the dog to go for those pretty little tits of yours. So if you want to be scarred for life, go slow and make my day.'

Siobhan began undoing her fly zip. Apart from the dog, it was like the nightmare, where she said, *I've got money and credit cards. Take it all. Look, I'm not wearing my glasses. I couldn't identify you, even if I did see you again.*

'The jeans,' Servus was saying. 'That's right. Leave 'em on the floor and just step out of 'em, darling. You can keep your pants on, for the time being. I prefer it that way.'

Siobhan put her hands over her breasts and stepped out of the jeans.

'Now sit, like a good little bitch. On that settee thing. Hands down at your sides. Good. We'll get along fine, you and me.'

The Alsatian was whining and pawing at the door leading upstairs.

'Who's up there?' Servus asked.

'No one.'

'That's not what the dog thinks.' He opened the door and peered up the stairs. 'While I'm gone, my furry friend will keep you company. Remember, one twitch and he'll go for your tits or your throat, depending on what your arms are protecting at the time. Hard choice, isn't it, darling? If I was you, I'd stay very still.'

Siobhan sat cross-legged on the futon settee, listening to him moving about in her bathroom and bedroom, then start up the flight of stairs to the attic. She heard him swear. Then Catriona gave a brief scream. The dog watched Siobhan, its tongue hanging out. Occasionally its nostrils flared, as though scenting her fear. Then two pairs of feet came downstairs.

'Naughty.' Servus moved back into Siobhan's field of view. He poked the cold metal of the silencer into her left breast and watched her eyes as he pretended to squeeze the trigger. 'You should have told me you had a friend up there,' he said softly.

Woken by a man with a gun just as she was falling asleep, Catriona was finding it hard to believe what was happening. The sight of Siobhan sitting nearly naked on the futon being threatened by Servus brought her back to reality.

'Let the girl go,' she said. 'Please! She doesn't know anything about the paintings. Keep me hostage if you want, but let her go.'

'Who are you?'

'I'm her mother.'

'Aah!' Servus recalled the time he had played Solomon, telling a woman in Zaire to choose which of her two children he should shoot. In the end he had shot them both and let her live, but the moment of her agonised choice had been a pleasure he still remembered.

The back of his hand connected with Catriona's cheek with a force that knocked her to the floor. 'Don't tell me what to do, lady,' he said. 'Now get that pyjama jacket off and sit down back to back with the girl.'

He laid the Scorpion down on the dining-table beside Siobhan's fiddle, and took a roll of black gaffer tape from the pocket of his car coat. With the dog standing guard, he taped the women's mouths closed and their hands behind their backs, then used up the rest of the roll taping them together around the waist.

'Wish I'd brought a camera.' He stood back, feeling pleased with his handiwork, and hoping that there would be time to have some fun later on.

The dog sat two metres away, never taking its eyes off the women it was guarding. Servus went into the kitchen for a drink. They heard him open the fridge, take out a pack of orange juice and pour some into a cup. When he returned, he was getting tense and the dog picked up his mood, fidgeting and whining quietly. Servus muttered a command in Afrikaans, and it went to sit in a corner.

Its master squatted down on his haunches, face close to Siobhan's. 'After this is all over . . .' He weighed her breasts in his hands, enjoying the revulsion in her eyes. She tried to pull away, but was immobilised by Catriona's body weight. '. . . you're going to wonder every night where I am. You won't chance going for a walk in the country alone ever again, in case I'm following you. And each time you go on stage, you'll be wondering if I'm in the audience, watching you. Think about it, sweetheart. I'm going to be with you for life – however long that is.'

.9.

Prince's two friends had taken off into the night with the excuse that their trade was housebreaking, not murder. Of the three cars in the garage, only the black Rolls had keys in the ignition, so Ken took that and drove up the ramp to street level. The disadvantage of such a car was its conspicuousness, but against that the heavily-tinted windows made him virtually invisible, should any neighbour wonder what Sir Terence's car was doing on the street at that hour.

He drove round Marble Arch and up Park Lane, hoping as never before in his life that his guess about where Servus had gone was wrong. It was tempting to accelerate to a hundred miles an hour, but the last thing he wanted was to be stopped or chased by a police car, so he stayed within the limit and sat fuming at each traffic light until it turned to green.

Irving watched the Rolls depart through the window of the study. 'Up,' he said to Sir Terence. 'You and I have some work to do. Get up off your arse and open the safe.'

'What safe?'

The blow from the metal butt of the Uzi left a scarlet weal across Savage's right cheek.

'Don't push me,' said Irving. 'I already have one good reason to kill you. You can open the safe now, or wait until I put a bullet in your left kneecap. Then you'll crawl to wherever it is so damned fast, you'd win a medal in the Olympics. If I'm wrong, there's always the right kneecap.'

Sir Terence got slowly to his feet, playing for time. 'If I were you, Bradley, I'd take off while the going's good. If Servus gets back here before Scott, he'll kill you. You haven't a chance against a man like that. I can't control him.'

'I warned you.' The anger that had been seething in Irving since the moment that he had *known* that the man in front of him was responsible for Mrs Prescot's death, was boiling over. He pressed the trigger. But he had forgotten about recoil during the years since he had last handled a firearm. The Uzi leapt in his hands and Sir Terence was left looking down at the hole in the silk Persian carpet on which they were standing. Involuntarily, he stepped backwards.

'Next time, I won't miss,' Irving promised.

With no intention of getting hurt if it could be avoided, Sir Terence led the way into the bedroom, where the chorus line of statues stood, frozen for ever in their attitudes of disdain, vanity or lewdness. One of the linenfold panels in the time-blackened oak head of the bed hinged open to reveal a wall-safe in the recess behind it.

'I don't keep any money here,' he said, dialling the combination. 'But I have things like the Strad which are worth far more than cash, Bradley. I admit I misjudged you, but we can come to some arrangement – you and I.'

Irving hit him again with the Uzi, and saw blood running down from the cut above Sir Terence's ear. A differently educated man might have thought it cowardly to land a blow from behind; as far as Scruff Bradley was concerned, he was back on the streets of Liverpool where there were no rules.

'I want the list,' he said. 'In fact, I want two lists.' Ken had reasoned that there would be one record of people to whom Savage had done favours over the years – and another of the handful of men or women who had bought one of Goering's paintings from him.

Sir Terence was frightened of the man standing behind him, but reasonably confident that Servus would be back soon. As slowly as he could, he turned the knurled knob in the centre of the safe door, going deliberately wrong so that he had to start again.

'Dammit,' he said. 'You're making me nervous.'

'You're right to be nervous,' said Irving. 'One more mistake – and your kneecap's gone.'

Ten seconds later, he was peering into the small cavity. He ignored the wads of currency and the three passports, and reached his rubber-gloved hand inside for the two slim notebooks.

'I warned you.' Sir Terence was sitting on the bed, dabbing the cut on the back of his head with a silk handkerchief. 'When you see the names, you'll realise the sense of the old saying: "If you can't beat them, join them."'

Irving ran his eye down the list of thirty-eight names in the first book. Most of the Asian, Latin and Arabic names meant nothing to him; they were the anonymous hyper-rich who rarely get named in the media. But the far longer list in the second book had many names he recognised, including that of Max Grayson, his agent.

Ken braked the Rolls to a halt on the yellow line by Siobhan's garage. There was no sign of any car in the mews. Irving's key opened the front door. The house was silent.

'Siobhan?' Ken called. 'Are you okay up there?'

There was no reply. He tried to tell himself that she could be asleep, and called again, louder, 'Siobhan?'

There was a muffled moan from the first floor, then Ken's heart dropped to his stomach as he heard Servus' voice: 'Come on up, Mr Scott. One step at a time, with your hands in the air.'

As Ken's head came level with the floor of the living-room, he saw Siobhan, gagged and sitting on the settee. From that low angle, she appeared naked. A step higher, and he saw Catriona and the tape that was binding the two women back to back. On the next step he saw the dog which did not even turn its head towards him. Servus was leaning against the wall with the Scorpion pointing straight at Ken's head. On the table beside him stood the missing briefcase.

'Evel Knievel,' Servus said. 'Don't just stand there. Come on up. Where's Bruce Lee?'

Ken took another step upwards, hands level with his head.

With the silencer on the Scorpion, Servus could kill them all in one burst and get away without waking the neighbours.

'I'll explain the rules of this game we're playing, Mr Scott. Penalty for a wrong move is a bad bite. But the dog won't go for you. He'll go for the women. Neat, isn't it?'

'You win.' Ken took one more step. He was trying to work out what state Catriona and Siobhan were in, and whether he could count on them. He decided the answer was no. They both looked to be in shock, breathing rapidly and shallowly with eyes staring rigidly ahead, so as not to see the dog or the man with the gun.

'What's that in your hand?' Servus asked.

'It's the film,' said Ken.

'What film?'

Ken hurled himself backwards down the stairs, throwing the spare gas canister at Servus. A spray of bullets hit the woodwork above his head and showered him with splinters. He landed badly and rolled to the bottom step, tearing open the leg wound and nearly winding himself. As he hauled himself upright with gritted teeth, grey fog was already spilling over the top step and down the stairs. He pulled the gas mask out of his pocket, put it on and raced upwards, three steps at a time with the Browning in his hand.

Through the green-tinted plastic of the eyepieces, the small room seemed full of contorted bodies, flailing about uncontrollably. Luckily, constrained by the tape, the two women could move very little, so there was room to deal with Servus and the dog. The dog had to come first. One shot from the Browning reduced it to a pile of fur in the corner of the room. The Scorpion was lying on the floor, where Servus had dropped it. For a brief but measurable period of time, Ken had the choice of merely disabling him and letting him live. Then through the distorting eyepieces, he saw Siobhan and Catriona with their legs desperately thrashing as they rolled helplessly on the floor, still taped together. In memory there was a third woman on the floor, whose head rolled over and presented the empty skull to him.

He had to act fast. Both women risked drowning in their

own vomit if he did not get the tape off their mouths swiftly. It was tempting to put a round from the Browning straight into Servus, but bullets fired from that weapon could be identified by ballistics and traced back to Kenneth Wilson Scott. He pocketed the Browning, stooped to pick up the Scorpion, checked that it was on *short burst*, and squeezed the trigger. Inaudible against the din the women were making, three rounds, slowed by the noise suppressor, slammed Servus back against the wall. His right hand closed on a Tibetan wall-hanging, pulling it down with him as he slumped to the floor, dead before he got there.

The room was suddenly much quieter. There was the rasping noise of the gas mask diaphragm as Ken sucked air into his lungs. And Siobhan was still kicking and struggling, but Catriona seemed unconscious. The window was soundproofed, to stop the noise of music from annoying the neighbours. Ken fought the sliding inner panes sideways and pushed the outer casement window wide open, then hurried into the kitchen for scissors to cut the tape. He cut Catriona free and dragged her, gagging and shivering, over to the fresh air first, then went back for Siobhan.

Finally he tore off the gas mask and was violently sick into the window-box of geraniums. A light went on in the house across the mews. A sash window slid up and a woman's voice called out, 'Oh, my God!'

Ken wiped his face on his sleeve and called across to her in a stage whisper, 'Sorry for the disturbance. Bit too much to drink, you know.'

The neighbour opposite seemed to have no inhibitions about waking the other residents. 'It's bad enough,' she said in the same deliberately loud, complaining voice, 'when the men from the pub widdle all over my potted trees by the front door, but this is disgusting.'

'The women will be feeling better in a minute,' Ken said. They were both lying half-in and half-out of the window, gulping oxygen into their lungs.

'I've a good mind to call the police.' The woman leaned further out, to see better. 'Is that girl not wearing any clothes?'

'We were having a party,' Ken said. 'Strip poker, you know.'

'Strip poker? You can tell Miss O'Riordan, when she sobers up, that I shall be raising the matter at the next management committee.'

'I'll tell her,' said Ken. 'Sorry we disturbed you. Good night.'

As cold air blew into the room, the gas was seeping down the stairs and out of the open front door. There was enough left to sting the eyes, but it was possible to walk through the living-room quickly without a mask. Ken pulled another Tibetan rug off the wall and put it over Siobhan's shoulders. Turning to him a face streaked with mascara, she managed to say, 'Thanks.'

'Good girl,' he said. 'I'll be back.'

Catriona's face was red and smarting from the gas, her eyelids so swollen that she could hardly see out of them. Like a blind woman, she let Ken lead her upstairs to the bathroom, not even seeing the man and the dog lying so neatly concealed by the rug on the floor. When he ordered her to take a good shower, Catriona nodded. He looked back a moment later, to see her still standing in front of the shower cubicle staring into space. He slapped her face and was caught off-balance when she began sobbing and collapsed against him, like a marionette whose strings have been cut.

'It's okay.' He hugged her for a minute, as a father hugs a child seeking comfort, patting her bare back soothingly.

'You must have a good shower,' he whispered when this had gone on long enough. Every minute she waited increased the risk of severe skin burning, especially on mucous membrane that had been exposed to the gas. 'Let the water wash all over you for ten minutes at least. Wash everywhere, as mother used to say. And don't use any soap, otherwise you'll have a bad case of sunburn all over your body. Understood?'

She nodded and he went back downstairs for Siobhan. Closing the window, he saw that the neighbour's light was out. Nobody else in the mews, it seemed, had noticed anything – not even the Rolls parked below the window.

When both the women were safely in the bathroom, Catriona in the shower and Siobhan in the bath, Ken washed his own stinging face and hands in the kitchen sink, and called the number of Irving's mobile phone.

'The Strad's fine,' he said. 'It's still hanging on the wall among Siobhan's instruments.'

'Fuck the Strad.' Irving's voice was tense. 'How's Siobhan?'

'They're both fine too.'

'They?'

'Catriona was here as well. And the man who was involved in Mrs P's accident is lying down. He's having a very long sleep.'

'Understood,' said Irving. 'I've got the lists.'

He replaced the mobile in his hip pocket and felt immensely tired. This was the end of the road. Within the last few hours, Liz and someone called Hallstatt had died. He had only met her for a couple of hours that evening, and never met Hallstatt at all. Mrs Prescot was six feet down in a Liverpool cemetery, but even that wasn't reason enough to shoot in cold blood the man bent over the four-poster bed, shivering with fear.

As the reaction to his adrenaline-high set in, Irving turned away, revolted with the blood-lust that had so nearly made him put a bullet into a man's leg.

'Drop it!' The quavering, cringing tone was gone from Sir Terence's voice. He was standing two paces behind Irving, holding in his right hand a silver-plated snub-nosed automatic. The neat little Davis Industries P-32 in his hand was the ideal weapon for a man who was nervous at night to keep beneath his pillow.

'Drop your gun,' he repeated. 'Or I'll shoot you dead!'

Irving held the Uzi as far out from his body as he could, spreading his fingers one by one until the weapon was held only by his trigger finger inside the guard. As he straightened that and the Uzi dropped, he spun round and put all his force into a kick aimed at Sir Terence's gun hand. A shot rang out, followed by another. Plaster rained down from the ceiling, and shards of glass from the chandelier, shattered by the second 7.65 mm. slug. Then Irving had his arms around the other man, crushing Sir Terence's gun hand against his chest, to stop him firing again. Locked together, they fell back on the bed and rolled from there onto the floor with a crash, Irving beneath. A life-size statue of Priapus, the Greek god of fertility, toppled from its plinth and 200 kilos of marble fell on the two men locked in struggle.

The grotesquely exaggerated and pointed penis of the Priapus bore the whole weight of the statue for a fraction of a second before snapping off at the base, but in that time it had penetrated Sir Terence's liver. The spasm of agony that gripped his whole body, tensed the trigger of the P-32, loosing a round that went through his chest wall and severed the aorta. With a noise between a yawn and a snore, the breath left the dead man's lungs.

Irving managed to wriggle from beneath Sir Terence and the statue. He rolled across the carpet to grab the Uzi, and only then realised that the other man was dead. Turning the body over with one foot, he saw the small red stain on the chest. Death had been virtually instantaneous. The P-32, with its mint-condition silver plating and polished hickory butt-plates, looked like a child's toy in the hand that was slowly unclenching.

.10.

As Ken came up to ground level from the basement garage, he was relieved to find that the CS gas had dissipated completely. Irving was slumped on the top step of the stairs that led down to the elegant white-marble entrance hall, staring at nothing.

After inspecting the corpse beneath the statue in the bedroom, Ken sat down beside him and put an arm around his shoulders. 'It's okay,' he murmured. 'It's okay.'

'It was self-defence.' Irving's eyes had aged ten years.

'Does it matter? Savage deserved to die.'

'All the same, thinking about killing a man and actually doing it are two different things.'

Ken could feel him shivering. 'Come on, let's get moving,' he said. 'I need your help to carry a Servus-size bundle up from the boot of the Rolls.'

He checked his wristwatch as they walked downstairs. His rubber gloves had got torn in the fracas with Servus, but he did not want to leave any prints in this house, so was wearing a pair of pink washing-up gloves that belonged to Siobhan.

'We have three hours before dawn,' he said. 'By then, I want us to be far away, having left behind a neat little scene of murder and suicide.'

'Can we fool the police that easily?'

'It used to be my job, remember? Amateurs panic. Pros take their time and clear up methodically.' Ken was making a mental list of the items that needed burning: the clothes and shoes that he and Irving were wearing, the gloves, the gas canisters, the rug and the plastic refuse sacks he had used to stop any blood getting on the immaculate carpet in the boot of the Rolls. The dog would be the biggest problem. With the bullet from the Browning inside its carcase, it would have to be incinerated in some out-of-the-way spot later on.

They dumped Servus' now rigid body in the entrance hall, peeling off the plastic bin-liners and unrolling the Tibetan rug in which it had been wrapped. It took longer to unfold Sir Terence's rapidly stiffening hand and get his prints on Servus' gun, which was then deposited halfway up the stairs by Irving, while Ken replaced the silver-plated automatic in Savage's hand. He did not think that the local CID would put in too many hours on this case, once they had seen the porn and the weaponry in Servus' apartment. There was a noise of dull hammering coming from the wine cellar where the cook had been locked up with the second dog. Ken ignored it; someone would let them out later.

Placing the notebooks was the hardest thing. He went alone back into the next door house, shutting his eyes to avoid seeing the mess of blood and brain tissue on the wall that had made up the sometimes infuriating but unforgettable personality of Liz Blantyre.

Ken knelt beside her for a moment and held her hand, but it was as cold as the statue lying across Sir Terence's corpse. He wished he could say some kind of a prayer for her, but he did not know any, so instead he murmured, 'It was a kind of love, Liz. It really was.'

He had to fight the instinct that made men in combat risk their own lives to save a dead comrade's body. It seemed heartless to leave Liz in that house, alone for ever. But a headstone was not memorial enough for the person she had been. He owed her the story, to be remembered by . . . and her lifeless corpse was one of the props that was going to get it on the front page.

He put all the papers from his briefcase on the settee beside the body and carefully sanitised them. The only thing that could incriminate him was Belasco's card. He put it in his pocket, together with Hallstatt's note. *Just in case, pal. Use it well.* The rest went into Liz's neat black attaché case.

With the street door open and left on the latch, Ken took a suitcase from one of the bedrooms and stuffed into it the blood-stained rug and plastic bags. He let Irving leave the house first and followed him to where the rental car was parked. There were still two hours to go before dawn, but there was more clearing up to be done.

Back at the mews cottage, the two women were looking better. Apart from where the rug was missing from the wall, there was no sign of the events of that night, but Ken added his briefcase, plus the mop and bucket Catriona had been using, to the things that he would later incinerate.

He let her pull him into the tiny kitchen and shut the door to give Siobhan and Irving some privacy. Having been torn open again, his leg wound was going to need stitches, but there was no time just yet, so he let her strap it up with adhesive plaster, then grabbed a cup of strong hot coffee and changed into a sweater and jeans that belonged to Irving.

At 6.25 a.m. he used Liz's mobile phone to call her editor, whose number was in the memory. The man was only half awake. Ken had to repeat twice the address of the house where Liz had died.

'Who's calling?' The voice at the other end was getting less sleepy by the second.

'A friend,' said Ken. 'Liz should have been back hours ago. She said to ring you if I didn't hear by now – and that you should go in person straight away, with a colleague to act as witness, to the address I gave you. And by the way, the paintings are in the house next door, on the second floor. Everything else is with her.'

He rang off and added the mobile to the items that had to be destroyed. Tiredness clamped him to the kitchen chair. He was unclear how much later Catriona was talking to him, but there was daylight outside the window. She had both her hands in his and was saying something about getting some sleep and medical attention. Lacking the energy to explain that he still had things to do, Ken shaved hastily and picked Servus' bunch of keys from the kitchen table.

After ten minutes of quartering the nearby streets, he found a grey Opel which the keys fitted, and drove it through the dawn traffic to within a couple of hundred yards from Brownlow Square, intending to walk the rest of the way. His leg was stiffening up, and every step was an effort, but he owed it to Liz to make sure all was going as she would have wanted.

Outside Sir Terence's house there was a small crowd standing behind the police line of green and white reflective plastic tape. Merging with them, Ken watched the ambulance men carry Liz's body out of the house on a covered stretcher. He recognised her editor from a photograph he had seen in the apartment overlooking the heath. The man was standing on the steps of Sir Terence's house with Liz's black attaché case in his hand. He and a colleague were arguing heatedly with a plainclothes police officer who had just ejected two Press photographers from the house, after finding them at work upstairs. All the turmoil of Liz's grab-it-and-print professional life was there in the scene. It was time to go home, so to speak.

Ken pulled up his coat collar and started to walk. It would have been bliss to sit down and rest his leg, or even fall asleep on the spot, but that was out of the question, and he did not want to be remembered by some cabbie as having hailed a taxi too close to Brownlow Square. Where was home? He wasn't sure he knew. It certainly was not at Le Farou, among the burned-out embers of a dream where he and Hallstatt would never again chew the fat through the night. There was Irving's cheque for £125,000 sitting in the bank account, and he wouldn't be asking for the money back. Of course, it could never have worked out with Liz. Ken wasn't sure why Catriona had come back – there had not been time to ask her – but perhaps that was the beginning of the thing called home.

Anne? Slender and elegant and exquisitely proportioned as the Mirova herself. And surrounding the house, woodland like a frame for a picture. Bower switched off the car's engine, and the night was filled with birdsong.

'I suppose you arranged that, too,' she said.

'Arranged what?'

'The nightingales. They won't sing for much longer, you know. Not even for Jay Bower.'

'You like it?' Bower asked.

'Like it? It's the most beautiful place I ever saw in my life. Whose is it?'

'Mine,' said Bower. Somehow she had been sure that that would be his answer. He put his arm around her, and she made no objection: it was a gesture of companionship, no more.

'I've had people in there working on it for six months,' Bower said, 'and now it's ready.'

'When do you move in?'

'Tonight,' said Bower, 'if you'll go with me.' His arm tightened round her, but she had made no move to leave him, and he relaxed.

'It's for my wife,' he said. 'That's no place for a bachelor.' He nodded at the exquisite house. 'So all I'm asking is that you jump the gun a little. That house can't wait any more than I can.'

Aunt Pen had given her clothes, a car, a Cartier leopardess, and at the end of the day a fortune, and now this man was doing it all again, telling her she could be the mistress of a house that was like a dream. But too far from Felston.

'I shan't say it's a compliment,' she said, 'although it is. But it's far, far more than that. It is absolutely the most wonderful thing –'

'But you're turning me down?'

'Not you,' said Jane. 'It.' For once Bower looked puzzled, which pleased her.

'Put it this way,' she said. 'I won't go into your *house* – not on the terms you offer. But you did once suggest I visit your – apartment did you call it? – in Fleet Street, and I wouldn't mind doing that.'

'It's second best,' said Bower, 'and I meant that. But I'll take it.'

It had been by any standards a remarkable night, she thought. Not just the sex, though that *had* been remarkable – far, far beyond anything poor darling John had ever done: the upper sixth after the junior school. Her instincts had been right about that: Jay Bower had been not only good at it, he delighted in sharing, and in teaching, too. And thoughtful. Delicately sounding her out on what means they should employ to prevent parenthood. When she told him that she had been to see her friend, a lady doctor, in anticipation of this very event, he looked first shocked and then delighted.

'Are you sure you won't marry me?' he'd said, but she'd been quite sure, and so he'd undressed her instead, and shown her what their bodies could do for each other. She'd been very happy to learn. And goodness how long you could make it go on, when you knew what you were doing. But it finished at last and he told her he could do no more, not that night anyway, which was perhaps as well. She did have to go home. So she'd used his shower, the first one she'd had since India, and he'd used it with her. That almost started him off again despite what he'd said, and then he'd driven her home, grumbling a little, but she wouldn't take a taxi, not at that hour. It was almost dawn when she climbed the stairs, and the servants were still sleeping, but she heard the clop of hooves and the clatter of bottles. The milkman had missed her by minutes and how Hawkins would have enjoyed it if she'd been seen.

When she awoke it was nearly ten but she always slept late after a ball and anyway Hawkins would assume it was champagne. As usual. She felt just a little sore still, but Jay had said that more of the same would take care of that, having assumed from the beginning that there would be more of the same, which wasn't surprising really after the way she'd behaved. Talk about abandoned women. . . . What fun we have, she thought, we abandoned ones.

Hawkins tapped at the door, came in with the tea tray, then drew the curtains quite ruthlessly.

'Ten o'clock, miss,' she said. 'You did say you were to be called by ten.'

And so she had. There was another Felston article to be written, and she'd promised to lunch with Georgina. Foch came in and waited for his biscuit. Neither he nor Hawkins seemed to have noticed any evidence of her shame.

'And Mr Warley phoned, miss. From South Terrace. He wants you to phone him there.'

'After I've bathed,' said Jane. 'Run my bath now, will you?' She and Foch settled down to their Rich Teas.

'What took you so *long*?' said Lionel.

'I was out late,' said Jane. 'That ball at the Piccadilly. I was gallivanting there.' And elsewhere she thought, but I'd better not gloat too much. Lionel could be very astute, especially about sex, even on the telephone.

'So you were,' he said. 'My dear, what a divine dress. The *Daily World*'s full of it. Some of the others have it too. How's the Felston fund?'

'Growing,' said Jane. 'I make begging speeches now and pass the hat round afterwards.'

'The *World* has that one, too,' said Lionel. 'What strange power have you got over that *dour* tycoon?'

Not strange, Lionel dear. Not at all strange.

'He thinks poverty's newsworthy, just at the moment,' said Jane. 'And the fact that I'm sort of rich gives it human interest.'

'Well *I* need your human interest too,' said Lionel. 'About South Terrace. I've been pacing and measuring like a lunatic. When can you come here?'

'After lunch any good?'

'Couldn't be better. Now you're quite sure you've told me everything you want?'

'There is one more thing,' said Jane. 'I want a shower. En suite with my bedroom.'

She took Georgina to the Brompton Grill. Georgina, she knew, loved the food there, and Jane had worked very hard on her article, which was about Dr Stobbs's clinic. She felt that she'd earned a treat. Besides, Medlicott had written to say that the South Terrace lease was now hers, so that lunch was a treat *and* a celebration.

'You looked gorgeous last night,' said Georgina.

'Another *Daily World* reader?'

'White's never an easy colour, but you looked stunning.'

'You look stunning now.'

'I've looked worse,' said Georgina. 'We both have. What's the betting those two foreigners in the corner try to pick us up. . . Who did you go with?'

'Jay Bower.'

Georgina looked up from her plate. 'Again?'

'It's only the second time,' said Jane.

'But so soon after the first.'

'Contain your excitement,' said Jane. 'We get on well together, that's all. I was chauffeur-driven both ways.'

A whopper, but she didn't want to share her secret with Georgina, or even Harriet. Harriet knew of course that there was a man, but she didn't know who. Nor would she. She would guess of course, but she wouldn't know.

'Quite a catch, Jay Bower,' Georgina said.

'I'm not fishing. How's Michael?'

'Working hard as usual. Worrying as usual.'

'Worrying?'

'In case his wife comes calling again. He wants us to move, but what's the point? She'd only hire detectives to find the new place. Maybe he should move by himself.'

'Could you bear it?'

'He could pop round to see me when he was feeling randy,' said Georgina. 'Or I was.' She cut into her food, then swallowed. 'This chicken is delicious.'

'It wouldn't be the same though, would it?'

'It's all I need,' said Georgina. 'I mean I love him madly and all that but his paints really do clutter up the place. I found some on the piano keyboard yesterday.'

Jane realised that it was all she needed, too, but that was because her feeling for Jay was nothing like her love for John.

'Do you really?' she asked. 'Love him madly, I mean.'

'As madly as I ever loved anybody. I've been offered a new job. At the BBC.'

'The what?'

'The British Broadcasting Company,' Georgina said. 'You know – the wireless.'

'You're going to be an announcer?'

'Of course not,' said Georgina. 'I'm going to play the piano and prattle merrily about how lovely it is to dedicate one's life to one's art.'

'Does it pay well?'

'Twenty guineas for the half hour. Mind you it's only for three half hours so far, but if it takes I can pay the rent indefinitely.'

'Does Michael like the idea?' asked Jane.

'What choice does he have? We need the mun.'

The head waiter came to them. 'The two Italian gentlemen in the corner would like you to join them for coffee and liqueurs, ladies,' he said.

Jane said, 'No, we won't do that. But give them an extra brandy each and put it on my bill. Tell them it's for having such good taste.'

Life rather fell into a rut after that: writing articles, making speeches, inspecting South Terrace, being under or over Jay Bower. No word from Mummy, and no word from Vinney either, though Medlicott swore that every effort was being made to trace her. Maybe she should send Mr Pinner to Bombay, Jane thought, and then one day Mr Pinner called her, most inappropriately, at a time when she was under Jay. Frantically busy though they were, Jane noticed, the telephone could not be ignored. Jay poised himself on his left elbow, reached out with his right hand, and scooped what Mummy called the instrument to him, juggling it so that he got the earpiece to his ear, and the mouthpiece was cushioned by her left breast.

'Bower,' he said.

Jane saw no reason why she should stop what she was doing, nor did she. Bower's next words achieved a certain urgency.

'Hold the wire,' he said. 'She's right here.'

He moved the mouthpiece to her left cheek and handed her the earpiece, then resumed what he had been doing.

'Yes?' said Jane. 'Who?. . . Mr Pinner?. . . Oh. . . .' And then again, 'Oh,' for Jay was showing no mercy. 'You've what?. . . Oh marvellous. . . . I said marvellous,' and Jay smirked. He would pay for that. 'And where is she?. . . Oh that's wonderful. . . . Thank you.' Jay smirking more than ever. 'Thank you so much, Mr Pinner. You're an absolute treasure.' Somehow she put the earpiece on its hook and got back to the matter in hand.

After the shower, she said, 'That was Mr Pinner.'

'What was?'

'The man who nearly interrupted our bliss. But he didn't did he?'

'Not mine, certainly. How did he know you were here?'

'I always tell Hawkins where I can be reached in emergencies. Another thing you taught me.' She put on her petticoat, then sat before the mirror and reached for a comb.

'Mr Pinner's an emergency?' Jay asked.

'Not really. Just good news. I have to go to Ireland.'

'Why, for God's sake?'

'He's found Bridget.'

'And who the hell is Bridget? A cook?'

'A horse,' said Jane. 'My horse if I'm lucky. She's in County Meath – just outside Dublin.' And she told him the story. Jay was entranced.

'Maybe we can use that,' he said.

'And maybe I'll let you. . . . I'm not sure about that yet.'

Perceptive as ever, Bower asked: 'Do I have a rival?'

'No,' said Jane. 'Only a yardstick to be measured by.'

'The one who was killed on 10th November, 1918?'

She had told the Hampstead tea swillers, and of course he'd spotted it at once.

'The very same,' she said. 'I really do mean to get that horse.'

'I wouldn't blame you,' said Jay. 'You're in a hurry, right?'

'I am indeed.'

'The week after next wouldn't do?'

'The week after next she could be sold,' said Jane.

'You wouldn't want to risk that.' She turned to look at him, but he was perfectly serious. 'The trouble is,' he continued, 'I want you in Paris next Thursday.'

'Want me?'

'Not that way,' he said. 'I want you that way every time I get my strength back. I want you to do a piece there.'

'About *Felston*? In *Paris*?'

'There are other places in the world than Felston,' said Bower. 'This is about a guy who drove an ambulance in the war. He's going to the Quart' Arts Ball. I thought maybe we should go too.'

'I'd love to,' said Jane, 'but I'll lose three whole days just travelling. And buying a horse isn't like buying a pound of carrots. One's expected to haggle.'

'You could fly there,' said Bower.

'So I could,' said Jane, 'but I don't happen to have an aeroplane.'

'I do,' said Bower.

'Of course you do,' said Jane. 'You have everything. And thank you. . . . I'd love to go to Paris with you – but you must let me pay for the plane.'

'On the house,' said Bower, 'if you'll let me print the story.'

She looked into the mirror, lipstick in hand, but what she saw was John on Bridget's back, learning to canter, and grinning his delight when he found that he could.

'Very well,' she said, 'but the editor's decision is final, and this time I'm the editor.'

'You've got a deal,' said Bower.

God alone knows what Jabber will say when he finds out, thought Jane, but I don't think John would mind. He was very proud of Bridget.

Bower had arranged everything. It would be all too easy to get used to the idea that Bower always arranged everything. Plane waiting at Croydon, landing field arranged in Meath, and a car to meet her and take her to Mangan Castle. For Bridget it seemed now belonged to an earl. But Bower took earls in his stride. He'd once told the Prince of Wales that he put too much vermouth in his martinis.

Jane hired the Rolls-Royce once more, said farewell to cook – who, Jane knew, would put her feet up the instant the front door closed – and sent Hawkins over to assist Lionel, a euphemism for resisting too much Bakst.

Bakst made her think of Hugh Lessing, who obviously didn't like Georgina, no doubt because he considered her a bad influence on Michael Browne. But Georgina wasn't a bad influence on anybody – or not deliberately. She couldn't help the way she looked. Even Mummy had admitted that she was a lady. Papa had been bowled over. . . . Mummy. . . . She searched in her handbag as the Rolls moved serenely on, and took out Mummy's letter. Mummy was writing at a furious rate, which was not in the least like her. And at length, too. Sheets and sheets. The latest was eight pages. And all about nothing, really. Except that Kalpur was lovely and the new maharajah had converted the cricket pitch into a polo lawn. And the people were delightful and she had been asked to play the piano everywhere. Stuff like that. Eight pages of it. And a PS to say that Miss Gwatkin was well though approaching obesity. Not like Mummy at all, except for the PS. Could she have gone out in the sun without a hat?

At Croydon the pilot came to meet her and led her to her plane, which was big indeed compared to the fighter her brother David had used that day he flew over to visit her. She even had a cabin all to herself. She still needed her fur coat of course – the heaviest one, the silver fox, and the travelling rug over her knees, but she was out of the wind. There was even a flask of tea.

The plane took off and climbed steadily, heading west. Jane looked down to see London sprawling in every direction, then thought of Jay once more. She had gone to bed with him, she supposed, because after Tony Robins had so disastrously taken her out she had realised that Jay had a sexual attraction for her that Tony lacked. And power. He had enormous power – aeroplanes and earls and aid for Felston, and she found that sexually attractive, too. He'd acquired another MP just recently. All newspaper owners had them, he'd told her; backbenchers who obliged with little 'think' pieces on 'The Modern Girl' and 'Can Socialism Work?' and 'The Greatness of Our Empire'. Until recently Bower considered three to be an adequate number, but then he'd got this bee in his bonnet about poverty, and that meant taking on a Socialist. They'd met in Jay's office where they were discussing the Paris trip. His secretary had announced that Mr Lambert was waiting.

'In a minute,' said Bower.

'Who's Mr Lambert?'

'An MP,' said Bower. 'One of mine as a matter of fact. Maybe you should meet him. He's a man of the Left. At least that's what he calls himself.' He flipped the intercom switch. 'I'll see Mr Lambert now.'

A colourless man, she thought, despite a suit of an unbelievable, almost an electric, blue, and a scarlet tie. Colourless and nervous. Or perhaps one was caused by the other. Bower made a lot of people nervous. . . . But a nice man, with a face more pleasant than handsome, and a surprisingly rich, deep voice, with a slight Yorkshire accent.

'Pleasure to meet you, Miss Whitcomb,' he said. 'Of course

I've read a lot about you.' He looked at Bower. 'In the *Daily World* of course. Hard to believe such an elegant lady could have done what you did in the war.'

'Felston,' said Bower. 'That's what we have to concentrate on now. What Miss Whitcomb's going to do for Felston. Or do you find that hard to believe too?'

'It'll take courage,' said Lambert, 'but as I say she's got that. And determination.'

'I'm very determined about this,' said Jane.

'I'm delighted to hear it. There's the charity stigma of course, and a lot of folk don't like that, but the way I look at it you're still a life saver, Miss Whitcomb, only this time it's in the class war.'

'Do you want to make a note of that one?' said Bower.

'I already have,' said Lambert.

Jay might call him 'one of mine', thought Jane, but he's his own man, nervous or not. She'd rather liked him.

The aeroplane was flying over fields now, pasture and stubble for the most part, with the occasional dark patch of wheat still waiting for the reaper – and then in the distance, she could see another town. Liverpool, would it be? Or that place where the packets left for what used to be called Kingston and was now called Dunleary? Nice not to have to take the packet, not to risk being seasick. Cunning, powerful, *lustful* Mr Bower.

The earl, it seemed, had a wife, and a family, a son and heir, and two other children, twins, a boy and a girl. He also had a mother, Bower had told her, who was very much a power in the land. Whatever happened, mother must be placated. . . . The sea appeared, and she looked down into a dark and angry green, ominously heaving. Definitely a good idea to avoid the packet.

She had two nights to negotiate for Bridget O'Dowd. The Irish loved horse trading and were rarely in a hurry, but surely two nights would do. Probably all it would take was too much money. Irish peers were famous for their poverty. But she must get Bridget back. There was no proper reason for it but it was more than a rich woman's whim, the imperious demand of wealth that insists all gratification be immediate. It wasn't like that at all. Bridget O'Dowd was her last link with the John who had died at La Bassée, the John who had belonged to her before she knew that his family were any more than names rarely spoken.

She wanted Bridget almost as a keepsake, a reminder of a time long past, but with a special quality that would never be repeated. If the earl declined to sell it would not be the end of the world, but she longed to persuade him; had packed two of her most persuasive dresses.

Another dark smudge on the horizon, that slowly turned into ships and a harbour, then streets and more streets: Dunleary, and then Dublin. They flew on until the houses dwindled then ceased, and the special greenness of Irish grass gleamed below them, a green far more friendly than that of the sea. They passed a small town, and the plane dropped lower, headed out towards a village where they were flying so low she could see the children running. Then in the distance a great house with formal parkland, and before it a scatter of fields in which horses grazed. One field was empty, and in one corner of it a flag flew, a great spread of blue with some heraldic beast or other embroidered in gold. The pilot circled the field once, and appeared to approve what he saw, for he put the plane's nose down, let it drift slowly in for an immaculate three-point landing.

The plane stopped at last and the pilot clambered down, produced a portable ladder to assist her out of the cabin, then reached inside to bring out her suitcase. Jane set out to walk to where two figures were seated on a fence, watching her trudge. Both of them wore macintoshes. This was Ireland, after all, and it was raining. A young man and a young woman, so alike that they had to be twins. The young man swung down from the fence.

'Miss Whitcomb?' he said.

'Yes.'

'I'm Piers Hilyard. This is my sister Catherine.' He offered his hand and she took it. A good-looking young man, quite arrestingly good-looking, more beautiful than handsome, and his sister another of the same. Black and waving hair, brown eyes, aristocratic little beak of a nose, firm mouth that held a hint of sensuality too.

'We thought,' said Catherine, 'that it might be fun if we drove you home ourselves.'

'To the castle?'

'It won't be exactly a giddy round of pleasure,' said Catherine. 'Daddy's had to go to see a man about an entail in London and taken Mummy and Desmond with him.'

'Desmond's our elder brother,' said Piers. 'Viscount Hilyard. It's all a bit complicated and Daddy hates to think – '

'I expect the lawyers just shake him till he wakes and show him where to sign,' said Catherine.

'That's probably the way they work it. Desmond, too,' said Piers. They began to walk down the road to where a Bentley waited. Thank God, thought Jane, that the hood was up, then turned to thank the pilot and confirm the time of the return flight.

'Do you do a lot of this?' Catherine asked as he left.

'A lot of what?'

'Oh – you know. Riding in aeroplanes and driving ambulances and helping chaps with shell shock?'

'You read the *Daily World* I gather.'

'Granny does. She laps it up. So do we, rather.'

'And what do you do?'

'Oxford,' said Catherine. 'We should be there now as a matter of fact but we much preferred to stay here and meet you.'

'Won't there be trouble for you?'

'We'll be fined,' said Piers. 'We quite often are.'

'Piers reckons it keeps the dons in port. His. . . . Not mine. He's at the House. I'm at Lady Margaret Hall. The House is Christ Church, by the way.'

'I know,' said Jane. 'My father and two of my brothers went to Oxford. I nearly went myself.'

'Only you went to war instead,' said Catherine.

'I do wish I wasn't. At Oxford, I mean,' said Piers. 'Oxford was a mistake.'

'What should you have done?'

'Army. Only I rather promised Granny and there we are. Still, this term isn't so bad. I've managed to get three days hunting a week.'

'Me too,' said Catherine.

They were still standing outside the car, and the silver fox was rapidly becoming sodden.

'Do you think perhaps we should get inside?' said Jane.

'Yes of course,' said Piers, who had been brooding so intensely that the rain held no meaning. Oxford and hunting. Hell and heaven, if she read his face aright. He opened the door.

'Shall I drive – or would you prefer to?' he asked.

'You, please.' She ached to drive that car, but she had no doubt that he did too, and Bridget O'Dowd was as yet unsold.

34

H E DROVE FAST and well, but took the most appalling risks, at blind corners, 'S' bends, and overtaking carts, or donkeys, or other cars. Jane willed herself to listen as Catherine prattled on, apparently unaware that there was any other way to drive, and at last the gates of Mangan Castle appeared, and Piers waited impatiently for the lodge keeper, and shot off again down the gravelled drive. Then the final stop, precisely in front of the main doors of the castle. Not that it was a castle. What was left of the original fortress was a couple of miles northwards, close to the village. This house was eighteenth century in every classical line. A butler appeared, followed by a footman who headed for the suitcases, and the twins walked in with her, into a massive hallway that was graced with the most elegant double staircase Jane had ever seen. All the furniture she could see was Chippendale or Heppelwhite, or contemporary Irish copies, the pictures looked at once beautiful and expensive – one surely was a Rubens? Even the carpet she trod on was a washed-silk masterpiece from China. There was no thread of possibility that this was the home of the poverty-stricken. Charm was all she had left. The Earl of Mangan was far, far richer than she.

'Granny says you'll probably want a rest and a bath and things,' said Catherine. 'I'll take you up.'

'Sherry down here at seven,' said Piers. 'We dine quite early. Granny doesn't like to be up late.'

What Granny liked was obviously what everyone else had to like, too, thought Jane. Strange that two such forceful youngsters should allow themselves to be dominated. She followed Catherine up the left-hand staircase.

'We've put you in the Blue Room,' Catherine said. 'It's rather your colour, I think you'll agree.'

A pretty room, really exquisitely pretty, padded furniture, deep-pile carpet, and a fire burning in the grate. One picture only, but the one was a Canaletto view of the Thames. And Catherine had been right about the blue. It was exactly the kind she liked; neither coy nor strident.

'It's heavenly,' she said.

'Granny and I think it's our best, though not for brunettes of course. Mucky little blighters like me. You are lucky being fair.'

And I was envying her that dark beauty she has in such abundance, thought Jane.

'Have we given you everything you need? Books? Cigarettes? Matches? I *think* so. Yes. All here.'

She looked at Jane's suitcases, brought ahead of them.

'Shall I send a maid to unpack?'

'Yes please,' said Jane. 'She can do it while I bathe.'

'Bathroom's just here.'

Catherine opened a door to reveal a vast and elegant bathroom. Not even the need to walk in one's dressing gown down a corridor whistling with draughts. Here were riches indeed.

'I'll let you rest,' Catherine said, then; 'Granny's dying to meet you. And I must say I'm glad we stayed on. Those dons need their port after all.'

She left then, and Jane took off her coat, then lit a cigarette and went to the window. From it she could see the grass and flowers of a formal garden, glittering in the rain, and beyond, a lake that gleamed, more silver than grey, then, as she watched, a flock of wild swans flew across it. Like a poem by Yeats, she thought, and all done by money.

At exactly seven o'clock she went downstairs to meet Granny, the Dowager Countess of Mangan. She wore yet another Paris gown, from Poiret. When she'd packed in London she'd worried because it had looked so grand, but now she needed it as a Crusader needed armour when he rode against the Saracens. Cream silk with an abstract pattern of blue, the same blue as her room. She walked down the sweep of the staircase, as elegant as a debutante's curtsey, and at the foot Piers was waiting for her. Black tie, she noticed, and the claret-coloured jacket of some Oxford dining club or other.

'Charming,' he said. 'Absolutely charming.' And then, 'Come and meet Granny.' There was no doubt about it, thought Jane. Here they were all horses, and Granny the only jockey.

Piers took her by the arm and led her into a small drawing room, – Aubusson carpet, Louis Quinze furniture, – where Catherine sat with an old and dumpy woman in grey, who looked, Jane thought, as Queen Victoria must have looked, if ever she had felt cheerful.

'Granny,' said Piers, 'this is Jane Whitcomb. Miss Whitcomb – my grandmother, the Dowager Countess of Mangan.'

'How do you do?' said Jane. 'I'm awfully grateful to you for asking me here.'

'It's us that are glad you came,' said the dowager countess. 'We don't often get the chance to entertain exciting folk like you. Aeroplanes indeed.' And she giggled.

This was something of which she'd had no warning. The dowager countess had not been born an aristocrat. Her accent reminded Jane very much of her Uncle Walter, but yet was not quite the same. A little further south perhaps? But she was every bit as sure of herself as Uncle Walter had been.

'Do you like sherry?' the dowager countess asked.

Jane had decided that honesty was the only chance she had. 'Not much, I'm afraid.'

'Get her one of your cocktails,' the dowager countess told Piers. 'I'll have one as well.' And then to Jane: 'I can't abide sherry.'

Piers poured, and the dowager countess said: 'You have a lovely life.' It was a statement rather than a question.

'More often than not,' said Jane, 'but I lost my father just recently – and an aunt I was very fond of.'

'She married Walter Nettles,' said the dowager countess.

'Why, yes, she did,' said Jane.

'Then I've no doubt she had her share of a lovely life too,' said the dowager countess, then stopped.

'Oh – do go on,' said Catherine.

'Not for you,' said her grandmother. 'But he was a lovely man.'

'Yes, he was,' said Jane. There could be no doubt that the older woman meant it. 'And he was a man who made things happen.'

'What things?' It was Piers this time, putting a glass into her hand.

Renting a stately home as if it were a weekend cottage, she thought, being bowled by Vinney because he couldn't read her off-break.

'He bought an ambulance and insisted I had to drive it.'

'He *made* you?' Catherine asked.

'Not me,' said Jane. 'The War Office.'

'That Walter,' said the dowager countess. 'His family and mine – we were in the same line of business. Light engineering. Only he went off to India.'

And married Aunt Pen, thought Jane. And you married an earl.

'I'd like it if you'd call me Emily,' said the dowager countess. 'Being a titled lady's all very well and I've never regretted it – but I was born Emily Parkin.'

'Parkin's Car Components,' said Jane at once. So that was where the money came from.

The dowager countess smiled. 'You would know, wouldn't you? Being a driver yourself.'

Catherine said, 'I should call her Emily at once before she changes her mind.'

'And that's enough sauce from you,' said the dowager countess, and then to Jane: 'Well girl? Not holding back on me are you?'

'We have business to discuss,' said Jane.

'We have not. That horse is yours.'

'Granny,' said Piers. 'She's Daddy's horse.'

'Do you think your father would deny me the chance to do a bit of good in the world? And anyway I told – asked him before he went to London. He was more than glad.'

'Of course I'll pay for him,' said Jane.

'You'll do no such thing.'

'But I must,' said Jane.

'All right,' the dowager countess said, and turned to the twins. 'How much? The truth mind.'

Piers said, 'She's in foal you know. And she had a filly with

– 354 –

her when Daddy bought her at that auction in Abingdon, and he bought her too. Do you want them both?'

'If I may.'

Brother and sister looked at each other. Jane had no doubt she was witnessing that telepathic quality that twins were said to possess.

'A hundred and twenty the two,' said Catherine at last, and Piers nodded his agreement.

'Bridget's a bit long in the tooth now but she's a damn good brood mare,' he said, 'and Bridie – that's her filly – could do very well indeed. A shade light, but she can go.'

'I'll write a cheque now if you like.'

'Sit down, girl,' said the dowager countess. 'You young people are always in a rush. Even watching you tires me.'

'Yes, Emily,' said Jane demurely.

'Oh super,' said Catherine, and Piers laughed aloud.

The dowager countess snorted. 'Because you're a celebrity you think you can say what you like, I suppose.'

'Indeed no,' said Jane. 'I'm trying to say what you like.'

This time the dowager countess smiled.

It was a pleasant evening, of a kind she didn't have all that often. Time spent with people older – and younger – than herself. Two who could hardly remember the war, and one who could remember long, long before it. And yet it was obvious that Catherine and Piers not only loved their grandmother but were perfectly at ease with her, as she was with all three of them. She had got what she wanted with no effort at all, but that wasn't it. The pleasure was in the people themselves.

The old woman's main preoccupation was power, but she was good at it, and handled it well, as she cajoled the twins into talking about themselves. They ate in the breakfast parlour, to the butler's rigid indignation. There was a guest present after all. But Granny was unyielding. 'There's twenty yards of mahogany across the way,' she said, 'and tomorrow I'll call a few neighbours in and you can show off another one of your frocks, but tonight we'll eat in comfort.' And indeed they did, thought Jane. Asparagus from their own garden, salmon from their own river. Even the most rigid patriots were drinking hock again, and Emily was not that. She enjoyed her hock too much.

'Are you enjoying Oxford?' Jane asked.

'It's all right,' said Catherine. Piers said nothing.

'What I mean is I'm reading history,' said Catherine, 'and I do read it – quite often, actually. Though not as much in the hunting season.'

'Naturally,' said Jane, and the younger woman gurgled her appreciation.

'What I mean,' Catherine said, 'is that it's frightfully interesting – all that stuff about Napoleon and Oliver Cromwell and Frederick the Great, but it won't ever get me anywhere. I mean it can't.'

All three men of action, Jane thought. Men of power. It seemed as if Catherine had acquired her grandmother's preoccupation.

'And do you read history too?' she asked Piers.

'When I must,' he said, then asked her how often she hunted. It was the only time that her friend Emily appeared less than content.

After dinner the twins declined coffee and went to sort through gramophone records. Jane and the dowager countess sat on.

'You seem to like my grandchildren,' the older woman said.

'How could I not?'

'There's a lot don't. They frighten some.'

'Frighten?'

'You should see them on horseback,' said the dowager countess – and she *had* seen Piers drive a car.

'The girl's all right,' the older woman continued. 'She'll marry some MP or other, and steer him to the top – but Piers,' she paused, then sighed. 'Piers is a problem.'

'You mean because he's a younger son?'

'Desmond's a good boy with a few more brains than his father. He'll manage the estate well enough – if our new masters leave us an estate to manage. And Piers won't interfere. It isn't that. He doesn't like Oxford.'

'I gathered that. What does he like?'

'The army.' The older woman sighed. 'He's always wanted the army. I asked him to try Oxford first and he agreed because he loves me. I hoped it might just be a passing fancy but there's no hope of that. The army will get him.'

'But whyever not?'

'The army got my husband too,' said the older woman. 'Or rather some bloody Boer farmer did. And I knew enough that died in the last one. And you must have known even more.'

'Two brothers – and my fiancé,' said Jane. 'But that was the war and it's over. Surely you can't think it will happen again? We're at peace.'

'Piers doesn't want to join the army to be at peace,' said the older woman. 'He'll find a war somewhere.'

Jane remembered the ex-officer in Jabber's waiting room, off to China to fight the war lords. It seemed as though men could always find a war if they needed one badly enough.

'Oxford will help him,' said Jane. 'He's bright anyway, but Oxford will make him think, and it's the thinking soldier who gets on.'

'I've just told you,' the older woman rasped. 'I don't want him to get on.'

'I was with the army for more than two years,' said Jane. 'I never once met a general who was shot at.'

Emily snorted. 'Good girl,' she said. 'And who taught *you* to think?'

'My father,' said Jane. 'He was an Oxford man.'

The older woman snorted again, as Piers and Catherine returned with a gramophone and records.

'We thought we might dance for a while,' said Catherine.

'What's the joke?' asked Piers.

'No joke taking care of the future,' said his grandmother, and Catherine put on a foxtrot. Piers went at once to Jane.

'May I?' he asked.

His dancing was as strong and skilful as his driving – unless one were in love with him, she thought, but I'm not. Any more than I'm in love with Bob.

Piers had an exhausting night of it, dancing with both ladies in turn, and even Lady Mangan insisted on a last waltz, dancing with intense concentration and counting audibly. One two three – one two three – *one* two three, and then looked at her watch pendant and announced that it was bedtime.

Piers said, 'I'll just take a look outside.'

'Well don't be all night about it,' said his grandmother.

He went off at once, and Catherine went to the window.

'Do come and look,' she said.

Jane joined her, and shortly she could see Piers, elegant in his dining-club jacket, and carrying a double-barrelled shotgun.

'What on earth – ?' said Jane. 'Poachers?'

'The IRA,' said Catherine.

'But I thought De Valera and Michael Collins had settled all that,' Jane said.

'The IRA won't be settled till it wants to,' said the old woman, 'and God knows when that will be.'

'Will they be armed?'

'If they come – of course they'll be armed,' said Catherine. 'They know Piers.' The thought seemed to please her.

'The local ones don't bother me,' said her grandmother. 'It's those loonies in Dublin I worry about.'

Then Piers came back in, the gun already put away.

'Nothing,' he said.

'How dreadful for you,' said his sister. 'Didn't you kill *any*body?'

'I never said I'd kill them,' said Piers. 'I said I'd shoot them. And so I will.'

'Oh go to bed you bloodthirsty young devils,' said their grandmother, and they obeyed her, but they kissed her before they went.

'I hope he doesn't spend too much time here,' said Jane.

'No more than I can help,' said Lady Mangan, 'but it is his home – and he loves it.'

'You really think he's safe from the local whatever it is – Chapter? Branch?'

'Battalion,' said her grandmother. She rose and took Jane's arm, moved to the door.

'Pretending to be soldiers?' said Jane.

'But their bullets are real. Still, they won't bother Piers.'

'Whyever not?'

'Parkin's Car Components,' said Lady Mangan. 'I've found jobs for half Mangan village there. They'd lose them quick if anything happened to Piers.'

Next day Piers and Catherine took her to the field where Bridget and her filly were out at pasture. They went in the Bentley, and this time Jane drove. A brute of a car, thought Jane, that needed all her strength: arrogant and assertive, frantic to excel. It reminded her of Jay Bower, and the way she had to use female cunning instead of male strength to achieve any kind of control reminded her of him too.

When they arrived, Catherine said, 'You really are good.'

'Better than me,' said Piers, but already his eyes were on the horses. She followed his gaze, and recognised Bridget at once.

A little longer in the tooth, she thought, a little more portly, but still so much the horse she knew that the field might have been in France. And beside her her filly, Bridie, a little lighter, as Piers had said, but with almost the same markings. Suddenly Jane amazed her host and hostess, and herself, by bursting into tears. But there was no thudding of guns, no vision of dismembered gun teams. Piers handed her a handkerchief large enough to satisfy even Jabber, and she dabbed at her eyes.

'It brought it all back, you see,' she said.

Piers produced a cigarette case and offered it round.

'Want to talk about it?' he asked. 'Because if you do we'd rather like to hear.'

'Oh yes please,' said Catherine.

And out it all came. Trooper O'Dowd and the Royal Northumbrians' first adjutant, and Goosey Gander and all the others, until it was John's turn, and John was the last, and he died.

'What a heartrending story,' said Catherine. 'No wonder you cried.'

'Rather wonderful though,' said Piers.

Oh dear, thought Jane. If my friend Emily hears it I'll never get Bridget. Or Bridie.

'I do wish I could ride her,' she said.

'You could ride Bridie,' said Catherine.

'I'd love to,' said Jane, 'but I haven't any gear.'

'Mummy's would fit you,' said Catherine. 'I'm sure she wouldn't mind.'

Nor did the dowager, and Jane found herself kitted out in very smart jodhpurs and handmade boots. Catherine and Piers rode with her and, like her, they took their fences straight and true. Bridie proved every bit as clever over the jumps as her mother, which was as well. Both Catherine and Piers were superb in the saddle, and with mounts that matched their skill.

'You ride well,' said Catherine, as they rode back to the stables.

'Very well,' said Piers.

'I had to, to keep up with you two.'

'Where did you learn?'

'India,' said Jane. 'There are wonderful places to ride.'

'Don't you miss it?' asked Catherine.

'I used to,' said Jane, 'but now I have so much to do I've no time to miss anything.'

'Those poor people?' He says it as one might say 'Those marmosets' or 'Those aardvarks', she thought. Creatures heard of, read about in books, but never encountered.

'What do you hope to do about them? Make them less poor?'

'Eventually,' said Jane. 'For the moment there isn't enough money for that. All I can do is help to make life a little better for the very worst off.'

'A lot of them were soldiers,' said Piers.

'Like my John. . . . Or sailors. But half of them are women.'

Catherine laughed. 'There's men for you,' she said, and turned to Jane. 'It must be worse for the women. Having babies. . . . Bringing up children.'

'Perhaps it is,' said Jane. 'But they bear it better. Maybe it's just our nature, or maybe it's because they have things to do, homes to run.'

'Poor devils,' said Piers. 'Why don't they start a revolution or something? I know I would.'

'Some of them are all for it,' said Jane. 'Perhaps there'll be more if things don't get better.'

The formal dinner that night was as dull and undemanding as such things usually are, except that on her left Jane found that she had an actor from the Abbey Theatre, and on her right an old Indian Civil Servant who had known Kalpur well. The dowager had gone to great lengths to see that she wouldn't be too bored. She'd been given by far the two most interesting men in the room. . . . As she undressed before the fire she thought: It's strange John is so close to me I feel as if he could walk in at any moment: as if we'd been married for years. And yet he'd never been in a house like this in his life.

That night she dreamed that the two of them were out riding together, in the maidan at Kalpur, but when the time came to turn back, only she rode off to the stables. John headed for the village, and the countryside beyond.

Next morning the twins asked if her aeroplane would be big enough for them, too, and she couldn't lie. How could she? They'd both seen it. At first the dowager was opposed to the idea, but in the end she gave in. At least it was a way of getting Piers out of Ireland. She hugged Jane warmly before she left.

'Catherine told me the story of Bridget,' she said. 'All those sad, brave young men.'

'I hope you didn't mind?'

'I don't suppose you had much choice in that matter,' the dowager said. 'Did Piers say how he'd get the horses to England?'

'He said your agent would handle it and send me the bill.'

'By far the best way,' said the dowager. 'Though I wish you'd come and fetch them yourself. I'd like to see you again. Will you come back?'

'As soon as I can,' said Jane.

'Good lass,' the dowager said. 'I'd like to hear some more about Walter Nettles.'

35

T HE PILOT ACCEPTED two extra passengers and luggage without a blink and took the aeroplane from a field in Meath to Croydon the way a bus driver might go from Marble Arch to Kensington High Street, but the twins didn't see it that way. Their eyes blazed with excitement throughout the flight.

Please God let them stick to horses, thought Jane, and when they got down at last, and found that the Rolls was waiting, she asked where she could drop them.

'Paddington,' said Catherine. 'If we get the first train to Oxford we can be back in our cells before they can lock us out.'

The car moved off. Jane offered cigarettes, and as Piers lit hers, she asked him cautiously, 'Have you decided on the RAF instead?'

'No,' said Piers, 'but they're fascinating things, aren't they? They can move you around so quickly, and they're bound to get bigger, wouldn't you say?'

'Oh don't be serious,' his sister said. 'There's a meet near Woodstock on Saturday.'

Foch was pleased to see her back, in a formal sort of way. Hawkins was more effusive. The house had been like a tomb, she said, though Jane rather got the impression that she'd spent most of her time at South Terrace, consulting with Lionel and bossing workmen, an impression confirmed by Lionel when she telephoned him.

'A tartar,' he said, 'a positive fiend. Though sound on plumb-ing.'

'I hope she didn't try to interfere with *your* ideas.'

'Well she did,' said Lionel, 'but she failed, because I'm even more of a fiend than she is when roused, and much, much more of a bitch. Come and see the work in progress tomorrow.'

'I can't,' she said. 'Not tomorrow. I have to go to Paris.'

'*Have* to? You're only just back from Ireland. You journalists do see the world.'

'It's the Quart' Arts Ball.'

'Is it indeed? You just watch what you're up to, Jane Whitcomb. We don't want you turning into a gadabout.'

Little chance of that, thought Jane. Gadabouts are supposed to enjoy their gadding. She slept late and was woken by a call from Bower.

'It's urgent, miss,' said Hawkins.

The ones from Bower were always urgent – for Bower. She yawned her way to the hall and the precise intersection of its two draughts.

'Yes?' she said.

'What a greeting. Ireland OK?' Then without a pause, 'It must have been since you didn't call me. You can tell me all about it on the plane.'

'Which plane?'

'The one that's going to Paris. I may not have time to stay long. You've got a costume fitting at Mutrie's. Eleven thirty.'

'Costume?'

'Certainly costume,' said Bower. 'The Quart' Arts is fancy dress.'

'And who am I to be?'

'Cleopatra,' said Bower.

'And you, I presume, will be Mark Antony?'

'Do I look that stupid? Julius Caesar, that's who I am. Wait till you see me in a toga.'

'He was bald,' said Jane. 'That's why he had to wear all those laurel wreaths.'

But Bower was already talking. 'Don't forget,' he said. 'Mutrie's at eleven thirty, Croydon at three. Or shall I collect you?'

'Collect me,' said Jane. 'I adore being collected.'

She hung up. As if I were a stamp or a cigarette card or something, she thought.

Cleopatra didn't exactly overburden herself with clothes, a fact she took up immediately she joined him in the car.

'I'd hate to take one of your photograph calls in that costume,' she said.

'You never told me you were a prude,' he said.

'The way you go on how can I be?' she said. 'But there'll be publicity photographs, I suppose? And in your paper? They read it a lot in Felston. Not many actually buy it,' she added nastily, 'but they go to the public library and read it. And in Felston they're prudes to a man – *and* woman, which is more to the point.'

'We'll get you a cloak,' said Bower. 'I'd hate to lose my big order in Felston public library.'

They moved on towards Croydon and she told him about Ireland.

'A good horse, you say?'

'She and her filly.'

'You think you could write me a piece about it?'

'I could,' she said, 'but it wouldn't be a very sad piece. And I'd still have to mention Felston of course.'

'Of course.'

'I can hardly mention Felston when I do my piece on the Quart' Arts Ball.'

'It'll be on your by-line,' said Bower. 'Now let me tell you about the guy you're going to meet.'

'Go ahead.'

'His name is Billy Powell,' said Bower. 'His wife's a relative of my sister's husband. The two of them live in Paris. He's sort of strange.'

'They live in Paris by choice?'

'Oh sure. I'm not saying my sister's husband's heartbroken, but they're in Paris because they like it there.'

'What does he do?'

'Writer,' said Bower. Of course every second American in Paris is a writer. The rest are either painters or musicians. But Billy at least works at it when he isn't getting drunk or smoking hashish or firing his revolver. . . . Or chasing women,' he added.

'Will he chase me?'

'Bound to,' said Bower. 'I'll be upset if he doesn't.'

'He sounds wild.'

'Wild enough.'

'Was he in the war?' said Jane. 'Was it that kind of wildness?'

'You catch on quick,' said Bower, as if she had just reinforced his faith in his taste in women. 'I guess you know all about that.'

'No more than you,' she said.

'God knows that's enough. Billy was like you. He drove an ambulance.'

'And was he blown up like me too?'

'Yes,' said Bower. 'He was.'

'I don't think I'm going to like this job very much,' said Jane.

'That's journalism for you,' said Bower. 'Half the time you hate what you're doing but you go right on doing it because that's what gets you your pay cheque and your name in the paper – or Felston's.'

He was right, and she knew he was right, and she couldn't tell him about the nightmares. She couldn't tell anyone. John and Bridget O'Dowd and the happy times, yes, but not the nightmares.

'I don't mean I won't do it,' she said. 'Of course I will, but don't expect me to enjoy it. Unless – is he good-looking?'

'A lot of women think so.'

'In that case I might enjoy the chasing bit,' she said.

They were staying at the Ritz in adjacent suites, which did not surprise her. Indeed it had a kind of inevitability about it. In so many ways Jay Bower *was* the Ritz. The American bar alone seemed designed as a setting for him. They bathed and changed, and went to dine with the Powells. When Jane said she assumed that they had been invited Jay said of course, and if the Powells had remembered they had a very good chance of being fed.

At that time they lived in the XVth Arrondissement, in the rue Scribe, in a tall, narrow house with a small, elegant garden and courtyard. Jay paid off the taxi and said, 'Billy's wife's called Florence. She has a claim to fame too.'

'She paints?'

'She invented the brassière,' said Jay. 'Or a lot of people say she did.'

'Then I shall be nice to her at least,' said Jane.

The Powells had remembered their coming, or somebody had; perhaps the admirable manservant who admitted them; lean, clean and elegant, and nothing at all to do with the vie de bohème. Both Florence and Billy were in the salon to meet them, Florence sober, Billy reasonably so. Florence still had the remains of what Jane would later realise was a typically American prettiness, fresh-faced, and with just a hint of athleticism. There was a suggestion of weariness too, as well there might be, thought Jane, if what she had heard of her husband was true.

Powell was very tall and very thin, and dressed, as he always was, in black and white, though not in a dinner jacket, as Bower was. Black jacket of what looked like doeskin and trousers of the same material, white shirt of heavy silk, and the sort of black tie one wore at funerals. Three carnations in his lapel; two white, the one in the middle dyed black. Black hair, too, much, much too black to be natural. Black like soot. He opened a bottle of champagne. Veuve Clicquot, Jane noticed. Well, widows had their own blackness.

'Champagne for the Philistines,' said Powell. 'They don't deserve it, but at least they're family.' He poured four glasses and the bottle was empty. The manservant passed them round and was told to go.

'Here's to the lady Philistine,' said Powell, and gulped down half a glassful.

'She's not a Philistine,' said Bower. 'She's a philanthropist.'

'She's the one you wrote about? The one who wants to prop up the existing social system?'

'That's the one.'

'Then she's an idiot.'

Jane put down her glass. 'What a fool you are,' she said easily. 'If you go on like this I shall slap your face very hard, and then either you will assault me or your wife will feel obliged to do so, and poor Jay, who is much stronger than you by the look of you, will be obliged to join in and knock you down.'

'I've got a revolver,' said Powell.

'I don't think anyone even as stupid as you appear to be would use it to shoot a female philanthropist.' Jane picked up her glass and sipped.

'Now wait a minute – ' Powell's wife said.

'No,' said Powell. 'That's OK.' He turned to Jane. 'You know you interest me.'

He says it as if it were a compliment, thought Jane, as though nobody had interested him in years. 'I'd like to write about you,' Powell continued.

'Snap,' said Bower, and then as Powell turned to him. 'I told you.'

'Hey, that's right,' said Powell.

'I think I've changed my mind,' said Jane. 'I can meet all the Communist champagne swiggers I want in Cambridge.'

'Who are you calling a Communist?' said Powell. 'Just because I spoke about the existing social system, I suppose?'

'Then what is going to take its place?'

'Nothing,' said Powell. 'It's all over; the whole stupid mess. Over and finished. Only it didn't end with that big bang we all expected; it's just winding down like a gramophone. Kind of friendly of God to leave us a little time to enjoy ourselves, but when the record's finished – we're finished too.'

'And how long do you reckon we have?' Bower said.

Powell shrugged, gulped down what was left of his glass, and took another bottle of champagne from the cooler.

'Who knows?' he said. 'Who could possibly know except God, and why should he tell? But my guess is soon, very soon. Maybe tonight.' He twisted the cork and it popped discreetly, as well-chilled champagne should, refilled his glass and turned to Jane. 'Let's you and I go somewhere and write about each other,' he said.

'Are you quite sure you'll be strong enough to write?' she asked.

'I've got pills you can take for that,' he said. 'I'll be OK. You too.'

'Aren't they dangerous?'

'What difference does it make?' he said. 'I already told you. It's all over. Why don't you listen?'

'Perhaps she doesn't share your simple faith,' said Bower.

Jane said, 'I've had enough danger for one lifetime. I prefer to go on propping up the existing social system.'

'Danger?' said Powell. 'You? *You* are going to tell *me* about danger? You sit there in your Paquin dress – '

'Worth,' said his wife. Taciturn she may be, thought Jane, but she believes in accuracy.

'She drove an ambulance,' said Bower. 'Like you.'

'Yeah. . . . You told me in your letter. But I was blown up.'

'So was she,' said Bower.

At once Powell looked like a child who had been robbed of its best toy. And so he had, thought Jane. It was his uniqueness.

'Were you hurt?' he asked.

It too had been part of her sickness, Jabber had said, but she would not tell him so, or the others, either.

'No,' she said.

'Nor me. Except – it's funny, and it certainly can't be defined as a hurt or any kind of wound for that matter – it was only after it had happened to me that I needed to write at least one good thing before the world ended. Are you sure you don't want to go somewhere and talk about it?'

'Quite sure,' said Jane.

'But whyever not? Florence will have Jay here for company.'

'He'll have me for company too,' said Jane.

The implications of Powell's remark had startled her, but she had no need to reply. The manservant came in and announced dinner.

Soup à l'oseille, medaillons de boeuf, green salad, apple tart, and Château Montrose to drink, bottles and bottles of it. Powell didn't eat much, but Bower and Florence tucked in well, she noticed, and so did she. The food was delicious. If she ate much more the Cleopatra costume would have to be stuck on with glue. The manservant handled the plates, but Powell poured the wine so that no glass was ever empty, including his own.

'Did you ever carry one of my countrymen in your ambulance days?' Powell asked.

She said at once, 'No. I never did. I wasn't near your part of the Front. I carried just about everybody else, though.'

'Who, for example?'

'Oh – British, Canadians, Australians, French.'

'No Germans?'

That question again. 'Them too.'

'Why, Miss Whitcomb? Why carry them?'

'Because they couldn't walk,' said Jane.

'I carried mostly French – and then Americans, when we finally got here. But I don't think I could have carried Germans. What do you make of that, Jay?'

Bower looked up, slow, unhurried, but a blow had landed and had hurt. 'Why nothing, Billy,' he said. 'What is there to make of it, except that you and Miss Whitcomb are very different people.'

Florence Powell began to talk of the ball they were going to next evening. Everyone, but everyone, what the French called le tout Paris would be there. She tried to question Jane about her costume, but Powell forbade it. Fancy-dress costumes, he insisted, should be a surprise. Well hers could well be that, thought Jane.

After dinner the men stayed on at the table, while Florence took Jane back to the salon. No port was produced by Powell, but he was already pouring more claret as the two women left. Most unusual in France, thought Jane, and then: Money. It must be that. To live in this kind of style even in Paris must cost a great deal of money, and Powell didn't look as if he could hold on to the stuff for long. He certainly looked incapable of making it. . . . The manservant brought coffee, and Florence Powell poured.

'You work for Jay, Miss Whitcomb?'

'Sometimes. But I'm not on his staff.'

'You're a freelance?'

'Why, yes,' said Jane. 'I suppose I am.' For some reason the thought was pleasing. 'But most of my time is occupied with charity work.'

'And do you enjoy that?'

'Enormously.' It was perfectly true, and yet quite obviously Florence Powell didn't believe a word.

'And you,' said Jane. 'Jay tells me that you are a creative person, too.' She saw that Mrs Powell was on to the use of the name 'Jay' rather than 'Mr Bower' in a flash. It could only mean one, or possibly two things, to her. Either she was rich, or she was sleeping with Bower, or both.

'Inventive rather than creative,' said Mrs Powell at last. 'I assume you are referring to the brassière?'

'I am indeed. How did one manage without them? How clever you are.'

'It's in the family,' said Mrs Powell. 'My grandfather patented a new kind of printing press.'

And is that where your money meets with the Bowers'? Jane wondered.

They talked about dresses then, until at last the men reappeared. Powell was looking pleased with himself, and not appreciably drunker than he had been when she had seen him last. He immediately offered brandy, which Jane declined.

'Tell you what,' said Powell. 'Let's drive over to Montparnasse. There are some great cafés there. The Dôme or the Coupole or somewhere.'

Bower looked at her, and she nodded slightly.

'Who's going to drive?' Bower asked.

'That's kind of a nasty remark,' said Powell. 'But I guess we can put our lives in Miss Whitcomb's hands.'

'Sure you can,' said Bower, 'but we haven't signed those papers yet.'

'Then let's do it and get in the car,' said Powell. 'Let's enjoy ourselves.'

Pleasure at any cost, thought Jane, but whatever papers were being signed, Florence Powell knew all about it. She didn't move as the two men went out once more.

'Pleasure seems to be my husband's only aim, wouldn't you say?' she asked.

'An Epicurean, certainly.'

'I suppose it's mine, too. Even inventing things. It's a pleasure.'

'More cerebral than most,' said Jane.

'Oh sure,' said Mrs Powell. 'But when you believe the world will end soon – I mean really, deep-down believe it – '

'And do you really believe that too?'

Mrs Powell said wearily, 'What does it matter what I believe? It's what Billy believes. It's what makes him the special person he is.'

You say that as a priest who had lost his faith might say the creed, thought Jane, but all she said was, 'I see.'

Mrs Powell said, 'If you don't mind, Miss Whitcomb, perhaps we should get our coats. Billy doesn't like to be kept waiting.'

'Certainly,' said Jane, and wondered if the Powell car, whatever it was, would prove driveable by a lady wearing a Worth dress, Uncle Walter's sable coat and evening sandals that weighed about six ounces apiece.

It was a Voisin, if anything rather larger than the Hilyards' Bentley, but rather less powerful, and much more amenable to female driving. Bower's faith in her had been justified, but Billy Powell sulked rather when he found that she knew the way to Montparnasse without being told. He'd looked forward to playing the old Paris hand helping out a tourist.

Still, the Dôme was packed with writer, amateur, professional, real, and in certain cases, quite unreal, and Billy revived at once. He knew them all, from the burly American who drank wine by the bottle the way other people drank by the glass, to the slight, acid Irishman who accepted two very large Napoleon brandies as no more than his due. But it was the Americans who drank the hardest, almost with dedication, and suddenly Jane remembered why. In America they had this thing called Prohibition, and so they had come to Paris to catch up, or at least, according to Bower, to drink the sort of stuff that didn't taste of the bath tub it had been made in.

It was fun for a while, but then Florence Powell returned to what Jane guessed to be habitual taciturnity, and Powell wandered from table to table, drinking at every one, and occasionally bringing what he considered a particularly choice specimen to them for inspection. They included a very drunk yet strangely prim young American with a wife, who, Jane saw at once, was in dire need of Jabber Lockhart, and a couple of grim females who would have made Fred seem positively girlish. All of them invited Jane and Bower to visit them, but as Powell had omitted to introduce them the chances seemed remote.

When Bower said that they would leave, Powell was incredulous. There was still so much fun to be had. He was still declaiming pleasure's necessity when Bower went out and hailed a taxi.

'Goodness, how exhausting,' said Jane.

'His kind of fun always is,' said Bower, then to the taxi driver, 'Ritz Hotel.'

'Do you still want me to write about it?'

'Him, them, the Arts Ball tomorrow. The works.'

'But why?'

'There's Felston,' said Bower, 'and there's Billy Powell – the other side of the coin, living over here because he can get a bottle

– 371 –

of champagne in Paris for the price of a Coca-Cola in New York for as long as the dollar stays strong.'

'He can also make his share of improper suggestions. More than his share.'

'He does his share of screwing I guess, and some of it may be fun. Most of it's more like necessity, because he's written his life like a novel, and that's the part he's going to play. You ever think about promiscuity?'

'Never,' said Jane firmly.

'The way I see it,' said Bower unheeding, 'it's more like ego than satisfaction. You take the girl for what she might be, without taking the trouble to find out what she is. It's like the Loterie Nationale. How can you be sure of winning unless you buy all the tickets?'

'And you only want one ticket? The winner? Is that what you're telling me?'

'Well maybe I've won a few smaller prizes too,' said Bower.

She nipped his wrist viciously and he yelled, and the taxi driver drove on stolidly. Americans. . . .

In the lift Jay Bower said, 'Now it's my turn to make an improper suggestion.'

'More than time,' said Jane, 'and I shall yield to your impassioned pleadings – but in my room, not yours. I've no wish to scurry about the hotel corridor in my dressing gown, fetching though it is.'

'I like your nightgown,' he said, and began to remove it. 'Not much of it but what there is is pretty.'

'Not like that,' she said, and wriggled. 'You'll tear the lace. There.' His arms came round her.

When they had done he asked for one of her cigarettes, a rare thing for him who smoked only cigars – but not in her suite. She lit up for both of them, cautious of their nakedness, and he drew on the cigarette just once, dragging the smoke deep down, before he stubbed it out, pulled back the sheets and looked at her body.

'The nightgown was pretty all right,' he said, 'but you're a lot prettier. You're beautiful.'

'So that's why you took it off?'

'That's why.' He began to stroke her in a way she liked very much. 'You could still be my winning ticket,' he said. 'My first prize.'

'If this is a proposal of marriage,' she said, 'you should stop what you're doing, delightful though it is, and get down on one knee.'

He got out of bed and knelt on one knee.

'Please marry me,' he said.

But she would not. She liked him very well, but she liked her independence better, and was rich enough to afford it, but how could she tell him so? Instead she coaxed him back into bed beside her, coaxed him into doing once more what he did so delightfully.

At last he said, 'Billy Powell reckons he's laid more than three hundred girls – but I bet he's never had this in his life.'

'Not even from Mrs Powell?'

'I guess she'd give it to him if he'd let her,' said Jay. 'Hell. She's given him everything else.'

'Her money?'

'Some. . . . A lot of it's in trust. But he's not a money-grabber – just asks for it when he needs it. And he spends his own just as fast.'

'What then?'

'Her first husband,' said Jay. 'Her children by him that she has to keep out of sight.'

'But that's awful,' said Jane.

'Pleasure can be like that sometimes.'

'Not ours.'

'No, not ours,' he said, 'even if you do force me to live in sin.'

'Just for that you can go back to your own bed,' said Jane, 'and close the door quietly when you go.'

36

G RANDMA LOWERED THE magnifying glass and looked at her audience. Only Bet and Bob were there. Stan had heard of a job at Tyneside Engineering and thought that this time it might be true. Andy had taken one look at the letter in Jane's handwriting and gone off to the library.

'I can't make head nor tail of it,' said Grandma. 'My eyes are getting that bad.'

'Here, let me,' said Bob, and got up to take the letter, but the old woman clung to it. To let go would be to admit the onset of blindness, and she wasn't ready for that yet, not by a long chalk. She raised the glass again.

'People can be very generous in London,' she read slowly, 'provided that you harass them enough. And I've started addressing meetings now and passing the hat round afterwards – and looking scornful if people don't give enough. They very often add a little more, especially the men.'

She lowered the glass and cackled her old woman's laughter.

'By, I wish our John had been spared to enjoy it,' she said. 'It must be a sight worth seeing. Where was I?'

'Especially the men,' said Bet.

'Trust you to remember that,' said Bob.

'Oh give over,' said Bet, and blushed.

'Now that'll do,' said Grandma, and resumed. 'Especially the men. So far I've raised in the vicinity of five hundred pounds more.'

'Another five hundred,' said Bob. 'I wish I lived in that vicinity.'

The old woman said, 'You mean that, don't you? You can't wait to get away.'

'John got away,' said Bob.

'You were all in work then,' said his grandmother. 'We wanted for nowt. But now whoever gets a start'll have to keep the rest.'
Bob said nothing.

'Well?' the old woman snapped. 'Am I right?'

'Yes, Grandma,' he said at last. 'I know. But there's no harm in dreaming.'

'Oh but there is,' said Grandma. 'You keep your mind on Felston. No sense in hankering after the Savoy Hotel. Just be content to hear it on that wireless of yours.' She resumed her reading.

'Give my regards to Dr Stobbs and tell him that a cheque is on its way.' She looked at Bet. 'That reminds me,' she said. 'Friday tomorrow. We'll have to go to the fish quay, pet.'

'Go by tram, will you?' said Bob.

'Bob will you give over,' his sister said.

Grandma ploughed on. 'And that's about it, really. I'll have to post this in rather a hurry as I'm off to Paris tomorrow. Your affectionate friend, Jane Whitcomb.' Carefully she folded up the letter. 'A real caring girl, that one,' she said.

There could be no greater seal of approval.

'Paris?' said Bet. 'What in the world would she want to go to Paris for?'

But this time Bob didn't tease her, just doubled up in an agony of helpless laughter.

Jay looked at Jane in her costume.

'I see what you mean,' he said. 'Just as well you bought that cloak.'

Jane looked into the mirror and saw herself clad in a skirt that didn't begin to hide her legs and left her tummy (and navel) clearly visible, a skimpy example of Mrs Powell's intervention covered in gold lacquer, and a head-dress that had taken the combined efforts of herself and two maids half an hour to put in place.

'All the same,' said Jay, 'it's got its own kind of appeal.'

He reached for her, but she swayed out of his way, smoothly and easily. At least in a costume like that the clothes didn't hold you up.

'Not a chance, my friend,' she said. 'There may not be much but it takes for ever to put on. Try again after the ball.'

'You can bet on it,' said Jay, and opened champagne instead. She watched him as he poured. The toga suited him, and the laurel wreath that looked like gold. He looked every inch the emperor in all but name, but then he was. He handed her a glass.

'Last night we were talking about Billy Powell, but we got sort of sidetracked,' he said.

'Is that what you call it?'

'Make the most of it,' he said amiably. 'Nothing lasts for ever. Not even the Quart' Arts Ball. Did I tell you his wife's money was sort of mixed up with ours? My family's I mean.'

'I sort of gathered it.'

'And from time to time he needs some. Like now. And somebody has to give it to him. Like me. Last night. And get a receipt.'

'The document you referred to.'

He lifted his glass to her. 'O Queen, live for ever,' he said, 'and always be as smart as you are now. So now he's loaded. Ten thousand dollars' worth.'

'Will it last long?'

Jay shrugged. 'Depends what he buys. Three months maybe.'

Ten thousand dollars, two and a half thousand pounds, would keep the entire Patterson family for the rest of their lives.

'I thought you told me drink was cheap here.'

'Cocaine isn't. Or friends. Not his friends anyway. His wife is sort of a relative by marriage.'

'So you said.'

'So naturally Billy knows my family pretty well. Our background. Our name.' He paused.

'I'm listening,' said Jane.

'My name is Joachim Manfred Bauer. That's B-A-U-E-R.' He waited.

'So I should suppose,' said Jane.

'Why should you suppose?'

'Last night he asked me if I ever carried Germans and I said yes, and he said he couldn't. There had to be a reason for it and you were the only reason there was.'

'Why me?'

'You'd just given him money – and asked for a receipt. '

'I said stay smart,' said Jay, 'but I didn't say too smart.'

'It's in the family,' Jane said smugly. 'My father was a scholar of his college; my brother is a fellow of his.' And then, as Jay looked worried: 'Jay, my darling. What's this all about?'

'You don't mind my being a German?'

'You're an American,' she said. 'You were on our side.'

His arms reached out for her, then dropped.

'Let's get this damn ball over with,' he said. 'I need to hold you.'

The ball was held in a vast hall at Luna Park in the Porte d'Auteuil, and to get in they had to fight their way through a mob that was mostly reporters and photographers. Jane's cloth of gold cloak, covered in what were supposed to be Egyptian hieroglyphics stitched on that afternoon, drew a crowd at once, but the cloak buttoned down the front and not too much leg was showing. When a sheikh and attendant belly-dancer arrived behind her, the photographers left at once.

'Good gracious,' said Jane. 'I feel positively demure.'

They went inside to find – because it was Paris after all – good food and good wine, and an orchestra that could match the Savoy's, but what caught attention at once, what it was for, were the set pieces ranged around its walls. Carefully, brilliantly built for one night and no more were miniature stages, each with its own mise en scène: Hell, Pompeii, a harem, Valhalla, and the rest, each with its own elaborate scenery, its elaborately costumed players. Jay marched firmly to the Roman Orgy stage, which at least explains our costumes, thought Jane.

'Who are we with?' she asked.

'This is the international press stand,' said Bower. 'The photographers won't bother us now.'

Most of the women around her wore even less than she did.

'I'd better take off my cloak then,' she said. 'I feel a positive dowd.'

And she did so, and was introduced to this one and that one: big in *Paris Soir* or the *Trib* or *La Stampa*. From time to time she danced with them or with Jay, but mostly she preferred to observe the merry throng as she reclined on her couch or whatever it was: it was draped in leopardskin which appeared to be real, and scratched rather. And then, bang on midnight, Billy Powell appeared. Billy and Florence, and one or two young men, and rather more young women.

What little the young men and women wore was designed to suggest the fairies of *A Midsummer Night's Dream*, Pease-Blossom and Mustardseed and the rest. The girl who played Puck was almost naked, and with an enviable body. Between them they pulled a sort of chariot that was designed like a lily, and in its cup sat Titania Florence, all in white, in translucent silk so fine it looked like moonbeams, and Billy Oberon, in black silk almost sheer and tight as a skin, and also silver boots and a wig of silver. They went to a bower of roses, forget-me-nots, moss and anemones, all real and already dying. By a rock pool a cascade played, glittering and frothing in the hall's relentless light; a cascade, she learned later, of champagne. But then what else could it be? At least, she thought, he has a sense of style. Not once did he look at her, let alone ask her to dance.

In the taxi Jay asked, 'Enjoy yourself?'

'Hardly,' she said. 'Got up like Theda Bara on an off-day and surrounded by men who could talk about nothing but their circulations.'

'Theda Bara was miles behind you on the best day she ever had.'

'I suppose you know her?' Jay nodded. 'Then mind I don't tell her so. And besides. . . . Quart' Arts. What Four Arts?'

'Music, Literature, Painting,' said Jay.

'And?'

He shrugged. 'Fornication maybe. Wasting Money.'

'Felston seems a long way away.'

'Four or five hundred miles,' he said. 'No more. That's the point I want you to make.'

'I'll be glad to.'

They drove on for a while in silence. 'Billy Powell was wasting money all right,' Bower said at last.

'He wasn't doing too badly at fornication either.'

In her bedroom Jane carefully removed the Cleopatra head-dress then turned to where Jay lay waiting.

'Hail Caesar,' she said.

She slept late, not knowing when Jay had left her, and became aware of a persistent tapping.

Breakfast, she thought. Good, strong coffee and the most delicious croissants. Suddenly she didn't mind at all being wakened.

'Un moment,' she called, and reached for her dressing gown to cover her nakedness, but the waiter was already in the room before she had finished fastening it. Except that it wasn't the waiter, it was Billy Powell, still in his Oberon costume and carrying her breakfast tray. He looked drunk but by no means incapable. Deliberately Jane continued to fasten her dressing gown, and found that her fingers were shaking.

'Mr Powell, what on earth do you want?' she said. Her voice at least sounded calm, she thought. For the moment.

'I think that under the circumstances you might at least call me Billy,' he said, in a voice of such sweet reason she could have screamed.

'Who let you in here?'

'The floor waiter,' said Powell.

'He can't have done. It will cost him his job.'

'I gave him five thousand dollars. With that kind of money he can start his own café.' He put the tray down. 'Five thousand dollars was part of what Bower brought me last night,' he said. 'I gave it to be with you.'

'I'm not flattered.'

'Why should you be?' said Powell. 'It's only money. We have to be together.'

'We do not,' said Jane. 'Why should we?'

'We saw it all,' said Powell. 'The dying and the dead. We were both blown up. We nearly joined them. When we make love it will be a fantastic experience. It may even be our last one. It could all end – once we have done. Because after we have come together, what else is left?'

Not only drunk, but mad as a hatter, she thought – or was it drugs? – and talking like a Gothic novel. She was terrified.

'Come on,' said Powell, and stepped towards her. 'It'll be wonderful. You'll see.'

Like a swimmer shouting to the beach 'The water's fine. You'll love it,' she thought. But I won't love it at all. And I'm not *going* to love it.

'And you're all white,' he said. 'White robe. White skin. That's perfect.'

She backed away to her dressing table, felt behind her with her hand as he lurched towards her, almost out of control but still very strong. Her fingers felt for the hand mirror her parents had given her on her sixteenth birthday, a solid lump of Indian silver, and when his hands reached out for her she swung it hard with all her weight behind it, edge on, striking his temple. He went down flat the way she had seen rabbits fall when one of her brothers had shot them with a twelve-bore, suddenly and completely, and without a twitch, then looked at the hand mirror. Unbroken, she thought. No seven years' bad luck: then picked up the telephone and asked for Jay's room. Powell made no move to prevent her.

'I wish you'd stop drinking coffee,' said Jay. He sounded pettish.

'I want coffee,' she said. 'I *need* coffee. It's what the text books all say you should have after a shock.'

Jay continued to hold Powell's wrist. 'At least he's alive,' he said.

She was in a panic at once. 'Of course he's alive,' she said. 'I only hit him once.'

'Have you seen the side of his head?' Jay asked.

'No.'

'I shouldn't.' He straightened up. 'We'll have to move him. I don't know what the text books say about that, but it's what we're going to have to do.'

'Move him where?'

'My suite,' said Jay. 'If anybody sees him I can always say we were fooling around pretending to fight or something. Get some clothes on then go to the door. When we're in the clear open mine and I'll bring him in.'

She took off her dressing gown as she went for the clothes she needed, saw her naked reflection in the wardrobe mirror. Her body that the whole black farce had been about. Jay didn't even look. As she dressed he asked, 'How the hell did he get in here?'

'He bribed a waiter.' Jane fastened Mrs Powell's invention.

'He must have paid the earth.'

'Five thousand dollars.'

'Half of what I gave him last night. He probably owes the other half for costumes and chariots and champagne in woodland glades. Do you feel flattered?'

'Not at all.'

'I wouldn't blame you.'

Jane went to her door, and looked out, saw no one there, then opened Jay's door and called to him softly. Bower appeared at once, carrying her victim as if he were no more than a clumsy parcel he was anxious to put down before it burst. As he crossed the threshold Powell's wig fell off. Jane picked it up and followed them in.

'Go back to your own place,' said Jay. 'You're out of this now.'

'Can't I help you?'

'No,' he said. 'You've done enough.' She flinched at that and Jay went on, 'Forgive me. Maybe I'm in a state of shock, too. What I meant was you did what was right and I admire you for it, but now you're out of it. Now it's my turn. . . . OK?'

She went back to her suite and stripped again, bathed, dressed once more, and rang for more coffee, listening hard. For what? The clatter of an ambulance? The tramp of stretcher bearers? A gendarme's whistle? There was nothing. She was finishing her last cup when Jay came in once more, bathed and shaved and dressed.

'You sure do like coffee,' he said.

'Shall I get you some?'

'Brandy,' he said. 'I know it's early but I need it. God knows I've earned it.'

'It's all right to ring room service?'

'Sure,' he said, and then came over to her and kissed her lightly on the mouth. 'I guess I'm punchy. *Every*thing's all right. I should have told you as soon as I came in. I'm sorry.'

She smiled at him. 'Just let me get you your drink,' she said, 'then I want to hear it all.'

He had begun by telephoning the *Daily World*'s Paris office, and demanding a discreet doctor who could deal with head wounds. They had provided one almost at once, Jane gathered, which gave some idea of the kind of people we journalists are. While the doctor went to work Jay had telephoned Florence

Powell who had arrived almost as quickly as the doctor, and brought some of his clothes.

'Wasn't she asleep?'

'Billy had disappeared before the ball finished,' said Jay. 'She didn't know where he was or what he was up to. You bet she wasn't asleep. So when she arrived I made her wait while the doctor fixed Billy up with a bandage and helped me dress him, then gave him a snort of sal volatile or something and he came round, just sort of lay there while I paid off the doctor and took him to the door. When we got there the doctor said to me, "I did not have a chance to examine him properly, but it is my impression that if he does not change his way of life soon your friend will kill himself," and I said, "That's the whole idea." Then he left with five hundred bucks which I stop out of Billy's next allowance. Five hundred. Funny, wouldn't you say? A waiter making ten times as much as a doctor?'

'Then what happened?'

'I went back inside and I told her, and at first Florence was good and mad.'

'With Powell?'

'With you,' said Jay.

'With *me*?' The rage in her voice made Jay smile.

'No need to go reaching for your mirror,' he said. 'They're on their way home by now. Sure with you. When it comes to love – sex anyway – those two make their own arrangements, but even so Billy's the biggest child she's got – and so she wanted to do unto you as you'd done unto him.'

'How did you stop her?'

'I said you wouldn't press charges.'

'What charges?'

'The French are all for l'amour and all that – at least they keep saying they are, but they're just a much against rape as any other civilised country.'

'I never thought of it like that,' she said.

'But Florence did because that's what it was. So we stuck his hat on top of his bandage and I helped him to the elevator, then out to that vast car of his and their manservant drove them off. I doubt if anybody even noticed, and if they did he was just one more casualty of the Quart' Arts Ball. Now, what would you like to do before we fly home?'

– 382 –

She took his brandy glass and finished what was left.

'I don't know why it should be,' she said, 'but I want you to make love to me, even though it means undressing for the third time this morning.'

'Wear your Cleopatra costume and you've got yourself a deal,' said Jay.

'All of it except the head-dress,' she said.

They were lying in each other's arms, weary and yet exultant, when the telephone rang and she reached out lazily.

'A call from London,' said the operator, and then it came, hazy but audible. 'This is Hawkins, miss,' the voice said. 'You've got to come home, miss. Quick. It's awful.' There was a sound like a crash. China? Crystal? And then the line went dead. She hung up. 'The most extraordinary thing,' she said.

'What now?'

'Surely Hawkins can't be drunk, and even if she were, why should she phone me?' She turned to face him. 'I'm most awfully sorry, but I have to go home.'

37

H E FLEW HOME with her, bitterly regretting an opportunity
missed to lunch at the Closerie des Lilas. And when they
got to Croydon there were thin wisps of fog; the tattered remnants of what in London was an impenetrable curtain. 'A proper
London particular,' Redman the chauffeur told them, not without relish. 'A real pea-souper.'

Jane went to a telephone, but there was no reply from Offley
Villas: no connection even, and so Jay phoned the *Daily World*
instead.

'Solid I'm afraid,' he told her. 'No visibility at all.'

'I don't mind giving it a try, sir,' said the chauffeur. He
sounded like a hussar volunteering for the front rank of the light
brigade. Jay ignored him.

'It might lift in a few hours they reckon,' he said. 'Let's go and
get a drink somewhere.'

'It's quarter past three and it's England,' said Jane. 'We can't
get a drink.'

'Tea then,' said Jay. 'God knows I couldn't face English coffee.'

It was nearly nine when the Rolls-Royce turned into Offley
Villas and the chauffeur got out to take her suitcases.

'I'll take those,' said Jay, and walked with her to the door.

'Why not?' said Jane. 'I haven't any reputation left anyway.'

Jay ignored it. 'There could be things in there he shouldn't
see,' he said.

'Oh dear God,' said Jane. 'The second time in one day. It just isn't bloody *fair*.' Then she inserted the key in the lock, turned it and went into the hall, with Jay close behind her.

It seemed all right, except for the absence of a large and very ugly vase from the telephone table, and a dark stain on the carpet nearby. Then she saw that the telephone, though neatly disposed, had had its wires wrenched from the skirting board.

She called out softly: 'Hawkins! Hawkins!'

A voice came from the kitchen. 'That you, miss?'

'Yes, of course it is. Hawkins, what's *happening*?'

Then came a sound which she later learned was Hawkins removing a chair from under a door knob, and then Hawkins appeared at last, straightening her cap.

'Oh, miss,' she said. 'I've been here ever so long on my own. It's been awful.'

'I came as soon as I could,' said Jane. 'There's a heavy fog. And what do you mean on your own? Isn't cook with you?'

'Cook did a bunk as soon as it started. There's only me and him.' Then she brightened. 'Unless he's scarpered.' And then the gloom returned. 'No. . . . I'd have heard him.'

'Heard *who*?'

Jane's sharpness got through to Hawkins, who made a massive effort to achieve coherence. 'A friend of Mr Francis came here this morning from Cambridge. He'd brought a note with him from Mr Francis saying he had permission to look through Sir Guy's papers.'

'He had no right – ' Jane began, and Jay pressed her arm, urging her to silence. 'But you weren't to know that, Hawkins,' she said at last. 'It wasn't your fault. Who was he? Not a Mr Willis?'

'Oh no, miss,' said Hawkins. 'Burrowes his name was.' A new one, thought Jane. 'He looked a bit untidy, not even clean, really, but I didn't think it was important. Some of those scholastic fellers tend to be like that.'

Scholastic. At a time like this.

'What was important,' Hawkins said, 'was he'd been drinking. Half past ten in the morning and he was half way home. Only he was in that quick – and he did have the letter, miss – and what could I do?'

'Nothing,' said Jane. 'Go on.'

'I showed him up to the study, miss, and he said that would

be all – and about an hour later he shouts down the stairs and tells me to bring him a bottle of whisky. So I took up the decanter, miss. And the siphon.'

'Yes, of course,' said Jane.

'Only he told me to take the siphon away again, miss. He said he didn't want no soda.' Then to Jane's astonishment, Hawkins began to weep.

'That's nothing to cry about,' said Jane.

'It isn't *that*, miss,' said Hawkins. 'It's the study.'

Jane began to feel the rage well up inside her. 'What about the study?'

'All that arranging and tidying you did,' said Hawkins. 'All them – those papers. He's chucked them about all over the place, miss. It's like a pig sty.'

Jane moved to the door, but again Jay's hand grasped her arm, holding her still. 'Finish it, girl,' he said.

'That was when I ran down to phone you, miss,' said Hawkins, 'only he came down after me and pulled the telephone like you see, only I clocked him one and he knocked the vase over and clocked me one. – "Tit for tat," he says. "Fair's fair. Clear up this mess," he says. "It's disgusting. And leave the phone the way it is. I don't like being disturbed when I'm working."'

Jane said, 'He didn't – he didn't – molest you?'

'Of course not, miss,' said Hawkins. 'I told you. He's a friend of Mr Francis. All he did was finish off the whisky.'

'How do you know?'

'I went upstairs and had a peep,' said Hawkins. 'Spark out, he was. Snoring his head off. Around teatime that would be.'

'And you stayed here by yourself all this time?'

'Yes, miss.'

'But why didn't you call the police?' asked Jane.

'I didn't think you'd want me to, miss.'

Here was devotion indeed. 'Well no, I don't,' said Jane. 'But even so – I'm very grateful to you, Hawkins.'

'You mean you'll still take me to South Terrace?'

'Indeed I will,' said Jane. 'One way and another I don't seem to be safe without you.' She turned to Jay. 'You'll come up with us?'

'Oh please, sir,' said Hawkins, suddenly aware how strong and aggressive Jay was.

'Well sure,' he said. 'Be a pleasure.'

Cautiously they all three climbed the stairs and Jane found herself remembering that piece of Gilbert and Sullivan, 'With catlike tread', and thinking how ridiculous they must seem. But no doubt she'd appeared ridiculous at the Ritz, running about in a flimsy dressing gown and using a hand mirror like a tennis racket. Twice in one day, she thought, and in two different capitals. . . . Then she looked round the study door, and realised that, ridiculous or not, it was serious too, just as Paris had been.

The study was a shambles. Papers, letters, photographs were thrown everywhere, some just crumpled, most of them torn in two, or in shreds. The tea chest that had held the stuff she had labelled miscellaneous had simply been stood on end and its contents strewn over the floor. There was cigarette ash everywhere, and there were cigarette stubs too, one even crushed out on the carpet, but mercifully there had been no fire. And in the midst of it all, flat on his back and gently snoring, Julian de Groot Burrowes, MA (Cantab) still clutching in his fist the empty decanter.

'Dear God,' said Jane, and put her hands to her face, and wept. Bower's arm came about her, supporting, comforting, until at last the tears eased and he gave her a handkerchief.

'No cops?' he said. 'Not even now?' She shook her head. 'What then?'

'Get him out of here.'

'Just throw him into the street? The state he's in that'll mean the cops anyway.'

'See if he's got an address we can take him to.'

Jay started forward, but it was Hawkins who bent over Burrowes and took out his wallet.

'There's his card, miss,' she said. '187, Gower Street. That's in Bloomsbury.'

'It would be,' said Jay. He looked down at Burrowes, and then to Jane. 'I guess I'm going to need some help this time,' he said. 'Your chauffeur?'

'He'll be OK,' Jay said, which meant he would keep his mouth shut, and sent Hawkins to fetch him.

'Tough for you,' he said, when Hawkins had gone. 'I remember you telling me how hard it was, collating all this.'

'*Why?*' said Jane. 'In God's name – why would he do it?'

– 387 –

'You won't find out tonight,' said Jay, 'but I sure would want some answers tomorrow if I were in your shoes. Still, by the state he's in, if you screech loud enough in the morning he'll tell you anything – just to give his head a rest.'

'I'll need to telephone my brother in the morning,' she said. 'Is it all right if I use the telephone in the *World* office? I don't want anyone else to hear.'

'I'll give you a note,' said Jay, and took out a note book. 'And that reminds me – I'm having a press card made out for you – and you'll be getting an application form for the NUJ.'

'For the what?'

'The National Union of Journalists,' he said. 'Don't you know anything? You're a woman of the Left. It's high time you belonged to a union.' He leaned forward and kissed her, a friend's kiss.

'It's tough on you,' he said, 'but you *are* tough. You'll make it. You'll see.' And then Redman arrived.

Together they picked up Burrowes, and he stirred at last and muttered something that Jay told her later was a quotation in Greek from Thucydides, and with hazy memories of his time at Harvard meant 'To famous men all the earth is a sepulchre'. Then he and the chauffeur carried him out, for all the world, thought Jane, like a couple of Tommies bringing in a wounded comrade.

'Do you want to do anything about this tonight, miss?' Hawkins asked.

'Not a thing,' said Jane, and looked again at the appalling mess, and reached a decision. 'Tomorrow we'll pack it all up in bags, and when Guy Fawkes night comes, we'll add it to the nearest bonfire.' Posy Sanderson was no more, after all, so why should the rest survive?

'Are you allowed to do that, miss?'

'It's mine,' said Jane. 'My father left it to me in his will.'

'But if it was left to you how could your brother – ?' Hawkins bit off the question. 'Beg pardon, miss.'

'Not at all,' said Jane. 'It's a fair question. But I don't suppose my brother ever expected anything like this. Are you hungry?'

'Starving, miss. I haven't eaten a thing since breakfast. I daren't. Not with him here.'

And I, thought Jane, have had nothing except coffee and

croissants in Paris and a cup of tea at Croydon aerodrome.

'Nor I,' she said.

'Shall I cook something, miss?' Hawkins asked.

'No.' There was a sort of brasserie in Dover Street that produced reasonably edible food until midnight. 'We'll go out.' And then she remembered something she should have thought of long before. 'Oh my God.'

'What's wrong, miss?'

'Foch. . . . I forgot all about him.'

'He's all right, miss. I had him with me in the kitchen. I even gave him a few dog biscuits. It's not what he's used to, but he's done better than us.'

'Hurry up and get ready then,' said Jane and went down the stairs. By the kitchen door she took out a cigarette, and found that her hands were shaking so much she dropped the lighter. She didn't cry, not then, but went into the kitchen instead and held Foch in her arms until it was time to go.

'I can't,' said the college porter. 'Honestly I can't. He'll still be asleep, miss.'

'You must wake him,' said Jane. 'There's been an accident. A very serious accident. His friend Mr Burrowes, and his sister. Go and tell him at once.'

'Yes, of course, miss,' the porter said. 'Will you hold on?'

'*Of course I'll hold on.*'

There was a silence, and Jane felt that she might begin to shake again, and picked up Foch instead, enjoying the comfort of his small, solid body and harsh, crisp-curling fur. Foch yawned – it wasn't yet seven o'clock – but snuggled to her, assuring her that she was loved before drifting back to sleep. Jane looked about her.

Not a bad little office, she thought. Leather swivel chair, generous desk, sporting prints between the filing cabinets. But the phone and the privacy were all that mattered. She yawned even more than Foch. Hawkins was still in bed. She'd told her to sleep late. The poor girl was as exhausted as she was, but she wouldn't be able to sleep, not until they had settled the thing. She'd enjoyed her meal, and looked pretty and smart in her best dress and the coat she'd lent her. Eaten nicely, too. A clever one,

Hawkins, one who watched and learned, but a nice one also. When she'd given her a tenner Hawkins had almost cried, and so had she. Loyalty and courage like Hawkins's were not things you could buy with money. The phone squawked and she picked up the earpiece.

'Yes?' she said.

'This is Francis Whitcomb,' said her brother. 'What's this about an accident?'

'This is Jane, Francis.'

'*Jane*? Hodges said you were hurt.'

'So I have been. And your friend, Burrowes.'

'Julian? Hurt?'

'He was unconscious when I last saw him,' said Jane. '*And* the house has been broken into.'

'I've got a lecture at eleven,' Francis said. 'I'll come as soon as it's over.'

Jane made her voice sound pleading and frightened. It wasn't all acting. 'You've got to come now,' she said. 'When I looked at Burrowes he could have been paralysed. *And* Hawkins was assaulted.'

'Hawkins?'

Neither he nor his friends ever seemed to know who Hawkins was.

'The housemaid, you bloody fool.'

And maybe that was what did it: the threat of violence in her voice.

'I'll come at once,' said Francis.

She had just finished lunch when Francis appeared: bacon and eggs that Hawkins had first fried, then served. She was taking coffee in the drawing room when Francis came in.

'Where's Julian?' he asked. And there's brotherly love for you, she thought. I'm supposed to be hurt, too.

'Have you eaten?'

'On the train,' he said. 'And look here – I thought you said Hawkins had been assaulted. Isn't she the one who let me in? And what's all this about a burglary?'

'Your friend Julian tricked his way in here yesterday, behaved like a vandal and assaulted Hawkins.'

'Jane – you can't be serious.'

Jane went to the bell. 'Let's ask her,' she said.

'No. . . . Wait. Tell me the lot. If getting me here was some sort of stupid joke – '

'I was away. In Paris as a matter of fact. Hawkins telephoned me in a panic. Thank God she got through to me before your friend Burrowes wrenched the telephone from the wall. I flew back to find he'd shown Hawkins some sort of letter – he claimed it was from you – '

'It *was* from me. I said he could have a look at those papers of Papa's. He's doing a piece about our administration of India. Or maladministration.'

'You had no right to do that. Those papers are mine.'

'Come on, Jane. Where's the harm? The letter I wrote was for you anyway. I had no idea you were jaunting off to Paris.'

'I was working,' said Jane, 'but even if I was jaunting, he had no right to go through those papers without my permission, and even less right to tear them up and crumple them and throw them all over the room.'

'Julian wouldn't do that.'

'Come and see,' she said, and they went to the study.

'Dear God,' said Francis, and then: 'Julian did this?'

'And the vase,' said Jane. 'I know it was a ghastly monstrosity and all that, but for some reason Mummy valued it.'

'Couldn't Hawkins have done that?'

'Why the devil should she? Hawkins was defending you property. It was your friend Burrowes who was trying to destroy it.'

'I wish you wouldn't keep calling him my friend like that,' said Francis. 'It sounds like – '

'Like what?'

'Like what it is,' he said, and again, fleetingly, she liked him.

'Whatever happened to Dennis?' she asked.

'He left me,' said Francis. 'I'm too serious, it seems. I suspect that I'm too poor, too.'

Unlike me, she thought.

'What do you want to do now?' he asked her.

'Go to see him.'

'But surely I'm the one to do that.'

'You can come too, if you wish,' said Jane, 'but I have to ask him why he did this.'

'He'll tell you he was drunk.'

'That's not an excuse,' said Jane. 'Not even a reason.'

'He can't help it, you see,' said Francis.

'You mean he's done this before, and you still sent him here?'

'Not this, of course not,' said Francis. 'But he's pretty wild, you see. I mean he tried for the navy but his health wasn't up to it, and even though he got a first there was no offer of a fellowship.'

'I expect his college prefers to keep its books inside their bindings,' said Jane, then before her brother could react: 'Have you heard from Mummy?'

'Not just lately.'

'I had a letter today. Masses. She's gone back to Bombay. Coming home, apparently. She and the Gwatkin aren't speaking.'

'Whyever not?'

'She wanted Mummy to accompany her at a concert when she sang one of those Amy Woodford Findon things. You know. . . . "The Indian Love Lyrics". "Pale Hands I Loved". All that. But Mummy refused.'

'Did she say why?'

'She considers Miss Gwatkin too fat to sing "The Indian Love Lyrics". "Like a haphazard collection of blancmanges wobbling in unison," she called her. But I rather think Mummy was too busy to practise. She's engaged, you see.'

'*What?*'

'Or as good as – whatever that means. Those are the words she used, but she didn't explain them. A Major Routledge. Late of the Puffers. He transferred in from the Gloucesters, she says.'

'What on earth are the Puffers?'

'The Punjab Frontier Force,' said Jane. 'A Puffer is considered quite a good thing to be.'

'I shall never understand India,' Francis said.

'In my day India wasn't there to be understood.'

'It was there to be enjoyed, I suppose,' said Francis.

'Yes, but enjoyment had to be earned.'

'And exploited.'

'In India the rich exploit the poor rather better than in most places. Part of Papa's job – the most important part – was to stop them. Let's call on Burrowes.'

'I don't want to see him.'

'I don't blame you. I'll go alone.'

'I mean I don't want to see him with you. But if I must – ' He turned to the door. At the foot of the stairs Hawkins waited.

'We're going to call on Mr Burrowes,' said Jane, 'to make sure this never happens again. My brother regrets it deeply. Don't you, Francis?'

'Oh yes,' said Francis. 'Deeply.'

'On the way home I have some other calls to make but I'll stop at an agency and find a cook. We can't eat eggs and bacon forever. Have you things to do?'

'Mr Warley telephoned when you were out, miss. About the drawing-room radiators.'

'You'd better go on over then,' said Jane. 'I'll join you if I can.'

She looked at Francis to see if the name 'Warley' had brought a reaction. There was none. His whole mind was devoted to the problem of Burrowes.

In the car she said, 'I'm moving into a new house.'

All he could manage was, 'I hope you'll be comfortable.'

She thought of Lionel, and radiators, and Bakst curtains and kitchen improvements and showers en suite.

'Sybaritic,' she said, and drove to Gower Street.

Handy for the British Museum, she thought, and for all the literary tea parties that Lionel spoke of with such horror, but not good for much else. Number 187 was a tall, narrow terrace house, its paint blistered, its bricks in need of painting almost as much as its windows needed cleaning. And yet it had once been an elegant house, before poverty and neglect had done their work. Not like Felston, she thought. In Felston there were no faded memories of grandeur, only poverty and neglect far worse than this.

Beside the door was a list of names: visiting cards, or scrawls on pieces cut from the backs of shoe boxes: everything from an ex-commander RN to a couple of obvious tarts. At least that's what Jay had said they were. Francis fidgeted about, looking for a bell, but Jane pushed at the door, which swung open to her touch, and went inside.

'Do you think we should?' said Francis, but he followed her even so.

Flat D, Burrowes's card had said. First floor. Up the stairs, treading on carpet worn thin as cotton, here and there a stair rod missing, past a lavatory and bathroom where the metal was beginning to show through the paint, and there was Flat D, with another of Burrowes's cards pinned to the door. Jane tried again, but this time the door stayed shut. She tugged at a bell pull, which by the feel of it was broken, then banged on the door with her fist.

'Jane, *please*,' her brother said, but the door opened at once and Burrowes faced them.

In a way, she thought, this was the first time she had seen him. Last night she had had eyes only for the havoc he had created. What she saw was a short man, shorter than Francis, and not so very much taller than herself, who was almost unbelievably beautiful, like some pre-Raphaelite vision of Lucifer before the fall. Black hair in curls that were not in the least effeminate, brown eyes at once loving and cruel, and a face that was perfect in its symmetry. He was clad in a dirty dressing gown, still unshaven, and stank like a polecat.

Oh Francis, my poor love, she thought. What have you let yourself in for this time?

Burrowes looked at her, uncomprehending, and then at Francis.

'Why sweety,' he said, 'how on earth did you escape from Cambridge? Do come in – you and your ladyfriend.'

Even his voice was deep and pleasant, without the least sign of homosexual affectation.

'This is my sister,' Francis said. 'Jane.'

'No matter,' said Burrowes. 'Bring her in. We're all men-of-the-world here. Except the ladies of course.'

Brother and sister followed him inside. The room stank rather less than Burrowes, but it still stank. And it too was a mess. Perhaps it's the only ambience he can live in, she thought, and looked from the divan bed still unmade to a table loaded with dirty dishes, books, letters and magazines. On the floor were more books, and a chair, once a rather splendid piece in buttoned leather, now scuffed and shabby and with one leg clumsily mended. The rest of the furniture looked as if it had been rejected by a junk shop, and competing with the feral smell of Burrowes and what she could only think of as his lair, was a strong and persistent odour of garlic. Empty bottles lay about everywhere, like booby traps.

'How do you like my little place?' said Burrowes, and then: 'What a question. I can see that you don't. But where do you live, one asks?'

'Where do I live?'

He looked at her. He seemed amused, yet slightly puzzled.

'It's a perfectly proper question,' he said.

'She lives at my mother's house,' said Francis. 'In Offley Villas.'

'Does she indeed? Kensington, I believe you said. The W8 bit. Not really my sort of place. All archdeacons and dowagers.'

'You enjoyed it well enough yesterday,' said Jane.

'I beg your pardon?' This time he merely looked puzzled.

'Or perhaps I'm wrong,' said Jane. 'Perhaps you didn't enjoy ruining my father's papers. Perhaps it's some new form of exercise.'

'My dear young lady,' said Burrowes, who must have been at least five years younger than she was, 'I've never been to your mother's house in my life.'

'I'm afraid that's not true, Julian,' said Francis.

'I'm absolutely bewildered,' said Burrowes. 'Is this a joke? Some new kind? Like your sister's concept of exercise?'

'Shut up and I'll tell you,' said Jane.

'By all means,' said Burrowes. 'But may I at least show some vestige of good manners and ask you to sit down?'

'No,' said Jane, and told him what he had done.

'But this is monstrous,' said Burrowes when she had finished. 'Do you have a witness?'

'I have three,' said Jane. 'Apart from myself.'

Burrowes turned to Francis. 'Your sister is not prone to hallucinations?'

Francis hesitated, and then said, 'No.'

'You paused there, sweety, before you answered,' said Burrowes. 'Definitely you paused. Are you sure your sister is quite as evenly balanced as a loving brother could wish?'

She hit him then, a round-armed, open-handed slap that caught him hard on the cheek and sent him sprawling into the leather chair.

'Jane – for God's sake,' said Francis, but all his sister could think was: Two in two days. But oh – how I enjoyed this one.

'Do you consider that an answer to my question?' Burrowes asked.

'Of course not,' said Jane. 'It was what you deserved and I gave it to you, as Francis seemed unwilling to do so.'

'I should like to stand up,' Burrowes said, 'but no more right hooks.'

'Then be careful what you say.'

Warily Burrowes got to his feet, then went to the only bottle in the room that still had drink in it. By the look of it it was gin and he drank it neat. He didn't offer it to either of the others.

'I must believe you,' he said, 'if only to avoid further assault, but I have no memory of it.'

'Oh, come on,' said Jane. 'Surely you can do better than that.'

'It's perfectly true,' said Burrowes. 'I take certain pills, you see – to alleviate the rather severe depressions that visit me from time to time.'

Jane turned to Francis. 'Are you sure,' she asked, 'that Mr Burrowes is quite as evenly balanced as a loving friend could wish?'

'Touché,' said Burrowes. 'Touché absolutely.' Then he continued: 'I also drink, dear lady. I drink far, far too much.' He gulped at his gin. 'The two combined do from time to time create a kind of amnesia, and so I accept your contention that I did the things you say.'

'Including your destruction of my father's papers?'

'Obviously I must, as I was seen doing it.'

'And the telephone and the vase and the assault on my maid?'

'All. All,' said Burrowes, with a kind of whimsical regret. 'Omnia mea maxima culpa.'

'And would you mind telling me why you did all this?'

'Ah, there you rather have me I'm afraid.' He thought for a moment. 'Your father was an Indian civil servant, I believe?'

'You must remember that at least,' said Jane. 'It was because Francis told you so that you talked your way in – to get material for an article. Or have you forgotten that, too?'

'My dear young lady, I can forget anything when I put my mind to it,' said Burrowes. 'But that I do remember, probably because they paid me for it. Five guineas advance, Francis dear – the cheque came this morning. We must dine soon. Definitely we must – before they find out I can't write it and stop the cheque.' To Jane he said: 'You should ask me why I can't write it.'

'It's of no interest to me,' said Jane.

'Oh but it is,' said Burrowes. 'I despise the British government's activities in India and the antics of their servants there disgust me so much I found I couldn't hold the pen. That may also be the reason why I treated your father's papers as I did, but I really can't remember.'

'I could take you to court for this,' said Jane.

'Oh, agreed. But you won't, surely? I mean think how upset your brother would be.'

'You have two choices,' said Jane. 'Either you pay for the damage you did or I'll take you to court.'

'I would gladly do so,' said Burrowes, 'but I'm broke, alas.'

'No, you're not,' said Jane. 'You have five pounds five shillings. You just told me so.'

'But it's all I have in the world.' Suddenly Burrowes's voice was a wail.

'It isn't nearly enough,' said Jane. 'But it will have to do. Make up your mind. I don't want to be late for my next appointment.'

Slowly, reluctantly, Burrowes produced a cheque and endorsed it over to her, then the resentment appeared to vanish and he handed it to her and bowed.

'I should treasure that if I were you,' he said. 'A cheque from Julian Burrowes is a rare edition indeed.'

Jane said to Francis, 'Can I drop you somewhere?'

'No,' said Francis. 'There are still a couple of things I have to settle with Julian.'

He wants to give him five pounds five shillings, she thought. Surely that must be it. He can't possibly want to make love to him amid all that stench.

38

BURROWES SAID, 'QUITE a card, your sister.'

'For God's sake,' said Francis. 'You upset her. What did you expect?'

'I had one of my amnesia attacks,' said Burrowes. 'Didn't you hear me say so?'

'I'm sorry,' said Francis. 'You never told me about them. Shouldn't you see a doctor?'

'Of course not,' Burrowes said. 'They don't exist – but they're a useful excuse, don't you think? I mean I don't suppose your sister believed it any more than I did – but it's not a thing you can disprove, now is it? I don't like your sister, by the way. Don't like her at *all*.'

'She was devoted to my father.'

'Of course she was,' said Burrowes. 'One rotten little bourgeois devoted to another. I read those papers before I tore them. Balls and tiger hunts and games of polo while an entire subcontinent starved. It was disgusting. It still is. . . . Don't tell me you admired your father?'

'I hardly knew him,' said Francis.

'Not a very brave answer, but effective.' He gulped more gin. 'One of these days you must tell me why you hesitated when I raised the question of your sister's state of mind. But not now. Now you slip the old tart the five guineas your sister stole from her, then she'll clean herself up and do her very best to earn it.'

Jane went first to the bank, and then to see Jabber. She hadn't wanted to while her brother was with her, and it was just as well he'd refused her offer of a lift, especially as that clever swine Burrowes had spotted his hesitation when he'd questioned her state of mind. But she'd made an appointment with Jabber and was determined to keep it, and not to talk about Burrowes. It was a suitably edited version of the Paris trip she discussed with him, and on the whole he was pleased with the way she'd handled it, but no more clouts on the head with hand mirrors, he'd warned her. She'd tried her limpid look. Had he never heard of death before dishonour? But in those cases it was the maiden who was supposed to die, he'd told her, then kicked her out. He might be in love with her, but he was a very busy doctor.

On to the agency then, and the promise of an adequate cook as soon as one could be found. Mummy preferred her cooks adequate: they didn't cost so much, and even an adequate cook would be better than eggs and bacon recurring over and over, or getting Hawkins into the habit of eating in restaurants she couldn't possibly afford. And then to Fleet Street to see Jay Bower by appointment – always by appointment, and say thank you and report.

'You're welcome,' he said. 'I guess it was pretty nasty for you.'

'I was very fond of my father,' she said. He nodded.

'Do you believe all that stuff about amnesia?'

'Of course not,' she said.

'But you didn't send for the police?'

'How could I?' she said. 'My brother was involved.'

'You did the right thing,' he said. 'That bastard will play every card he's dealt.'

'You know something about him?'

'I've had a little work done.'

For the first time she found herself wondering how much work he'd had done on her. 'And what did you find out?'

'Good family. Eton and Trinity. His father was in the navy – killed in the war – but Burrowes still hates his memory. Highly intelligent, an aggressive drunk, totally unreliable, and queer as they make them.'

'No wonder his college didn't give him a fellowship.'

'He's a Communist too – at least he says he is every chance he gets. Not too many people believe him.'

'Why not?'

'He buggers too many bourgeois. What are you going to do about your father's papers?'

'Get rid of them.'

'Good in bed,' he said, 'marvellous to be with, stunningly attractive, and smart, too. Why won't you marry me?' And then – 'Don't answer that. My ego couldn't stand it.' His desk telephone sounded, and his secretary's voice quacked.

'Three minutes,' said Bower, and motioned Jane to stay, then hung up and turned to her. 'I've got a couple of things for you.'

The first thing was her application for the NUJ, already filled in. All she had to do was sign it. The second was her press pass.

'One more thing,' he said. 'That office you were in this morning. It's yours whenever you want it.'

She looked at him warily. 'Do all your employees get offices like that?'

'You know they don't,' he said, 'but you're good for the *Daily World* right now.'

'And when I'm not you'll throw me out?'

'Sure.'

'Then I'll take it. But only for working in.'

'That's all offices are for.'

South Terrace then, and tea in the kitchen with Lionel and Hawkins. The rest of the house had reached that stage of heroic disorder that looked as if it could well be permanent, and was swarming with workmen. Together the three of them went over it, and she oohed and aahed gratefully as the two of them showed off the shower, the radiators, the kitchen already installed. Another cook, she thought, but rather better than adequate if the cook was to match the kitchen. Then Hawkins went off to rebuke a plumber because it was good for him.

Lionel said, 'She's good you know. Really awfully good.' And then, 'She told me about your visitor.'

'I told her she could.'

'He's a bad one. Vicious, cruel, unscrupulous. Did he try to get money from you?'

'I got some from him. For the damage he'd done.'

'But how marvellous,' said Lionel. 'That makes you unique – though of course you always were. Your brother is – emotionally involved, I take it?' Jane nodded. 'Such a pity,' said Lionel. 'Why couldn't he have stayed with dear little Dennis?'

'Dennis was rather too expensive – and altogether too frivolous.'

'The course of true love never did run smooth,' said Lionel. 'How right the Swan of Avon was. As usual. . . . Burrowes will hate you, you know.'

'For showing him up in front of Francis?'

'For besting him. He'll try his utmost to hurt you. You should be on your guard against that. He's awfully good at hurting people.'

'I met a man in Paris,' she said, 'who is utterly convinced that the world is going to end soon and that the only thing left for him is to have a good time, no matter who gets hurt. He doesn't set out to hurt people. It just doesn't bother him. But you're saying that Burrowes enjoys it.'

'He does,' said Lionel. 'It's what he does best. Believe me I know.'

You too, poor darling, she thought, though indeed Burrowes was extremely beautiful.

'Tell me,' she said, 'why does he smell so much of garlic? Is he afraid of vampires?'

'Hardly,' said Lionel. 'He's almost one himself. He just likes the stuff – as so many of us do. But Julian of course can like nothing in moderation.'

'But doesn't it put his chaps off?'

'Some,' said Lionel. 'Some have been known to be too fastidious to stand it. But there are those among us who have shall we say specialised tastes. And of course he will clean himself up if you offer him enough money. Julian has a very large circle of admirers. What are you doing this evening?'

'Georgina Payne has invited me to dinner at the Etoile.'

'In that case would you mind very much if I took Peggy to dinner?'

'Peggy?'

'Hawkins to you,' said Lionel.

'But are you sure you want to?' said Jane. 'I mean forgive the snobbery, but she is a parlourmaid.'

'Well of course she is,' said Lionel. 'But she's the only parlourmaid I ever met – possibly the only one who exists – who wishes to have the Romantic Movement explained to her. The urge to take her to dine was irresistible.'

'You intend to explain the Romantic Movement in one dinner?'

'The dinner was my idea. After such a request, how could I not? You don't mind?'

'Of course not,' said Jane. 'But not the Etoile. We'd both be embarrassed.'

'I thought the Savoy,' said Lionel. 'Or somewhere sombre like that. Oh – and she says she will go only if you'll lend her the same coat she wore when you took her to the brasserie.'

'Anything except Aunt Pen's leopardess,' said Jane.

Georgina Payne said, 'Lionel's taking your maid to the *Savoy*?'

'Why not?' said Jane. 'You've taken me here.'

'But she's your maid.'

This was pretty well what I said to Lionel, thought Jane. But Lionel's right. Hawkins is special.

'She's a very pretty girl.' And it was true, she thought. Suitably made up and dressed, Peggy Hawkins was very pretty.

'She's been a great help to us over South Terrace,' she said. 'And anyway they share an interest in what you might call cultural history. Lionel says it will be a treat for him.'

'I hope I don't sound like a snob,' said Georgina, 'because I'm not. Honestly. I mean la vie de bohème and all that. It's just that I'm astonished, that's all.'

'Talking of la vie de bohème,' said Jane, 'how is Michael?'

Their chicken Kiev arrived, and they waited while it was served.

'Michael is prospering,' said Georgina. 'But not in my humble abode. Not any more. Not in Lilian Browne's magnificent abode either, with its Metcalf and Richards studio.'

'Where is he?'

'Carcassonne, so I believe. Or is it Rimini? Taormina was mentioned, too. *And* Paris. Anyway it's somewhere really rather nice, wherever it is.'

'He must have sold a vast number of paintings.'

'He hasn't done too badly – including that rather lush one of me. It went for pounds and pounds, apparently.'

'Who bought it?'

'Some gallery. Acting for a client. Oh Mikey did make a bob or two, but not enough for Carcassonne, never mind Taormina.

He got a scholarship. A travelling scholarship – and so he's travelling.'

The idea had been, thought Jane, that he would take Georgina with him.

'He didn't want you with him?'

'Certainly he did. Rather went on about it as a matter of fact. I turned him down.'

'But Georgina. . . . Why?' Jane asked. 'I mean Paris. . . . Rimini. . . .'

'The BBC,' said Georgina, and then reproachfully: 'I told you. Only they've changed their minds.'

'Oh I'm sorry.'

'Not at all. After my audition they signed me up for six months. That's how I can afford to bring you here. They're going to make me into something called a celebrity, not the little woman trotting behind her great big talented man.' She smiled at Jane. 'We really are alike, you and I.'

It was what Jane had thought at the Brompton Grill after all, but she couldn't just leave it at that. 'Why do you say that?' she asked.

'Paris,' said Georgina. 'The Quart' Arts Ball. Jay Bower. That must have been fun.'

'Oh frantic,' said Jane. 'But it was work as well.'

'Work?'

'I'm doing a piece about it,' said Jane.

'Oh. . . . That's all right then,' said Georgina. She meant it, too. Then she signalled the sommelier to pour more burgundy.

It was time and more than time for her to go back to Felston. Not all the speeches and articles in the world – and she had done many – could compensate for being there. Not for Felston, but for her. She discovered, little by little, that she was beginning to need the place at least as much as it needed her, and so she took a taxi to King's Cross. Foch barked when she bent to pat him goodbye. He knew she was leaving him, and perhaps she should take Foch with her, she thought. But how could she take him to a place where a dog would eat better than the people who lived there?

An easy journey of it. Five hours to Newcastle. Much less than the Riley would take, and lunch on the way, then a hunt for the garage she had been told about, where she hired a Wolseley, a bigger car than her Riley, much bigger, but there was a strong possibility that she would have passengers if she knew Dr Stobbs. . . . The garage proprietor had not been all that keen until she had sat him in the passenger seat and driven him around for a while. When she left he had seemed almost cheerful, though the twenty pounds deposit might have helped.

She drove out of the city, and through the sad, ugly little towns that led to the sea. First Cambridge, then Ireland, then Paris, and now this, she thought. Ireland reminded her of Bridget and Bridie, and the fact that they were on their way to Oxfordshire, to a stable where Piers and Catherine would see them, exercise them, until she could decide what to do about them. It looks as if I am a spoiled, rich brat after all, she thought. I buy two living creatures and don't even think where I shall keep them. But I had to have them. I had to.

Before she could once more think about why, she was in Felston, and the car was at once conspicuous because it didn't belong. It was too big, even for a doctor. This was a toff's car, and toffs of that magnitude seldom visited Felston.

She reached John Bright Street and stopped at Number 36, and at once a swarm of children appeared, but fortunately Bob appeared too, and drove them off with a machine-gun burst of that guttural yet strangely sing-song dialect that she was only just beginning to understand. He looked at the car in admiration.

'Bought a new one, have you?' he said.

'Hired,' she said. 'It's good to see you, Bob.'

'And you,' he said.

'How are you? How's everybody.'

'Canny,' he said. 'Bet's courting. Andy and me's still out of work, but Da – he got a start at Tyneside Engineering.' He makes it sound as if poor old Stan had joined an expedition to the North Pole, she thought, so unlikely did it seem.

'And Grandma?'

'Her eyes is bad,' said Bob, 'but you'd better come in and see for yourself else there'll be ructions.'

They went inside and climbed the stairs.

Stan was still at work, and Andy was at a meeting – where else? – but both the women were at home and delighted to see her. Dr Stobbs's clinic was doing well and Canon Messeter was back driving the Armstrong-Siddeley that was even bigger than the Wolseley though he wasn't near as good a driver as Jane. And her idea of starting a kitchen was working a treat. They had all the stretcher bearers they needed, and all eating regular. And *they* were all eating regular too.

'On account of Stan getting a start, you see,' said Grandma. 'Rarer than rubies – jobs round here.'

'Mind you Andy doesn't think much of it,' said Bob.

'Whyever not?'

'Minimum wages,' said Bob. 'No piece work. No overtime. Da's not scabbing – he would never do that – but that's the best you can say.'

'It's still a job,' said Grandma.

'And that's more than the rest of us have got,' said Bob. 'I know.'

'Your turn will come,' Grandma said, but she'd said it so often that all conviction had gone, thought Jane.

Aloud she said, 'How are your eyes, Grandma?'

'Canny,' the old woman said. That useful non-commital word that could mean anything from not bad to splendid.

'Oh you fibber,' said Bet.

'You watch your tongue, me lady,' Grandma said.

'But Gran, this is Jane,' said Bet. 'She's one of us. You said so yourself.'

'All right,' Grandma said, and turned to peer at Jane. 'If you must know,' she said, 'I'm nearly blind and getting worse.'

'I've found a man who can cure you,' said Jane.

At once the old woman said, 'That's very thoughtful of you but I'm not going to London, not at my age. And where's the money to come from I'd like to know? Our Stan does his best but he couldn't manage that.'

'He wouldn't have to,' said Jane.

'Somebody would.'

'Well of course,' said Jane.

'And I won't have charity,' said Grandma. 'Any more than I'll leave here.'

'John would have paid – if he'd lived,' said Jane. 'But since he didn't, I'll pay instead. It's the same thing after all.'

'Don't talk so daft. How can it be?'

'Because if he'd lived I'd be Mrs Patterson,' said Jane and held out her left hand. 'And there's his ring to prove it. Besides, you wouldn't have to go all the way to London. There's a very good eye surgeon in Newcastle.'

'You've a tongue in your head all right,' said the old woman.

'And when you're in this mood I need it,' said Jane.

'Bella Docherty wil make a mess of things on her own,' said Grandma, fighting to the last.

'She won't be on her own,' said Bet. 'I'll be there. You've shown us how. And besides – you won't be any good looking at stuff till you can see again.'

'There, you see,' said Grandma to Jane. 'You've got our Bet at it an' all.'

'It's for your own good,' said Bob, but still the battle raged, until at last Grandma said she would think about it, which the whole room knew meant surrender, but with full military honours to the vanquished. Which was just as well, thought Jane, as I've already booked the surgeon.

Soon after that, Andy came in, and then at last Stan, back from the fettling shop at Tyneside Engineering, his boiler-suit scarcely marked, since fettling shop work demanded the kind of devoted and patient precision which was his whole nature. Nevertheless there was hot water ready for his wash before he would shake hands with Jane and pan hagglety to be fried for his tea, which he ate in solitary splendour, after he had said his grace, for he was the sole provider and king in this his kingdom.

And so at last she learned what pan hagglety was: bacon and sausage fried with potatoes and onions according to a formula known once only to Grandma, and now entrusted to Bet. Stan offered her some to taste, amazed that anyone alive should be ignorant of what it was. Cautiously she swallowed, and found that it was delicious.

'Better than caviar?' asked Andy.

'No,' said Jane at once. 'But caviar is rather special.'

'You had your picture in the paper the other day,' said Andy. 'At some do or other. In Paris it was. More chance of caviar than pan hagglety there I reckon.'

'There was neither,' said Jane. 'Not if you mean that ball where I dressed up as Cleopatra.'

'What in the world did you do that for?' asked Grandma.

'It was fancy dress,' said Jane.

'Big gold cloak with picture writing on it and a head-dress like a heathen idol,' said Andy. Stan looked up from his food.

'Only she wasn't an idol,' said Jane. 'She was just a woman who happened to be a queen. Not that there were any Christians then. It was before Jesus was born.' Stan went on eating.

'She's in Shakespeare, too,' said Jane. 'As a matter of fact, Shakespeare was well represented. Titania and Oberon were there too – from *A Midsummer Night's Dream*, you know.' Mention of Shakespeare would invoke not merely respect, but the threat of boredom, too.

'Still, I bet you enjoyed yourself,' said Bob.

'Very well. The band was excellent. But I'd really gone there to get material for an article.'

'You've done with Felston then?'

'Not at all,' said Jane. 'Rich and poor is what the article's about. The Four Arts Ball and Dr Stobbs's clinic.'

'And do you condemn the rich?' Andy asked.

'No,' said Jane. 'I don't condemn the poor, either. It's up to the reader to decide.'

'I wish I'd been there,' said Bob. 'Shakespeare or no Shakespeare.'

Jane said, 'Are you still looking for a job, Andy?'

'Well of course I am,' Andy said.

'I think I know where I can get you one.'

'And where might that be?'

'Parkin's Car Components,' said Jane.

'Never heard of that one,' Stan said.

'But I have,' said Andy. 'It's in the Midlands somewhere, isn't it? Coventry would it be?' Jane nodded. 'And how could I ever go to Coventry? I'm needed here.'

'John went to Bradford,' said Grandma, 'and sent money home. We managed champion.'

'It's not just us here,' said Andy. 'It's the Party. I'm needed in Felston.' He looked at his family. 'You know I am.'

'Suit yourself,' said Bob. 'I wish it was me, but they don't need printers. Not in a machine shop.'

Bet got up to pour out tea for her father. Jane rose.

'I'd best be off,' she said. 'I want to leave my suitcase at the Eldon Arms and then go on to Dr Stobbs's.'

'Can I come with you?' asked Bet. 'There's something I want

to ask you about.' She looked at once at Bob, but all he did was wink.

'Aye,' said Grandma. 'You go with her and have a bit crack. Since Jane's made up her mind she's one of us she'll have to be told sooner or later.'

Bet loved the car, the first she had ever travelled in, and indeed once it must have looked well enough, but now the leather was cracked, the bodywork needed polishing; but Bet sat in it as if it were the Coronation Coach.

Jane said, 'What is it you want to tell me?'

'It's sort of personal,' said Bet.

'Well I should imagine it would be,' said Jane, 'but I can keep a secret you know.'

'I suppose it started with you showing me about make-up,' said Bet. 'It does something for you, doesn't it?'

'For one's morale, you mean?'

'I'm sorry,' said Bet. 'I don't know that word.' And the shyness that always hovered close engulfed her, and she said no more.

Jane Whitcomb thought, what a snob I am. Thoughtless arrogant scribbler of an intellectual snob. Show-off, too.

Aloud she said, 'I mean it makes you feel better.'

'That's right,' said Bet, and then: 'Oh. . . . We're here. It goes so fast. Not like the trams.' And then for some reason she blushed.

Jane said, 'Come in with me. We can talk while I unpack,' as the porter came hurrying out. The manager was waiting with the register, and as she signed she asked Bet what she would like to drink, so that as she stowed away her clothes in the massive mahogany drawers and wardrobe, she drank sherry and Bet lemonade.

'All that silk,' said Bet in wonder, and then, 'You'd have thought they were expecting you here.'

'They were expecting me,' said Jane. 'I telephoned from London and booked.'

'I never knew you could do that,' said Bet.

Really she is too vulnerable, thought Jane, but she's looking prettier, *and* more positive. She even risked drawing Grandma's fire.

'Can you tell me now?' she asked.

Bet rose and handed the garments from the suitcase to Jane, and talked as she did so. 'Is it *all* silk?' she asked.

'Mostly,' said Jane. 'Now stop dodging the issue and tell me your secret.'

'It isn't a secret, exactly,' said Bet. 'It's just – I've got a chap.'

'I beg your pardon?'

'You know. A young man. Not that he's that young. He's thirty-three. And he's a widower. Da isn't too keen on that.'

'Whyever not?'

Bet shrugged. 'Da says one marriage is all that's needed.'

This could be religion, thought Jane, or it could be prudishness. Very possibly it was both, but whatever it was, it was best ignored.

'Has he any children?'

'There was one,' said Bet. 'A girl. She died of TB. And so did his wife, poor thing.'

'That's very sad,' said Jane.

Bet shrugged. 'It happens all the time round here.'

The poor have their own armour, Jane thought, and my God how they need it. 'What's his name?' she asked.

'Frank,' said Bet. 'Frank Metcalfe.'

'And has he got a job?' Really she thought, this is like pulling teeth.

'Yes,' said Bet. 'He has. He's a tram driver.' Unexpectedly she giggled. 'Bob says it was the glamour of the uniform. Bob's a terrible tease.'

'Tell me about him. What he's like,' said Jane.

'He was in the army during the war,' said Bet. 'Royal Artillery. And he can play the mouth organ. He doesn't drink – well not all that much – and he lives in Lord Collingwood Street. And he makes two pound five a week without overtime.'

'Tall? Short? Handsome? Fair? Dark?' asked Jane.

'Sort of fair,' said Bet. 'But his eyes are brown. Not as tall as Bob or Andy – but tall enough.'

'And he loves you?'

'He doesn't talk like that. – Like the pictures I mean. "I love you." He couldn't say that – any more than I could. But he does.'

'And do you love him?'

'Oh yes,' said Bet. 'I can say it to you. I worship that man.'

'And when's the wedding?' Bet shrugged. 'But if he's got a job – '

'Oh he can afford us,' said Bet. 'I mean tram driving's a steady job. It isn't that.'

'What then?'

'It's Bob and Andy and Da and Grandma. Who's going to take care of the other Pattersons if I get wed and move away?'

'Couldn't Frank move in with you?'

'He wouldn't hear of it,' said Bet. 'He told us straight. He wants a wife. Not a share in a housekeeper.' The tears welled then. 'Oh Jane,' she said. 'What am I going to do?'

Jane took Bet in her arms and rocked her as Aunt Pen had once rocked a much younger Jane. 'There there,' she said. 'We'll think of something, you'll see,' and offered her a silk handkerchief which Bet resolutely refused to use. So Jane drenched it in perfume and gave it to her for her bottom drawer, as proof of her optimism, then drove her back home in style before going to the clinic.

39

D R STOBBS WAS busy as usual, so she went into the kitchen
for a chat with Bella Docherty, a kitchen still redolent of
stew, before she heard the characteristic thump of the
Armstrong-Siddeley's gear change, and stood in the hall to watch
as a couple of sturdy-looking men carried in a woman on a
stretcher, a woman prematurely aged, her body wasted. Her
idea to feed helpers seemed to be working, thought Jane, even
though the burden they carried appeared beyond help. She
watched as they lifted her into Stobbs's surgery, then a voice spoke
behind her.

'Cancer of the breast, I fear,' said the voice, 'and quite in-
curable.'

Jane turned to face a man in a superbly cut, if ageing grey suit,
and a dog collar.

'You must be Miss Whitcomb?' he said.

'Canon Messeter?' she asked, and offered her hand.

He was of medium height, but so lean as to look taller.
In almost every way he looked the conventional upper-class
Englishman: sprucely shaved, grey hair neatly cut as if he had
been to Tramper's that morning, hand-lasted shoes. Nose the
required aristocratic beak, she noticed, chin and mouth firm.
Only the eyes departed from the norm. They were of the deepest,
most shining blue she had ever seen, and with more than a hint
of madness.

Messeter took her hand and bowed over it with a kind of
studied nonchalance, and she knew at once that in his day the

canon had had more than his share of success with the ladies.

'You drive my car much better than I do, so I'm told,' he said.

'It's not the easiest car in the world to drive.'

'Never was,' said Messeter. 'But then neither was a field ambulance.' He looked at her. 'You know it's a pleasure to meet you. I had my doubts about that, but it is.'

'Doubts?'

'We get them here from time to time. Mostly women. Ladies, I suppose one must call them. They come here oozing sympathy and beef tea, and sometimes a little money if we're lucky, but after their first encounter with someone like that poor soul in there – ' and his head bobbed towards the surgery, ' – they take the wings of the morning as the psalmist says, and away they fly. But you, I perceive, are back, just as Stobbs said you would be.'

One of Bella Docherty's helpers came in with tea and biscuits, and he took her to a room off the hall, a room that was all books and battered furniture, and a crucifix on the wall. Canon Messeter's room.

'A parson gets used to drinking tea,' he said. 'Occupational hazard. Before that I was a soldier. They drink tea at all hours, too.'

'Which regiment?' Jane asked.

'Rifle Brigade. . . . I enjoyed my time as a rifleman.'

'You must have been in France?'

'Lord yes. I was in India when it started, but they got me back to France in time for first Ypres, and I had the good fortune to be carried by colleagues of yours on a couple of occasions. Pity it wasn't you. It would have been more appropriate, somehow.'

'Did you say *good* fortune? To be wounded twice?'

'Oh good heavens yes,' said Messeter. 'I got better, you see. Or rather considerably better than I had been, but as a rifleman I was rather surplus to requirement then. I regretted it bitterly at the time – I was a major, you see, and next in line for the battalion. Vanity of vanities, you will say, but one is but human after all – though I do pray for forgiveness of course. The sin of pride is very terrible. I should warn you that I do pray rather a lot.'

'So I should suppose,' said Jane.

'On account of this?' Messeter touched his collar. 'Because prayer's my trade, so to speak?'

'Because of the kind of man you are.'

Messeter bowed once more, this time sitting down.

'Prayer is very necessary in Felston,' he said. 'The devil has such a strong hold. I cannot understand how a man can turn his back on God and live in this place – though Stobbs seems to have achieved it.'

'When did you go into the church?' Jane asked.

'In 1918. After I received the second one. . . . A shell burst. . . . I have rather a lot of German iron in me still. All the best authorities were agreed that I should be dead, and one day it occurred to me that as I wasn't – dead, I mean, – God must have had some further plans for me – and what they were seemed obvious. I took orders and did rather well – vanity again, you observe, although this time I speak no more than the truth. A curate in Mayfair, then rector in a quite delightful village in Hampshire, and then a canonry. The rank of major you see, and the battalion the next step up, by which of course I mean a bishopric.

'But God hadn't spared me to enact the same vainglorious foolishness a second time. Perhaps he gave me a reminder. Certainly it was His will, insofar as everything is His will.'

'What was?'

'I was ill again. A piece of shrapnel became dislodged after I fell when out hunting. Once again I nearly died. Once again I was spared, and obliged to ask myself why. . . . All the medicos were convinced that I would never work again, so I resigned my living and asked a politician I know what he considered would be the greatest contrast to a village in Hampshire, and he said Felston. So I sold up and came here and met Stobbs – and I haven't stopped working since, except for an occasional spell in hospital, which is why I missed you last time. You are a journalist, one gathers.'

'On the *Daily World*,' she said, not without pride. Almost she produced her press pass.

'Vanity, lust in a small and ineffectual way, belligerence, snobbery and occasional good works – mostly yours.'

'I covered the Four Arts Ball for the paper not long ago,' said

Jane. 'It was all the things you mention. And it will make money for Felston.'

'You accept money from such a source?'

'I'd take money from the devil himself,' said Jane, 'if it would help the poor people here.'

'Which is precisely why the devil won't give you any. You've raised rather a lot already, Stobbs tells me.'

'I seem to be good at it,' said Jane. 'I came out of a crisis of sorts not long ago. Nothing like yours, but important enough – to me at any rate. And after it was over I just sort of got involved. Largely because the man I was engaged to once lived here.'

'So Stobbs told me.'

'After I – felt better, I started to find out things about myself. And one was that I wasn't afraid to ask for money – not when the money was for Felston.'

'I thank God for it,' Messeter said; and he means precisely that, thought Jane. Then Stobbs came in.

'Miss Whitcomb,' he said. 'Nice of you to look in. Have you brought another cheque?' Then to Messeter: 'Mrs Elstob's dying. I've banged enough morphine into her to calm a platoon, but she's still conscious. She wants a prayer, she says.'

He says it as he would say she wants a corned-beef sandwich, thought Jane. Messeter left them at once.

'So now you've met,' Stobbs said. 'What do you make of him?'

'I like him.'

Stobbs looked at her. 'Not everybody does,' he said. 'He frightens people. Goodness often does.'

'I'd no idea he'd been so ill,' said Jane.

'Whalebone and leather that one,' said Stobbs. 'He should have died years ago. But he reckons God won't take him until he's outlived his usefulness. He gave me every penny he had the first day he came here. What a man.'

He began to go through his pockets, and produced a pipe at last. Jane lit a cigarette.

'Did you bring a cheque?' he asked.

'Have a heart,' she said. 'I've just about had time to cash the last one.'

'I know,' he said. 'But this place eats money.'

'I'll go back soon and raise some more.'

'The sooner the better,' said Stobbs.

'Just as soon as I see Mrs Patterson into hospital,' said Jane.

'Cataract?' Jane nodded. 'Who've you got?'

'A man called Hannay,' said Jane. 'At the Royal Victoria Infirmary.'

'Then you've got the best,' said Stobbs. 'That lad'll end up in Harley Street soon. But you don't have to stay here.'

'I want to be sure she's all right.'

'She's got a son. She's got grandchildren. She'll be all right. But I need the money you can raise now. This minute.'

'You can wait a week,' she said.

'The poor can't.'

You sound just like my very nearly brother-in-law Andy, she thought.

'Yes,' she said. 'They can. Because they'll understand why. I love that old woman and I think she's beginning to love me. Certainly for the moment she needs me, not just for the love, but for the way I can make her do things in a way her own family can't. If I go now she'll think I've deserted her, and what kind of love is that?'

Behind her Messeter said, 'She's right, you know. . . . Love first, and then good works. First Mary, then Martha, and perhaps this young lady is both. I think Mrs Elstob is dying, by the way. She would like me to take her home for more prayers before she goes.'

'We need your car,' said Stobbs. 'There are still patients to see.'

'I'll drive her,' said Jane. 'Just tell me where I have to go.'

There was uproar, of course, when Grandma found out that her operation was already arranged, and getting her to Newcastle a heroic labour, but she went in style in the Wolseley, with Bet and Andy and Bob in attendance, as well as Jane, and Stan swore to visit her as soon as he'd finished work and washed and changed.

The private room alarmed her: she had never felt so isolated in her life, but the others stayed on and there were flowers and fruit, and Bob had brought his crystal set. I should have thought of that. She won't be able to read for some time, thought Jane. And next day, when the operation was over and they all went back to see her, she took the latest and most expensive wireless she could find, and the old woman, eyes bandaged, body vulnerable still after the anaesthetic, listened enchanted to Peter Dawson singing 'Glorious Devon'.

'By, you certainly splash your money about,' she said.

'When it's in a good cause,' said Jane.

'So I'm a good cause, am I?' Grandma Patterson asked.

'The best.' Jane leaned over to kiss her.

'That means you'll be leaving us, I suppose?'

'I have to,' said Jane. 'I've had my marching orders. I've got a lot of money to raise.'

Mostly it was talks again, and mostly to women's groups. Middle-class women, she discovered, had a voracious appetite for being lectured and hectored, especially by another woman, provided she was rich and famous enough. And then there was the Quart' Arts Ball article. That went down very well. Disraeli's two worlds in a column and a half, Jay called it, and she told herself that she must ask Lionel what it meant. She thought of it as treacle, but the amount of correspondence – and even money – it generated was very gratifying.

'You can't beat righteous indignation,' said Jay, 'provided you cut it with Hearts and Flowers.' She'd done that, all right. Mary Pickford would have been proud of her, or even Charlie Chaplin.

Then there was the ball. Lady Twyford had been approached by Jay and her fee agreed. It was outrageous of course, but she would make sure she sold enough tickets to pay for it. The Berkeley to hold it, and the right band, the right caterers. Décor by whoever was fashionable at the moment and a dance programme that alternated pictures of the London season with pictures of Felston.

'But we've done that already with the Quart' Arts Ball piece,' Jane objected.

'Always repeat a success,' said Jay Bower. 'It's only with a failure that you pretend it never happened.'

There was a lot to do. Andy – or Francis for that matter – would have dismissed it as frivolous, but Jane treated it with the necessary importance. It was a means of making money, after all, and caterers and band leaders and entertainers – Bower had insisted on a cabaret; had even insisted that services be donated free for Felston's sake – were as important as medicines and drugs for Dr Stobbs's clinic. The one financed the other after all. At five guineas each the ticket price was astronomic, but Bower argued that all the snobbish rich and social climbers would clamour for tickets just because the price was astronomic, and he was right. On the other hand, she noticed, quite a lot of people wanted tickets because they thought that helping her – or Felston – was a good idea. All her fellow ambulance drivers, for instance. Bower promptly had an editorial written about it, and earmarked Sarah for the cabaret.

Suddenly South Terrace was finished. Lionel telephoned and she went over to 'ooh' and 'aaah' more than ever, while Lionel and Hawkins stood by and looked smug, and rightly so, she thought. The central heating worked so well that the fires were lit only as part of the décor; the Bakst curtains glowed in a drawing room that was white with touches of black, like shadows, the dining room was sumptuous and traditional. The shower worked.

'Would you like tea, miss?' Hawkins asked.

'Champagne,' said Jane. 'There should be champagne. But I forgot to buy some.'

'I didn't,' said Lionel. 'In the refrigerator, Peggy darling.' A refrigerator too!

Hawkins set off, and Jane called after her, 'Bring three glasses,' then turned to Lionel. 'I've had no time to ask,' she said, 'but how did the Romantic Movement go?'

'Very well,' Lionel said. 'She taught me quite a lot.'

'Lionel,' Jane said, 'darling. Please tell. What is Hawkins up to?'

'God knows,' said Lionel, 'but whatever it is she's working at it.' Then Hawkins came in with a bottle and three glasses, and they drank to a house brought to life, and Jane toasted the other two for having done it.

'I think I may have found a cook for you, miss,' said Hawkins. Jane noticed that she was handling her champagne glass far more elegantly than Pardoe had ever handled his.

'Mrs Barrow, miss. She used to be with Lord Carberry. You know – the one who owns all those ships.'

'Good gracious,' said Jane. 'He's incredibly rich. Whyever did she leave?'

'He didn't pay enough, miss.'

'And I will?'

'Enough isn't all that bad, miss,' said Hawkins.

'I'm delighted to hear it. Perhaps you'd better engage the rest of the staff as well – but make it a week's notice – just in case.'

'Very good, miss.' From the tone of her voice Jane gathered that Hawkins already had.

'It's this damn ball,' she said defensively. 'I'm frantically busy.'

'Of course,' said Lionel. He was maddeningly soothing.

'And when am I to be allowed to move in?' she asked.

'On Monday if you like, miss,' said Hawkins. 'All we have to do is pack your things and move the Mount Street stuff out of storage.'

'Then Monday it shall be,' said Jane.

Until then she spent most of her time in Fleet Street, where Foch lorded it over a following of devoted slaves and she harangued and cajoled to sell more tickets, raise more subscriptions. Sunday she spent mostly in Jay's bed, in the flat he called the penthouse. Living above the shop, she called it, and the expression was new to him. When she explained it he was delighted.

'It's the only place to be,' he said.

'Except Berkshire.'

'Not yet,' he said. 'Not while we're like this. If you won't marry me – above the shop will have to do.' His arms came round her, gentle yet pleasing. She knew that one. He was up to something.

'I have to go to New York,' he said. 'California too.'

'Before the ball?'

'No. But soon after.'

'How soon?'

'As soon as you're ready.' She stiffened against his coaxing hands.

'You want me to meet your family? Is that it?'

'That's not it at all,' he said. 'You'll meet them, sure – but I think you'll like New York. *And* California. And I want to be there when you do. That's *all*. Honestly.'

She believed him and relaxed, and let his hands resume their pleasing.

On Monday evening she ate a solitary and adequate meal prepared by the agency's adequate cook. Next day an equally new
parlourmaid would begin work at Offley Villas. Mummy couldn't
possibly take much longer to return home, and she wanted the
place to be comfortable for her.

Jane went into the drawing room and tried the new cook's
coffee. It was less than adequate. While she sipped it cautiously
and read the *Morning Post*, Hawkins appeared.

'There's a taxi at the door, miss,' she said.

'Anyone we know?'

Hawkins looked puzzled. 'It looks like her ladyship, miss.'

'Good God,' said Jane.

'And with a gentleman.'

'Go and let them in,' said Jane, 'then warn cook that we may
need extra dinner.' She put down her coffee cup and went into
the hall.

There could be no doubt that it was Mummy. A little thinner,
but still with a magnificent carriage, and scarcely darker than
when she left England for India. Shady hats and parasols,
thought Jane, and how attractive both can be when handled
adroitly, which could well explain the attendant gentleman.

'Mummy, darling,' she said, and went forward to embrace her.

Lady Whitcomb looked long and hard at her daughter, and
then, 'Well!' she said, and that one word said it all. That she had
changed very much and not necessarily for the better, that she
was much, much too self-sufficient, and far too well-dressed for
a Monday in Kensington. Even so she returned Jane's embrace.
Her arms about me are still familiar, thought Jane, and she smells
as always of lavender, and when I move I shall miss her, but I
shall be content.

'My daughter Jane,' said Lady Whitcomb. 'This is Major Routledge.'

'How do you do?' said Jane, and offered her hand to a man as
tall, slender, spruce as Canon Messeter, but with none of the
madness in his eyes. 'Are you staying for dinner?' she asked.
'I've warned cook – '

'We ate on the train,' said her mother. 'Really the prospect of
sitting down to a meal while not in motion has all the charm of
novelty.'

Major Routledge chuckled appreciatively.

'Kind thought on your part, but I must be off,' he said. 'I wired ahead and booked a room at my club. Digging in there for a while.'

'Major Routledge is a member of the Travellers,' said her mother. 'Not wholly inappropriate for one who has been to India and back seven times.'

Again the chuckle. It seemed the major had had a lot of practice.

'Hope I don't get lost on the way there,' he said, and this time it was her mother's turn to laugh. It was like being at a concert party behind the lines, thought Jane.

'Taxi's waiting so I'll say au revoir,' said Routledge. 'Just come along to see your mother's kit got in safely.' He turned to Lady Whitcomb. 'I'll telephone you tomorrow if I may, Honoria.'

'Certainly you may, George,' said her mother, then waited, implacably the only word, as Routledge bent to kiss her mother's cheek, and shake her hand, and go.

'Let us go into the drawing room,' her mother said.

'Shall we see to your luggage first?'

'The heavy baggage will be delivered tomorrow by van,' said her mother. 'Doubtless there will be men to help carry it upstairs. I see Hawkins is still about the place. No doubt she can take my overnight case upstairs and unpack it – if she's careful, of course.'

They went into the drawing room.

'Would you like anything?' Jane asked. 'Coffee? Sherry?'

'Nothing at all,' said her mother. 'And if I did I am perfectly capable of requesting it.'

'Of course you are, Mummy,' said Jane. 'I merely thought that the journey might have tired you.' She said it easily and without strain, and her mother was satisfied.

'That was kind,' she said. If only she didn't sound so surprised, thought Jane. 'You will have observed that little scene in the hall,' said her mother. 'George and Honoria, the shared jokes, the kiss on the cheek.'

'Yes of course, Mummy,' said Jane.

'The conclusion, need I say it, is obvious.'

'That you're now engaged?'

'Not quite that. I have been invited to become so, not once but on numerous occasions.'

Like daughter, like mother, thought Jane.

'At my age it is flattering, to be sure,' said her mother, 'but one does not accept such an invitation lightly, and technically it could be argued that I should still mourn your father.'

'That is entirely your own business,' said Jane firmly.

'A just and friendly observation,' said her mother, 'and I thank you for it. You have been busy while I've been away?'

'Yes, Mummy.'

'With that newspaper, no doubt. Tell me about it. You may smoke a cigarette if you wish.'

Jane lit up at once. The *Daily World* business was all right, and so were suitably edited versions of Ireland and Paris, but Felston, and her reasons for being involved with it, were high hurdles indeed. She had no glib story prepared: there was nothing she could offer but the truth.

'The Royal Northumbrians,' her mother said when she had finished. 'I attended a ball they gave once, in Simla, in the year I married your father. George was in the Gloucesters before he transferred to the Puffers, but I believe I informed you of that in my letter.'

'Yes, Mummy.'

'And so your captain was killed?'

'On the 10th November, 1918.'

'And decorated, you say?'

'DSO. Military Cross.'

'And it never occurred to you that I might be interested in hearing of all this?'

'It occurred to me very often,' said Jane. 'But I couldn't. I couldn't tell anybody.'

'Whyever not?'

'Because I was mad.'

'You were, my poor child, and I'm beginning to understand why. If you'd told me – '

'I wouldn't have been mad,' said Jane.

'You didn't tell your father?'

'Of course not.' The vehemence of the answer pleased her mother.

'But you're telling me now,' she said. 'Do I take it that means that you are cured?'

'According to Dr Lockhart I'll never be cured,' said Jane. 'But for the moment at least I seem to be able to control myself.'

'Very much so,' said her mother. 'How is your house hunting?'

'Finished,' said Jane. 'I bought one in South Terrace. I was supposed to move in tomorrow.'

'Then I beg that you will do so,' her mother said.

'Don't you want me to stay till you're settled in?'

'You told me before I left that there could only be one queen to a hive,' her mother said. 'You haven't changed your opinion, I'm sure. Please go. I have been settled in here as you call it for fifteen years.'

'I promised to take Hawkins with me,' said Jane.

'Really there is no end to your kindness,' her mother said.

'I have a replacement for her. She starts tomorrow. With your approval. And you have a new cook, too.'

'You have appropriated the old one?'

'She ran away,' said Jane.

'I suspect the beginning of a saga,' said her mother, 'and I am rather too tired for narrative at the moment. Let us save it for breakfast. How is your brother?'

'Well,' said Jane, 'but he's part of the saga too.'

'Then I shall bid you good night,' said her mother, and kissed her and left. Jane found it necessary to have a little brandy before she went to bed.

Next morning she told her mother about Francis's friend. She made no reference to the sexual nature of the friendship because she found it impossible to do so.

'He sounds a most unsatisfactory young man,' her mother said when she had done.

'He is, Mummy.'

'And what do you intend to do with your father's papers?'

'They will form part of a Guy Fawkes bonfire.'

'I congratulate you on your decision. It cannot have been an easy one,' said her mother, and added: 'He broke that vase in the hall, you say?'

'I'm afraid so.'

'It was a wedding present from a colleague of your father's,' Lady Whitcomb said. 'I always disliked it.'

'But I thought you adored the thing.'

Her mother smiled.

'I may have given you that impression,' she said, 'but that was merely to annoy your father, who detested it. At what time do you intend to leave me?'

'I'd like to be at South Terrace before lunch, if that's all right?' said Jane.

'Why not?' said her mother. 'It is your house after all. I am to be privileged to see it?'

'As soon as it's presentable,' said Jane.

'And in the meantime I shall remain here,' said her mother, and smiled. This time the smile seemed to be without malice. 'Unchaperoned.'

'You could always invite Miss Gwatkin to visit you,' said Jane.

Her mother nodded as one acknowledging a hit.

'Did I not say that Gwendoline and I had quarrelled?' she asked.

'Something about her being fat, and her need to sing,' said Jane. 'It sounded the merest tiff.'

'It was nothing of the kind,' her mother said. 'Words were spoken. Unforgivable words.'

'And yet you shared a cabin on the way back?'

'We did not,' said her mother. 'We did not even share the same boat. I had a single state room.'

'Golly,' said Jane, and then: 'Forgive me, Mummy. But wasn't it expensive?'

'The money at Cox and King's took care of it,' her mother said. 'Really a most pleasant surprise. So like your father to forget about it.' She paused, and then, for her mother, became almost furtive. 'You remember Cox and King's office in Calcutta?'

'Quite well,' said Jane. 'In Chowringhi, wasn't it? Always a crowd of people.'

'A hotbed of gossip,' said her mother. 'A positive hotbed. Still, it enabled one to keep in touch, which is not always an easy matter in India.'

'You met someone there?'

'I had news of someone,' her mother said. 'An old acquaintance of yours. Perhaps rather more than an acquaintance. Miss Vincent. Vinney I believe you called her.'

'You saw her?' Jane asked.

'That was not possible,' her mother said, and then: 'I'm sorry, Jane, but there seems to be no way in which I can spare you this. Miss Vincent died. Two years ago. Of cholera.'

'Oh,' said Jane. 'Oh dear God how awful,' and she covered her face with her hands. Her mother got up from the table and came to her, patting her shoulder.

'It's as I thought,' she said. 'Miss Vincent was rather more than just your governess.'

'Yes,' said Jane. 'She was. . . . And her orphanage? Did that die with her?'

'No,' said her mother. 'It continues. A group of Eurasian women Miss Vincent recruited have stayed on. They are determined. Really quite determined. Able too, so I am informed. Though short of funds of course.'

'You have their address?' Jane asked.

'You wish to send money?'

'Aunt Pen left Vinney rather a lot for the orphanage,' said Jane. 'I'll add to it.'

'I've already done so,' said her mother, and this time her smile glittered with malice. 'That windfall from your father. Wherever he may be, he can hardly object to my helping a Eurasian woman or two. You have a telephone?'

'The number is in your book, Mummy.'

'Then be so good as to inform me on the instrument as soon as it is convenient to call on you. I should very much like to see your new home. And the major too, of course.'

Jane rose. Her mother embraced her and she returned the embrace.

'I think that I can understand your loss,' her mother said. 'I honestly think I can. From everything I heard, Miss Vincent was a remarkable woman. . . . I'm sorry.'

Jane left Offley Villas soon after. There was nothing to keep her there, apart from her mother's astonishing expression of affection, and that she thought had been shown simply *because* she was going away. She left her mother to her new parlourmaid, her adequate cook, and her major, talking on the instrument.

40

HER OWN NEW staff were there to greet her, presented by
Hawkins: the cook, Mrs Barrow (why was it that all cooks,
whether married or single, were Mrs?), the kitchenmaid, and
the second parlourmaid, Brown, already, Jane noticed, firmly
under Hawkins's thumb. Such unimportant creatures as char-
woman and jobbing gardeners were not it seemed thought
worthy of presentation. What would Andy think, she wondered,
if he knew that it took four grown women working full time to
take care of me, and others working part time too? And even so
she didn't have a lady's maid to do her hair, manicure her nails,
look after her dresses. Ladies' maids were all very well when one
felt lazy, but they were great ones for prying, and gossips every
one. Impossible to have a lady's maid *and* Jay.

Lionel came over for cocktails soon afterwards, and to fuss
while Aunt Pen's cherished pieces and pictures were installed,
and when it was done they relaxed. The house was a delight
and she'd told him so, and Hawkins. Now it was time to test the
other creative artists in the establishment. From the first taste of
Mrs Barrow's vol-au-vents, Jane knew that she was enslaved.
The word 'artist' was by no means overdoing it. Lionel was
already using words like 'minor genius'. Over coffee which was
not like English coffee at all, he told her earnestly, 'You must
never lose her.'

'Lord Carberry did.'

'Carberry doesn't know a soufflé from a syllabub,' said Lionel.
'Of course she left him. Her cooking for Carberry would be like

setting Raphael to paint railings.' He turned to her. 'You look sad,' he said.

'I've just learned that a friend of mine has died,' she said. 'A friend I haven't seen for years. If you'll excuse me, I'll have to do something about it.'

She went to the little room Lionel had designed for her when she wanted to be alone to work, or think, or gossip on the phone with friends. The phone was there, already installed, an elegant affair of brass and ivory. She called Mr Medlicott. It seemed that he knew.

'Yes,' he said. 'That chap Pinner got on to it. I wrote to you just now to tell you so. He had the idea of writing to Cox and King's direct. Bright chap, your Mr Pinner. . . . You want me to go ahead with the legacy?'

'I want you to double it – if that's possible.'

'If you're sure. . . .'

'I have never been more certain of anything,' she said. 'As quickly as possible, please.'

'Yours to command, of course.'

He sounded puzzled, but she could not bring herself to tell him that she had lost a friend. She went back to Lionel.

'So now it's done,' she said.

'Now it's done. . . . You'll give a party to warm your little house?'

Georgina without Michael she thought, and the Lessings to see what they would make of it. Tony Robins if he would come, because he would tell Pardoe and that would annoy him extremely. Dennis because he was sweet and Francis because she must. All the girls from the ambulance corps, and then she could ensnare Sarah and tell her how important it was to do her bit for Felston. And darling Lionel of *course*. And Jay, if he would come. He wasn't very keen on parties that didn't sell his paper, especially if there weren't a lot of nobility present. And the only lady of title she knew was Louise (she could hardly count the Lessings, even suppose they accepted) and one by herself he would consider paltry. She knew no other nobility, except for Lady Twyford, who would probably want a fee for coming. But then she remembered that she did know some nobility. Well sort of. The Hilyard twins. Catherine was Lady Catherine after all, and Piers was the Honourable. She would ask them.

'I really must give a party,' she said. 'Drinks and canapés?'

'Caterers,' said Lionel firmly. 'We don't want Mrs Barrow prostrate. We'll hire a butler and footman, too. Add to your consequence. Shall I do it?'

'Would you, darling?'

'Well of course,' said Lionel. 'I adore parties. And you will give lovely ones, I'm sure.'

More talks, more and more talks, and more passing round of hats. She was now quite brazen about it, and of course she was in her way quite famous now, and that helped. More articles too, because Jay needed a stockpile. They would be off to America in the New Year, he told her, and he needed a supply of her work to appear while they were away. About the party he wasn't sure at all, until she mentioned Louise, and the Hilyard twins, and then he said he'd try.

Every evening she spoke to Grandma Patterson on the telephone, and heard the tired whisper of a voice after the operation grow stronger and stronger, until the bandages were removed: her right eye had regained its sight. 'And now they tell me I have to go through it all again with the other one,' the old woman said. 'By – you know how to make a body suffer, Jane Whitcomb.' And then: 'When am I going to see you? I *can* see you now, you know.'

'Soon,' said Jane. ' I promise.'

'Well mind you do,' the old woman said. 'I feel starved for the sight of you.'

It was time to invite her mother, and her major of course. Honoria and George. Impossible to explain to the minor genius in the kitchen that her mother's lack of interest in food was almost total: adequacy her only criterion. Instead she allowed Mrs Barrow full rein, because she would have to eat the stuff too, and Lionel. The chance of eating a meal cooked by Mrs Barrow more than overcame his dread of meeting Lady Whitcomb, so there was a menu of consommé and sole, partridges and soufflé, Riesling to drink, and burgundy, because there were gentlemen present.

They arrived punctually to time, but Lionel was already present, summoned early so that they could gulp a cocktail together before Lady Whitcomb arrived.

'Liquid courage,' said Lionel, and poured the last dregs of the shaker into his glass, then stiffened, listening hard. 'Oh my God,' he said.

There was the rattle of a taxi and Hawkins scurried in, scooped up the shaker and glasses, then scurried out again and was only just in time to open the door when the bell rang. Jane and Lionel rose as Lady Whitcomb entered with her major, already alert to the fact that his Honoria might make a joke at any moment.

Jane performed introductions, and her mother looked about her, an imposing presence in black with silver lace, and an emerald set that Jane had not seen for years, and which had been recently cleaned, too. Mummy was definitely courting. No doubt about it. And why not? Her father would never have wished her to do otherwise.

'Would you like me to show you round the place?' she asked.

'I would,' said her mother. 'It will be interesting to see the kind of environment you envisage as being appropriate to yourself.'

The two of them went out, and the major eyed Lionel warily. His evening suit was well enough, but Lionel wore his black and white like the plumes of a peacock.

'You and Miss Whitcomb friends?' he asked.

'I like to think so,' Lionel said.

'Known her long?'

'We met at the Lessings' party. The one they gave for the Mirova.'

'For the what?'

'The Mirova,' said Lionel. 'The Russian dancer. Lady Lessing wore a dress that was inspired by Bakst – if that's the word I'm looking for. Still – it gave me the idea for those curtains.' He nodded at the drawing-room window, ablaze with red and green and blue.

Major Routledge ceased looking wary, and looked appalled instead.

Come come, Lionel admonished himself. This really will not do. Talk about something manly, you silly old queen.

'Which regiment were you in?' he asked.

'The Gloucesters,' said Routledge. 'And you?'

'The Royal Flying Corps,' said Lionel, and Routledge looked relieved. No doubt he expected me to say the Women's Land

Army, Lionel thought, but he persevered, and poured out another glass of sherry which Routledge accepted, because, Lionel was quite sure, Lady Whitcomb was out of the room. When she and her daughter rejoined them the two men were discussing a château near Amiens where they had both, though at different times, attended performances of the same concert party. The fact that both performances had been dreadful rapidly became a bond between them.

Lady Whitcomb cut in ruthlessly. 'It is modern, of course,' she said. 'Extremely modern. But then Jane is modern, too.' Routledge looked severe, and Lady Whitcomb continued, 'I am however coming round to the opinion that Jane's kind of modernity has a rôle to play in society.' Routledge's frown vanished; a nod of approval replaced it. 'I refer to her charitable works, naturally. A distinctly modern approach. Publicity and so on. The newspapers. But their existence was known even in India, was it not, George?'

'Oh decidedly,' Routledge said.

'And even Gwendoline Gwatkin was impressed by what you had achieved.' She closed her eyes for a moment at the memory of a faithless friend. 'This house has a style all its own. Light, airy, fully of charm. I gather I am to congratulate you on that, Mr Warley?'

'One did one's poor best,' said Lionel.

'Well done, old chap,' said Major Routledge. It was rather a relief when Hawkins announced dinner.

Her mother ate sparingly, but made no adverse criticism, which was about as much as Jane had dared to hope for. She refused the burgundy, but had accepted the Riesling: again a sort of victory. Major Routledge made no effort to hide his delight at what was offered, and ate and drank almost as much as Lionel. When they had done, Hawkins brought in a decanter of port, Lionel opened the door, and the two ladies left for the drawing room.

'I am no judge on such matters, as I have no doubt you know,' Lady Whitcomb said, 'but I have eyes in my head, and I can see that you have hired an excellent cook.'

'I'm glad you think so, Mummy.'

'It's of no consequence to me,' her mother said, 'but a lot of people do set store by such things, I know, and it is thoughtful of you to indulge them, although of course money cannot be an object with you.'

'Precisely so, Mummy,' said Jane. 'May I offer you coffee?'

'I thank you. No.'

'It is very good coffee,' said Jane, and her mother smiled. In her own way, Jane knew, her mother was enjoying herself.

When the men joined them, they both accepted coffee, Routledge rather as if he needed it, thought Jane. Lionel took his and sipped and said, 'Delicious.'

'It is the best,' said Lady Whitcomb. 'It has to be. My daughter has such exacting standards.'

Game and set to you, Mummy dear, thought Jane. But not match. Not yet.

When at last a taxi was summoned for Lady Whitcomb and her major, Lionel was already wearing his coat and scarf, but he took them off again as soon as he heard the taxi's gears engage.

'I must,' he said, 'I simply must have some brandy.'

'Help yourself,' said Jane. 'I felt the same the night that Mummy came back to Offley Villas.'

'Every possible respect to you, my darling,' said Lionel, 'but what a tartar.'

'Do you suppose I don't know?' said Jane. 'But she does rather keep one up to scratch, wouldn't you say? And what about the major? What *did* you find to talk about?'

'Not the Russian Ballet,' Lionel said, 'and certainly not Bakst.'

'What then?'

'The war, what else? Who I was with. Where I served. All the usual trivia.'

'Who were you with?' Jane asked. 'How odd that I never asked you.'

'Not odd at all,' Lionel said. 'I go to great lengths to avoid such questions. I mean do I look as if I were ever in arms? I began in the Sussex Yeomanry, as a matter of fact, but transferred into the Royal Flying Crops as soon as I could. Very hearty, the yeomanry, but in the RFC I could at least be by myself from time to time.'

'You were a pilot?' Lionel nodded. 'Like my brother David.'

'Well hardly, my dear,' Lionel said. 'I survived.' He looked into his glass, swirled the golden liquid round. 'I can't think why.'

Lady Twyford was every bit as formidable as Jane had thought she would be, with a mind like a calculating machine, but at least that mind was being put to use for Felston, once a fee had been agreed. But even with Lady Twyford running the show, there were still things which needed her attention: points of protocol, sensitive egos. That was because a ball involved so many artists, said Lionel, all of whose egos were sensitive. This was largely because of the cabaret, of course. Bower's solution to finding performers for a cabaret was to tell them the date and time and make sure they did their best, or else incur the *Daily World*'s displeasure. It worked of course, but it meant that afterwards Jane had to take them out and soothe them: lunch after lunch at the Ivy, the Caprice, L'Apéritif. In the end she rebelled and told Bower at least to moderate his language. Or buy her a new wardrobe.

Mummy rang up to invite her to lunch, or dinner, and to bring her 'young man'. Jane assumed she meant Lionel, and begged off on the grounds that she was working every day, but accepted an invitation for tea. All the adequate cook would have to do, she was sure, would be to boil the water. The cakes would come from Fortnum's. And so Jane drove Lionel and Foch to Kensington in the Riley. Mummy had requested Foch's presence, as well as Lionel's, and for the life of her Jane could not think why, but the question was answered as soon as they came in.

'There,' said her mother to Major Routledge, 'doesn't he look exactly like that chaplain in the Cameronians we met in Delhi?'

Routledge laughed his distinctive laugh, at once hearty and dutiful, and agreed that Foch did, and they sipped their Earl Grey.

'My daughter,' said Lady Whitcomb to Major Routledge, 'is too busy to dine with her mother – or even to lunch. Even tea one must assume to be a kindness, the interruption of an all-too-demanding schedule. What are we to make of it, George?'

Major Routledge looked saddened but reproving.

'Young people, Honoria,' he said. 'Always obsessed with their own affairs.'

'This particular young person,' said Jane, 'is being modern –

in the most respectable way of course. I'm organising a charity ball – or rather Lady Twyford is, but I am expected to help.'

'In aid of Felston, perhaps?'

'Well – yes,' said Jane. 'We're rather hoping that you will come. And the major, of course. It should be really rather grand.'

'We're hoping for two good friends of Jane's,' said Lionel. 'The Countess of Hexham *and* Sarah Unwin. – The actress, you know.'

'Certainly I know,' said Lady Whitcomb, and it was obvious that the major knew too. 'They and my daughter spent a rather convivial afternoon together not so very long ago. But I fear it would not be appropriate for me to attend. My bereavement is rather too recent for quite such a public appearance.'

Jane said at once, 'Then you must come to my house-warming party instead.'

'House-warming?'

'A few friends to drink a little champagne and say nice things about my new house. Not exactly a public appearance, Mummy.'

'I hardly think – '

'Oh come, Honoria,' Major Routledge said. 'No one could possibly object to your taking a glass of fizz with your own daughter.'

And Mummy capitulated without even a skirmish, let alone a battle.

'Very well,' she said. 'A brief appearance would be permissible, I suppose. Thank you, Jane. We have lived rather sequestered lives lately, George and I.'

'Not like India,' said Routledge.

'Ah, India,' Lady Whitcomb said, and sighed.

'And just what do you suppoose they got up to in India?' Lionel asked as she drove him home.

'Church, a little bridge, theatricals, polo, musical evenings.'

'How can you be so sure?'

'Because that's what it always is. And balls of course. But she couldn't go to a ball so soon after Papa's death.'

'India sounds like one mad round of dissipation,' said Lionel. 'I don't think I could stand the pace.' And then: 'I say. . . .'

'What do you say, Lionel dear?'

'That major of hers. He seems rather smitten.'

'He proposes marriage from time to time.'

'Will your mother say yes, once she's out of her mourning?'

'She very well might,' said Jane. 'Why do you ask?'

'Blest if I know,' said Lionel. 'I mean he's a perfectly presentable chap. The Gloucesters, the Puffers, all that.' And then he said again, 'Blest if I know.'

She dropped him in Chelsea, then drove over to Fleet Street for a tête-à-tête with Jay Bower. He had some criticisms of her latest article, but she defended herself vigorously. They went to bed together, then resumed their argument over supper.

'I still think it's too long,' he said at last.

'Then cut it without altering the sense,' she said. 'I bet you can't.'

He grinned at her. 'You might win at that,' he said. 'You're a fast learner. Marry me?'

'No.'

'Then tell me about the ball.'

She told him and he approved. 'If it works out right we'll do a big spread,' he told her.

'I have an idea for a follow-up,' said Jane.

'Let's hear it.'

'Let's see if it works out right first,' said Jane.

'That's my girl,' he said. 'Nothing on approval, right?'

'Right.'

'Then tell me about your party. Who's coming?'

'Everybody,' said Jane.

'Including your countess friend?'

'*And* her husband. *And* the Hilyard twins.'

'Did I ask about them? Now did I?'

'I just thought you might be interested,' said Jane. 'And did I tell you my mother's coming? She's got a title, too. She's Lady Whitcomb.'

Suddenly Jay grabbed her, put her over his knee and slapped her, then turned her to face him and put his arms about her.

'I love you,' he said.

She rubbed her bottom solicitously. 'You have such an elegant way of showing it,' she said. The slap had been meant as a joke but it hadn't felt like one.

'I got mad,' he said. 'I'm sorry. It's just – there are times when I find that I can't reach you – and that never happened to me before.'

Francis didn't come, but even he telephoned at the last moment and apologised. A Fabian Society meeting, and he had been asked to take the chair. But all the others came. Louise with her husband whom she had picked up at the House of Lords, taking his dinner jacket with her, because otherwise, as she explained, he would certainly have forgotten to change and very probably forgotten to come: but he was a plump and cheerful peer, and full of information about the novels of Surtees, and India, where he had once been ADC to the viceroy. Harriet too came early, together with her husband Neil who looked more like a bank manager than the research scientist of fiction, and danced, as she later discovered, extremely well; Sarah Unwin arrived alone: Beddoes, her current husband, was being difficult. Fred arrived alone too, in a very daring black and white trouser suit of her own design that Lionel applauded instantly. 'I *must* have one just like it,' he assured her, and Fred blossomed. More and more people arrived, as the hired waiters served champagne and Hawkins carried round the canapés. The Hilyard twins came early too, despite the fact that Piers had been hunting all day and Catherine had hunted *and* attended a tutorial. At Oxford, she assured Jane darkly, four days hunting a week was not enough. She was expected to learn things as well. Just as well she had persuaded the dean to let her loose for the night so that she could see her dentist in the morning. Piers never had *any* difficulty in persuading his dean to let him loose for the night.

Until Catherine arrived, thought Jane, Louise and Sarah had been far and away the most beautiful women in the room, but now there were three, and all of them groomed with an unerring sense of their own beauty, Louise in silver, Sarah in scarlet, and Catherine in a simple, smooth-flowing white dress that only a young and very pretty girl could wear. And then Georgina arrived, in a new and very expensive blue dress, and that made four. Sir Hugh and Lady Lessing next, he uneasily aware of Georgina, and she once more gowned in what looked like remnants of ballet scenery, but this time all muted silver and pearly grey: a classical piece – *Coppelia* perhaps, or *Les Sylphides*.

Mummy and the major arrived, and Mummy was at once monopolised by Lord Hexham. They had never met, but he had heard a great deal about her, and demanded at once the true account of Sir Guy's exploits against the maharajah who cheated at cricket. Mummy was only too happy to oblige, and poor Major Routledge looked so sad that Jane took him over to Georgina and introduced him. That done, she looked about her. All safely gathered in, she thought; except Bower.

Lionel strolled over to her. 'Counting the house?' he asked.

'All here, I *think*,' she said. 'Except Jay.'

'Bower always likes to come last,' said Lionel, 'if he comes at all.'

And after that wallop he gave me perhaps he's too ashamed to come, she thought, but that was nonsense. Bower had never been ashamed in his life. Then the door opened, and Hawkins ushered in not one man, but two.

'Who on earth – ?' Lionel asked.

'The one who looks like a prize-fighter is a Cambridge don called Tony Robbins,' she said. 'The one who doesn't is Richard Lambert.'

'And what is he?'

'A Labour MP.'

'Not a gatecrasher then,' said Lionel.

'Of course not,' she said. 'Rather an afterthought, that's all,' and went forward to greet them.

'How kind of you both to come,' she said.

'I was delayed at the House,' said Lambert. 'There was a division.' His eyes were already searching the room. According to Bower he would be looking for other politicians, because that was what MPs always did at parties. Impossible to say whether he was relieved or disappointed to find that there were none.

'And did you drive down all the way from Cambridge?' she asked Tony.

'Without you to drive me back,' he said. 'Certainly not. I came by train.'

Jane eased them into the mob, and looked about her. Going well, she thought. Enough to eat and more than enough to drink. Soon they would be dancing, but not too soon, please God. Her mother came up to her.

'It is time that we left,' she said, 'although I find it hard to leave Lord Hexham. A most perceptive man. Will your party be in the newspapers, I wonder?'

'In the *Daily World*, certainly,' said Jane. 'If you would like your name excluded – '

'I think not,' said her mother. 'In fact I am quite sure not. Gwendoline Gwatkin is a voracious reader of the *Daily World*. Come George.'

She moved to the door and the major followed, calling out over his shoulder what a wonderful time he had had. Jane went with them, and Hawkins opened the door. There, facing them on the doorstep was Jay Bower. Jane hastened to introduce them.

'The *Daily World*,' her mother said. 'You work there with my daughter?'

'I'm her employer, Lady Whitcomb,' said Bower.

'I should not be too sure of that if I were you,' her mother said.

She was aglow with the attentions of Lord Hexham and Bollinger, but even so Jane could have kissed her. When they went back inside, Lionel was already rolling back the carpet while Piers dropped the needle on to a record. 'Get Out And Get Under' began and Jay's arms came round her.

'I would have come sooner,' he said, 'but I couldn't get away.'

'It doesn't matter,' she said.

'Doesn't it?'

'Oh so touchy,' she said. 'All I meant was I know how busy you are.'

'You've forgiven me then?'

'There's nothing to forgive.' He stiffened, but she pulled him to her, forced him to keep moving. 'By which I mean that it's over and done with, so stop looking like a wronged husband.'

'Stupid of me even to try,' he said, 'considering that I'm neither. Wrong adjective. Wrong noun. . . . You're very like your mother.'

This time it was she who nearly stopped, he who pushed her on.

'That's the first time anyone's told me that,' she said.

'All the same it's true,' he said. 'Tough as old boots, and with a cold eye for realities. Your employer indeed. She was dead right to question it. Employer suggests control. Ownership even. Who could own you? I might as well try to pick up a handful of mercury.' He danced for a while in silence. 'I wish we were in bed together.'

'It would certainly liven up the party.'

She danced with Dick Lambert then, who was competent, but rather lost concentration if one tried to speak, and then Piers, who wanted her to tell him about the war, and then, as a reward, with Sir Hugh who danced divinely, as usual.

'I took your advice,' he said. 'About Michael Browne.'

'So I heard.'

He looked to where Georgina danced with Lionel. He was making her giggle almost uncontrollably, yet she never missed a beat.

'I trust she's not too heartbroken?' he said.

'It seems unlikely.'

'You think perhaps I did the wrong thing?'

'If you did,' she said, 'it was because of my advice. But as it happens I don't think you did do the wrong thing. Michael has to paint no matter what. And you made it possible for him to do it. His private life is precisely that. Private. You never met his wife, I suppose?'

'I never did.'

'I did,' said Jane. 'If you're taking on Michael, you should prepare yourself for a little more action when he gets back from abroad.'

Neil Watson claimed her then, an even better dancer than Lessing, perhaps the best dancer in the room.

'Wonderful party,' he said at once. 'I don't go to nearly enough, according to Harriet.'

'Whyever not?'

'Busy,' he said. 'Always busy. Like your pal Robins over there. And Pardoe. Not that he's likely to be a pal.'

'Most unlikely.'

'He'd like to be, you know.'

'Indeed I do know,' said Jane.

'Ah,' said Watson. 'He seems obsessed with you if you don't mind my saying so. Always asking questions about you – because of Harriet, you see. I keep telling him I hadn't even met you but he wouldn't listen. Obsessive. But then he *is* an obsessive. Quite a lot of us are. It's the only way things get done. Do I have to come to this ball of yours?'

'That's rather up to you.'

'No,' said Watson. 'It's rather up to Harriet. Which means I'm coming. I shall enjoy the dancing – you'll save me one won't you? – but there's an experiment at the Cavendish that day and I have to be at Cambridge.'

Jane noted that the Cavendish, which sounded like a club, was in fact a laboratory.

'I shall have to leave early,' said Watson. He made it sound like quitting Paradise.

Tony Robins next, and last. He was still a terrible dancer, but he didn't let it interfere with his conversation.

'I'm glad I came,' he said.

'I too.'

'I didn't think I would be,' said Tony. 'After the way I behaved last time – and you turned me down, too. But I'm glad I came. Does me good to be in an environment other than Cambridge now and again.'

How these dons love to analyse each other, and themselves, Jane thought. Still, he was rather sweet about it.

'Besides I now know that there was a *reason* why you turned me down,' said Tony. 'So much better when there's a reason, as opposed to just a general distaste.'

'And what is my reason?'

'You're promised to another,' said Tony. 'I knew it as soon as I saw you dancing together.'

'My dear man,' said Jane. 'That's Neil Watson. He's married to one of my oldest friends.'

'Not him,' said Tony. 'I've known Neil for years. Of course it's not him. I mean the other chap when I first arrived. The one who affects an American accent.'

'The only one here with an American accent *is* an American. His name is Bower and I write for him sometimes. He owns the *Daily World*.'

'That's the one,' said Tony, and left it at that, to Jane's relief. But she couldn't help wondering how soon it would be all over Cambridge, and whether anyone there would believe it, especially Francis.

The party was ending. In ones and twos, people were leaving. 'Darling, how marvellous,' they all said, and 'Such a *lovely* house.' Jane looked at the little French clock on the mantelshelf, Aunt Pen's favourite clock. Lionel said it didn't belong, but she'd put it there anyway. Nine thirty-seven, the clock said. Not bad for a six to eight party. The hired men had cleared away the glasses, and the room looked rather less like a pub with pretensions. Too many cigarette stubs in too many ash trays, and much too much cigarette smoke, but it was a nice place to be, now there were only the Hilyard twins left, and Georgie, and Lionel, and Dennis, and Jay.

Jay said, 'Can your cook make Melba toast?'

'She can make anything that can be made,' said Lionel, who didn't seem quite sober.

'Can you get some?'

'You're not feeling well?' asked Jane.

'Never better,' said Jay. 'What I want is Melba toast for everybody.'

Jane rang for Hawkins. When she came back, Jay was dancing with Catherine, Lionel with Dennis, and Piers with Georgina: beauty to beauty, Jane thought. Innocence and experience, too. Piers kept looking at Lionel and Dennis: Georgie did not; probably was only vaguely aware that there was anything odd in the fact that they were dancing together. After all it was obvious that they liked each other.

Jane turned the record, and Piers took Georgina to her seat then came to Jane, and danced with her easily and yet respectfully, somehow. He hadn't danced with Georgie like that.

'How pretty your friend is,' he said.

'Yes, isn't she?'

'And talented too,' said Piers.

'Did she tell you so?'

'Of course not,' said Piers. 'But she's Georgina Payne.'

'Actually I do know that,' said Jane.

'Oh do stop ragging,' said Piers. 'What I mean is she's on the *wire*less. Surely you must have heard her?'

'As a matter of fact I haven't,' said Jane, trying not to sound too contrite. 'I've been rather busy lately – '

'Another talented lady,' said Piers. 'Sweet of you to find the time to give such a wonderful party. She's promisd to let me take her to tea some time. Then on to the studio where she broadcasts.'

'That should be fun,' said Jane.

'I should just about think it will,' said Piers.

The dance ended, and Hawkins came in with the Melba toast, then cleared the ash trays and opened one window, just a little.

A jewel, thought Jane, a positive jewel, and wondered when Lionel would have to lunch her at the Berkeley to discuss the Peloponnesian War. . . . Jay got up and left the room, then in a little while they heard his car-door slam, and he came back with the biggest pot of caviar Jane had ever seen. Goodness he must be feeling ashamed of himself, she thought. He knows how I adore caviar.

'I was going to suggest supper somewhere,' said Jay, 'and then I thought why not let's have some of this instead, if there's any champagne left? We can always go on somewhere afterwards if we feel like it.'

'Oh,' said Catherine, and clasped her hands, rolled her eyes heavenwards. 'There *is* a Santa Claus.' She looked about twelve years old.

The party began again, and the dancing. This time it was Jay's arms that embraced Georgina. When they had done Georgie came over to Jane, and spooned caviar on to a piece of toast.

'Numbered among the elect,' she said.

'I think I've had too much champers to cope with that,' said Jane.

'I had a Scots governess once,' said Georgie. 'Bit of a slave-driver, especially on the Sabbath. She was a Calvinist or something. She said that if you were numbered among the elect you were saved. At the top table. Up there with the cherubim and seraphim. That's the way I feel now. Among the chosen. It was sweet of you to let me stay.'

'No,' said Jane. 'Not sweet at all. I like having you here. Besides, I *may* want a favour from you soon.'

'If I can I will,' said Georgie. 'You know that.' And then: 'I say. That young friend of yours is sweet.'

'Piers?'

'Of course Catherine's sweet too,' said Georgie, 'and *so* pretty. But I do rather prefer the male, sweet old-fashioned thing that I am. He's of the noblesse, I believe?'

'Younger son,' said Jane. 'His father's the Earl of Mangan.'

'Irish,' said Georgina, 'but not impoverished, not if his sister's dress is anything to go by.'

'Not in the least impoverished,' said Jane, and then: 'Georgie. . . .'

'No no,' said Georgie, and laughed. 'Not marriage. Not me.

Not even for the chance to live in Ireland. I say – your friend Bower's making rather a hit with my boyfriend's sister.'

Jane looked to where Catherine smiled up at Jay.

'Santa Claus is always popular,' she said.

He danced with her next, and she thanked him at once for the treat.

'Not enough for everybody,' he said, 'which is why I hung on to it for so long.'

'But more than enough for the deserving,' she said. 'You are sweet.'

'I am when you say so. I want to phone for a photographer if that's OK. Of course we've got library shots of Hexham and his wife and Sarah Unwin – but I could do with a picture of those twins. They're really something.'

'I think so too,' she said.

'And I'd like a picture of your mother – if she wouldn't mind.'

'I think I can find one,' said Jane, 'and she won't mind at all.'

She found a photograph, and the *Daily World* photographer came, and the second party began to drift to a close. Lionel and Dennis knew of a place where they could practise the tango together, and Piers had offered Georgina a lift, which was really too bad of him since he'd arrived in a two-seater, thought Jane, though quite understandable. Jay suggested that they all go to a nightclub, but Jane was far too tired for nightclubs, and a day of hunting and tutorials and champagne was beginning to make Catherine yawn, so Jay offered to drive her home, instead, to the family house in Curzon Street. Jane went to the door with them to watch them go. Redman was at the wheel of the Rolls-Royce. Well of course he was, she told herself. Jay brought that caviar for *me*.

41

THE PIECE IN the *Daily World* was gratifying enough: she was 'the popular and philanthropic girl about town', the 'well known', the 'eager supporter of those less fortunate', and, as always, the address to which the charitable should send their money was prominently featured. All of which was pleasing, if predictable: Jay Bower had spent a couple of hours there after all. What did astonish her was the length of the piece – almost the whole of 'This Wicked World' devoted to her party, and Mummy, and Sarah and Louise, and the twins, all of whom were described with an almost endearing disregard for the truth. Really this time Jay had gone too far, she thought, until she looked at the other papers: the *Express*, the *Mail*, the *Morning Post*, and there she was again: not in quite such detail, perhaps, but she was there. And so was Mummy, and her major, though sometimes described as Captain Rutledge, or even as Colonel Coolidge, but he was there every time: 'a gallant upholder of the Raj'. Nothing wrong with that, she told herself, after all he *was* an upholder of the Raj and presumably gallant enough since he'd been through the war; what baffled her was how the other papers had found out, and since they had found out, why they had bothered to pursue in such detail an enjoyable, but decidedly trivial evening. Even the caviar was mentioned in one column, but not that Bower had brought it. Bower himself must have passed on the story, she thought, but why she could not begin to comprehend – except that it would be to Bower's advantage, and perhaps to Felston's too.

Mummy telephoned. It was imperative that she see Jane, she said. There were things to be said that could not be discussed on the instrument. Jane went, but left Foch behind. Mummy had sounded upset, and Foch was never conciliatory.

Offley Villas was chilly that morning, its trees already stripped bare, and the new parlourmaid was a poor hand at building a fire. Jane reached for the coal tongs. Mummy was just back from India after all. By the time her mother joined her, the flames were already leaping, the coals beginning to glow. Jane kissed her mother, who looked at once at the fire.

'You must find it chilly indeed in a room without central heating,' Lady Whitcomb said.

'I cannot allow you to die of pneumonia because of a parlour-maid's carelessness,' said Jane. Her mother smiled.

'It would be a pity,' she said, 'now that we both enjoy such social triumphs.'

'You're pleased?'

'Delighted,' said her mother. 'A photograph too. And so many words. Most gratifying. Gwendoline Gwatkin has already telephoned.'

'*Miss Gwatkin?*'

'She has social aspirations too, it appears. She wishes me to – "use my influence" was the expression she used. I told her nothing was possible until she had lost at least two stones. George also telephoned. It would seem that he was not pleased with our success. On the contrary. He referred to it as notoriety.'

'I thought the *World* did him proud.'

'Friendly, but not fulsome,' her mother agreed, 'and yet George was not happy.'

'Whyever not?'

Her mother fidgeted. 'Would you care for coffee?' she asked. 'It is early for sherry.'

'No thank you, Mummy.'

'No indeed,' said her mother. 'Unpleasantness is always best tackled head on.'

So there was to be unpleasantness.

'George is a man very conscious of his family,' her mother said. 'They are apparently conscientious and hard-working. They are also dedicated to the ideal of service and disapprove of frivolity. They all, it would seem, share a pride in this.'

'The proud house of Routledge,' said Jane.

'I suspect a quotation,' said her mother. 'Some literary game you journalists play?'

'A misquotation,' said Jane. 'Lord Macaulay. *Lays of Ancient Rome.*'

'And apt,' said her mother. 'Macaulay is exactly the sort of poet the Routledges would approve. So worthy.' She paused, then hurried on, 'You may perhaps have noticed that George is – shall we say – malleable?'

Bullyable was more the word, thought Jane, but he seems to enjoy it.

'In the past he has been influenced by members of his family. Now of course he is more inclined to heed what I say.'

'Naturally.'

Her mother smiled her special smile: the one that signified enjoyment. 'It is good of you to say so. However this – what he considers to be frivolous notoriety – has alarmed him.'

'What are his family like, Mummy? Have you met them?'

'I have not. George has three brothers. A backbench MP – Liberal of course – an archdeacon and a county-court judge. Of modest achievement, I think you will agree, but eminently worthy, like George himself.'

'He doesn't sound much like Papa.'

'He is not in the least like your father.' Lady Whitcomb sounded appalled. 'Your father was a scholar of his college, a double first who declined a fellowship to take the ICS examinations which he passed with – what is that Balliol phrase? – effortless superiority. He administered a province bigger than the United Kingdom and advised a maharajah. He was a fine shot, a superb polo player, and as promiscuous as a monkey. George is none of these things.'

'Mummy!'

'You thought him faithful, no doubt, apart from one brief, romantic idyll with the Sanderson creature?'

'Well of course I did,' said Jane.

'Then you were wrong,' said her mother. 'Anything in skirts, provided it achieved his standards of prettiness, which I admit were severe. Colour he did not consider a handicap – but then you're aware of that.'

'Mummy,' said Jane, 'why are you telling me all this now?'

'You feel I should have spared you?'

'It isn't that at all,' said Jane. 'It's just – you've kept it bottled up inside you all these years.'

'As you did with your engagement,' her mother said. 'We are more alike than you might think.'

'Somebody else said that last night,' said Jane, 'and I accept it. But why now? That's all I'm asking. I assume it's the major but I don't understand why.'

'*Very* like me in your perceptiveness,' said her mother. 'It's *because* George is so different that I intend to marry him.'

'You are quite sure that he will be faithful to you?'

'Quite sure,' her mother said. 'I have observed him very closely – of course I have – and I'm sure.'

'But that's not a reason for matrimony.'

'I was as clever as your father,' her mother said, 'but being female I was never allowed to advertise the fact. George is not clever at all. Competent, but of moderate intellect. This time I shall do all the thinking that marriage requires – and George is quite happy to allow me to do it.'

'He is able to support you?' Jane asked. Really, she thought, I'm beginning to sound like a Victorian father, but this is my mother after all, and I'm beginning to realise how much love I have for her.

'Together we shall manage,' her mother said. 'I shall let this house which will supplement our income, and George has his pension. He has retired, of course.'

'Can he get a job?'

'He's skilled in the breeding of horses,' her mother said. 'He would make an excellent manager of a stud farm.'

'And will you enjoy being a stud-farm manager's wife?' Jane asked.

'I shall enjoy being George Routledge's wife,' said her mother, and sounded suddenly like a much younger woman, the woman who had taught her the future perfect tense of the verb venir.

'I wish you good fortune,' said Jane.

'I honestly believe you mean that,' said her mother. 'Will you forgive me if I say that I'm surprised?'

'But why on earth should you be?'

'I am aware how very much you loved your father.'

'I always will. He was that sort of a man,' said Jane, 'the sort of man one can't help loving, but every time you let me, I love you too.' Again her mother smiled that special smile. 'And it's your life, Mummy. You must live as you think best. Is there any way in which I can help? Financially, I mean.'

'I do not intend to become your pensioner, said her mother.

'Of course not.'

'But the Indian trip proved rather more expensive than either of us had envisaged, despite the windfall at Cox and King's. If I might request a loan of fifty pounds – '

'Gladly,' said Jane. 'I'll write you a cheque now.'

'I should prefer cash if that's possible,' said her mother.

'Of course,' said Jane. 'I'll stop at the bank and have someone send it round. . . . Did Aunt Pen know? – About Papa, I mean?'

'She never said so,' said her mother, 'and she had her own preoccupations – but she must have known. Everyone else did. Perhaps that was another reason why she and Nettles were so willing to make a home for you.'

'What about Francis?' Jane asked. 'Will you tell him?'

'About your father – or my intention to remarry?'

'Both,' said Jane.

'I shall endeavour to do so,' said her mother. 'The difficulty will be to persuade him to listen to a word I say, particularly when he discovers that George is not an intellectual.'

Next day was the day of the Oxford telephone calls, first from Piers, then the principal of Catherine's college.

'She doesn't approve of hunting, you see,' said Piers, referring to Catherine's principal, 'and she's not all that keen on inherited wealth either, so you can see poor old Catherine's on a hiding to nothing.' (Catherine was the elder twin, Jane had been told, by twenty-seven minutes, and Piers liked it to be known.)

'But what on earth has it got to do with me?' said Jane.

'Your ball,' said Piers.

'What about it?'

'We want to be there,' said Piers, 'but it means coming down a day early. I've already told my chap – he's no trouble – but Catherine's dragon may be a bit sticky. She told Catherine so as a matter of fact so I said I'd phone you.'

'But why didn't *she*?'

'Gated,' said Piers. 'She went out to take a look at Bridget with me and forgot to ask permission. I must say women's colleges are a bit much. Might as well be chained to an oar in a galley. You'll tell the right lies for her, won't you? She's a deserving case really.'

'Do my best,' said Jane. 'How's Bridget?'

'Looks well,' said Piers. 'Could drop the colt any day. I took Bridie for a canter. Is that all right?'

'Most kind,' said Jane. 'I'll tell my best lies for both your sakes.' She went back to the cost of printing programmes, until once again the phone rang.

'Miss Whitcomb?' said the voice. 'Miss Jane Whitcomb?'

It was a voice Vinney had mimicked many times. Dry, precise, academic. The Oxford female don's voice. Jane replied in kind.

'This is she.'

'This is Dr Caswell. I think you know a pupil of mine. Lady Catherine Hilyard.'

'Certainly.'

'Is there any possibility that you will be in Oxford in the immediate future?'

'None,' said Jane.

'What a pity.' The voice continued to be precise, but now with a hint of condescension, too. After all, Dr Caswell was already *at* Oxford. 'Perhaps we may discuss the matter by telephone.'

'Matter? Catherine is not unwell I trust?'

'Catherine is never unwell,' Dr Caswell said, a little regretfully, Jane thought. 'She tells me that you have invited her to a ball on the eleventh of December. To do this she needs my permission to go down a day early.'

'A charity ball,' said Jane. 'For a project which is important to me.'

'Charity?'

Not a good word to Dr Caswell either, it would appear. Jane crossed her fingers.

'In the present state of society there is no other way to achieve my aim,' she said. 'This is regrettable – to me at any rate.'

'May I enquire the nature of this – charity?' A little more warmth in the voice this time. Lie away, Whitcomb. It's in a good cause.

'A town called Felston in the North East of England,' said Jane. 'It's poor and neglected and abandoned, and neither our present government nor anybody else seems prepared to do anything about it. There is a clinic there that should be the responsibility of the state. It is the responsibility of no one, and will be obliged to close if my ball is not a success. Frivolity to the rescue of necessity, you will say – but there is no other solution, not in our present state of society. And so I'm giving a ball, just as I lecture and write articles for the *Daily World*.'

It rolled off her tongue without giving her the slightest cause to think. Old stuff, most of it, bits and pieces of articles and talks.

'And Catherine can assist you in this?'

'As an aide de camp she would be invaluable.'

'Aide de camp? Do I take it that she will be working?'

'Flat out,' said Jane.

'Then of course she must assist you. I'll send her to you on the tenth, if you wish.'

'Too kind,' said Jane.

'You said lecture?' Oxford's most sacred, most talismanic word.

'On the present state of Felston,' said Jane. 'Its suffering and needs.'

'I am chairman of a small society interested in such matters,' said Dr Caswell. 'We call ourselves the Two Worlds Group. – The overtones of Disraeli will be obvious to you, of course.'

'Of course,' said Jane.

'We would be delighted if you could find the time to address us.'

'I too,' said Jane, 'though I must warn you that it is my invariable rule to pass the hat round afterwards.'

There was a pause, then, 'Quite so,' said Dr Caswell. 'Quite so.'

This time Jane did phone Lionel to find out why Disraeli should be obvious, before she returned to programme costing.

As a treat, when the programmes were finished, she made time to work on the piece she had promised to write for Sarah Unwin. Sarah had agreed at once to take part in the cabaret, and her agent had been delighted, even though there was no fee. The publicity, he was sure, would be greater than even Bower had promised. The problem was the material. Sarah had wanted to do something about Felston, and nobody had ever written anything about Felston except Jane, so Jane it would have to be.

The trouble was it would have to be a monologue, not a piece for Bower's paper: dramatic, simple, short. And all she could remember was John's story about Private Walker, so Private Walker it would have to be.

Catherine came down on the tenth, determined to convert Jane's lies to truth and work as aide de camp. Dogsbody was more like it, thought Jane, but there was no doubt about it; Catherine worked: answered the telephone, ran errands, collected packages, and told lies about Jane's unavailability with an astonishing and somehow worrying fluency.

The day of the ball dawned cold and clear and crisp, which was perfect. Furs always felt better on a cold, crisp day, and taking them off in a warm room would add a sense of gratification that every woman in the place would enjoy, and so be just a little better disposed to giving. Bower had promised to escort her, but at the last moment had been delayed, which did not surprise her, and sent Dick Lambert instead, and the *Daily World* editor, Don Cook, a harassed and nervous man who became even more harassed and nervous when confronted by Jane in the Fortuny gown. ('It must be wonderful to be old,' Catherine had said, 'and allowed to wear dresses like that.') With it she had worn sapphires left to her by Aunt Pen, and the sapphire ear-rings that had once been Papa's cuff-links. The trouble was that Jay had sent her a present that afternoon, and with it a message.

'I don't know why I'm sending you these,' he had written. 'A thank you for so many things, the thought that they are right for you, the fact that Christmas is near. I think it's just that I felt an overwhelming need to give you something, and these are the best I could find to give. I look forward to seeing you again above the shop. Oh boy, do I. Jay.'

Very nice. Gratifying even. But 'these' were a pair of diamond ear-rings that were splendid indeed, so splendid that she had no diamonds to match them.

The editor came to collect her and was confronted not only by Jane, but by Catherine, slender and elegant in rose-pink, wearing the pearls lent to her for the evening by Lady Mangan, and standing behind Jane in a sort of lady-in-waiting pose. ('Pearls,' Catherine had said. 'It would be. And I came out two years ago.' 'What's wrong with pearls?' Jane had asked. 'So virtuous,'

Catherine had said. 'So inadequate.' They were three feet long at least. . . .)

Don Cook took one look at the two of them and added incoherence to his nervousness, and envied the lot of an MP, even a Labour MP, who could claim parliamentary business as an excuse. Still Lambert arrived at the Berkeley in time, and took his place by the ballroom door to help shake hands as the major domo bawled out names, sometimes correctly, sometimes not. Next to him stood Lady Twyford in a gown of unrelenting mauve and a garnet set that clashed with it so violently Jane assumed that she had done it on purpose. And yet people had come at her bidding; masses of people. If a crowd was a sign of success, then the Felston ball would be a triumph.

Her arm was limp when eventually she went to her table, and was able to look about her. The Lessings had booked a table and filled it, and so had Louise and Lord Hexham. Georgina, she noticed, was sitting with the Lessings: a plea for forgiveness on Sir Hugh's part, and Piers was already hovering beside her when he should have been sitting next to his sister. The moth and the flame may be the greatest cliché of the lot, thought Jane, but that's because there's no other way to describe it. Then the band struck up 'After You've Gone', and Dick Lambert asked her to dance, no doubt because Jay had told her that he was supposed to do so.

On to the floor they went, and Jane forced herself to prattle merrily because after all they were supposed to be enjoying themselves and people were watching, photographers hovering, and poor Lambert was quite incapable of talking and dancing at the same time. On the way back to their table he said: 'Well at least your ordeal's over quickly.'

'Ordeal?'

'Your duty dance with the amateur Trappist. I'm sorry, Miss Whitcomb, honestly I am. But I have to concentrate or else I go wrong.'

And that would never do for Dick Lambert, she thought.

Aloud she said, 'I think Jane would be more appropriate, don't you?'

'I don't know about appropriate,' he said, 'but I'd like it. Thank you.'

'Do you find these affairs a strain?'

He grinned. 'Give me a political meeting every time. You won't find me tongue-tied then.'

'I'll look forward to it,' said Jane, 'but if it's such a strain – why do you do it?'

'Felston,' he said, promptly. 'Never mind this talk about charity not being the answer. We all know that, but it's all there is, and if there's money going then Felston must have its share.'

'No matter how many Charlestons it takes?'

'For Felston I'd even make it a tango,' said Lambert, 'even if it does mean looking like a Tory.'

Her next partner was Lionel, and that of course meant only dancing and laughter. Lionel was enjoying himself, which meant he talked even faster than she had talked with Lambert. Only at the very end did he ask: 'Is my chum the major still courting your mama?'

'To the best of my knowledge,' said Jane.

'It's none of my business,' Lionel said, 'of course it isn't, and yet – better from me than anyone else.'

'Better *what*, Lionel darling?'

'Cheltenham races,' said Lionel. 'He was there, so I am told, keeping the bookies in champagne and accompanied by a lady. Quite an elegant lady. Your mother's not a gambler, I take it?'

'Not in the least.'

'The Cheltenham lady was. . . . Sorry to tell you now, but I was afraid that somebody else might.'

'Not at all,' said Jane. 'I'm grateful to you.' And so she was, but not just at that moment. She needed all her mind for Felston.

Piers next, and the course of true love. It was true that he was just turned twenty-one, he told her, but he was a very mature twenty-one, and after all Georgina couldn't be *that* much older, surely? And so sweet and feminine and *young*. All of which meant that Georgie too would have to be thought about. But not *then*. And still Jay hadn't appeared. Really it was quite a relief to dance with Sir Hugh, and Neil Watson, neither of whom was interested in anything but the dance.

Supper, and then the cabaret. Singers and dancers, and Sarah last of all. Sarah the star, in the sketch that Jane had written. The improvised stage in the centre of the ballroom went black, and Jane realised that she was terrified. Every word of what was to come had been written by her. The lights went up to reveal Sarah in the uniform of a VAD nurse – the kind worn at the front in 1917. The band's drummer thumped his bass, softly and insistently, and here and there the lights of the ballroom flickered: a crude enough imitation of shell fire, but real enough to create a kind of tension in every second man there.

'I want to tell you,' Sarah said, 'about Private Walker of the Royal Northumbrians. He was married and had two sons – and he was very shy, and like a lot of shy men he made jokes, sheltering his shyness behind a barrage of laughter.

'In 1917, at Passchendaele, he won the Distinguished Conduct Medal, for rescuing a comrade under fire, and sustaining severe wounds. He should have been dead, of course, quite a lot of those who won the DCM *were* dead – and the rest were lucky. That time Private Walker was lucky.

'His friends congratulated him, and bought him beer, smuggled into the hospital behind the Line, but all Private Walker said was, "I should have rescued an officer, and then I'd have got the Victoria Cross." And his friends all laughed and thought "Good old Walker. Always ready with a joke." But for once Private Walker had been serious. With the VC you got a pension, and he could have put the money by for his wife.'

Sarah's voice went on, calm, precise, the voice of a nurse remembering the words she had heard on night duty: Walker sane and Walker raving, remembering the days of peace and his work as a riveter in the shipyards, until at last he had gone home on sick-leave, home to his wife and sons.

'The wound was a bad one,' Sarah said, 'a Blighty one we used to call it. Bad enough to send him back to England – to Blighty – for weeks and weeks. Private Walker had three months, and arrived back with his wound stripe and his medal ribbon just in time for the next big push. A shell burst got him before he'd gone ten yards, and that was how I had the pleasure of Private Walker's company a second time.'

'Because it *was* a pleasure. He was so patient, even cheerful, and so concerned about me, even then, because of the humiliating and degrading things I had to do for him, the things he could no longer do for himself. He was dying of course, and we both knew it, though it was never mentioned. But once a day he would ask me to look at a photograph in his wallet: his wife and his sons: his "bairns" as he called them.

'One day his Company Commander came to see him. Captain Patterson. Like Private Walker he was a Felston man, and together they talked about their town, their home, how busy it was and thriving, and what a future Private Walker would have there. But both of them knew that they were lying. Private Walker had no future at all. When the captain had gone I went to him and he said, "You heard all that?"

'"Yes," I told him. "I heard it."

'"Sounded a bit of all right, didn't it?" he said. "But it's what I wanted, you see. What I was hoping for. It isn't what I'm going to get."

'"Now now," I said.

'"Oh give over," said Private Walker. "Don't you start looking on the bright side. There isn't time." He settled back in his pillows and looked, for the first time, relaxed, and I knew that he was ready for death.

'"Felston was all very well in its way, " he said. "Playing football on the sands when I was a lad. A pint with your pals before Sunday dinner. But I can't say I'll miss getting up at half past six on a February morning to be in time for the half-past seven hooter, and the wind cutting up the river like a butcher's cleaver. I've had my share of that – and the others can have the rest.

'"But I'll miss the wife – lying warm and snug beside us at a quarter past six and me waiting for the alarm to go off and my arms around her. Aye . . . I'll miss that – wherever I'm going. I hope I'm not speaking out of turn, sister."

'"Of course not," I said.

'"Aye well," said Private Walker. "It takes a bit of thinking about. . . . I'll just close my eyes for a few minutes. I mustn't keep you, sister."

'And so I left him, because he wanted me to leave. But I hadn't reached the end of the ward before he spoke again, and this time the voice was strong and young, the voice of the man who had rescued a comrade under fire and had the Distinguished Conduct Medal to prove it.

'"I won't leave them," he said. "I won't. How can I? I'm all they've got." But by the time I got back to Private Walker he was dead.'

The applause was deafening. First the men rose, the ones who had been there, and then the others, and the women too, and Sarah curtseyed and became no longer a VAD but an actress in costume. At last she held up her hand for silence, and when it came, said: 'You're very kind. But remember all your kindness tonight is for Felston. And just one more thing. I'm delighted to see how much you were moved by what I've just done – I know I was, when I first read it. So I'd like to let you into a secret. It was written by a good friend of mine, a fellow ambulance driver who carried many a Private Walker in her day. – Our hostess for this evening. Jane Whitcomb.'

Her arm reached out, pointing into the darkness to where Jane sat, and a spotlight obeyed the gesture, then swung across the dance floor to pick her out at last. More applause, prolonged, ecstatic, for this was not just a piece of entertainment: this was an experience shared. She got to her feet and bowed, over and over, until at last the lights of the ballroom came on and the band played 'Dardanella'.

Jane looked about her. Her entire table was staring at her as if she'd just turned lead into gold, but it was all Sarah's doing, and John's. All she'd had to do was remember. She looked away, towards the door. Bower was standing there, and as she watched he began threading his way among the dancers to the vacant chair beside her. For once nobody seemed to have noticed him.

'Mr Bower,' she said. 'How good of you to come.'

'I promised I would,' said Bower. 'I hope you got my present.'

'Very nice,' said Jane. 'Extremely nice in fact. But not with sapphires.'

If he did not mind being overheard, then neither would she. The band began to play 'Ramona', and he rose.

'I should very much like to dance with you,' he said. She rose too.

'Just as well,' she said. 'You are one of the hosts after all.'

'I hope Don Cook did his best,' said Bower.

'It's hard to tell,' she said. 'The poor man's so nervous.'

'That's because I pay him three thousand a year on a day's notice.'

'Good gracious,' said Jane. 'Is he worth it?'

'He must be,' said Bower. 'He hasn't had the day's notice yet.'

They began to dance. 'You really liked the ear-rings?' he asked.

'I really did.'

'Will you take them with you to America?'

'And tell everyone that you gave them to me?'

'No. . . . Not unless you want to,' said Bower. 'Just take them.'

They were beginning to like each other again, she thought.

'What made you so late for your own ball?'

'Politics,' he said. 'There's a strike brewing. A big strike.'

'There's always a strike brewing.'

'Not like this one,' said Bower. 'This one's going to be *big*. If it happens – but maybe it won't. Still if it does – I want the *World* to be there first. You too.'

'In Felston they don't have to strike,' said Jane. 'There's no work anyway.'

'Maybe it's time you moved on from Felston,' said Bower. She stiffened.

'I don't mean get rid of it. You couldn't do that. And anyway it would be bad for the paper. I mean cover other things as well. This could be just what you need.'

He wasn't going to tell her, she knew that: and so she wouldn't ask.

'Does it mean postponing New York?'

He shook his head. 'We'll be back before the balloon goes up. If it does. . . .' He danced on then said, 'Hey, that reminds me – why were you taking a bow when I came in?'

'I thought you'd never ask,' she sasid. 'A little piece of mine has been most kindly received by the public.' She told him about Sarah – and Private Walker.

'You should have saved it for the paper,' said Bower.

But he was pleased for her, she knew.

The ball was a success, inasmuch as it made even more money than she had dared hope for, even after Lady Twyford had been paid. Bower stayed till the end, and did his duty nobly: that is to say he danced with a great many women who were rich and plain as well as Louise and Georgina and Sarah and Catherine. Jane knew her duty and accepted invitations from wherever they came – every man there had contributed after all – but found time for another dance with Dick Lambert, though she avoided Mr Cook.

As they left the floor Lambert achieved speech at last. 'I'm glad Mr Bower managed to get here,' he said.

'It was his ball as much as anybody's said Jane. 'He *had* to get here.'

'Hamlet without the prince otherwise,' said Lambert, and smiled. 'Did he say why he was so late?'

'He had a meeting,' said Jane. 'You'll find when you've worked for the *World* a little longer that he very often does.'

He blushed a mottled, unpleasing red that reminded her of her mother.

'I wasn't trying to be rude,' he said.

'Of course not,' said Jane. 'Just inquisitive. But it won't do, you know. Not with Jay Bower.' Sarah came up to her then. She had changed back into her ball gown, fresh powder, new lipstick. She looked as if she had just arrived and the time was half past nine instead of ten to two.

'Darling,' she said, 'I must have a word.' And then to Lambert, 'Do you mind, darling?' Lambert fled. 'Who was that?' Sarah asked.

'Don't you know?' said Jane.

'Should I?'

'You called him darling.'

'I call everybody darling,' said Sarah. 'It saves having to re-member names. That piece of yours went well, I must say.'

'Because you did it well.'

'That was part of it,' said Sarah, and sounded quite objective, for this was work. 'But a lot of it was the writing. There's a new revue coming up shortly and I've been asked to be in it. I want to do "Private Walker". May I?'

'I might want something in return,' said Jane.

'Well, of course.' The famous smile appeared: happy and eager, and yet intimate – a smile only for one person, the one who looked at her. And she doesn't even know she's doing it, thought Jane.

'Darling, I must fly,' said Sarah. 'I have to get home and be nice to poor old Beddoes. I just remembered he's putting money into the review. Now remember, *you promised*.'

It was time to go. Jay offered a lift, so she sent Catherine home in her car, and left Piers among the group offering to escort Georgina home. She really must talk to Georgina, she thought. And Mr Pinner. That was not a nice thought, but it had to be faced. Major Routledge had been seen with another lady, and

Mummy needed fifty pounds in cash and she would have to find out why, because Francis would be hopeless, even if he could be made to see the necessity. . . . She found that she was yawning, and apologised.

'A tough day,' said Jay.

'Adequately so.'

'I wish I could share your bed,' said Jay. 'Just to sleep.'

'So do I,' said Jane. 'But you can't. Sorry.'

'At least you didn't make a joke about it.'

'Well of course not.'

'Last time you did. Last time you said, "It would certainly liven up the party."'

'Well so it would,' said Jane, 'and anyway last time, a: there was a room full of people, b: you weren't talking about sleeping –'

'And c: I'd just smacked you far too hard,' said Jay.

Her hand covered his. 'Tonight's different,' she said.

'You're right,' said Jay. 'Everybody's crazy about that piece of yours.'

'Sarah wants to do it in her new revue,' said Jane. 'I told her she can – only I want her to do it in Felston first.'

'*Felston*? Sarah *Unwin*?'

'And Georgina Payne,' said Jane. 'And anyone else who'll go. So far all Felston's been given is medical aid and nourishing soup. I think they deserve rather more than that. They deserve a party, too.'

'Toys for the kids,' said Jay. 'Beer for the men. Scent for the women.'

'Golly,' said Jane. 'That'll cost a bit.'

'The paper will launch an appeal,' said Jay. 'If we do it right it won't cost a cent. You sure you don't want Don Cook's job?'

'Not even for three thousand a year would I want to be as worried as Mr Cook,' said Jane, and then remembered her other host.

'Dick Lambert coped quite well,' she said.

'I'm glad,' said Jay. 'He wasn't too keen at first and I don't blame him. A Tory charity ball won't do his reputation any good with his Party – unless he sells them the idea he was keeping an eye on what the capitalists were up to.'

Perhaps he had been, thought Jane. Aloud she said, 'Was it Tory? The ball I mean.'

'The guests certainly were. I had to lean on Lambert to make him go. I told him it sort of went with the job.'

'Will he know about this strike you were talking of?'

'He'll know,' said Jay. 'He's a union-sponsored MP. But he doesn't know that I know.'

Clever Mr Lambert, thought Jane, and Jay echoed her words.

'He's a very smart guy,' he said.

'Likeable, too,' said Jane. She meant it.

'Oh sure,' said Jay. 'But he's a guy to watch.'

42

M R PINNER DIDN'T like it, and said so. In fact for Mr Pinner he was quite vehement about it. It never did any good, he told her, for other people to get involved in what he called 'matrimonials'. Jane remembered the policeman, and Mr and Mrs Michael Browne, and was inclined to agree with him, but pointed out in the interests of accuracy that the major was unmarried. Mr Pinner said darkly that that remained to be seen.

'Oh dear,' said Jane, 'I do hope you're wrong.' The truth, she thought. There's nothing else for it. 'It's my mother, you see, Mr Pinner. She considers herself engaged to him. In fact I rather think she'll marry him as soon as she's out of mourning.'

'Lady Whitcomb?' said Mr Pinner. 'Well now that's different, miss. You'd better tell me all about it.' He smiled. 'You know our motto: Discretion Guaranteed.'

And so she told him. About the courtship in India, and the need for cash, and the furtive visit to Cheltenham races with a lady most definitely not her mother.

'I know it doesn't sound like much,' said Jane, 'and yet I have a feeling. I most certainly don't want her deceived or made a fool of. I'm very fond of my mother.'

'Yes, of course, miss,' said Mr Pinner, 'and that makes it different, I must say. I'll get on to it straightaway. If I may ask – how's your horse coming along?'

'She should foal any day,' said Jane. 'I'll be off to see her soon.'

'And your other business?' said Mr Pinner. 'That went off all right?'

'Splendidly, thank you,' said Jane.

Getting the Christmas treat together involved the kind of staff work they should have had at the Somme, she thought. Availability of artists, cash for Christmas puddings, toys by the gross, paper hats, mistletoe, beer. And most difficult of all, who should go to the treat, and hence who should be excluded. That was a terrible choice, and one that she didn't feel in the least qualified to make. In the end, after furious arguments by telephone, she left it to a committee composed of Grandma, Corporal Laidlaw and Canon Messeter. Between them they could assess the wealth – and poverty – of every family in Felston. There was a hall to book, too, the Mafeking Hall, the only one big enough to hold the crowd – and the entertainers, for Jane had found no difficulty in obtaining offers of help. Jay's free publicity had seen to that. It was only getting them all there on the same day that was the problem. Once again she called in Catherine Hilyard to run errands and smile sweetly and tell lies, and once again Catherine was invaluable.

At last they fixed the day, the twenty-eighth of December, and Jane and Bower between them booked the entire cast of a Newcastle pantomime as well as Sarah and Georgina, and a dance band complete with male and female singers. Not even a London variety theatre could top that, Bower's professional adviser told them, even supposing they could find one that could afford it.

But before that there was Christmas. Its eve she spent with Jay. They dined at the Ritz, and danced, and went back to his flat for midnight and an exchange of gifts: for him a box of cigars and a Longines wrist-watch; for her a pot of caviar and a diamond necklace.

'Now you can wear those ear-rings,' he said, then added, 'I wanted to buy you a steamer ticket as well, but I guessed maybe you'd prefer to buy your own.'

Again that sudden and quite surprising sensitivity. Bower was quite right. Diamond necklaces were one thing, keys to state rooms quite another. She put hers on, despite the fact that she was wearing nothing else.

'I like your outfit,' said Jay. 'It suits you,' and put on his watch. 'But don't expect me to light a cigar. There are some risks I just won't take.' She was still giggling when his arms came round her, easing her to him.

Christmas Day, rested and demure, she took lunch with her mother and the major and Francis. Foch was in attendance, wearing a new collar of black and white, which Mummy insisted made him look more like the Cameronians' chaplain than ever. They dined on pheasant, which the adequate cook had cooked adequately, and a Christmas pudding bought at Fortnum and Mason. Jane had brought champagne, and Francis a couple of bottles of his college claret, and afterwards there were gifts: a bracelet for Mummy, cigars for the major, a pair of briar pipes for Francis: and Jane became in her turn the owner of a phial of the sort of perfume she detested, from the major, a riding crop from Mummy, (what convoluted ironies did that involve, she wondered?) and a copy of R. H. Tawney's *Religion and the Rise of Capitalism* ('Pretty basic, most of it,' said Francis, 'but after all you have to start somewhere, and it may help you to get your work in Felston into perspective').

'Far above my head, that sort of stuff,' said the major. 'Ruff's *Guide to the Turf* is about all I can manage these days.'

Lady Whitcomb smiled at him indulgently. 'You have other qualities George,' she said. 'Even Francis would not expect us all to be intellectuals.'

'Good Lord, no,' said Francis. 'The workers come first, you know. Always.'

'Surely darling,' said Lady Whitcomb, and turned her smile on Francis, the *other* smile, 'you can find room for one grasshopper among all those ants?'

The major said he would like to hear Lady Whitcomb play the piano, something jolly and perhaps seasonal, and they went to turn over the sheet music together.

'I'm most grateful for the pipes,' said Francis. 'They're absolutely first-rate.'

'You're very welcome,' said Jane.

Francis said, 'There's something I should tell you.' Jane sipped at her coffee, and waited.

'I've broken with Burrowes,' Francis said at last. 'After what he did to you – I just couldn't go on any more.'

'I'm delighted to hear it,' said Jane.

'That's all I want to say about it really,' said Francis.

'That's all I want to hear.'

'So now we're friends again?' he asked her.

'Yes please,' said Jane.

'Tell me what you're up to in Felston.'

It was a question deliberately designed to please, and she was touched by it, and told him at length, until at last the major came to call them. He had prevailed upon Lady Whitcomb to play a little Chopin, and afterwards he had allowed himself to be persuaded to sing a couple of songs: 'Goodbye Dolly Grey' and 'God Rest You Merry, Gentlemen'.

'But it must have been too exhausting,' said Lionel.

He had come to South Terrace that evening to deliver her present: a set of records by a new American band leader called Paul Whiteman, and to be persuaded to accept a little more of Jay's caviar, though this time she didn't tell him that Jay was the donor.

'It was a *little* trying,' she said, 'though he did hit the note more often than not. But he expected us to join in the chorus of "God Rest You Merry, Gentlemen".'

'Probably because it was seasonal,' said Lionel. 'Dear dear. The times we live in. All that *and* R. H. Tawney. Nothing was mentioned about Cheltenham, I suppose?'

Jane said firmly, 'Not a thing.' Cheltenham must wait on Mr Pinner.

Lionel rose to his feet. 'I must away to Santa's Grotto where all the other fairies await me,' he said. 'Thank you so much for the present, *and* the caviar.' His present was a Charvet scarf he had put on immediately.

'I'll drop you off if you like,' said Jane. 'Louise and her husband are giving a party in Eaton Square.'

'How grand you have become,' said Lionel. 'Positively magnificent.'

They went by train. She had arranged for the Wolseley to meet them at Newcastle, but Don Cook had gone further than that. He'd had toys and gifts and food sent up by goods train, and loaded on to lorries to await Jane's arrival, and waiting at the station were Bob and Bet with Grandma, soon to be the subject of a *Daily World* article. (Stan had had to go to work; Andy had refused to come.) But Grandma was there, and Jane had rushed down the platform to embrace her, while the flash bulbs popped. Bob stood transfixed, staring at the three young women who walked down the platform to follow Jane. He was still staring when Jane turned to embrace Bet, then shake his hand.

He had never in his life, Jane was sure, seen anything like Georgie, Sarah and Catherine walking towards him. Separately each one would have passed for a very pretty girl, but together all three achieved a kind of magic that transformed them into a picture: a modern Three Graces perhaps. And they were dressed and made-up as no women in Felston had ever been dressed and made-up. Bob, who prided himself on a kind of imperturbable sophistication, was gawking like the veriest yokel.

One of Cook's minions appeared and began to marshal the procession: Jane and Grandma and her three friends crammed into the Wolseley, and Bet and Bob riding in a bus with the musicians: another wonder; riding with a band that had played on the wireless. There were more cars to bring up the rear: loaded with reporters, mostly from the *Daily World* and the agencies, but there were stringers from the other papers too. Like an army convoy, thought Jane, as they assembled outside the Central Station: an army whose sole objective was the distribution of happiness; a rare thing in the life of any town, and probably unique in Felston's, and all because Jay had had the idea that it would sell newspapers.

It was clear and fine when they moved off, Jane leading, driving the Wolseley, then the four loaded lorries, and the bus, and last of all the shoal of reporters' cars. Even in Newcastle heads were turning, but it was outside Felston that Cook's man had organised his master stroke. Another lorry was waiting, but this one was decorated like a float at carnival time, all bunting and streamers and balloons. The band climbed on to it, and began to play, and on each side of the bus a painted message appeared: 'The Daily World Wishes Felston A Merry Christmas.'

The sound of the band brought the children running before the convoy had even crossed the borough boundary, then in ones, in twos, in groups, their elders appeared, lining the pavements, silent at first, then roaring their approval as their children taught them how to shout aloud for happiness. Round and about and through the town they went, and finished at last outside the town hall where a mayor in a cocked hat and chain, and a fur-lined robe designed for a man six inches taller, read out a painstaking message of welcome, Jane told them how happy they were to be there, and the band played 'Jingle Bells'.

The lorries went to the Mafeking Hall then, to be unloaded under the careful eyes of Grandma and Bella Docherty and their helpers. Every item would be counted twice, Jane knew, and nothing would be missing, not with those two watching. The others went off to the Eldon Arms to change for the concert. The hotel was crowded with bandsmen, and Jane, Catherine, Georgie and Sarah had the four best rooms in the place. If the rest of the town thought of her as a benefactor, to the manager of the Eldon Arms she was Santa Claus incarnate. He even produced champagne when Canon Messeter and Dr Stobbs came to call. Stobbs still did not believe that money spent on Christmas pudding would not have been better spent on medicine, but the priest would have none of it.

'To the poor people here, Christmas pudding is a medicine,' he said.

'And a lot of them won't get it,' said Stobbs.

'Then we must pray to God to guide Miss Whitcomb's endeavours so that it will,' Messeter said, and his blue eyes looked from one to the other of the women about him.

'God has been good to you today, Stobbs,' he said. 'And to me. Stop grousing, for goodness sake, and enjoy your company.'

They finished the champagne, and Jane drove them to Dr Stobbs's clinic, so that the three young women could see for themselves the misery that Felston endured. She sat, waiting, as Messeter showed the others what she had seen so often, and Bob came up and sat beside her.

'Are they all like that in London?' he asked.

'Like what?' said Jane.

'Those three.' He gestured to where the three heads, two dark, one fair, nodded obediently to the point that Messeter was making.

'Not all,' she said. 'No,' and remembered the work that Harriet did. 'Quite a lot of them are like the people here.'

'But where you live,' said Bob, 'the people you meet. I'm not asking if they're all like you – because you're unique. But are they all like them?'

Jane thought, first the flattery, then the demand for knowledge. Even Jay would have been pleased with that one, but even so Bob was almost frantic with the need to know.

'Some of them are men, you know,' she said, 'the people I know. But most of the ladies dress and talk like that. Not all of them look like that of course. But then they are far and away the prettiest girls I know.'

'Aye,' said Bob. 'They would be. The tall one in the yellow's Sarah Unwin. I've seen her picture in the paper many's the time.'

'And the fair one is Georgina Payne,' Jane said. 'You must have heard her on that crystal set of yours.'

'On the one you gave Gran,' said Bob. 'Gran thinks she's lovely. . . . She's right an' all. And the other dark one?'

'Her name is Catherine Hilyard,' said Jane. 'She's the daughter of an earl.'

'She's never.' Bob was by now in a world that transcended even the cinema.

'She studies at Oxford and spends most of the rest of her time in Ireland,' said Jane, 'and she's helped me organise this little jaunt rather well. *And* the ball at the Berkeley.'

Bob said, 'You could do us a favour.'

'If I can.'

'Introduce us,' said Bob, 'so I can shake hands with them. That's all. Just shake hands.'

'That's easy,' said Jane. 'They want to meet all the family, and I've promised they will. But not here. Not now.'

Bob looked at the crowded surgery waiting room, so many of them women, so many with sick children. They too were staring at her friends, like a flock of half-starved sparrows, she thought, visited by a flight of kingfishers.

'Aye,' said Bob. 'I see what you mean.'

He left her then, and soon after Bet took his place.

'Like a kid in a sweet shop,' she said, and Jane looked puzzled.

'Our Bob,' said Bet. 'I had to go to the kitchen to see the meat was ready for tomorrow's dinner for the helpers, and when I came back, there he is. Goggle-eyed.' She was clearly enjoying the fact: a small revenge for the teasing she had endured.

'Don't tell me Frank Metcalfe doesn't goggle at you like that,' said Jane.

Bet said, 'That's different.' And indeed it was.

'How's it going?' Jane asked.

'The same,' said Bet. 'Nothing's changed. Frank says we'll just have to wait – but you sharp get sick of waiting,' she sighed. 'But what else can we do?'

Obviously not what Jay and I do, thought Jane, and even to suggest it would be lunacy.

'I'm sorry,' she said, and Bet turned to her.

'Oh no,' she said. 'You mustn't say that. It isn't your fault. And anyway – you've done wonders for us here.'

It all seemed so damned unfair that Jane wanted to cry, which wouldn't achieve a damn thing. Two damns in one sentence, she thought, and even inside my own mind that's one damn too many. High time I took a long sea voyage, with or without Jay Bower.

The concert was a blend of familiar classics and music-hall entertainment that the band had done a hundred times, and Georgie said wasn't all that different to playing in the cinema. But her gown was blue and silver, designed by Molyneux, and someone had found her a hairdresser who could set her hair just right, and the applause was deafening. A little Chopin, Brahms's 'Lullaby', Sinding's 'Rustle of Spring'. Not quite Pachmann, but the best that Felston had heard for many a long day. The applause was deafening: as it was for the dance music – 'Running Wild', 'Lady Be Good', 'Yes We Have No Bananas'. And then Georgie came back again, in black, with pearls, and played with the band this time, the songs that they loved best of all, even though they reminded each singer of a time of nightmare – except that they didn't, thought Jane. They were reminders of leave, and rest camp, and comfortable route marches. 'Tipperary', 'There's A Long Long Trail A-Winding', and last of all, 'Pack Up Your Troubles'. Georgie coaxed them into song like the pub pianist she once had been, and the band, towards the end, stopped being a dance band and became as military as the band of the Coldstream Guards. Trumpets blared, side drums rattled and swaggered and, as Jane looked around her, the women's hands touched the sleeves of their menfolk, the men's shoulders straightened. All that was missing was the rhythmic crunching sound of a battalion marching at ease.

> What's the use of worrying
> It never was worth while – so!
> Pack up your troubles in your old kit bag
> And smile – *smile* – *smile*!

Then the applause, tumultuous, deafening, Georgie making curtsey after curtsey, and the band leader bowing, then gesturing to where Jane sat, beckoning to her. Once more she rose in her seat and faced a crowd, and the applause grew louder still, then one by one men rose to applaud, and women too, until at last the entire audience was on its feet, clapping and cheering till they could do no more.

Messeter leaned over to Dr Stobbs. 'Don't tell me that's not medicine,' he said, but Stobbs made no answer. He was too busy yelling.

Grandma put her hand on Jane's arm. 'Eh, me bairn,' she said. 'I'm proud of you.'

There was a reception of course, in a sort of ante-room behind the stage. Always there were receptions afterwards, because how else could triumphs be relived? But Don Cook's representative had done his work well. There were sherry and whisky and beer and lemonade instead of champagne, and the sandwiches were substantial. Jane kept her promise and introduced the Pattersons to everyone in sight. Georgie looked elegant and bewitching even when drinking pale ale, and Sarah was all smiles and congratulations because she knew her turn would come next day. Catherine divided her time between checking notes and urging Jane to eat (she'll be telling me to sit down and put my feet up next, thought Jane), but all the time she could have said which woman Bob was watching. Bob was a very good-looking man, but then so had his brother been.

The mayor was there, being gracious, for even though his politics were as Red as the robe he'd worn that afternoon, he knew a contented voter when he saw one, and that evening he'd seen a hall full of them. So he thanked Jane and the *Daily World* and the band leader and Georgina. It took him rather a long time to thank Georgina, Jane noticed, and wondered if she'd *ever* failed.

The presence of the mayor had not surprised her – after all he needed votes the way a horse needs hay – nor did Andy's absence.

Bet sounded indignant about it, but for Jane it was a blessing.

'All those songs from the war,' she said. 'How could Andy have endured it after what he went through in prison?'

Frank Metcalfe said, 'Miss Whitcomb's right, you know, pet. Andy would have hated it. Better for him to keep away.'

Jane had decided from the start that she liked Frank Metcalfe, shrewd and solid and reliable, though maybe with a touch of the Puritan about him. But then Bet could be puritanical, too. They really ought to be married, she thought. They'll never be happy until they are.

Manny Mendel was there, which did surprise her. He had a girl with him, slender and pretty and Jewish, and much more expensively dressed than any other woman in Felston. This was not a night for shrinking violets. She went up to him.

'How are you, Mr Mendel?' she asked.

'Miss Whitcomb,' Mendel said, but did not answer her question. 'May I introduce my fiancée – Miss Perlman – Bernice – this is Jane Whitcomb.'

'Oh Miss Whitcomb,' Bernice said. 'I've been absolutely dying to meet you.'

'No. Really?' said Jane.

'Bernice is very interested in women who do things,' said Mendel.

'One of these days I'm going to write a book about them,' said Bernice Perlman, 'and if you don't mind, I intend to put you in it. At the moment I write bits and pieces for women's mags. Bottling Fruit, Removing Stains from Tablecloths, Does Love Really Conquer All? You know. But we have to start somewhere.'

'Yes indeed,' said Jane. 'I started here in Felston.'

'And now Manny's leaving it,' said Bernice.

'Are you?'

'I've got a job,' said Manny. 'Based on a new idea from America. It's called doing market research. For a pharmaceutical company in Slough. Rather a good job. – We're getting married, you see.'

He smiled down at Bernice, and Jane knew exactly how Manny Mendel was. He was wonderfully, deliriously happy.

'Of course,' he said. 'I shall still support the Labour Party.'

'Of course,' said Jane, and thought: Poor Andy. Another reason why he didn't come.

That night she dreamed of John. They had been making love, and now they had done, and he wanted to hold her in his arms and talk and make jokes, and look at her lying there, naked, because although he was shy about it, much shyer than she, he enjoyed her nakedness. Sooner or later he would always say the same thing. 'By – you are a bonny lass.' But this night she couldn't stay. There was an alarm. A strafe, or a big raid perhaps, or the Germans were attacking. Whatever it was she had to get up and dress and John couldn't understand why. She tried to explain, but he couldn't understand.

'You're always in a hurry,' he said. He looked so young.

Jane woke up thinking; But then he was young. He was only twenty-six when he died.

Next morning at breakfast her three friends could talk of nothing but the clinic and the horrors they had seen there, which was as well, thought Jane. They would work all the harder for Felston. And work they did, and all the other people that the *Daily World* had hired. There was a potted version of *Cinderella* performed at break-neck speed by the company from the Theatre Royal so that they could be back in time for the evening perform-ance, but including, even so, a splendid comedian dame whose jokes were in dialect and well-nigh unintelligible, and a trans-formation scene that included a carriage and Shetland ponies, which had taken a score of skilled craftsmen all day to arrange. Afterwards there was a high tea, the first Jane had seen, and a very high tea indeed according to Grandma; tinned salmon and tongue and boiled ham, *and* potted meat. Tomatoes even, in late December. And cream cakes and Christmas cake and biscuits to take home. And balloons. And presents. Toys and scent and beer. And after that there was Georgie to play for them, the songs they liked so much to sing, and when they had sung themselves hoarse, there was Sarah to tell them the story of Private Walker and make them weep. 'Not a dry eye in the house,' she told Jane in triumph. 'It went even better than at the Berkeley.' Even Catherine dabbed at her eyes.

'And I never snivel,' she said, 'but it was all so sad. You're jolly clever, the pair of you.'

Georgina was in floods, Jane noticed, yet still looked beautiful.

Last of all there was dancing: after the children left, each one presented with an orange and a boiled egg. (Vitamins *and* nutrition, Harriet had told her, and Dr Stobbs agreed.) The band was far better than the floor of the Mafeking Hall, but the caretaker had done his best with French chalk, and even the heaviest boots could slide a little. It was not just the modern dances either. There were old-fashioned waltzes too, and the Bradford Barn Dance and the Military Two Step. Canon Messeter led out Jane for the first dance to thunderous applause, and for a complete turn of the room they danced alone, while the rest of the dancers watched and clapped.

'And all for you,' Canon Messeter said. 'They know what you have done, and they bless you for it.' He smiled. 'If you asked them to invade France they'd form fours and march off this very minute, so long as you marched in front.'

'Then I shan't ask them,' said Jane. 'I shall remember what the slave told the conquering Roman general instead.'

'Remember that you are but mortal,' said the canon. 'It's a good thing to remember.'

He danced on, and gradually others joined them, Bob among the first, leading out Georgina, and so already a hero.

Canon Messeter danced well, surprisingly well for a man who had such a quantity of what he described as 'German iron' inside him, but others took his place: Stan, nimble and inventive in the Military Two-Step, Bob, whose Charleston matched anything in London, and even the mayor, like Dick Lambert, waltzed in silent concentration. Could it be something to do with their politics? she wondered. The night sped by, and the whole room danced, Grandma revolving cautiously in the arms of Dr Stobbs. Bet, predictably, danced only with her Frank, but Bob danced with everyone, and especially Georgina, Catherine and Sarah. By now he had become the stuff of which legends are made.

But it ended at last, and the band played 'God Save The King' and everyone sang; then Canon Messeter called for three cheers for Jane, and the roof, according to Georgina, only just failed to lift. The bus and a car came for the band and Georgie and Sarah, who were catching the sleeper to London for appointments the next day. *She still hadn't talked to Georgina about Piers.* But that would have to wait for London. So many things would have to wait for London. For now there were questions to be answered, people to talk to; Bella Docherty, Grandma, Dr Stobbs, reporters; all with the need to know, until at last Catherine dragged her off to the Eldon Arms, and a sleep with no remembered dreams.

43

O N THE TRAIN next day, Catherine said: 'I enjoyed our little outing. I thought it would be just good works, but it wasn't. It was fun as well. You are marvellous.'

'Don't you start,' said Jane. 'I saw something that needed to be done and I'm trying to do it, that's all. Just like you.'

'But you make it happen,' said Catherine. 'If it weren't for you I wouldn't even be here. You must be exhausted. Why don't you put your feet up? Nobody will see.'

Just as I predicted thought Jane, then said aloud, 'Certainly not.' She lit a cigarette. 'What did you think of the Patterson family?'

'The one they call Grandma's a devil to go,' said Catherine. 'She could even give my granny a game.'

'And Bob?'

'He's a very good-looking boy,' Catherine said, and added hastily: 'Don't you think?'

'Well of course I do,' said Jane. 'He looks exactly like my John.'

'*Does* he?' said Catherine. 'How marvellous.' She was silent for a moment. 'Forgive me,' she said. 'I was trying to imagine Bob in a captain's uniform, instead of that terrible suit.'

His best one, thought Jane, the trousers ironed by Bet specially for that evening, the tie bought that day with the money his father had given him for Christmas.

'Imagine two medal ribbons and a wound stripe too,' said Jane.

'He must have looked marvellous.'

'He did,' said Jane, but now it was becoming difficult to imagine exactly how John had looked. She could think of Bob of course. She hadn't been wrong: the resemblance was there. But it was Bob she saw in her mind and not John. John had been different, but now she couldn't remember the difference.

'If I may ask,' said Catherine, 'how old was your captain when he died?'

'Twenty-six,' said Jane.

'That's just Bob's age now,' said Catherine, then blushed, but prettily, the colour becoming.

'Is it indeed?' said Jane.

'We were talking about ages,' said Catherine. 'You know how one does. I'm twenty-one.'

'Did he ask?'

'Of course not. He's not gauche, you know. I just told him. He's a jolly good dancer.'

'Almost as good as Lionel.'

'Almost,' said Catherine, and giggled. 'But not in the least like him.'

'Not in the least,' said Jane.

'It's a pity he's poor,' Catherine said. 'With a proper haircut and a different accent and some decent clothes he could go simply anywhere.'

'Perhaps he will, one day,' said Jane.

Catherine shook her head. 'Not if he's poor. I know it's a perfectly ghastly thing to say but I could never not be rich. I just couldn't stand it.'

'Don't worry,' said Jane. 'It's hardly likely to happen.'

The train slowed down for Durham, and once again she saw the massive splendour of its cathedral.

'Are you sure you don't want to rest?' said Catherine.

'Thank you no,' said Jane. 'I was wondering – if you give me the support of your arm – whether I could totter as far as the dining car. I thought I might stand us both a gin and It before lunch.'

One more talk that year, to a group of women in St John's Wood who met once a month to assure each other that the world would be a better place if everyone was nice to everyone else, and they might well be right, thought Jane, and set out to convince them that a good way of being nice was to give a lot of money for Felston. Seventeen pounds seven shillings and sixpence. That made them really very nice: nothing less than half a crown. And afterwards a call on Mr Pinner, even if it was New Year's Eve. Mr Pinner didn't hold with New Year's Eve, which was all very well for Scotsmen, but this was London. There was work to be done.

The typist brought in tea, and Jane, who thought she must have drunk about half a gallon of the stuff in St John's Wood, nevertheless accepted it. Mr Pinner was embarrassed, and tea would at least help to get him started, tea and the pipe which he asked permission to light almost at once. Then came questions about her Felston concert, and she doubted whether he even heard the answers, for Mr Pinner could no more evade an unpleasant issue, than could her mother.

'About Major Routledge,' he said.

'Yes?' said Jane.

'He did go to Cheltenham Races with a woman,' said Mr Pinner. 'No doubt of it.'

'Oh dear,' said Jane. 'Woman' made it even more ominous.

'No,' Mr Pinner said. 'Nothing like that.' He sounded stern.

'Then what was it like, Mr Pinner?'

'I do a bit of racing myself, miss,' Mr Pinner said. 'So I know a few people. Otherwise it wouldn't have been easy.'

'I'm obliged to you,' said Jane. 'Of course. And I've no doubt some of the people you talked with wanted a thank you. It's only natural. I understand.'

'Thank you, miss,' said Mr Pinner. 'The woman's a Miss Dawson. Lives in Camden Town. Your major picked her up there. They went by train – came back soon after the race meeting.'

'But there was nothing – irregular?'

'Not a thing, miss,' said Mr Pinner. 'There couldn't be.' Jane watched, and knew that he was bracing himself for a storm to come. 'Miss Dawson's his half sister.'

'What?'

'Not legitimate, miss, unfortunately, and not all that bright, either. A bit tenpence in the shilling as they say. What the Aussies call "Not the full quid".'

'I remember,' said Jane, 'but do get on, Mr Pinner.'

'Sorry, miss.' Mr Pinner sought comfort in his pipe. 'The major's father was the squire – in a modest sort of way, but he was very clever with the horses, and the major's sort of inherited that.'

'Is this relevant, Mr Pinner?'

'You'll have to be the judge of that, miss,' Mr Pinner said.

Bitch, thought Jane. Arrogant, supercilious bitch.

'I'm sorry,' she said. 'Of course it is or you wouldn't have mentioned it. Do go on.'

'Yes, miss.' Mr Pinner blew out smoke. 'Miss Dawson's mother was a housemaid, miss. Lucy Dawson. Same as her daughter. Of course she left when – ' He waved his hand.

'Quite,' said Jane.

'But he paid up like a gentleman,' Mr Pinner said. 'Left a bit of money in trust. Miss Dawson's mum married again, had another daughter – and she's the one who looks after Miss Dawson now. You'll be thinking it's the money and it probably is, but from what I gather there's sisterly feelings too.'

'But why on earth did Major Routledge take her out?'

'She loves racing, miss. The crowds. The excitement. And the horses most of all. The major took her because it's a treat for her.'

'Oh,' said Jane. 'But why Cheltenham?'

Mr Pinner said, 'Major Routledge is not well off, miss.'

'Majors on half pay seldom are.'

'Major Routledge is skint,' said Mr Pinner, then added darkly, 'investments. Always a mistake for a military man.'

'Oh dear,' said Jane.

'Get rich quick,' said Mr Pinner. 'Double your income. . . . I don't think. He's got the price of a room at the Travellers and that's about all he has got,' said Mr Pinner, 'except the nags.'

'Are you telling me that Major Routledge is a professional gambler?'

Mr Pinner looked shocked. 'The major's a gentleman, miss, but from what I gather he can pick 'em. Fifty quid at Cheltenham is what I'm told.'

'And that's all?' said Jane.

'All I know, miss.'

Fifty pounds profit and fifty pounds in cash for stake money.

'Good gracious *what* a relief,' said Jane. 'The major emerges without a stain on his character.'

But Mr Pinner was a realist. 'He's hardly in a position to support Lady Whitcomb,' he said.

'Then I must think of something,' said Jane. 'I owe him that much at least.'

From Falcon Court below them there came the sound of singing. Mr Pinner went to the window, and Jane joined him, to look down on a group of ragged men, huddled beneath a gaslight, who sang to a mouth organ and banjo. All of them wore medals, and one of them carried a small placard that read: 'Ex-Servicemen. We Wish You A Happy New Year.'

Oh the moon shines bright on Charlie Chaplin, [they sang]
His boots are cracking for want of blacking
And his little baggy trousers they'll need mending,
Before we send him to the Dardanelles.

'Last time I heard that was outside Amiens,' said Mr Pinner. September 1918 that would be. Just before the last big push. . . . If you don't mind, miss?' He nodded at the window.

'Of course not,' said Jane, and Mr Pinner opened the window and whistled clear and shrill. At once the men below looked up, and Mr Pinner threw down a shilling, and Jane opened her bag and threw down another, before Mr Pinner closed the window and shivered.

'A bit cold for open-air concerts,' he said.

'Yes indeed,' said Jane, and held out her hand. 'Happy New Year, Mr Pinner.'

Dinner with the Watsons. That meant something simple, she thought, but by no means abject. A discreet little confection in blue and white silk by Vionnet, and Jay's diamond ear-rings, though not of course the necklace. Far too grand. As she hooked in the ear-rings she thought of Jay. Time, more than time, that they shared a bed together again. The sort of satisfaction that they could create for each other was rare – she was quite sure of it – and should not be neglected.

Hawkins came in and looked her over, critically the only word. 'Very nice, miss,' she said, and somehow Jane managed to suppress a sigh of relief. Really it was like being married, without the fun.

'Thank you,' she said.

'There's a car outside, miss,' Hawkins said. 'Driver says you ordered it.'

'So I did,' said Jane. 'Is it very grand?'

'Rolls-Royce, miss.'

'The thing is,' said Jane, 'there may be rather a lot of champagne. My host is a Scot.'

'I see, miss.' I might as well have said he's an Eskimo, thought Jane.

'Don't wait up,' she said. 'Or do if you feel like it. Its New Year's Eve after all.'

Harriet was delighted to see her, and yet contrite too. The Millingtons had let her down. 'Flu, both of them. Not that it wasn't raging . . . Still, they had only been six to dinner in the first place, and now there were four.

'Like the ten little niggers,' said Jane.

'Good Lord I hope not. There were none of them at the end. But Keith's here, bathed and shaved, and how he tore himself out of his lab I'm blessed if I know.'

'Of course you know,' said Jane. 'You look gorgeous.' And indeed she did, in a dress of orange satin that set off to perfection her dark, clear skin.

Harriet giggled. The drinks must have started early and it's time I had one, thought Jane.

'Come and meet your dinner partner,' Harriet said. '*He* hasn't caught 'flu, thank God.'

She was introduced to a man called Lovell, Charles Lovell, who had that same neat and well-brushed air she had seen in Canon Messeter and Major Routledge, but his eyes, though dark, were more reminiscent of the canon's than the major's: not that they looked mad, but they glittered with intelligence which he did his best to hide, almost as if it were bad form. About thirty-eight, she thought. Jay's age. And then: Why on earth make such a comparison? Jay's as clever as they come and doesn't give a damn who knows it.

Watson was saying, 'Charles and I met in the war.'

'Just like Jane and me,' said Harriet. 'Really without the war we'd have had no social life at all.'

'Which regiment?' Jane asked.

'Rifle Brigade,' said Lovell.

'He saved my life,' said Watson, and offered Jane a glass of Bollinger.

'Nonsense,' said Lovell.

'Not nonsense at all,' said Harriet. 'You got a medal for it.' She turned to Jane. 'It wasn't Keith's turn to die, you see. I hadn't finished with him. Hadn't even started on him actually.'

Lots and lots of champagne before I got here, thought Jane. To Lovell she said: 'Did you by any chance know a Major Messeter?'

'Teddy Messeter?'

'No doubt. I always referred to him as the canon. He's a parson now, you know.'

'*Messeter?*'

She had surprised him, astounded him even, and for some reason she was glad of it.

'You hadn't heard?'

'I knew he'd been badly wounded – and discharged, I believe. But I never thought – Messeter? A *parson?*'

'He's sort of retired,' said Jane. 'He gets ill from time to time – but when he's well he works in a voluntary clinic in Felston. Why is it so surprising?'

'He was the most thorough-going ladies' man I ever met,' said Lovell.

'I can believe it,' said Jane. 'And the charm's still there, believe me. Though he uses it for good works now.'

'I've read about you and Felston,' said Lovell. Like everybody else, thought Jane, but at least you don't look at me as if I had two heads.

'Everybody should read about Felston,' she said. 'It's important.'

He smiled, but left it at that, which was a pity, she thought. If he'd been in the Rifle Brigade he was bound to have money.

The parlourmaid came in and announced dinner. Cockaleekie soup, but no haggis. Watson wasn't that sort of Scotsman, and even if he had been Harriet would have been firm. But there were grouse, and cheese, and a sorbet, and a burgundy that the men approached with a respect bordering on reverence.

Jane grinned at Harriet. 'Better than poached eggs on toast

washed down with gin,' she said, and Harriet grinned back.

After they had left the men to their port and Harriet had admonished them not to dawdle, she learned a little more about Charles Lovell.

'He really did save Keith's life,' Harriet told her. 'It was in an advanced dressing station. The Germans shelled it – more bad luck than malice, Keith reckons. He'd just finished plugging a damn great hole in Charles's side and gone on to the next case. The first shell knocked him flat. The second one didn't go off. Keith just lay there and looked at it sticking out of the ground, because now his leg was broken, and Charles sort of shambled over and picked him up and carried him out, and all Keith could do was nag him about what would happen if Charles's dressing slipped. Keith reckoned they must have made about twenty yards when the damn shell went off and knocked them both over. Charles got a Military Cross for that one.'

'I should hope so.'

'He got other things as well. A Croix de Guerre, even. Keith seems to think he's quite mad.'

'What does he do now?'

'Lives elegantly. Hunts. Shoots things.'

'Hardly a sign of madness.'

'Oh he's sane enough in peacetime,' Harriet said, and then: 'Damn that champagne. I didn't mean to be offensive.'

'You weren't,' said Jane. 'I'm sane enough in peacetime too. For the moment.'

And then the men came back in and they danced, Lovell remarkably well for a man with a hole in his side; but then Canon Messeter too had ignored German iron when he wished to dance. 'I Want To Be Happy' was the record they played, and happy they were in the movement of their bodies.

When skies are grey and you're lonesome and blue
You'll see the sun shining through Pom-Pom-*Pom*
I want to be happy still I can't be happy
Till I've made you happy too.

But it really doesn't apply, thought Jane. I haven't been lonesome since I went to Felston. Or blue either . . . Keith Watson went over to the gramophone and lifted the needle, and Jane glanced at the clock on the mantelshelf. One minute to midnight.

'If you don't mind, Charles,' said Watson.

'Of course,' Lovell said, and walked out of the room.

'You have everything?' Watson called after him.

'Of course,' said Lovell over his shoulder. 'My nurse came from Inverness.'

Jane turned to Harriet, eyebrows lifted.

'Barbarism,' said Harriet. 'Sheer barbarism. But he couldn't get through the year without it.'

The clock on the mantelshelf wheezed, then began to strike the hour. When it had done Jane could hear a distant church clock chime, and then a measured knocking at the front door. Watson went to it at once, and Jane and Harriet followed as Watson opened the door to a Lovell dappled white with the fall of the first snow of the year.

'Happy New Year,' he said, and gravely handed over a silver sixpence, a twist of salt and a piece of coal to his hostess, then kissed her on either cheek, before shaking hands with Watson and kissing Jane.

'Happy New Year,' he said.

'Happy New Year.'

It was like an incantation, a rite, and even though they might not be true believers, they observed the form.

Watson bustled them back into the drawing room, and champagne for the women, whisky for the men. For a man at this time, he said, a dram was the only possible drink.

'Barbarous,' Harriet said again.

'Not at all,' said Watson. 'We North Britons are a practical and scholarly lot on the whole. We get all our superstititions over in one go on the thirty-first of December, and a lot of our drinking, too.'

'Charles here is our first foot. No offence to the suffragettes, but the first foot over the threshold in the New Year has to be a man, and preferably a dark man like Charles – bringing money and fuel and the savour for our food that represents the food itself. The promise that we'll neither starve nor freeze nor fall into poverty.'

'I damn near froze on your doorstep,' said Lovell. 'Still, let me give you a toast.' And then to Watson, 'Oh don't worry. It's a Scottish toast. Scottish regiment. Argyll and Sutherland Highlanders would it be?' He lifted his glass and said in creditable

Glaswegian, 'Here's tae us. Whae's like us? Damn few.' And they drank.

Harriet said, 'Jane and I know one, too,' and turned to Jane. 'That château in Picardy, you remember? We had a leave there in 1917.'

Jane nodded and went to her.

'I looks towards you,' said Harriet.

'I catches your eye,' said Jane.

'I bows.'

'I likewise bows.'

And then together: 'We links and drinks according.' And they linked arms and sipped their champagne.

There had been snow in Picardy, Jane remembered, and champagne too, and later had been the first time that she had danced with John – and all so long ago that it might have happened to a completely different woman . . . Then Keith wound up the gramophone and asked her to dance, after which it was Lovell's turn and the record was 'Roses Of Picardy', and she thought she might cry, but only because she had drunk too much champagne.

Lovell said, 'I'd like to hear more about Felston. Perhaps we could lunch some time.'

'A donation would be better,' she said.

'Maybe I could manage both.'

And then it was two o'clock and the hire-car came, with the news that the snow was still falling, and beginning to lie in the sidestreets.

'Not a lot of taxis about I take it?' said Lovell.

'None, sir.' The thought seemed to cheer the driver enormously.

'I'll give you a lift,' said Jane. The driver looked reproachful.

In the end Lovell escorted Jane to South Terrace first, before going on to Eaton Square, where he was staying with friends.

'I really should get a flat in London,' he said. 'The trouble is I'm lazy and I've got lots of friends who can just about put up with me. And being on one's own can be ghastly – in London, I mean. But you don't find it so?'

'I scarcely ever am alone,' said Jane. 'Nor would you be – with all those friends.'

'Probably not,' said Lovell. 'I think perhaps the truth of the matter is that if I bought a place I should feel obliged to use it –

and I do so like the country.' They drove for a while in silence, the snow in the windless air drifting like blossom in the car's headlights.

'Harriet said you were engaged to a chap in the Royal Northumbrians,' he said at last. 'A chap called Patterson. Do you mind if I talk about him? I knew him, you see.'

'You did? How marvellous. Of course I don't mind.'

'Well I didn't exactly know him – but I met him. We took over the Northumbrians' section of the Line in 1916 – and he saved my life.' He chuckled. 'I know what you're thinking. It's a big night for life-saving. All the same it's true – without any hyperbole I mean. Captain Patterson gave me some advice. If I hadn't taken it I'm quite sure I'd be dead.'

'Please go on,' said Jane.

'I carried a revolver,' said Lovell. 'A damn great brute of a thing that would stop a charging rhino if you could get close enough to hit it. Almost all officers carried revolvers, come to that, so that when we went over the top the Germans, being a logical people, killed the chaps with revolvers first, and left the other ranks leaderless. As I say – logical.'

'So what did John advise you to do?'

'Carry a rifle, like everybody else. It seemed a bit infra dig at first, but when I thought about it it made sense. I mean I had no objection to running the same risks as my men, but there seemed no point in running more . . . So I did what he suggested. It caused a bit of a stir in the mess at first, but it was surprising how many of the survivors came round to my point of view. After all we were the Rifle Brigade, not the Revolver Brigade. He seemed an awfully nice chap, your fiancé.'

But he's still dead, and you're still living. Not that it was his fault – or yours.

'Yes,' said Jane. 'He was.'

Well of course he was, thought Lovell. How could he not be, since you accepted him.

The Rolls moved on into the swirling whiteness. In the side streets the snow was already lying.

'I meant what I said – about giving you lunch,' Lovell said at last.

'Then you must telephone me. I'm in the book,' said Jane, and again there was a silence, a silence that felt like anger. But how could it be anger against her?

The car pulled up in South Terrace, and Lovell got out, walked with her on the snow to her door, and offered his hand.

'Happy New Year,' he said again.

'And the same to you.' In the schoolroom her brothers had invariably added, 'With knobs on.'

'I'll call you soon then.'

'Please do,' she said, and thought, Really if I annoy him that much why all this frantic haste to buy me lunch?

She went inside quickly. Her shoes were of fine kid, and already wet.

There was a light on in the drawing room: a black mark for Hawkins. Dead against waste was Hawkins, as she'd told Jane herself. Lights burning in empty rooms were like burning pound notes. Wicked waste. Jane went into the room and was confronted by a tableau. Bob Patterson, wrapped in a travelling rug, sat in an armchair drawn up close to the fire, and hovering in attendance were Mrs Barrow with a bowl of soup, Brown with an extra cushion, and Hawkins with the whisky decanter, for all the world, Jane thought, as if Bob were already preparing to take over Teddy Messeter's vacant throne.

'What's this?' she said aloud. 'Charades?'

Bob began to stand up, remembered he was in his underwear, and sat down again.

'He says he knows you, miss,' said Hawkins. 'He's just come from Felston.'

That 'he' said it all. Hawkins at least remained unsmitten.

'Certainly Mr Patterson knows me,' said Jane, and then, turning to the pasha himself, 'I didn't know you were planning a visit, Bob. You might have warned me.'

'By sea, miss,' said Brown. 'He came by sea, the poor feller.'

'Half starved,' said Mrs Barrow. 'And soaked to the skin. We've got his clothes drying in the airing cupboard, Miss Whitcomb.'

'A jolly good idea,' said Jane. 'And I see you're feeding him, too. Which bedroom have you chosen for him?'

'The pink room, miss,' said Hawkins.

The smallest, darkest room in the house, and pink was *not* Bob's colour.

'No,' said Jane. 'The bed's too small. Move him to the blue room.'

'Yes, miss,' said Hawkins. She looked annoyed, but Mrs Barrow and Brown were smirking.

'And go to bed,' said Jane. 'Don't you know what time it is? I have a meeting tomorrow.'

They turned, and then she remembered her manners, and called out to them, 'No wait.' There was port in the decanter, a drink, according to Beau Brummell, fit only for the lower orders, so her father had told her, but she poured a glass for herself too, and lifted it in a toast.

'A Happy New Year,' she said.

'You certainly keep them in order,' said Bob.

'All those innocent females,' Jane said, 'and a man loose in the place. Somebody had to keep them in order.'

'And they all work for you?'

'When you let them. Bob – what on earth is all this stuff about a sea voyage?'

'I told you,' said Bob. 'Don't you remember? The cheapest way to get to London is on a collier.'

'Yes,' said Jane, 'I remember.' She quoted him. 'A ten-bob note and bring your own food.'

'That's what I did,' said Bob. 'Food for three days, but the weather turned nasty. It took us nigh on five. Not that it mattered. I was seasick most of the time.'

He was foxing. Trying to hide something. She was certain of it.

'And why did your harem tear your clothes off?' she asked. 'What happened to your overcoat?'

'I pawned it,' he said. 'The price of my ticket.'

'Bob,' she said. 'It's late. I've had rather a long day.'

'Me an' all,' he said. 'It's a fair step from Rotherhithe.'

'You *walked* here?'

'By the time we docked I had ninepence left. I squandered half of it on beer and bought a tram ticket. When they put us off I *had* to walk.'

'In the snow?'

'Uncle Tom's Cabin wasn't in it,' he said.

'But why, Bob?'

'I came to do you a favour.'

'You're very kind.' She said it without irony, and Bob knew it.

'It's Andy,' he said, and gulped at his whisky. 'God knows I don't want to shop him –'

'Is that what you're doing?'

He shrugged. 'What I'm telling you – it wouldn't put him in prison. Nothing like that.'

'If it did I wouldn't want to hear it,' she said, but he wasn't listening.

'Another spell in the clink – I doubt if even Andy could stand it . . . But it isn't that. He's just out to harm you. I don't like that.'

'How?' Jane asked.

Bob flushed, seemed almost embarrassed. 'You went to Paris,' he said.

'You know I did. The Four Arts Ball.'

'Aye,' said Bob. 'There was a chap came up from London to have a word with Andy. He never let on to the rest of us – but I saw the two of them going into the Boilermakers' Arms. Into the saloon. What you might call the posh end,' he explained.

'Now our Andy never goes into pubs,' said Bob, 'so I went into the Boilermakers' meself and bought a half – in the public bar. There's a hatch there between the bar and the saloon, and if you ease it forward a bit you can hear very nicely. So I –' he hesitated.

'Eased it forward a bit?'

'Aye. You might think I was just being nosey, but you'd be wrong.'

'You've no idea what I think.'

'No more I have. What I thought was our Andy was heading for trouble. One look at the toff he was with and I knew it was trouble.' He smiled. 'Poor Andy. Drinking his lemonade, and thinking he was putting the world to rights.'

'What were they talking about?' said Jane. 'Or don't you want to tell me?'

'I *have* to tell you,' said Bob. 'They were talking about you.'

'What about me?'

Bob hesitated, then said, 'I'm only telling you what that toff said.'

'Of course.'

Bob braced himself. 'You were a tart,' he said at last. 'A prostitute. And they had a picture to prove it. A picture from Paris.'

'But you saw that picture yourself,' said Jane. 'In the *Daily World*. I wore that Egyptian head-dress and cloak. That doesn't make me a tart.'

'In this one you weren't wearing the cloak,' said Bob, and waited.

At last Jane said, 'Go on.'

'Andy asked if the toff had the picture – and the toff showed him. I didn't see it,' Bob added hastily. 'Didn't want to. But Andy said it was very bad. Felston couldn't take the charity of a loose woman like that.'

'What will they do?'

'There'll be copies made,' said Bob. 'Sent out to different organisations . . . Churches. Women's groups.'

'Will it have any effect?'

'Bound to,' said Bob. 'They're a straightlaced lot in Felston. Da . . . Bet . . .'

'And Grandma?'

'Not her,' said Bob. 'But she's a bit whacked just now. She couldn't put up much of a fight, even for you. It's true then?'

'Of course it's true,' said Jane. 'But I wasn't indecent. At least I didn't think so. I went as Cleopatra.'

'Depends what you mean by indecent,' said Bob. 'In Felston that's showing your knees.'

'How long have I got?' Jane asked.

'A week, mebbe,' said Bob. 'All the toff had was a print. They have to wait for the negative.'

'This toff,' said Jane. 'What did he look like?'

Bob gave her an accurate description of Julian Burrowes.

'I see,' she said, and then: 'Does Andy know you're here?'

'I'm not that daft,' said Bob. 'I told them I was off after a job in Coventry.'

'All of them?'

'The whole family. Aye.'

'And what did Grandma say?'

'Nothing,' said Bob. 'But she didn't believe a word of it. I know she didn't. Just wished us luck and told us not to forget to write when I was settled. What are you going to do, Jane?'

'What do you suggest?'

'Well we're nothing to you, are we?' said Bob. 'I mean if there's scandal and name-calling – why should you put up with it? You've done your whack. More than your whack. I mean look at Christmas. If a lot of narrow-minded old biddies want to make your life a misery why should you bother? Like I say – you've done your whack. Take yourself off to Paris or somewhere.'

'Is that what you want me to do?'

'Of course not,' he said. 'But the folks up there – they're not like me. They'll hate you. They'll say you let them down.'

'You talk as if I were some kind of saint,' said Jane.

'Well you are to them,' said Bob, 'and saints don't go around with no clothes on.'

Jane said, 'I'm obliged to you. Now what can I do in return?'

'I thought –' said Bob. 'I mean it just crossed my mind – you must know this feller Bower.'

You know I do, Jane thought. You heard Burrowes say so.

'We've met,' she said.

'He must use a lot of printers,' said Bob.

'And now you want him to use one more?'

'They pay good money, the press,' said Bob. 'If he took me on I could get myself a room and still send money home.'

'I thought you'd told the family you'd gone to Coventry?'

'If I was sending money home,' Bob said, 'they wouldn't care if I was in Timbuktu.'

'I'll speak to Mr Bower,' she said, and rose. 'Finish your soup, then up the stairs, second door on the left. Don't forget to turn the lights off. Hawkins is very fussy about turning off lights.' For the last time that day she held her hand out.

'Happy New Year,' she said, 'and thank you.'

44

By next morning the snow had blanketed the whole of mainland Britain. Only in Ireland were the horses running, and that was much too far for the major to travel. She phoned him at his club, and he was at once wary and evasive. Only the mention of Cheltenham brought him to heel. On the second her dear mother had an appointment with her dentist, he said, which would make it convenient, *most* convenient, for him to come to lunch. Jane wondered which was the greater incentive: the threat of Cheltenham or the lure of Mrs Barrow.

He ate well. Jane had told him that this lunch was a private matter, between the two of them, and so he drank well, too. Bob took his lunch in the kitchen: as he told her, he'd have eaten it in the coal-house so long as Mrs Barrow did the cooking. Throughout lunch the major talked of horses. He knew they were the reason he was invited, and so he talked about them, fluently and knowledgeably enough even to impress the Hilyard twins, she thought.

And so she let him talk, and was impressed herself, but even so, she thought, a man who could make fifty quid at one meeting at Cheltenham had more than knowledge. He had luck, too. She offered him coffee in her little sitting room, where they would not be disturbed, and permitted a cigar, lit a cigarette herself.

'Someone saw me at Cheltenham, I take it,' he said at once. 'Saw me with a lady not your mother.'

This was getting down to business indeed, but by far the best way.

'Saw you with your half sister,' said Jane.

He looked at her sharply, and for the first time, with dislike.

'How do you know that?'

'I hired a detective to make enquiries,' said Jane.

'That was a monstrous thing to do,' said Routledge. 'You had no right – '

She interrupted him. 'Monstrous, certainly. But as for no right – '

'You refer to your mother?'

'Of course,' said Jane.

'You intend to tell her?'

'I think you should do that.'

'I?' said Routledge. 'The knowledge would appal her, surely?'

'Why should it?'

'She has a particular horror of marital infidelity,' said Routledge. 'She told me so herself.'

Oh Mummy, Mummy, thought Jane. Am I not to have a secret either?

'My mother is a realist,' she said. 'She would understand perfectly well that it wasn't your fault. She also has a great respect for discretion. You seem to have shown that rather well – till now.'

'Lucy – Miss Dawson – needs her little outings,' Routledge said. 'They wake her up, you might say. I've taken her racing every leave I've had in England. I just can't abandon her.'

'Of course not,' said Jane. 'Just explain it all to Mummy.'

'I might lose her.'

'I don't think so,' said Jane. 'But if you don't tell her somebody else will.'

'Yourself?'

'Certainly not,' said Jane. 'But sooner or later you'll be spotted. Some of Mummy's friends are very well-informed.'

'That damn Gwatkin,' said the major. 'She was a one-woman intelligence unit even in India.' Jane waited. 'What do you know about me?' he asked at last.

'That you were a major in the Gloucesters,' she said.

'I was a captain in '14,' he said. 'A forty-eight-year-old captain. And I was about to retire when the war came. After Mons and Le Cateau and first Ypres they could find a use even for forty-eight-year-old captains. I even had the battalion for a while

– when they made me a major. Then I got pneumonia. My war ended in 1915. – Before yours had even started.'

'How did you know about that?' she asked.

'Your mother told me,' Routledge said. 'She's very proud of you.'

Jane willed herself not to look astonished.

'I was useless in France but I wangled my way into the Puffers,' Routledge said. 'A good life. Useful too. Left the younger men free for the Western Front. Kept things going. . . . Took my discharge in 1919 and came home and lost all my money.'

'How did you?'

'Backed a feller who knew how to find oil in the North Sea,' Routledge said. 'All he really knew was how to take the life savings of middle-aged fools like me. So I went back to India.'

'Why did you?' asked Jane.

'Pension goes further there. And I could make a bit – horse trading. That's how I met your mother. I'd got a couple of polo ponies the maharajah wanted to buy. And that was it.'

'I'm sorry?' said Jane.

'I fell in love,' said the major simply. 'For the first time in my life. Sixty years old and smitten like a subaltern. Only – '

'Yes?'

'I'm broke,' he said. 'And I gather that your mother's not all that well off either.'

'No,' said Jane. 'She's not. I'm the rich one in the family.' She waited.

'There you are then,' said the major, and Jane knew it would be all right.

'Mummy thinks you might make a living breeding horses,' said Jane. 'Suppose I bought a stud farm – could you manage it for me?'

'I could try, I suppose,' said Routledge. 'The trouble is you see – what I can do with horses is pick 'em. Breeding them's another matter. I'm not a dashed vet. And anyway – your mother doesn't like the country.'

'She'd do it for you, but I think it would be a mistake.'

'I must do something,' said the major. 'We can't live on my pension.'

'Of course not,' said Jane. 'What you should do is become a racing correspondent.'

All of which meant that she had to see Jay Bower very soon. Jane Whitcomb, the threefold suppliant: for Bob, for Major Routledge – and for herself. It didn't seem to her that there was a damn thing to be done about that *bloody* photograph, but if there were, it would be Bower who would know what to do. If not, he could certainly do something for Bob, and very possibly the major.

Surprise, so her military friends had never tired of telling her, was the essence of attack, and so she went to call on Bower one evening at the penthouse, without telling him so. She wore simple, easily removable garments, a lot of French perfume, and Uncle Walter's sables. It really was very cold, so cold that she left Foch behind with Hawkins; so cold that he didn't even sulk.

But the Riley started without too much nonsense, and the main roads were easy enough, all the way to Fleet Street. The doorman knew her at once, and she went to the lift, which was empty, and pressed the button that would take her to what for most people was the top of the building, but not for her. She had a key that opened a scarcely visible door to another lift: 'the elevator', Bower called it, a luxurious affair in black and ivory that went up one floor only, to another door that opened with a key, and beyond the door Bower's penthouse.

She went in, calling out his name, but there was no answer, which did not surprise her. Day or night Bower always was aware of someone who had information to give, at lunch, or dinner, or a party. Even at breakfast. She went into the drawing room, ugly and comfortable as it always was, except that against one wall a painting had been rested, a painting covered with a piece of sackcloth. She lifted it up, and found that she was looking at her friend Georgina Payne, whose body was every bit as scrumptious as the last time she'd looked at it. Sackcloth, she thought, was the last thing to cover Georgina with, then she left, locked the door, and went down to her own office, and sat at her desk. This was going to take a bit of thinking about, but not yet.

The thing was that she needed Bower, whatever that picture meant. If she were going to go on helping Felston, she really needed Bower, to get off the hook of that *bloody* photograph. Not to mention Bob, and the major. *They* were what she had to think about, she realised, before ever she could *begin* to speculate on that fruit salad upstairs; the delectable Georgina, all peaches and cream and a couple of cherries for garnish.

What Bower was after was obvious, even if he'd chosen a damn funny way to go about it. But the point was did it matter? – or rather, did it matter enough when compared with Felston and Bob and the major, or even Jane Whitcomb's continued social acceptability – for she was in no doubt that whatever first became known in Felston would spread, rippling out in ever-widening circles until even Knightsbridge and Chelsea were encompassed; even Miss Gwatkin would know. Poor Mummy. . . . And poor Jane, too, she thought. For her reputation wouldn't stand that kind of revelation. It would mean purdah for her: the Italian Lakes at least.

But it wouldn't be good news for Bower, either, she reflected. The *Daily World* had backed her, made her into the kind of shining heroine she neither could be nor wanted to be, were it not for Felston. The other newspapers would never forgo such a chance. It would be against their every principle. Jay Bower would have to fight for her, whether he wanted to or not.

She put paper into the typewriter, and pecked away with two fingers and a thumb for the space bar, putting down on paper Bob's account of his sea voyage south. Jay hadn't asked for it, might well reject it out of hand, but it was better than sitting in South Terrace wondering if that picture really meant that Jay and Georgina had done it while she was delivering a lecture.

When at last the telephone rang she heard it with a sense of relief. For her, action had always been better than brooding, no matter what the outcome – at least until they'd had to pack her off to Jabber Lockhart.

'What the hell are you doing down there?' said Jay.

'Working.'

'You've got something?'

'I think so,' she said.

'Great,' said Jay. 'Want to come up and talk about it when you've finished?'

'I'd love to.'

'When will that be?'

'Say another half hour,' she said.

'See you then.' He hung up first. He always hung up first.

She would have to go to bed with him, she thought, and it

would have to be good, whatever she knew or thought she knew about Jay and Georgina Payne, because he had to be grateful. Unless he was grateful she hadn't a hope.

It seemed that he was grateful. He even liked the piece about Bob's journey, which he insisted on reading as soon as he had done. She must have been good, she thought, though for her there had been little memory of pleasure: she had been far too busy concentrating on what one might call the job in hand.

'I like this,' he said at last. 'It's a good piece. I'll use it. We'll put it with the rest of the stuff for while we're away. Is he still here – this Patterson guy?'

'He's staying with me.'

Jay nodded, that feminine streak of his assuring him that Bob was no threat. 'Why did he come?'

She got up and walked naked across the bedroom. Jay liked to watch her do that, but that wasn't the only reason. She had to know if Georgina's portrait was there, and so she walked on across the hallway and into the drawing room. No Georgina. No sackcloth, either. Not on Georgina anyway. She picked up a table lighter, turned to go back, then paused. There was snow on all the roofs she could see below her, and yet naked as she was the room was warm. In his own way Jay knew all about pleasure.

He appeared beside her, a dressing gown belted about him.

'Now what are you up to?' he asked.

She took a cigarette from the box and lit it.

'Admiring the view,' she said.

'Me too.' His hand reached out, began to fondle. 'Why did young Patterson come here?'

'To warn me,' she said.

'Warn you of what?'

She told him.

'Oh boy,' he said. 'Somebody doesn't like you.'

'Julian Burrowes doesn't like me,' she said. 'He doesn't like either of us.' His hand moved away.

'Go on doing that, if you please sir,' she said. 'You know I enjoy it.'

She knew the request would please him, and besides it was true. What he did was soothing.

'I can't do this and think,' he said.

'Of course you can,' she said. 'You're Jay Bower.'

She turned to find an ash tray, and his hand moved with her.

At last he said, 'It'll be rough.'

'What will?'

'Getting you off the hook.'

'I expect every fish thinks that at the time. Tell me what I have to do.'

He told her, and first she smiled, and then she laughed, a full-throated chuckle that went on and on.

'You don't mind?'

'I love it,' she said, 'but will it work?'

His hand moved down and squeezed. 'Bet your ass,' he said.

She turned to face him then, loosed the knot on his dressing gown.

'Let's celebrate,' she said.

'Go back to bed?'

'I can't wait that long.' She lay down on the couch and Jay joined her. At least Georgina wasn't there to watch.

Bob had been no problem. Jay would send a chit to the printers' father of the chapel, who owed him a favour, and that would be that. But the major was another matter. Jay was all for racing tipsters, provided they gave a winner now and again. The trouble was so many of them didn't. But she'd been ready for that, and brought the major's profit and loss account over the jumping season. Even Jay was impressed.

'I'll give him three months' trial,' he said. 'Fifty a week.'

She'd been expecting six weeks at best.

'You must think he's good,' she said at last.

'He's good so long as he does this,' he said, and tapped the sheet of paper, and then: 'He'll need a name, I guess. I don't think he'll want to use his own. Any suggestions?'

'How about "The Major"?' she said.

'Hell why not?' said Jay. 'I like it. You hungry?'

'Ravenous,' she said.

'Then why don't we go out and eat?' said Jay. 'Unless there's somebody else you want me to find a job for.'

They went to the Embassy, so that they could dance as well.

Bob was delighted and grateful, and told her so many times. Indeed his delight was such that she opened champagne, and he was delighted and grateful all over again. No question of pretence, she knew: no hankering after Northern beer behind a feeble, unconvincing smile. This was Bob's first champagne ever and he adored it. The one thing needed to make his happiness complete was to thank Mr Bower in person, it seemed, and she could even do that for him, beneficent fairy godmother that she was. Bower had been asked to dine at the American Embassy and bring a lady, and she was the lady. He called for her in South Terrace, and she introduced him to Bob.

They got on well, which surprised her at first, until she realised that they both had the ability to project a seeming frankness that was in truth not frankness at all, but a mask for a deviousness more appropriate to Bengal, or Kerry perhaps. Each recognised it in the other, and responded to it. Then Hawkins called her to the telephone, which was irritating. She had enjoyed watching them: an immensely tortuous yet hugely enjoyable music-hall turn.

It was Lovell. They still hadn't had their lunch, and even if it sounded a little presumptuous, he would like to arrange a time and place. She hesitated for a moment: Jay's plan held all the excitement and wit imaginable, but there was no written guarantee of success. On the other hand Lovell had not seemed the sort of man to be bothered by either scandal or convention. It would be interesting to find out if she was right, and so they settled on the Ivy in two days' time. Just a week before they sailed, she realised. Her tickets for the *Mauretania* had arrived that morning.

When she got back Jay and Bob had settled whatever it was between them, and Bob was trying to explain the finer points of English soccer to Jay, who wanted to know why it was forbidden to tackle a guy just because he wasn't holding the ball. Each man was as devious as ever, and enjoying himself hugely.

Dinner with the ambassador was dull by comparison, though her diamonds – or rather Jay's – were much admired. When at last they left Grosvenor Square, Redman was still waiting to drive them; so she was to sleep alone, it seemed, and perhaps as well. She was lunching with Mummy the next day.

'You were a big success,' Jay said.

'Your diamonds were.'

'I'm glad,' said Jay. 'That night at the Felston Ball when you didn't wear them – it really bothered me. You know that? But it wasn't the diamonds, it was you.'

'I wonder if it will still be me when our story breaks?'

'Of course it will,' said Jay. He seemed utterly certain. 'It's every woman's dream. A chance to act like a courtesan without having to be one.'

'All those tiresome gymnastics,' she said.

'Is that what you do with me?'

His voice was light, but the vulnerability was there. She knew precisely how to hurt him if the need ever arose. But oh you bitch, she thought, you silly, silly bitch.

'Of course not,' she said. 'But that's for us – for affection. You were talking about courtesans, and what are they after all but very expensive tarts?'

If he didn't mention her diamonds, she was home and dry.

'Oh my God,' he said. 'I'm sorry. I didn't mean – '

She too could be devious, it seemed.

'Of course you didn't mean,' she said. 'Go on about me acting like a courtesan.'

'It'll be a sensation,' he said, then added: 'It'll sell one hell of a lot of newspapers.'

'So you are suggesting that George becomes a kind of tout,' said her mother.

'Exactly,' said Jane. 'But an anonymous tout.'

She took another spoonful of her only just adequate soup. Careful, she admonished herself. Don't muff your lines. The major had met her in Harrods, taken her to tea, discussed his talent for picking winners, and he had told his Honoria, but of course he knew nothing about Jane's plan to utilise his talent.

'Anonymity of course would be an advantage,' said her mother.

'It's absolutely vital,' said Jane. 'Otherwise you would be plagued by all sorts of persons.'

'Very true,' said her mother, and rang the little table bell for the parlourmaid.

After the lamb had been served she said, 'What kind of remuneration is contemplated?'

'Fifty a week,' said Jane, 'for a three-months' trial.'

Her mother looked startled: gratified too.

'Of course,' said Jane, 'if Major Routledge is a success – and I see no reason why he should not be – he could always ask for a little bit more, from time to time.'

'Like Oliver Twist, in fact,' said Lady Whitcomb.

'I hope not, Mummy,' said Jane. 'Oliver Twist was refused, you will recall.'

Over coffee Lady Whitcomb said, 'You seem on good terms with this Mr Bower.'

Careful, Jane told herself. Be very, very careful.

Aloud she said, 'Not really. Bower is a very shrewd and very successful newspaper publisher. His entire life is devoted to selling more newspapers. When it was discovered that I had a talent for journalism – '

'How did that come about?' her mother asked.

'Quite by chance,' said Jane. 'A sort of happy accident.'

'Serendipity,' said her mother, delighted. 'I have always enjoyed that word.'

'He devised this – plot, I suppose you would call it, in which my destiny and Felston's were interlinked. It helped him sell more newspapers, but it was also good for Felston, and so I agreed.'

'And was it good for Jane Whitcomb?'

'Indeed it was. I enjoy what I do, Mummy, and so long as I do it well he will continue to publish me. Because he believes that I have inherited at least some of my mother's intelligence he will also listen to me. When I told him of the major's ability he saw at once that it would help to sell newspapers – and so he made the offer.'

'Suppose George fails?' her mother asked.

'Then he will be got rid of. But I see no reason why he should fail.'

'Can't you? It has perhaps escaped your notice that George is a rather timid person?'

'Of course he is,' said Jane. 'But he has you, Mummy.'

'You are suggesting that I too should become a tout?'

'Not a tout, precisely. No,' said Jane. 'A tout's mate, perhaps.'

This time her mother did not smile. She threw back her head and laughed.

At last she said, 'Why did you do this?'

'Because I couldn't believe that you would be happy in the country, helping the major to breed horses.'

'You are perfectly right,' said her mother, 'but I should have tried. It would have been my duty to do so. Except that – ' she hesitated.

'Yes, Mummy?'

'George did not think he could have made a success of it either, once I had discussed it with him. But he will make an excellent tout, I'm sure of it.'

'The word is tipster, Mummy.'

'Whatever it is,' said Lady Whitcomb, 'we are both most grateful to you.'

Jane tried to say something modest, but her mother motioned her to silence. She was doing sums in her head.

'Fifty a week is two thousand five hundred a year,' she said, 'which is what your father left me. So we can double that and add in George's pension and the money we will get when we rent this place – and you say George can ask for more, later. I shouldn't be suprised if we were worth seven thousand a year quite soon.'

'You think the major will be a success then?' Jane asked.

'I'm quite sure of it,' said her mother.

Bower fired his first salvo in the 'Wicked World' column next day. Jane Whitcomb To Visit America? queried the headline, and the answer could only be yes. Jane Whitcomb was indeed going to visit America, and the good fortune was all America's, for the gracious Miss Whitcomb was taking with her not only her un-rivalled beauty, grace, charm, writing talent and compassion for those less fortunate than herself (try as she might, Jane still found that she winced at that one) she was also to confer with certain heads of the entertainment industry not only in New York, but on the West Coast also, and the West Coast, as devotees of the 'Wicked World' column knew only too well, meant Hollywood.

She poured one last cup of coffee and lit a cigarette, waited for Hawkins to come and clear away. That Hawkins would have a comment she was quite sure. Hawkins might prefer *The Times* these days, but she always looked into the *Daily World*, especially the 'Wicked World' column. But when she appeared, it was Bob that she wanted to talk about.

'Had his breakfast early, miss,' she said. 'Eggs and bacon. Two eggs. Five rashers. *And* a sausage. I toasted half a loaf for him too.'

'Eating well is still a novelty to him. Let him enjoy it. Did he say where he was going?'

'To find a room, miss. He's getting a start next week.'

'So he is. Did he say where he would look?'

'High Holborn, miss.'

'Nice and handy for Fleet Street,' said Jane.

'Yes, miss. I got – I have a sister there, miss. She's a widow. Got a room to let. He's gone to have a look at it.'

'I see,' said Jane.

'She's a respectable woman, my sister,' said Hawkins.

'Well of course she is,' said Jane.

'Lost her husband two years ago,' said Hawkins. 'Lung trouble it was. On account of he was gassed in the war. She gets a pension of course but it isn't all that much. Renting that room'll be a Godsend if Mr Patterson takes it. Not that she can afford to serve him half a pig for his breakfast every morning.'

'Will you miss Mr Patterson?'

'He's good company. He can always make you laugh,' said Hawkins. 'Of course a lot of it's that funny accent of his, but he has his own kind of wit if you follow me, miss.'

'Indeed I do,' said Jane. 'He's very like his brother.'

'I didn't mean to be personal, miss,' said Hawkins.

'Oh we are touchy this morning,' said Jane. 'You read about Captain Patterson in the *Daily World* half a dozen times at least.'

'Yes, miss,' said Hawkins. 'But Bob – *this* Mr Patterson – he's not an officer, miss. He's got his way to make in the world. Just like me.'

'And do you think he will?'

'Oh yes, miss,' said Hawkins. 'I mean just look how he got here. Turning up on your doorstep more like a drowned rat than a human being – and inside a week he's got a thumping good job. I only hope my sister can cope, that's all.'

'I'm sure she will,' said Jane, smiling, 'if she's anything like you.'

Hawkins chuckled. 'She can look after herself all right,' she said. 'Well you have to if you're a widow renting a room in Holborn.'

There was a dress she very much wanted to wear for her lunch at the Ivy, a sequinned georgette dress by Chanel in the palest possible blue, with a top that tied to the dress in a bow, and a hat that wasn't for once the inevitable cloche, but a Gaby Moro masterpiece that was brave enough to sport a brim, and no jewellery at all except a thin gold necklace. No diamonds, and certainly no coloured stones. The trouble was the shoes. Satin with ankle straps was the only possible answer, and the snow outside was still thick and frozen hard. It would have to be Russian boots and change when she got to the restaurant, she thought. Only when she was inside the Rolls-Royce and huddled into her sables did it occur to her that this was going to a very great deal of trouble to take lunch with a man who might and only might be good for a twenty quid subscription for Felston. But by then it was too late to start examining motives.

At least he appreciated the dress, and very right that he should, she thought. Even in the Ivy that dress was really something special. He had read the piece in the 'Wicked World' column, and that too was gratifying, as was the fact that he didn't want her to go to America, though he did his best to hide it. He was also dying to know why she was going to Hollywood, and Jane found that she was dying to tell him, only she couldn't: not without ruining Jay's oh-so-carefully contrived effect. Not the best atmosphere for a companionable lunch. And yet it was companionable at first.

Perhaps she had Canon Messeter to thank for that. Lovell had said he wished to know about Felston, and the canon was his only link with the place. He shook his head in wonder as Jane told him about Messeter's work as hospital chaplain, ambulance driver, orderly.

'St Paul on the road to Damascus was nothing to this,' he said at last. 'And did you really drive that damn great Armstrong-Siddeley?'

'When I had to,' she said. 'Don't for heaven's sake think I enjoyed it.' And then: 'Tell me about yourself.'

'There isn't an awful lot to tell,' he said.

'Gentlemanly modesty? The reticence of the sahib? The Balliol cult of effortless superiority?'

'I was at Magdalen,' he said. 'In my day we were effortless –

in the literal sense – to the point of inertia, but I'm damned if we were superior.'

'You were in the army.'

'So was everybody else. The Lovells have only two talents – for being rich, and for staying out of the public eye. They made a lot of money in the eighteenth century, and have hung on to it ever since. It's mostly in banking now – and land. I have a place in Sussex – and I rent another in Northumberland – for the shooting, you know. And a little box of a place in Leicestershire.'

'For the hunting?'

'Precisely.' He was perfectly aware of the irony in her voice. 'And that is how I fill my days. Shooting game birds, chasing foxes, counting dividends. This last is not a gentleman's business, but it's what we Lovells do because we have a talent for it. Maybe that's why we have always refused a peerage.'

'Always?'

'You are right to rebuke pretension,' he said. 'We have declined a peerage on both the occasions when one was offered.'

'Do you know Sir Hugh Lessing?'

'Quite well,' said Lovell. 'We are friends for the most part. Rivals occasionally.'

'He was in the Artists' Rifles.'

'He's a much better banker than he was a soldier. Will you take dessert?'

'Apple tart,' she said.

'With Calvados if I may suggest it,' said Lovell. 'This kind of weather rather justifies it.' And when she had finished it he asked, 'Do you plan to stay in Hollywood for long?'

Oh clever you, she thought. First you ply a girl with spirits, *then* you ask her questions. Every barrister in England would jump at the chance.

'It depends on circumstances,' she said. 'Believe me I know how feeble that must sound, but this time it's true.'

'I've been invited to visit Los Angeles,' he said. 'We have investments there. What they call real estate. If you're there for any length of time then I shall go.'

'And if I'm there only briefly?'

'Then I shan't.'

'Goodness,' said Jane. 'You really are the head of the firm.'

'Yes.'

The monosyllable was pleasantly spoken, and utterly assured.

'There is always one,' said Lovell, 'in every generation. For the moment it's me – or is it I? I never remember.'

'"It is I" is correct,' said Jane, 'but rather pompous.' Suddenly and without warning, the Calvados struck. 'You should marry, you know. Think dynastically.'

'I am married,' said Lovell.

She suddenly felt very foolish. 'Nobody told me,' she said.

'Not many of my friends know,' he said. 'Keith Watson certainly doesn't. My family knows of course, but not my friends.'

'Whyever not?'

'She's mad, I'm afraid,' said Lovell. 'Has been since 1913. She's been in a place in Switzerland ever since. Not exactly what I wanted to tell you – but how could I not tell you?'

Oh no you don't, thought Jane. Not yet. Perhaps not ever, but certainly not yet.

'What's wrong with her?' she asked.

'They don't know,' said Lovell. 'Twelve solid years – and they don't know. She won't tell them, you see.'

'Tell them what's wrong?'

'Tell them anything,' said Lovell. 'She simply refuses to com̲municate. I. tried. The doctors have tried. It isn't any use. The specialists seem to think that life simply became too much for her – and so she left it as best she could without actually dying.'

'And this was before the war?'

'1913,' he said. 'I told you, and I know what you're thinking. So many of us went mad because we were in it – but even more of us didn't. Keith. . . . You. . . . Me. . . . But for Anthea it wasn't like that at all. She was doomed from birth, you see. Ypres Salient or a hunt ball; it wouldn't have made the least difference. She was doomed, it seems.'

'How awfully sad.'

'For her parents while they lived, certainly. For me, to this very day. For her – it's impossible to tell. She smiles a lot. She has a very beautiful smile.'

'I don't think you should tell me any more of this,' said Jane.

'I wish you would explain to me why.'

'You've known Keith and Harriet for years and they aren't even aware that you're married – and yet you tell me at our second meeting.'

'Ruthlessness,' said Jane. 'The utter certainty of the rightness of one's cause. It sounds more like religion than politics.'

'That isn't the way my Stan worships,' Grandma said.

'This has nothing to do with Stan.'

'Well of course not.' The old woman paused for a moment. 'It's begun already. . . . Gossip. Sniggering. Dirty talk. Only they call it "seeking after truth" and "no smoke without fire".'

'Who do?'

'The ones that's doing it. You've a good body on you, they tell me.'

'Not bad,' said Jane, 'considering how little exercise I take.'

The old woman chuckled. 'Good lass,' she said. 'You'll fight them?'

'Well of course,' said Jane. 'I'm told I'll beat them.'

'You must,' said Grandma. 'Only the folks that live here could think Felston can manage without you.'

'It's lies, you know,' said Jane.

'Well of course it is,' said Grandma. 'Anybody that spent ten minutes with you knows that. Anybody with any sense that is.' And then: 'We're a bit short of people with sense up here. Maybe sense is something you get when you eat properly.'

'Does Bet believe it?'

'Not to say believe,' Grandma said. 'More like interested. What's the word? Fascinated. She'd have more sense if she was married.'

In this, as in every other field, doing, for Grandma, was infinitely more important than talking.

'I'm going back into hospital soon,' the old woman said. 'They reckon the other eye's about ready. I'll be glad to get away from here. . . . Dear God.'

'Grandma,' said Jane, 'what's wrong?'

'To think the day would come when I'd be glad to go to hospital. . . . You sure you can get out of this?'

'I must,' said Jane. 'I have a piece of good news for you.'

'I could do with it.'

'I raised another hundred pounds for Felston yesterday. I wore my prettiest dress and flirted and smiled and said "thank you" ever so prettily while he wrote it out and signed. But that's all I did, Grandma. And it was for Felston. Not for me.'

'A lot of silly cats,' said Grandma. 'Just wait till I get my strength back.'

Somehow Jane knew that Bella Docherty was one of them.

'I'll be in America by then,' she said.

'So you will. But you'll come back to us, won't you?'

'Well of course,' said Jane.

'Word of honour?'

'Cross my heart,' said Jane, 'and hope to die.'

'That's all right then,' said Grandma, and hung up.

Jane looked at her watch. There was still time to phone Medlicott and tell him to take care of Grandma's hospital bills, and then go back to her brooding about Charles Lovell.

This time it had been she who had lost her temper, and for very much the same reason: because Lovell had a wife who somehow had managed to insinuate herself into the restaurant, silent and smiling beautifully. Now simply wasn't the time to go into all that. There was simply too much happening. That morning Bower had struck again. 'Cleopatra – the truth' – the 'Wicked World' column had trumpeted. 'Jane Whitcomb to consult with world-famous experts to learn the facts about Egypt's Queen of Beauty on the eve of her departure for Hollywood.' And so on and on and on and on.

The *Mauretania* was incredible. Every bit as vast as she had expected, and with a certain elegance despite its old-fashioned Edwardian solidity. Her state room – was it? in a hotel it would have been a suite – contained every possible comfort, including a writing desk, so that she embarked almost at once on a letter that was almost a journal – events, thoughts, imaginings all written down just as they occurred to her. But there was nothing intimate of course, or even personal. No mention of that well-groomed Rochester who had converted Switzerland into an attic for his wife to rave in. How could there be, when she avoided thinking about him? But there was nothing about her own problem either, at least not directly. Grandma's eyes might not be well enough to read by the time the letter reached her, and if someone else read it to her there would be no secret. Still, there were ways. Bower's success was living proof that there were always ways.

I had a very nice lunch with a gentleman from Oxford, a professor no less, who told me all about Cleopatra – or as much as he could during one lunch. It seems that she was much more than a mere beauty, if indeed any woman can be called mere, who lolled about in flimsy skirts. (Though as the professor said, why wouldn't her skirts be flimsy? Egypt is a *very* hot country and there is simply no demand for tweed.)

However, she was also a very clever woman, and a very patriotic one, not at all keen on seeing her countrymen exploited by the Romans, and determined to do her best for them. I won't go on about it now, but I hope to have more news about C. when I get to Hollywood.

She crossed out the word Hollywood, making sure that it was still legible, and inserted the words Los Angeles. Just the sort of thing Jay Bower enjoyed. She found that she enjoyed it too, and was quite sure that Grandma would.

The rest of the voyage appeared to be vast meals – incredible menus for lunch and dinner, and even breakfast, cocktail parties with canapés, and beef tea served on the sunny side of the deck where one reclined on a folding chair after being tucked up in a steamer rug. In between the feasts there were deck tennis and dancing and bridge and parties, official and unofficial. There was even a palm court where a trio played the kind of music Miss Gwatkin liked so much. Even Amy Woodford Findon.

She was lucky. The Atlantic Ocean, for January, was calm, far calmer than the North Sea had been for Bob. By avoiding every second course on the menu and not eating at all at parties, she managed well enough, despite the huge ship's hurtling speed. Jay of course was fine, circling the promenade deck lap after lap, winning at bridge, sweating in the Turkish bath: treating the ship like a huge toy specially chosen for him alone – and yet delighting in sharing it.

They slept apart. The stewards were far too zealous and Jane was by no means sure that her tummy would stand the strain of the gymnastics involved. There was also the problem of Georgina – and of Charles Lovell, come to that, neither of which she looked like resolving, and certainly not by discussing them with Jay. But they danced a lot, and drank a lot at parties and enjoyed it all, even the fancy dress ball, for which, forewarned by Jay, she wore her sari again, successfully enough to be awarded a prize. But then so many people were awarded prizes.

'The closer we get to New York,' she wrote to Grandma, 'the more the Americans drink. But it isn't because they think their country's awful – on the contrary. It's because they have this thing called Prohibition in America, which means that the sale of alcoholic drinks is forbidden from one end of the country to the other. Poor darlings, what do they do when they want to celebrate? . . .' Jay had told her that after Prohibition came in the American people had done nothing *but* celebrate. She decided to save that till she'd seen for herself, and told Grandma about the fancy dress ball and the sari – 'another flimsy skirt. Bare midriff too. But it can't be too naughty. Scores of millions of women wear them every day.' She considered telling how they dined, because of Jay's eminence, at the captain's table, if only because it would annoy Andy, but decided against it. They were fighting a war, not a vendetta.

At last Jay spotted what to him was a very familiar smudge on the skyline, and he dragged her up on to the deck, swathed in furs, to watch New York slowly, inevitably emerge. A cold day, much, much colder than London, and for the time being no snow, but a sun that looked small and clear and almost white, and coloured the city like no other city she had ever seen. And such a city. Towers that soared like arrows, that statue on the island that she was quite sure would be a cliché until at last she saw it, and everywhere people, working, talking, shouting, ants in an ant hill that soared to the sky. And the cars and lorries: automobiles and trucks, Jay said she must call them. And why not? It was his city after all.

Porters came aboard, some of them black men; the first negroes she had ever seen outside a circus, and not at all like Indians, not even Tamils, though Tamils were often far blacker than some of those she saw. And then it was time to tip her steward, and the stewardess who had acted as her maid, and venture into the enormous customs shed, and be confronted by some of the rudest men she had ever met in her life: customs and immigration officials. Prohibition would have no terrors for them, she thought. They were drunk with power from the moment they put on their uniforms.

Then Jay came to collect her, and two very Irish-seeming men with a trolley piled their suitcases on to it, and followed them out to where a line of cars stood waiting, and headed at once for the biggest one, a car that was quite enormous, far, far bigger than the Hilyards' Bentley. Outside it a waiting chauffeur, boots polished, every button gleaming, snapped to attention and saluted as soon as he saw Jay.

'Herr Joachim,' he said, and the rest made no sense at all. He spoke in German, and in German Jay replied, and called him Karl. The two Irish-seeming men looked on as if they were watching a movie that might turn out to be rather good.

'I never heard a chauffeur talk foreign before,' said one.

'He's never a chauffeur,' said the other. 'He's an admiral.' He thought for a moment then added, 'At least.' The chauffeur called them to him, and they began to load trunks and bags into the enormous boot.

'What a huge motor car,' said Jane.

'It's a Cadillac sedan de ville,' Jay said. 'Belongs to my father. I said he should get a Bugatti for a change, but he doesn't like Italians. Says they're all gangsters – even the accountants.'

'Do all your servants speak German?'

'Yes,' said Jay. He hesitated, then added: 'He doesn't even spell his name the same way I do. He and Mom are a little set in their ways.'

'But they do understand that you and I are just good friends?'

'They don't understand how good.'

'No jokes,' said Jane. 'Not now. I'm serious.'

'They know that you're a colleague,' said Jay, 'as well as the daughter of a distinguished man, and a distinguished person in your own right.'

'You're very good,' she said.

'No I'm not.' The words came quickly: almost angrily. 'I told them these things because I believed them to be true.'

Karl appeared once more, and spoke in German, and they got into the Cadillac. On impulse Jay picked up the speaking tube and gave instructions.

'I told him to drive us around for a while,' he said. 'Give you a chance to get used to the city.'

The Cadillac moved off: a softer, more yielding ride than a Rolls-Royce, but even so the power was there.

The city would certainly take some getting used to, even the cramped, restricted city which was the only one Jay thought important: the city of Manhattan. Cars everywhere, people everywhere: policemen bundled up like bears, women in fur coats. Men, too. Buildings that grew higher and higher, the more one drove. In Wall Street (where Jay told her that money was invested and reinvested, but never actually spent) the buildings pushed so high that from inside the car she could see no sky. But in Central Park the view seemed to stretch forever, the sky was limitless, and the skaters swirled on the lake in a cold that seemed unending. But not in the Cadillac. In the Cadillac she perspired with the heat, and loosened her furs. Jay spoke again into the tube, and the car set off into the city, down another long driveway, as straight as anything the Romans made, then turned and turned again into somewhere called 8th Avenue, and suddenly the light was dimmed from above. She looked up, and a train swooped above her in a great arc, swerving like a fairground switchback into somewhere called 53rd Street.

Jay chuckled. 'The El,' he said. 'The Elevated Railroad.'

'No Underground?'

'Oh sure,' he said. 'But we call it the subway.'

The car slowed, and from its window Jane could see an ugly box of a building: dirty red brick six storeys high, with a zig-zag fire escape down its centre. Jay followed her gaze.

'Tenement,' he told her. 'Walk-up. That's about as far down as you can get unless you sleep on the street, and if you try that at this time of year you die.'

'But it's so close – ' she said, and he knew what she meant. To Madison Avenue, and 5th, and Park, and the rich hotels and theatres and shops.

'We're different,' he said. 'You see that now. It's like our elevators compared with yours. With us up and down is a hell of a lot faster.'

The great car moved on, heading northwards, and at last even New York came to an end, and all she could see was farm land under snow.

'Where now?' she said.

'My parents' place. I told you.'

'Yes, but where?'

'Connecticut,' he said. 'Near New Haven.'

'Difficult to say and impossible to spell. Like Massachusetts. New Haven is a good place to live, I take it.'

'It's the best.' He sounded amused, she thought, but he also sounded surprised that she had asked.

'Tell me about it,' she said. 'Tell me about *them*.'

'Well,' he said. 'They're rich. You're probably thinking that's a banal thing to say – but just give me a minute. They've always been rich, that's the point. My grandfather was rich back in Düsseldorf, Germany, and the only reason he came to the United States was he wanted to be richer.'

'What did he do?'

'He was a banker. He came here in the Eighties and brought my father with him. He got in on the grain boom, then went on into oil along with Mellon and Rockefeller and a whole lot more. He was rich and he got very rich. And powerful.'

'Like a maharajah,' she said. 'If you're so rich you have power whether you want it or not.' And you always win your cricket matches, she thought.

'Like the king of a small country. Right. And maybe not all that small. . . . He liked me. Hell, he must have done.'

'Why is that?'

'When I was twenty-one I told him I wanted to be a journalist – and he let me – and made my father let me. In spite of the fact that I was supposed to be a banker, like everybody else. Then when I made a success of it – ' he turned to her. 'I did, you know. Make a success of it. I was good.'

'Well of course,' she said. 'I've watched you. You taught me.'

'When I proved myself – when I was twenty-five, he bought a newspaper and made me editor in chief. And when I was twenty-eight – ' Again he hesitated. There were some things that were too much, even for Jay.

'Go on,' she said.

'I *made* that paper,' Jay said. 'Doubled its circulation – but I didn't *own* it. So on my twenty-eighth birthday he gave me a million dollars and told me to buy one of my own. Only the war came and I went off as a war correspondent instead. He loved the United States but it seemed he still loved Germany too, and when they went to war with each other – it killed him. Heart failure they called it. He had a heart like a lion. He died of grief.'

So much poetry from one so prosaic, she thought. And yet it hadn't sounded like a lament for a million-dollar donor.

It began to snow. . . . The house was called the Towers, and there were plenty of them, from attenuated pepper pots to a sullen great brute by the stables that would have heartened Sigmund Freud, if she had understood Lionel correctly. A damn great schloss of a place, as German as the Brothers Grimm, especially in the middle of a snow storm. And vast. Really quite enormous. It would take an army to run a place that size, but then the Germans were rather good at armies. . . . Now now, she admonished herself. At least wait till you've met them.

Jay took her by the arm and led her inside, into a vast hall two storeys high, and everywhere one looked, antlers and stags' heads and black oak furniture, and a vast open fire that seemed to be burning an entire orchard, so that the room smelt of apples. But it wasn't the fire that made the room so warm. Double windows, she thought, and steam radiators, then loosened her coat, and at once a maid-servant appeared to take it from her, as Jay was confronted by a – butler, would one call him? in frock coat and stiff collar and a cravat instead of a tie: like an ambassador in a musical comedy, she thought, all foreign accent and mispronunciation before the chorus tripped on in bathing suits to sing about the delights of Deauville; except that this one didn't speak with a foreign accent, he spoke German, and in German Jay replied, before taking Jane's arm and following the butler to a flight of stairs, and on into a drawing room where three women and two men drank coffee and ate cake. Jay's parents, she decided at once, and three others. Both his father and mother were stout – the cakes they were eating were oozing cream – but otherwise he resembled both of them. Perhaps they were related as well as married? Of the rest, both the women looked like Jay, and the young man looked vaguely and tantalisingly familiar. And then she remembered.

Jay was saying, 'Jane my dear, I should like you to meet my mother and father.'

She went forward at once, and held out her hand. There could be no compromise on this. 'How do you do?' she said to Mrs Bauer.

'So nice to meet you, my dear.' A voice at once pleasant,

cultured, and American. No hint of Teutonic overtones. She turned to the man.

'Mr Bauer?' she said, and offered her hand once more.

'How do you do?' said Bauer, in a voice very like his son's, then added: 'You don't speak German?'

'I'm afraid not,' said Jane. 'I can manage a little French.' Or Urdu, she thought, or Hindi. Gujarati at a pinch.

'No, no,' said the elder Bauer. 'We will continue in English. German is for the game we play. The nostalgia game.'

'Nostalgia?'

'We pretend we are there,' said Bauer. 'In the Black Forest maybe and it is all as it was. German servants, German food, German wine.'

'As it was?' Jane asked.

'In the game,' said Mrs Bauer, 'the year is always 1911, and nobody knows that the war will ever begin. Would you like some coffee?'

'Oh yes please,' said Jane, and the butler wheeled over a trolley. Jane took coffee only, but Jay allowed his plate to be filled. As he did so, his father said, 'May I present my daughters? This is Erika, who stays here with us to help her mama to run this place – and this is Louisa, who is married to Joe here. Joe Ballantyne.' More handshakes, and the chance at last to drink her coffee.

'We haven't met,' said Ballantyne, 'but I believe you're acquainted with my sister and brother-in-law, Florence and Billy Powell? In Paris?'

'We did bump into each other,' said Jane. 'Quite briefly.'

'That's what most people say,' said Ballantyne.

'Joe!' His wife sounded stern, but sympathetic too. 'It's not your fault, Joe. It could have happened to anyone.'

'Yeah,' said Joe. 'But it happened to me.' He turned to Jay Bower, and began to ask questions about the London stock market.

Erika said, 'You work for my brother, Miss Whitcomb?'

'I write articles for him from time to time,' said Jane, 'for which of course he pays me, but I doubt whether either of us would call that working for him.'

Jay interrupted to say 'Certainly not', then at once went back to discussing the impending British miners' strike and its probable effect on British steel shares.

'Just as well I should think,' said Erika. 'I don't think my brother would be all that great to work for.'

'Yes and no,' said Jane. 'He's a bully of course, but he does make things happen, and he turns out a wonderful paper, even if I do write for it myself.'

'You are a writer, Miss Whitcomb?' Louisa Ballantyne asked.

'A journalist, anyway.'

'And is that a rewarding thing to be?' Jay's mother asked.

'In money terms barely adequate – but it's exciting, and it has its own sense of achievement.'

'And these things are important to you?' Jay's father asked.

'I think so.'

'You don't sound very sure,' Jay's father said.

'She should be.' Ballantyne, bored with the future prospects of gilt-edged, plunged in with relish. 'Miss Whitcomb drove an ambulance in the war and got herself blown up, just like brother Billy.'

The elder Bauer acquired a sort of glazed look: the two sisters looked appalled. Joe Ballantyne had broken the first and great commandment: Thou shalt not talk about the war.

'Oh that was all ages ago,' Jane said. 'Ages and ages.' She looked about her. 'What an incredible room this is.'

And indeed it was, with its overwhelming furniture, and tapestries that looked and probably were medieval, and a chiming clock like a miniature fortress, that looked as if it could only be wound by direct assault.

'It is what we like,' said the elder Bauer.

'Of course,' said Jane.

'It is – conservative. I use the word in the sense of traditional. It is what my father liked, and so we keep it as it was, to honour his memory.'

'Your son has told me a little about him,' said Jane. 'He appears to have been a remarkable man.'

'Very remarkable,' said the elder Bauer. 'Everything he did was on the grandest scale. Even his mistakes were vast.' He did not look at his son, but Jane was in no doubt that it was Jay for whom the words were meant. He spoke in German, but his father said at once, and in English, 'No, no. You must not be impolite to our guest.'

This to the man who was impolite to everybody. But this time it was meant to wound, and did.

'Perhaps you would like Erika to show you over the house?' said Mrs Bauer. 'I don't know whether that is the English custom?'

'Sometimes,' said Jane. 'I should like it very much.'

Erika rose at once, to conduct her through what was like nothing so much as a very well-maintained series of museums: the library a museum of books, the music room a museum of instruments, the dining room a museum of furniture: each selection the very best, the most expensive of its kind. She was a good guide, the younger Miss Bauer, knowledgeable and fluent, if not particularly enthusiastic. And not particularly young, either, thought Jane. Pushing thirty rather hard. Soon she'll be middle-aged like me. She examined a wheel-lock musket, hung, for no reason that she could discover, in the morning room.

'Made for the Duke of Bavaria in 1618, the lock plate chiselled with a bear hunt.' Erika rattled it off. 'The stock inlaid with flowers and leaves in white stag horn.' She paused – for breath.

'What did your brother say to your father?' Jane asked.

'The stock is signed by Hieronymus Borstorffer,' said Erika, and then: 'I don't think you should ask me that.'

'Was it so very dreadful?'

'Heck no,' said Erika Bauer. 'It wasn't dreadful at all. One point three million is what he said. I guess they were talking about money. This family often does. You saw for yourself. Joe Ballantyne. He couldn't wait.'

'In a way they were talking about money,' said Jane. 'One point three million is the latest circulation figure of the *Daily World*.'

'Sounds a lot.'

'It is a lot.'

'My God,' said Erika. 'That means that everything you write is read by one million three hundred thousand people.'

'More like four million,' said Jane. 'They reckon that for every one who buys a newspaper, two more people read it.'

'My God,' said Erika again, and then: 'How I envy you.'

Suddenly the plain face became attractive; a transformation brought about by nothing more than animation.

'I've been lucky, I suppose,' said Jane.

'You certainly have,' said Erika. 'You wear pretty clothes, too.'

Well I'm damned if I'm going to apologise for it, thought Jane.

'Paris mostly,' she said at last. 'One has to be careful in one's choosing. That's the trick. Not to let the designer bully you.'

'I've never been to Paris.'

Oh God, thought Jane. Does she want me to apologise for that, too?

'It's much, much easier for me,' she said. 'Living in London.'

'Father still wouldn't let me go.'

There was nothing to be said, and so she said nothing.

'I know what you're thinking,' Erika said at last. 'I'm a grown woman. My life is my own. Well maybe it is – but my money isn't. It's all tied up with father's. I can't even get a couple of dollars for a book unless I ask.'

Still there was nothing to be said, and yet this time she had to say something.

'Couldn't you visit your brother?'

'I couldn't visit Joachim if he lived in the next house down the road,' said Erika.

'Whyever not?'

'Because my father hates him. You see that little Madonna next to the gun? It's from Augsburg. Father's experts say it dates to around 1519. It's probably by Hans Holbein the Younger and if it is it'll be worth a lot more money than if it isn't. But nobody can say for sure.' The last statement seemed to please her greatly.

'How much longer do you intend to keep me here?' Jane asked.

They were in the conservatory, the only place that Erika had not shown her, perhaps because it contained no tapestries or arquebuses or Meissen china, though the plants too looked expensive – and nasty too, quite often.

'It was a mistake,' said Jay, 'and I apologise for it, but my mother went on and on about it – and if I didn't bring you here, people might get the wrong idea.'

'Your people, you mean?'

'Not just them.' He took her arm and turned her to face him. 'Our relationship's important to me,' he said. 'I wish it was even more important. – But I don't want gossip about you. And if I was seen with you in New York without coming home first – oh boy would there be gossip.'

'I'm obliged to you,' she said. 'I mean that. After all I've seen your father in action. This can't have been easy for you.'

'It wasn't meant to be.' Jay stared moodily at an orchid, as well he might, she thought. It looked like decaying flesh.

'I'm not a banker,' he said at last. 'I make a hell of a lot of money, but I'm not a banker. When father goes there won't be a Bauer to take over.'

'What about Ballantyne? Couldn't he change his name?'

'He's in wood pulp,' said Jay. 'That's where his business mixes with mine – and Florence Powell's. He's OK I guess – but he'll never make a king. Not even a crown prince.'

'There's only Erika left,' said Jane. 'She'll have to marry.'

'She nearly did, once,' said Bower. 'Second gardener. Good-looking lad from Saxony. Very fair. Father fired him. I don't think he minded all that much – father also slipped him a thousand bucks. The price of a farm – but Erika did.'

'I want to go away from here,' said Jane.

'Two more days,' said Jay. 'That's the minimum sentence. In this place they never even heard of remission.'

46

Two days later she and Jay left in the Cadillac for New York. Bauer senior was attending a meeting in the library, and his wife had a migraine, but Louisa and Joe Ballantyne joined her for breakfast, and told her how very much they had enjoyed Jay's account of her rudeness to Billy Powell in Paris. Verbal rudeness only, she gathered. Assault with a deadly hand mirror was still a secret.

'It was a pleasure,' she told them, and they begged her to come and dine with them, any time, at least any time except the immediate present. There was trouble at a saw mill across the border in Canada, and Joe simply had to go up there and put it right.

She was going to an apartment instead of a hotel. It had been Jay's idea, and she thought it a good one. An apartment rented by the week for a two-week minimum: small and expensive, but on Park Avenue, and with a couple of servants included.

'And where will you be?'

'Near,' said Jay. 'But not too near.'

She waited for him to move closer at that, but instead he nodded towards the front of the car. Karl's duties, it seemed, included spying on the young master.

'Il parle français, le conducteur?' she asked.

'Pas de tout,' said Bower.

They talked in French all the way to New York.

Jay, it seemed, had meetings there: with banks, with investment companies, with brokers and finance houses; because whatever his father thought of the way that Jay chose to run his life, his grandfather had thought highly enough of him to make it difficult, maybe even impossible, for his father to administer the Bauer millions without his son's active participation. Jane was delighted to hear it, even though it meant that Jay would not be free to show her New York.

'Still you'll be comfortable,' Jay said. 'That apartment's really good, and the servants – ' He paused, suddenly.

'What's wrong with them?'

'Nothing,' said Jay. 'They're as good as our own. I really mean that. Only – '

'Only what?' said Jane.

'They're black,' said Jay. 'I forgot to ask you. Does it bother you?'

'My dear Jay,' she said, 'I never even knew white servants existed until I came to England. But who's going to show me New York?'

'All taken care of,' said Jay. 'I've talked to Barry Golding.'

'Who's Barry Golding?'

Jay chuckled. 'Don't ever let him know you said that,' he said. 'Barry Golding, my dear, is New York's answer to Lionel Warley.' He reached into an inside pocket, and pulled out a sheet of paper. 'I almost forgot,' he said. 'This came this morning.'

She found that she was holding by far the longest telegram she had ever seen, and that quite a lot of it was about her. The 'Wicked World' column once more. 'Will Jane Whitcomb accept the challenge?' it demanded. 'Will the glamorous and intrepid champion of the unfortunate succumb to Hollywood's pleadings and take on the rôle of CLEOPATRA, sultry temptress, serpent of Old Nile?' For it was no longer a secret that Miss Whitcomb had already tested for the part in Paris, where she had worn a costume perhaps a little startling in its brevity, but *absolutely correct* in historical detail.

'Was it?' she asked, intrigued.

'You'd better ask Mutrie's,' said Jay. She read on.

Cleopatra, Jane read, had been famed as much for her patriotic fervour and steely dedication to duty as her gorgeous looks, which was yet another reason why Jane Whitcomb . . . etc., etc. It went without saying that every penny she earned would be donated to her favourite charity, the people of Felston. But there was inevitably a price to pay. If Miss Whitcomb were to dedicate herself to this – and perhaps other – rôles for Felston's sake, then Hollywood would claim her for years and years. Perhaps for ever. She handed back the Western Union sheet.

'You're taking the devil of a risk,' she said.

'How so?'

'Suppose they – what's the word they use? – suppose they call me? Give me a test? Have you any idea how badly I can act?'

'What difference does it make?' he said. 'I own the studio. At least grandfather's trust owns a lot of the bank that owns fifty-one per cent of the studio's shares.'

The 'small apartment' had no more than five rooms, including a master bedroom with a shower en suite. Jay's memory really was remarkable. The two servants were a woman cook, and her husband who served as butler. They seemed clean and capable, and Jay left her with them after seeing her in. He would be back soon, he said, with Barry Golding, then went to check that the apartment's drawing room contained a piano before he left. Jane went to confront her entourage.

'Mr Bower was in such a hurry,' she said, 'that he forgot to tell me your names.'

'I'm George, Miss Whitcomb,' said the butler, 'and my wife is Martha.'

Jane blinked. 'You must forgive me,' she said. 'I'm English and perhaps not as well aware as I should be about your country's history, but George and Martha – surely there's a reference there.'

'The first president of the United States was George Washington,' said the butler.

'And his wife's name was Martha,' said his wife.

'Is this something that was forced upon you?' Jane asked.

'Oh no, miss,' said Martha. 'It just sort of happened.'

Serendipity, thought Jane. Mummy's favourite word.

'So you don't mind?'

'Not at all, Miss Whitcomb,' the butler said. 'For good or ill, most people tend to remember our names.'

'I should think they would,' said Jane. 'Now I must go and unpack. Mr Bower will be back soon.' She hesitated. 'I have a feeling that there ought to be cocktails.'

'Yes, miss?' George said this as if he were absolutely certain that there ought to be cocktails.

'What I mean,' said Jane desperately, 'is where do I go to buy the gin?'

'Some blue-jewelled individual in a white fedora with a dubious bottle wrapped in a New York *Daily Mirror*,' said Barry, who had turned out to be a smaller, younger version of Lionel Warley. Jay had told her that he played the piano rather well.

'What did George do?' Jay asked. 'Laugh?'

'Certainly not,' said Jane. 'George is a butler and a gentleman. But a man more obviously not laughing I never saw in my life.'

'What *did* he do?' Jay asked.

'Showed me the drinks cupboard,' said Jane. 'What he called the cellarette. Four kinds of whisky, three kinds of gin, cognac, Calvados, every liqueur I ever heard of.'

'What did you expect?' said Jay.

'She expected to be shown the bathroom,' said Barry Golding. 'Because that's the place where we're supposed to make the gin.'

'*What?*' said Jay. He not only sounded surprised: he sounded outraged, too.

'Well, of course,' said Jane. 'Isn't it all supposed to be illegal?'

George came in with a shakerful of martinis, and Jane discovered the importance of ice, and exact proportions in the blending.

'Delicious,' she said to George, and continued, 'But it's all illegal, surely? As illegal as morphine or cocaine? Of *course* I expected a blue-jewelled gangster.'

'Al Capone's in Chicago,' said Jay.

'And of course they do tend towards a certain lack of polish in Chicago,' said Barry. 'Though he did begin his career in New York, one must admit.'

'So you do use gangsters here?' said Jane.

'*We* don't,' said Barry, 'but a lot of people are obliged to, poor dears.'

'And go blind? And die of alcoholic poisoning?'

'It rather depends on one's supplier,' said Barry. 'The worst thing that most of them can do is give you the most ghastly hangover. Could I have another one of these before I play?'

So he not only expects to play, he insists on it, thought Jane.

All the same he is rather sweet. . . . George replenished his glass.

'Do you like your apartment?' Jay asked.

'Yes,' she said.

'You seem a little blue.'

'I'm missing Foch,' she said, and then to Barry: 'Foch is my dog. He's a Scots terrier.'

'With a prodigious appetite for the fleshpots,' said Jay. 'In his canting, Calvinistic way.'

'We Americans are often like that,' said Barry. 'Disapproving and desirous at the same time. Booze may be sinful, but we couldn't possibly be expected to do without it – so we make it squalid, and then it's all right.'

'You wouldn't care to do me a piece on that?' Jay asked.

'I'd much sooner play the piano.'

He took his glass and went over to it, picking out chords at first, selecting and choosing as a woman might select and choose a hat.

Jay said, 'I got your picture.'

'Which one?' She was listening to Barry play a tune at last, 'What'll I Do?' He played it very well.

'Cleopatra,' he said. 'Want to see it?'

'I suppose so.'

He took a photograph from an inside pocket and handed it to her, and there she was sprawled out on a scratchy tigerskin and leaving little to the imagination.

'I must say,' she said, 'I don't look too bad, considering my age and the amount I eat.'

'It doesn't bother you?'

'It'll bother some people I love,' she said. 'Mostly older ladies like my mother and possibly Grandma and Lady Mangan.' She thought of Bet. 'It may bother some young ones, too. But there's not a great deal I can do about it except to say that I did it all for art, just as you suggest. Burrowes really is a swine, isn't he? But one day I'll catch up with him. You'll see.'

The melody had changed to something she hadn't heard before. Very softly Barry was singing

> I'm just a little boy who's lost in the wood
> I wish I could always be good

With one who'd watch over me. . . .

to a melody as delicate as gossamer. Jay tried to speak and she motioned him to silence. Barry sang on.

Won't you tell her please to put on some speed,
Hear when I plead. Oh how I need
Someone to watch over me.

The music died at last.

'Who wrote that?' she asked.

'Gershwin,' said Barry. 'Who else?'

She reached for her handkerchief. Gershwin and martinis were a lethal combination.

'He told me once,' said Barry, 'that he wrote his music for young girls sitting on fire escapes on hot summer nights in New York and dreaming of love.'

'He did,' said Jane. 'Oh dear God he did. Come and look at my naughty picture before I burst into tears.'

Barry came and looked. 'My,' he said. 'Are you going to work for Mr Ziegfeld?' and then, answering his own question: 'Well of course not. He couldn't afford you. You look good, Jane.'

'Thank you so much,' she said.

'Now,' said Barry, 'I guess we ought to get started. We have at least three parties to go to, and then dinner and Jack and Charlie's and the Stork Club.'

'Goodness,' said Jane. 'How many days will that take?'

Jay said, 'That's it?' Barry turned to him, eyebrows lifted. 'Jane's picture,' Jay explained. 'You look good, Jane. Let's go to five or six parties. . . . That's *it*!'

'Well,' said Barry, 'what else can I say? When it comes to what you might call a Baby Bunting sort of costume, some girls can get away with it and some can't, and Jane's obviously one of those who can. *And* it's for art's sake. I mean I know you're worried about what Jane's fellow countrymen will say, but goodness – that won't matter.'

'Won't it?' asked Jane.

'Well of course it won't,' said Barry. 'Because as soon as that photograph appears in the press you'll be denounced by some of *my* countrymen, and if there's one thing that's guaranteed to make your fellow citizens forgive you – cherish you even – it's the fact that you'll have been blackguarded by a bunch of Yanks. You'll be a national heroine, my dear. Baring all for Britain.'

'Well not quite all,' said Jane. 'But I do see what you mean.'

'So we go to some of these parties?' Jay asked.

'We go to all of them,' said Jane firmly.

Two more Manhattan apartments, and one small (so Jay said) but beautiful house near Central Park, with the most comprehensive collection of eighteenth-century French paintings Jane had ever seen: Fragonard, Watteau, Boucher, Chardin, de la Tour. And at each one Barry played Gershwin, or Kern, or Berlin, or that new young man called Richard Rogers, and Jane began to drink lemonade instead, because this was not the time for tears. Then on to Jack and Charlie's Luncheon Club on West 49th Street, a speakeasy where to Jane's delight the ritual was scrupulously followed: the elaborate knock on the door, the sliding panel that allowed two hard grey eyes to survey you, and then the spoken formula: 'Harry said it would be OK.' And then in to crowds of people and real champagne, and the kind of sandwiches that only Americans dare attempt.

Jane seemed to spend at least an hour there saying 'How do you do?' and accepting invitations to parties, tomorrow, next week, next month (this last to a party which had already been going on for several days). New York City, perhaps even the whole of the United States of America, had decided that it was time for a party, and only the Bauers had not been invited. Jay had, but then he wasn't a Bauer, after all, he was Bower, hard at work even at Jack and Charlie's bless him, showing off her picture and telling all and sundry it was art, while she at last was allowed to converse, rather than simply accept invitations, and found herself discoursing, apparently simultaneously, on Coco Chanel and the Prince of Wales, Braque and Joyce and the Russian ballet, but that was merely champagne on top of martinis, she thought, then regretted the 'merely'. It was a word she must learn to use sparingly.

On then to the Stork, with Barry and Jay, and a girl called Thelma who did nothing but lament the fact that she had never been to Venice and must do so at once, before she became old.

'How old is old?' Jane asked.

'Twenty-four,' Thelma said. 'That's what I'll be next year.'

Jay chuckled. 'You leave that photograph where it is,' said Jane.

The Stork Club was not disappointing exactly, but it was predictable. For this sort of thing she preferred the Embassy in London. But it was a speakeasy – no ritual to be recited, but a careful scrutiny of membership cards – and it did have music. ('Not Paul Whiteman,' Barry told her. 'Not this time. He's down in Florida selling real estate.' In other words, she gathered, Whiteman and his band were the sugar on the pill of a Florida land sale.)

They joined a group of theatre people who had already begun their supper. Was it so late already? And indeed it was, but all the same she had to dance – with Jay, with Barry, with the jeune premier among the actors, and the play's director who talked the whole time of Shakespeare and Dryden and Shaw, all of whom, she remembered, had written plays about Cleopatra. To dance was sobering, but it was also tiring. Jay's publicity machine had done its work already: wartime heroine, indefatigable charity worker, even her offer to strip with Marigold Ledbitter at her brother's college. But all of it wholesome. The good sport, the patriot, the pretty pal. Everything that filled out a Chanel suit.

'You're a success,' said Barry. 'Un succès fou.' They were sitting out for once.

'Are you surprised?'

'Not at all. But it's always gratifying to find one's prophecies fulfilled.'

The theatre director leaned across to them. 'I doubt if Cassandra found it so,' he said. Barry pouted. 'It's far too late at night to try to remember the stuff they used to tell me at Princeton,' he said.

'Do you remember the Serpent of Old Nile?' the director asked.

'If there are marks out of ten for that then I want some,' said Barry. 'That was Cleopatra.'

Jane said, 'I must have met about two hundred people tonight – and it's just too many names. If anybody told me yours I've forgotten it.'

'Tom Waring,' said the director, and offered his hand. 'Nobody introduced us.'

'How do you do?' said Jane. 'I should explain that when people are talking about me – however obliquely – I like to know their names.'

'You reckon I'm talking about you?'

'I think that's what Jay Bower hired you to do.' She looked across to where Bower danced with the ingénue of the play. He was talking. Of course he was.

'Am I right?' she asked.

'Quite right,' said Waring.

'Could we leave it till tomorrow?'

'Sure we could.'

'Because my feet have recovered you see, and Barry needs the exercise.'

The band played 'Ain't We Got Fun', and Barry danced it well, but not so well as Lionel.

He escorted her home too through air he described as being as cold and crisp as the frosting on a daiquiri.

'I like to scatter these little gems around,' he said, 'in the hope that somebody more energetic than me will steal them – and then I can claim co-authorship. Do steal that one.'

'Do my best,' said Jane, 'though they don't drink many daiquiris in Felston.'

'Speaking of the written word,' said Barry, 'shouldn't you be escorted home by Jay? I mean I'm charmed – utterly charmed – but all the same you were his date.'

'Jay,' she said, 'is watching the print of the bulldog edition of the New York *Herald*. Does that make sense to you?'

'No,' said Barry, 'except that it sounds exactly the sort of thing he would do. He doesn't own it, does he?'

'No,' said Jane, 'but it's a newspaper, and it's printing, and if he doesn't see a newspaper at work at least twice a week he has one of his turns.' The cab stopped by her apartment building.

'You like him, don't you?' Barry said.

'Enormously,' said Jane, and he kissed her cheek.

'An acquired taste, dear Jay,' he said. 'So glad you acquired it.'

An acquired taste is right, she thought as she lay in bed, and there's no doubt that I've acquired it, but do I still love him (or more precisely want him) as once I did, after all that hard labour to buy jobs for Bob and the major and a way out of trouble for me? In Felston they had a word for that sort of hard labour, and no doubt they were right, but life was never quite so simple as that. Take George, for instance. George had been waiting up for her when she came in, and was vaguely surprised, no more, at her anger that he should do so. Indian servants, as she remembered, would have fallen asleep and stayed asleep until somebody began to shout and swear.

She slept well: alcohol for a sleeping draught, good bed, warm room, and when she woke a shower en suite so that all she had to do was take off her nightdress and stagger under the deluge. But it reminded her of Jay, and his room above the shop. If his desires were carnal, and when were they not, how would they achieve fruition? Mercifully that was his problem. She telephoned George on the internal telephone (would Hawkins permit an internal telephone in South Terrace, she wondered?) and asked for breakfast. Fresh orange juice, George suggested, and ham and eggs. Fresh orange juice pressed from Florida oranges it seemed, where Paul Whiteman serenaded, and quite delicious. And Virginia Ham like no other ham she had ever eaten. Fed on peaches, George assured her, and George would know.

By eleven thirty she was dressed in a sweater and skirt and sitting by the window, watching the snow fall, which it did in a busy and determined kind of way that was somehow very American. Soon, Jay had told her, she would take a train to California, something called the 'Super Chief' and, when she got there after several days of cocktails and steak dinners, the sun would be shining. Which was very nice. She liked the sun. But what would she do? Jay had muttered something about a screen test, but they both knew that was nonsense. Or did they? If it was nonsense, why was she seeing Tom Waring?

George came in, with the dreaded tabloids that Jay had warned her about: McCormick's *Daily News*, Hearst's *Daily Mirror*, and McFadden's *Graphic*. All three of them, Jay had told her, were friends of his. They weren't friends of hers – or perhaps McFadden was. He certainly made a lot of fuss about the body beautiful, and included hers in that category. But gracious how he did go on. The other two were simply old-fashioned lechers disguised as moralists, but all three had printed the picture. If Barry's theory was correct, England would rise to her defence to the last man. . . . The telephone rang, and George came in to tell her it was Jay.

'You've seen the papers?' he asked her.

'I can't remember when I've had more fun,' she said. 'What have you in mind next? Tar and feathers?'

'I heard what Barry told you,' said Jay. 'He's right. This is the way to lick this thing. You believe me, don't you?'

'Well of course I do,' she said. 'You're the expert. This is what you're for.'

'OK then,' he said. 'Just go along with me and enjoy yourself.'

'Aren't I going to see you?'

'Not where you are,' he said. 'I haven't given out your address but they'll find you soon enough.'

'Where then?'

'I've got a suite at the Waldorf,' he said. 'If you would care to see it.'

'I should adore to see your suite at the Waldorf,' she said. 'Would four o'clock be convenient? I'm promised to Barry at seven.'

'Four is fine,' he said. 'Enjoy yourself till then.'

She spoke quickly, before he could hang up. 'Any message for Tom Waring?'

'Just listen to him,' he said.

'My pleasure,' she said, then for the first time since she had known him, she hung up first. It must be the air, she thought.

Tom Waring was prompt, and looked sober and rested, but just a little apprehensive. She offered him a drink, and he asked for a Manhattan – rye whiskey, Italian vermouth and bitters over cracked ice, plus a Maraschino cherry. She asked for a glass of Chablis for herself, and George produced both without a blink. Waring raised his glass.

'Your health,' he said.

'And yours.' Jane raised hers.

'You've heard from Mr Bower?' She nodded. 'What did he say?'

'That you were to talk and I was to listen.'

'Yes, of course,' said Waring. 'I understand. For him that has to be the simplest way.' He sipped his drink. 'You know I directed this play on Broadway?'

'*Summer's Lease*? Of course. I look forward to seeing it.'

'I also work in Hollywood from time to time. Most directors – once they go to Hollywood they stay there – but I like to come back East occasionally. It isn't just the theatre. It's things like the seasons. That.' He nodded at the window where the snow now gyrated like feathers from an exploding eiderdown. 'But when I am in Hollywood I usually work for Worldwide Films. Do you know about that?'

'I know that Mr Bower's family owns quite a lot of it.'

'Yeah,' said Waring. 'Quite a lot.' He finished his drink and Jane poured him another. There was no point in bothering George, not when he was helping Martha prepare their lunch.

'He wants us to make a film,' she said.

'Not a film,' said Waring. 'Not right off. Just a test. But if the test's good – '

'The idea's preposterous,' said Jane. 'I've never acted in my life.'

'Eighty per cent of Hollywood's never acted in its life,' said Waring. 'The camera acts for them.' He gulped again at his drink. 'Look, Miss Whitcomb – it isn't going to last because any year now there'll be talking pictures and then people will *really* have to act – but just for now a person who looks good and can project the way they're asked to feel. That's all it needs.'

'And you think I can do that?'

'Oh boy. Look, Miss Whitcomb – I've seen your picture.' He hesitated. 'I'm sorry. Maybe you – '

'My dear man,' she said. 'Half of New York has seen my picture. Tell me about this projection business. And do call me Jane.'

'Projection's just looking the way I ask you to look. I mean if I say look sad – could you do that?'

'How?'

'By thinking of something sad. And happy the same.'

'I'll try,' said Jane. 'Just give me a moment.'

Suddenly her sadness was there; wounded, heartrending.

'Great,' said Waring. 'Now happiness, please.' And she duly obliged. 'Fantastic,' said Waring. 'How on earth did you do it Miss – Jane?'

'For sadness I thought about my dog and how much I miss him,' she said. 'For happiness I imagined that I was present as an observer while a man named Burrowes was mercilessly thrashed by a man named Pardoe. They were both arrested for disturbing the peace. Mr Waring this is all a very great nonsense.'

'But it pays,' said Waring earnestly. 'I get twenty grand – that's twenty thousand dollars for every picture I make. That's the heck of a lot of money.'

'I've got the heck of a lot of money,' said Jane.

'For you it would be more. Maybe even fifty thousand. More than twelve thousand of your pounds for just ten weeks' work.'

'Ten weeks?' said Jane. 'Jay expects me to prance around in that ludicrous piece of peau de soie for ten whole weeks?'

'You could give the money to that town of yours,' said Waring. As if I owned it, she thought. Felston. My town.

'Tell me why,' she said. 'I'm over thirty. I've never acted in my life – oh you say that's not important and I believe you – but I've never even wanted to act. So why pick on me?'

'First I must tell you that you're an unusual woman,' said Waring. 'Almost unbelievably so. America is full of people who want to be in pictures: to be stars. Especially young and pretty women.'

'Over thirty,' said Jane. 'And I didn't even tell you how far over.'

'It doesn't matter,' said Waring. 'It's all in the lighting. We could make you eighteen or even eighty-three if we wanted to. I could have a queue from here to Times Square if I said I was looking for a girl to play Cleopatra – in Hollywood it would be half way to San Francisco – and you tell me you don't want to do it.'

'I don't,' said Jane, 'but let's have lunch while you tell me about it.'

Lunch was lobster bisque and lamb chops and a soufflé, and all of a kind that Mrs Barrow would have approved. While they ate Waring told her about the movies in general, and his plans for Cleopatra in particular. To him Hollywood meant money: the kind of money that would subsidise the work in the theatre he loved but could by no means afford, what with an ex-wife and a fiancée, and a Packard coupé he liked so much that he had two of them, one in Los Angeles and the other in New York. But it wasn't only money. There was a kind of crazy ingenuity involved in what he did that he found immensely stimulating.

'Every picture I make I'm Pearl White tied to the railway track,' he said, 'and I never know till the last reel whether the express is going to hit me or not.'

'And the prospect doesn't terrify you?'

'Every time I think it might I come back here,' he said, 'and take anything that's going, even summer stock. But to do that I need Hollywood for half the year at least.'

'And Jay really wants us to do this?' Jane asked.

'Yes, mam.'

'Where Shakespeare and Dryden and Shaw have triumphed, you and I will triumph too?'

'What we'll do is a carnival really,' said Waring, 'although the critics will call it an epic. You know the kind of thing – Roman legions, chariots, toiling slaves. Mark Antony at war with Caesar Augustus, and you as sort of a warrior queen. Ben Hur, you know. D. W. Griffiths stuff.'

'It sounds quite wholesome,' she said, 'if rather violent.'

'Most of it will be.'

'Most?'

'She was the kind of woman who could break one of the world's great rulers and captivate another. A woman who used sex as Mark Antony used his sword.'

'You should approach Pola Negri,' said Jane.

'Mr Bower wants you,' said Waring.

And indeed he did, she thought, in that grand and rather pompous suite at the Waldorf. First he wanted me and then he had me, and it was still pleasant enough, and only afterwards did they talk.

'What's this about seeing Barry?' he asked.

'He wants to show me Harlem,' said Jane. She had showered, and was drying herself on the fluffiest, most luxurious towel she had ever used.

'You should see it all right,' said Jay, 'but you could have problems.'

'Why should I?'

'The gentlemen of the press. . . . They didn't bother you at the Stork Club last night?'

'No.' She reached for her comb, and the towel slipped.

'They will tonight,' said Jay. 'Even if you got to the YWCA.'

'Then I must remember to stay away,' said Jane. She wandered into the bathroom, leaving the door open, and found the box of talcum powder she had brought for the occasion, and the huge powder puff that went with it.

'Tell me about Waring,' she said.

'Don't do that,' said Jay.

'What nonsense,' she said. 'You know how much you enjoy it.' She began to powder her breasts.

'He's a good director,' said Jay. 'He likes money so he does what he's told. . . . Come here.'

'Without even a please? Tell me about this screen test.' The powder puff moved lower.

'It's a gag,' said Jay. 'A publicity gag. It gets you known. Good for Felston – and good for the *Daily World*.'

Her body wriggled as she applied more powder.

'He doesn't believe that,' she said.

'Tom Waring believes what I tell him,' said Jay. '*Please* come here.'

And so she went. It was nice to know that she could have such an effect on a man, she thought, but not nearly so fulfilling as their early days together. More like General Knowledge, really: the Principal Rivers of Europe, perhaps, or how to get a stone out of a horse's hoof. When they had done he said, 'You must be feeling pleased with yourself,' and it was true that he had performed prodigies. But all she did was smile. It was better than saying, 'Not really.'

47

'I THOUGHT WE'D start at the Hotsy-Totsy,' said Barry, 'and then lower the tone a little. The Sligo Slasher's or somewhere like that. And then supper somewhere and on to the Cotton Club.'

'Aren't I just a little overdressed for roughing it?' Jane asked. 'I mean a Paquin dress *and* sables?'

'If I'm being rebuked for not admiring that *exquisite* gown then so be it,' said Barry. 'My dear, such a blue. But for the rest – fear not. The proprietors of these dens of iniquity are all friends of mine. My God they should be – the money I spend there. You will notice that I'm wearing a tuxedo.'

'I have indeed.'

'Well let me tell you that I could go into Tony's on East 53rd Street clad in no more than a derby hat and an athletic support and be perfectly safe.'

'My poor love,' said Jane. 'Are they all blind?'

'Martinis will be the death of me,' said Barry. 'I don't even listen to what I say any more. Shall we go?'

'Play a little Gershwin first.' – What with one thing and another, it seemed a good time to be sad. As he played, she said, 'What makes Jay think that Cleopatra was a blonde?'

He was playing his own version of the 'Rhapsody in Blue', and almost missed a beat. 'Does he?' he asked.

'You *have* noticed the colour of my hair?'

'Oh that,' said Barry. 'Colour isn't the thing. Really it's not. Blonde and brunette. All that. A femme fatale, that's what Jay's after. That's what wigs are for, surely?'

'Let's go to a den of iniquity,' she said.

They went to many, starting at the Hotsy-Totsy, then Tony's, then the Sligo Slasher's, and then on a downward spiral to the sort of place where you either sat on a box or stood at the bar, and whatever you drank was served in a cup, and after one sip of her drink she marvelled at the resistance of New York china. Not that she drank much: she had come to watch, and there was a lot to see. A clientele mostly male, listening to music on a gramophone, a radio, or from a group of musicians, and at the same time telling each other which stocks had risen highest that day. Stockbrokers, bank clerks, cab drivers, barbers, it didn't matter. They all knew which stocks had done best. Even the bartenders knew it; in fact they knew it best of all.

They went to a supper club then, and on to Harlem, in north east Manhattan, which turned out to be a district inhabited largely by middle-class blacks, and so to the Cotton Club, which was every bit as much an institution as the Brigade of Guards, she thought, and with the same high standards of discipline and physical perfection. Except that these were chorus girls, tall, elegant, and with a colour never darker than milk chocolate; what Barry told her was called 'high yellow'. Slender and lovely and aloof, they danced to the music of a black orchestra to amuse an audience entirely white on whom black waiters attended. Like the Raj, she thought, but it wasn't like the Raj. Brown men waiting on her had never seemed a problem, but this did. And then the music reached her, and she forgot everything else. Strong, rhythmic, inventive; she heard brass and woodwind played as she'd never heard them before.

'Like it?' Barry asked.

'It's incredible,' she said. 'How do they do it?'

'I've asked them often enough,' said Barry, 'but they can never tell you. You just do it, they say. I expect Rachmaninov and Heifetz would give you the same answer.'

The girls danced again: every one of them a much more probable Cleopatra than she.

'Would you like to go to a party?' Barry asked.

'Now?'

'Why not now?'

'Isn't it rather late?'

'It's never too late for a party in New York,' Barry said. 'You should know that by now.'

But before they could leave they had to fight their way out. The press had caught up with them at last. Seven men and two women, not counting cameramen, whose flashlights blinded like flares, while the questions came at her like gun fire. 'Miss Whitcomb, have you a comment on yesterday's article?' 'Miss Whitcomb, do you approve of semi-nude pictures?' 'Do you regard yourself as a corrupter of morals?' 'If you were a mother, would you like your child to see you like that?' and even, 'Do you believe in God, Miss Whitcomb?'

And all the time she smiled like a maniac seeking an axe, and kept on repeating over and over, 'Such a happy place, New York, and the people so helpful and friendly', until Barry came up with a taxi-cab, and they rode off at last.

'Rough?' he said.

'I've seen worse,' said Jane. 'But not for eight years.'

The party was in a penthouse of an apartment in 64th Street, and she could hear the music from two floors below. When they left the elevator Barry led her at once to a door where two men stood like sentries, and gave his name, and hers. One of the men consulted a list, then nodded, and the other man opened the door. They went inside.

'Just like a speakeasy,' said Jane, and for some reason Barry smiled.

Inside, the apartment was more like Bedlam on a bad day, she thought, or perhaps like 'The Rake's Progress', Barry suggested, except that everyone was having such a good time. And indeed they were. They ate, drank, smoked, embraced, in a conglomeration of bodies; man with woman, man with man, woman with woman, black with white.

Jane blinked. 'Well well,' she said. 'Didn't I just tell the press that in New York the people are so helpful and friendly?'

'Come and meet our host,' said Barry. He led her up to a man who simply had to be a gangster, she thought. Blue jowls despite a close shave, draped tuxedo and diamond ring. With him with was a girl of maybe thirty, who was very beautiful and very black, and who might well be the reason for the racial mixture.

'Frank Cardona, this is Jane Whitcomb,' said Barry.

Jane offered her hand. 'How d'you do?' she said.

'Miss Whitcomb's from England,' Barry explained.

'Pleased to meet you.' His hand touched hers then let go very quickly. 'This is Maebelle Barton.'

The black girl smiled. 'Enjoying the music, Miss Whitcomb?'

'I've never heard anything like it,' said Jane.

'You never will,' said the black girl, 'not anywhere else in New York. Chicago maybe, but not New York.'

'Get my guests a drink,' said Cardona, and a young man near him took off like a greyhound out of a trap, and came back with a bottle and glasses. The bottle was Dom Perignon, and Jane and Barry toasted Cardona, then went to dance.

'I think I know why you smiled when I mentioned speakeasies,' she said.

'Doucement, petite,' said Barry, looking about him.

'Because a certain gentleman owns them,' said Jane. Barry winked.

On and on went the dancing, and the drinking and smoking and loving, until at last the black drummer left the others – white banjo player and clarinettist, black pianist and trombone player – and searched around the room until he found a neat, contained white man asleep in a chair, a ring of empty glasses around him. The drummer shook the white man gently but firmly until he awoke. He blinked at the drummer, then fumbled to his feet, picked up what she thought was a trumpet, and lurched with the black man over to the band. The banjo player at once provided a seat, and then, without any apparent signal, they began to play together.

'"Jazz Me Blues",' said Barry. 'Oh what bliss.'

And indeed it was. The neat contained man could conjure sounds out of a brass instrument she would not have believed possible, even though he was obviously very drunk.

'Who is that trumpeter?' she asked at last.

'Cornet player,' said Barry. 'When you go back to London you can tell them you heard Bix Beiderbecke.'

'Is he always so drunk?'

'Very often. He should be in Florida with Whiteman. He's been offered a job in his band.'

'Why isn't he?'

Barry shrugged. 'He probably forgot to go.'

'Poor lamb,' said Jane.

Maebelle Barton joined the band and began to sing in a rich yet husky contralto, and Beiderbecke's trumpet wove variations around it. It was like no other blending she had ever heard.

Another late morning. Did anyone *ever* go to bed and get up at the right time in New York? she wondered. But that was ridiculous. Everybody did except the rich parasites, but what a lot of them there seemed to be. How happy Andy would be here, she thought. So much scope for righteous indignation.

George said, 'Mr Bower telephoned, Miss Whitcomb. He says he'll call here at around noon.'

I ought to go out, she thought. How dare he *say* he'll call. He should ask. But Jay never asked. He didn't know how.

He looked angry, and she wondered why. She had done nothing after all except to go to parties and clubs and dance with Barry.

'You went to Cardona's,' he said.

'The most marvellous music,' she said. 'There was a dear drunken man called Bix – '

'Never mind,' he said. 'You shouldn't have gone.'

'Because he's a gangster?'

'How did you know that?'

'Because I looked at him,' said Jane. 'Of course he's a gangster. It couldn't be more obvious if he wore a label with "Gangster" on it. He served the best champagne I've had since I got here.'

'You could have been seen by the press,' said Jay. 'What would have happened to that wholesome image then?'

'I was seen,' said Jane, 'at the Cotton Club. They took enough bites out of me there for one night.'

'You played that quite well,' said Jay. He sounded grudging. 'Helpful, friendly New Yorkers. But Cardona. He's what they call the head of a family. Big-time crook. Booze, gambling, prostitution.'

'Like Al Capone?'

'Cardona despises Capone,' said Jay. 'He makes too much noise. Cardona likes things discreet. That way he makes more money. But you keep away from him.'

'We'll see,' she said. 'I liked his music and I liked his girl. If I'm invited again – '

'You won't be,' said Jay. 'Barry won't take you – '

'You seem very sure.'

'Of course I'm sure,' said Jay. 'He owes me money.'

'He's also very fond of you,' she said, but he didn't hear. He was talking.

'And anyway Cardona – ' he said, then hesitated.

'Owes you money too?'

'Not owes,' said Jay. 'And not me. . . . But he'll do me a favour even if you won't.'

'Not you?' she said. 'Your father perhaps. Does Mr Cardona get him all that lovely hock and Moselle he's so fond of?'

'You're still a smart one,' he said.

'When I can be bothered. . . . I see in my newspaper that your mother's giving a reception in that schloss of hers tomorrow. All New York is going, it says. Have you brought my invitation with you?'

'You're not going.'

'Why not? You are. The paper said that, too.'

'I didn't have my picture in the tabloids,' said Jay.

'You bastard,' she said.

'Not at all,' said Jay. 'We discussed the whole thing – remember? You knew what the *Graphic* and the rest of them would say. So you must have known how my mother would feel about inviting you.'

She chuckled. 'Touché,' she said. 'But tell me just one thing. Does your mother know she's living off Mr Cardona's immoral earnings?'

He was up on his feet at once, fist pulled back. She chuckled again.

'Mummy's boy,' she said. 'You know that's interesting. I'd never have suspected it.'

He said stiffly, 'You know how to hurt, but then you always did. I guess that's part of your charm.' He went through his pockets, and at last came up with a cigar.

'We've had letters,' he said. 'At the *Daily World*. About you going to Hollywood. At the moment they're running at twenty-three to one asking you to stay. When the great British public reads about what the New York tabloids have said about you it'll be fifty to one. At least.'

'And so?' she said.

'And so you have a choice,' he said. 'If for any crazy reason you want to know what I think, then I'll tell you. Whether you go or stay, at least go to Hollywood and do the test. Make it a cliff-hanger.'

'I told you I would go to Hollywood,' she said. 'I don't go back on my word.'

'OK then, we'll go,' said Jay. 'Thursday suit you? We'll be there on Monday of next week. Drawing room. Take all your warm clothes. Those trains are cold till long after Chicago.'

She understood very little of what he was saying, but she nodded. 'And where am I allowed to go until then?' she asked.

Jay winced. 'Theatres,' he said. 'The ones that show improving plays. Carnegie Hall. Art galleries. And stay way from speaks.' And then incredibly, 'Just one thing more. You still haven't changed your mind? You still won't marry me?'

'What an extraordinary man you are,' she said. 'Of course not.'

For three more days she shopped at Saks and Tiffany's and the little places Barry recommended, and went to see *Rose Marie* and *Showboat* and *What Price Glory?* Barry took her to all three, but never again mentioned Jay. And then at the appointed time the most enormous motor car arrived, to take her and her luggage to Grand Central Station, and to leave behind two servants whom she knew she would miss for a long, long time. The Century was only the Century as far as Chicago, after which for some reason it became the Super Chief, perhaps, she thought, because one had to change stations. But there really was a drawing room, and a place to wash, and a bed, and a flock of white-jacketed negroes who provided their own bootlegging service and made the beds as well.

Jay had the drawing room next to hers, but for most of the journey he stayed in it and worked his way through the pile of telegrams that seemed to be waiting for him every time the train stopped, or even slowed; though from time to time he did join her to drink martinis or eat an enormous steak called a tenderloin. While he ate and drank he told her all about the world's news.

When they got to Chicago there was another enormous car waiting to help them change stations, and more negroes in white jackets to bring them martinis. Chicago was even colder than Manhattan, and she felt very sorry for the negroes, because it was cold on the train, too. But at least there were letters, waiting for her in her drawing room, brought across from England in the liner *Aquitania*. A few, a very few, from lunatics who denounced her immodesty, shamelessness, lust: and a very large number from people who begged her to reconsider, stay out of America, come home to the rescue of those who needed her. There was a picture postcard from Lionel, a portrait of Britannia, and on the back he had written: 'Britons never never never. . . . Come back soon you idiot. Love. Lionel.' There was a letter from Mummy too, which said the same thing at much greater length.

The major was, of course, deeply upset, but with brothers like his what could one expect? The costume was perhaps a *little* exiguous, but one had been assured of its historical accuracy. On the other hand, while the lure of Hollywood was doubtless wildly exciting to impressionable minds (Gwendoline Gwatkin had placed Offley Villas under a state of siege since first she read of it) there were other and perhaps more cogent reasons why it should be rejected. Felston needed rather more than her money: it needed her presence.

Grandma wrote to say the same. The latest operation had worked, God be thanked, but eyesight was a blessing of God to allow us to look at the ones we loved – and not on a screen or in a newspaper either. Bet had been dubious at first, but now she thought the same. And she, Grandma, had had a big row with Dr Stobbs for saying that Jane could go where she liked so long as she sent money.

Jay came in. 'There's a bunch of entertainers in the club car,' he said. 'They'll be singing soon. Do you want to hear them?'

'Why not?' she said, and folded up her letters.

'Nice mail?' he asked.

'About what you told me. A little over twenty to one – not counting the lunatics.'

'There's one from your mother,' he said.

'My mother is sane,' Jane said, 'and, as far as I can gather, on my side.'

'I didn't mean to suggest she wasn't,' said Jay.

'Of course not. Let's go and listen to your entertainers.'

A ukulele and a mouth organ, a blonde who sang and a brunette who danced. But it was pleasant and relaxing: 'Show Me The Way To Go Home', 'Me and My Shadow' – without any suggestion of the emotional demands made by the music at Frank Cardona's.

'The weather will be better tomorrow,' said Jay.

'Oh really?'

'We're moving south all the time. Soon it'll be too warm for snow.'

'Very nice.'

Jay slammed his hand down on the bar counter.

'I'm trying to make conversation,' he said.

'You can usually do better than the weather,' she said.

And then at twelve o'clock [sang the blonde]
We climb the stairs. We never knock
'Cos nobody cares.
Just me and my sha-dow,
All alone and fee-ling blue.

'Do you own them?' Jane asked.

'Just the brunette,' said Jay. 'The others are under option for when we switch to sound.'

Touché, she thought, and went back to her drawing room to read her letters and drink a Sidecar (one third cointreau triple sec, one third brandy, one third lemon juice) prepared by one of the black bootleggers. Reading and drinking were about all one could do – the Middle West from her window seemed one vast, flat field in which nothing ever happened. And so she read. Not just her fan mail but books about Cleopatra that Waring had sent her: almost every book about Cleopatra that had ever been written, or so it seemed. She didn't much like what she read.

Then somewhere south of Kansas City, Missouri, the weather became warm, and for no other reason than that she need no longer spend all day in a fur coat, she began to feel more cheerful. She finished all her Cleopatra books too, and began on a novel called *The Great Gatsby* by someone called Scott Fitzgerald. There was a photograph of him on the back cover, and she discovered that she had met him in Paris. She enjoyed the book very much.

Jay she saw only at meal times. He made no further attempt to share her bed. There were others who had joined the Super-Chief in Chicago, bankers for the most part, and a newspaper owner. He spent a lot of time with them, but made no effort to persuade Jane to join them, and she was glad. She enjoyed her privacy and her reading, and if she needed conversation there were always the black bootleggers. But she didn't much. All the self-improvement, 'how-to-be-a-nicer-person' books would stress that this was a perfect time for what they liked to call 'a period of quiet reflection', 'a chance to think things through': but she found that she couldn't do that. She could *remember* effortlessly: Michael Browne's wife and Georgina Payne's picture, the feel of Burrowes's skin under her palm when she walloped him, Jay's house in the country, taking a fence on Bridie's back. And Felston, endlessly. The slums, the market place, and most of all the clinic. And even further back than that. With the girls in the Ambulance Unit, and her first dance with John; and beyond that even, to India and Mummy and French irregular verbs. It was all as clear and accurate as if it had been recorded on film: but quiet reflection must lead to decisions, and she wasn't yet ready to make decisions. Certain events had still to take place, but when they did she would know.

One morning she woke up to find that the scenery too had improved. The vast field had ended in the night, and in its place was one of the Americas that one saw in the cinema, the Wild West of Tom Mix and Hoot Gibson. Desert and grass land and distant mountains, but no stage coaches and no Indians, though once she was almost sure she saw some cowboys.

Jay joined her for lunch.

'We'll be in this evening,' he said.

'You say the nicest things,' she said.

He looked contrite for once. 'It must have been lonely for you,' he said. 'The thing is I was going to arrange some company but it didn't work out.'

'Please don't apologise,' she said. 'After New York I needed some peace and quiet.'

'A chance to think things over?'

'Exactly,' she lied, and then: 'I take it that there won't be much peace and quiet in Hollywood?'

'There'll be none at all,' he said.

And he was right. The first crowd of reporters was waiting for them at the station, and at first their questions were directed at Jay, and what they asked was not *if* he would make the picture, but when. And how much would the budget be, and who were the co-stars, and was it true that Tom Waring would direct? Jay was polite, anxious to help and extremely vague, but they wrote down every word. After all he owned one newspaper already, and one day he might own theirs. Then it was her turn, and she braced herself, but they were surprisingly gentle, after New York, even friendly in a weird sort of way. What were her impressions of California? Was she looking forward to working in Hollywood? Was she ever homesick at all? How did it feel to be a heroine?

She tackled them in turn. Your state is magnificent, she said, and the most delicious oranges. To work here is the fulfilment of my wildest dream, but I miss my dog. I'm not a heroine, merely a woman who was lucky enough to have the chance to serve.

Then an earnest and rather stout girl asked her: 'Is it true that you believe a beautiful body to be a gift of God?'

Jane flicked a glance at Jay. 'Indeed it is,' she said, 'and it must be treasured as such.'

The black bootleggers carried her luggage to another enormous car, and she gave them money, far too much, according to Jay, but she had been glad of their company.

'You might have warned me about that beautiful body nonsense,' she said as the car pulled away.

'We Americans are a religious-minded people,' he said. 'If we can plant the idea that to look like you is a burden then we'll all feel good about it.'

'Where am I staying?' she asked.

'You mean I forgot to tell you?' She nodded. 'And you didn't ask.'

'I was too busy thinking,' she said, 'and anyway I'm quite sure it'll be the best. It always is.'

'Why thank you,' said Jay. 'You're staying at the Garden of Allah.'

'You're usually wittier than that.'

'I'm perfectly serious. It's a hotel. Surely you know that?'

'The only hotel I know to stay in is the Eldon Arms at Felston.'

'You used to know the Ritz,' said Jay.

' – And the Ritz in Paris,' said Jane. 'Who could ever forget the Ritz?'

They arrived at this vast and quite extraordinary hotel which didn't look as if it had been designed at all: rather written by a screen writer adapting a novel by Ethel M. Dell. Jane looked about her, awestruck. 'Golly,' she said. But Hollywood was having one of its better December days, with hard, clear sunshine, and the palms and the orange trees looked green, the roses still bloomed. She and Jay walked into the foyer, and a flock of Mexicans came out for her luggage as reporters swooped. They were different reporters, but their questions were the same. There were more letters waiting for her too, brought over to New York in the liner *Berengaria*, then on by train. She was obviously an important person. When she signed the register there was almost a round of applause.

Jay went with her to her suite and inspected it personally: the living room, the dressing room, the bedroom with its quite heavenly bed after the joltings of the Super-Chief, and the bathroom that had everything, including a telephone, but no delicious shower close to the bed. A chapter, it seemed, was ending.

'Seems OK,' said Jay.

'Of course,' she said. 'Didn't I say you always choose the best? My mother tells me it's the only standard I'm used to.' And then she smiled. 'Thank you,' she said.

'You're welcome.' He hesitated. 'There is just one thing. I hired you a maid. Now don't get sore.'

'I'm not,' she said. 'Not yet, anyway. Please go on. Tell me why I need a maid.'

'Because this is Hollywood,' said Jay. 'Here everything depends on status. You start with the kind of car you have. Ford, Buick, then on up to Packard, Olds, Cadillac.'

'That's the summit? A Cadillac?'

'Hell no,' said Jay. 'After that you start on foreign cars. Rolls, Bugatti, Isotta-Fraschini.'

'I drove a Voisin once,' she said.

'Sure you did,' said Jay. 'I was there, remember? And tomorrow you'll drive a Hispano-Suiza. But for now you're beyond cars. You're a suite-at-the-Garden-of-Allah lady. That's almost the tops.'

'Only almost?'

'Your own maid is the clincher,' said Jay, 'and so I got you your own maid.'

'Is she nice?'

'Judge for yourself,' said Jay. 'If you don't like her you can always change her.'

She hated that, but in fact Amparo seemed fine; about her age, with a restful prettiness and a golden skin that seemed designed to be exactly the colour to set off her glittering dark eyes. Jane offered her hand at once, and Amparo took it warily, before Jay sent her to unpack.

'She's a Mexican,' he explained. 'They're never too easy with us gringos.'

'Why not?'

'Because we exploit them,' said Jay.

'You too?'

'I'm different,' said Jay. 'I exploit everybody. But remember this. I could have got you a French girl or a fraulein, but I chose Amparo – because she's the best there is. Would you like to rest for a while?'

'I would,' said Jane. She meant it.

'Why don't you nap for an hour then change and I'll pick you up around eight thirty? There's a party I want us to go to. A lot of important people I want you to meet.'

'Must I?' she asked.

'Sure you must,' said Jay. 'It's to impress the good people of Felton when they queue up at the public library to read about you in the *Daily World*.'

'I'll be ready,' she said.

48

S HE WAS AS good as Jay had promised she would be: evening
clothes laid out exactly as she would have done it herself.
She had even suggested a massage, and very refreshing Jane
had found it, the only possible thing to put enough life in her
body to get her through another party. She was the best, all
right. Jane wondered if she could also be Jay's spy.

He was prompt – he was always prompt – and she hurried
down to join him at once after telling Amparo not to wait up.

'Yes, Miss Whitcomb,' said Amparo. Even her voice was
pretty, with the distinctive 's' sound that makes the Spanish
language so pleasant to listen to.

'Whose party is it?'

'David Greenglass. He's a big producer these days. I knew
him before the war when he was just a writer.'

A writer, she gathered, was a very unimportant thing to be.

'I worked out here for a while,' he said.

'In the movies?' She felt rather proud that she had said movies
rather than films. Et in Arcadia ego, her father would have said.

'Hell no,' said Jay. 'On the *Los Angeles Times*. The only thing
to do in the movies is own a studio. The rest is just as boring as
any other salaried work.' He looked at her and grinned. 'Unless
you're an actress, of course.'

'Will there be actresses at this party?'

'Sure there will. And actors. And directors. Maybe even a few
writers – if they're foreign and over here on a visit.'

'And the press of course.'

'Of course. But only to see who came and who didn't.' He went through his pockets, seeking a cigar. 'Your dress is just great.'

'One does one's best. So does Amparo.'

A midnight-blue velvet dress that showed a lot of skin, and over it a beaded evening coat that deepened in colour from pale grey to black, and trimmed with midnight-blue velvet. Not that he would know, or even care, but he would and did know at a glance how good it was.

'Paris?' he asked.

'Yes.'

'If anybody asks, mind you tell them so,' he said.

'But almost every woman you introduce me to buys her clothes in Paris.'

'No,' he said. 'They buy clothes *made* in Paris, but mostly they buy them in New York or LA. You *buy* in Paris. That's the tops too.'

They turned into a driveway, and a road through a garden that was mostly hibiscus and oleanders and roses. There should have been bulbuls, she thought, until she saw the house, which was what Californians called Colonial. By that they meant Spanish Colonial, Jay explained, and indeed it did look vaguely Moorish, and rather like a film set, though once inside she could see that it was substantial enough. There were perhaps fifty people there already, and to judge by the number of glasses, at least as many more expected. A hired butler who looked precisely what he was, an actor out of work, enquired their names, and a hovering flock of reporters ticked them off against their lists.

'Miss Jane Whitcomb, Mr J.M. Bower,' he called, in a voice that could have cracked windows.

An eager, bustling little man scurried across to them, beckoning to a waitress as he came.

'Jay, good to *see* you,' he said. 'And Jane – how nice of you to drop by.'

To her certain knowledge they had never met, but this was Hollywood after all: to admit ignorance of her identity would be the deadliest of insults. She took a chance.

'David,' she said. 'It was sweet of you to invite me.'

The waitress offered yet more champagne. Jane wondered what Americans had drunk before prohibition.

'Let me introduce you to my fiancée,' said Greenglass, and beckoned once more, this time to a girl about half his age. She was a very pretty fiancée, just as the waitress was a very pretty waitress, but then every woman in the room was pretty, except for a very few who all had that air of being indissolubly wedded to wealth. The fiancée seemed oddly reluctant to join them, Jane thought, and looked at Jay, who for once seemed startled, and then she realised why.

'This is Thelma,' Greenglass said, and of course it was. When last seen she had been lamenting the fact that she had no hope of seeing Venice before she became old next year. That was Venice, Italy, she'd explained. Venice California she had seen too often already.

'How do you do?' said Thelma and offered her hand. There was a frantic look about her eyes that made instant sense.

'How do you do?' said Jane. 'So nice to meet you.' The frantic look faded a little.

'Thelma was in New York too, last week,' said Greenglass. 'Had to go to visit her poor old mother. Thelma's a real mother's girl.'

'Really?' said Jane.

'You didn't run into each other in the wicked city then?' The eager look was still there, but now it was a shrewd look too.

'How could we?' said Jay. 'I doubt if Thelma's mother belongs to the Stork Club.' He turned to Jane. 'Would you care to dance?'

They went to a drawing room where the furniture had been pushed back to leave the parquet clear. In an alcove a quintet led by a cornet player attacked 'Way Down Yonder In New Orleans'. The cornet player did his best, and he seemed sober, but he was not Bix Beiderbecke.

'Why are we lying?' Jane asked.

'About what?'

'About Thelma what's-it?'

'Tanagra,' said Jay. 'She's Thelma Tanagra.'

'Golly,' said Jane.

'Well she is now,' said Jay. 'Greenglass reckons he's going to make her a star and Thelma Schultz didn't have the right ring to it. Trouble is he wants to make her an innocent, sweet kind of star like Mary Pickford. None of this Pola Negri bad-girl stuff – so speakeasies and clubs are out.'

'And did she really go to New York to see her mother?' Jane asked.

'I guess so,' said Jay. 'When she could spare the time from the Sligo Slasher's.'

'And will Mr Greenglass succeed in making her a star?'

'Maybe,' said Jay. 'She moves well – and she even talks well. Come next year she'll be in with a chance – but she'll never be in your class, naturally.'

'I want to talk to you about that,' said Jane.

'Not now,' said Jay. 'Half the people here can lip read, and all the agents.'

From time to time the brass-hinged butler roared out more names: famous names most of them, the Hollywood royalty who never arrived early. 'Miss Theda Bara', 'Miss Mabel Normand', 'Mr Ramon Navarro', 'Mr Arbuckle', 'Mr Fairbanks', 'Miss Pickford'.

Like living inside a movie magazine, she thought, as Jay introduced her to this one and that one, not forgetting Tom Mix.

She sipped champagne and chatted and danced when asked, which was fairly often. Jay's influence, she supposed, and dutifully told the three men who mentioned it that she bought her dresses in Paris. None of the women mentioned it all. Waring was there and danced with her, and she told him at once that they were not to talk business on account of the lip readers. He looked puzzled and relieved at the same time. When the supper interval came she went out into the garden instead. No nightbirds sang, but the scent of roses persisted, the air seemed warm after New York, and there were lights in the trees by the pool – and nobody to ask her where she bought her clothes and offer to buy her some more. There had been two, so far. Not bad for an elderly person when it wasn't yet midnight. Then she caught a glimpse of movement by the oleanders and turned too late to go back in. She had been seen.

'Miss Whitcomb,' Thelma Tanagra called. 'Give me a minute, will you?'

Jane went over to her. There was a stone urn with a broad base near the shrubs: on it were a bottle of champagne half full and two glasses. Only one glass was being used.

'I needed some air,' said Thelma Tanagra, then added: 'Also

I needed a drink. Mr Greenglass doesn't like it when I need a drink.'

'So I gathered,' said Jane.

'Who told you? Jay Bower?'

'Why yes,' said Jane. 'But it wasn't gossip, you know. He was just explaining to me why we couldn't say we met at the Stork Club.'

'Was that what Jay says he was doing for me? Protecting me?'

'More or less,' said Jane. 'But it was nothing, really. A few tactful lies.'

'Jay's good at lies,' said Thelma, 'but I never heard him called tactful before.'

Jane thought, she must have gulped that champagne awfully quickly, and then remembered that one did sometimes, when one was miserable.

'Have a drink,' the younger woman said. 'I brought an extra glass. I guess I thought I might get lucky.'

She laughed then, shrill and mocking laughter at the suggestion of Thelma Tanagra of all people thinking she might get lucky. Jane allowed her to pour champagne into the other glass.

'Here's to us girls,' Thelma Tanagra said, then gulped down her drink and promptly poured another. 'Jay was crazy about you,' she said.

'Indeed?'

'Indeed,' said the other girl. 'Hey – maybe that's why.'

'I don't understand you,' said Jane.

'The way you talk. That English-rose voice . . . . Indeed . . . .' She tasted the word.

'We're colleagues, no more,' said Jane.

'It's not what he wants you to be,' said Thelma Tanagra. 'A partner's what he wants you to be. His partner in a double act.'

'Even if it were true,' said Jane, 'it's hardly your business.'

'If it were,' repeated Thelma Tanagra. 'You see? Not even "If it was". He gets the hots for a voice.' She paused then, her glass half way to her lips. 'My God yes,' she said at last. 'That's what it must be. The way you all talk.'

Jane said, 'I honestly think we ought to go back inside. You'll be missed.'

'Who would miss me?' asked Thelma Tanagra.

'Your fiancée surely?' said Jane.

'By now David will be in the library talking money,' said Thelma Tanagra. 'The library – that's a hot one. Twenty yards of phoney leather and a half a dozen scripts, and him on his knees to Jay Bower saying "Of course you keep Canada, Jay sweetheart. But maybe I could have Peru?"' She gulped once more.

'All the same,' said Jane, 'I made him promise to take me back to my hotel by twelve thirty and you know how prompt he is.'

'I used to,' said the other girl, and added: 'I've been drinking all day.'

'So I should suppose.'

'I'm that bad?'

'I'm afraid so,' said Jane.

'There's a pool hut here with a shower,' said the other girl. 'If I go in there for a while I'll be OK. I've done it before.'

'Do you want me to keep watch for you?' Jane asked.

'I don't think I could bear for you to do me another favour,' said Thelma Tanagra. 'I'm sorry about that but it's true.'

She turned, and lurched towards the pool hut, and Jane poured the champagne out on to the soil of the urn and hid the bottle and one glass beneath it, then took the other glass and walked back into the house. Neither David Greenglass nor Jay Bower was present, but this was neither the time nor the place for quiet reflection: the quintet had just begun on 'Japanese Sandman'. She allowed Gary Cooper to dance with her instead.

Jay emerged with Greenglass at exactly twelve thirty and held the beaded coat for her as if it were the pleasantest task he had performed all evening. Greenglass looked round the room and spotted his fiancée at once, sipping a glass of non-alcoholic fruit punch. He came back to Jane and Jay, his arm about Thelma Tanagra's waist.

'I wish you could have stayed longer,' he said.

'I promised Jane,' said Jay. 'It's a punishing trip all the way from New York.'

'You're telling me,' said Thelma Tanagra.

Greenglass laughed, and kissed her cheek. She stood as still as stone, but at least she seemed sober.

'You'll think over what I said?' Greenglass asked Jay.

'Oh sure,' said Jay. 'There could be a deal here once you cut your costs a little. I'll call you in a couple of days. Goodnight.'

Then all the goodbyes were said, and Thelma Tanagra called out: 'Goodbye, Jane. It was just great to meet you.' They went out to the car.

'You and David's girl have a chat?' Jay asked.

'No.' A lie, a real whopper, but now was definitely not the time.

'Then why did she say it was great to meet you?'

'Maybe it was,' said Jane.

He laughed, and took her hand. 'I was crazy for you the first time I ever saw you,' he said. 'And I can't think of anybody who'd be surprised by that.'

'Except your parents.'

'Except, as you say, my parents. But then I never fail to surprise them. But don't interrupt me – not when I'm talking about you. . . . One of the million reasons why I feel this way about you – '

'Love me, you mean?'

'Love you then – is that you can always make me laugh.'

He had said he loved her, probably for the last time. Tomorrow he wouldn't even remember he'd said it, but it had been said.

'Do you like my voice?' she asked.

'Sure,' he said. 'It's a beautiful voice.'

'Is there something in English voices that you find specially attractive?'

'No,' he said. 'Just yours. Once the movies start to talk you'll be an even bigger star.'

'Will Miss Tanagra really be a star? That's what you and Mr Greenglass were discussing, I take it?'

'You wouldn't listen at a keyhole,' said Jay. 'You're British.'

'I also have eyes in my head,' said Jane. 'I saw the way he made a beeline for her the instant the two of you appeared.'

'I'll never try to hide anything from you,' he said. 'It can't be done. Yeah. . . . He needs money for a picture, and my father's bank can let him have it – if the price is right.'

'The price of money.'

'It always comes high,' said Jay. 'Still – as I say – the girl's not bad: I've seen her tests – and the script is good. His little Thelma could turn out to be a star this time next year.'

'If she does she'll leave him?' said Jane.

'What makes you say so?'

'I watched her when he kissed her.'

'Maybe you're right,' he said, in the voice of one who didn't care much either way. 'Still, if she gets to be a star she won't need him any more.'

Jane found herself willing the car to go faster. She wanted to be in her bed, alone. She wanted to cry.

Next morning she still felt rotten, so she wore the Cartier leopard pinned to the lapel of a white silk suit by Worth. 'Are all your clothes made of silk?' Bet had asked her, and the answer seemed to be, well almost. But there were the fur coats, of course. The suit was simple, with a pleated, unfussy skirt. Shoes were of white kid with an enamel buckle, and a cloche hat by Martine Callot. Much too good for Worldwide Studios, she thought, but only just good enough for Cleopatra. But the brooch made her feel better. As she pinned it to her lapel she heard Aunt Pen's voice. 'It'll be all right,' it said. 'You'll see. Only try not to fret too much, my lovely.' And then, it was gone. But it had been there – for as long as it takes to say fifteen words. It helped quite a bit.

She was going to the studios with Waring, but for once he wasn't driving his Packard: this time she would be driving, an enormous great beast like a scaled-down version of a clipper ship, according to Jay, a Hispano-Suiza that he had acquired by some intricate deal or other. Jay Bower, she had observed, rarely bought things: he acquired them. That way he could make a profit. Waring arrived, looking nervous, and with him yet another batch of post, which was awkward. There were far too many to take with her, and Waring was fretting. He'd borrowed his best lighting cameraman from a feature, and couldn't keep him for long. Jane flipped through them and found only two with handwriting she recognised. She locked them in a drawer, then called for Amparo, who came at once.

'Have you ever been to a studio?' she asked.

'Once I work as an extra. Two days,' Amparo said.

'Would you like to go to Worldwide?'

'Oh yes, miss.' There could be no doubt that she meant it.

'Then get your hat,' said Jane. 'And mine.' Amparo fled.

Nice to make someone happy, thought Jane. And if she's with

me at Worldwide she can't be going through my letters here. . . .
Garden of Allah, indeed.

'It's not really a big production,' Waring was saying. 'But we
can let you have a dresser too.'

'I like Amparo with me,' said Jane. 'I feel more comfortable.'

He didn't argue: he'd been coping with female stars for years:
ladies who insisted on having their hairdresser with them, or
their love-birds, or their pekinese. Once it had been a chimpanzee
in a dinner suit. A maid was nothing at all. A cloche hat, brisk
but not too businesslike, with a spray of feathers to one side,
and she was ready. They went out all three. Just like the movies,
she thought. The star, her director and her personal maid.

The Hispano-Suiza brooded in the sunlight, looking as if it
were about to set sail from Australia with a load of grain. Beside
her stood its chauffeur, dressed like a uhlan lancer who had
decided to exchange his helmet for a peaked cap. He waited
uneasily by the driveway of the hotel as Jane walked towards
him, pulling on a pair of white, gauntletted gloves as she did so.
I mean Mr Bower said she'll be OK, he thought, and she surely
looks OK, but this car is unique.

'Good morning,' said Jane. 'Perhaps you'd better tell me a few
things before we start.'

He began to do so, and around him camera flashes flared, a
movie cameraman cranked away. This time Cinderella was going
to drive the coach herself – or crash it. And either way, it was
news.

At last she interrupted the chauffeur's nervous gabble in
mid-sentence, and motioned Amparo and Waring into the back.
The Hispano-Suiza's body was curtained and flower bedecked
and far from visible, but the chauffeur's place was open and
uncovered and on display. No wonder that cunning so-and-so
had decreed that she should drive. The chauffeur swung the
handle and got in beside her, and she did what he had said and
the whole contraption took off, moving easily enough. Not as
friendly as the Voisin, but not nearly as antagonistic as the
Bentley. She patted the little leopard for luck and drove out
through the gates.

But she didn't need luck. Not really. The car was far too vast
an object for the transportation of four people, but not as big as
an ambulance, and a damn sight easier to drive. All the same the

chauffeur didn't begin to relax till they reached Sunset Boulevard, and even then he started twitching again when a truck appeared alongside them, with another movie camera aboard to take more pictures.

But at least they arrived at Worldwide Studios, and Waring flourished his pass and was waved on by the guard, so that Jane could drive beneath the arch surmounted by a globe on which a winged figure perched, rather uneasily she thought. A symbol for David Greenglass? She drove to the front office and parked, and the chauffeur smiled at last. His car was being returned to him. Jane went in to meet the president.

Her memory of such things was hazy, but for her presidents had names like Washington, Lincoln, Roosevelt. Murray Fisch was a surprise, and so was Waring's attitude towards him. Presidents, she thought, were there to be grovelled to, but Waring's attitude to Fisch was polite, yet firm, and Fisch took it without a blink. Another twinkler like Greenglass, but older and fatter, with more of a survivor's look, and not in the least resentful when Waring explained in detail exactly the back-up that he and Jane needed. And then she realised why. Of course. Waring was there as Jay's man, and Jay controlled the money. So of course he got everything he demanded – or rather requested. Waring was a very polite young man.

Fisch's attitude to her was puzzling, too. When it came to eager bustle he was every bit as good as David Greenglass: ash tray, coffee, turn down the air conditioning, anything you want just ask, anything at all; it was all there, and yet behind the pleasing there was something else, something she found it difficult to define. Almost a sense of transience. He had a hard time masking his relief when at last they left him for the Hispano-Suiza.

This time the chauffeur drove them to a bungalow near the stage where they were to work. Amparo was already at work, blissfully bossing a couple of workmen she had commandeered. The shower dripped, and the dressing-table mirror had stuck.

The drawing room was prettily furnished, she thought, and all the furniture elegant, except for one large sofa that was sturdy indeed. The place where the stars relaxed, she thought. Singly or in groups. . . . Waring brought her a slim folder of yellow typescript.

'Your script,' he said. 'Look it over. Want a drink?'

'Will you?'

'Not when I'm working,' Waring said.

'Then I'll wait.' She began to read: Mid Shot Cleopatra, at ease in her palace, reclining on a divan. . . . . A slavegirl enters.

2 Shot. Slavegirl and Cleopatra.

Another Angle. The slavegirl prostrates herself before the queen.

Close Shot. Cleopatra. Her lips move. 'Well?' She signals to the slavegirl to rise.

Mid Shot. Slavegirl rises, speaks. Caption: 'O great queen, Mark Antony approaches.'

Close Shot. Cleopatra. Her eyes blaze at the news, her bosom heaves. She is ecstatic.

'I think perhaps I will have that drink,' said Jane. 'Gin and Italian vermouth if they've got it.'

Waring opened a cupboard and she went on reading. It was all pretty much of a muchness. Mark Antony entered in Roman armour and they rolled about on the couch a bit – though first, she noticed with relief, she helped him out of his breastplate and things. Then he told her he had to return to Rome and live with his wife again for reasons of politics, and Cleopatra's bosom heaved even more. . . . Jane took the drink Waring offered.

'Will this really work?' she asked.

'If you and the slavegirl and Mark Antony do it right it will.'

'But it's all so simple,' she said. 'So – crude. Forgive me – '

'I've heard it before,' said Waring. 'But you're forgetting one thing. What you've got is words on a page, and that's not what we're after. What we're after is pictures on a screen. Do you want to try it?'

'I don't think I can,' she said.

'Of course you can,' said Waring. 'What's your problem? All this mid-shot and two-shot stuff? I'll take care of that.'

'It's not that,' she said. 'It's just – doing it. I know it sounds silly, but I'm shy.'

'We'll try it here first,' he said, 'and don't let it bother you. A lot of people get camera fright.'

'Even before they see the camera?'

'Miss Whitcomb,' he said, 'you know damn well we've got to do this, so finish your nice drink and let's get on with it.'

She finished her drink and imitated his gestures, and was so stiff and wooden that for once Waring looked worried.

'I don't get it,' he said. 'Back in New York you had no problem. Yet. . . . Wait a minute.'

'Oh God what now?' she said.

'Nothing. Relax. In New York you were thinking of your dog – and two guys you couldn't stand the sight of.'

'So?'

'So now you've got to think of Mark Antony. Don't tell me you haven't had one in your life, Miss Whitcomb. The way you look.'

So now it seemed she was going to have to act out her farewell to Jay Bower in his own studio, and record it all on film for posterity.

Amparo was waiting for her in her dressing room to help her out of the Worth suit and twentieth-century underwear, and into the minimum amount of material the front office thought they could get away with, then they wrapped her in a motor rug and drove her to the stage where the camera waited. It must have been all of a hundred yards. Thank God the head-dress thing isn't so heavy this time, she thought. But it did have a tendency to slip. Make-up next on face and body, and goodness what a nasty colour it was, and then on to the stage and this weird new brand of purgatory. There was the couch or whatever it was, and on it a tigerskin that scratched every bit as much as the one in Paris. Suddenly she was back there, Jay was making her laugh and that idiot Powell was prancing about as Oberon, and soon they would make love, and later she would clobber Powell, and Jay would come charging to the rescue. Really, Mark Antony wasn't all that far away. . . . Enter slavegirl.

She missed her marks a couple of times, and responded to the wrong cues, but at least Waring and his cameraman and crew treated the whole episode as a job, and not as some sort of comic treat. At last Waring said, 'That's the one. We'll print that one. Lunch break. – Thank you, Jane.'

To her amazement she discovered that they had been filming for over two hours.

Jane and Waring went back to the bungalow, where he telephoned for food, but he sent Amparo to the commissariat.

'She looks after you well,' he said. 'She deserves a treat,' then laughed at her bewilderment. 'Half the stars of Worldwide will be there,' he said. 'She'll be able to talk about it for weeks.'

They went over the remainder of her test, with him as Mark Antony. His grip was disappointingly tentative, she thought, and then she remembered whom he worked for.

'I've got Guy Fielding to play Mark Antony,' he said.

'I don't know him,' she said. 'Is he nice?'

'He's OK,' he said. 'Not quite at the top but better than most. He's a faggot. You don't mind, I hope?'

'I beg your pardon?'

'You know. A homosexual. Like your friend Barry.'

She looked down at her costume. 'I hope I don't put him off,' she said.

'He's an actor,' said Waring, 'so he'll act.'

He did, too. Very ardent and warlike, and with a splendid profile, even if it was only a test, and he knew how to take hold of a girl, or at least he acted as if he knew.

Then at last Waring said it was over and Guy kissed her cheek and went off not quite mincing, and telling everyone who would listen how lucky the Romans were to be able to wear skirts and not get arrested.

49

SHE SHOWERED AWAY the make-up, and Amparo helped her dress (really, it was like being back in the nursery), then drove back to the Garden of Allah and the two letters that she recognised: one from Charles Lovell, and one from Georgina Payne. Strange that she should recognise Lovell's so easily, she thought. She had only received one note from him before, and a very brief scrawl it had been, to tell her how much he regretted the way in which their lunch had ended.

He was not a good letter writer: or at least he was not good at writing a letter of this kind. Spelling and punctuation good, even VGI or Very Good Indeed, according to Vinney's system of marking. The letter had been carefully planned too: point followed point; argument evolved from argument. But it was never him speaking, reaching out to touch her. . . . Close Shot heaving bosom would have made far more of an impression – if men did have bosoms. But of course they did. Abraham had one, according to the Bible. But did it *heave*?

She said aloud, 'Now that's enough. Get on with your letter,' in a voice like Vinney's. Which wasn't surprising really. She had often tried frivolity as the way of dodging something unpleasant. It had never worked with Vinney.

'Essentially what I am trying to say is that I have never been more miserable in my life than since your departure. Perhaps you realise what an overwhelming effect you had on me when I was privileged to meet you at the Watsons': as a mere male I have no way of telling. What I do know is that I grossly mishandled our luncheon engagement, my only excuse being that from the beginning there would be no deception between us. I had deceived many people: for reasons of shame perhaps, or self-disgust, or mere secretiveness, but I could not deceive you. I admire you too much.'

And so on. At very great length indeed.

Admire. Not at all the word she'd wanted to read. Even Jay had admitted that he loved her, when she'd finally resorted to the forceps. Well either Charles did or he didn't, but he'd never put it in writing. She'd have to face him if she really wanted to know. But if he didn't love her, why write all this screed? All this admiration and need to see her, and 'my fondest hope is that we can meet again'? Suddenly she longed very much to be in South Terrace, where she could at least telephone him at Eaton Square. It was, she decided, time for decisions, then realised almost at once that hers had already been made.

Best tell Jay face to face, she thought. They were due at another party that night – when money came to town it seemed that Hollywood was always en fête – but a party was not the place. She went to the telephone, but before she could reach it the doorbell rang, and Amparo came in, then to the hallway. There was a murmur of voices, both female, which was a pity. She had hoped it would be Jay, and was in no mood for a lady reporter. Amparo came back in.

'A lady to see you,' Amparo said. 'I told her not without an appointment, but she says you know her.'

'Well of course you know me,' said Georgina Payne.

'Hello Georgina,' said Jane. 'Yes. . . . I rather think I do know you.'

'Darling I did write to you,' said Georgina. 'Don't tell me you didn't get it?'

Jane held up the letter. 'You were next on the list,' she said, then turned to Amparo. 'Can you make martinis?' she asked.

'Yes, Miss Whitcomb.'

'Make us a shaker then,' said Jane, 'and telephone room service for some canapés.'

'Yes, Miss Whitcomb.' Amparo left them.

'What splendour you live in,' said Georgina, 'but then I live in splendour too.'

'Where, may I ask?'

'The suite above yours.'

Suddenly Jane burst out laughing, and got up from her chair to embrace Georgina.

'That's better,' Georgina said. 'At first I detected a distinct nip of frost in this mild California air.'

'No darling,' said Jane. 'Just shock. A couple of days ago you'd have encountered frost, Antarctica in fact, but that was all my own foolishness. Or almost all.'

'Oh,' said Georgina. She wore a pink silk suit, and shoes of pink dyed glacé kid, and looked as edible as she always did.

'Am I on the carpet?' she said.

'Certainly not,' said Jane. 'You're one of my chums. Oh by the way, Amparo my maid is a spy of Bower's I think, so if you don't want anything to be reported you'd better give me some sort of signal.'

'Finger to lips sort of thing?'

'Something like that.'

'I'd much sooner have a girlish chat,' said Georgina, 'and if you should need written evidence there's always my letter.' Amparo came in with the shaker and poured two drinks, her face expressionless. Jane raised her glass, then drank as Amparo left them.

'I really needed that,' she said, then added smugly, 'I've been filming all day.'

'Never mind the glamour,' said Georgina. 'Tell me all.'

'It started with your picture,' said Jane.

'The one of me in the altogether?' Jane nodded. 'You saw it at that terrible house in Fulham, the day Mrs Browne popped in to borrow a bread knife, I remember.'

'I saw it again after that,' said Jane. 'In a rather grand penthouse in Fleet Street.'

'Oh,' said Georgina, and Jane waited. 'But I didn't know he belonged to you then, honestly I didn't. I mean I knew he'd fed you from time to time, and he was printing your collected works, but I didn't know that you – ' She hesitated. 'You know.'

'He bought me some ear-rings, and I wore some others instead,' said Jane. 'Nothing personal. It was just that his didn't go with my dress. But we quarrelled, rather foolishly, and it wasn't entirely his fault, and being the sort of man he is he felt he needed a little consolation.'

'It was more like revenge,' said Georgina. 'And only the once, I promise you.'

'Of course.'

'Made it up for a while, did you?' Georgina shook her head. 'Sorry. Not my business. But why did he buy my picture? I mean I didn't own the thing. Unless – '

'Go on.'

'He *said* it was so a lot of randy little bastards – '

'Randy?'

'Horny was the word he used, but he meant randy – he said he didn't want them gawping at me. This was nonsense and I told him so and he said that the picture would hurt my career at the BBC so he'd bought it as a favour to me.'

'My God yes,' said Jane. 'The British Broadcasting Company. What's happened to them?'

'Still there so far as I know,' Georgina said. 'I'm the one who upped and left.'

'To come here?' Georgina nodded, her martini on its way to her lips.

The canapés arrived, a whole trolley-load, and Jane gave its trundler a dollar, then turned to Amparo, who was serving the canapés. 'I think we'll have another batch of martinis,' she said.

'Yes miss,' said Amparo. 'Mr Bower said he'd stop by at eight, miss.'

'Just the martinis,' said Jane. 'For the moment.' Amparo took the shaker and left.

'Goodness you are stern,' said Georgina.

'Are you going to the Ogden party tonight?' Jane asked.

'A man called Waring was supposed to take me,' said Georgina. 'I hadn't even met him. It's weird. Then I bumped into Michael in New York and thought I might be delayed so I wired this Waring at the studio and told him not to bother – only I wasn't delayed after all. Michael's got this new girl he met in Rimini who says she's a contessa.' She smiled. 'What fun for him if she is. Only besides being a contessa she's an American widow with oodles of money so I arrived here on time anyway.'

'Have you got a maid yet?'

'A Swede,' said Georgina, 'but she starts tomorrow. You are lucky having a brunette.'

'Go and get your evening dress and bring it down here,' said

Jane. 'We'll talk while we change. Amparo will help you.'

'But if she's a spy – ' said Georgina.

'Then she'll tell it all to Jay and save us a lot of trouble.'

Georgina said, 'This is rather important to me.'

'I know,' said Jane. 'But it will be all right. You'll see. Just trust me.'

Georgina left, and Jane rang the bell for Amparo, who looked if anything even more impassive.

'I want you to telephone Mr Bower,' she said, 'and tell him I've been delayed – that I shan't be ready till nine o'clock. Then I want you to telephone Mr Waring – the studio will know where to reach him, and tell him to be here at nine, too. He's to collect Miss Georgina Payne. Will you do that?'

'Yes, Miss Whitcomb.' Bewilderment replaced the impassive look, but she went to make the calls in the bedroom, and Georgina came back with a small travelling bag.

'What now?' she said.

'Amparo makes a couple of telephone calls, then we bathe and change. . . . Jay told you half the truth about that picture. It was to avoid embarrassment, but it wasn't the BBC's, it was his. Or rather Worldwide's. He's offered you a contract, I suppose?'

'Well yes,' said Georgina, then dropped her voice. 'Has he got some kind of a weird thing about voices?'

'Talking pictures,' said Jane. 'In the future the likes of us will have to sound nice as well as look nice. Or rather the likes of you will. You knew I was being tested for Cleopatra?'

'My dear the whole country knows it. Especially the ones who read the *Daily World*. Will she, won't she? Too bad you weren't there to see it.'

'And did they show my picture?'

'Well yes,' said Georgina. 'Such a lot of fuss about nothing.'

'Nothing?'

'No no,' said Georgina laughing. 'You were more than adequately covered.' Jane gathered that a little discreet art work had been done. 'Not like me.'

Jane said, 'I tested for the Cleopatra part today, and I *think* it was adequate. Just about. The whole thing was a put-up job, anyway, to get me out of a nasty situation. Bower at his best. But at some point while it was happening he got the idea that there might be money in it – '

'Bower at his worst,' said Georgina.

'Maybe. But you're the one he wants to replace me, I'll bet. That's why he signed you up'

'Oh my God,' said Georgina. 'Me? Are you sure you won't mind?'

'Not in the least,' said Jane. 'Do you think you'll enjoy it?'

'At least I won't be playing the piano,' said Georgina, 'and it's far more money than the BBC.'

'Tell me,' said Jane, 'how did Bower get you out of their clutches?'

'Bower had nothing to do with it,' Georgina said. 'I handled that myself.' Somewhere in the British Broadcasting Company there worked a man in need of sympathy.

Amparo warned them that it was their last chance to change.

Their gentlemen were impressed. The quality of her gown suggested that Georgina was receiving either a dress allowance or an advance on her salary, and it was the first time that Tom Waring had seen her and it was pretty to watch, Jane thought. She was wearing her Fortuny dress, as it was very possibly the last time that she would attend a party with Jay as her escort.

'You look beautiful,' he said, and she curtsied. He had brought her an orchid, and Waring had brought one for Georgina. The problem was where to pin them, but Amparo managed it.

'Tell me about Ogden,' Jane asked.

'Rick Ogden is the highest-paid star at Worldwide,' said Jay. 'He's also the meanest son of a bitch I ever met. In fact he's so damn mean we had to put it in his contract that he gives four parties a year, and somebody else does the catering. They tell me that when he got the bill for the first one he cried. Now are you going to tell me how you and Georgina met up?'

'Serendipity,' she said, and he nodded.

'What's that?' asked Waring.

'Discovery by happy accident,' said Jay, and she discovered that there were occasions when she still liked him very much, then told him how Georgina had walked in on her.

'Georgina was to have been my surprise companion on the Super-Chief, I take it?' she said.

'That's right,' said Jay. 'But she got delayed in London as well as New York.'

'The BBC were rather reluctant to let me go,' Georgina said.

'I don't blame them,' said Waring. 'Whoever they are.'

They went to the party.

Jay danced with Georgina first. There was a protocol in these matters, and the first girl that the representative of the owners of Worldwide danced with was thereby proclaimed the important girl, the one on the way up, the one to watch, just as the one he didn't dance with was the girl on the way down. So Jane danced with Rick Ogden instead. He was under contract after all, and had had his orders. As they danced he talked of nothing but the escalating price of grapefruit. Waring was scarcely better. When she danced with him she tried to talk about her test, but he was evasive. He hadn't finished cutting. Much too early to say. Obviously he wouldn't tell her a thing until Jay had told him what he was *allowed* to say.

The third dance was Jay's, and he said: 'I saw your test.'

'What about the lip readers?' she asked.

'They may as well know it now.'

'But Tom Waring said he hadn't finished cutting it.' For some reason, now that she could know, she didn't want to.

'It's not the fine cut but it'll do,' he said, and then, 'Relax. You were OK. Not sensational, but better than most.'

For some reason she felt enormously relieved. Adequacy for once was all she had wanted. The band began to play 'Horsey Keep Your Tail Up' and Jay stopped dead.

'If you don't mind,' he said, 'I'd rather talk.'

'Of course. Shall we take a walk by the pool?' She hadn't seen it, but there was always a pool.

'OK,' he said. 'We won't run into Thelma this time. She and Dave are at Mack Sennet's party.'

'I looked Tanagra up,' she said. 'It was a town in ancient Greece famous for its terra-cotta figurines, also called Tanagra. Why would anybody be called after a terra-cotta figurine?'

'Because it's better than Schultz,' said Jay. 'Where did you look it up?'

'In a dictionary.'

'Where in God's name did you get a dictionary at the Garden of Allah?'

'Room service,' said Jane. 'You can get anything at room service.' They were out in the garden, which Ogden had been forced to maintain under threat of suspension, and so it looked pretty. Other couples were strolling too, but as soon as they saw Jay they moved away.

'I'm sorry you missed Georgina,' he said.

'She's going to take my place, I gather?'

'Now wait a minute – '

She laughed, a low, gurgling sound, and he was surprised and relieved to note that it held nothing but amusement. 'As Cleopatra you ass.' He said nothing, and she added, 'That *is* the idea, isn't it?'

'Well yes,' he said. 'If you don't want it.'

'Oh come off it,' she said. 'I'm sure her test will be much better than mine. But I *don't* want it.'

'What do you want?'

'To go home,' she said. 'I gather the jury's in and I've been found Not Guilty and without a stain on my character. Well nothing visible anyway.'

'Back to Felston?'

'Sort of,' she said. 'Hollywood was fun and I adored New York, but the hols are over, my dear.'

'And I'm part of the hols?'

'Obviously,' she said.

'You going to tell me why?'

'On account of Miss Terra-Cotta Figurine.' He nodded. He had known it was coming after all.

'It started last year when I came out here,' he said. 'Then she met David Greenglass and I thought that it was over. Then I met her again in New York and found out it wasn't.'

'I was in New York,' she said.

'But you didn't want me, except that one time.'

'I was still there.' They walked on and strolled round the edge of the pool.

'Did you tell Georgina about Thelma?' he asked.

'Not her business.' A few more steps, and an amorous couple scurried into the shadows.

'I don't suppose I'll see you again,' she said.

He said at once, 'You mean you're quitting the paper?' He sounded amazed.

'Not if you don't want me to.'

'Of course I don't want you to.' He was impatient, which

meant that things were back to normal. 'Your stuff's good now. Your features are going over big. I want more.'

'Then I won't say goodbye.'

'I should say not. When are you planning to leave?'

'Three or four days. As soon as I decently can. It wouldn't look too good if I scuttled off back home tomorrow.'

'It would not. I thank you for that. Maybe I could arrange a trip or something?'

'Some other time,' she said. 'I have about five thousand letters to write. But I would like to see my test if I may.'

'Be a pleasure. Shall we go back inside?'

The agenda was completed: there was no point in wasting further time. 'Why not?' she said.

More dances, with Jay, with Tom Waring, with the men who had been told to dance with her, until it was time to go home in the Hispano-Suiza, which she let the chauffeur drive. It was if she'd tipped him a hundred dollars. On the way Georgina told her that her screen test was due in two days' time, and that Tom Waring would be working on it with her at the Garden of Allah the next day. Jane advised her to order plenty of Sidecars. She was so tired her whole body ached.

In her suite Amparo was still up, and as impassive as ever.

'You didn't tell me to go to bed, miss,' she said.

'Just as well,' said Jane. 'I'm dying for a massage – if you're not too tired.'

'Be glad to.'

Her hands were as strong and sure as the first time, and Jane wallowed in it.

At last Amparo said, 'What you said about my spying, it was all true.'

'Of course it was,' said Jane. 'I hope he paid you in advance?'

Amparo chuckled. 'Cash on the barrel,' she said. 'Two hundred dollars. It's the only way to do business.'

'Quite right,' said Jane. 'So we're both all right. I didn't tell you anything I didn't want anybody to know, and you've got two hundred dollars. What could be nicer? But – forgive me for prying – but why did you tell me?'

'I never did it before, Miss Whitcomb,' said Amparo. 'And the first time has to be a lady I find I like very much. And now I'll have to tell it in confession. Would you like a shower, miss?'

'No,' said Jane. 'I'll take a bath.'

There was thunder during the night, and sheet lightning, but no rain. Jane dreamed of Passchendaele. She was in the château, lying in John's arms. Together they listened to the guns.

Next morning while Amparo helped her to dress (really she must stop getting used to this nonsense) she thought about the dream and decided that Jabber would be as happy with it as she was, then ordered breakfast and looked at the papers. The *Hollywood Reporter* had discovered Georgina. 'Graceful yet glamorous English rose', 'Worldwide's latest beauty', 'centre of attraction at Rick Ogden's delightful party'. She was there too, at the end of paragraph three. 'Jane Whitcomb, talented and fashionable friend of the beautiful Miss Payne'. She had been demoted to the rank of friend. She was safe.

It was time to begin on the letters. She sorted out the obvious fan mail first, dividing it into two groups: adoration and abuse, and found herself wishing there had been more abuse, since she had no intention of replying to it. For the rest she devised one standard letter which replied to every possible point raised, and stated in three different forms of words how happy she was, and how she had no intention of abandoning her trust. Then she rang the desk and enquired if she could hire a typist and was asked how many she would need. Three would do, she said. They came up to collect her standard reply and she asked for three hundred and seventy-seven copies. No carbons. The girls treated it as part of a perfectly normal day's work.

Then she read Georgina's letter, which told her nothing Georgina had not already told her, and began on the others. One from Bob, congratulating her on the way folks was all on her side, and how a bloke in a pub off King's Cross had got a punch on the nose for saying she was no better than she should be, 'and not' (heavily underlined) by me either. Though I would have done if I'd been there.

A letter from Bet. She had seen the photograph of Jane in fancy dress and couldn't understand what they were all on about. (She simply must see what the *World* had done to it, she thought.) Everybody was fine but they all wished she was back except Andy and he kept going on about how nobody listened to Andy, not any more, even though times were bad and getting worse and Da had been paid off, so there didn't seem like much chance of wedding bells this year. There was a PS from Grandma. 'Bet's right, me bairn. Things are bad and getting worse, and the clinic's working full blast already. But there's trouble brewing. I can smell it. It's time you were back. Lucky for us Bob's in London and sending money back regular. There's lots of folks here don't have that luck. From your loving Grandma.' I must pass the hat before I leave Hollywood, thought Jane. Another picture postcard from Lionel. It depicted a Christian martyr (female) fearlessly confronting a Roman gladiator (male). 'If I had wanted to take an interest in the Perils of Pauline,' Lionel had written, 'I should have gone to the cinema. Do come home.' Acha, Lionel. I hear and I obey.

She went up to Georgina's suite then, to help with the rehearsal. This time she was the slavegirl. From star to bit player overnight – but what were best friends for? Georgina worked at it as a miner might search for gold, striving to give each gesture meaning, even reality. 'O great queen, Mark Antony approaches,' she said, and my God did that bosom heave. But then why not? It was why she was here. Georgina really did want to be a star.

She lunched with them, rang the desk again, and found that she could hire a car and took charge of something called a Buick Six which she'd come across in England too. In it she drove out into the California countryside, that was all canyons and mountains and orange groves, and down to the ocean to watch the great surf pounding, along a seemingly endless coast until she even reached a place called Venice, but not the one that Thelma yearned for.

Next day she called on Jay at the studio, and he promised her a copy of the photograph, and showed her the test. She knew at once that Georgina would be enormously better, and said so, and asked for the film test as a gift. It seemed that for a studio executive to give up film was a far more serious matter than to give up arterial blood, but in the end Jay yielded and it was hers. Her very own three-minute reel.

'Can you fix me up with a drawing room on the train?' she asked.

'Be a pleasure. When do you want to go?'

'The day after tomorrow.'

'I envy you,' he said. 'It's always a good idea to get out of this town.' Her eyebrows rose. 'Movies,' he said. 'Dreams on a production line to order. My God what a way to make money.'

'When are you going back to the paper?'

'Soon as I can,' he said. 'Week after next at the latest. Murray Fisch will be glad to get back to work. He likes it.'

He took her – and Georgina – to one more party, one last lunch, and at this he handed her an envelope, which contained train tickets and a ticket for a suite on the *Aquitania*, too. This time she let him pay. She was going back alone after all.

'You're very kind,' she said, 'but there is just one more thing. . . . A donation for Felston.'

'From the *Daily World*?' Bower sounded horrified.

'From Worldwide Studios.'

Bower grinned. 'I'll get Murray Fisch to send you a cheque.'

And that really was the end of it: a tearful farewell from Amparo, and her promise that next time she came to Hollywood she would send for her at once, a promise she was sure she would have no difficulty in keeping; then breakfast with Georgina who couldn't come to the station because she had a lesson with her movement coach, but who kissed her and wept a little, and said to be sure to give her love to that dear sweet youth at Oxford. She must mean Piers, thought Jane, and wondered how he would take it. She went down to pay her bill, but Worldwide had paid it all, including the Buick, and there was money for her: a cheque for twenty-five thousand dollars from Murray Fisch, and her photograph from Jay.

It was time to go to the station, and Worldwide had taken care of that, too. They had sent a Cadillac – the Hispano-Suiza was taking Miss Payne to her movement coach – but it was nice to see the black bootleggers again, and to be alone, because now, she thought, I really do need time for quiet reflection, all the way to Chicago. Just south of Kansas City she had to put on her fur coat again, and by Chicago the cold was brutal, but there was another Worldwide Cadillac waiting there to take her to the 'Century'. At the Grand Central Station Barry was waiting, and there was time for neither reflection nor quiet. They went to speakeasies instead, or stayed indoors while the snow fell so that he could play more Gershwin. When it was time to leave, Barry drove with her to Pier 13, where the *Aquitania* was berthed, and took her to her suite, the Gainsborough, that was filled with flowers – from Georgina, from Jay, from Tom Waring, and all those delightful people she'd met at Jack and Charlie's, and the Hotsy-Totsy and the Sligo Slasher's. Quite a lot of them came aboard to see her off, and it was really a very nice party until the stewards began beating gongs and shouting 'Visitors ashore, please'. After that she was alone again

But not for long. She had been placed at the captain's table. More Jay Bower manipulation, she wondered. But whether or not, she was a celebrity, she was known, the famous Jane Whitcomb who had turned down Hollywood and written about Felston and dressed up as Cleopatra. She had studied that photograph dozens of times, not for any reasons of narcissism but to try to work out how it differed from the one she'd first seen. It was the same photograph, and yet it wasn't. Elegant, feminine, even dashing: it was all of those, but it displayed and indeed promised far, far less than the original. The point was, as Jay had written on the note he sent with it, that everyone would believe that this one *had* been the original. After all it had been in a newspaper, hadn't it? Anything more revealing would be the one that had been tampered with, the work of malicious persons motivated by grudges unknown. And so far there had been no attempt to display the other photograph, which was why she was so often asked to dance and invited to passengers' parties, and applauded so heartily when she won a prize at the Fancy Dress Ball by wearing her sari yet again. So that in the end she had to give a party too, or her steward and stewardess would never have forgiven her. Not that the Gainsborough suite was such a bad place for a party: the vast drawing room like a section of a country house, with a copy of Gainsborough's portrait of the Duchess of Devonshire on the wall, heaps of room for dancing, and endless champagne.

And the dinners! Gargantuan to the point of caricature. One night perspiring stewards rolled in a vast chafing dish about the size of an Austin Seven, on which was a sort of herd of grilled antelope grouped round a hillock of foie gras and surmounted by peacock fans. Quiet reflection was impossible, the more so as she detested venison, but on the other hand, she thought, perhaps I've done enough. Action is much more my thing.

50

LONDON SEEMED MILD after New York, though the snow still lay on the side streets. Even so she thought of the California orange trees without regret. She picked up Foch and hugged him as soon as she reached South Terrace (some divining mechanism of his own had brought him to the door as soon as the hired Rolls drew up) and she continued to hold him as the Rolls's driver unloaded her luggage while Hawkins supervised. Almost she could have done the unthinkable and hugged Hawkins too, but she wandered about from room to room instead, and said hello to the other servants, who, if not exactly overjoyed at having to work again, appeared less than appalled. Mrs Barrow seemed positively glad, but then Mrs Barrow was a creative artist who would shortly resume her creativity.

She telephoned her mother, and found her at home. Major Routledge and she were dining the vicar, it appeared. They wished to know when, with propriety, they might announce their engagement, and the vicar struck them both as one who would know.

She remembered the funeral, and Dr Dodd's voice saying, in tones of utter certainty: 'I am the resurrection and the life, saith the Lord.' And now he was to advise the widow on when she might be married.

'How is the major?' she asked.

'In good health,' said her mother, 'but he has not as yet embarked on his literary labours. The weather has not been conducive to horse-racing. On the other hand – '

'Yes, Mummy?'

'We have worked together on the way in which he will conduct this – ah – enterprise, and I think he will do well. And I must say, child, that shared employment can be most gratifying.'

Was there a barb there? It was certainly not a request for corroboration.

'I'm delighted to hear it, Mummy,' said Jane.

She telephoned Lionel, who promised at once to come round and dine provided Mrs Barrow was still with her and said he'd be round in a jiffy, which meant in fact an hour and a half, and gave her ample time to bathe and change. Hawkins came in to help her dress.

'I've just about finished your unpacking, miss,' she said, 'and I must say somebody looked after you very nicely.'

'The maid on the ship, but the one at the hotel was better,' said Jane. No point in stirring up trouble.

'Do you mind telling me which hotel, miss?'

'The Garden of Allah.'

'Oh gorblimey,' said Hawkins, then instantly flushed scarlet. 'I'm sorry, miss – but did you really stay there? No that's daft. Of course you did. But what was it like?'

This was not a girl one could lie to, and Jane had no intention of trying.

'A year or so ago you would have thought it wonderful,' she said. 'Now I rather think you'd find it vulgar.'

Hawkins looked at her, the flush marks fading. 'Thank you, miss,' she said at last.

'Button me up will you?' said Jane, and as Hawkins did so, asked, 'Is Bob Patterson still at your sister's?'

'Yes, miss.'

'Could you get a message to him? Tell him I want to see him?'

'Certainly, miss. Any particular time?'

'Tomorrow. Soon as he can. I'm going North again.'

Lionel said, 'Always so restless. Now you're back can't you stay back, for heaven's sake?'

'Don't worry, darling,' said Jane. 'I'll invite you to dinner again as soon as I return.'

'Well I must say Mrs Barrow hasn't lost her touch,' said Lionel, and sipped at his brandy. 'That was the best meal I've had since you deserted us for the fleshpots.'

'That reminds me,' said Jane, and hunted about her, handed over a parcel labelled Saks Fifth Avenue. Lionel unwrapped it cautiously, then gave a soft trill of delight. It was the most splendid, most *American* cocktail shaker he'd ever seen.

'As used at Jack and Charlie's,' said Jane.

'Who or what are Jack and Charlie?'

'It's a speakeasy. I told you.'

'A speakeasy!' said Lionel. 'Oh what bliss.' He looked towards her drinks cabinet.

'Not now,' said Jane. 'You're drinking cognac.'

'Then as soon as you get back,' said Lionel. 'You must be the first. Until then I'll practise on my own.' He put the shaker down. 'You didn't say how dear Jay was.'

'No,' said Jane. 'I didn't, did I? The short answer is that he is well. He has also discovered a new star to add to his particular firmament.'

'The delectable Miss Payne?'

Jane nodded. 'You knew that Jay and I were lovers?'

'The thought had crossed my mind,' said Lionel.

'Of course it had. You and my mother are the two sharpest people I know, and I've no doubt it crossed her mind, too. Well now we're not. But not on account of Georgie.'

'Another girl?'

'Rather a pretty girl, quite young, who drinks just a little too much because otherwise thwarted ambition would choke her. He'd decided to give her up once he met me, I gather. But suddenly she was available when I wasn't.' She thought for a moment. 'I honestly think there are certain excuses I might accept for unfaithfulness,' she said, 'but availability isn't one of them.'

'Did you weep for him?' Lionel asked.

'No,' she said. 'I wept for Captain Patterson.'

On the train to Newcastle she thought a little longer about Lionel, postponing for a while the time when she must think about her mother, and Bob. Lionel had wanted to know all about her trip, and made her tell him about the Cardona party twice, and the screen test. She hadn't dared tell him that she had a copy of the test. He'd have dragged her off to a cinema then and there and bribed everyone in sight. About other things, about what was going on, he had absolutely no idea. All the seriousness, the interest in the world of affairs, had been burned out of him in his two years flying a Sopwith fighter.

Her mother was better informed, of course. Her mother read *The Times* right through every day, including the racing pages now. She had embraced her daughter with more warmth than Jane could remember for many years, then looked at her and said, 'Hm,' without further comment. It seemed that she was satisfied. They took coffee together, and Jane put her questions.

'Of course there will be trouble,' said her mother, 'and almost certainly it will begin with the miners. They sustained another wage cut while you were away. Doubtless you will see its effects when you visit Felston. You have money for them?'

'Yes, Mummy.'

'They will need it, I fear. Some of them are very close to starvation.'

'But how – ?'

'Incredible as it may seem,' her mother said, 'the Poles and Germans can produce coal even more cheaply. The miners are understandably – if irrationally – incensed.'

'They'll strike?'

'Of course,' said her mother. 'But not yet. There are some men of sense among them. They won't strike till the weather's warmer.'

'Will they win?'

'No,' said her mother. 'How can they? They may drag others into it with them – railwaymen and the like – but they cannot possibly win unless they drag in the army and the police also.'

'Revolution?'

'Precisely,' said her mother. 'But revolution in this country is never easy. Without an Oliver Cromwell it will be impossible.'

They began to talk of more personal affairs, and especially of her mother's engagement.

'Dr Dodd proved rather difficult to pin down,' her mother said, and smiled her smile of pleasurable malice. 'One understands why, of course. To set a date for me would be to create a precedent. Perhaps he feared a positive stampede of widows determined on *secondes noces*.'

'But he gave a date?'

'Ultimately. Late summer, he thought, would be in order. I – *we* decided that mid July was quite late enough, and we shall marry in the autumn. In the meantime we go racing, taking care of course to conceal the fact that George is employed.'

'That's where you come in,' said Jane. 'The major will be with you and you provide the camouflage. The right sort of clothes are essential, Mummy.'

'Then I hope and pray that you will advise me.'

'Tweeds,' Jane said at one. 'Tweeds all the way till the flat season starts. I should get the Donegal kind if I were you. Harris is far too heavy. In fact when I come back from Felston I should like to buy you some if I may – just till the major's in funds.'

To her amazement her mother had said 'You're very kind', and nothing more. But why be amazed? she wondered. She too had learned about the need for love and money.

Bob had been brisker. There was a hell of a row coming, no doubt about it. Once the summer came. . . . In 1914, she remembered, it had been a question of waiting till August when the harvest was in.

'You'll be in it?' she asked.

'Might be,' said Bob. 'If I'm still in this job. But it mightn't get as far as the print unions.'

'What mightn't? And why do you say *if* you still have a job? Are you likely to be sacked?'

'Sacked?' said Bob. 'No fear. I need to work to send the money home. You know that. I just might get a change of job, that's all. And as I say – there's talk of a big strike in the summer.' He shrugged. 'But it'll be the miners who start it. It always is.'

'But you'll be all right?' she asked him.

'I didn't come all this way to strike for the bloody miners.' He paused. 'Sorry for the language,' he said. 'But I didn't. . . . You'll be going up there?'

'I heard from Bet when I was in Hollywood,' she said.

'"When I was in Hollywood,"' he quoted. 'It's grand to hear you say that.'

'Your dad's out of work again.'

'Yes,' said Bob. 'Grandma wrote and told us. Poor old Da! My bit money's all they've got now barring the dole.' He smiled. 'Andy'll be in his element.' Suddenly he changed the subject.

'Do you happen to know if Mr Bower's still in America?' he asked.

'He'll be sailing back soon,' she said. 'He doesn't like Hollywood.'

'Well I'm blest,' said Bob. 'What does he like?'

'The *Daily World*.'

She should have spoken to Dick Lambert of course, but there simply wasn't time, not if things were as bad as that. There hadn't even been time to see Charles Lovell, though she had written to him, suggesting that they meet when he was next in London, then dashed off to King's Cross. Indecent haste, Lionel had called it, and he was just about right. Foch had watched her departure appalled. If a dog could be said to do such a thing, he washed his hands of her. But he, and Lionel, were wrong. Felston was all the excuse she needed.

'But didn't you read about it in the papers in America?' Grandma asked.

'In New York they're too busy making money to worry about what's happening in England,' said Jane. 'And in Los Angeles they don't even bother what's going on in San Francisco, unless it's an earthquake.'

'Well I'll tell you what's going on,' said Grandma. 'Starvation's going on. Not everywhere mind you. But it's started. For the miners anyway. Since them last wage cuts. The rest is mostly like us – jogging on the best way we can and lucky if they've got somebody working away and sending money home.'

'I was going to bring some stuff up with me but I hadn't the remotest idea how to shop for you so I brought this instead.' She opened Grandma's worn leather handbag and stuffed bank notes into it.

'Thanks, pet,' the old woman said. 'There was a time I'd have chucked it at you – but not now. We're going to need it.'

You and Mummy seeing sense at the same time, thought Jane, and was glad of it.

'How about the clinic?'

'That doesn't change,' said Grandma. 'More clients, that's all. But that money of yours still feeds the helpers, thank God.'

'How's Bob?' Stan asked.

'Working hard,' said Jane. 'He asked me to tell you how sorry he was that you'd lost your job.'

'Aye,' said Stan. 'Me an' all.' His mother clucked her disapproval.

'How's Andy?' Jane asked.

'At a meeting,' said Grandma. 'As usual.'

Jane wasn't surprised. Once Andy knew she was coming he'd have *called* a meeting, if one wasn't available. She turned to Bet, who sat busy and abstracted, knitting a scarf.

'And what does he think of what's happening?' Bet sat silent.

'Tell her girl,' said Grandma, and this time it was the voice that there was no denying.

'It's got him all excited,' Bet said reluctantly. 'You'd think it was Christmas. He says this is going to be our chance.' She rose to her feet. 'It's time I was off to the clinic,' she said.

'I hired the Wolseley again,' said Jane. 'I'm going there too. Let me give you a lift.'

'That's all right,' said Bet. 'You stay and finish your tea.'

'I almost have,' said Jane, but the younger woman had already put on the coat that had hung behind the door, and was adjusting her hat before the mirror.

'It's all right, honestly,' she said, and kissed her grandmother. 'Ta-ra,' she said, and hurried out.

'She's in a hurry,' said Stan.

'After a tram ride, likely,' said Grandma.

'There's more to it than that,' said Jane. 'Bet wrote to me in America and she was fine then. She isn't fine now.'

Grandma sighed. 'That Bella Docherty talks a lot about morality,' she said. 'There's times you'd think she'd invented it – and our Bet's a good listener. Then there's that fiancé of hers.'

'You don't tell me he disapproves?'

'She's worried he might,' said Grandma. 'Oh I know it's daft but when a girl has to wait too long she does get daft ideas.'

'I see,' said Jane, and turned to Stan. 'And what do you think, Mr Patterson?'

'I prayed for you,' Stan Patterson said. 'And then I listened. And it seemed the good Lord was telling me that you might not be over-modest but you understood compassion.'

'And the good Lord was right like always,' said Grandma. 'Now you take yourself off to your clinic and never mind about our Bet. She'll be all right once she's married and got a few bairns to worry about.'

It wasn't that Stobbs and Messeter weren't glad to see her. They made all the right noises and asked all the right questions, but they treated her as if she were someone who'd brought comforts to the Front Line just before a big push. They were kind and they made her welcome, but their minds were elsewhere. Both of them wondered if she had brought money this time, but Messeter was too polite to ask. Stobbs wasn't.

'I'm sorry,' he said. 'I know it's rude and uncouth. All that. But I can't help it. If you haven't brought money I'll have to close.'

'I've brought money.' Both men looked up at her. 'Twenty-five thousand American dollars and three thousand English pounds from the ball.'

'That's over eight thousand pounds,' said Messeter. 'We can survive for quite a while on that.'

'Two years,' said Stobbs, 'and into a third.' He turned to Jane. 'I'm obliged to you. It can't have been easy.'

'Some of it was fun,' she said. 'Like the ball – and the concert here. And some of it wasn't, but it had to be done.'

'Duty, stern daughter of the Voice of God,' said Messeter. 'How irritating of Wordsworth to be so often right. I'm grateful too, dear Jane.'

She smiled. 'I'm in the way, aren't I?'

'There'll be a clinic soon,' said Stobbs.

'I have the Wolseley – if you need another car.'

'Cars are no longer a difficulty,' said Messeter. 'There are certain businessmen who live in rather large houses in Northumberland and have social aspirations, as indeed do their wives. It occurred to me that if I could arrange for them to dine with a duke or a marquis they might feel grateful. . . . We now have a bus and an ambulance.'

'So much more convenient than an Armstrong-Siddeley,' said Jane, and rose, then said: 'Oh – I almost forgot. Do you remember a Charles Lovell?'

'He has a house quite near, has he not?' said Messeter. 'But he was of no use to me. He's a commoner.'

Stobbs said, 'If you'll excuse me I have things to do. I'll leave you to your gossip,' and left.

He isn't even aware that he's been rude, thought Jane. How I wish he could meet Jay Bower.

'But do you remember Charles in the war?' she asked Messeter.

'Of course,' said Messeter. 'A very gallant officer.'

'He said the same of you,' said Jane. 'But since the war?'

'A little adrift, if you will excuse my saying so. No sense of purpose. Not like you – or me, thanks be to God.'

There was the rattle of a motor vehicle outside, and Messeter was on his feet at once. 'If you'll excuse me,' he said.

'Of course.'

They went outside together. The hall of the clinic was already beginning to fill up with the chronically sick, who sat or lay in dreadful contrast to the fit young men who helped them, the glittering clean nurses who were already beginning their business. It was like a casualty Clearing Station in the middle of a battle, except that this time the wounded were women and children, as well as men.

She left Messeter to his work, and made for the door, easing her way through the growing crowd, until she collided with a woman carrying a tray of empty cups. It was Bella Docherty. She looked at Jane angrily as Stobbs appeared at the door of his surgery.

'Oh it's you,' she said. 'What you're doing here getting in the way of decent folk I don't know. You've no business here. You're not wanted.'

'Then I won't stay,' said Jane, and went out of the door. Behind her she could hear Stobbs's furious roar. 'Mrs Docherty, you damn fool. What in *hell* do you think you're doing?'

It was the first time she had heard him swear, but she continued walking to where the Wolseley was parked. She could hear footsteps behind her, but she continued to stride out.

'Miss Whitcomb.' It was Messeter's voice. 'I wonder if I might ask you to stop? Or at least slow down.' She turned to face him. 'Thank you,' he said. 'I'm afraid all this German iron is rather a handicap when one wishes to walk off a rage as you are doing.'

Jane waited.

'For some reason,' Messeter said, 'I find it difficult to talk in the street. There is a church nearby. Could we go inside, do you think?'

'You're needed at the clinic,' said Jane.

'This will not take long,' said Messeter. 'Besides, it's possible that you may need me too.'

She walked with him past the Wolseley to the church of St Andrew. It was a small church of raw, red brick and quite the ugliest ecclesiastical building Jane had ever seen. Inside was no better: whitewashed walls, chipped and grimy chairs instead of pews, an even uglier table, partly covered by a purple velvet cloth, for an altar, that bore only a cross and two candlesticks, and two bunches of chrysanthemums begged no doubt from someone like Stan. Messeter knelt at once to pray, and she joined him. She had no words to say, but the act of kneeling helped to calm her, just as the angry walk had done.

Messeter said, 'Mrs Docherty insulted you, and Stobbs rebuked her.'

'Dr Stobbs,' said Jane, 'would swear at anyone who imperilled his goose that lays the golden eggs.'

'Can you blame him?' Messeter asked.

'No more than I blame you for doing something much the same – though rather more practical.'

'Stobbs would have run after you too, but he was needed where he was.'

She said nothing.

'Forgive me,' Messeter said. 'I must ask you this – '

'I'll go on asking for money,' said Jane. 'Of course I will. But don't expect twenty-five thousand dollars every time.'

Messeter brushed that aside. 'And you'll come back to us?'

'No,' said Jane. 'I shan't do that. I have it on the authority of two good women that I'm not wanted.'

'As if that mattered,' said Messeter.

'It matters to me,' said Jane.

He was looking at her deeply: the look of a man beyond sexual love, but who remembered well its demands and its rewards.

'I shall pray for you,' he said.

'Heaven knows I need your prayers,' said Jane, and rose. 'Good night.'

As she went back to the Wolseley she thought, at least when Stan prays, he tells me what God's answers are, then stopped. Andy was waiting by the car. She went up to him.

'Yes, Andy?'

'I've got to talk to you,' Andy said.

'Not here,' she said. 'It's far too cold to talk out here. Shall we go back to John Bright Street?'

'No,' he said. 'Da's there. And Grandma. This is private.'

'The Eldon Arms then?' He shook his head. 'Some pub? *Any* pub?'

'It'll have to be here,' he said. 'There's nowhere in this town you and me can be seen and not set tongues clashing.'

'Get in the car then,' she said.

'Where will we be going?' he asked.

'Nowhere,' she said. 'We'll just drive round until you've told me what you have to say.'

He got in, and listened as the engine fired, the car eased forward.

'Nice engine,' he said.

'It would be,' said Jane, 'if the plugs were cleaned. Did you come to talk about motoring?'

'I came to talk about you,' said Andy.

And why not? she thought. Everybody else is talking about me.

'Go on,' she said.

'I reckon I owe you an apology,' Andy said, and she almost lost control of the car. It was the one thing she had not been ready for.

'Indeed?'

'You know about that picture,' Andy said. 'I reckon Bob must have told you. He disappeared fast enough after I got it, *and* landed himself a good job.'

She said, 'It isn't Bob's peccadilloes we're discussing at the moment. It's yours.'

'Peccadilloes,' Andy said. 'That's little sins, isn't it?'

'It is.'

'Well I don't know about the size of Bob's sins,' said Andy. 'But I don't reckon mine was all that little.'

He was silent as she drove towards the coast road, dark and empty on that bitter cold night.

'Do get on with it, Andy,' she said. 'We can't drive round for ever.'

He said stiffly, 'I'm sorry. . . . It's about that photograph.'

'Of course.'

'Not the one the *Daily World* fixed up. The real one. The original. A chap brought it to me from London. A posh chap.'

'Did the posh chap have a name?'

'He didn't give one and I didn't ask. But he knew all about you and your charity.'

'And disapproved of me because my good works got in the way of the revolution?'

'That's right. And I agreed with him. I still agree with him. You have to be stopped. Only – '

'Only what?'

'Not like that. Not with indecency. Dirt. That's not the way.'

'What is the way, Andy?'

'To fight you,' said Andy. 'Head on. That's the way. It's the road you took. Flaunting yourself, off to Hollywood our English Cleopatra and will she never come back and keep the people in subjection with a Christmas concert and a cracker? I might hate what you're doing, but you did it fair.'

'And you didn't?' Her question was a torture deliberately applied.

'You know fine well I didn't. And I'm sorry. Honestly I am.'

'Tell me one thing, Andy?' said Jane.

'If I can.' His voice was wary. Loyalty, thought Jane. One of your favourite virtues.

'This posh chap,' she said. 'Did his breath smell of garlic?'

'Would that be like very strong onions? Aye, it did.' He thought for a moment. 'You know him?'

'He's a friend of my brother's.'

'Well I'll go to France,' said Andy. Jane drove him home.

She had gone back to London almost at once, stopping off only to say goodbye to Grandma, choosing a time when she thought that Bet might be at the clinic. She was lucky. Grandma was on her own, cosy by the kitchen fire with her shawl around her. She made tea at once.

'So you're off back, are you?' she said. 'Can't say I blame you. Tongues like Gillette blades, the folks round here.'

'I can't help with the driving any more,' said Jane, 'now that the canon's got his clutches on a bus *and* an ambulance. And I can't work indoors, not with Bella Docherty there.'

'Bella Docherty doesn't have to be there,' the old woman said.

'Be sensible, Grandma,' said Jane. 'Bella Docherty's indispensable. What use would I be in a kitchen? And it isn't only Bella Docherty.'

'Our Bet?'

'Her. . . . Perhaps others. The rest of the country think I'm innocent – but not the whole of Felston, it seems.'

'We owe you too much, said Grandma. 'That's never an easy thing to forgive. But you and me are still speaking, I hope?'

'How could we not be?' said Jane. 'You'll write to me sometimes?'

'If you'll promise to write back I will.' She brooded over her tea cup. 'I'm due at the clinic tonight,' she said. 'I'll be having a word with Bella Docherty.'

'Please Grandma,' said Jane. 'Not on my account.'

'Accounts,' said Grandma darkly. 'The Meat Account, the Fish Account, *and* the Vegetables.' Suddenly she cackled. 'If my Stan was here he'd give you a text,' she said. 'Let him that is without sin among you cast the first stone.'

London had begun to thaw, the dark grey snow turning into a squelching mess as the rain began. She telephoned Charles Lovell in Hampshire, and was told that he had gone to Switzerland. As February gave way to March, she spent a lot of time dancing in nightclubs with Lionel. Then one morning Hawkins came in and woke her. It was eight o'clock: she'd had five hours sleep.

'Hawkins, what on earth – ' she said.

'It's Mr Bower, madam. He says if I hang up he'll just go on ringing back. Best to call it force majeure, madam.'

Jane was too tired to argue. She got up and went to the telephone.

'I need an article,' Bower said

'I think I've rather had enough of Felston just for the moment,' she said.

'There are other places,' said Bower. 'Get yourself over here and we'll talk about them.' He hung up.

It seemed, she thought, that they were still speaking, or at least he was.

51

WHAT HE WANTED, it seemed, was more Two Worlds stuff. Elegance and Deprivation.

'It's a steady market, you see,' he told her. 'The rich seem to have discovered the working class the way they discovered appendicitis in Edward VII's time. And anyway, how can you enjoy being rich if you don't know about the poor?'

'Is that what I'm doing?' she asked. 'Helping the rich to enjoy themselves?'

'They don't need any help,' said Bower. 'What you're doing is helping the poor. Get yourself around the East End for a change, then tell us all about your snob friends.'

'I'll need someone to show me round the East End. A reporter perhaps.'

'Not a reporter. They'll think they know what I want, and maybe they do. But they won't know what you want. You can have Dick Lambert.'

'Does he know?'

'It's all arranged.' His hand reached out for a sheaf of type-script. She stood firm.

'How's Georgina?' she asked.

'Fine.' His hand moved again towards his papers.

'Don't be so bloody silly,' said Jane. 'Tell me how she *is*.'

He scowled. 'Her test was good. I'm leaving the Cleopatra picture written for her. Fisch thinks we ought to let her talk in the last scene, and I'm beginning to think it's a good idea.'

'And the terra-cotta figurine?'

'She's playing the slavegirl.'

Despite herself Jane was moved to comment. 'You bastard,' she said.

'Not at all,' said Bower. 'It's a nice little comedy cameo. She's got to start somewhere. Now will you kindly let me work?'

Dick Lambert invited her to lunch at the House of Commons 'to discuss the whole thing'. Discussing the whole thing largely meant getting a good table so that others could see Dick Lambert lunching with a pretty woman for once, instead of having sandwiches and a half of bitter in solitude. She was still noteworthy, it seemed. Several members made some excuse to come over and talk to them, including at least one junior minister. All of them knew who she was.

'Sorry about that,' said Lambert, who had enjoyed every minute of it. 'We'd better get on with it before any more come.'

Poplar, they decided, the Elephant and Castle and the Isle of Dogs. Lambert knew Labour Party workers in all three, and every one was a connoisseur of misery.

She took him in the Riley, and it irked him rather, being driven by a woman, and he said so.

'But you can drive if you want,' she said.

'That's just it,' he said. 'I can't drive.'

'Then you should learn,' she said, 'instead of grousing at those of us who can.'

'I'd learn if you'd teach me,' he said, and then: 'No. That's not true.'

'Why not?' she said. 'It would be a pleasure to teach you.'

'But I wouldn't learn how to drive,' he said.

'Whyever not?'

'I wouldn't want the lessons to end.'

Best to say nothing, she thought, and drove on down the Blackfriars Road.

'I'm a Yorkshireman, Miss Whitcomb,' he said, 'and we're rather proud of our direct way of speaking. Too proud, maybe. That last remark of mine – '

'You wish to withdraw it?'

'No I don't,' said Lambert. 'What I wish to do is rephrase it – some other time. If you'll let me.'

And what was she supposed to say? Oh I'd much rather you didn't? Once again it was best to say nothing.

'My party's the party of idealists,' Lambert said at last. 'There's times we go on about it a bit too much. Complacency you might say. Still, by and large it's true. Poverty, sickness, class distinction, the inferior status of women – we're determined to tackle them all – and we will, too. But I know which one will come last.'

'And which will it be, Mr Lambert?'

'The status of women,' said Lambert at once. 'If you ask me, that won't happen until there's enough women activists to vote it through.'

'I'd like to use that some time, if you've no objection,' said Jane.

'I'd be honoured,' said Lambert, and sighed. 'I'm as idealistic as the next man,' he said, 'but – '

'Not when it comes to sex equality?'

'That's just it,' said Lambert. 'Once you got that through – you wouldn't be our equals. You'd be our superiors. It may not have dawned on the chaps down here, but up in Yorkshire we've always known that.'

And in Felston too, she thought, because in Felston at its worst only a woman could strive to hold together a family, and far more often than seemed possible they succeeded.

She turned on to the London Road and the Elephant and Castle, and the sort of streets that could give even Felston a game when it came to the kind of poverty that stopped so tantalisingly short of death. It was time to go to work.

She got far more material than she could possibly use. Each Labour Party activist had his own particular horror to display, as if poverty were a sort of competition and a mention in the *Daily World* the prize. But then it was the prize. Those men and women knew precisely what Jane had done for Felston, and hoped that she would do it for them. Their attitude was different, Jane noticed. They were, every one, as dedicated and idealistic as Andy, but for them the revolution would have to wait until the troops had had at least one decent meal.

Sarah Watson, when she visited her for scrambled eggs and gin, could not quite agree. The poor she treated – though admittedly they had not reached the appalling poverty that Jane had just seen – still had one more fight left in them, and were indeed looking forward to it with a sort of grim relish. Jane asked for names, and the ones she talked to all bore out Sarah's theories. Jane wondered why Dick Lambert hadn't shown her them, too. But for Lambert, she realised, no amount of ardent love could imperil his idealism.

The rich, she thought. Now is the time to visit the rich, but where do I begin? It was Dr Caswell who solved her problem, calling to remind her that she had promised to address her little group when Jane had returned from more exotic climes. She wants to ask about Hollywood, thought Jane, and accepted at once. Gilded youth would be just the thing, and she reminded herself to look up Catherine and Piers.

She drove up in the Riley, and took Foch with her, telling Hawkins no more than that she would be away for a night, perhaps two. She had no wish to be badgered by Bower and his 'Wicked World' bloodhounds. This was serious stuff; and so she booked in at the Mitre and bribed enough people to keep Foch with her, then took him for a walk to look at the High before dinner. Together they approved the soaring beauty of St Mary the Virgin and Magdalene's manifold charms, but it was at the solid dignity of the Queen's College that Foch lingered. 'Puritan to the last drop of your blood,' she told him. 'But I can't take you to Cambridge every time.'

She dined alone with only Foch under her chair for company. Best leave reunion with the Hilyards until next day, when she would have the strength to cope with all that youthful energy. She went to bed early, and had an early call, then scribbled notes to Piers and Catherine before, dressed in riding boots and breeches, she set off for the farm where her horses were kept. Foch sneezed once, but he enjoyed the run. Oxford in the half dark of a March morning, brooding and damp, had lost a fair proportion of its frivolity. The countryside too seemed sunk in gloom: soggy fields, dripping hedgerows, but Hyde's Farm, where her horses were, seemed cheerful enough: grey stone unsullied by smoke, blue-grey tiles, a cobbled courtyard between farmhouse and stables. Its owner came out to greet her himself. Mr Benson had written often enough to Jane, even telephoned when Bridget had finally given birth – to a foal this time: not a filly.

He was a big and cheerful man, instantly crestfallen when she made her request. Mr Benson, she saw at once, hated to deliver bad news.

'If only you'd thought to write to us, Miss Whitcomb,' he said. 'We'd have known what to do then – of course we would. But the young lady came so bright and early the way she usually does – '

'Lady Catherine Hilyard?'

'Exactly so, miss. And with her having the gentleman with her, and Bridget and Bridie both needing the exercise – '

'Quite all right, Mr Benson,' said Jane. 'But I'll take a look at the foal if I may.'

'But of course, Miss Whitcomb,' said Benson, and led the way to the stables.

She liked what she saw. Three months old now, a chestnut with one white stocking and a white blaze on the forehead, already strong, yet elegant in his shape.

'Well *well*,' she said.

'You're right there,' said Benson, who approved of taciturnity in others. 'He'll be a real good un to go when he puts his weight on. Good hocks and shoulders, and just right for size. Fifteen hands or a bit over – and a real good goer, I'll bet.'

'He certainly looks it.' She put out her hand, and the foal nuzzled into her.

'Have you decided on a name for him yet, miss?'

She felt the push of the foal's head, already strong, determined.

'Bridget's Boy,' she said. 'What else?'

'Would you like a bit of refreshment, miss?' Benson asked. 'Though I doubt if my wife has coffee – '

'Tea,' said Jane firmly, 'will do very well. And a biscuit if possible.'

Benson brought them himself into a parlour that glowed with polished mahogany, and did his best to entertain with stories of his days in the yeomanry – out in South Africa that had been, a cruel place for horses – but left them at last. Foch snorted as the door closed.

'I quite agree,' said Jane. 'But at least he's keeping my new horse in good trim.'

Foch yawned. Horses bored him; always had.

'Then what shall we talk about?' said Jane. 'My lecture to the bluestockings this afternoon? You know that almost as well as I do. What about my piece for Mr Bower? We mustn't call him Jay any more, I'm afraid. That would show a lack of respect.'

He had been great fun when one lacked respect, she thought. Eager and inventive – if vaguely surprised that a female too could be having such a good time. She wondered if Charles Lovell – Now that's enough, she told herself, and gave the last biscuit to Foch. He's gone to Switzerland, remember, and he can only have gone to Switzerland because of his wife. And anyway, he's pompous. But she knew that wasn't true. His letter may have been pompous, but that had been because his emotions were too much for him. Emotions like that always were too much for an English gentleman. Except for Papa, of course.

She had been drowsing when the sound of hooves woke her, hooves that slithered on the cobbles outside. Foch sat up, and barked sharply. He too had been dozing.

'Oh be quiet,' said Jane. 'You've met Catherine before, and Piers is just like her.'

She got up and went outside, and reluctantly Foch followed. The fire's heat had been pleasant.

Jane looked at Catherine astride Bridie. She was slender and elegant, even in jodhpurs. Beside her, astride Bridget, was Jay Bower.

'Why Jane,' said Catherine. 'This is a surprise.'

'Yes, isn't it?' said Jane.

'But why didn't you tell us you were coming?'

'It was one of those spur of the moment impulses that one so often regrets afterwards,' said Jane. 'If you'll excuse me, I must get on.'

Catherine said, 'But we've only just seen you. Can't you stay?'

'No,' said Jane. 'I'm afraid not. I've an awful lot to do. Come along Foch.'

She walked to the Riley, then turned.

'Catherine darling,' she called. 'Are you quite sure that Bridget is up to Mr Bower's weight yet?'

Then she drove away.

She had told Catherine and Piers where she was staying, so that it was necessary to drive to the Mitre at once, change, and stay out of sight by driving around the Oxfordshire countryside with Foch beside her. The awful thing was that she didn't know how to react. Twice in as many months really was a bit much, she thought, but even so, *how did she feel* about it? Surely to God she should know. But she didn't. Should she laugh or cry? Give way to disgust, despair, righteous indignation? She simply didn't know and couldn't force herself to find out. All she did know was that she wished it hadn't happened.

She lunched on bread and cheese at a pub in Banbury, (Foch had a ham sandwich) then drove back to Dr Caswell's cottage and a collection of what Jane thought of as sort of Hampstead women assembled in her rooms, though they would have been outraged if they'd known it. An old campaigner now, she kept the text-book references to a minimum, and played up her rôle as an ambulance driver both on the Western Front and at Felston. It was because of her stint in the war, she told them, that she had missed her chance to come up to Oxford herself. My goodness that went over big. For good measure she threw in Private Walker at the end, and the reaction could only be described as ecstatic. The odd thing was that she really had enjoyed giving her performance, despite what had happened that morning, and enjoyed even more the fact that she'd gouged twenty-three pounds eleven shillings and sixpence out of them. Then came tea, which she swallowed affably – it was in fact rather good tea – and a further barrage of questions before she was free to go and wonder whether she should see Piers; not because of Bower's article, but because of Georgina. He had a right to know, after all. But it was Bower she found waiting for her, beside the Riley. For the first time since Foch had known Bower, he growled at him.

'Even your dog hates me,' he said.

'Whatever emotion he shows is the one he senses in me,' said Jane. 'And I don't hate you.'

'How do you feel?'

'I've no idea.' It was true enough. 'Please get out of my way.'

'If we could sit down and talk for a minute or two – '

'For God's sake will you get out of my way?' He saw he had no choice, and moved, and Jane unlocked the door: she and Foch drove off at last.

At the Mitre Piers was waiting, every bit as elegant as his sister.

'Sorry to be so late,' he said. 'There was a meet today. I've only just got back and your note was waiting, so here I am.'

'Would you like a drink?' Jane asked.

'Enormously,' said Piers, 'but I'm what is called in statu pupillari, little more than a microbe, less than the dust in fact, and so I can't drink strong waters in bars. But there's a club in Walton Street I belong to. We have sort of a guest bar that lets females in. We could have one there. We could have a dozen if we felt like it.'

'One,' said Jane. 'At a time, anyway.'

The guest bar had once been a breakfast parlour and they had it all to themselves, whether because of taste or shyness Jane had no idea. But the martinis were at least adequate, even by the Hotsy-Totsy's standards. Jane sipped and began to answer a barrage of questions about Hollywood. At last she could put it off no longer.

'I saw Georgina there,' she said.

'Oh yes?' At once Piers looked away.

'It seemed to me that she may be thinking of making her career there.'

'Not coming back you mean?'

'Not for a long time.' To her amazement he seemed relieved. 'You're not sorry?' she asked.

'Sorry? Well no. . . . Not really. I mean I liked her enormously –'

'You must have done,' said Jane. 'You wanted to marry her.'

'Oh do stop ragging. As I say I liked her enormously but I'd forgotten something really frightfully important. I mean it just goes to show what an effect you women can have on a man.'

'Ought I to apologise on behalf of us all?'

'This is serious,' he said severely. 'I'd quite forgotten that in any decent regiment subalterns aren't allowed to marry. I mean it isn't a rule or anything – but you just don't.'

'You had a lucky escape,' she said.

'Jane!' Was it the resilience of youth or its censoriousness she found hardest to endure? she wondered. The club steward came over to them, followed by Catherine.

'Your sister's here, sir,' he said.

'I should just about think I am,' said Catherine, and then to the steward: 'I think we'd better have another lot of these.' Piers nodded, and the steward took the shaker and left as Catherine turned to Jane.

'I've been looking all over for you,' she said. 'Just as well that I remembered Piers's pompous club.'

'They make jolly good martinis,' said her brother. 'But isn't it a bit late to be wandering about on your own? Shouldn't you be in purdah?'

'I told the dean Jane had asked me to dine,' said Catherine. 'I'm afraid you'll have to do it if only to lend verisimilitude or whatever it is.'

'Delighted.'

'I must say,' said Catherine, 'that the dean was no trouble. Positively worships at your shrine.'

'I think it's mostly Hollywood.'

'Very likely,' Catherine said. The martinis came, and she took one. 'But I didn't spend my time scouring Oxford just to talk about the dean. It's about Bridget and Bridie.'

Not Bower? Jane wondered. 'Nothing to talk about,' she said.

'What's wrong with them?' Piers asked.

'Nothing's *wrong*,' his sister said. 'It's just that Jay Bower was in Berkshire yesterday.'

Checking on that fairy-tale country house of his? Jane wondered.

'And he asked if he could see Jane's horses – I was going to ride this morning anyway – and he appeared in this vast Rolls, right outside the door of our nunnery.'

'Was he driving?' Jane asked.

'Chauffeur,' said Catherine. 'Anyway, he was wearing riding kit and when we got to Benson's farm he asked if he could see how Bridget went – just hacking about, you know. And I said yes.'

'*You did what?*' Her brother was furious. '*Without asking Jane?*'

'Oh dear,' said Catherine. 'I knew I'd done wrong.' She turned to Jane. 'You were furious, too.'

'Well yes,' said Jane. 'But not any more. And not at you. He had no business to ask you.'

'And you had no business to let him,' said Piers.

'Perhaps we'd better go and eat that dinner,' said Jane. She had no wish to endure a sibling quarrel to round off what had already been a very trying day. Besides, while feeding them she could ask them about the more gaudy aspects of Oxford life: the parties, the Common balls, the hunting. First of course she had to warn them why she was asking her questions. They couldn't wait to tell her.

They had eaten at the Mitre, and once they had gone she sat with Foch beside her, making notes on what the twins had told her. There was enough for two pieces at least, if Bower wanted them. Suddenly Foch grunted, and she looked up. Bower, wearing a dinner jacket, was standing by her chair.

'Hello,' she said, and went back to her notes.

'I've come to apologise,' he said.

'That's all right,' she said, 'but please don't do it again without asking.'

'I want to explain,' he said.

'There's no need,' she said. 'It happened and it's over. Let's leave it at that.'

'Damn it I have to explain,' he said.

'Then sit down and do so,' said Jane. 'But try not to shout.'

'I've been dining at Oriel,' he said. 'Hence the dinner jacket. There's a don there who works for me sometimes. I didn't have to dine at Oriel and I didn't want to dine at Oriel but I had to kill time while I found out where you were – so I did. You should have told me you were coming to Oxford, Jane.'

'You should have stayed off my horse,' she said.

'OK, maybe I should, but – '

'Not maybe.'

'All right then. I should.' His hands searched his pockets and found a cigar, and he prepared it for lighting. 'But I didn't. I asked Lady Catherine if it was OK to let me ride – only I asked her in such a way she couldn't refuse. You believe that?'

'You Americans have an expression for it,' she said. 'Taking candy from a baby.'

His hands shook for a moment, the match flame fluttered as he lit his cigar.

'It was a stupid thing to do,' he said. 'It was a crazy thing to do. She'd have told you – of course she would. There was no way of avoiding this little talk we're having – '

'And yet you did it anyway.'

'You and that horse,' he said, 'and the story of it. There's some kind of mystique about it.'

'There's John,' she said. 'There was no mystique about him. He rode that mare and a machine gun got him at La Bassée and we loved each other. That isn't mystique. That's just life and death.'

'To you, maybe,' Bower said. 'But not to those who know you. The way things happen with you – there's a sort of, I don't know – almost a magical quality. It's rare. Very rare.'

Indeed I hope so, she thought. It's called going mad then becoming sane, again. And perhaps being grateful for one's sanity.

'So I thought,' said Bower, 'that if I rode the horse – this isn't easy for me, Jane.'

'You thought you might find out what John was like?'

'It was the man on the horse you'd loved,' he said. 'For that brief while I was the man on the horse.'

'Oh dear,' she said.

'Well now you know,' said Bower. 'Is there anything you'd like to do about it?'

'No.'

'I'll leave you to it then. When can I see your copy?'

'Thursday,' she said.

'Thursday will be fine.' He got up and left with no other word.

As she undressed she thought about how simple her life had been in wartime. She'd met a man and loved him until he was killed, knowing with each day that passed that the odds against his survival increased, knowing, too, that there was no choice. He was there in the trenches and he stayed there till that last machine-gun burst, till the biography of John Patterson was no more than the inscription she had seen once on a headstone in a graveyard: a whole family mourned, recorded, tidily buried, and then, carved in the only space left vacant, the name of a twenty-year-old boy, Killed in Action, Ypres, 1917; and the words 'His country called. He answered with his life.'

That was war. Peace was Jay Bower, Jay Bower of all people, behaving in a stupidly romantic way – love and despair and the Horse As Sexual Symbol – it sounded like an article by Burrowes. And she still didn't know how she felt about Jay, except that she didn't want to share his bed, ever again. On the other hand it seemed as if he were still in love with her, Thelma Tanagra notwithstanding. And Catherine? Catherine had given no sign of wanting him, but that didn't necessarily mean that this year next year sometime, she might not have a place in Bower's plans. . . . Jane got into bed and fell asleep at once.

The article appeared, and was good enough for Bower to demand another, and she took Mummy to Harrods and bought her tweeds and hats and shoes. Mummy had suggested brogues, but Jane was firm. 'If you're seen in brogues everyone will know you're in disguise,' she said, and took her instead to a shop in New Bond Street that sold French silk scarves to soften the tweed's hard line. Lady Whitcomb was delighted and said so, and even more delighted when there was racing at Newton Abbot and a rear admiral tried to pick her up. 'George,' she told Jane on the telephone, 'is furious.' She sounded in ecstasies.

For the rest there was Lionel, and there were occasional men to take her to dances, to wrestle with in a taxi on the way home and the occasional lecture and hat-passing. She missed Felston. Sending off a cheque to Stobbs and Messeter, writing to Grandma, weren't the same. She missed the place. But there was nothing she could do about it. Grandma needed her presence: Felston didn't. She turned to the newspapers instead. The *Daily World* was utterly certain that some kind of confrontation between Capital and Labour was on the way, and so was Mummy, when she could be dragged away from thoughts of the Cheltenham Gold Cup, which wasn't often.

'Unavoidable,' her mother said. 'Some writers even talk of Armageddon. Though how they can do so after the Somme is beyond my comprehension. . . . I saw Gwendoline Gwatkin the other day, quite briefly. At Fortnum's. She was buying cream cakes, poor thing. She asked me why I travelled so much these days. I told her that widows are notoriously flighty.'

The the major tipped an unlikely horse for the National and it won at 66 to 1. Not only that but he backed it himself and bought a motor car with the proceeds; a quite capacious Hillman. The *World*'s circulation improved considerably because of the tip, and he received a substantial fan mail which Mummy answered personally. He also received a bonus and a rise in salary. Small wonder that Mummy had little time for Armageddon.

Dick Lambert had, but then he had little time for anything else. She invited him to a dinner party with Harriet and Neil

Watson and Sarah – once again not speaking to her husband. Sarah she thought would be adequate bait for any man, but he telephoned in an agony of remorse on the day of the dinner, and said he had to go to a meeting in Wapping. She had to call in Lionel instead. Lambert called next day, still remorseful.

'My dear man,' said Jane, 'I've no doubt that what you had to do was far more important.'

'If it had been anybody but you,' said Lambert. One in the eye for Sarah, thought Jane, but how could I possibly tell her?

'It's coming then,' said Jane. He nodded. 'An all-out strike? What they're calling a General Strike?'

Lambert said, 'I love you. I think you know that. But I must ask you this. Will you keep secret what I tell you?'

'Of course.' She smiled. 'I'm a woman, and by your definition inferior – for the moment, but I don't chatter.'

'They'll all come out,' he said, 'and soon. It's like a bottle of champagne. You twist the wire off and let it get warm and give it a good shake – the cork'll come out like a bullet.'

'The miners?'

'The unlucky ones,' said Lambert. 'Again. They're never anything else. You've seen them.' She nodded. 'Down underground, deeper than a grave, and danger and hard labour and black when they come home.'

He must be quoting from a speech she thought, and a good speech at that.

'So they'll start, and the rest will follow.'

'Like sheep?' she asked.

'I didn't say that,' he said. 'Like Kitchener's Army. The Pals' Battalions. The miners'll go over the top and their friends'll follow: railwaymen and transport workers, shipyard men and steel men. . . . And then the others because they think it's right, or because their mates are doing it, or even because it's a bit of a lark – if they're young and unmarried. And none of them will want to scab.' And then, more softly, almost with regret: 'It'll be rough on scabs, this one.'

Jane said, 'And will it be only about money? The miners' pay cut?'

'That's where they're weakest,' said Lambert. 'They can't make up their minds what it's about. The extremists want to make it political, but – '

'But what?'

'They'd have to storm the House of Commons,' he said. 'And what chance would they have? It's not as if it were the Winter Palace in Leningrad.'

'More coffee?'

'It's the best I ever tasted, but I can't stay,' he said.

'Mrs Barrow made it,' said Jane. 'She cooked the dinner you missed.'

She smiled, but he'd been too busy to remember what one did about jokes.

'I told you I love you,' he said.

'Yes,' said Jane.

'But you said nothing.' He waited, but again she found there was nothing she could say.

'I'm probably the only man in London who'll be glad when this bloody strike starts,' he said. 'At least it'll keep me busy.' He hesitated. 'Bower wants you and me to cover this strike together,' he said. 'The places you wrote the articles about. Are you going to?'

'Yes, of course,' she said. 'Are you?'

'You'll have to drive again,' Lambert said.

52

THE MINERS STRUCK on 26th April. All across the country they finished their shifts and refused to go back, and Jane's thoughts went at once to Felston and its five collieries, the wheels of their cages no longer spinning, the men in their allotments, or fishing from the pier, eking out the money they had put by; the handful of notes and silver that was all they had to keep them alive. And still they didn't want her.

Bob called, but this was Bob transformed: pin-striped suit, blue shirt and collar, blue and red striped tie.

'Good gracious,' she said, as Hawkins showed him in. 'How successful you look. Printing must pay well.' He waited till Hawkins closed the door behind her.

'I'm not working at the press any more,' he said. 'Mr Bower's given me an office job. Liaison he calls it. He sent you this.' He handed her a sheet of paper that bore no address, simply M.J. Bower across the top.

'I want you to cover this business with Dick Lambert,' it said. 'I gather he told you and he said it was OK. Bob'll go with you when Dick's too busy. Use your own office when you need it, but get out and about as much as you can. This thing will be happening everywhere. Every street corner a movie set. I want an epic. Bower.'

Jane said, 'Liaison?'

'That's what he calls it,' said Bob. 'More like being nosey. Finding out what's happening. I'm good at that.'

'My photograph,' she asked.

'Aye. You might say that was luck, but some of us have to make our own.' He paused, tried to think of something more to say. 'The money's canny.'

'Will you work with Mr Lambert, too?' she asked.

'Just with you,' said Bob. 'When Lambert's got you I work on my own.'

'And do you like what you're doing?'

'Chance of a lifetime,' said Bob.

There was now, everywhere, a sense of inevitability in what would happen, almost as if everyone wanted it to happen, thought Jane, despite the moderate voices that called for more talks, more bargaining: for in the main both sides had done with talks, and were demanding action instead.

'Just like 1914,' said her mother, and Jane had no doubt that she was right. A General Strike was announced for the third of May.

Lionel was sunk in gloom. His cook, it seemed, who was Extremely Red, had announced her intention of picketing Harrods throughout the strike. Jane told him that he could lunch or dine at her house whenever he wished, since Mrs Barrow held no discernible political convictions, and Lionel was himself again, then suddenly he grew bored with the high-camp posturing and came down to earth.

'Some of this will be nasty,' he said.

'Lionel,' said Jane, 'this is a strike for heaven's sake. People are bound to get angry.'

'Some of them will do more than that,' said Lionel. 'The country's split in two, chosen sides. . . . Usually when there's a strike they negotiate, don't they? I can't give you a shilling but I might manage sixpence. That sort of thing. Not this time. One lot's got to win. Or more significantly, the other lot's got to lose.' He sighed. 'Dear God. I thought we'd finished with all that eight years ago. Would you like to go to the Embassy?'

On the morning of the strike a *Daily World* car brought Lambert to South Terrace: not a bus, not a tram, not a tube was running. Lambert got out and the *Daily World* car sped off, and Jane was ready and waiting for him. Lambert was pale and on edge.

'Where do we start?' Jane asked, and then: 'Oh, I'm sorry. Would you like coffee first?'

'No thank you,' he said. 'I'd rather get on with it. Elephant and Castle?'

'Why not?' she said. 'Then on through to Poplar and the Isle of Dogs. . . . Shall we take a look at the West End first?'

'Still hankering after the Two Nations?' he asked her. But it was a good idea. 'All right.'

She was drawing on her gloves when the telephone rang, and she picked it up at once. If it was Bob doing his liaison tricks, she didn't want Hawkins announcing the fact to Lambert. He was nervous enough as it was. 'Hello?' she said.

'Miss Whitcomb?' said the voice. 'Jane?' And she knew at once who it was, that day of all days.

'This is Charles Lovell.'

'How kind of you to call.'

'I'm in Eaton Square,' said Lovell. 'When may I come to see you?'

'Not now,' she said. Oh God how could he choose such a time? 'I'm really frantically busy. This strike – '

'You're not involved in that, surely?'

'I'm writing about it. . . . May I call you when I'm free?'

'Yes of course. I have rather a lot to tell you. At least I hope I have.'

'The instant I'm free,' she said, and hung up. Lambert was looking at her. There could be no doubt he was aware of her feelings. 'Shall we go?' she asked.

Along Knightsbridge, past Hyde Park, now firmly closed to the public, its gates guarded by police. It was a good depôt, said Lambert, and nobody could come in without a pass. She pulled up as a lorry loaded with crates swerved suddenly across their path and chugged towards the park gates. It was driven by a young man wearing a Balliol tie.

'What on earth – ?' she said.

'A volunteer. There's hundreds of them. Came up at the weekend. Doing their bit, they call it.'

'I expect they'll enjoy themselves.'

'The workers won't.'

She drove on down Piccadilly to the Circus, then back to Belgravia, and Eaton Square, where there was no more exciting spectacle than housemaids polishing doorknobs, and over to Chelsea: Sloane Square and the Embankment. In the whole drive there was nothing to indicate a General Strike except the absence of buses. Shops were open, taxis plied for hire. There were perhaps more policemen than usual on their beat, but not *so* many more. And then she noticed something. The news-stands were deserted: the newsboys who usually worked the area by the tube stations were not there. She had begun her day too early to bother about her own newspapers, but apparently it was as well. There weren't any. Not even a *Daily World*.

She drove on, past the Oval to Kennington and on to the East End, past Southwark and the Borough to Kennington Causeway, and on to the Elephant and Castle, and at last she believed in the Revolution.

Heaven knew what she had expected in Mayfair and Belgravia: fat profiteers in top hats hanging from lamp-posts perhaps: anything other than that air of preternatural calm; but the Elephant and Castle provided everything a good journalist could wish. The great square was thronged with people on foot – here of all places, not a bus or a tram would be tolerated, although Lambert told her that volunteers were going to drive them too. But not in the Borough, not in Newington. She eased the car: pedestrians that day were using the road, as well as the pavement, and she could see that men and women alike were far more animated, more alert than the last time she'd been there. They were even smarter in their appearance: many of them wore their best clothes, as if they were on their way to attend a great occasion. All of them wore a look of savage expectancy. All that's missing is Madame Defarge, she thought, then grimaced in self-disgust. To them at least this was real and overwhelmingly important.

A policeman pushed his way through the crowd to them – the whole area was saturated with policemen. He was a vast man with a row of medal ribbons, and made his way through the crowd as if wading in pygmies.

'A bit far from home aren't you miss?'

She produced her press card.

'I see miss,' he said. 'Well you can stay if you like, but there won't be nothing happening here till the evening. No speeches till then. Nothing.'

'Then what on earth are they all doing here?'

'What else have they got to do miss?'

They went on to Poplar and the Isle of Dogs, taking in Limehouse on the way. And still there were no buses, trams, carts or delivery vans, in an area where only the doctors had cars – and not all of them. Instead, the people were there on foot, by the hundred, the thousand, and she heard the first jeers as she turned down the West India Dock Road into a scene of pure fantasy. In the dock a detachment of the Brigade of Guards was unloading bags of flour, and while they did so the Band of the Coldstream Guards was playing 'Poor Little Buttercup', from *H.M.S. Pinafore*. She found it very hard not to laugh. Lambert was almost incoherent with rage. A guards subaltern came over to them.

'Sightseeing?' Once again Jane produced her pass. The guardee read it carefully, and changed at once from a six-foot whiplash of inherited authority to a devoted admirer. '*The* Jane Whitcomb?' he said. 'Cleopatra? . . . Gosh.'

'May we get out for a little while?' she asked.

'Yes, of course,' said the subaltern, and turned to Lambert. 'Mr . . .'

'Richard Lambert. I'm the MP for Leeds West.'

'Help yourself, Mr Lambert,' the subaltern said, then turned once more to Jane. 'I'm glad you came back,' he said simply.

They went on to the dock side where the guardsmen grunted and heaved, and experimented with equipment rather more complex than a 303 Lee-Enfield. They were doing their best, but the work was new to them, they were slow. Even so a steady trickle found its way to where the lorries waited in a row, ringed round by pickets five, seven, ten deep. Slowly, irresistibly the lorries filled, and the band moved on to Ketelby's 'In A Monastery Garden', a tune, Jane thought, even more wildly inappropriate. She glanced at Lambert. The rage was returning.

'Not yet,' she said. 'Don't waste it. There'll be far more important things to be upset about before this is over.'

His face relaxed, but he didn't smile. 'Look at the lorry drivers,' he said.

There were three to a lorry: one equipped with a street map to find the way, one to drive, and a policeman for escort. Nearby another squad of policemen watched the crowded pickets. All big men, she noticed: at least a head taller than the men they watched. Even so they were twenty against what – five hundred?

a thousand? and yet they didn't seem in the least apprehensive, standing easy and relaxed in the hazy spring sunshine.

A guardsman dropped a bag of flour and it burst on the pavement, and the crowd cheered ironically. The guardsman looked at them, glaring his hate, then went back for another. Not the way to bring on the Revolution, she thought. The trick is to subvert the military not antagonise them. The lorries were almost ready to leave when a voice from inside the picket called out: 'Stop it, soldiers. Don't do no more. It's your mates you're hurting. Your comrades.'

The guardsmen laboured on with the mindless application of men on fatigue, but the inspector in charge of the police squad growled to his men, they stiffened to attention as the last bags were loaded, and the guards' band still thumped on.

The lorry crews in groups of three began to climb in to their lorries. One driver, she noticed without too much astonishment, was Piers. He had never looked happier.

One by one the engines fired, and the first lorry moved forward to the final gate where the picket waited. Deliberate, unhurried, moving like soldiers, the police squad marched past the lorries and lined up as the gates swung open. The inspector in charge moved in front of his men, one step, then another, then another. An insanely courageous thing to do unless one were utterly sure, she thought. But how *could* one be utterly sure?

'Stand clear of these gates,' he said.

The crowd made no move to obey. Instead there was a low and angry growl, like some large beast waking from sleep.

'I'll say it again. Stand clear.'

The growl grew louder. From the crowd came whistles, cat-calls, jeers.

Behind his back the inspector snapped his fingers and a sergeant caught the signal, rapped out an order. At once every policeman produced his baton. Jane glanced over to where the guards' fatigue men stood waiting. They stood at ease, but in that way of drilled relaxation that only guardsmen can achieve, and on their faces was a look of anticipation, enjoyment even. As if they were at the cinema, thought Jane. . . . The band stopped playing.

'Have you got a spokesman?' the inspector asked.

Beside her Lambert said, 'Not a leader, you notice. Pickets are mobs, and mobs don't have leaders.'

A grey-haired man came forward. He was small, wiry, bespectacled, and he wore his Sunday best. Like the inspector he took three steps forward, matching courage with courage.

'Tim Potter,' he said. 'I'm a shop steward here.'

'Tell me what you intend to do.'

'Peaceful picketing,' Potter said. 'That's all we intend to do. What the law says we can do.'

'Two men to each lorry,' said the inspector. 'And keep away from my constables.'

'The law doesn't say that,' Potter said.

'I'm saying it.'

He snapped his fingers again, and again a sergeant barked orders. The police squad moved in close to the inspector.

'I have my orders,' the inspector said, 'and you may be sure I'll obey them. And so will my men here.'

The voice that had called to the guardsmen shouted, 'Don't listen to him, lads.'

The inspector's voice went on, unheeding: 'These lorries are coming out,' he said. 'Now it's up to you, Mr Potter. You can let them through, or else I'll clear the way for them first. And believe me I'll do it.'

The shop steward stood impassive, but his face was sweating.

'You have no right,' he said.

'I have my orders, Mr Potter. That's all the rights I need.' His voice grew gentle, almost, Jane thought, compassionate.

'You can't win, man. Not with this lot.' His head gestured to the policemen behind him. 'Get out of our way. . . . Don't make us hurt you.'

Potter said, 'You're right. We can't win. Not this time. But there'll be others.' He turned to face the picket. 'Let them through,' he called.

The picket stood firm for a moment, then again there came a sound from them, one sound, the moan that said they had lost. Reluctantly the ranks parted, and the first lorry moved forward. As it did so the whistles and jeers began again. Jane looked for Piers. He was driving with such concentration that the lorry could have been his Bentley doing ninety, and he was still bursting with happiness.

'So we lost a skirmish,' said Lambert.

She watched the police put away their batons. Were they disappointed, she wondered, or was there relief that they hadn't had to club down men who were very like themselves after all?

'But you'll win the battle.'

'Not this battle. . . . Not this strike. And I'll tell you why not?' Under the stress of emotion his Yorkshire accent had grown more pronounced. 'Because the government were ready for it and we weren't. See for yourself. Troops to move food supplies, drivers to take care of distribution. And folks still getting to work.'

'Scabs?'

'Lower-middle-class folk,' he said. 'Office workers. You saw them. On bicycles. Sharing lifts. Walking. Miles and miles some of them. They'll keep business going till we wear ourselves out. You'll see.'

'Is that bound to happen?'

'Of course it is.' For the first time he was impatient with her. 'It's like I told you – we don't know what we're fighting for. But we will next time – and by God we'll win.'

The last of the lorries went through the gates, and the pickets moved away: slouching, disconsolate.

'Where now?' she asked.

'House of Commons,' he said. 'I've a meeting there. I hope it isn't out of your way?'

'Of course not,' she said.

She took him back to Westminster and left him by the House of Commons. Extra policemen on duty, she thought, but not so many more, and the customary flow of MPs and visitors. Business as usual, in fact. She drove on along Birdcage Walk, past St James's Park, to Constitution Hill and still the place seemed as if it had always been: gleaming motor cars, well-dressed pedestrians, many of them exercising superior kinds of dogs. On Knightsbridge she saw a small queue, and she parked the Riley and joined it. It was a news-stand with three newspapers for sale, *The Times*, a single sheet, the *Daily Mail*, proudly announcing that it had been flown in by air from Paris, and something called the *British Gazette*, which she had never heard of.

She turned to the paper seller, an ageing gentleman who wore a suit that a duke might envy.

'What is it?' she asked.

'Issued by the government,' the paper seller said. 'Edited by Winston Churchill.'

'No *Daily World*?'

'Sold out,' said the paper seller, and even at that stage of their relationship she was glad for Bower's sake. And for the *World*'s, she thought. The paper was beginning to demand her loyalty. After all it was almost a family affair.

She returned to South Terrace to find that it was only just lunchtime. Hawkins came into the hall at once.

'Mr Warley's here, miss,' she said.

'Yes,' said Jane. 'His cook is out supporting the strike.' Suddenly she remembered something. She had consulted Mrs Barrow about her feelings, thinking perhaps that all cooks might have leftist tendencies, but she had ignored Hawkins.

'I should have asked you before,' she said. 'Are you quite happy working while this goes on? I shan't hold it against you if you say no.'

'Perfectly happy for the moment, miss,' said Hawkins. 'I haven't got on to Politics yet.'

When she went to join Lionel he was looking at his watch.

'Don't worry,' said Jane. 'You'll be fed soon.'

'All this upset makes me nervous,' said Lionel. 'And when I'm nervous I feel hungry.'

'What upset?' said Jane. 'There wasn't a sign of trouble here – or in Chelsea. Make me a cocktail, there's a love.'

Lionel picked up the shaker and began mixing: handed her the results.

'A Bronx,' he said. 'But I warn you – my heart isn't in it.'

Jane sipped. 'Nonsense,' she said. 'It's delicious.' She sipped again. 'Do tell me why you're fretting so. If you want to, that is.'

'Of course I don't mind,' said Lionel. 'I'm a frivolous person, you see – and all I'm really good at is frivolity. All this stern purpose stuff gets me down. I suppose you think that's bad of me –'

'Well yes,' said Jane. 'I do rather.'

'And so do I,' said Lionel. 'But it's as I told you. I used up a lifetime's supply of seriousness in the two and half years I was in the Royal Flying Corps – I was thinking of going to Paris till it's over.'

'How would you get there?'

'Drive to Dover of course, then cross on the steamer. Oh . . . I suppose the Merchant Navy's on strike too?'

'Of course,' she said.

'Not a sailor to be had,' said Lionel. 'What a fate for a queen. . . . I'm losing face, aren't I?'

'What a question,' said Jane. But he was.

'In fact there's rather more to it than that,' said Lionel.

'Do tell,' she said. 'You know I'm good at keeping secrets.'

'The man I'm in love with's rather keen on all this class-war stuff.'

'Oh my God,' she said. 'Not another Burrowes.'

'Oh no no,' he said. 'As a matter of fact he's a plumber – and awfully sweet. But he wanted me to *do* something about it all.'

'Do what?'

'I've no idea,' said Lionel. 'I asked him if there was any sort of fund I could subscribe to and he got awfully angry and said he couldn't be bought and stormed out. And considering I'd just bought him dinner at the Ritz I thought that was a bit much.'

'Perhaps he did too,' said Jane. 'People don't like being bought. They don't mind being treated, but that's different.'

'Oh Lord,' Lionel said. 'How right you are. What on earth am I going to do?'

'You could try telling him that all sorts of people have been pestering you to volunteer to drive buses and lorries and be a special constable and you've refused.'

'A bit negative,' Lionel said.

' – And all your friends are furious with you.'

'He'd like that,' said Lionel. 'He's dead against us toffs. Bless you, my sweet. I didn't know you did the Advice to the Lovelorn bit as well.'

Hawkins came in to announce lunch, but she told her that there would be a short delay. Advice to the Lovelorn applied to her as well, and she suddenly wanted very much to hear Lovell's voice that instant instead of waiting until after lunch. She went to telephone.

The butler of his friends in Eaton Square told her that he was out on business, and would not be back till evening.

Lionel ate a good lunch, and set out to find his plumber, and she settled down to make her notes. It would be a strong piece;

very strong, she thought. Maybe too strong even for Bower. 'Labour's Last Big Push?' she wrote, then wrote down the facts haphazardly, as she remembered them. The pattern would emerge in time – after she had gone back to the East End, with or without Dick Lambert. At night perhaps Bob would be better. He wouldn't be inhibited by the thought of trouble. She left a message at the number she was told would get him, and telephone Charles Lovell again. He came to the telephone at once.

'May I see you now?' he asked.

'I have to go out,' she said. 'Work. . . . How about later?'

'I have a dinner engagement.'

'Oh damn,' she said. 'How about very late?'

'Of course,' he said. 'Where?'

'My parlourmaid's a bit of a prude,' she said. 'How about Eaton Square?'

'My friends are all away,' he said.

'If you're sure that's all right.' The doorbell rang.

'Eleven thirty,' she said.

It was Bob, in a sports jacket and grey slacks and a flannel shirt. He had the fit and confident look that only a very young man who is eating well can achieve, and his eyes showed some of that same excitement that she'd seen in the eyes of the guardsmen at the docks.

'Where are we going?' he asked.

'The Elephant and Castle to start with.'

He nodded. 'Lively there. Will you be taking the car?'

'Yes of course. How else – '

'I could phone the *World* and get one.'

'We'll take mine,' she said. 'We don't want anything too grand.'

There was the same stark contrast of West End and East End. The West End still living its elegant life: theatres, cinemas, restaurants, bars all open; even the occasional bus erratically driven by volunteers. Only the big electric signs were missing, switched off, Bob told her, to save electricity. But otherwise the West End was as it always was: except that perhaps the people there seemed to be enjoying themselves rather more than usual: as if pleasure were a form of defiance.

As they drove eastwards, Bob said, 'We got word the Honourable Piers Hilyard's driving a lorry.'

'Who's "we"?' she asked.

'The "Wicked World" lot, of course. I pass on things I hear to them.'

'As a matter of fact I saw him,' said Jane. 'At the West India Docks.'

'Doing his bit,' said Bob. The thought seemed to amuse him. 'There's a lot of them at it.'

'Bob,' she said. 'Doesn't it make you angry?'

'No,' said Bob. 'He's doing what he wants to do. Same as me.'

No time to ask what that was. They had reached Newington Butts and already the press of people was so strong that the car had to crawl. She turned off into a side street and parked beside a police van after Bob had got out and had a word with its driver, then they moved back into the crowd. There were policeman everywhere, but they weren't moving singly as they had been that morning: now it was like the docks, with small, compact groups stationed here and there, each one under the command of a sergeant or inspector.

'Trouble?' she asked.

'Not yet,' said Bob. They moved on further into the square. There was a sort of makeshift rostrum by the pub, with its sign of an elephant bearing a howdah, and round it a crowd stood grouped, packed in tight, staring up at the speaker. It was Dick Lambert.

'We can win,' he was saying. 'Only be patient. There are five million of us. A bigger army than ever Marshal Haig had. How can we not win?' The crowd listened, but what they heard was not what they'd come for, and Lambert knew it.

'What we're doing is right,' he said. 'The bosses are trying to cheat us, but our demands are just. A living wage – that's all we ask. Is that so unreasonable? Of course not. It's the very foundation of a free and just society – and we'll get it, comrades. This strike is our show of strength. Overwhelming strength. Five million of us united as one. Let the rich men in Mayfair think of that, and tremble. Brothers, comrades. I promise you. Only let us stand firm and we shall win.'

He left the rostrum, and there was a mutter of applause, no more. Among the crowd, the 'Red Flag' began to be sung, tossed backwards and forwards from one activist to another, until at last the whole great audience responded:

> Let coward flush and tyrants cheer,
> We'll keep the Red Flag flying here.

Jane looked at the squads of police. They still stood easy, relaxed. It seemed that Bob was right.

'Is it over?' she asked.

'For tonight it is.'

She looked at her watch. Almost nine thirty. Still a couple of hours to go.

'I wonder if we could go and get something to eat in that case?' she said.

'There's a sort of artists' caff in Chelsea,' said Bob. 'We could get a bite there.'

'Will they let you in like that?'

'They'll let anybody in,' said Bob.

And so it proved. Not a bad meal either. Onion soup and lamb chops with basil and cheese brought over from Normandy. There wouldn't be any more of that till the strike was over. She asked for wine, and so, to her surprise, did Bob: a rough and cheerful red that he seemed to enjoy.

'What do you do for Jay Bower?' she asked.

'Find things out,' he said. 'I told you. Mr Bower's the sort of chap that needs to know things.'

'So you spy for him? I'm sorry if that sounds rude, but –'

'Quite all right,' he said. 'What I do could upset a lot of people. It didn't do you any harm though.'

'Me?' she said, then: 'Oh. . . . Of course.'

'Of course,' he said. 'Cleopatra – Queen of the Sunday School. . . . It's best to be forewarned in this life.'

'And is that what you do? Forewarn Mr Bower?'

'That's it,' he said. 'It's better than printing. Pays better too.'

The bill came at last and she offered to pay it, but he settled it himself. 'All on expenses,' he said. His tip was generous, and she wondered if he had informers among the waiters.

The next day she would spend with Lambert, and Bob was relieved, if anything. Nothing would happen on the next day. It was the day after that when the excitement would begin. . . . She agreed at once to share it with him. She didn't want Lambert where there was excitement. He was strong enough, but he had too much to lose.

53

At Eaton Square, Lovell answered the doorbell himself.
'Where's the butler?' she asked.
'Night off.'

She moved at once into his arms. Later she thought that they
might have rehearsed it, so inevitable was it. He tried to talk to
her, to explain what had happend, but she kissed him into
silence, made him take her up to his bedroom, where it was all
most satisfactory. Not like Bower: neither better nor worse, only
different – and just as worthwhile. Except that when
they finished he had a tendency simply to lie there and keep his
hands to himself. But it was early days, and he *did* have a lot to
tell her.

'That dreadful letter I wrote,' he said.

'Awful.'

'I wanted to tell you everything.'

'And you ended up by telling me nothing,' she said. 'Certainly
you never gave me any idea that you ever felt like this.'

She gestured across the bed and touched him. It really was
time he began to learn.

'I couldn't marry you,' he said. 'Still can't.'

'Did I ask you to? Did it never occur to you that I like my
freedom too? For the time being at least.'

'I went to Switzerland because I was told my wife might be
dying. God help me I – '

'That's quite enough of that,' she said. 'This is here. This is
now. Just enjoy it.'

Her hand moved again. 'What on earth are you doing?' he said.

'If you don't know,' said Jane, 'there's no hope for either of us.'

He was still laughing as he embraced her.

But she couldn't see him the next day. The omnipresent butler was back, and she needed an early night anyway. She hadn't got into her own bed till three, and Lambert called at nine. It was the day for attending committees in Lambeth. Strike committees, hardship committees, ways and means committees. And here Lambert was at his best; cajoling the waverers, restraining the hotheads, and always holding out to them that shining vision of the day when they would win. And in small groups at least it seemed to work.

'You did well today,' she said, when it was over.

'Oh yes,' he said. 'Give me a classroom full and I can reach them.' His voice was bitter. 'I used to be a schoolteacher, you know.'

'I didn't know,' she said. 'But what's wrong with that?'

'I'm trying to teach the grown-ups now,' he said. 'I didn't do so well last night at the Elephant and Castle.'

'Didn't you?'

It would have been an appalling cruelty to say that she had heard him.

'No I damn well didn't.'

'But surely you must have made speeches in Yorkshire – in your constituency?'

'Preaching to the converted,' said Lambert. 'Solid Labour my lot. Fifteen thousand majority. If a bulldog could make the right noises he'd walk it.'

'Didn't you make the right noises last night?'

'I thought I did,' said Lambert, 'but my audience didn't agree with me. I was preaching moderation. What they wanted to hear was revolution.'

They walked back to the car. On the way they passed a news-stand where a couple of young men were distributing copies of a newspaper called the *British Worker*. Working men in shabbily respectable clothes queued up to receive their copies.

'We seem to be fighting back,' said Lambert.

'We do indeed.' The two young men, Jane noticed, were

dressed exactly as Piers would have been dressed if he'd ever decided to distribute a Socialist broadsheet.

'That work "fight",' said Lambert. 'It's a tricky one. The Marxists keep saying we should arm the workers, but how the hell can we? I wouldn't know where to put my hands on a blunderbuss, never mind a rifle. We can't fight that way – though there's some that keep saying we must. On the other hand there are limits – and we've started going beyond them already.'

'What limits?'

'Over at a tram depot in London,' he said, 'they held a football match this morning. Police versus strikers. They've been out less than two days and they're playing football. . . . *And* they lost.' He saw her lips twitch. 'It isn't funny.'

'No indeed,' she said. 'But it's human. And it's better than handing out blunderbusses.'

'I keep trying to tell them how serious it is,' he said, 'but they just won't listen.'

'*And* you keep telling them they mustn't fight,' she said. 'But these are simple people. If you say it isn't a war, why shouldn't they play football?' As she drove home, a fog was beginning to form. It seemed the perfect comment on the day.

She slept long and late, and was awakened just in time to prepare for Bob. As she ate breakfast she put on the headphones and listened to the wireless news bulletin, which was remarkably impartial, she thought, considering that the government owned the BBC. But it might not stay like that if things began to go wrong from the government's point of view. The unions should have thought of that. The unions should have thought of so many things.

'I thought we'd have a look at the toffs this morning,' said Bob, 'then maybe we could go and have a look at a few diehards this afternoon.'

Really, she thought, he might have been an ornithologist showing off his rarer species.

So in the morning they went to *The Times*'s offices, to watch a row of debs led by Lady Diana Cooper folding the single, flimsy page of that day's issue, then on to the *Daily World* where Bob took off his jacket and helped Jay Bower and a couple of executives set that day's edition in type. Bower, she noticed, was covered in printer's ink to the eyebrows and sublimely happy, like a small boy at Christmas who had received the Meccano set he'd always wanted. They went on then to a Territorial Army drill hall in the city, special constables whose uniform consisted of an arm band, a whistle and a truncheon, were receiving instructions in crowd control, and finished up at Euston Station, where only one train waited, and a man in a bowler hat assured everyone who would listen that he was the engine driver, and he hoped to take them as far as Manchester. In fact, Jane learned later, the train was derailed at Harrow, a few minutes's ride away. Even so she was beginning to realise that the government was at least a match for the strikers in determination, and streets ahead in efficiency.

The next morning was Bob's. He arrived prompt to the minute, wearing the same grey flannel slacks and brogues, and another and very elegant sports jacket. He carried a bag like an army pack.

'Fancy a little excitement this afternoon?' he asked.

She eyed him warily. 'What kind of excitement?'

'What you lot in Hollywood call a hi-jack,' he said. 'Or a try at one anyway.'

'By all means. Where is it?'

'Bethnal Green. Just off the Whitechapel Road.'

'We can't possibly get there till eleven,' she said.

'Take your time,' he said. 'It isn't due to happen till eleven thirty.'

She looked at him. 'How the devil do you know?' she asked.

'I get about,' said Bob. 'I talk to people.'

'Have you told Jay Bower?'

'Not this time,' he said. 'I don't want to tell him all I know. You and me's going to find this one by accident.'

'Serendipity,' she said.

'How much?'

'Never mind,' she said. 'You silly ass. Bower would want a reporter there – and a cameraman.'

'You're a reporter,' said Bob. 'At least you've got a card that says so. And I've brought a camera. I can work it an' all.'

'Does he know you've got it?'

'It was his idea.' They set off for Aldgate.

'Guess who's come up to town?' he said.

'How can I possibly?'

'Andy,' he said.

For a moment her hands tightened on the steering wheel, then she relaxed. 'Andy? But why? Hasn't he enough to do in Felston?'

'Felston's chock-full of Andys,' said Bob. 'His lot decided he'd be more use down here.'

'His lot?'

'The garlic chewer's lot,' said Bob. 'I reckon that means the comrades, don't you? . . . He wants to see you.'

'When?'

'After the hi-jack. Pub I know. Will you come?'

'Certainly,' she said. 'But why did he come to you?'

'Blood's thicker than water,' said Bob. 'At least Andy reckons it is. Redder, too.'

They drove to Aldgate East, and on to the Whitechapel Road. The cars became fewer and fewer, until there was only theirs, but everywhere, as usual, men and women were walking, and here and there a cyclist skimmed past, or a horse and car grimly plodded.

'Turn left at Brady Street,' said Bob. 'There's a bit of waste ground there.'

She did as he bade her, and found herself a place to park in front of a couple of ruined houses that seemed to have collapsed from sheer exhaustion.

'How did you know about this?' she asked.

'I came over on my bike first thing this morning,' he said. 'To do a what d'you call it? Like the war.'

'To reconnoitre,' she said. Suddenly he looked very like John in the early days.

At eleven twenty he looked at his watch. 'Time to go,' he said. 'Just round the corner.'

'Aren't you perhaps a little worried?' she asked. 'Taking a mere female into possible danger?'

'You?' he said. 'Do me a favour.'

Which was flattering in a way, she thought, but only in a way. The danger remained. Nevertheless she had to follow him. He moved swiftly and easily ahead of her. He'd removed his brand-new jacket and was carrying the bag that must have held the camera, easing his way through the crowds. She wore her oldest clothes, but still she knew she must look conspicuous. Tomorrow she must borrow some from Hawkins. Fair's fair, she thought, and then her mind went back to Bob. For him the General Strike was his great opportunity and he was grabbing it with both hands. 'Do me a favour' . . . . Even his speech was changing. . . . The crowd grew thicker and he waited for her, helping her to a street corner where a flight of steps led up to a house.

'This'll do,' he said, and looked at his watch. 11.28. But it was ten minutes later before he heard the sound he had been waiting for, the clattering yet rhythmic beat of a motor engine in bottom gear, doing its best to move in a crowded street.

'What's supposed to happen?' she said.

'You'll see.' Bob had that same absorbed, excited look, as if he were in a cinema and the Apaches were preparing to attack.

A lorry came up to their corner. It was heaped with bags of what looked like vegetables, and as usual had a crew of three: a driver, a map reader and a policeman. The driver was Piers, cautiously edging the lorry forward. Suddenly from the houses round about men appeared, dozens of them, moving with the disciplined speed the army had taught them. One group stood unmoving in front of the lorry, the rest flowed round to the sides and back. Piers braked, and at once the men at the back of the lorry climbed on to it, cut at the ropes that held them and began throwing the bags of vegetables into the crowd. The men at the sides joined in, all except a few who stayed on as guards. One of them, she noticed incredulously, was Pardoe. Well at least he practised what he preached. Suddenly from Brady Street came the sound of police whistles, and the watching crowd began to heave like a sea as the men on the lorry jumped clear, and the men at its sides began to push at it.

'Heave – heave – heave,' cried the crowd, and at last the lorry began to tilt; the men in the cab had no choice but to jump clear. The policeman had already drawn his truncheon, the map reader held a starting handle, but Piers had nothing but his fists. He used them as well as he could, until he found himself matched against Pardoe, who at once began to beat him in a cold and scientific sort of way to which Piers could find no answer. Beside him Bob was frantically taking pictures. She tugged at his sleeve.

'Help him, can't you?' she said, but he looked at her bewildered. 'The driver,' she yelled. 'He's Piers Hilyard. He's a friend of Jay Bower's.'

– 618 –

'Oh my God,' said Bob, and handed her his camera, then leaped into the fight. Pardoe saw him coming and turned to meet him, fists up, right arm protecting his belly and chin, left arm extended, in the scientifically correct boxing stance. Bob, two stones lighter, three inches shorter, stopped just out of the left arm's range and kicked Pardoe in the testicles with his brogue-shod foot. Jane took the picture with Bob's camera and wound on as the crowd beside her split suddenly, like a paper bag, and a squad of police charged in.

Lady Mangan said, 'I don't know how to thank you.'

'It's Bob Patterson you should thank,' said Jane. They were in the drawing room of the Grosvenor Square house.

'I've done that,' said Lady Mangan. 'He's a useful lad, that one.'

'He is an' all,' said Jane, and Lady Mangan grinned.

'Cheeky,' she said. 'But I really am grateful. From what Piers said, the chap that was hitting him was a boxer. Knew what he was doing.' Jane nodded. 'Then how did that lad manage to beat him?'

Jane told her, and the old lady wheezed in delighted laughter.

'The only way he could win,' she said. 'Oh I do like that lad.'

'Where is he?' Jane asked.

'Using the telephone. Who does he work for?'

'Jay Bower.'

'Well of course,' Lady Mangan fidgeted. 'Are you and Mr Bower still friends?'

'Not as close as we were,' said Jane.

'I see. . . . He's been seeing quite a bit of Catherine off and on,' said Lady Mangan. 'Especially since you both came back from America. Is that a good idea, would you say?'

'He wouldn't try to seduce a virgin, if that's what you mean,' said Jane.

'I should hope he'd have more sense. What I do mean is why is he?'

'He wants to marry,' said Jane. 'It's not surprising. He's of an age for it.'

'He's too old for my Catherine,' said Lady Mangan. 'He's rich, of course. I know that. But how rich?'

Jane thought of the house in New England, the platoons and companies of servants, the bank and the studio.

'Enormously,' she said.

'Oh dear,' said Lady Mangan. 'Come and have a word with Piers before you go.'

He was lying on a bed, his face painted with arnica. Already one eye was darkening, and his face was heavily bruised.

'It looks as if I should learn to box,' he said.

'Much better ask Bob to give you kicking lessons.'

'Don't make me laugh,' he said. 'It hurts. . . . How did it end?'

'The lorry went over just before the police arrived,' she said. 'They cleared the crowd rather quickly.'

'With truncheons?' She nodded. 'The text-book way,' he said. 'If you must go in, go in hard. But – '

'But what, my sweet?'

'I've driven down those streets where those people lived,' he said. 'I never had, before. The "great unwashed", we called them at Oxford. How can they wash if there's ten of them to a tap? And horse dung all over the streets where the children play without shoes? They call it the class war, don't they? Well now I've seen the casualties.'

'Do you wish you hadn't driven that lorry?'

'Of course not,' he said. 'There has to be discipline. But when it's over there should be some compassion, too.'

She bent to kiss him, then left. Best not to tell him that the man who beat him was a Cambridge don, she thought. He had enough to think about without that.

Andy was waiting for them in a gloomy cavern of a pub near King's Cross Station. A typical Andy pub, she thought, totally without cheer. In front of him was a half-finished glass of lemonade, and he declined another. Bob went to fetch her a port and lemon, which was the only woman's drink she could think of. This was not the pub for cocktails.

'How's Grandma?' she asked.

'Fine,' he said. 'The eyes is no trouble. Da's fine too. They both send their regards.'

'Please give them mine. How's Bet? Still busy at the clinic?'

'That clinic of yours has never been busier,' said Andy. 'Bet's engaged.'

Bob came back with her port and lemon and a whisky for himself. Another change.

'Taking the plunge, is she?' he said.

'She's already done that,' said Andy.

'Oh aye?' said Bob.

'Aye.'

And that seemed to be it, because all Bob said was, 'What does Da say?'

'Da says once she started walking out with a widower we could expect nowt else. Blest if I know what he meant.'

'Got the habit,' Bob suggested.

'Watch your mouth,' said Andy primly. 'Frank Metcalfe's a decent chap. But he's human.'

'When's the wedding?' Jane asked.

'Soon,' said Andy. 'It has to be.'

'Will they accept a present from me?' Jane asked.

'They will if they've got any sense,' said Bob, and Andy agreed.

'That wouldn't be charity,' he agreed. 'It was her first said you were part of the family. Presents in a family – what could be more natural? But I didn't ask you here for that.'

'What then?'

'Bob said you're doing a lot of writing about the strike. For the *Daily World*.' She nodded. 'I asked to meet you because I wanted to ask you something. A favour you might say.'

'Ask and we'll see.'

'I asked if you'd give our side a fair look-in. No more, no less. . . . Now that wasn't my idea. The way I look at things you've very often been wrong, but you've always been fair. But others – chaps I'm working with – they said I had to ask. So I'm asking.'

'I'll be as fair as I can, Andy.'

'That's good enough for me.' He dashed off his glass of flat lemonade as if it were the wine before a battle, then Jane offered her hand and he took it.

'So that's it then,' he said. 'I'm making a speech next week. Bob'll give you the details when the time comes.' He hesitated. It was as hard as it always had been for Andy to ask a favour. 'I'd like you to come and write it up the way it is,' he said. 'If it isn't too much trouble.'

'It's my job,' she said. 'Of course I will.'

In the drawing room she rang for Hawkins, and asked to borrow some clothes.

'Be a pleasure, miss,' Hawkins said. 'At least it was when I borrowed yours.' She hesitated. 'There's something I have to say, miss.'

'Yes?'

'It's sort of a favour.' She hesitated. 'No, not really. It's hard to say what it is.'

'Take your time,' said Jane.

'I'll be giving notice in September, miss – and I want you to say it's all right. That's why I said it's a favour.'

'But it isn't all right,' said Jane. 'I shall miss you dreadfully. And I must say it's a bit much leaving me for somebody else. I thought we go on well together.'

'So we do, miss,' Hawkins said. 'I didn't think I could be so happy in service. I wouldn't leave you for anybody else, miss.'

'Why then?' said Jane. 'Oh my God! You're not ill, I hope?'

'Course not, miss,' said Hawkins. 'I'm going to London University.'

'What?'

'My gran died couple of years back,' said Hawkins. 'She had a corner shop. My share was five hundred quid. – Pounds, I should say. So I put it in the bank and went to night classes. They have a special exam for what the University call mature students and I took it while you was – were in Hollywood. Today they telephoned and told me I'd passed. They had to do that because there's no postmen working. I hope you don't mind, miss.'

'*Mind?*' Jane took Hawkins in her arms, and hugged her and hugged her. 'Hawkins I'm so proud of you.'

'Thank you, miss.' The two women parted at last. Both of them were crying.

'What will you study?' Jane asked at last.

'We don't specialise till the second year,' said Hawkins, 'but Mr Warley reckons I should have a shot at languages.'

'Oh Hawkins it's all too marvellous,' said Jane, and then: 'Will five hundred be enough?'

'If I'm careful, miss.'

'Don't be too careful,' said Jane. 'It never works. I'll tell you what – I'll pay the tuition fees and books and things, and you keep the five hundred to live on. Although how you can live on five hundred pounds over three years – '

'I'll manage, miss.'

'No you will not. I'd better double it and then we can all relax. I'll tell you what – I'll make it a scholarship. In memory of my father. You'll be the first Sir Guy Whitcomb Memorial Scholar.'

'But I couldn't, miss. It's too much.'

'Please don't say that.' Jane's hand reached out to touch her. 'You kept all my secrets in the dark days. One night when I was drunk – if you didn't save my life you most certainly saved my reputation. Please, Peggy.'

Somehow Hawkins achieved a smile. 'Thank you, miss,' she said, and would have wept again but for the fact that the telephone rang. She picked it up.

'Miss Whitcomb's residence,' she said, then covered the mouthpiece. 'Mr Lovell,' she said.

'Thank you, Hawkins.' Jane went to the telephone. 'I tell you what,' she said. 'Mr Warley's dining with us again tonight. His cook's still out picketing. Why don't you put some champagne in the fridge – something vintage – and we'll drink to our new scholar?'

Hawkins left then, and she picked up the telephone.

'Yes, Charles?'

'I've got a service flat,' said Lovell. 'In Bruton Street. It seems very nice except that I'm not too sure whether the bed's comfortable or not. I wondered if you'd come and advise me.'

'When?'

'I thought now might be a good time.'

'Not now,' she said. 'I mean not precisely now. I have a date to drink champagne with my maid which I'll tell you all about later. Would eight o'clock to too late for bed testing?'

'Eight o'clock would be splendid,' he said. 'And perhaps supper at the Berkeley afterwards for those of us who can stagger that far?'

She broke the news to Lionel before the champagne arrived.

'But I can't possibly,' he said. 'How can I dine here alone?'

'You won't be alone,' said Jane. 'You'll have Hawkins with you. You can mug up a few French irregular verbs together. She'll need all the irregular verbs you can teach her when she starts in October.'

Lionel jumped to his feet. 'You mean she passed?'

'Indeed she did,' said Jane. 'And what's more she's the first Sir Guy Whitcomb Memorial Scholar.'

'Dear Jane,' said Lionel. 'Thank you.'

And that, she thought, is Lionel. Abstractions bored him so much that he fled them, but give him a human being to worry about and he was marvellous.

'What a clever Pygmalion you are,' she said.

'No tutor could wish for a better Galatea. . . . *Why* are you going out?'

'Love,' she said.

'What better reason? You may rely on me to tell any necessary lies. Which reminds me – I took you advice about Fred.'

'Fred?'

'My plumber. I told him how staunch I was in my refusal to strike break or whatever one calls it. He's really quite proud of me.'

Let him stick with his irregular verbs, she thought. That way he'll come to no harm. Then Hawkins came in with the champagne.

The bed had proved adequate for its purpose, and now they rested on it.

'You never came to America,' she said. He grunted. 'You said you would.'

'Only if you stayed there a long time. You didn't. I'm awfully glad you didn't.'

'Me too.' She turned into his arms.

'Are you staying the night?' he asked. She nodded abstractedly: her fingers were busy trying out something that had just occurred to her.

'Bit tricky for you?'

'Not at all,' she said. 'All you do is tell the right lies. *This* is what's tricky.'

Later he said, 'Are we still going to the Berkeley?'

'Certainly,' she said. 'I'm ravenous.' She kissed him. 'Don't worry. If you're too exhausted I'll carry you. . . . Fireman's lift. They taught me in the Girl Guides. And then when you're refreshed and strong, we'll come back here and test the bed again for comfort.'

And that was the way the next week went. Bed testing and the General Strike. She'd told Hawkins she was visiting a sick friend. Hawkins didn't believe a word of it, but at least she'd be convincing if she had to talk to Mummy, thought Jane. But Mummy too was in love, and it was spring. She didn't call for a week, and then caught Jane just before she left to watch with Lambert another football match between strikers and policemen at Tower Hamlets. Poor Dick Lambert was in despair. 'They'll be organising a league table soon,' he said. Jane told her mother what he had said.

'I do not think so,' her mother replied. 'According to that ludicrous sheet of paper that calls itself *The Times* these days, Sir John Simon has declared that in his opinion a General Strike is illegal. He is a Liberal of course, but he is also a most able lawyer, – and the Liberals would err on the side of weakness on this issue, surely? It is their invariable rule.'

'But would the strikers worry about what Sir John Simon thinks?'

'Probably not. They are far too busy rioting and playing football. But their leaders might. I have yet to read of one cast in the heroic mould.'

That is because I haven't yet written about Andy, thought Jane. But it was true.

'But my reason for calling is quite other,' said Lady Whitcomb. 'I should like us to dine en famille.'

'I'd love to Mummy.'

'There are matters to be discussed. Family matters.' Lucy Dawson? Jane wondered. 'Could you bear to receive us at South Terrace? Dear George has never ceased to talk about your cook.'

'Delighted Mummy. I am rather busy at the moment. But if the twelfth isn't too late – '

'The twelfth will do admirably,' said her mother. 'Please do not apologise. I can imagine nothing more time-consuming than observing a General Strike.'

As so often after a telephone call from her mother, Jane had to resist the impulse to mop her brow.

On the 11th May Bob called her. Andy was due to make his speech that evening. It was time to borrow Hawkins's clothes. They were going back to the Elephant and Castle, it seemed, and the same makeshift rostrum next to the pub. On the way there what Bob told her made her sure that her mother was right.

'There's a lot of talk among the leaders about giving in,' said Bob. 'Respect for law and order! All that. Our Andy doesn't give a damn for law and order. Bloody revolution, that's what Andy wants. That's why they're putting him up there. Very Red around the Elephant and Castle. If you ask me, it's the last chance they've got.'

They left the car in a side street, then found a doorstep, as they had in Bethnal Green. The crowd moved in, tighter and tighter, so that Jane and Bob were imprisoned on their doorstep.

Exactly at four, two figures climbed the rostrum, Andy and his chairman, a small and earnest man whose voice was no match for the murmurs of the crowd. 'Fraternal delegate,' Jane heard. 'Down from the North East. . . . Workers' Rights. . . . Staunch Fighter.' Then he stepped back and Andy moved at once into the attack in a voice of effortless power, the voice that she had last heard in Felston market place.

'Comrades,' he roared, 'I come here to tell you that the miners and shipyard workers and steelmen of Tyneside send you their greetings. The miners especially say thank you for this display of solidarity, for no men have suffered more than the miners, comrades. And no women more than their wives. And yet they fight on. As you fight on. And for why?

'Because we see a vision. We see this country transformed into a fair and shining land where there is justice for all and fair shares for all, and an end to poverty and wage cuts and lock-outs, a country where a man can stand up and be free.'

He paused, and the crowd stirred and seethed like a giant flexing its muscles – 'No means tests,' Andy roared. 'No Guardians. No Charity. Never again. No yes sir no sir let me lie down in the mud so you won't have to reach too far when you kick me sir. That – is – over.'

The murmur grew louder.

'Take a look around you,' said Andy. 'Go on. . . . Take a look.' Half embarrassed, they did so. 'What do you see? The great army of workers, that's what you see. But not the whole army. Not a division. Not even a brigade. Just one regiment – but look at the numbers of it. The might of it. . . . The unions will tell you that unity is strength – and so it is – but numbers is strength too. Numbers is power. And it's high time we used that power!'

This time the giant lifted his fists above his head and roared, and then Andy raised his hands. The giant grew still.

'But not here,' he said. 'Power's not needed here. Here among the dirt and the poverty and the stink – that's where *we* are. Where our friends, our comrades are. And that's where the bosses want to keep us. Are we going to let them?'

'No!' the giant bellowed.

'Or are we going to go out there – ' and suddenly Andy's arm stabbed out, pointing to the west – ' to demand what should be ours by rights, and to take it if we have to?'

'Yes,' the giant bellowed.

'Now is the time for the haves to yield to the have-nots,' Andy thundered. 'Time and more than time, for I tell you this, comrades, if we don't show the bosses our strength and show it now, our leaders will betray us. We'll have suffered in vain.'

A man on the edge of the crowd, a big, red-shirted man, called out in a voice that rivalled Andy's. 'He's right, comrades. Let's go and get what's ours before somebody with more guts does it first.'

A plant of course, thought Jane, but none the less effective for that. The big man strode off down the London Road, and the crowd surged after him. Andy swarmed down from the rostrum to be with them.

'Well I'll say this for our Andy,' said Bob, and his voice was admiring, 'there's never any doubt whose side *he's* on.'

And still the crowd surged past, then suddenly it stuck, jammed fast like a cork in a bottle. From ahead there came the sound of screaming, then suddenly the crowd split, funnelling into side streets or racing back the way they'd come.

'Police,' said Bob. 'It must be.'

The crowd was running hard, breaking up. Now the roadway and the tramlines were visible once more. Andy stood in front of one group, roaring at them to stand firm, be brave, but they swept him aside, not even hearing, and the next wave knocked him off his feet.

'I'd better get him,' said Bob, but she had been listening hard, and now grabbed his arm.

'Leave him,' she said. 'He's safer where he is.'

The sound she had heard was like no other sound in the world: the sound of horses at a full gallop.

They came down the road like a cavalry charge, the heavy horses held well in, but moving strongly; their riders helmeted, silver buttons glittering against dark-blue tunics, and swinging in their hands the long baton of the mounted policeman. And suddenly Jane realised what it was that they looked like. She was back in India, watching Papa and his friends play polo, but this time with a human head for a ball.

One by one they galloped past where Andy lay, but the last horse reared and its rider paused to regain control, and as he did so Andy, dazed, bewildered, staggered to his feet. The policeman turned his horse to follow the others, kicked it into a gallop, then casually, almost lazily, struck Andy with his baton as he galloped by.

'Oh God!' said Bob, and ran to his brother, and Jane ran off to fetch the car. The police would be back soon enough searching for enemy wounded.

Between them they got Andy into the back seat of the car. His face was a mash of blood, more blood poured from a gash in his scalp, and he made the snoring noise that Jane knew meant concussion.

'What are we going to do?' said Andy. 'What the hell are we going to do?'

'Take him home,' said Jane.

'Home?'

In the state he was in, the only home Bob could think of was Felston.

'South Terrace,' said Jane.

'But he needs a doctor.'

'Of course he does,' said Jane. 'We'll get him one from there. Now hold on to him, Bob. I'll have to drive fast.'

She drove very fast indeed, on to the Embankment and heading west. Only once did a policeman stop her, and that was a special who turned out to be Mr Pinner, immaculate as always in bowler hat, dark suit and arm band. He took one look at her face and waved her through, holding up everyone else in sight. Somehow she and Bob and Andy between them got Andy upstairs and on to a bed and Hawkins found a towel to replace Bob's blood-sodden handkerchief as Jane telephoned Harriet Watson.

'She'll come at once,' she told Bob, and then, before he could speak: 'Don't worry. She's a friend of mine. She won't betray him.'

He was ill, of course, Harriet told them, but not nearly as ill as she had expected, and looked at Bob. 'Heads like mahogany where you come from,' she said. 'Or is it just in the family?'

'He'll be all right then?' Bob asked.

'Of course,' said Harriet. 'He'll need rest and nursing for a couple of days at least – '

'I'll do that,' said Bob.

'Nothing else?' asked Jane.

'Aspirin,' said Harriet. 'He'll ask for rather a lot of that. . . . I'll look in tomorrow.'

Jane took her downstairs.

'Is there a warrant out for him?' Harriet asked.

'I've no intention of asking,' said Jane.

'Very wise.' Harriet kissed her on the cheek. 'No rest for the wicked, is there?'

As Jane came in, the telephone was ringing. It was Bower.

'I'm told you were in the thick of it again,' he said. 'You and young Patterson.'

'I'm writing it up now,' she said.

'Good,' said Bower. 'I could use some copy.'

'In the middle of a strike?'

'We'll be printing next week – but that's only for your information. . . . How did Patterson find out about this one?'

'His brother told him.'

'The Red? Did you know he'd disappeared?'

'No,' said Jane. Nor did she.

'Keep away from him,' said Bower. 'Don't go looking. You've watched one victory and one defeat – fine. But we don't need any more. Not from you. It would look too much like inside information. No more serendipity. I've told Patterson the same. Still I'm grateful for what you've got.'

'There's masses more,' she said. 'Enough for a book.'

'Then write it,' said Bower. 'And if it's any good I'll serialise it. When am I going to see you?'

'When I bring my copy in.' He hung up.

Next day the strike was over, but Bower had been right, as usual. The dockers, transport workers and printers stayed out for another five days. (The miners stayed out for another six months and gained not a thing. But then a pitman only has three hobbies, Bob said. Whippets, leek shows and strikes.) He proved a remarkably good nurse for Andy, and Mrs Barrow found time to make him broth, despite her preparations for that night's dinner party. When Jane visited the brothers, Andy was already sitting up in bed. He demanded his clothes at once. He couldn't inflict himself on her, and in any case he had work to do.

Gently she said, 'I'm afraid you don't, Andy. . . . The strike's over.'

'I know that.' She looked at Bob.

'Not me,' he said. 'Well not really. We borrowed your wireless.'

'That doesn't mean there isn't work to do,' Andy said.

'Not by you,' said Jane. 'I don't think there's a warrant out for you yet, but there could be. You're said to have disappeared. Why not leave it at that?'

'But if they find me here – you'll be in trouble, too.'

'They won't find you here.' Andy looked at his brother.

'You bide where you are till you're better, kidda,' said Bob. 'We'll get you back to Felston then.'

And so she left them.

She and her mother and the major were drinking sherry when Harriet arrived, briskly apologetic for her lateness: a crossbirth, a broken leg and an outbreak of measles all in the same street. She had no time for sherry, but went at once to her patient, and scrawled a prescription for something she thought would be more effective than aspirin. She became even more brisk when Andy asked to get up, then hurried away. Jane went back to her guests.

'One of the servants is ill?' Lady Whitcomb asked.

'No, Mummy.' She told them what had happened. The major was appalled.

'But he's a Red,' he said. 'You can't harbour him.'

'I can't turn him out,' said Jane. 'He's ill. Anyone would be who was clubbed down like that.'

'He should have thought of that before he started inciting people to riot. Your good name's at stake here. And your mother's. You must – '

'George,' Lady Whitcomb said. Her voice was gentle, almost

caressing, and yet the major was silent at once. Like switching off a wireless, thought Jane.

'George dear,' Lady Whitcomb said again. 'This man is from Felston.'

'I don't see that – '

'*Felston*, George. . . . Because of my daughter's literary efforts, the *Daily World* takes a particular interest in Felston. *Mr Bower* takes a particular interest in Felston. Mr Bower is our employer, George. Why don't we simply accept the fact that this man's presence here is no business of ours, and leave it at that?'

Hawkins came in then to announce a dinner that did much to calm the major, and the port that Jane produced afterwards would intensify the treatment she was sure. None of it would be wasted. Harriet had suggested port, and Jane was determined that Andy should drink it, even if she had to use a funnel. . . . She and her mother left the major with his decanter.

'You will have observed that George's intellect is limited,' said her mother, 'and that it is tenacious besides, which is unfortunate.'

Here was frankness indeed. 'Yes, Mummy,' said Jane.

'However he is also morally admirable – far better than I am I fear – and affectionate, which is more than adequate compensation. It is also why his conscience has been troubling him, poor lamb.' Then she told Jane about Lucy Dawson.

'What will you do, Mummy?' Jane asked.

'Take her racing of course,' said her mother. 'What else can one do? Oh – you are referring to the moral aspect of the problem. I have decided that it does not exist. As I told George at the time, if there is one lesson that my daughter has taught me it is how to be broadminded.'

And make of that what you will, thought Jane.

'Which reminds me,' her mother continued, 'that we have decided to ignore Dr Dodd's advice. We intend to announce our engagement next week and marry as soon as possible after the Derby.'

'Congratulations, Mummy.' Jane rose and kissed Lady Whitcomb.

'I am tired of living alone,' said her mother, and then: 'You do not have that problem?'

Ambiguous to the last, thought Jane, who had no doubt what her mother was asking.

'No, Mummy.'

'I'm glad,' Lady Whitcomb said, and changed the subject at once. 'You have seen a great deal of this disturbance?'

'I have indeed.'

'And now you harbour one of its instigators, even though he is from Felston?'

'I saw what was done to him,' said Jane.

'And yet he is from Felston and, from things you have told me in the recent past, I rather gathered that you had washed your hands of Felston.'

'I thought that too,' said Jane. 'I was wrong.'

'You intend further involvement?' Jane nodded. 'You're very like me, you know. You cannot tolerate being directed. For us the need is always to direct. Consider dear George.' Lady Whitcomb put down her coffee cup. 'Perhaps the saddhu was right.'

'Saddhu, Mummy?'

'The one your ayah consulted all those years ago. Perhaps you will achieve greatness, as Shakespeare says. Or perhaps it will be thrust upon you.'

'Nonsense, Mummy,' said Jane.

'Not at all,' said Lady Whitcomb serenely. 'It would take a strength of purpose far beyond my capacity to put a town like Felston to rights.'

Nonsense yourself, thought Jane. Between the three of you, Lady Mangan, Grandma Patterson and you, you could square the circle. But she didn't say so aloud.

When her mother and the major had gone, Jane drove to the all-night chemist in the King's Road to have Andy's prescription made up, then went back into the car and sat. She was tired: far too tired for bed testing, but that was all right. She would see Charles next afternoon. Dear Charles who had been so conventional in his love-making, until they had started sleeping together, and now unhesitatingly followed wherever she led. . . . Oh my God, Mummy's right, she thought, and yawned.

She had a right to be tired. Football matches and victories and defeats, an aristocratic blackleg rescued, a wounded warrior in her house. Andy would fight on, of course. Andy would fight on till he died. He would fight and he would lose, she thought, because he wants everything now, this minute, and the only sure way is one piece at a time.

The pubs had emptied. Across the street a man was walking, not quite steady on his feet. Suddenly he began to sing in a true, pure tenor, and the war came back at once; almost she could feel John's hand touch hers.

> When this lousy war is over
> No more soldiering for me.
> When I get my civvy clothes on
> Oh how happy I will be. . . .

The drunken man turned the corner, and his voice faded. . . . The war I'm in now isn't over, she thought, whatever the wireless says. It's hardly begun. And no more have I. She started the car. It was time to go home.

A selection of bestsellers from Headline

FICTION

A RARE BENEDICTINE	Ellis Peters	£2.99 □
APRIL	Christine Thomas	£4.50 □
FUNLAND	Richard Laymon	£4.50 □
GENERATION	Andrew MacAllan	£4.99 □
THE HARESFOOT LEGACY	Frances Brown	£4.50 □
BROKEN THREADS	Tessa Barclay	£4.50 □

NON-FICTION

GOOD HOUSEKEEPING EATING FOR A HEALTHY BABY	Birthright	£4.99 □

SCIENCE FICTION AND FANTASY

RAVENS' GATHERING Bard IV	Keith Taylor	£3.50 □
ICED ON ARAN	Brian Lumley	£3.50 □
CARRION COMFORT	Dan Simmons	£4.99 □

All Headline books are available at your local bookshop or newsagent, or can be ordered direct from the publisher. Just tick the titles you want and fill in the form below. Prices and availability subject to change without notice.

Headline Book Publishing PLC, Cash Sales Department, PO Box 11, Falmouth, Cornwall, TR10 9EN, England.

Please enclose a cheque or postal order to the value of the cover price and allow the following for postage and packing:
UK: 80p for the first book and 20p for each additional book ordered up to a maximum charge of £2.00
BFPO: 80p for the first book and 20p for each additional book
OVERSEAS & EIRE: £1.50 for the first book, £1.00 for the second book and 30p for each subsequent book.

Name ....

Address ....

....

....